AFTER THIS OUR EXILE

AFTER THIS OUR EXILE

Aubrey Malone

PENNILESS PRESS PUBLICATIONS
www.pennilesspress.co.uk

Published by
Penniless Press Publications 2019

ISBN 978-1-913144-09-8

The years are a unit of memory. The hours and days, of experience.

Cesare Pavese

1

He remembered the nights of spring. He ran as if possessed through the valleys, a moth trapped in light. The evenings made shadows through the trees but then the moon came along and obliterated them. He heard voices resounding like the whinnies of horses but he could never pinpoint the sources, dodging in and out of the crevices. He carved his name on the trees and scaled the peaks of the hills, the ridges bearing down on one another like giant animals.

After he came home he skipped rope into the twilight, calling names to the boys who had girlfriends, the single unpardonable sin. If it was your birthday you got dunked in the water and if you were a cissy you were stripped. He made rude jokes about the girls in the convent and everyone tried to get a look at Eithne Melia undressing at the swimming pool.

The beach was like a paradise to him. Old men bent with a hundred winters staggered along the pier, black-gabardined and gaunt. He cycled there every week, freewheeling down the hill as he spotted the first dunes. Afterwards he'd make smart comments to the girl in the sweet shop, annoying her for loose cigarettes. Cycling home in the dying light he felt like Superman. He stopped at the all-night petrol station for toffee bars, talking tough and dreaming of things like motorbikes and waves that drowned the universe.

An old woman who lived in the farmhouse down the road put a spell on him. She had arthritis and a hump and an uncle who was the seventh son of a seventh son. She read palms and cackled at news when it was bad, visibly delighted. No beautiful women or grand fortunes were on his horizon, she told him, only deep sea monsters and a life of cold, unstoppable terror.

Every night when his parents went to sleep he used to get out of his bed and look out his window at the sky. He was fascinated by spaceships and astronauts and men from Mars. If you landed on the moon you could jump as high as you wanted.

He fought the aliens every night with guns that turned them into dust. They were trying to take over the earth. If they succeeded he'd have to go to Saturn or some other planet to survive. He could raise plants there and feed himself. He'd travel in a giant capsule with all his friends. He'd be the captain. Women and children would be let in first. If the aliens tried to come after them he'd bomb them with explosives.

When he was twelve the local cinema closed down. There were rats in it. People were too busy going dancing now anyway, or to the rugby club over the bridge. The old woman who was a witch died so there were no more spells put on him anymore. He was able to walk out late.

New businesses opened up in the town. People in sharp suits blew in, official-looking men with cruelty in their eyes. He watched them in the banks and business places with their attaché cases. They were always rushing to get somewhere but when they got there they didn't seem to have anything to do. They dangled their car-keys in their hands importantly as they talked to you. Then they said, 'Birdie must fly.' They had dark coats that stretched all the way to the ground. When they were leaving they brushed past him like the wind, their minds on more sensible things than his own wild daydreams.

The years passed by like so many mirages. Before he knew it he was in long pants and styling his hair like a rock star. He took his first alcoholic drink one night in a snooker hall and it was an explosion to his insides. Afterwards he was bland about it all, affecting a knowing casualness.

'You'd want to watch it with the drink,' his mother said, She had dreams he'd be a priest and for a while he had these dreams too. After he finished school he'd go to a seminary and learn the prayers he needed to and then he'd be ordained. Every day he'd say Mass and afterwards he'd visit the sick and the poor. He'd also do weddings and funerals. When he died he'd go to heaven with the other priests and meet God. God lived in heaven. It was high in the sky behind the clouds. He made the world and died for all the people he created. They could make up to him by praying and becoming priests.

2

One Saturday evening he was in the Capri, a cafe he liked in the town. He didn't usually go there at the weekend but the Grand National was on and everyone got merry. His father had a few drinks too many after it was over. His mother was playing the piano. She was able to play a song after hearing it once. When she played she went into another world, the world of her childhood.

'Bartley is in bed,' she told him. That was his father's name. He spent more time in bed these days than he did out of it.

He was supposed to go to confession but he didn't feel like it. There was a debate on in the college about milk but he didn't feel like that either. He knew he'd get hell for that on Monday but he didn't care. He'd just been at a James Cagney film and that always made him feel tough.

Tommy Glynn was with him. He was in his class. Tommy often got into trouble for poaching salmon from the river. He never did a stroke of work but he got away with it.

Brian liked hanging out in the Capri café. Most of the time he sat at the window nursing a cold plate of chips doused in tomato ketchup. He made wolf-whistles at the girls passing by.

Tommy had a girl with him. Brian knew her from Primary School. When she went to the convent he used to see her walking down Priory Grove with her friends. That was where the convent was. Sometimes he muttered hello to her if he felt brave enough. She always smiled shyly at him in reply and then looked at the ground. He used to watch her until she turned the corner for the road home. Her name was Jennifer. She reminded him of the actress Ann Blythe. She was very good-looking. She always wore slacks and low-cut dresses when she wasn't in her uniform. She wasn't aware of her beauty. He thought that made it more desirable.

Tommy was drunk. He sat down beside Brian, falling into the seat. Brian smelt whiskey off his breath. He had a small bottle of it in his pocket. He offered Brian some.

He took it neat. It stung his insides. He pretended he was used to it but Jennifer sussed that he wasn't. She laughed as he sucked in his breath. After he handed the bottle back to him she had a swig too. She seemed better able for it than he was.

'I wish I could drink like you,' he said to her.

'Stop talking to her,' Tommy said, 'She's my girl.'

'Is that true?' he asked her.

'No.'

'What about getting some salmon?' Tommy asked him.

'It's too cold,' he said, 'Another night maybe.'

Tommy gave him a funny look. He knew he was exaggerating the cold so he could be longer with Jennifer.

The cafe revolved around him. He got giddy. He put vinegar in a glass of water Tommy had. When he took a slurp of it he started to choke.

'What the fuck is in this?' he said.

'Vinegar.'

'You're dead when we get out of here,' Tommy said. He made a sign of slitting his throat with his hand.

Jennifer laughed. A few minutes later he put salt in her cup of tea instead of sugar.

'You bastard,' he said after tasting it. She spat it onto the floor.

They started getting dirty looks from the waitress so they decided they better go. Tommy wanted to do a runner without paying for the tea but Brian left a few coins on the table.

'Wimp,' he said as they went out.

They walked towards Tommy's house as the night came down. Brian was walking funny because of the whiskey.

'This is a footpath,' Tommy said to him, 'It's what people walk on. I mean civilised people, not shitty farmer's sons.'

Brian went to hit him but Jennifer got in the way.

'Don't mind him,' she said.

'Why did you stop him?' Tommy said. 'If he hit me he'd get two back. He knows that.'

'I'm not afraid of you, Glynn,' Brian said. Tommy just laughed.

He got Brian in a headlock for the vinegar offence. He wrestled him to the ground. Jennifer came to his rescue. She dug Tommy in the ribs until he released him.

'Ouch,' Tommy said, 'You're stronger than he is.'

They got to the bridge.

'Adios amigos,' Tommy said, 'This is where I take my leave of you beautiful people.'

'Don't do anything I wouldn't do,' Jennifer said.

'See you,' Brian said.

He thought she might have gone with him. He was relieved she didn't.

He asked her if she wanted him to walk her home. She shrugged her shoulders as if she didn't mind either way. He was excited to be alone with her. He felt his insides tingling.

'I'd kill for another drop of that hootch,' she said as they walked down by the church.

They shared what remained. Afterwards everything swam before him – the church, the bridge, the lake. Clouds massed themselves in the sky like bundles of cotton wool. They seemed to be about to fall down on him.

He had a cigarette in his pocket that he was saving for times like this. He offered it to her. She grabbed it as soon as she saw it. He lit it for her. She took a drag of it. Then she offered him a puff. As he drew on it he started to cough. She laughed.

'If you don't mind me saying so,' she said, 'You look even more stupid when you're smoking than when you're drinking. I'm half afraid you'll set yourself on fire.'

He knew she was right. Anytime he smoked he got more nicotine on his hands than in his lungs.

They walked towards her house. With the Dutch courage of the whiskey he found himself taking her hand. He was surprised she didn't withdraw it. Then he kissed her.

She slapped him playfully.

'Tommy will have something to say about that if he finds out.'

'I thought you said you weren't his girl,' he said. She just giggled.

He looked into the lake. His hand shook with excitement as he held her. He didn't want her to see he was nervous but she probably knew he was anyway. Maybe she was flattered.

She put her arms round him. A car passed by. The driver honked his horn. Was it someone who knew them? Brian didn't know. They were always doing that if they saw a boy and girl together. It annoyed him.

'Why don't we go to Broomfield?' he said.

It was where he played football sometimes. At this time of night he knew they'd have privacy there. Jennifer didn't seem to know if she wanted to go or not. He could see her eyes drooping. She looked beautiful in the moonlight. He wondered if he was falling in love with her. Maybe he'd been in love with her without knowing it since the first time he saw her.

They walked up the hill. There was a tennis court on the other side of it. Nobody had played on it for years. There was grass growing up through the tarmac.

They came to a field that had goalposts on it. There was a ball in the goal. Jennifer kicked it but it was hard and it hurt her foot. She let out a scream. Then she fell down laughing. Brian threw himself down beside her. She let him feel her breasts. Then they started kissing. She moved under him on the grass. He opened her blouse. She smiled as he undid the buttons. He couldn't believe she was letting him. He lay on top of her. She was still kissing him. He felt dizzy all over. He didn't know what was happening to him.

'What's wrong with you?' she said, 'Do you not like me?'

She got out from under him.

'Of course I do,' he said. 'I'm just a bit dizzy.'

He rolled over on his side. The sky suddenly seemed far away. The clouds were gone but the night was getting darker.

'Would you prefer it to be Tommy instead of me that was with you?' he asked her.

'Tommy has B.O.'

'He thinks he's the cheese.'

'He can think what he likes. I'd run a mile from him.'

He put his arms around her as they lay on the ground. After a few minutes he found himself nodding off. She fell asleep too.

He didn't know how long it was before he woke up. He looked up at the sky. The clouds were darker. He thought it might rain. The weather had got much colder.

He stood up. She opened her eyes.

'You look funny, she said.

'I drank more than I thought. My head feels as if there's a drill inside it.'

'I'm freezing,' she said, 'Get me something, will you?'

There was a changing room beside them. He wasn't sure if it would be open or not.

'Try it,' she said, 'I'd kill for a blanket.'

He walked over to it. The door opened. It was a tiny dressing-room. He got as stale smell from it, a smell of sweat and unwashed clothes. He saw a piece of tarpaulin beside one of the lockers. He took it out to her.

'Good yourself,' she said, 'Just what the doctor ordered.'

He lay down beside her. It wasn't big enough to go over the two of them.

'This is no good,' she said.

'You take it. I'm not cold.'

'Liar.'

She saw a car on the road about ten yards from them.

'Look,' she said, 'That might do.'

'It's probably locked. Or maybe there's someone in it.'

'You're an awful pessimist.'

They went over to it. She looked inside. There was no one there. Then she tried the back door. It opened.

'See?' she said, 'You don't know everything.'

She got into the back seat. He sat in beside her. He felt he was going to fall asleep again.

He looked out the window. The moon was racing through the clouds. He enjoyed looking up at it. He'd never been out this late before. He wondered if he'd have been missed.

She smiled at him.

'Do you like being with me?' she said.

'Of course.'

'You're a man now.'

He felt she was making fun of him.

'Can I see you again?' he said.

'What do you mean? Are you asking me for a date?'

'If I am, will you come on it?'

She laughed again. Did that mean yes or no? He didn't know how he'd be with her the next time he saw her. It was different when you were alone with someone than when they were in a crowd. Most likely she'd be in Priory Grove surrounded by all the other girls from the convent. He wouldn't be able to talk to her if that was the case. His mouth would dry up.

'I'll see you at Mass tomorrow,' she said.

'That's a funny place for a date.'

'Are you saying you won't come?'

'Of course not.'

She sat up.

'I'm going to go home now,' she said, 'Will you walk me, Sir Lancelot?'

Her eyes were droopy. She fell back on the seat.

'Do you know what time it is?' he said.

'Is that all you can think of? Were you not excited by me?'

He didn't know how to reply. He felt she was out of his league. He blamed Tommy and the whiskey.

He looked at her. Her hair was in her eyes. He parted it. She smiled.

'Thank you,' she said.

He smelt the leather of the car, the wet grass of the dawn.

'I could stay here forever,' he said.

'Me too. At least if I didn't have a mother who's probably got the police out looking for me at this stage.'

She started laughing. She laughed so much she fell off the seat onto the floor. Brian dropped down beside her. The two of them lay squashed in a heap.

'We'll choke if we don't get up,' she said.

They sat up. Her hair was back in her eyes. Her dress was crumpled too. She straightened it.

He looked at himself in the car mirror. His eyes were bloodshot.

'Let's go, partner,' she said.

They got out of the car. They walked down the hill and onto the street. They passed by the garage and the sweet shop. He was dragging his feet. Everything was an effort. His head was still throbbing.

They turned onto Leafwood Lane. That was where she lived. He'd have given anything to go in with her. Imagine if there was nobody there except the two of them. It would be too much to hope for. He wanted to marry her and have children and live all the days of his life with her.

Her house was the last one on the street. It was in darkness. She started to walk more quickly as they got close to it.

'What's your hurry?' he said.

'I don't want my parents to see me. If I'm lucky they'll be asleep.'

'Of course they're asleep. If they weren't they'd be lights on.'

'You'd never know,' she said. 'If Daddy sees you there'll be hell to pay.'

He wanted to kiss her again but he knew she wouldn't let him.

'Can we go to Broomfield some other time?' he asked her.

'If you're good.'

'I will be.'

She stood on the threshold looking him up and down.

'A lot of people think you're stuck up,' she said.

'I know. It's because I'm shy.'

'You weren't too shy tonight.'

He didn't know what to say to that. She stood there enjoying his awkwardness. Then she gave him a peck on the cheek.

'You better go,' she said, 'It's bedtime for young boys.' She put her hands under her head to mimic a child asleep. Then she was gone.

He couldn't remember going back to the farm. He woke up hours later wondering if his time with her had really happened. He was a man now, as she said. Or was he? Maybe he was only a boy pretending to be a man.

He heard the peal of a church bell. It was Sunday, He remembered her saying she'd see him at Mass. His head was still throbbing. He dressed himself.

The floorboards on the stairs creaked as he went down the stairs. Why did they always do that when you stepped lightly on them? They seemed to make more noise when you walked slowly on them than if you raced down.

He opened the door. He put the key in the lock from the outside so he could close it gently. He got the bus to Loughrea. When it reached the terminus he walked to the church.

Mass was about to begin when he got there. He knelt down. The priest came out. It was Fr. Finnerty. He started praying. Brian tried to concentrate but he couldn't.

The sermon was about chastity. He thought Fr. Finnerty was looking at him as he gave it. Was it being directed at him? Maybe it was. But then he talked about chastity most Sundays.

After a few minutes he felt someone tapping him on the shoulder. It was Tommy. He was grinning. He was always grinning

'Did you do the bold thing last night?' he said.

'What are you talking about?'

'I heard about you and Jennifer. I knew it was a bad idea leaving you two alone.'

Brian felt he was bluffing. He moved away from him to one of the other seats. Tommy kept staring at him.

When it came to the Communion Brian stayed in his seat. Tommy came over to him.

'Why are you not receiving the body of Christ?' she said.

'Shut up,' he said. Tommy laughed.

'Did you save any whiskey for me?' he said Brian didn't answer him.

The Mass went on. Brian looked around him at the other people in the church. It was mostly old people who were there. Most of them had grey hair. Or no hair. He yawned. He thought he was about to fall asleep again.

Finally Fr. Finnerty said, 'The Mass is ended, go forth in peace.'

Tommy said, 'Thanks be to God.'

They left the church.

Brian saw Jennifer at the railings. Her parents were with her. They looked like bodyguards. He waved to her but she didn't wave back. A few moments later she went off. He wondered if she'd told them anything. He thought they were looking at him strangely.

Tommy was gone. He started to walk home. It was a fine day. The sun had come out. He went across the bridge and up the street that ran parallel to the lake. Everyone around him seemed to be looking at him. The sun stung his eyes.

He walked as slowly as he could, dragging his steps to delay the moment when he got home. What would he do for the rest of the day? Would he be thinking of her? Would she be thinking of him? Would he still be attracted to her?

Tommy appeared from nowhere. He dug him in the ribs.

'It's Lucozade for you from now on,' he said.

Brian tried to laugh but he couldn't. He felt empty inside. He didn't know why. It was as if something magical had been disappeared from his life.

3

School continued to be dull. He did all the things he'd done up to now but without conviction. The teachers told him he was living in a dream world. He was hardly bothered by that. He didn't think he was missing much.

When he got close to the Leaving Cert he became tense. Life seemed to be closing in. He felt his childhood was gone. He blamed his father for a lot of that. People whose fathers drank grew up too fast.

One day Tommy Glynn said to him, 'Your old man is a drunkard.' Brian hit him. He didn't think it was in him to do something like that. Blood spurted out of him. He didn't retaliate. Maybe bullies were always like that. In the past he'd shied away from fights with Tommy even though he told Jennifer he didn't. It was a watershed for him.

He didn't feel he owed his father any loyalty. When he thought about it, Bartley had never done much for him. He was closer to Declan, Brian's older brother.

He could never confide in him about things. He looked bored if he ever talked to him about things that were worrying him. His mother was different. She listened to everything he said. Bartley thought she mollycoddled him.

'He's not a baby any more,' he'd say to her, 'Why do you treat him like one?'

'Life is hard,' she'd reply, 'Why make it worse?'

Brian lay awake at night sometimes trying to work out his future. What was he going to do after he left school? His mother still hoped he was going to be a priest. Some other people thought it too. They tended to say that about anyone who was quiet. He didn't think he had a vocation. He wasn't even sure what a vocation was.

15

He asked Fr Finnerty once. 'It's just a feeling that you'd like to be a priest,' he said. That didn't solve the issue one way or the other for him. It left him scratching his head.

Religion dominated his house. There was a statue of the Little Child of Prague on the mantel-piece in the living-room in the living-room and one of the Sacred Heart on the stairs. It always made him nervous. In fact religion in general did that. If he decided to be a priest he thought it would have been more from duty than anything else. He wouldn't have wanted to disappoint his mother.

'Maybe I'll become a social worker,' he told people. It was like a concession, a way of making up to her, a second best.

After Declan left the college he started dating a girl called Yvonne. They'd met at a tennis social and got serious fast. They saw each other almost every night. Brian hardly missed him. They'd never had much to say to one another. Declan enjoyed needling him the same way Tommy Glynn did. He picked on him for stupid things.

But he liked Yvonne. She always made something of him. 'Why are you so mean to Brian?' she'd said to Declan. 'Because he's an idiot,' he'd say.

They got engaged after a few months going out together and married a few months after that. It was a lavish affair, too lavish for Brian's liking. He filled himself up with whiskey to get through it, drinking more than he'd ever done. Bartley got drunk too. That was less surprising.

They moved to Newbridge after the wedding. Declan was working in a computer firm there. He bought shares in it and moved up the ladder fast. He had a quick mind for deal-making. Bartley admired that in him. He wanted Brian to be more like him. He tried to get him to follow Declan into the firm but Brian wasn't interested. He said he'd prefer to stay on the farm.

Declan used to drive the family car when Bartley wasn't using it. It was an Austin. It only moved when you coaxed it. Brian started driving it after Declan left home. He spent most of his time in it, driving it along the back roads of Loughrea to get the hang of it. He even drove it across the fields if he was out inspecting the cattle.

'You'll be bringing it up to bed with you yet,' Bartley said.

Sometimes he brought Rusty into it with him. That was his dog. He used to sit him in the passenger seat and speak to him as if he was a person. Rusty always barked at him when he did that, wagging his tail wildly. Bartley didn't like Rusty being in the car because he got his hairs all over the seats when he was shedding. Brian thought Bartley was hard on him most of the time. Like the Austin, he was getting on in years. He wasn't as good at herding sheep as he used to be. The sheep were gone now anyway. He wasn't even good as a watchdog anymore according to Bartley. 'If he saw an intruder,' he said, 'He'd probably run the other way.'

When Brian was in his Leaving Cert year he got serious with Jennifer. She'd left Loughrea to do teacher training in Limerick after doing the Leaving Cert. Brian still had a year of school to finish.

A lot of their dates at that time took place over the phone.

'You should marry her in the telephone exchange,' Bartley said.

People had them pegged for marriage almost from the time they met. It was like a foregone conclusion when people talked about them. Brian didn't like that kind of talk. It led to conversations about jobs and houses, the kind of conversations that wore him down. Most of the married people he knew seemed to lose their jizz after they went up the aisle. A lot of them were also in trouble with mortgage repayments. They were trapped in jobs they hated trying to keep up with them. Some of them had been living together before they got married. He couldn't understand why they didn't go on as they were. It didn't make sense to him.

He didn't know if he wanted to marry Jennifer or not. It was nothing against her, just his fear of commitment. He didn't like being tied to things. He envied people who knew what they wanted in life, people who moved in a straight line from school to career to having children. He wasn't like that. He'd always been confused, even about the simplest of things. He'd go into a room and forget why he was there. Or he'd start to say something and then stop suddenly as if it didn't matter.

'You'd forget your head if it wasn't stuck onto you,' Bartley used to say to him, the old cliché.

His own world was straightforward. His view of Brian was straightforward too. 'If he married Jennifer,' he often said, 'he could move to Newbridge and get something going with Declan.'

Brian's mother didn't like it when Bartley picked on him.

'Leave him alone,' she'd say, 'He'll make his decisions in his own time. Why are you putting so much pressure on him?'

'I'm not. He's putting pressure on himself. Look at him. Is that the face of a happy boy?'

He didn't want to live in Loughrea forever. It was too dead for him. Everyone knew everyone's business because the population was so small. The young people made off for Galway in increasing number each passing year. The tourist industry was almost non-existent. Most of the visitors to the area were people visiting their relatives. 'Tourists here,' Bartley liked to say, 'are optical illusions.'

The people who stayed tended to follow in the footsteps of their fathers. They married someone known to the family and settled down to a predictable life. You could almost set your watch by their activity at a given time of the day. They etched out their lives without stress, content to be exactly what they were. Many of them may have harboured ambitions to buy a house off the main road or to send their children away to college. Others just took each day for itself and made do. When they met in the bars it was the evils of materialism they discussed, the fact that it was harder for a rich man to get to heaven than for a camel to pass through the eye of a needle.

Sometimes an unusually bright student got a scholarship. Whenever that happened, Brian thought, there was resentment. It was as if he was getting ideas above his station.

Brian had got enough points in the Leaving Cert to go to university but he didn't. He stayed put. Bartley wanted him to move to Newbridge to work with Declan. He got fed up of his nagging about that.

'I'd sooner fly to Mars,' he said to him. Bartley snapped back, 'Then you might as well stay on the farm.'

He wasn't sure he wanted that either. It was all right to pass the time but he couldn't conceive of a lifetime at it. A lot of the time his concentration drifted, just like it did in the college. If he was milking the cows or saving hay it might be a million miles away. Bartley wasn't able to understand that and Brian didn't talk to him about it. He talked to his mother but she didn't really understand what his problem was either. By now she'd given up on her dream of him being a priest. She tried to console him by telling him that everyone was restless in some way, that very few people were totally happy in their jobs. He accepted that. He told her he'd continue doing what he was doing until something better came along. The fact that she spoke kindly to him helped him deal with his restlessness.

'That's the best idea,' she said, 'None of us knows what's around the corner.'

Her words were prophetic. One day not long afterwards without any warning she fell down in the kitchen. She had a pain in her leg for a while but she'd played it down. She did that with all the things that went wrong with her health over the years. She was a strong woman but she'd never taken care of herself. She'd had a mastectomy one year and a hysterectomy two years later. Both of the operations she seemed to regard as minor inconveniences.

She acted like this was another triviality but Brian feared it wasn't. Despite spending the rest of the day in bed the leg swelled up like a balloon.

'It's nothing,' she said when she saw the worried look on his face. Bartley got concerned too. They wanted her to call the doctor but she refused. She carried on doing her work around the house. But later that night she fell in her bedroom, narrowly avoiding gashing her head on a bedside lamp. Bartley was with her at the time.

'That's it,' he said, 'We're bringing you down to A&E whether you like

18

it or not.'

Grudgingly she agreed. She was in bad humour as they led her out to the car a half hour later.

'Leave me alone,' she said, 'The pair of two are treating me like a cripple.'

They sat into the Austin. It came to life after a few turns of the ignition. It coughed and spluttered as they drove to the hospital. It sounded like it was about to give up at any moment but it still kept going somehow.

'It's great old beast,' she said, 'It'll see us all down.' She'd often compared it to a human thing, doing its best against the odds.

'They don't make them like that anymore,' she said.

'It's you that's the problem now,' Bartley rasped, 'not the car.'

'I don't know what you're on about,' she said, 'I wish I hadn't agreed to come with you in the first place. If you left me alone I'd have been fine.'

They got to the hospital. Bartley took her in as Brian parked. The A&E ward was packed. Many of the patients were in a bad way. One man was bleeding from the head. He had a motorbike helmet beside him.

'Is there any healthy person in this blessed town?' Bartley said.

Brian came in a few minutes later. Because it was Saturday he felt they'd be there a long time. The doctors were giving priority to the emergency cases.

He watched his mother looking at them all. He knew she'd have more interest in their diagnoses than her own. Maybe that was why she was here tonight, he thought. It pained him to think of the near-impregnable body she'd been given, how she'd let it get to the condition it was in now.

She grimaced at one stage when she went to cross her legs. It was so unusual to see her doing that.

'Why did you not have this dealt with before now?' Bartley said, a sudden anger rising in him. He was slow to see things but when he did, he became fiery.

'I didn't think it was anything,' she said tamely.

It was midnight before an intern appeared. His hair was mussed. He looked as if he'd just got out of bed. He was a good-looking man, one of the junior doctors. To Brian he looked like he wasn't long out of school. If he'd chosen another career path, he thought, he'd probably have been at a party tonight instead of spending it in a manic A&E unit listening to the groans of people in pain.

He put on a look of high importance as he examined her. Brian and Bartley were told to wait some distance away. When he was ready he summoned them over.

'It's not a clot,' he said.

Bartley gave him a rueful smile.

'I don't know much about medicine,' he said, 'but even an idiot could see her leg is like a rock.'

'It's probably fluid retention,' he said, 'That often has the same effect.'

'I don't agree,' Bartley said, 'I want a second opinion.'

'We could get that,' he said, 'but not tonight. It's mad here. I have a man in the next room that we're about to bring down to theatre. It's a bad time.'

'What time would suit you for her to have a relapse?' Bartley said. 'I can see your eyes are falling out of your head. How can you give her a proper appraisal?'

'I'm sorry that's the way you feel about it. We can run some tests on her if you like. She could have an ECG.'

'There's nothing wrong with her heart.'

'You'll have to be patient. Whatever it is we'll get to the bottom of it. I have to go now.'

Before he went away he put her down for a more thorough examination the following Monday. They left the hospital in a daze.

4

She had a good weekend. Maybe that was the worst thing that could have happened to her. Brian tried to make a fuss over her but she wouldn't have any of it. Bartley had to go to a mart to sell some cattle so he wasn't there most of the time.

'It was a false alarm,' she said to Brian when he woke her up on the Monday, 'I don't think I'll bother with that old appointment.'

He'd seen her like this often before. She was like a child trying to get out of going to school.

When he looked at her leg it was as stiff as a board.

'You won't be happy until you have yourself destroyed.' he said.

'All right, I'll go,' she grudged, 'but it's a storm in a teacup. Will I be putting you out driving me to the hospital?'

'How can you say something like that?'

'You have your life to be getting on with.'

It pained her to have him leave the work to drive her in. It always pained her to have people do anything for her. She'd have walked to the A&E if her legs were up to it.

When they got to the hospital she told him to stay in the car. He wanted to go in with her but she wouldn't have it.

'You have Bartley's work to do as well as your own,' she said, 'Be off with you now. And tell Bartley not to worry.'

There was no talking to her when she was in a mood like that. She tried to hide her limp as she walked through the swing doors of the hospital but she couldn't. Brian saw the pain on her face.

When he called for her later that evening she was sitting on a bench at the end of the corridor. She was deep in chat with the woman sitting beside her. It had always amazed him, this ability she had to get to the depths of people this soon, to immerse herself this readily in their problems when she had so much to worry about herself.

He sat down beside her.

'This is Maura,' she said, 'She's really been through it.'

He said hello to her. He tried to make small talk but he was never good at that. A doctor came along later a few minutes and took her away.

'Well,' he said to his mother, 'How are you?'

'Good. They think it's a clot all right. That young doctor had another look at it. He thinks something must have developed over the weekend.'

He felt his blood boiling.

'Over the weekend? That's ridiculous.'

'Relax. They seem to have located the problem.'

The doctor appeared a few minutes later. He had an important-looking man with him.

'That's the man who found it,' she said pointing to him.

He stood over Brian.

'Good evening,' he said, 'I'm the consultant. I presume you're Mrs Kilcoyne's son.'

'I am. What's happening?'

'We're taking your mother in.'

The solemnness of his tone seemed to act as a kind of defence against any annoyance he might have been able to show.

'Taking her in?'

'Yes. The situation has become exacerbated since Saturday.'

'What does that mean?'

'She's worse than she was.'

'Yes.'

He knew he was covering for the young doctor beside him.

Brian said, 'It must have been all the dancing she did over the weekend.'

The consultant gave a wry smile. Brian's mother kicked him under the bench.

'I'm sorry if you think we missed anything. She's in good hands now. A bed is being prepared for her. We believe she's in the VHI. Perhaps you could give in her details at the desk.'

He went off.

Brian was ready to explode.

'If you weren't in the VHI,' he said, 'They'd probably have turfed you out on the street. '

'Stop talking like that. It won't do either of us any good.'

'It's true, though, isn't it?'

She gave him a hard stare.

'Why did you insult the doctor?' she said.

'Because he deserved it.'

'I wish you wouldn't embarrass me like that.'

'I'm sorry. I'm boiling mad. If they're all like him we might as well call it quits now.'

'Don't be negative. They're doing their best.'

'He mis-diagnosed you.'

'Maybe it wasn't as bad on Saturday as it is now.'

'Why are you defending him?'

'I have a bed now. That's the main thing. It's really hard to get into a hospital these days with the long waiting lists. Once you're inside the door you're elected. They do a thousand and one tests on you,'

'That's the kind of attitude that has you into this situation in the first place. If you were pushier you'd have been in a ward two nights ago.'

'I don't want to argue with you. Will you tell Bartley what I'm having done?'

'Of course. He's in a state about you.'

It wasn't strictly true. He'd made a few calls but he was too keyed up about the cattle to do any more.

'The poor thing. Tell him not to worry.'

'Okay.'

She went down to the desk and signed in with the secretary. He'd brought her nightdress in the car with him. He went out to the Austin to get it.

'You're an angel,' she said when he came back in, 'How do you think of things like that?'

'Because I know you won't.'

A few minutes later a nurse came out. She had a form in her hand. She sat on the bed.

'Any allergies, Mrs Kilcoyne?' she asked her.

'Hospitals,' she said.

The nurse smiled at Brian.

'I can see we're going to have fun with this one.'

'Oh yes, she's a riot.'

He said goodbye to her. She gave him a kiss.

'I'll be in to see you when you're settled,' he said.

'Don't come in until I get some news.'

When he got outside he rang Bartley on his mobile. He was on the motorway so the signal was bad.

'How did it go in the hospital?' he said.

'There's no news yet.'

'Those gombeens. They couldn't be more stupid if they tried. Have they given her any idea?'

'Not really. They're going to run tests on her.'

'I don't know how that hospital stays open. If I had a penny for all the horror stories I've heard I'd be a millionaire. It's like Fawlty Towers.'

After he put down the phone he went into the café. He tried to read a newspaper that was there but he couldn't concentrate. After a while the nurse came over to him. She told him he could go up and see her.

When he got to the ward she was having her pulse taken. She looked disoriented. She always looked disoriented when she was being waited on. She preferred to do the waiting.

'How are you?' he said.

She brushed the question aside.

'You hear some wicked coughs in here. The women at the end has emphysema.'

He could see the way her stay would develop: Each day she'd have a new story for him about another patient, using anything she could to get the talk away from herself.

'You'd be better off thinking about your clot rather than someone else's emphysema,' he said.

'What can I do about that,' she laughed, 'It's out of my hands now. They'll get to the root of it, don't worry. Is Bartley back from the mart yet?'

'He's on the way.'

'Tell him not to worry about anything.'

'Okay. I'll be in tomorrow.'

'There's no need to.'

'Please don't talk like that.'

'I'm taking over all your lives.'

'If you say that again I'll scream.'

'I hate it when people worry about me. Make sure you get a good night's sleep. And Bartley too.'

5

Bartley was sitting in the kitchen when he got home. He asked him what delayed him at the mart.

'It wasn't the mart that delayed me,' he said, 'I had to stop at a garage on the way back. I need the engine of the tractor re-bored. I know I shouldn't be talking about tractors with what's going on. Sometimes you need things like that you keep you functioning. How is Teresa?'

'They got her a bed.'

'About time. I'm worried about the tests you mentioned.'

'What can we do? She has to have them.'

'So they still don't know what's wrong with her?'

'They think there could be a clot.'

'What? You didn't say anything about that on the phone.'

'I couldn't talk properly. There was static on the line.'

'Fuck it.'

'They didn't say for sure. They're not ruling anything in or out.'

'I have a bad feeling about this.'

'Don't panic. I'm sure she'll be fine.'

Bartley stood up. He walked to the cabinet where he kept his whiskey. He took a slug out of it. It was his medicine for every celebration, every tragedy.

'Did you let them know how you felt?'

'In a way.'

'I want to go in and see her.'

'Don't. She's tired.'

'I want to give them a piece of my mind.'

'Don't do that either. Please.'

'How is she taking it?'

'She's casual enough about it.'

'That's half the problem. She plays everything down.'

'I know. Anyway she's in the right place now. Have your drink and get a good night's sleep.'

'That sounds like her talking.'

'It's what she said to me.'

'She said for me to have a drink?'

'No, the other bit. About the sleep.'

'I feel bad about not being in there. I hope she didn't think I was putting the blasted mart before her.'

'She'd never think that. Stop worrying. Did you sell any cows?'

'I couldn't concentrate. She was in my mind too much.'

The doctors found nothing over the first few days. They seemed to be more interested in getting the swelling down instead of trying to find out what caused it. She was on anti-coagulants now. They spent most of the time taking blood samples from her.

Her arms were as pockmarked as the arms of a drug addict when they went in to see her. She looked like she was getting a fix as she held them out. It was as if a syringe could give only pleasure, not pain.

'What are you going to do when you run out of veins?' she asked a nurse one day.

'Don't worry, Mrs Kilcoyne, you still have some lovely ones left.'

He could see how much they liked her. Why wouldn't they?

At the end of the week they found a shadow on one of the x-rays. Brian was with her at the time. They didn't say anything to her. They called him into a room and told him.

'What does that mean?' he said.

'A tumour,' the doctor said matter-of-factly. His blood froze.

'Do you think it's cancer?' he asked him. It was a word he feared almost as much as the disease itself.

'Possibly. We have no way of knowing until we open her up.'

He didn't go back to her room because he knew he wouldn't be able to hide his shock from her. Instead he drove home.

Bartley was out in the fields when he got there. He drove out to him. He tried to sound hopeful but Bartley got hysterical.

He drove him back to the farm. At one stage he reached into the glove compartment and pulled out a naggin of whiskey. It was one of his many hiding places for it.

'I'm not able for this,' he said as he took a drink from it.

When they got home he sat at the kitchen table drinking the whiskey. He emptied the bottle long before the night was over. Brian tried to stop him but he didn't get anywhere.

'We should keep our strength for her,' he said.

Bartley wasn't listening. He was locked away in some inner world.

They visited her the following day. A decision to talk of other things than health had to be abandoned when she greeted them with the words, 'The consultant told me about the tumour.'

Neither of them knew what to say. She looked at Bartley.

'Have you been drinking?' she said.

She made him come closer to her so she could smell his breath.

'You have, you rascal. I suppose you're using me as an excuse.'

'Didn't I always?' he said, putting on a childish grin.

She sat up in the bed. Bartley put a pillow behind her head. She looked at Brian.

'Why the worried face?' she said.

'They might have to take your kidney out.'

'I know.'

'Are you not bothered?'

'I can function perfectly on one.'

She said she didn't want to talk about it. She asked them about the farm, plying them with a series of questions. Were the cattle well? How did Bartley get on at the mart?

The conversation turned to Declan afterwards. Brian had been on the phone to him. He hoped to get up to see her if work cooled down. There was always pressure there.

25

'I wish he wouldn't,' she said, 'but I know I can't stop him.'

'Stop fretting about him,' Bartley said, 'You need to wind down. You're facing a serious operation. Don't wear yourself out thinking about stupid things.'

'They're not stupid. They keep me going.'

He didn't talk for the rest of the visit. She knew he wanted to get away. When a nurse came in to take her blood pressure she saw an opportunity to end the visit.

'You can go now,' she said to them, 'They don't like it when people are here when they have work to do.'

He was quiet on the way home in the car. He was annoyed with himself that he hadn't made a point of asking someone official about her.

'I think I'll go back,' he said to Bartley, 'I need to talk to one of the head bottle washers about her.'

'You've talked to them already. They won't be able to say anymore until they operate on her.'

'I don't care. I want to go back.'

They were passing the pub Bartley usually drank in. He stopped the car.

'Why don't you go in and have a pint,' he said, 'I'll be back in no time.'

Bartley agreed. Brian felt he would. He'd never seen him turn down a chance to go into a pub.

He doubled back to the hospital. When he got there he asked the nurse on duty to page the surgeon.

'He's run off his feet,' she said, 'His own wife can't even get through to him.'

But not too long afterwards she said, 'You're lucky. He's in the next ward.'

He came in after a few minutes.

'Well, Mr Kilcoyne,' he said, 'What can I do for you?'

'I'd like to know some more about what's happening to my mother.'

'We've told you everything.'

'What are the chances the operation will be a success?'

'100%,' he said, 'at least if we get the whole tumour.' There was always a catch.

'Why wouldn't you be able to?'

'A part of it may have invaded the artery going to the heart. We won't be able to touch it if it has.'

That put a new complexion on things.

'Were you not going to tell me that unless I asked?'

'There are complications with every operation. It's better not to worry people.'

'I don't understand that. What if something went wrong on the

26

operating table?'

'That wouldn't happen. I won't operate if I can't.'

'If you don't, is there a Plan B?'

'What do you mean – chemotherapy?'

'I don't know. You're the doctor.'

'Let's meet that bridge when we come to it.'

'If you don't operate, how long will she live?'

'I can't answer that question.'

'What if you didn't operate at all?'

'That wouldn't make sense. As far as we can see she has no secondaries.'

'Are you sure of that?'

'As sure as anyone can be,' he said. He was tempted to say, 'As sure as the intern of last Saturday night?'

Bartley was sitting at the counter when he got back to the pub. He could see he was well on.

'Well,' he said looking up from his drink, 'How did you get on?'

'I asked him as many questions as I could think of. He's hopeful the operation will be a success.' There was no point in saying anything else.

'Obviously. So you went all the way back just to hear that? Why didn't you grill him more? I should have gone with you.'

'That wouldn't have been a good idea. You get too worked up.'

There was a time he wouldn't have been able to say something like that to him but he took it.

'When are you going to ring Declan?' he said then.

'There's no point worrying him unless we have to.'

'You're right. I envy you your clear head. It's like you're the father and I'm the son.'

'I don't know about that. I'm just about holding myself together.'

She was due to have her operation the following day. They talked about trivial things to try and keep their minds off it. Bartley prayed and drank. He had a rosary beads in one hand and a bottle of Jameson in the other.

Brian rang Jennifer to tell her what was happening.

'Please give her my best,' she said, 'And your father as well. Let me know if there's anything I can do.'

'I know you're always there for me. It means a lot.'

He phoned Declan then.

'When is the op?' he said.

'Tomorrow morning.'

'I didn't know it was that soon. I was hoping to get up for it but that cuts it a bit tight. What's the prognosis?'

'Nobody is saying much. They're keeping their hands close to their chest. At the end of the day they don't know any more than we do until they open her up.'

'We've been thinking about her all day. Yvonne is hoarse saying prayers.'

'So is Dad.'

'I was on to him last night. He sounds in a bad way with the gargle.'

'In another way it's keeping him going.'

'Thanks for calling me. How are you feeling yourself?'

'Trying not to think. '

'It's the only way.'

6

It was almost dawn before Brian closed an eye that night. Soon afterwards the alarm went off. When he went in to call Bartley he found him sitting up in bed staring at the wall. For once he wasn't drinking. There was a bottle of whiskey beside the bed but it hadn't been touched.

'I was afraid to start it in case I finished it,' he said.

They didn't speak on the journey to the hospital. When they got there they went into the oratory to say a prayer. Brian tried to bribe God to make her well. That was what his prayers consisted of now. Bartley sat with his hands clenched.

As they walked towards the operating theatre He avoided the lines on the panelled floor. It was a kind of superstition to charm the fates. When they got to the waiting area beside the theatre a nurse gave them a cup of tea. Bartley's hands shook as he drank it. On any other morning Brian would have thought it was the DTs but today it was fear, naked fear. His own fears he kept locked inside him. If he let them out he was afraid of where they'd go.

The morning was endless. One cup of tea led to another. They drank it without tasting it. It was just something to have in their hands. The clock on the wall ticked like a metronome, inching its way towards a reprieve or bad news.

He tried to tell himself the operation would be a success but it didn't work. He was never much good at optimism. Expecting the worst, he thought, gave a situation more respect. If he worried enough he believed he could make bad things go away.

But when the surgeon came out of the theatre he only had to take one look at him to know his worrying didn't do any good this time.

'It's bad,' he said, 'It's very bad.'

Brian started to shake. Bartley looked like a ghost. He tried to say something but the words wouldn't come out.

The surgeon had his mask in his hand. He threw it on the table like you would a worthless cloth.

'The tumour was too big,' he said.

He hit the table with his fist.

'It was that hard,' he said, 'We just opened and closed her.'

Brian felt he was going to throw up but then the nausea went away and he became almost relaxed. He had nothing to hope for now.

'So you didn't remove the tumour,' he said. As he spoke it seemed the words were coming from outside himself, that someone else was saying them.

'She would have haemorrhaged if I did. She'd have died on the table. I'm sure of it. I'm sorry.'

He slumped down in his chair. The clouds started to part for him, the picture widen into a casual finality. He thought of how radiant she'd looked in the first few days after she was admitted, how ridiculously healthy she looked for a woman in her condition. What absurdity was there in the world that you could be eaten alive with cancer and still look that good? Anyone could have it.

He remembered the way she'd get one kidney infection after another, occasionally a flow of blood. So that was what was behind it. The old problem returned for revenge sixteen years after her original mastectomy. A decade after the supposed danger of recurrence period.

'So there's nothing more you can do for her,' he said, words that had to be said even though he knew the answer to them.

The surgeon didn't answer. He just looked at the ground.

'How long has she got?' Bartley asked.

'That I can't tell you,' he said. 'It depends on too many things. I would advise you to make the most of her while you have her.'

'So you're not going to put a time on it.'

'I don't have a crystal ball. She might go on for quite a while.'

It was the cushioner that would have come with all the years of being the harbinger of grim revelations. How many families had he given this kind of news to, Brian wondered. Had he developed a pattern of how he'd say it, leading in with the brutal part and then leavening it a bit?

Bartley was more angry.

'You've stitched her up without doing anything,' he said.

'I'm afraid so,' the surgeon said, 'She's basically the same as she was before the operation. But there'll be a reaction to her having been opened up. Once the air gets at cancer it can play havoc with it.'

'Can we see her?' Bartley asked.

'You'd be better off waiting till tomorrow. She's asleep now.'

The clock kept ticking. It seemed louder. How many more hours would it give her? How many more days?

'I'm really sorry,' the surgeon said, 'I wanted to do my best for her but

I couldn't. My hands were tied.'

He put those same hands out now in a gesture of hopelessness. He looked genuinely upset.

There was nothing more to say. He walked away.

A nurse came over to where they were sitting.

'She's such a lovely lady,' she said. She had tears in her eyes.

She offered them more tea but they didn't hear her. They just sat there in the silence. Time stood still. The clock kept ticking but nothing changed. Nobody moved. Brian felt his mind going blank. It was like a protection. He wanted to cry but he couldn't.

It was a long time before they stood up. There was nobody around them now. They walked to the exit. Bartley was staggering.

They got to the car. His hands were shaking as he started the ignition. Bartley took the whiskey bottle from the glove compartment again. Brian didn't grudge it to him this time. He had a drink of it too.

'I don't know if I'm going to be able to face her,' Bartley said, 'What will we tell her?'

'As little as possible,' Brian said, 'What she doesn't know won't hurt her. Let's play it by ear for the moment. She mightn't want to know anything.'

Bartley rang Declan when they got back to the house. He let his tears out now. The call ended in under a minute.

He drove up from Newbridge the next morning in his Skoda. Brian and Bartley were sitting in the kitchen when he arrived. He didn't say anything as he came in. He hugged Bartley for a long time. Then he hugged Brian.

The three of them spent the morning in a daze. Conversations were reduced to a minimum. They drank endless cups of tea and cried. There was laughter in the middle of the tears as they recounted stories about her. Each of them had a different one than the others.

'We're talking about her as if she's already gone,' Brian said at one point, 'Let's not do that.'

In the afternoon they went back to the hospital. Declan drove to give Brian a break. He insisted in bringing the Skoda. When they got to the ward she was sitting up. She didn't seem to recognise them. She started fidgeting at the tubes that were coming out of her.

'Well Mam,' Declan said, 'You look great as usual.'

She stared at him without saying anything.

He said a few more things to her about how his job was going but she didn't respond. Then he went over and put his arms around her. She didn't respond to that either.

He gestured to Brian that he wanted to see him outside. They walked out to the corridor. When they got around a corner he said, 'What the fuck is going on?'

'I don't know. Maybe the surgery caused the tumour to get worse.'

'Who told you that?'

'No one. I read it somewhere.'

'She's like a different person.'

'We'll have to take it for what it is.'

'What's going to happen to Dad?'

'Dad is the last thing on my mind now.'

Over the next few days she stayed the same. Nothing came out of her except babble. She repeated things that were said to her like a child. One morning after waking up she said, 'I dreamt I was in Spain.' When he asked her to tell him about the dream she just looked at him.

Most of the time she sat there motionless. She looked drugged. The nurse said she was on a lot of pills. Sometimes she started to talk and stopped in mid-sentence. Anytime she was asked a question she looked puzzled, uncertain what it meant. It was draining for them all to have to watch her like this.

But then one day she came back to herself. They knew as soon as they looked at her.

'What happened to me?' she said.

She was confused, unaware of how much time had elapsed since the operation took place. Brian felt elated even though he felt it was an illusion. He thought the recovery would only be the postponement of a later relapse.

'They cured your cancer,' Bartley said, 'They got it all out.' She nodded vaguely. Then she said, 'That old cancer.' It was as if it was a human thing, a kind of trivial nuisance you swatted out of the way every now and then.

Declan asked her how she felt.

'Like a new woman,' she said. It had always been her answer to every question no matter what condition she was in. 'I can't believe you came all the way up from Newbridge just to see me. How is Yvonne?'

'Fine. She's killed asking about you.'

'I love Yvonne.'

Nobody mentioned anything about how slow she'd been to come out of the anaesthetic, about how she'd been raving. Brian wondered what she might have suspected.

She was almost proud as she showed them all the scar that ran across her stomach.

'Look at that,' she said, 'a straight line.'

Brian thought of the surgeon opening and closing her. It was like you'd open and close a handbag, running the zip across.

'He has a wonderful skill,' she said, 'He should have been a tailor.'

'How are things with you all?' she said then, 'How is the house?'

'Believe it or not it's still standing,' Bartley said. 'Despite three destructive individuals inhabiting it.'

'Are you eating well?'

'Like horses. We're looking forward to having you home.'

'They better let me out soon or I'll be climbing the walls. I hate being cooped up. I'm dying for a smoke.'

'No more cigarettes for you, missus,' Bartley said, 'Those days are gone.'

'Don't worry. I'll find a way to sneak a few when you're not looking.'

'Do that and I'll have you back here in five minutes.'

The days went by with no change. They were in and out to her all the time. Sometimes Jennifer went with them. She was devastated. Yvonne rang every night. She cried into the phone.

Very little work was done on the farm. Nobody talked much. They walked in and out of rooms without knowing where they were going. Even Rusty looked as if he knew something was wrong. He sat quietly by the fireside, occasionally yelping in his sleep. Arguments erupted over the slightest things. They all seemed to be looking for someone to blame that things had got to this.

Brian confided his fears for the future to Jennifer. She consoled him, telling him not to let his imagination go into overdrive, to just stay in the moment. That was easier said than done.

His mother didn't ask anything about the operation afterwards. She was too intelligent not to suspect something happened but she didn't enquire what. She spent most of the time talking about the farm, asking them the kinds of questions she always had about 'the three strong men in my life.' They felt far from that now.

For a while everything seemed normal. They talked to her as if they were sitting in the kitchen together instead of the spectral silence of this terminal cancer ward.

Then one day as Brian sat by her bed she shattered that illusion.

'How are you getting on with Jennifer?' she said.

'What do you mean? We're still as tight as we ever were if that's what you mean.'

'Do you not think of settling down with her?'

'We talk about it all the time. No doubt it will happen some day. We're a bit young yet. Why do you ask?'

'Bartley and Declan think you're too dependent on me.'

'What's that got to do with anything?'

'I'm not going to be around forever, you know.'

Her words shocked him. Had she been told about what happened to her? Or what didn't happen?

'I wish you wouldn't talk about things like that.'

'I'm talking about them because I've had an operation. And because I'm no spring chicken.'

'You can live to be ninety if you mind yourself.'

'That's enough about that,' she said, 'Let's talk about something else now. You haven't any news for me at all these days.'

He tried to be natural with her but he couldn't. He was shaking now with anger as much as fear.

'You're tired,' she said after a few minutes, 'Go home now. Don't think about things too much. That always tires you. You need to give your mind a rest.'

After he left the ward he had the surgeon paged again. It was the same nurse who did it. She didn't talk to him this time.

He arrived as quickly as the last time. When he saw him he looked tense.

'Come into my room, please,' he said.

They sat down. He was different now to the day he'd done the operation. The compassion he showed then was gone.

Brian went straight into it.

'Did you tell her how sick she was?' he said. .

'Yes.'

'Why?'

'She asked me a straight question and I gave her a straight answer.'

'So what was the question – was she dying?'

It was a few seconds before he replied.

'Yes.'

He felt like hitting him.

'It was the hope that was keeping her going.'

'That's a matter of conjecture.'

He stood up. He went over to where he was sitting.

'You bastard,' he said.

He gave a kind of smile. He said, 'I'd ask you to watch your language if you don't mind.'

'I'll use whatever language I want.'

'It's hospital policy to be frank with our patients. The day your mother was admitted she told me she'd been smoking since she was five. She's done rather well to get to the age she is. She knows that. In fact she said it to me one day.'

He stormed out of the room. He felt his heart going a mile a minute as he drove home. He wanted to write a letter of complaint to the hospital. Was life this discardable? Were people's feelings less important than 'hospital policy'?

He didn't tell Bartley about his conversation. He knew he'd have been tempted to go up to him and punch the surgeon's lights out.

His mother was a different woman in the following days. Her energy level was depleted she barely roused herself to speak to any of them now. The pounds fell off her. Her wedding ring became loose on her finger. She couldn't keep food down.

Brian went into the hospital a few times every day. He sat by her bed doing little but changing her oxygen mask. Jennifer was usually with him. Declan got emotional every time he saw her so he didn't go in much. 'I can't take it,' he said. Bartley was too out of it to visit her. He was drunk almost all of the time now, the whiskey his comfort blanket. On every visit she asked Brian how he was. Sometimes she fell asleep as they talked. She drifted in and out of consciousness.

One night a call came from the hospital telling them she was sinking. They'd been expecting it for some time now. There was no reason to hope for anything else. Bartley was drunk on the sofa. He had to be led to the car.

Brian drove. They didn't talk on the journey. Declan was breathing fast. He held on to Bartley trying to sober him up.

There was no parking space in the car park when they got there. Brian ran the car onto a grass verge. A security man approached them as they got out.

'You can't do that,' he said, 'I'll clamp you.'

They ran up the stairs to her ward. Bartley was gasping heavily. A nurse led them to her bed. Her face was in shadow. It was half under a pillow. The light of the moon shone in on it.

Brian sat on the end of the bed. Bartley clung onto the end of it for support. Declan was on the point of tears. 'Mam,' he said but she didn't respond.

They put Bartley sitting on a chair.

She looked at them quizzically for a moment. Then she closed her eyes. Declan said to the nurse, 'What should we do?' She said, 'I don't know.'

They sat there wondering what to do. The moon disappeared behind a cloud. The nurse came over and fixed her pillow.

Now and then she opened her eyes. She smiled faintly. Brian wanted to hold her hand but it was swollen. The nurse said it was from the injections.

She opened her eyes again.

'I must be bad when you're all here together,' she said.

Brian tried to smile at her. He said, 'You'll be fine.' Declan couldn't speak. Bartley got up out of the chair and hugged her. 'I love you, Teresa,' he said.

The nurse came over. 'It's better if you stay in the chair,' she said. She got a second chair for Brian.

The minutes ticked on. She was breathing heavily. Then she fell asleep. She started to snore. Bartley sobered up. Declan was still crying but trying to hide it. 'It doesn't matter,' Brian said to him, 'She can't see you.' He sensed she was fading away from them.

She stopped snoring. She even seemed to stop breathing. Brian jumped up. He went over to the nurse. She came over and felt her pulse. She looked up at a monitor.

It was a long time before she spoke.

'I'm afraid she's gone,' she said.

'Don't say that,' Declan said to her.

Bartley dug his fingers into the pillow. He kept saying, 'I love you, I love you.' Declan put his head in his hands.

Brian didn't cry. He was full of a kind of abstract shock. He'd been preparing for this moment from the day she entered the hospital. He told himself he'd be able to deal with it but he knew now he couldn't. All he could do was pretend it didn't happen, that she was just asleep again.

Her face was serene. He kept looking at its purity, its innocence.

Bartley hugged her. He buried his face in the pillow. Declan recovered his composure. 'It's all right, Dad,' he said, lifting Bartley away from her, 'It's all right.'

The nurse was crying. 'I can't tell you how sorry I am,' she said.

Bartley and Declan went over to a seat. Brian sat apart from them. They were saying things to one another through their tears. He couldn't make out the words.

He started to hyperventilate. The nurse asked him if there was anything she could do for him.

'I need some air,' he said.

He walked down the ward. Declan disengaged himself from Bartley.

'Where are you going?'

'I can't breathe.'

He went down the stairs and out the front door. His breath started to come back to him. He walked over to where the car was. The security man looked at him but he didn't approach him.

She was gone. He kept saying it to himself to try and make himself believe it. He wanted to go back into the ward and look at her face again but he knew that wouldn't have done him any good. Nothing would have.

The night was clear. He looked up at the sky, the sky where heaven was. She imagined it to be a physical place behind the clouds. He used to think that way too. He didn't know what to think now.

God took him away from her. It would be easy to lose his faith. Was blaming God better than stopping believing in him?

Declan had a strong faith. So had Bartley. Her death wouldn't weaken it for either of them. They'd see it the same way his mother would have seen it, as a test of faith rather than a threat to it. It was the will of God. He wanted her to be near him. People died and then they went to heaven. That was all there was to it. It was a simple philosophy, the penny catechism one. He envied people who had it. He wanted to be one of them.

He walked around the quadrangle wondering if it could have ended any other way. He listened to the wind whistling through the trees. It was like a voice, a human thing. Somewhere in the distance there was the wail of an ambulance. Was it heading towards another person in the town, someone else who didn't know they were in danger? It held no terror for him now, no portent or fear.

He heard Declan calling him but he didn't reply. A few minutes later he saw him walking towards him with Bartley. He looked up at the window of the ward where she'd died. He saw the silhouette of the nurse at her bed. Was she removing her from it already?

He called Jennifer. He expected her to know what he was going to say. When he said it she broke down.

'Is that Jennifer?' Declan said. He was crying too. So was Bartley. Everyone was crying except him. Did that mean he was a cold fish?

They drove home in silence. The roads were empty. A lone crow stood on a telephone wire above the north field.

Bartley made straight for his bottle of whiskey as soon as they got in the door. Declan phoned Yvonne to tell her what happened. He bawled into the phone like a baby.

Brian went up to his bedroom. He lay on the bed in his clothes. He didn't want to sleep. Going to sleep meant he would wake up tomorrow with the knowledge that she was gone. He wanted to stay awake all night to prevent that.

His last thought was of the serenity of her face. It comforted him.

7

Jennifer was at the farm most of the next day. She was the only one he was able to talk to. He felt a sense of suffocation. It was as if the sky was closing in on him.

They drove out to the lake and sat in the car. It was raining. He listened to the drops plopping down on the roof. They blotted out his thoughts, soothing him with their repetition. Afterwards the sun came out like an apology.

Back at the house the depression hit him again.

'We have to be strong,' Declan said. But how could you be strong when you weren't in control of your thoughts?

Yvonne came up for the funeral. Brian couldn't remember her arriving. Everything was a fog to him now.

There was a huge turn-out at it. People arrived from far and wide, people he hadn't seen for years. He didn't even know some of them were still alive. When they saw him they talked about how wonderful a woman his mother was, how memorable she was even to those who'd only known her slightly. He tried to sound grateful when they praised her but their words floated above his head. Why did people always turn up in droves to salute the dead? Why did they not salute the living?

He was dreading the funeral Mass. Fr Finnerty said it. He asked Brian if he wanted to give a eulogy but he said no. Neither Declan nor Bartley were up to giving one either. Fr Finnerty gave it instead. He said, 'Teresa will have gone straight up. I bet she's already with the saints in heaven.' She was surely that but what good were they up there? It was on earth they were needed.

Bartley sat at the end of the pew. It was customary for the chief mourner. Declan and Brian were beside him.

Brian sat with Jennifer in the second pew. He was conscious of people looking at him. A man opposite him poked his wife. He heard him whispering, 'That's the younger one. He was very close to her.'

Bartley had an expression on his face that was half way between anger and grief. Declan held his hand.

Fr Finnerty talked about 'Teresa's brave struggle.' Brian was lost in his thoughts as he spoke. He tried to think of her life rather than the way she died. Her childhood growing up on a farm in Wexford. Meeting Bartley on a train one day and the whirlwind romance that followed. How beautiful she looked in photographs of her that survived from that time, how full of joy and expectation.

Marriage didn't bring her what she wanted. Bartley's drinking problem had already gotten hold of him by the time they walked down the aisle. It drove a wedge between them. It was a wedge not even her love for him could broach. And she had a lot of love.

Declan was born a year later. His arrival gave her some relief from Bartley's binges. So did Brian's birth two years further on. It was commonly thought that a most of a mother's love went to her first-born but she was closer to Brian than Declan. Declan was wild. He wasn't a child you could lift up. He became Bartley's buddy as he grew up.

Most of the memories Brian had of his youth were tied up with his mother. The day he fell off his bicycle and broke his leg. The first time she found him with a packet of cigarettes in his pocket. Sitting with her in the kitchen so many nights as they waited for Bartley to roll in drunk.

Then there was the day he told her he'd stopped going to Mass. She had a pained look on her face as he told her. He thought it would be the ultimate shock to her. It seemed like that at first but she weathered it. Everything that went wrong in her life afterwards was met with the same resigned acceptance – including her cancer.

The Mass ended. Declan had to give him a nudge to stand up. The two of them carried the coffin with Bartley and a friend of his. A woman with a beautiful voice sang 'Nearer My God to Thee' as they went down through the church.

A crowd gathered outside. The coffin was put into the hearse. Rain hinted. People huddled into little groups. Brian heard some people talking in hearty tones as they remembered her. Already the mourning had subsided. Anecdotes about her life replaced the tragedy that had just unfolded.

'It's a blessing for her to have been taken out of her pain,' an old farmer said to Brian at the door. He was a drinking friend of Bartley's. Another one said, 'You gave her a great send-off. She'll already be at the Pearly Gates if I know anything.'

Bartley recovered his composure. The anger he had in the church was replaced by a look of dignified sadness. People came up to him to offer their condolences. It seemed to do him good to hear their words of comfort. He basked in the glow of bereavement.

Brian wandered over to a tree that was in the grounds. Jennifer followed him.

'Are you all right?' she said. He nodded. Declan stared at him. He was among a group of people standing at the church door. He beckoned Brian over to him but Brian didn't respond. A few minutes later he came over to him with Yvonne.

'What are you doing over here?' he said.

'I need some time alone.'

Declan frowned. He was about to say something but Yvonne made a sign to him to stop.

'Don't worry,' she said to Brian, 'Stay here as long as you want.'

He went off shaking his head.

'One of these days…' he said.

'Don't mind him,' Yvonne said, 'He can be hard to take sometimes.'

'It's okay. I understand him.'

'He's cut up too in his own way.'

'I know that.'

When he looked at her it struck him how beautiful she was. She was wearing too much make-up but then she always did. He figured that was to please Declan. He would have wanted her to look glamorous even on a day like this.

She went back to him. They saw her giving out to him.

Brian felt numb on the journey to the graveyard. Neither Bartley nor Declan spoke to him. Declan was still holding Bartley's hand. A light rain had started to fall. He tried not to look at the house when they passed it. He remembered her last night in it. She was putting a plaster on a cut he'd got when he was fixing a fence.

The cortege passed Kelly's hardware shop, Sinnott's boutique. They went up Grealish's Hill and past the Devil's Bend. He looked at these places in a different way now that he was passing them on the way to the graveyard. They wouldn't be just places to him anymore, they'd be benchmarks on her last journey.

The hearse stopped. They walked to the graveside. The sky turned dark. He fought back tears as the coffin was taken out. He tried to block thoughts from coming into his head, either of her or anything else.

Prayers were said. Bartley went down on one knee as the coffin was being lowered. He threw a bouquet of flowers onto it.

Declan helped him up. Brian always felt out of things at times like this. He knew it was Declan he would have wanted to lift him up instead of himself.

Some of the mourners went back to the house after the burial. He wasn't sure who a lot of them were. People who hardly knew his mother gave lengthy attestations to her character. More genuine ones said a few words and went off.

Bartley played the role of the bereaved husband like one to the manor born. He sat with his hands gripped tightly around a glass of whiskey. He looked like he was going to crack it open. His eyes were on fire.

'How do you think you'll be?' a farmer said to him.

'I wish it was me that was in the ground instead of her,' he said.

Declan's friends came up from Newbridge. He stayed with them for most of the day. Brian heard him saying to one of them, 'She's gone to a better place. God took her out of kindness.'

Like Bartley he was saying all the right things. Brian could never think of the right things to say. It seemed to him that some people performed well at funerals in the same way they did at various other occasions one could think of, wedding and parties and general social occasions. He wasn't able to react to the people who praised her mother over-lavishly. They said so much there was nothing for him to add.

At a certain part of the day their tears turned to laughter. He'd only been at a few funerals in his life but it was a pattern he'd seen before. Just as people were devotional at weddings when they were in the church and then became jocose at the reception, the same principle held true of funerals after the body was laid to rest and the condolences given. Once the food and drink appeared, a different atmosphere took hold.

People forgot the tragedy. Instead they focussed on the feast of food that lay before them, on people they hadn't seen in a while that they were anxious to talk to so they could catch up on their news. The obligation to mourn the dead person had passed. Now they could be themselves again. There was no need to go around with long faces anymore.

There was a pecking order in it. Distant relatives could drop the mask sooner than close ones. Casual acquaintances didn't have to wear one at all. The immediate family were expected to have sad faces for most of the day, at least until late evening when the dismalness was replaced by humorous anecdotes. That was the worst part of the day for him, having to put up with stories from people who annoyed him. He was relieved when the last of them shuffled out of the house a few hours later. It was only then that the reality of what happened sunk in.

He started to feel unwell. Jennifer noticed it. She asked him what was wrong with him.

'I think I'm going to be sick,' he said. His stomach felt like a stone.

He went up to the bathroom. His head felt light. He wet his face with a facecloth. He felt like throwing up but he stopped himself. It was something he always did. He had a horror of it all his life. He did everything he could to stop himself when he felt he might be about to.

He turned on the tap in the wash basin. He put his head under it until the nausea passed.

His mother's bedroom was next door. He went into it. He hadn't been able to since she got sick. Her dressing-gown lay on the bed. He wondered if Bartley left it there. Why would he have taken it out of the wardrobe? He lifted it up. The smell of her perfume was on it.

There was a hair clip on her dressing-table. It was sitting on top of a little box where she kept her make-up. He took out a stick of lipstick. She only wore it once in a blue moon. She didn't think it suited her. Bartley disagreed. Beside the box there was a packet of cigarettes with just one cigarette in it. Behind the cigarette packet was a little statue of Jesus she got from Knock one year. He put it in his pocket.

The room felt strange without her. Even though she hadn't been in it for months there was always the hope she'd come back, at least during the first few days of her hospitalisation. He'd stayed out of it because he was superstitious. Now it didn't matter.

He opened the wardrobe. Her clothes were lined up neatly. All the fashions of the years, fashions she chose with such care. Now they'd probably be stuffed into some binliner.

He went downstairs. Declan was standing in the hall. He had his hand on the banister rail.

'Where were you hiding yourself?' he said.

He felt he was being cross-examined.

'I went into the bathroom to freshen up.'

'Did I hear you in Mam's room too?'

'Is there a law against that?'

'Is there a law against talking? You need to lighten up.'

'What does it matter where I was?'

40

'It doesn't. Dad was asking about you. I didn't know what to say to him'

'Sorry. I'm on edge.'

'No problem.'

They went into the main room. The talk was of practical things now, not his mother. Declan said he was going to stay for a few days to take care of Bartley. Yvonne wanted to stay too but Declan wasn't in favour of this. Brian wondered why. Was he uncomfortable about the way she was so friendly to him?

'Can she not stay?' he said.

'No. She's going now,' he said, 'Maybe you'd like to say goodbye to her.'

He went out to the car. She was just sitting there. He didn't know whether she was waiting for him or not.

'Sorry to be rushing off,' she said. He could tell by her face that she didn't want to go.

'I'll be on the phone to you,' he said.

'Will you be all right?'

'I'll be fine.'

'Mind yourself, won't you?'

'I will. And you too.'

Declan came out. He sat into the car with her. His expression suggested he was saying something serious to her. He looked bothered when he got out.

They went back inside after she drove off. The crowd had thinned by now. Only a few people were left. Declan started talking to Bartley. Brian told Jennifer he was going out for some fresh air. She said she'd join him in a minute.

He went outside. The day was fine, too fine for a funeral. It seemed ages since the burial. People were already gone back to their lives.

He went over to a tree that was at the back of the house. There was a tyre hanging from one of the branches. It was from a tractor that gave up on Bartley some years before. Declan and himself used to take turns swinging around in it when they were young. They'd always be dizzy when they came off. Declan always got to stay longer in it because he was older. Bartley used to urge him to swing higher and higher. His mother was always worried one of them would fall off and injure themselves.

Jennifer came out to him as he was squeezing himself into it.

'How are things in there?' he said.

'Not too bad. How are things in where you are?'

'I needed to get away from the pressure cooker atmosphere in there. Do you not find it like that?'

'Maybe it isn't so bad for me.'

'I don't know how to talk to anyone. They all seem to be more comfortable with the situation than me. For some of them it seems to be just a day out.'

'Maybe they're putting on a brave face.'

'I wish I could believe that.'

He got out of the tyre.

'Are you ready to go back in?'

'I suppose so.'

They went in. He felt Declan's eyes on him.

'Can I get you a drink or anything?' Jennifer said.

'Why don't we go upstairs? It would give us some time on our own.'

'If you want to.'

They went up to his room. He didn't feel like talking and she didn't press him to. She always knew when he was like that. They looked out the window. The day was already getting dark.

They listened to Declan and Bartley talking downstairs. Glasses clinked. They were laughing and crying, sometimes both together.

After a while they heard Declan's footsteps on the stairs. He knocked on the door.

'Is that you?' Brian called out.

He popped his head in.

'How is Dad?' Brian said.

'He's after nodding off. I'm going to sit with him for a while in case he falls into the fire.'

<h2 style="text-align:center">8</h2>

Declan and Bartley spent most of their time in deep consultation over the next few days. They seemed to be re-building a relationship that was always strong. It was even stronger now that there was no third party in the middle of it.

Brian went into a shell. Jennifer tried to take him out of it.

'It's no good,' he said, 'I feel like hitting someone.'

It was as if he was taking her death out on them, punishing them for how he felt.

'You think you hold the franchise on suffering,' Declan said to him, 'You think it gives you the high moral ground to diss the rest of us.'

The longer he stayed in the house, the more they got on each other's nerves. It brought back the old days to him. They argued about everything then. After he moved to Newbridge they'd stopped, at least for a while. When he wasn't seeing much of him he found him easy enough to take. Now that he was with him all the time the old conflicts started off again.

Bartley became an unlikely referee for their arguments. More often than not he tended to take Declan's side of the story. If his mother was alive, Brian knew, she'd have taken his. It wasn't a level playing field anymore.

'Dad is keeping it together, isn't he?' he said the day before he was due to go back to Newbridge.

'Not only is he keeping it together, he seems to be getting off on it.'

'That's a strange thing to say.'

'It's the way I see it.'

'Are you saying he's putting on a show?'

'I don't know.'

'How do you think he'll be down the road? Do you think he'll miss her more and more or will time help?'

'He'll probably block it out. The way he blocks out everything he doesn't like.'

'You don't think much of him, do you?'

'I don't think well or badly of him. He's working his way through it. I admire him for that.'

'You give with one hand and take away with the other.'

'Maybe. I don't think we should analyse it too much.'

'Sometimes I feel we have different fathers.'

'Maybe we have.'

'You don't think he treated Mam very well, do you?'

'Do you?'

'I never saw much of the stuff you give out to him for.'

'You were away a lot.'

'I think I know my own father.'

'Maybe I'm being too hard on him. He probably treated her the only way he could – by being himself. After a while she stopped expecting anything different.'

Declan smiled at him. It wasn't a friendly smile. It was one that said: 'I hate you because you think you know more about my parents than I do.'

'We know how lost you are without her.'

'You think I was tied to her apron-strings, don't you?'

'It doesn't matter about that. I care about your future.'

'Do you? Maybe if I live it your way.'

'That's not fair. I want you to live it whatever way brings you happiness. Your own one doesn't seem to have worked so far.'

'What makes you such an authority on that?'

'Everyone knows you've been walking around like you found a penny and lost a pound since Mam died.'

'Sorry for being such a bore.'

'You need to man up, Brian.'

'Does loving your mother makes you a wimp?'

'Why do you twist everything I say? I don't want to fight with you.'

'Why do you provoke me then?'

'I'm trying to help. Obviously I'm not making a very good job of it.'

'It's okay. I understand you. I shouldn't fly off the handle.'

The comment softened him.

'Look, I'll be gone tomorrow. Maybe you'll lose some of your aggression against me then. Don't they say absence makes the heart grow fonder?'

'Yes, whoever "they" are.'

'Why don't you come down to Newbridge for a visit? It would get you away from the atmosphere here. Yvonne thinks the world of you.'

'It sounds like a good idea,' he said but he felt it was unlikely. He couldn't really talk to her while Declan was around. If he knew her independently of him he would have had a totally different relationship to her.

'We've done the place up. I'm sure you'll like it.'

It was a bungalow outside the town. There was a stone fireplace in the middle of the living-room. They had art deco effects everywhere. Most of these were Declan's doing. He'd employed an interior decorator who almost charged as much as they paid for the house.

'Let me think about it.'

'Great.'

He always felt on display any time he went down there. He was expected to rhapsodise about everything he saw around him – the kitchen with the magic presses, the circular bath, the split level living-room.

'We live for your visits,' he said, 'You never mind if things are in a mess.'

This was amusing. Yvonne always had the house like a palace. Every few days a cleaner woman came in. Brian was always terrified he'd knock over something every time he as much as turned around.

'I'll go down to you as soon as I get my head straightened out,' he said.

'Good on you.'

Suddenly there was nothing more to say. Each of them knew they could never be close. The best they could be was polite with one another. The silence grew tense between them. It was a few minutes before Declan spoke again.

'I know you're annoyed with me for not keeping in touch with Mam more,' he said.

He tried to think how many times he phoned in the average year. It was probably about a dozen. On most of the calls he spoke mainly to Bartley. There were usually only two visits – Christmas and Easter.

'She missed you a lot. She was too proud to say it to you.'

'I suspected that. I'm annoyed at myself about it. It always gnawed at me. You don't think these things will affect you until it's too late.'

'There's nothing you can do now. Don't beat yourself up about it.'

'I won't.' He went quiet for a few seconds. Then he cleared his throat. His voice became thick. It always did when he was tense. He said, 'You probably would, though.'

'What do you mean by that?'

'You brood too much about things.'

'Do you think so?'

'You should get out more.'

'Really? Is there anything that wonderful I'm missing? Like your computer friends, for instance. Out on the piss in Newbridge, falling into lamp-posts?'

'It's better than disappearing up your arse with a book every night of the year.'

They were trading insults like they used to. In a way it made him feel more natural with him. It was better than the patina of civility that was more usual for them these times.

He drove him to the train station the next morning. Having the exchange of words cleared the air between them. There was no tension now. They talked about ordinary things - people they knew in the town, who got married, people who emigrated, the things every family talked about. Their mother was gone. Life was beginning again.

'What doesn't kill you makes you stronger,' Declan said to him as they got to the station. 'I know it's a cliché but some clichés are true.'

The train was in. They got out of the car. Brian handed him his case. He went into the depot to get his ticket. He was sitting on the platform when he came out.

'Everything done now,' he said.

He stood there with his case in his hand.

'You better get on,' Brian said, 'It'll be going in a minute.'

'I hope I see you in happier circumstances the next time.'

'Sorry for anything I said out of line.'

'Me too. I love you, you little bastard. You know that, don't you?'

'Likewise.'

He put his arms around him.

'And I'm holding you to that visit. Yvonne will never let me hear the end of it if you don't come down.'

He got onto the train. It started moving. Brian watched him looking for a seat, putting his case down. He waved to him and he waved back.

'Take care of that father of mine,' he shouted out.

'I will.'

The train picked up speed. It whistled off, receding into the distance. In a few moments it was nothing more than a speck.

He walked back to the car. He sat in but he didn't turn on the ignition.

He started to feel emotional again.

He took the statue of Jesus out of his pocket and looked at it. It made him want to cry. Maybe he'd have been better off to leave it in her room, better not to have anything to remind him of her.

He drove home in a daze. Bartley was still in bed when he got to the farm. He didn't know whether to wake him or not. Sometimes it did him good to sleep off his hangovers. He decided he wouldn't tell him Declan had invited him to Newbridge. He'd only keep nagging him about when he might go down.

He thought about Jennifer. She'd gone back to Limerick. What was going to happen to them now? Tragedies were supposed to bring people together. Maybe they did, at least for a while.

He turned on his mobile. There were some missed calls from her. She'd sent a few texts as well. They all said the same thing. How was he? He couldn't answer that question.

He spent as much time with Bartley as he could in the next few days. He was drinking all the time but he didn't say anything to him about it. He had a licence for it now – grief.

He tried to think of the happy times with his mother but only the blackness came back. The longer he spent around the house the worse it got. Each plate he lifted stung him with her memory, each picture he looked at on the wall. He thought of the way she was always there for him as he went through his various crises growing up, how she busied herself quietly in the background. Her life was never about herself and neither was her death.

People kept coming up to him commiserating. He tried to be polite to them but he didn't encourage them to prolong their conversations. He feared involvement with them. Loughrea was a goldfish bowl. Sooner or later he felt it would grind him down.

Sometimes as he lay in bed trying to sleep he heard sounds that reminded him of her: the purring of the fridge in the kitchen, a kettle boiling, even the sound of a creaking step on the stairs. He thought of her pottering around the kitchen washing dishes or darning socks. He remembered the way she shook her head when she was asking him a question, the way she threw her head back when she laughed. He knew these memories were no good for him but he couldn't stop them.

He tried to be like Declan, a man who had little truck with memories.'What good are they?' he'd say, 'They can't bring her back.' And of course he was right. But what did being right or wrong matter when the person who meant most to him in the world was gone?

Eventually he came out of his gloom. Work became therapy. Doing jobs around the farm revived him. The nights were starry and moonlit. Leaves fell from the trees in the garden and he raked them into clumps.He drove around in the tractor surveying the fields. The secret was not to think, not to feel.

Life could be good again, he told himself, if he let it.

9

Bartley came out of his gloom in time as well. It was about a month after the funeral. Brian felt he could almost have pinpointed the moment. It was a sunny day. He was shaving at the kitchen mirror. The way he looked over at him seemed to say he'd recovered. It was as if he made a choice to live instead of die.

'I'm going to plant a tree in her memory,' he said.

He also formed the ambition of going off the drink. He went down to Fr. Finnerty. He hadn't seen him since the funeral.

'How are you bearing up?' he said to him as he entered the church.

'I don't think the drink is helping.'

'It doesn't take a genius to know that. Where do I come in?'

'I want to take the pledge.'

He often joked that he'd taken more pledges than drink in his life. Brian wondered how long it would last. A week? A month? Maybe it didn't matter. The will to live was enough.

He made a special effort to get on with him. It was easier, of course, when he was sober. They worked together but they didn't talk much. When they were busy they were fine but in the idle times Brian couldn't help being angry with him. He couldn't help thinking his behaviour had been a factor in his mother's final illness.

Then something happened to make that anger a million times worse. He was in McDonagh's one night when he heard two farmers talking about Bartley. He was behind a pillar so they hadn't seen him. One of them said he saw Bartley in what he called a 'compromising position' with a woman. Her name was Angela Curley. He'd known her for years. He also knew her parents. They were killed in a car accident when she was in her twenties.

The rumours grew in subsequent days. One word borrowed another. Eventually people started saying he'd been seeing her before Brian's mother got sick.

She used to call to the farm now and then to buy vegetables for a shop on the outskirts of Loughrea. Sometimes he thought he saw Bartley looking at her in an over-familiar way, even flirting with her. It wasn't obvious but in a way that made it worse.

She was almost ten years younger than him. A big woman with a voluptuous figure, she wore dresses to emphasise that fact.

She didn't have too much respect in the town. There were rumours she'd been with other married men besides Bartley.

She'd been a stunner in her day. Nobody knew why she never married. Maybe she was too busy playing the field. She was what was known as a 'man's woman,' someone who seemed to be as comfortable sitting at a bar counter as she was carrying vegetables from a farmyard. .

When Jennifer came up from Limerick on a mid-term break he gave out to her about Angela almost non-stop. She said, 'You're eating yourself up with this stuff. It's not good for you. You have no proof. Your mother wouldn't like you thinking that way.'

'My mother?' he said, 'That's what this is about. She's hardly cold in her grave. I can't believe you're saying that.'

'You took me up wrong. What I meant was that she wouldn't want to see you upset.'

'I can't help it.'

'Let it go. It's driving you crazy.'

'I have to get out of this place.'

'Are you serious?'

'I've been thinking about it for a while. It's doing my head in.'

'Where would you go?'

'I don't know.'

He wanted to go to university in Dublin but he didn't think there was any chance it would happen. He doubted Bartley would fund him.

Jennifer disagreed when he said that to her.

'I'm sure your father would help out,' she said.

'Are you joking? How could I ask him for anything with all that's going on? It would be blood money.'

'He's lonely. Maybe Angela is just company for him.'

'You always think the best of people, don't you?'

'It doesn't do much good to think the worst.'

'You're not like everyone else around here.'

'Why do you think I left?'

She always had a way of cooling him down. She was like his mother that way. He said he'd think about what she said.

He was quiet with Bartley the following day. He couldn't bring himself to say anything to him. It was noon before he got his courage up.

Bartley was bent over the Austin at the time. He was trying to dry out a spark plug that was flooded.

'People are saying you were seen with Angela Curley before Mam died,' he said.

He didn't react for a few seconds. He took the spark plug out and stared at it. Then he threw it on the ground. He stormed off in a temper. Was that from guilt? Brian wasn't sure.

Anytime he went into Loughrea afterwards he was aware of people's eyes on him. They seemed to know something he didn't. When he walked by them their voices got lower or they stopped talking altogether.

He would have preferred if people were upfront with him. They whispered when there was no need to. It made everything they said sound that much more important.

'I don't know if I can live in this town much longer,' he told Bartley at the end of the week. He was lugging a milk pail to one of the stables at the time. He dropped it on the ground.

'Why would that be?'

'People are still talking about you and Angela Curley.'

He dropped the pail on the ground.

'You were never much good at ignoring gossip, were you?' he said.

'Is it gossip or are they telling the truth? There's no smoke without fire.'

'In this case I'm afraid there is but I'm not going to defend myself if some dogsbodies are spreading dirt about me. Let them. It hurts me that my son believes them.'

'I didn't say I did. I just said I don't know if I can live here any longer.'

'If you want to go, go. If you do you'll only fuel nonsense like that. People will say you went off as a result of it.'

'That may be so. Anyway I've said what I said. That's the way it stands.'

Bartley was quiet for a few seconds. Then he said, 'If you left, what would you do?'

'I was thinking of going to college.'

'College? Who's going to pay for it, might I ask?'

'I don't know. Maybe I could borrow some money from you. I could pay you back when I graduate.'

'How much were you thinking of?'

'Whatever the fees are, and a few bob for a flat. I could get a part time job to help out.'

He drummed his fingers on the milk pail.

'Let me think about it.'

A few hours later he was reading in his room when Bartley knocked on the door.

'I've been thinking about your idea,' he said. 'I know how tough the last few months have been for you. I'm going to help you.'

Brian sat up in the bed.

'Do you mean it?'

'Yes, but I'd like you to know what you plan to study.'

'English and French.'

'English and French? What would they get you?'

'I could teach with them.'

'You mean do the H.Dip? That would be another year after graduation, wouldn't it?'

'If you don't want to help me, don't bother. I'll find a way.'

'I'm not saying I won't. We're just talking.'

Angela was in the house a lot over the next few days. He knew Bartley talked about everything with her. She probably knew about the university already. He thought he was using her as a kind of hostage to his future. She was a bargaining chip that said, 'I'll let you go to the university if you're nice to her.' He refused to play that game. If anything he was more cool with her than he might otherwise have been. He hated set-ups.

When he conveyed his suspicions to him he dismissed them out of hand.

'You must have got out of the wrong side of the bed this morning,' he said, 'I haven't said a word to her. Even if I did she wouldn't have any interest. She has more to do with her time than worry about you.'

In the end he agreed to it all. There was no lead-up. He came up to him one day when he was feeding the cows. He put his head in the door of the stable and said, 'Have you a minute?'

They walked back to the house. When they got into the kitchen he took an envelope out of the dresser. It had a blank cheque inside it.

'What's this for?' Brian asked.

'Anything. Everything. Make it out for whatever you want.'

He was dumbfounded.

'Why are you doing this?'

'I owe it to you.'

'In what way?'

'Think of it as backpay for injustices of the past.'

'I don't know what you mean.'

'I'm talking about favouritism.'

'Favouritism?'

'Declan got everything growing up. Now it's your turn.'

'I never said that.'

'Whether you did or not it was true. Fathers don't realise they're doing things like that unless it's brought to their notice. Anyway, that's neither here nor there. I've been putting a few bob aside for the rainy day.'

'I don't know what to say.'

'Don't say anything. Just take it. Have a good time on it. We'll be dead long enough. There's no point in it gathering dust in a bank account.'

'What about paying you back?'

'You can do that whenever you like – or not at all. I'm not pushed.'

'This isn't like you talking.'

'Money used to be important to me once but now it isn't. Not since Teresa died.'

'I really appreciate this. I thought I was going to be putting out the begging bowl.'

He flattened the cheque on the table and handed him a pen.

'Make out an amount,' he said grandly.

'What will I make it out for?'

'Whatever you like. There's more where that came from, as the woman said when she peed in the ocean.'

He thought for a moment, putting the pen in his mouth.

'Would 10,000 euro be too much?'

Bartley let out a whistle. Then he said, 'Okay, we wouldn't want you singing for your supper.'

'I'll pay you back every penny.'

'Don't worry about that. When you're a university lecturer I'll probably be coming to you for a dig-out.'

'I hope you won't end up in the poor house.'

'I'll be all right. We mightn't be able to have three course meals for a while but so what?'

He rang UCD the next day. He had enough points in the Leaving Cert to do English and French so he registered for those subjects.

Jennifer was quiet when he told her. He wondered if she regretted her advice to him now. It meant they'd be seeing a lot less of one another.

'You don't sound too delighted,' he said.

'I'm fine'

'Are you angry with me?'

'How could I be? Wasn't it me who advised you to make up with your father?'

'This changes nothing between us. You know that, don't you?'

'Of course.'

She went quiet for a second. Then she said, 'I bet you'll be tempted by all the Dublin girls.'

'I could say the same about you and the Limerick men.'

'You must be joking. Most of the ones I meet are eejits.'

'So you say anyway.'

'When are you off?'

'Soon enough.'

'This is very sudden, Brian.'

'We'll still have the holidays to see each other. And I have a bit of time before I go. We'll make the most of it.'

Over the next few weeks he saw her most nights. They went to the pictures or for a meal. Sometimes they just went walking down by the river. He tried to steer their conversations away from his plans, quizzing her about her life in Limerick instead.

She was bored silly by the lectures.

'The stuff they make you learn is ridiculous,' she said. 'Who needs to read *Deoraíocht* to teach four year olds "Tá Daidí sa ghairdín"?'

'It's the same with everything. Just stick with it. You'll be in the classroom soon enough. Then you'll be able to forget all that nonsense.'

'How are things with your father now? Are you okay about Angela?'

'Sort of.'

'Wasn't he very good to give you the money?'

'I couldn't believe it.'

'Can he afford it?'

'He said he had a nest egg put aside for me.'

'Is he going to retire soon, do you think?'

'He's at the age for it anyway.'

After he walked her home he thanked Bartley again.

'Don't think I take this for granted,' he said.

'Forget about it. How is Jennifer?'

'Good. She was ringing your praises.'

'She always sees the best in people – like Teresa.'

'How will you be on the farm without me?'

'I'll survive, Don't over-rate yourself.'

He was only doing casual work now. Bartley covered for him as he prepared for Dublin. One day he put a new lock on the henhouse. Foxes had been getting in. Another day he moved cattle from one field to another so he could vet them for sale.

'Don't take too much out of yourself,' Brian said to him, 'You're not the man you used to be.'

'It keeps my mind off what happened.'

He saw Jennifer every day. He tried to act casual with her but as they went on walks they'd been going on since childhood he felt different. Had something changed? He had no reason to think that. Maybe she was just quiet because he was going away.

As the day of his departure approached he became doubtful about the whole idea. It was going to be a culture shock for him moving away from everything he knew. Bartley told him it was right for him to go but he wasn't sure he meant it.

Every other night he heard him on the phone to Declan. They talked in a code he couldn't understand. It had always been the way, this secret language he was excluded from.

One of the calls was cut short a few nights before he was due to go to Dublin.

'Here,' he said, handing him the phone, 'He wants a word with you.'

'I'm not in the mood for talking.'

'Go on. He wants to wish you well.'

He took the phone.

'I believe we're about to have an intellectual in the family,' Declan said, 'University, mind you. It's a long way from snaggin' turnips.'

'It's no big deal.'

'I'd never have thought it. So it's English and French, is it?'

'That's what I'm thinking of.'

'I never knew you were into that stuff.'

'Neither did I.'

'Are you looking forward to it?'

'I don't know what to expect. We'll see how it goes.'

'Keeping your hands close to your chest as usual. Anyway, the best of British luck to you. Or should I say the best of French luck.'

'Thanks.'

'Come down to us the first chance you get, won't you? I meant that about the offer.'

'I said I would.'

'That's great. I'll let you go now but Mademoiselle wants a word with you.'

Yvonne came on.

'I'm delighted for you, Brian,' she said. 'I'm surprised you're not going in for veterinary. Or Ag.' It was her short for Agriculture.

'That's what everyone says. I needed a break from that kind of thing. It would be like bringing coals to Newcastle.'

'I know what you mean. Are you nervous?'

'Not really. After the first few days I'll probably settle.'

'That's the attitude to have. I'm sure you'll miss Jennifer. Will you be able to fit in your trips home with hers from Limerick?'

'I'm sure we'll work something out.'

'Have a great time for yourself. I hope we'll see you here soon.'

'You will.'

'We're on the road to Loughrea. There's no excuse for you not dropping in on your way.'

'I told Declan I would.'

'I'll be watching for the car. The CCTV cameras will pick you up if you try to escape us.'

'I wouldn't dream of it.'

After he hung up, Bartley said, 'What was all that about?'

'Nothing. You know Yvonne. She rambles a bit.'

He went down to McDonagh's with Bartley for a farewell drink the following night. He was glad Angela wasn't with them. He knew she'd like to have been there but she couldn't make it. It clashed with a girl's night out at the local bridge club.

There were only a few stragglers there. They gave Brian a big cheer when he walked in.

'I should have known,' he said to Bartley.

'Ignore them. You have to get over that self-conscious streak in yourself. They're only people. They won't bite you.'

They got a seat in the corner. Bartley ordered a pint of Guinness for himself and a large whiskey for Brian.

'A small one would have done,' he said.

'Don't make a big deal out of it. You can nurse it. It's a special night.'

He sipped at it.

'I'm surprised you're not on the hard stuff yourself,' he said.

'Angela has me on strict orders to be on my best behaviour with you.'

After a few minutes he felt a tap on his shoulder. It was Bill Delaney. He used to play football with him in the college.

'Fair play to you, man,' he said, 'Off to the big smoke. The rest of us fuckers save hay while you're sitting on your arse with the intellectuals.'

'It's not as glamorous as it sounds.'

'Do you know what you'll do after?'

'Give me a chance. I haven't even got there yet.'

He went off.

'Let's get out of here,' Brian said to Bartley, 'There'll be people coming over annoying us all night.'

'Relax, will you? That's your problem. You can never wind down.'

He took a slurp of the Guinness.

'I want to say something to you,' Brian said.

'What?'

'I think you disapprove of me going.'

'What gave you that idea?'

'I don't know. I just sense it.'

'Well you sense wrong. It took me a while to come around to your way of thinking but I know now it's for the best. It's what Teresa would have wanted.'

'Thanks for saying that.'

He became more relaxed as the night went on. Bartley had two more pints. With each order he bought Brian another whiskey.

'You'll have me on my ear,' he said after the third one.

'That's the general idea. Maybe we'll get the real Brian then.'

'I'm afraid there's no other one. What you see is what you get.'

'You were always deep. Deeper than the ocean.'

'I hate that image people have of me. It puts a wall up.'

'Do you not want that wall? Every time the doorbell rings you run upstairs.'

'I hate it when people are tense with me.'

'You can't have it both ways.'

'I know.'

'Maybe you'll come out of your shell in Dublin.'

'You'd never know. It might drive me deeper into another one.'

Bartley gave a dry laugh.

'If that's your attitude I think I'll take back the cheque.'

'I'm sorry. You wouldn't want to take me too seriously these days. I always hated change.'

'We all do. Just give yourself over to whatever happens. You'll be fine.'

'I hope so. What about yourself?'

'I'm going to sell some more stock if the market picks up,'

'Don't leave yourself too short.'

'I don't care if they all go. I want to give more time to Angela. She's been very good to me lately.'

'I'm glad to hear that.'

'I hope you don't find her too intrusive.'

'Not at all.'

'Sometimes I think you're awkward with one another.'

'Maybe a bit.'

'I hope that improves.'

'So what if it doesn't? I'll be gone a lot of the time now anyway.'

'I'd like you to get on.'

He fixed his eyes on him.

'Do you still think I was seeing her behind Teresa's back?'

'No,' he said. He didn't know what he believed but he didn't want to get into it. Whatever happened happened. He couldn't change the past. There was no point torturing himself about it.

'Don't let what people say about us get to you, Brian. They don't want anyone to have a life.'

'I know that.'

They were quiet for a few moments. Then Brian said, 'Do you think you'll marry her?'

He hadn't intended saying it. It just came out. If he hadn't drunk so much whiskey it probably wouldn't have.

'Who knows what's down the road? I'm not a saint like your mother. I need company. The nights are long on your own.'

'I wouldn't grudge you your happiness.'

'Some people don't approve of her. I can't do anything about that. We care for each other. That's all that matters. After that, everyone can go and fuck themselves.'

10

Jennifer stayed in Loughrea in the days coming up to his departure. She couldn't resist advising him about things – what to bring with him and what he mightn't need. He'd prefer to have made his own mistakes but he didn't like to say anything to her. He knew she'd be sensitive if he passed even the slightest negative comment.

'I feel guilty about you missing your lectures,' he said to her one night when they were out for a meal together.

'Don't worry,' she said, 'I have a friend taking the notes for me. I can make up when I get back.'

'We might both end up as teachers yet if I get my B.A.'

'That would be nice. We could borrow each other's sticks of chalk in emergencies.'

'If we were married we could meet in the staff-room to prepare our shopping list for the week.'

'I don't think that'd go down too well.'

'What do you think will happen to us?' he asked her.

'How do you mean?'

'We were supposed to tie the knot after you graduated, weren't we?'

'There's no rush on it.'

'The last few months have been the worst of my life. You got me through them.'

'That's over-stating the case. I was only a small help.'

'And now I'm repaying you by going away.'

'Don't feel bad about it. Get your degree. If you don't do it now you'll regret it later. We'll be in touch all the time. It's not as if you're going to Outer Mongolia. I'm just down the road if you need me.'

'You're very understanding as usual. With Bartley and yourself being so supportive I don't know what hit me. I feel I'm covered in clover.'

'How are you getting on with him at the moment?'

'I still can't believe he gave me the money. He's always been careful with it. It would have been harder for him than for most people. He pretends he doesn't care about things like that anymore but I know he does. A leopard doesn't change his spots.'

'Don't analyse him too much. You're set up for your future. What do you care if he gave it with a bad grace or not?'

'You're right. In the last few weeks I've started to understand him more. We had a drink together one night and talked things out.'

'I can't remember you ever going drinking with him before.'

'I rarely did. I was too young for starters. Even if I wasn't I doubt he'd have been interested. Declan was always a likelier candidate.'

'Maybe that'll change now that your mother isn't there anymore.'

'He feels guilty about Mam. It's a pity he wasn't like this when she was alive. If he was she might still be with us.'

'Don't think like that. It's too late for it.'

The meal arrived but neither of them were hungry. They picked at it more out of duty than anything else.

'How are you getting on with Angela?' she asked him.

'We don't have too much to do with each other. I'm terrified he'll go up the aisle with her.'

'What do you not like about her?'

'I think she's using him.'

'For his money?'

'That and everything else. He's vulnerable at the moment. She's jumping into the breach.'

'You haven't had words with her, have you?'

'No. Maybe it'd be better if we had. It might get things out into the open.'

'What kinds of things?'

'She's trying to fill Mam's shoes. That will never happen for me. She needs to know it.'

'I don't know why she bothers you so much. You're not going to be around her much even if she marries your father.'

'That's not the point.'

'You should tell her how you feel.'

'It wouldn't do any good. She's here to stay.'

He stopped eating. He looked at her.

'Actually I'm more concerned about us.'

'How do you mean?'

'People are saying we're breaking up.'

'Good for them. If it's the same people who say your father was having an affair with Angela while your mother was alive. I'm not really interested.'

'It's hard to escape them. You know the way rumours fly around a small town.'

'Don't mind them. I know how I feel about you. That's all that matters, isn't it?'

'Of course, but you know me. I'm always looking over my shoulder at what's coming behind me.'

'They say don't look back, don't they?'

'With me it's a permanent habit. Maybe that'll change in Dublin.'

She became thoughtful.

'You'll probably have loads of girls after you up there.'

'That's the second time you said that. Why do you keep mentioning it?'

'Because you're good-looking. And you're nice. I'm sure they'll be interested in you. Especially when you start reading all those fancy books.'

'Don't worry, I'll always be a bogman. Even if they put me in a top hat and tails.'

'Bogmen can be sexy too. You'll be a novelty to the Dubs.'

'I don't think I'll fit in up there. It's just a stopgap for me.'

'That's what all the men say when they're running away from their women.'

'Stop that talk or I'll give you a smack.'

'The alternative would be to use your father's 10,000 euro for a deposit on a house. We could move in together.'

'That sounds nice. The only problem is I'd have to hide for a few years so he didn't suspect I was misappropriating his funds.'

'That could be arranged. I'd build a bunker for you and put you in the Witness Protection Scheme.'

'I'm beginning to like the idea already.'

11

Bartley drove him to the train the following day. Rusty was in the car with them. He looked at him as if he knew he was going away for a long time.

He was going to be staying in a flat in Ranelagh that was owned by a neighbour of theirs. His name was Martin Geraghty. It was above a Centra shop. Martin had left farming some years before to become a businessman. Bartley thought he was secretly rich even though he drove a banger of a car.

'I don't know why I'm doing this,' he said as he handed him the piece of paper with his details on it.

'I know you have things against him.'

'He sold me bad stock when he was getting out of the farming lark.'

'Maybe he didn't know they were bad.'

Bartley smirked.

'And maybe Hitler didn't know he was killing six million Jews. Never give that fellow the benefit of the doubt. He'd take the eyes out of your head and come back for the eyelashes.'

'I don't like making my mind up about people before I meet them.'

'Have it your own way. The flat is above the Centra anyway. That's all you need to know for now.'

They waited for the train. Brian was feeling nervous. He was already missing Jennifer. She wanted to go to the station with them but he didn't encourage her. It would have made him too emotional.

The closer he got to going the more nervous he became. He wondered if he was doing the right thing. He'd always been like that. He made decisions impetuously and then started to regret them even before he put them into action. He was worried about everything – the break in his routine, trying to make new friends, not having Jennifer to share things with. She'd been someone he could run to with his problems ever since Primary School.

'Penny for your thoughts,' Bartley said to him.

'I don't know if I'm making the right decision.'

'It isn't the far side of the moon. You can come back in a week if it doesn't suit you.'

'I know.'

'And don't get your head too cluttered with all that book stuff.'

'I'll try not to.'

'You need a bit of a social life. Think of that first. If you fail your exams you can always repeat them in the autumn. I won't give you a hard time about it.'

'It's nice to know that.'

'I just want to put your mind at rest. I know how much you worry about things.'

The train pulled in. He walked towards it. Bartley put his arms around him.

'Goodbye so.'

'Goodbye. Thanks for everything.'

'We'll see you soon. Angela said to give you a kiss.'

'I hope you're not going to do that.'

'She meant from her.'

'I know. I'm joking.'

'Mind yourself.'

He patted Rusty. Bartley handed his case to him. He got on the train, Rusty started to whine.

He found a seat. He tried to open the window but he couldn't. He made a miming gesture to Bartley indicating he'd be on the phone to him. Bartley nodded. He lifted up Rusty's paw to give him a wave.

The train pulled away. His head was still in a muddle as it picked up speed. He watched the town disappearing behind him. In leaving it he seemed to be leaving everything it represented.

That included Jennifer. He told her his going didn't change anything between them but deep down he knew it did. His mother's comments about her had affected him. Instead of drawing him towards her they pushed him away. He'd lost is mother. Maybe he'd lose Jennifer too.

He hadn't mentioned any of his misgivings about her to Bartley. As far as he was concerned they were going to pick up where they left off after he graduated. Brian knew he'd have been a good father-in-law to her. He wasn't so sure he'd be a good husband.

A woman with a pinched face sat down opposite him. He knew her from seeing her around the town but he couldn't put a name on her. She tried to engage him in conversation.

'I know your face,' she said. 'Where are you off to? I wish I could remember where I know you from. Are you a local?'

Towns passed by. They all looked similar. He was only vaguely aware of them as the train clattered on. He'd brought a book with him. He tried to read it but he couldn't. He was too aware of the woman staring at him, waiting to ask him more questions.

He picked up a magazine someone left behind them on the seat. It was one of those celebrity ones with lots of photographs. He flipped through the pages without reading them, just looking at the photos. After a while he nodded off.

He was still asleep when the train got to Dublin. The woman nudged him awake. 'We'll be there shortly now,' she said. He thanked her.

He looked out at the city. All he could see were the backs of houses, dirty clotheslines, spray-painted walls. Was this what was facing him? Maybe every city was like that in its outskirts. Trains always seemed to come into them from the bad end.

They pulled in at Heuston. There was consternation everywhere. He walked along the platform. The noise was deafening. When he got out onto the street it was a relief. He started to walk.

The buildings were huge. The Liffey stank. It looked like coffee.

He saw a beggar with a cup in his hands. He threw a coin into it. The man nodded without looking up. Was he a drug addict? An alcoholic? Maybe it didn't matter. He might just have been homeless. Bartley told him to expect to see people on the streets. 'Dublin is a city,' he said, 'Everyone will be looking for something off you.'

The sun beat down on him. He got to O'Connell Bridge. His skin felt clammy.

He saw a taxi passing by. He hailed it. A rough-looking man was chewing gum at the wheel. He had the window open. His elbow was sticking out.

'Yeah?' he said.

'Do you know where Ranelagh is?'

'If I don't I shouldn't be in this job. Do you want me to bring you to it?'

He sat in. The driver went very slow. He stopped at every yellow light instead of going through it. Was he trying to push up the fare? That was something else Bartley warned him about.

'What do you think of Dublin?' he said. How did he know he'd come off the train? It was probably the case.

'It looks nice.'

'You'll have other ideas about it after being here a while.'

'Do you think so?'

'It's a cesspool. Look around you.'

They drove through the traffic. There was chaos everywhere. It was like the bumpers at a carnival.

The driver kept asking him questions. Where was he from? Who was he going to? What was his business in Dublin?

He answered him politely without saying too much. He felt the same way as he'd felt about the woman on the train. He hadn't expected such curiosity. Weren't cities supposed to be impersonal? He thought it might be to distract him from looking at the meter. He couldn't stop staring at it. It clocked up a new amount every minute.

They ground to a halt at a set of lights.

'This place is turning into a permanent traffic jam,' he said.

'That should be good for you.'

'I suppose that part is.'

'Are you not doing well?'

'Not really. There's a lot of stuff that goes on in this game.'

'Like what?'

'There are a lot of chancers putting up false plates.'

'I didn't know about that.'

'They'd put us out of business if they could. A lot of them have second jobs. They're squeezing the life out of the legit drivers.'

They drove on. The sun went in. It started to rain. The driver kept chewing his gum, giving out about everything – the weather, the unregulated drivers, a man who threw up on his seat the night before.

Eventually he stopped.

'We're in sunny downtown Ranelagh, my friend,' he said, 'Or should I say pissing-from-the-heavens Ranelagh. How far more is it?'

'I can walk from here.'

He paid him and got out.

He started walking. The rain got worse. He tried to keep himself dry by walking close to the buildings. A lot of them had awnings or some other kind of cover.

He took the piece of paper out of his pocket where Bartley had written the directions to the Centra shop. It was soggy from the rain. He could barely make them out.

After a few minutes he spotted it.

There was a young girl behind a counter. She looked very pretty. A man was talking to her. He had a face like a bull but there was a kindness in it too.

'Hello,' he said, 'I'm Brian Kilcoyne. I'm looking for Martin Geraghty.'

'That's me. Pleased to meet you. Lovely weather, isn't it?'

'Fantastic.'

They shook hands.

'That hand doesn't feel like it dug too many spuds,' he said, 'Are you sure you're Bartley's son.'

'You must be Mr Geraghty.'

'Martin.'

'He always says I had my head buried in a book whenever he asked me to do any work.'

'You were as well off.'

He looked him up and down.

'Welcome to the city. How was the journey?'

'I slept through most of it.'

'You were only a nipper the last time I saw you. You probably don't remember me.'

'Not very well I have to admit.'

'How are things in the old homestead?'

'Good enough.'

'How is Bartley? He's been on the blower to me.'

'Already?'

'Probably five minutes after you got on the train. How do you like Dublin?'

'It seems nice. It'll take me a while to get used to it. It's good of you to offer me the bedsit.'

'You won't say that when you hear what I'm charging for it.'

'Is it expensive?'

'I'm only joking. Don't worry, I won't put the boot in. I wouldn't want to upset that father of yours.'

He looked him up and down again.

'So you're going to be a scholar.'

'Yes.'

'You don't sound too happy about it.'

'We'll see how it goes. I like reading books but I'm not sure I'll enjoy studying them.'

'Don't knock education. Not too many people from our neck of the woods have two brain cells to rub together.'

'I'm not sure if I'll last the pace.'

'Don't tell Bartley that or he'll pull you out.'

'I won't.'

He slapped his hands together.

'Okay. Let me show you the room.'

'Is it only one?'

'I'm afraid so. You're not in Loughrea now. Every inch is precious here.'

'No problem.'

'Let's go then.'

He tapped the girl on the shoulder.

'I'll be back in a few minutes,' he said to her.

They went up a staircase. It had a frayed carpet on it.

'Wear and tear,' Martin said, 'Too many students.'

There was a door off the landing. It was only half painted.

'The last fellow that was here started painting it,' he said. 'He left before he had it finished.'

'Why was that?'

'I think he failed his exams. He's pumping petrol somewhere now. What a waste. His old lad spent his life savings putting him through. Let that be a lesson to you not to follow in his footsteps.'

'Now you have me worried.'

'I believe he was a nightmare student.'

'It doesn't look like he was much of a painter either.'

'Do you want me to fix it for you?'

'Don't bother. I like it like that.'

He screwed up his eyebrows.

'Whatever turns you on.'

He brought him inside. It was a large room. There was a sofa in the middle of it. An en-suite bathroom was on the left. The bed was in the corner. A tiny television sat on a coffee table in front of the sofa. There was a poster of Che Guevara on the wall.

'I don't know who that bozo is,' he said, 'Probably one of those revolutionaries students go for.'

'It's Che Guevara,' Brian said, 'His grandmother was from Galway.'

'Are you serious? You learn something new every day. I'd have taken him for a foreigner.'

'Most people do.'

He sat down on the sofa.

'What do you think of the room?'

'It's very nice,' Brian said, 'It has everything I need.'

'The rent is 1000 a month. What do you think of that?'

'It sounds fair. Do you want me to pay you now?'

'If you're Bartley Kilcoyne's son you can pay me whenever you like. I don't think you're the type to do a runner.'

'Thanks for the vote of confidence.'

'You're welcome.'

He stood up.

'Okey dokey. I'll leave you to get settled in. Let me know if you need anything.'

'I will.'

He took a sheaf of paper out of his pocket.

'This is the lease, by the way. It means I can't throw you out without notice. Sign it when you have a minute. You can leave it with Denise when you're finished. That's the sexy-looking one at the counter. Don't tell her I said that or she'll want a raise.'

'Okay.'

He looked at his watch.

'Jesus, it's five o'clock. I better go. I was supposed to be somewhere an hour ago.'

'You're a busy man.'

'One of my other flats is after flooding.'

'You have more than one?'

'Did Bartley not tell you I'm a millionaire? Richard Branson might come to me looking for a few quid yet.'

'Is it a bad leak?'

'There's water leaking all over the place. The tenant is tearing her hair out. You know women. They tend to get a bit hysterical about things.'

'Tell me about it.'

'That's the thing about being a landlord. There's never a day you can sit back. People think I have a cushy number but I'm working harder now than I ever did at the farming.'

He went to go.

'Do I have to give you a deposit as well?' Brian asked him.

'I usually ask for a month's rent in advance and a month's deposit. If that's too much for you we can talk about it.'

'No, it's fine.'

'Good. Well it's been nice talking to you. I hope you'll be happy here.'

'I'm sure I will once I get settled in. Everything is a bit strange at the moment.'

'Don't worry about that. In a few days you'll feel you've been here all your life.'

He paused for a moment. Then he said, 'I'm sorry about your mother, by the way.'

'Thanks. It's a while ago now.'

'The pain never really goes away. She was a lovely lady. Anytime I ever went in to see Bartley she was very nice to me.'

He took his car keys out of his pocket.

'Okay. The best of luck to you. No wild parties now. I know what you students are like.'

'Don't worry.'

'I'm only having you on. Bartley tells me you're quiet.'

He went out. Brian heard him whistling as he walked down the stairs.

He looked out the window. He watched him getting into a car. It looked like it hadn't been washed in a month. The engine didn't sound too great either. He spluttered off in it.

He sat down on the sofa. It had obviously seen better days. As soon as he sat on it he knew there was something wrong with it.

He decided to ring Bartley. The phone was answered immediately. He sounded excited.

'Did you meet Geraghty?' he asked him.

'Yes. He's just gone.'

'How did you find him?'

'Fine. He was asking for you.'

'What's the flat like? Don't let him pawn a dump off on you.'

'It's very nice. There's only one room but it has everything in it.'

'One room? I'm not surprised. That fellow is as mean as muck. He'd squeeze twenty people into a shoebox if he could get away with it. What's he looking for in the rent?' '

'1000 euro a month.'

'Jesus Christ. That's daylight robbery.'

'Not in Dublin it isn't. It's half nothing the way things are going these days.'

'I wouldn't call 1000 smackers half nothing.'

'It's well below the market rate. Anyway I'm not going to argue with him.'

'What's it like?'

'Basic, I suppose you'd say.'

'Don't take it if it isn't suitable for you.'

'If I don't like it after a few weeks I can get somewhere else.'

'Did he give you a lease?'

'He left one for me but I didn't sign it yet.'

'Don't until you have it well read. He could tie you to it and not give you your deposit back if you left.'

'He didn't sound like that. He said it was for my protection.'

'They all say that. If you want to move inside the year he could screw you. He didn't get to be a millionaire for nothing.'

'Okay. I won't sign it. I better go now.'

'I'll be on to you. Angela sends her best. We're glad you arrived safe.'

After he left down the phone he unpacked his things. It was just as well he hadn't brought much luggage. He'd have had nowhere to put it.

He sat down on the sofa again. The springs were so jumpy it was more like a trampoline. He looked around him. It was good to just sit there in the silence and not be answerable to anyone. He felt relaxed for the first time all day.

He put the kettle on and made himself a cup of tea. There was a transistor on the coffee table. He switched it on. Somebody was talking about the EU. He switched it off again.

There was a bookshelf on the wall. Every kind of thing was in it – cookery, sailing, tourism. He took one of the books from it at random. It was by Herman Hesse. He'd never heard of him.

He opened it. The first page had a message on it. It said, 'Conleth Ferguson, UCD, 2010.' He wondered if he was the person who painted the door the two colours.

He sat down again. He didn't know what to do. When a lot of things happened and then they stopped it left you at a loose end. He wanted the activity to continue.

He decided to go for a walk. He went back down the stairs and into the shop. Denise was still at the counter. She was reading a Stephen King book. Yes, he thought, she did look sexy.

'Do you like the room?' she asked him.

'It's lovely. Have you worked here long?'

'I'm only out of school a year,' she said.

'How do you get on with Martin?'

'He's a dote. What do you think of him?'

'The same.'

'Are you organised up there yet?'

'I think so. I'm going to go for a walk now. It might help me to get my bearings.'

'Have fun.'

He went out. The traffic was crawling all the way up the street. Everyone seemed to be coming home from work. It was so different to Loughrea where you mightn't see a car from one end of the day to another. He thought of Martin's words: 'You're not in Loughrea now. Every inch is precious here.'

He looked around him. Which way would he go? It didn't really matter. He started walking.

He was tempted to ring Jennifer but he didn't. It was too soon. He needed to let some time pass for both of their sakes. If Dublin didn't work out and he had to go back he'd have felt like a fool.

He went into a bar. It was one of those kinds of pubs that seemed to be crowded at all times of the day. As well as drink you could get food. There was a huge television set above the counter.

There was a football match on. Everyone sat transfixed watching it. Nobody spoke to one another. They sat there like zombies.

He brought the drink over to a table. The match got to half-time but nobody moved. They just sipped their drinks. They gazed at the screen as if the game was still going on.

He didn't stay. The bar depressed him. It felt like a crypt.

When he got out to the street again it was getting dark. The traffic had eased a bit but there were still a lot of cars. The drivers all kept looking for gaps. They inched into them, stopping for a few seconds until another gap was created. Now and then someone honked a horn in temper.

He crossed the road, threading his way between the cars. A few minutes later he was back at Centra.

He waved at Denise but she didn't see him. She was serving a customer. He went upstairs. As soon as he turned the key in the lock he felt at home. Going out and back did that for him. It was a small thing but it was still important to him.

The flat was his now. This was his new life. He had no expectations. That made everything somehow possible.

12

He woke up early the next day. For a few seconds he didn't know where he was. He looked around him at the fridge, the cooker, the poster of Che Guevara. Everything seemed strange.

He put on tea and toast for himself. The clock said 10.20. There was a lecture he should have been at but he was too late for it now. He didn't care. It was good not to have to worry about things like that. It wasn't like the college in Loughrea where his absence would have been noticed.

He got a bus to Belfield. That was where the university was. There were mainly students on it. He listened to them talking. They were all excited. That was different to Loughrea too. People were in control of their destiny. They were here because they wanted to be rather than because they had to be.

Some of them were speaking on mobile phones. A girl sat at the back with earphones on. She seemed to be in a trance.

They reached the campus. 'Terminus!' said the driver. He got out. Everyone collected their things and shuffled along after him.

Belfield spread out before him like a secret city. The first thing he noticed was a lake. He hadn't expected that. But it didn't look like a lake. It was square like a swimming pool. It had a fountain in the middle of it.

It was an artificial lake. Would the university be artificial too? And the students? The buildings around him looked like they were made from Lego. There were no colours. It was all just concrete. It wasn't like the brownstone ones he'd seen in American universities in films. It was more like a factory. He told himself not to be so negative, to give it a chance.

He went into the main building. The corridor was huge. He felt like a midget in it. He watched the flow of students walking up and down. They all seemed to know where they were going. A lot of them had folders in their arms. Others carried hard-covered books. One of them passed by him on a skateboard. He thought he smelt cannabis off him.

A group of people were talking animatedly at a seating area. He watched them enviously. How did they know each other so well? The term hadn't even properly begun. Maybe they'd been to secondary school together. That would have eased their path into the university. He didn't have that advantage.

He'd never been a joiner. If he didn't get to know people fast he'd stand out. It would be embarrassing sitting alone in the restaurant or at the lectures. He'd stick out like a sore thumb. You could get away with it in the library but not anywhere else.

That was the downside of being anonymous. You could be too much out of things. Friendships were forged automatically in Loughrea without you having to work at them. You were put sitting beside people you knew. Conversation was automatic.

Here he'd have to work at it. It was a melting pot. If he was in a flat with other students it might have been easier. They could talk about their day together even if they were in different faculties.

That was another negative thought. He told himself to stop it. Maybe his isolation would be a kind of adventure. Maybe he'd get stuck into reading. Maybe he'd become lost in his books.

He looked through a door that had a porthole on it. It was built like an amphitheatre. The words "Theatre L" were emblazoned on it.

He went in. There were rows of seats descending towards a rostrum at the bottom. It reminded him of an arena he'd seen once in a Biblical film where gladiators were fighting. There was a blackboard behind the rostrum but it wasn't black, it was green. There was a lot of writing on it that he couldn't understand. It was like hieroglyphics.

He came out. People were still streaming by, still talking excitedly. Some of them went into a toilet. He followed them in.

A message outside one of the cubicles said, 'Flush twice, it's a long way to the restaurant.' Underneath it someone had written in marker, 'Oedipus – call your mother.'

It was a far cry from the messages in toilets in Loughrea. These usually carried drawings of sexual parts. He wondered if everything here would be so clever.

He went outside. The sun was high in the sky. It stung his eyes. The people from the corridor were heading towards the restaurant. He followed them. They were talking about a lecture they'd been at. One of the girls said she fancied the lecturer. Everyone laughed.

The restaurant was enormous. Half way across the floor there was a staircase leading down to a basement area. He walked down.

He ordered a coffee. He went over to a desk to pay for it.

'Very warm, isn't it?' the waitress said.

'Roasting.'

She was the only person he'd seen on the campus who wasn't a student. There was something reassuring in that. She had an ordinary accent. It contrasted with the posh ones of the students. That was reassuring too.

He sat down with his coffee. The conversations around him were unceasing. It was as if people who hadn't seen one another for a long time were suddenly thrown together and had things to catch up on. They were like electric currents.

Some of the talk was about books. Some of it concerned more practical things like people having to move their belongings in and out of bedsits.

The voices seemed to be coming from far away. He felt he was in a film, as if he was watching things that weren't really happening. What if all these people were actors, he thought, instead of real people. Sometimes he got weird ideas like that.

He walked back to the Arts Block. Another lecture was after finishing in Theatre L. People were coming out.

'What did you think of it?' a girl in a ponytail said to her friend. 'Bollox,' the friend replied. They laughed.

He listened to half a dozen conversations going on at the one time. He could have been in the middle of O'Connell Street during rush hour.

Then suddenly they stopped. Everyone was gone and the corridor was quiet again. He wondered where he'd go now.

He decided to register. Maybe he should have done that first. Maybe he wasn't even entitled to be in the building if he wasn't registered.

He went through a glass tunnel. There was a sign saying 'Library' at the end of it. He walked through it. It had a pleasant view on both sides – the playing fields, the bar, a reservoir shaped like a goblet.

He went through a turnstile. There were lots of people behind desks. He presumed they were staff rather than students. They were taking down details from the people they were talking to, clicking details into machines as they did so.

There was a man behind a desk at the bottom of a staircase. He walked over to him. He had a bald head.

'I'd like to register,' he said.

'What faculty?'

'Arts.'

It made him feel important saying the word.

'You have to fill this in,' he said.

He handed him a form. It looked very intricate. He brought it over to a desk. After a few minutes he had it all filled in. He brought it back to the man. He put it into a drawer with a lot of other forms. Then he reached into another drawer. He whipped out a sheet of paper. It had a booklist on it.

'You'll have to buy these,' he said. 'If they're in the library you can read them there.'

'How will I know if they are or not?' Brian asked him.

He pointed towards a desk where a lot of students were sitting looking at machines. Some of them had headphones on them.

'Computer search,' he said.

'Thank you.'

Before he went away he was given a key. It had a number on it.

'That's for your locker,' the man said, 'Don't lose it. They're hard to replace.'

He walked out of the library. The day was still warm. Some of the students were sunning themselves at the lake.

They fanned their faces with the pages of books. It was pleasant sitting there going through the booklist. He didn't recognise any of the titles or even the people who wrote them.

He lay on the edge of the lake. The day had made him sleepy. He could live his life like this, he thought, reading books that had no relation to his life or even to anyone else's, books that were set in past centuries in foreign countries. Such an indulgence was decadent in a way. What relationship had it to anything? What would it lead to? It didn't seem to make sense and yet he was seduced by it.

He went back to the library. On the way he passed by the man with the bald head. He nodded to him but the man didn't respond. He didn't know if he remembered him or not. There were so many registrations.

He went upstairs to the library proper. It was the largest one he'd ever seen in his life. There must have been hundreds of people in it and yet they were as quiet as mice. He might have been in a church. All he heard were occasional whispers, the scratch of pens here and there.

He took a book from a shelf and started to read it. It was a poetry anthology. It had a poem by a man called Wallace Stevens in it. He was vaguely familiar with the name. He read the poem but didn't think much of it.

He put it down. He took up another one. This was a collection of literary criticism. Some of the pages had comments from previous readers on them. They'd been engaging in debates with the writer.

One outraged person had written 'This is shit!' in black marker. Elsewhere there were underlined paragraphs. Beside one paragraph someone had written, 'That's a total misrepresentation of what Lawrence meant.'

He was amused. How could anyone get that worked up about a book? Maybe he'd have to as well if he was to get his exams.

He sat at one of the tables. He felt like talking to someone but you couldn't. It was like being in a church.

There were windows everywhere. He went up to one of them. He looked out at the lake. It didn't look too mechanical now. Many of the students were still sitting beside it. They had drinks in their hands.

He went back down the stairs. His head felt light. He thought of the days on the farm when he was up to his knees in mud, feeling he was using every sense as the elements did their worst.

Everything was neutral here. It was internalised. Could that develop another part of him?

There was a wind blowing when he got outside. Everything was quiet. It struck him that he'd hardly spoken to a soul the whole morning. The only people he'd communicated with were the waitress and the bald man.

The sun was strong on his face. He closed his eyes and sat at the lake. A few moments later he heard a voice. It said, 'How interesting you look.'

He opened his eyes. A young girl was looking at him. She was pretty. She had pink lipstick on her. She was wearing a blouse that reminded him of one he'd seen in a cowboy film once. It had frills and was half way down on one shoulder.

'Sorry?' he said.

'You look like a character from a Russian novel.'

He wasn't sure if it was an insult or a compliment.

<h1 style="text-align:center">13</h1>

He attended his lectures in a daze over the next few weeks. Some of them were unfathomable to him. Texts were dissected like corpses by people who looked for meanings in them that they might just as easily have put there themselves. It was as if they were subservient to the lecturers' views of them.

He liked the mystery of books. He preferred not to fully understand what they were about. When he got to a point where he did he often discarded them.

He sat in tutorials listening to people coming out with obscure statements about the hidden meanings of poems. He imagined a lot of them were probably stolen from other writers. The idea was to sound more impressive than the person sitting beside you.

He had no interest in those kinds of competitions. As far as he could see, the students were apeing the bad habits of the lecturers, trying to create an a language for themselves to appear as intelligent as they were. Was that intelligence? If they dragged up the name of an author nobody else had heard of it was a coup. If it was someone with a foreign name with lots of syllables in it. That earned them extra brownie points.

Whenever a poem was being discussed, his tutor had a habit of describing it as 'an insight into the human condition.' He never explained what that was. Was it the experience of being human? If that was so, why was it such an exceptional thing?

Everyone tried to give perceptive answers to the questions they were asked. It became too intense for him. He wished one of the other students would stand up and make a fool of themselves. He wished they'd say something stupid instead of sensible. Insights were only welcomed when they were the ones other people had before them. They were recycled.

Behind all the pretensions to non-conformity he felt his fellow students were going to end up being pillars of the establishment instead of radicals. He looked at them taking down notes and he thought: They're sheep. It wasn't that different from Loughrea really. One of his lecturers said, 'When in Rome, do as the Greeks,' but he doubted if he'd put it into practice. Maybe it was easy to say it when you weren't living in Rome.

He bought a bicycle. It was enjoyable cycling in to the campus instead of taking the bus. Feeling the wind in his face freshened him up for the day ahead. It also relieved him of the pressure of having to talk to the people he met on the bus every day. Such conversations had become jaded over the months. They'd degenerated from the meaning of life to how long a Rambler ticket lasted.

They were given assignments to complete every week. He tried to get his one in early so he could forget about it. He felt his work was under-valued as a result. The students who were looked up to were those whose projects became delayed. That seemed to make them more important to the tutors. Obscurity was good too. Alain Robbe-Grillet beat Henry James hands down.

The people in the class gave lip service to the magic of books but he wondered if they enjoyed reading at all. As far as he could see, Denise was getting as much enjoyment from the Stephen King novel she dipped into at her desk in Centra than the superbrains discussing 'Ontological Substructures in the Shorter Fiction of Guy de Maupassant.' What did 'Ontological Substructures' have to do with life? In the news stands on the way to the campus each day he'd see headlines about Dublin's growing street crime. When people were being shot in the head in drug wars it made nonsense of such discussions.

He didn't like people who were obsessive about books. They tended to wear long faces when they were talking about them. Did being intelligent mean you had to be miserable as well? If that was the case he thought he'd prefer to be stupid.

The French classes didn't have that problem. The focus there was on learning the language rather than being obscure for the sake of it. He liked the French students better. They were more natural than the English ones. They had nothing to prove.

After a while he started acting the fool to try and shake them up. One day they were discussing Ernest Hemingway's *The Old Man and the Sea* in the tutorial. The tutor asked Brian what he thought it was about. He waited a few seconds before saying, 'I think it's about an old man...and the sea.' There was silence in the room after he spoke. Then one of the other students began to titter. A few minutes later everyone was in convulsions – except the tutor.

Brian felt he hated him after that. Maybe he was threatened by him. Sometimes he wanted to scream at him. He wanted to shake him to find out if there was anything inside him besides data.

The university was supposed to be a centre of learning but he saw it more as a laboratory, a laboratory breeding mice. The mice ran around in circles chasing their own tails. The lecturers were so many forensic scientists analysing them.

He rang Jennifer every week or so. He didn't tell her how he felt about things. It was easier to just say everything was going fine.

He didn't know if he was growing away from her or not. He was becoming a different person to the one he'd been at home. He wasn't sure how he'd feel about her when he saw her again. The feeling that she was going to be different frightened him but it also gave him a kind of excitement. He loved unpredictability.

He only rang home rarely. He told Bartley even less than he did Jennifer. He'd become increasingly fussy.

'I worry about you,' he said to him on one phone call, 'You may not believe that. I know I probably didn't say it to you when you were growing up. I felt it was Teresa's role.'

'I'm a big boy now.'

'You've had a sheltered life. Now you're in a city where you hardly know anyone. It must be a bit of a wrench for you. I don't know if you're equipped to deal with it.

'Don't worry,' he said, 'I know how to take care of myself.'

'What about violence? We hear stories all the time about people being beaten up. Would you be able to defend yourself if you were attacked in one of those no-go areas?'

'I don't go into them,' he said. But he did.

By the end of October he'd stopped going to the tutorials. He skipped a lot of the lectures as well. He started to read books that weren't on his course. He became infatuated by them.

He hung around second-hand bookshops picking up rare ones. Some of them were falling apart. He liked the smell of them, the binding.

He found it hard to read in the library as the term went on. Many of the other students read kindle books. They had iPods, USBs. He watched them downloading books on their computers. For him that debased them. It made them into products. He remembered the film *Fahrenheit 451*. Books were seen as dangerous things by a totalitarian state in it. The tutor talked about it in one of his classes. Books weren't so much dangerous as irrelevant now. They took up too much space.

He thought he might fail his exams because of the way he was going on. Falling out with the tutor wasn't going to do him any favours. He wasn't studying much now either. Some days he just stayed in the campus bar playing pool and drinking. He'd come back to the flat at teatime half-soused.

Martin called around one day. 'You look like the back of a bus,' he said, 'Are you trying to turn yourself into that Che Guevara fellow?'

'I don't know if "trying" is the right word. You don't have to make an effort to be scruffy. The effort comes in when someone tries to stop you.'

Bartley kept phoning him. He mentioned Angela a lot on the calls. Brian wondered if she'd moved in with him. He didn't like to ask.

She came on the line one night.

'How are you getting on up there?' she said, 'Are you enjoying yourself?'

'It's not too bad.'

'What about the social life? I bet you have to beat the women away.'

He hated her over-familiarity with him, her lame attempts at humour. On many calls he avoided talking to her when Bartley said he was going to put her on.

'I have to rush,' he'd say, 'I have a lecture.'

It was a lie. He rarely went to them now. They were about the same subjects all the time – what a writer was trying to get at, why he wrote a book, how it slotted into the sociology of the period.

He preferred immersing himself in books that weren't prescribed. They spilled off the shelves in the flat. He read them on park benches, on the top storeys of buses.

He developed a passion for the German poet Rainer Maria Rilke. He read him so much the pages started falling out of the books. That made them more attractive to him.

He learned some of his poems off by heart. He recited them to himself sometimes when he was walking down the street. They became like food to him.

He ate little enough actual food, just scraps he picked up in the Centra shop, pre-cooked dinners he heated up in a micro-wave. They made him feel sick but they filled a gap.

'Are you minding yourself?' Bartley asked him one night on the phone.

'Why wouldn't I be?'

'You sound different. You're not on drugs or anything, are you?'

'Just cocaine,' he informed him, 'and a bit of heroin. Nothing serious.'

'I wish you wouldn't make those kinds of jokes. They're childish.'

'I don't like being interrogated.'

'I'm not interrogating you. I'm your father. Is it a crime to ask you how you are?'

'Sorry for being touchy.'

'Maybe you're working too hard.'

'Or not hard enough.'

Some days he went to films instead of to the university. Often he didn't bother checking what was showing before he went in. The plots of the films didn't matter to him. It was enough for him to be sitting there watching images revolve in front of him, watching scenes unrelated to his life.

He began to write poems now, carving words out of his head like a sculptor with stone. He had some of them published in the campus literary magazine. That gave him a certain standing with some of his classmates. Others resented him for it. They'd have preferred him to just study poetry rather than write it. He thought his tutor felt the same. Scholarship was preferable to creativity for him. He suspected he was going to give him poor grades at the end of the year. When you didn't like someone it was hard to hide it. With them it was mutual.

He didn't know where the poems came from. A lot of them were about his mother. He was told he used a stream of consciousness style. He didn't even know what that term meant the first time he heard it.

One of the people in his class said, 'I see Ezra Pound in your work.'

'I'm glad you noticed,' he replied. He'd never read a word of Pound. By now he was tired arguing with them. Nothing was ever resolved by it. Everyone left the tutorials with the same views they had coming into them. They always went back to their own points in the end.

When he had enough poems compiled for a collection he sent them off to a publisher, He expected them to be rejected but a few weeks later he got a letter saying they were going to be published. 'You have a unique voice,' the publisher wrote in his acceptance letter, 'a kind of negative energy.'

He met him to discuss the book. They went to a café in Dawson Street. He was a small man in a corduroy jacket. It had a hole in one of the sleeves.

'We're thinking of a spring launch,' he said. The idea filled him with dread. He hadn't thought about things like launches.

'You'll read, of course, won't you?' he said then.

That prospect became another kind of dread for him. He imagined a sea of faces looking up at him on a podium as he tried to look tortured enough for his 'negative energy.'

He told him there wouldn't be any money in it for him. Even

recognised poets were lucky if they sold a few hundred copies of their books. That didn't surprise him.

'I don't care about money,' he said.

'Then you'll die broke,' the publisher said, 'like most poets.'

Jennifer was thrilled when he told her. He didn't mention it to Bartley.

The completion of the book emptied him creatively. Afterwards he started attending the university again. He didn't go to the lectures. He just liked the atmosphere.

He enjoyed talking to the other students as long as they didn't discuss the course. That was difficult in the English faculty. He spent more time with the French students for that reason. He had chats with them about everyday things. There was no snobbery in it.

In the afternoons he usually got a bus into town. He hung around the coffee-houses of Temple Bar. In an army surplus shop he bought a long coat. He felt like the Russian novelist the student had compared him to that first day.

He stayed up late most nights. He listened to music into the small hours, keeping himself awake with endless cups of black coffee. Sometimes he topped them up with whiskey. He played the songs over and over, letting them flow into him like a drug.

On other nights he just sat at the window looking out at the people outside, people darting into shops for cigarettes or bottles of milk. Often there were couples courting across the street. It made him feel lonely. He listened to them arguing, making up, making love.

Sometimes he tried to write their life stories in his head. He always thought he lived more in his imagination than in the real world. In his mind he could have many lives but in the real world only one was available to him. Happiness was being removed from everything he saw but still being a part of it. He got that from his perch at the window. It made him feel free. He could stay up all night looking out if he wanted.

He liked to have music playing in the background when he did that. He listened to every type - rap, heavy metal, soul.

He didn't mind when the songs were written. His favourite decade was the sixties: Bob Dylan and Leonard Cohen in particular. People told him Cohen was a depressive but he never saw it like that. He thought of him as a prophet, a prophet with a sense of humour. His lyrics entered his soul like mini-oracles, pointing him the way to some new kind of identity. Dylan was hypnotic in a different way. He listened to him when he felt fired up with anger.

The days became grim and rainy. He walked past dead leaves on the way to the campus, arriving in at different hours every day. Sometimes he went into lectures in the middle of them. He felt more in charge of things that way.

As he looked around him at the faces in the lecture-halls he saw them as ghosts, ciphers. He listened to them scraping their pens across pages as the words of the lecturers were transcribed into folders. He felt superior to them, superior to the snobs. Maybe that was another kind of snobbery, the dictatorship of the proletariat.

He went clubbing every so often. He didn't intend to be unfaithful to Jennifer, it was just something to do. He didn't try to chat up the women he met but that seemed to make them come on to him more. The best way to get a woman, he concluded, was not to try.

Now and then he brought them back to the flat with him. That usually happened when he was drinking. If he was drunk enough he couldn't remember how they got there. Drinking got him into fights as well. One morning when he woke up there was a girl in bed with a gash on her forehead.

'You really need to get yourself sorted out,' she said.

'What happened?' he said but she refused to tell him. She didn't wait for breakfast.

He became involved with two students from his English class as Christmas approached. Adrian and Dominic were their names. They shared his disenchantment with the way the course was being taught. Adrian was from Rathangan. He was the older of the two. He'd been out in the world a few years before going to College. He left home after his parent's marriage broke up. Dominic was from the inner city. He'd got to UCD on a scholarship.

Brian saw them as misfits like himself. They seemed rootless. When he asked Adrian where they lived he said, 'Wherever becomes available.' They slept rough a lot of the time, grudging any money they had to pay for rent. When one of them got a place, the other moved in with him. Otherwise they bunked down in the homes of friends or even on the street. For a while Brian thought they were gay. .

Sometimes they found disused buildings to inhabit. They didn't mind how uncomfortable they were. Many of them had rats in them.

They slept on mattresses on the floor. Newspapers were used for curtains. They pinned them onto the windows with sellotape. On cold nights they wore their overcoats to bed with them. They usually put a few jumpers on them as well.

Adrian used to work for the Simon Community before he went to the university. Now he looked more like someone that could do with being helped by them. He had holes in his shoes. He filled them with the pages of a book by Marcel Proust. He hated Proust.

Adrian and Dominic were disliked by most of the people in the class. Maybe that was why Brian was drawn to them.

They stole books from the campus shop. The idea of being caught was like a challenge to them. They didn't really want them. They threw most of them away afterwards.

One day Adrian arrived at a lecture with twenty postcards in his pocket. They were all of the same scene.

'Why would you buy twenty postcards that are exactly the same?' Brian asked him.

'I just liked it,' he said. Dominic burst out laughing. He'd obviously stolen them.

They went on train journeys without paying, hiding in the toilets if a ticket inspector got on. They used to put the door on 'Vacant' instead of 'Engaged' so he wouldn't check to see if they were in there. They went to places they didn't want to for fun. Then they came back again.

Adrian got Brian a job doing night security in one of the abandoned buildings they used to squat in. The money he got from Bartley was running out now. It was a shady firm. Sometimes he turned up for work with a sleeping bag and an alarm clock. Nobody asked any questions.

One night he was put guarding a factory. He slept there too. He set the alarm for shortly before his shift was due to end. Then his replacement arrived. He wouldn't have known if the whole place had been cleaned out by burglars.

He wasn't studying at all now. The days drifted by without him being aware of them. He enjoyed not knowing what each one might bring.

He rang Jennifer.

'See you on the Christmas tree,' he said.

'I'm afraid not, she said, 'A few of us are going to Kerry.'

He thought that was unusual.

'Is everything okay?'

'Of course.'

She sounded cool. He didn't know if she was going off him or not. Maybe she was giving him some breathing space. It wasn't her style to play hard to get.

14

He didn't go home until Christmas Eve. He still didn't know if Angela had moved into the house or not. From a few comments Bartley made on the phone he thought she might have. He put her on to Brian on nearly every call now. That made him less inclined to ring. He hadn't picked up the last few times Bartley rang him.

They met him at the station.

'It's good to see you, Brian,' Angela said, 'You look great.'

'You too,' he said.

Bartley got straight into it.

'Why have you been ignoring my calls?'

'I was busy.'

'Bullshit. Nobody opens a book before Christmas in university. Even I know that.'

'I've been reading around the course.'

'What's that supposed to mean?'

'Books that haven't been prescribed.'

'What good is that going to do you?'

'It's all grist to the mill.'

'Is it going to help you in the exams?'

'I hope so.'

They walked to the car. Angela tried to get in on the conversation.

'Are you doing any protesting up there?'

'How do you mean?'

'Isn't that what students are supposed to do?'

'Maybe in the old days, when they cared about things. The only things they'd protest about nowadays is the cost of their dinner.'

'So they're not likely to be storming the gates of government anytime soon?

'Not unless the Minister for Education cuts their grants.'

They got to the car. Bartley took his case. He was surprised to see how light it was.

'You haven't got the Crown Jewels in here anyway,' he said.

'Sorry. I didn't bring either of you presents.'

'I didn't mean that.'

'I just brought my toothbrush, as they say.'

'It must be a big toothbrush,' Angela said.

They sat into the car.

'Declan will be up later with Yvonne,' Bartley said, 'They're looking forward to seeing you.'

He'd only rang Brian once or twice since he left. They didn't have much to say.

'How are things going for him?'

'Mighty. He's expanding like you wouldn't believe.'

'Good for him.'

'He'd like to have you with him. He'd make you a partner if the university didn't work out for you.'

'A partner?'

'It'd be a handy number for you, wouldn't it?'

'If I wanted it.'

'In other words you don't.'

'Give the boy a break,' Angela said, 'He hardly has his feet wet in the university and you're grilling him about other things.'

'I'm trying to tell him there's something else out there.'

He drove along a back road. The Austin puffed its way along.

'How is Geraghty treating you?' Bartley asked.

'I don't see much of him.'

'You're better off. That's the way to keep it.'

'He's never given me any problems.'

'Don't ever relax with him.'

'Why do you say that?'

'The more relaxed he is with you the more likely he is to rip you off.'

'Don't be so hard on him,' Angela said, 'He can't be that bad.'

'Believe me, he's worse.'

'Why are you so against him?' Brian said.

'You don't know what he's like. If he raises the rent I want you to leave.'

'You can't be serious about that.'

He didn't want to argue with him. It was too ridiculous.

'Have you been on to Jennifer?' Bartley asked him.

'Of course. She's going to Kerry for Christmas. What about you?'

'She calls up to see us when she's around. She's always asking about you. She worries that you're not taking care of yourself.'

'In what way?'

'Food-wise.'

'You look under-fed,' Angela said, 'We'll have to do something about that.'

'You must be joking. I've been eating all around me.'

He saw the farm in the distance. It gave him a comfortable feeling. He didn't think he'd be nostalgic but he was. He felt as if he'd been more than a few months away.

Bartley kept pumping him with questions.

'Tell us a bit about the kind of stuff you're studying. Just a few details so we have the gist of it. It'd probably mean nothing to me anyway.'

He rolled off the names of some high-sounding books.

'We'll have to show you off to the neighbours with all that stuff. You can be the resident professor of Connacht.'

'I'd prefer to be a scarecrow on the north field,' he said.

'You're a queer class of a lad, to be sure.'

When they reached the farm he got a fright. All the plants in the driveway were gone. They were replaced with cobblelock paving.

The house was painted a bright yellow over the original stonework. The ivy that had been on the walls was gone too. It made them look naked. Double-glazed windows had been put in.

'Home sweet home,' Bartley chirped as they pulled into the driveway.

'What happened?' Brian said.

'To what?' Bartley asked.

'The whole kit and caboodle.'

'You mean the bit of painting?'

'The place looks like it's been revamped. What did you do with all the plants?'

'There was too much maintenance on them.'

'You should have told me. I'd have taken care of them.'

'That wouldn't have worked. We were getting the driveway paved. They were in the way.'

'So it wasn't the maintenance.'

'It was a few things. The work would have stopped unless we got rid of them.'

'I should have been consulted.'

'How could I? You never picked up the phone. It wouldn't have made any difference anyway once the work was started. One thing led to another.'

'How do you mean?'

'The roof was falling in. We had to get a fellow to do that in a hurry. It was affecting the electricals.'

'You're telling me all these things as if I'm a stranger.'

'I didn't think you'd be interested. You were all fired up about your books anytime I talked to you.'

He got out of the car. He felt like he was on another person's property.

'Who did the roof?'

'Some doxy from the next parish. I can't even remember his name now. He ripped us off, needless to say. He probably made the problem ten times worse than it was. They always do that when they have you over a barrel. If I could have got up there myself I'd have put manners on him. Those days are gone, I'm afraid.'

'So the roof was the first job. What happened then?'

'You know yourself. Once you get one thing done, everything else looks bad. You get yourself into a trap. Before you know it the whole house is torn apart. And you're bankrupt.'

He stood there looking at it, still not able to take it in.

'I still think I should have been told.'

'You told us you wanted to be left alone.'

'Not for things like that.'

'Decisions have to be made in a hurry when people aren't around. You can't be ringing them up for every little detail.'

'I wouldn't call destroying a rock garden a detail. It was there since the day I was born.'

'I said I was sorry. We could be going round and round with this all day. You can plant another one if you like. It'll only take a year or two to grow.'

He sighed.

Bartley went over to him.

'Is this going to put a damper on your visit?' he said.

'No. I just need a while to get used to it.'

'If there's anything else happening down the line I'll bring you in on it. How is that?'

'Thanks.'

They went into the house. Rusty was sitting in the corner. When he saw Brian he jumped up. He ran over to him excitedly.

'Look at that,' Bartley grumbled, 'I feed him every day and he treats me as if I don't exist. Then *mo dhuine* waltzes in and he goes doolaly.'

There was a Christmas tree in the centre of the room.

Decorations lined the walls. The mantelpiece was bedecked with cards. A fire had been set.

He put a match to it.

'You can't beat the old turf,' he said. He warmed his hands.

'Sorry for flying off the handle,' Brian said, 'I just need time to get used to everything'.

'I'm sorry too. Let's not get worked up about things. We'll have a nice Christmas for ourselves.'

'Good idea.'

'You'll see a few more changes as you move around the house. I hope they won't bother you as much as the outside ones.'

'I'll try not to let them.'

'Most of them came about by accident. It started with a pothole in the driveway. Angela was driving over it one day when she got a puncture. I filled it in with cement but it looked a sight. That led to the cobblelock. Then we thought we should look at everything else – after the roof I mean.'

'Was it expensive?'

'I wouldn't like to tell you how expensive. We had a local man on it at the beginning but he went off on us. The work was only half done. I wasn't paying him that much. I think he got a better offer down the road. That's what you're up against. We had to get some Poles to do it in the end.'

'I believe they work very cheaply.'

'If you can get them to understand what you're saying. That's a day's work in itself. You'd think they'd take a few classes in English before coming over here.'

'Their English is a lot better than my Polish,' Brian said.

'Maybe, but you don't live in Poland. Or paint houses for a living.'

He went over to the window. He pulled the curtains aside. .

'What are you looking at?' Bartley asked.

'The fields look bigger,' he said.

'I sold some cows. That could be the reason.'

'How many?'

'As many as I could. At least that bastard Geraghty didn't get them this time.'

'I wish you'd lay off Martin.'

'Oh, so it's Martin now, is it? Very cosy. You'll be inviting him over for dinner yet.'

'Let's just agree to differ on that subject. What does it matter anyway? He's not in your life now.'

'I suppose so.'

It wasn't like him to give in so easily. He was surprised.

He looked around the room.

'What's up with you now?' Bartley said.

'I see you got strip lighting too.'

'What do you think of it?'

'It's nice.'

'Hallaluah. He likes something. Wait till you see it at night-time. It's like the Starship Enterprise.'

Angela came in. She stood in front of him with a smile on her face. She had a box in her hand.

'What's that?' he said.

'It's your Christmas present.'

She courtseyed before him like a little girl, 'See what Santa brought you.'

'What is it?'

'Open it and you'll see.'

'Can I not wait till Christmas day?'

'No.'

He took it from her. It was heavy. He pulled the paper off.

It was a computer.

'You can't be serious,' he said.

'We thought it might come in handy for the study,' Bartley said.

'This is insane. You must have paid a fortune for it.'

'Not at all. You can get these things for half nothing these days. Do you like it? It was Angela's idea. I wouldn't know a computer from a hole in the wall.'

'You're too kind,' he said, 'Both of you. I really appreciate it.'

'Will you use it?'

'Of course. I'll never come off it.'

He didn't want to appear bad-minded by saying he didn't like computers.

'We heard you were writing some poems,' Bartley said then. He pronounced it 'pomes.'

'Who told you that?'

'Jamesie Gildea. He's doing Social Science up in UCD. He knows you to see.'

'Jesus Christ.'

'It's a small world,' Angela said.

'He said they were going to be put in a book. Is that true?'

'Yes.'

'Have you got a copy for us so we can have a goo at it?'

'It's not out yet.'

'Who's publishing it?'

'You wouldn't have heard of him. He works on a shoestring.'

'I don't care if he works from a shoebox. It's going to be a book, right?'

'Yes.'

'And he's a regular publisher.'

'He is.'

'Well that beats Banagher. I didn't know I was raising Seamus Heaney. What's it about?'

'I can't say.'

Anytime he talked about his writing he found he couldn't write afterwards. He remembered something he read from Nietzsche, 'We only speak about that for which we have lost respect in our hearts.'

He wouldn't back off.

'Give us an outline,' he persisted.

'It's just the thoughts of a man who lives in his head.'

'That sounds interesting,' Angela said, 'I could see myself liking that.'

'Why don't you write about the world *outside* his head,' Bartley suggested.

'That doesn't interest me.'

He put on a face.

'What doesn't interest you?'

'Reality.'

'Did you hear that, Angela?' he said, 'He's not interested in reality.'

She shrugged.

'Which of us are?'

He screwed up his features.

'I never heard you talking that way before.'

He looked at Brian.

'Can you show us some samples of the poems that are going to be in this unreal book?'

'No.'

'Why?'

They were in his case but he didn't want to take them out.

'Go on,' he pressed, 'Show them to us.'

'I can't. I only have the galleys at the moment.'

'The galleys? What is it, a ship or a book?'

'You get galleys before a book is printed.'

'You're showing our ignorance of the literary world,' Angela said.

'Okay,' Bartley said, 'Show us the *galleys* then.'

'I don't have them with me.'

He was determined not to show them to him. He couldn't have faced all the questions.

'Go on out of that. I know you have. You probably think we wouldn't understand them.'

'Don't be ridiculous.'

'Why don't you write a book about the government, how they're mismanaging the country. I bet it'd be a best-seller.'

'I'm not interested in politics.'

'Too fancy for that, are we?'

'I didn't say that. Don't put words into my mouth.'

'All right. But let us read it, will you?'

'Of course.'

'When?'

'Some other time.'

'That means never. I know you.'

'You might be surprised.'

'Give him a rest,' Angela said, 'You haven't stopped grilling him since he walked in the door. Can I get you something to eat, Brian?'

'No thanks.'

He wanted to be out of the room. He felt Bartley's eyes boring into him. He could see him warming up for his next enquiry. It wasn't long coming.

'Tell me more about what you're studying in the French course,' he asked, 'I suppose the lads there would be over my head too.'

'Not necessarily.'

'Give me the name of one of them till I see.'

'Do I have to?'

'You do.'

'Okay,' he said, 'Rimbaud.'

He looked confused.

'Who's he when he's at home?'

'A writer.'

'Is he not someone to do with Sylvester Stallone?'

'No. That's a different person.'

'Didn't Sylvester Stallone play Rambo?' he said to Angela.

'About twenty times,' Angela replied.

'There you go,' Bartley said, 'I could knock spots off those bozos in that French department.'

He poured a glass of whiskey for himself.

'How long are you home for?' he said.

'It depends. The university doesn't open until the new year.'

'We'll have you well countrified by then. They'll be able to smell the shit off your shoes in the lecture-halls.'

'That's been there all along.'

'Good. I'd hate to see you turning into a yuppie.'

'There's no fear of that. Anyway, I think I'll go up to my room now if you don't mind. It's been a long day.'

'Do that. Hopefully we'll have a few people in over Christmas. It'll save you looking at our two ugly mugs all the time.'

'Speak for yourself,' Angela said.

He laughed.

'Will you join me in a drink?' he said to Brian.

'I don't know if I feel like one at the moment.'

'It's Christmas Eve. Are you Irish at all?'

'Have you anything besides whiskey?'

His eyes lit up.

'That's more like it. Angela, where's that bubbly you bought?'

She went over to the cabinet.

'There's a bottle of Prosecco in here. Is that what you were talking about?'

'The poor man's champagne. What do you say, Brian?'

'It sounds good.'

She took it out. Some of it spilled onto the floor as she popped it.

'Watch it, woman,' Bartley said, 'Don't waste it,'

'I'd like to see you trying to open it. There'd probably be more on the floor than in the bottle.'

'Just a small glass,' Brian said. She handed it to him.

'*Sláinte,*' she said.

'Should that not be for Guinness?'

'You're right,' Bartley said. He looked at Angela. 'He's getting all posh on us, Angie.'

Why was he calling her Angie?

'Actually very few people bother with Guinness round here anymore,' she said, 'We're very sophisticated these days.'

'Have a glass yourself,' he said to her.

'I don't think so. I have some work to do.'

'The work will be there after you. Have a feckin' drink on Christmas Eve, for feck's sake.'

'Okay. Just one.'

'Jesus, I've landed myself with two yokes from the Pioneer's Association.'

'He's desperate, isn't he, Brian?' she said.

She poured a glass for herself. Bartley took another swig of the whiskey.

Brian wondered how much he'd taken already. He remembered Christmasses of yore when he'd be on it almost from dawn.

Any occasion was an excuse to over-imbibe. Christmas was better one than most of them.

He sat on the couch savouring it. Every time he finished a glass he went over to the table and filled it again.

Brian looked at Angela to see if she seemed concerned. If she was she didn't show it.

He continued to ask Brian questions about the university. Brian knew he wasn't really interested in the answers. Having him there as a drinking companion was enough.

He yawned. Angela looked at him sympathetically.

'You're probably tired after all the travelling,' she said.

'Maybe I'll turn in early. We can continue the celebrations tomorrow.'

'Fuck that for a game of cowboys,' Bartley said, 'It was never the Kilcoyne way to let a Christmas Eve go by without wetting your whistle. Dammit, we deserve it. Especially this year.'

He looked sad for a moment. Brian looked at his mother's picture on the wall. Then he looked away from it. One of the reasons he hadn't wanted to come home was because of it.

'I shouldn't have brought that up,' he said.

He seemed to sober suddenly. He put down his glass.

The three of them sat in silence. Then Angela said, 'Why don't you show Brian the rest of the house?'

The suggestion revived him.

'That's a great idea,' he said, 'Why didn't I think of it? Are you on, Brian?'

'I was going to wait till tomorrow.'

'come on. There's no time like the present.'

He put some more whiskey in his glass.

In his enthusiasm he spilt it.

Angela laughed.

'He gets more on the carpet than down his gullet these days.'

'If that's the case,' he chortled. 'maybe the carpet will get cirrhosis of the liver and I'll escape.'

He went out of the room with Brian.

'Let's start with the Blue Room,' he said, 'Angela will be along later with the tour guide.'

The so-called Blue Room was what used to be the study. It was where the piano used to be. He opened the door with a flourish. Cabinets lined the walls.

He felt sad as he looked around. He thought of his mother playing the piano, the expression that came into her eyes as her fingers glided over the keys. It was a world away from her pain for her, a world away from Bartley. He remembered how she'd almost go into a trance as she played. Did she play because of a love for it or to get away from Bartley? He never knew.

Neither did Bartley. He didn't understand music. It was 'that high-falutin' thing.' Brian remembered her having to stop playing when Bartley rolled in from the bar. If she didn't he'd pass some smart comment about her. Brian hated him on nights like that. He wanted to hit him but he was too young to.

The floor was wooden.

'What happened the carpet?' he said.

'I got rid of it. It was in bits.'

'I liked it.'

'Wood is all the rage now.'

'It makes the room look cold.'

'I don't agree.'

The furniture was honeypine. The walls had been papered with a gaudy design over the original *terra cotta*.

'It'll take you a while to get used to it,' he said.

'You can say that again.'

He brought him round to the other rooms. They were similarly furnished. The house didn't look like a farmhouse anymore. Its identity was gone.

'I see Angela has been busy,' he said.

'You were hardly out the door when she started. Her brain goes into overdrive whenever she sees something she doesn't like.'

Why had he given her that power?

She appeared beside him. It was as if she'd been reading his mind.

'I hope you don't think I'm taking over,' she said.

'Not at all. You've done a great job. Everywhere looks fantastic.'

'I don't know about that. There's a lot of dust around.'

'I can't see any of it.'

'Don't look too close.'

They went upstairs. The bathroom was re-tiled. Its shelves were full of her perfumes and facial creams. He needed no further evidence that she was living with Bartley now.

Bartley got embarrassed.

'Angela,' he said, 'You left some of your things here.'

'Did I?'

'She was here last weekend,' he said. Angela blushed.

The bath had been taken out. A power shower stood in its place.

'Another one of Her Ladyship's inspirations,' Bartley said.

'It looks well.'

'You'll probably miss the bath. You always spent hours in there.'

'That was years ago.'

'Angela thinks it's unhygienic lying in your own dirt.'

'That's a bit dramatic, isn't it?'

'I don't think people bother with baths anymore,' Angela said, 'The world is moving too fast.'

They went into Bartley's bedroom. Not much had been done to it except for the installation of an en-suite toilet.

'It's far from that I was reared,' Bartley said.

Brian sensed his discomfort. A picture of his mother had been removed from the wall.

'They're handy when you get short-taken,' he said, 'You don't have to go down the corridor to the bathroom. You have to be thinking of things like that at our age.'

'We're not quite that decrepit yet,' Angela said.

They stood in the silence. Nobody seemed to know what to say.

'We'll show you your own room now,' Bartley said eventually, 'The grand finale of the tour.'

They went down the corridor. The carpet was gone from there too.

When he saw it he got a shock. Everything was exactly as he'd left it – the wardrobe, the tallboy with the drawer missing, the poster of James Dean on the wall. They'd even kept a glass bottle he'd had from childhood. It made it look like it was snowing when you turned it upside down.

The sameness of everything gave him an eerie feeling. He thought of homes where sons had died and their parents kept their room as a kind of shrine to them.

The words of a Philip Larkin poem he'd studied in the university came to him. They concerned a house that was kept the same after the children went away: 'Shaped to the comfort of the last to go/As if to win them back.'

'We didn't have the heart to move anything,' he said, 'It might make up to you for all the other changes we made.'

'That was thoughtful of you.'

'So that's it then. Unpack your things and then come down to us for a nightcap. Do you want me to bring your case up?'

'That would be great.'

They went out. He went over to the window. There were a few cows still in the fields, the few that hadn't been sold. They were like a threatened species now.

Bartley came up with his case. He unpacked what little things he'd brought with him. Apart from his clothes he had the proofs of his book, the proofs he pretended he didn't have.

Angela had left the laptop on the tallboy. He put it into a drawer. He doubted he'd ever use it.

He went back down the stairs. Bartley and Angela were in the kitchen. Angela had an apron on her. Bartley was wedged into a chair.

'Tell us about Dublin,' he said, 'We hardly got a dickeybird out of you so far.'

'I told you everything I could think of.'

'You should be in the IRA. You'd never say where the bodies were buried.'

'Give him a break,' Angela said.

He put a funny hat on his head.

'Pull a cracker with me,' he said then 'Just to get into the spirit of things.'

Brian wasn't in the humour but he pulled it anyway. Bartley won.

'Ha ha,' he chortled, 'I'm stronger than you are.'

He tried to read the message that was inside it but he wasn't able to.

'Why do they make the writing on these fucking things so small?' he said.

Brian was bored.

'Would you mind if I turned in early?' he said, 'I'm exhausted from the travelling.'

Bartley looked deflated.

'Do exactly what you want,' Angela said, 'You're here to unwind.'

'I feel bad going up when you've gone to such trouble for me.'

'Divil a bit of trouble. Get your sleep. We'll chat in the morning.'

She put on the kettle for a hot water bottle for him. His mother used to do that. It disturbed him to see her doing it. When she handed it to him he said he didn't need it.

'Are you sure? It's a freezing night.'

'I don't find it too bad.'

'None of that nancyboy stuff for the Kilcoynes,' Bartley said.

He went up to his room. A bright moon shone over the fields. It made him feel peaceful looking out at it. He'd spent his life looking out at such nights but not seeing them. That's what going away did to people. How many more of them would there be?

He listened to Angela washing the dishes downstairs. She was part of the house now. If Bartley married her, as he was sure to, he couldn't see himself coming back home again.

She finished her work. Bartley went upstairs. He put his head in Brian's door.

'Angela and myself are off to midnight Mass,' he said, 'I don't suppose you feel like coming with us.'

'I don't think so. I hope you're not driving.'

'In the condition I'm in, we'd hardly make it to the gate.'

'Okay. See you tomorrow then.'

'Sleep tight and don't let the bedbugs bite.'

'Say one for me.'

'I will, and I'll get Angela to say one too. Her prayers reach the target much quicker than mine.'

He had the contrite nature of most alcoholics. At Mass he always kept his head down. Tonight he'd keep it lower than ever.

God would forgive him for his indulgences because he loved sinners. Bartley knew that. It was the cornerstone of his faith.

For Angela Mass was more like an opportunity to take the high moral ground. She'd sit in her pew and pass silent judgment on all the sinners across from her, safe in the knowledge that she'd never be tarred with the same brush as them.

15

Brian woke up early on Christmas Day. He thought back to his childhood when he'd see the presents his mother would have put on the end of the bed. Bartley used to get Declan's ones. They were always more showy than Brian's.

Bartley was at the cooker when he got down to the kitchen.

'The bloody turkey,' he said, 'It never works out right for me. It'll probably be midnight before it's cooked. Happy Christmas, by the way.'

'Happy Christmas.'

'What would you like for your breakfast?'

'A cup of tea will do me.'

The kettle boiled. Bartley poured it. Brian buttered a slice of bread. He put jam on it.

'Would you not like something more elaborate?' Bartley asked.

'No, this is fine. Were there many people at the Mass?'

'They were spilling out the doors. You'd imagine the Pope was there. I never saw such a crowd. You go in there the other 364 days and it's empty. What brings them out?'

'Probably the night that's in it.'

'Half of them didn't even know the responses. It was embarrassing looking at them. Mass is just a fashion show here now. Everyone looks at what everyone else is wearing instead of concentrating on the responses.'

'It's the same everywhere. A lot of people go to one Mass a year and that's it.'

'You reckon?'

'That's the way it looks. It's a kind of atonement for the times they're not there.'

'You're probably right. Do there be many people at the Masses in Dublin?'

'Not that many. Mostly grey heads, I'm afraid.'

'Like myself.'

'I didn't mean it that way.'

'Don't worry about it. I'm not sensitive. '

He dug him in the ribs.

'You didn't tell us much about yourself last night.'

'What did you want to know?'

'Anything that's going on. What's the social life like at UCD? Have you made any friends up there?'

'Not really. I keep to myself a lot of the time.'

'You're as well off. Some of those city slickers can be right arseholes.'

He started to cough. Brian asked him if he was all right.

'I had a few drinks after the Mass. And a few smokes. It's not a good idea to mix them. It makes the hangovers twice as bad. You can write the next day off.'

'I hope you didn't drive Angela home.'

'I'm not quite that mad. She got a taxi.'

'Have you any plans for today?'

'Declan and Yvonne will be down later. Angela is staying the night, by the way. Is that okay with you?'

'You didn't say anything about it before.'

'Did I not? Sorry. You don't mind, do you?'

'Why should I?'

'I know it's very soon since...'

'You don't need to say that.'

'I get lonely, Brian.'

'I understand.'

'You don't dislike her, do you?'

'Why would you think that?'

'I don't know.'

'I've never said anything against her, have I?'

'She's good for me – and to me.'

'I know that.'

They heard a car pulling up in the driveway.

'That'll be her now,' he said.

Brian saw her getting out of the car. She waved in at him. .

'She's an early bird,' Bartley said, 'unlike yours truly.'

She came in. Her overcoat was open even though it was a cold day. Underneath it she had a dress with a plunging neckline.

'Look at her,' Bartley said, 'To what do we owe the honour?'

'I thought I'd make a bit of an effort for the day that's in it.'

'You look very nice,' Brian said.

She was drowned in perfume. When Bartley kissed her on the cheek he started coughing again.

'What in the name of God have you on your face?'

'It's a thing called perfume. Women use it sometimes to smell nice. You probably don't recognise it after all the years smelling pigs.'

'You could kill a fellow with that.'

'I wouldn't like to tell you what it cost.'

She took off her coat.

'I heard you had a few drinks after the Mass,' Brian said to her.

'*Someone* had a few. No names mentioned.'

'I wonder who that was,' Bartley said.

She went over to the cooker.

'Why don't the two of you go off and look at the land? I'll check the turkey.'

'Are you sure?' Bartley said.

'Of course. Have you been round the farm yet, Brian?'

'No.'

'You have a treat in store,' Bartley said, 'I don't think.'

'Make sure you put on your wellies. It rained earlier. The ground is going to be soggy.'

'The voice of reason,' Bartley said.

'She's right, though.'

'I'm glad someone appreciates my advice.'

Bartley got the wellingtons. They put them on.

'Don't be in any hurry back,' she said.

'Will we bring the car?' Brian said.

'After all I've sold? A spider could make his way across it now.'

They went outside. Rusty tagged along beside them wagging his tail. The day was crisp and clear. Brian was glad to be out of the house.

They went across a ditch towards the first field Bartley owned. There was a bull at the end of it. He always looked as if he was about to explode with rage. Bartley pretended to charge at it. When he did that, the bull did likewise.

He laughed heartily at the little charade.

'Stop working him up,' Brian said.

'He likes me doing that.'

'One of these days you might bite off more than you can chew.'

'If I do, you can read about me in the local paper: "Farmer Dies Playing

Matador".'

He picked up a piece of grass. It looked scraggly.

'See how bad this is?' he said, 'That's why I'm getting rid of it.'

'How much have you sold?'

'Not as much as I'd like. Nobody is buying these days. It's the wrong time. They can name their price.'

'Why don't you wait till things pick up?'

'That'd make more sense, wouldn't it?'

'Then do it.'

'I can't. I hate everything about the spread these days. It sickens the life out of me. It's a drain on me even looking at it. Too much work for too little reward.'

'Would you not get someone to help you manage it?'

'What's there to manage?'

'I don't care. Even for an acre it would be worth it.'

'There aren't that many around here that know what they're doing. I took on this fool after you left and he made a pig's ear of everything. I had to let him go after a week. The only thing he was good at was looking for money. He said I had no right to sack him. I said, "What do you think of my right to give you a large kick in the arse?" He went quiet enough after that.'

'It's hard to get good people nowadays.'

They trudged along. He couldn't believe he was spending Christmas Day walking across a waterlogged field discussing the sale of land.

'Will are you going to contact Jennifer?'

'She's in Kerry. I thought I told you.'

They got to the end of the field. There was a gate they had to climb over to get to the next one.

Brian went over it first. Bartley struggled to climb it. He sat at the top of it trying to get his legs through the bars.

'Does it not open?' Brian asked from the other side.

'The lock is rusty. I keep meaning to break it off.'

He jumped awkwardly. There was a pool of water under him. He fell straight into it.

'Bollox,' he said, 'I'm half drowned.'

'What happened you?'

'I thought I'd be able to clear the pool.'

'You should have listened to Angela about the soggy ground.'

'I feel like I've pissed myself. It's gone up above the wellingtons.'

'Do you want to go back and change?'

'I'll be all right. I knew that fucking pool was there. Sometimes I can't think straight. I'm not myself today.'

He sat on the grass. Brian never saw him looking so vulnerable.

'You're not well, are you?'he said, 'I mean apart from being wet.'

'To be honest, I have the a pretty bad hangover.'

'Let's go home then.'

'I wanted to show you the stock I have left. You mightn't be seeing them for long more.'

'We can do it some other time.'

'Okay. Maybe I'll go back to the old hacienda and have a hair of the dog.'

'That's not what I was thinking of. Why don't you sleep it off?'

'And sacrifice Christmas? No dice.'

There was a spring in his step going back. Brian watched him licking his lips in anticipation of the whiskey. It took his mind off the trousers.

They got to the farmhouse in half the time it took them for the outward journey.

Angela was surprised to see them.

'Back already?' she said, wiping her hands on her apron as they came in.

She looked at the water dripping off Bartley.

'Glory be to God. What happened you?'

'I fell off the blasted gate.'

'It'd take you. I'm always warning you about that gate. Go around it the next time.'

'The ditch is too high.'

'Then let Brian lift you over.'

'Where are my other pants?'

'What did your last servant die of? Have a bit of patience.'

She found a pair hanging on a chair.

'Will these do?'

'They'll have to.'

She gave them to him. He started to take the wet pair off.

'Keep your eyes averted,' he said, 'unless you want to see something that might give you bad thoughts.'

'Thanks for warning me.'

He put them on.

'You can look now,' he said.

'You're anyone's fancy.'

'I'm going upstairs to freshen up.'

'Good man. We'll await your re-appearance with bated breath.'

Brian went over to the cooker to see how the turkey was doing.

'The smell is making me hungry, he said. 'You seem to be making a nice job of it.'

'You never know with turkeys. It's hit and miss.'

Bartley came down the stairs. His eyes looked watery. Brian suspected he'd already had his hair of the dog. He was wearing a jumper with a picture of a reindeer on it.

'Here's Father Christmas,' Angela smirked, 'Ho ho ho.'

'Is that Rudolph?' Brian asked.

'Don't laugh. I saw it in town. I thought it'd be seasonal.'

'It certainly is that,' Angela said.

He did an imitation of a reindeer prancing along in front of a sleigh.

'How do you like my Rudolph impersonation?' he said.

They didn't react.

'To look at you two,' he said, 'You'd think it was Good Friday instead of Christmas Day.'

He went over to the hi-fi.

'We need a bit of music to get this show on the road,' he said.

He slotted a CD into it. A group of carol singers came on. They sang 'Deck the Halls with Boughs of Holly.' He clapped his hands as he duetted with them.

'Have you been drinking?' Angela said.

'Just a little one.'

'There's no such thing as a little one with you. Come on, where's the bottle?'

She frisked him. There was a bulge in his pocket. She tapped it. It made a clinking sound.

She took it out. It was a naggin of whiskey. She put it on the table.

'I might have known. Don't say you're going to make a disgrace of yourself with your son just home.'

'Why would I do that? Don't always be expecting the worst of me.'

'I know what you're like.'

He took it off the table. There was a determined look on his face. He had another sip.

'If you have any more of that,' Angela said, 'I'm going to hide it.'

He ignored her.

'I think I'll ring Declan,' he said, 'He's late.'

'Declan is always late,' Angela said.

'I'm going to ring him anyway.'

'Don't put me on,' Brian said.

'Why not?

'I'm not in form for him.'

'I'll never understand you. Your own brother.'

He went next door to make the call. His voice sounded excited.

'Where are you? Portumna? Do you know what time it is?'

'Keep your voice down,' Angela shouted in at him.

'A breakdown? How could your car break down on Christmas Day?'

The call ended, He came back to the living room.

'What's the story?' Angela said.

'He's having problems with the car. I couldn't hear him properly. It was one of those hands-free yokes.'

'What kind of problems?'

'The baffler is gone. He says the exhaust pipe is hanging off the car. It's breaking the sound barrier. You can get yourself hauled into the cop shop for that kind of stuff. I better ring him back.'

'Leave him alone,' Angela said, 'We'll have some fun ourselves till he gets here.'

'If I don't hurry him up, the day will be gone.'

'It's not his fault. You'll only annoy him by nagging him.'

He went next door. He got onto Declan again.

'Where are you now?' he said.

Brian heard Declan roaring at him. He heard the sound of the car in the background. It was like the engine of an airplane.

'Jesus,' said Angela, 'He never lets up.'

She prattled on about this and that. He found it hard to talk to her. He heard Bartley putting down the receiver.

He came back in.

'What's the latest?' Angela said.

'There's no change. He's going about two miles an hour. The exhaust pipe is sparking like fuck.'

'Language.' Angela said.

'Is that blasted bird cooked yet?'

'It won't be long now. Sit down and hold your whist. Some people have to wait till seven or eight o'clock for their dinner. Do you think of anything besides your belly?'

'Now that you mention it, no.'

She took the turkey out of the oven. Bartley ran over and cut a piece off for himself.

'Keep your greedy paws off that until it's cooked,' she said, slapping him on the wrist, 'You'd have it gone all on your own if you were let.'

He sat on the sofa. By now he'd retrieved the whiskey. He waved it in the air.

'Anyone for a belter?' he said.

Angela looked despairingly at Brian. They shook their heads.

He took a swig of it.

'It's not much fun drinking on your own,' he said.

'I thought you were going to go easy on that stuff till Declan got here,' Angela said.

'I was. I got fed up waiting for him.'

'There's always something.'

'What did you say?'

'I don't believe you.'

'You bitch. That kind of attitude makes me want to get bladdered.'

'Have as much as you want,' she said, 'I'm not bothered. Drain the bottle if it makes you happy.'

It was the first time Brian saw her getting annoyed with him. She usually bit her tongue.

He continued to knock it back.

'I hate Christmas,' he said.

He stood up, waving the bottle around.

'All these people who can't stand each other's guts the other eleven months, cosying up to each other with kisses and presents. The only reason we put up with it is because we have short memories. We forget how miserable we were the same time last year.'

'Yourself and Scrooge would get along great,' Angela said.

'Scrooge made a lot of sense. That's why people don't like him. They're afraid of facing the fact that it's all bullshit.'

'You hate Easter as well, and Halloween. Is there anything you like? '

'Yes – taking down the tree so I can see the wall again.'

'I give up,' she said.

He turned his attention to Brian.

'Am I right or am I right?' he said, 'Is Christmas the greatest con game known to man or am I missing something? It's insane. We do it every year. I send cards to people I wouldn't be seen dead with, hoping they don't reply so I won't have to repeat the performance next year.'

He staggered up to Brian.

'I bet you do the same,' he said. He was spitting the words at him.

'Well, do you?'

'Of course I do. It's a money-making scam. Everyone knows that. Don't think too much about it or you'll get depressed.'

'I *am* depressed. Dammit, I'm entitled to be depressed. So is everyone else. They just won't admit it. I was reading the other day that more people commit suicide at this time of year than any other.'

'If you don't shut up,' Angela said, 'You won't have the opportunity to kill yourself. I'll do it for you.'

He started laughing. He laughed so much he fell onto the sofa.

'Be careful,' she said, 'You'll do an injury to yourself.'

'You see?' he said, 'I'm not a total Scrooge. I like a laugh.'

The bottle was nearly empty. It fell out of his hand. She picked it up.

'What are we going to do with you?' she said.

He didn't reply. His eyes were gone back in his head.

'Don't say you're falling asleep on us,' she said.

She shook him but there was no response. A few seconds later he was snoring.

'I've seen him at this crack before,' she said.

'Do you think I haven't?'

'If I know anything he's out now till the morning. We better make our own arrangements about the turkey.'

'Okay,' Brian said. He put a blanket over Bartley.

'Rudolph will probably surface around midnight,' she said.

She cut the turkey. The rest of the food was already on the table.

'Sit anywhere you like,' she said, 'Dig in.'

He sat in Bartley's place at the top of the table.

'The new man of the house,' she said.

He knew she was trying her best to be friendly but he couldn't warm to her.

They ate in silence. He'd lost his appetite. There was a feast in front of him – turkey, potatoes, vegetables heaped on his plate with a separate plate for the stuffing. Even looking at it made him feel full.

'Have you enough there?' she said.

'There's enough for ten men. If you put any more on the plate it would be touching the ceiling. There's no way I'll be able for this.'

'Nonsense, you're a growing boy. It'll put hairs on your chest.'

He could only pick at it. Angela ate nearly all hers, shovelling it in.

'I can see how upset you are,' she said.

'It reminds me of the old days.'

'I bet you really miss your mother at times like this.'

She started talking about her, saying how lovely she was to her anytime she met her. He might have been able to appreciate her comments if she wasn't sitting in her place serving him the food.

'Do you think of her a lot?'

'I try not to.'

'Sorry for bringing her up. Let's talk about something else.'

'How do you think Bartley will be when he wakes up?'

'I don't know.'

He stood up from the table.

'I'm afraid I can't eat anymore.'

'But you've hardly taken anything.'

'I know. I'm sorry.'

'Don't be. I'll put tin foil over the turkey. We can have it tomorrow. You'll have some pudding at least, won't you?'

'I don't know.'

'Come on. You're not going to let me down, are you?'

'No.'

'How about a cup of tea to go with it?'

'That would be nice.'

She put the kettle on. They listened to Bartley snoring. Rusty sat by the fire. He looked at them curiously.

She started talking about her life before she met Bartley. He tried to look interested.

The kettle came to the boil. She poured the tea.

Bartley woke up as they were drinking it. He almost fell off the sofa, clutching the arm at the last second.

'Jesus, ' Angela said, 'Are you all right?'

He looked as if he didn't know where he was.

'What time is it?'

'Seven o'clock.'

'What are you talking about?'

'I'm talking about the time. It's seven o'clock.'

'In the evening?'

'Yes. And not a child in the house washed.'

'How can it be that?'

'You've been asleep all day. You conked out with the whiskey.'

He sat up.

'Did Declan get here yet?'

'No,' Brian said, 'It's just as well.'

He started blinking his eyes. He shook his head from side to side.

'I feel weird.'

'You'll get your bearings after a minute.'

'Have the two of you eaten?'

'Yes. We had a good chat too, didn't we, Brian?'

'Yes,' he said faintly.

Bartley stood up.

'Any chance of a bit of turkey?'

'Of course.'

She started to make him a sandwich. Brian put his head in his hands.

'Sorry, Brian,' he said.

'There's nothing to be sorry about.'

'You're just saying that to be polite. I've wrecked everything.'

'No you haven't. Relax.'

Angela gave him the sandwich.

'The poor man's Christmas dinner,' she said.

He ate it clumsily, dropping bits of turkey onto the floor. He tried his best to stay awake but his eyes were droopy.

'It's lovely,' he said.

He didn't finish it. Halfway through it he started to get sleepy again. He put it down. A few seconds later he threw his head back on the sofa.

Brian thought he was still drunk. He wondered if he'd wake up before Declan arrived.

He turned the television on. A religious film was showing. It was centred on the crucifixion.

A man with piercing blue eyes was playing Jesus. He was at Calvary.

'I think I've seen that one before,' Angela said, 'Have you?'

'I can't say for sure.'

They sat watching it for a few minutes without saying anything. Jesus fell under the cross. Angela sighed.

'They always go on too long,' she said, 'Don't they?'

'Sorry?'

'These kinds of films. They always go on too long.'

'Agreed.'

'And the acting is terrible.'

She looked over at Bartley. He was snoring again.

'I think I'll go home,' she said, 'He's out for the count.'

'I thought you were staying the night.'

'Not now. It wouldn't make sense.'

'Sorry about this.'

'I'm sorry too. It's not much fun for you either.'

'I don't mind. I'm used to it.'

'You are?'

'I remember Christmasses when he was out of it for the whole twelve days.'

He thought it was only fair to let her know. Or was he trying to scare her off?

'That's desperate. He hasn't been drinking that much lately.'

'It's always waiting to come out.'

She put her overcoat on.

'I hope I see you before you go back,' she said.

'No doubt you will. Thanks for cooking the turkey.'

'It was nothing. Maybe the pair of you can have some more sandwiches from it. At least if himself does us the courtesy of waking up.'

She stood at the door.

'Goodbye then. Try not to let this upset you too much. He'll probably be back to himself again tomorrow.'

'I know,' Brian said, 'That's what I'm worried about.'

She laughed.

'It's great that you can see the funny side of it.'

'If you didn't you'd go off your rocker.'

'Very true.'

She went out. Brian heard her car starting up outside. The sound woke Bartley. He jumped up.

His body was twitching.

'Where am I?' he said.

'At home.'

He looked around him.

'Where's Angela?.'

'Go back to sleep.'

He heard the sound of the car.

'What's happening?'

'Angela is going off.'

'What? She can't. I have the room made up for her.'

He tried to get up but he couldn't. He got a cramp in his leg. He sat there writhing in pain.

'Angela!' he called out.

The car drove off. They listened the sound of the engine getting fainter.

'Fuck it,' he said.

'What's up with you?'

'I have a cramp.'

'Relax. It'll be gone in a minute.'

'Where's Declan?'

'I don't know and I don't care.'

'Give me another drop of whiskey. I spilled the bottle.'

'No. You've had enough.'

Usually he would have put up a fight but he didn't say anything this time. He fell into another sleep.

Brian sat there looking at him. The lights on the Christmas tree twinkled. He looked at all the dishes on the table. He couldn't be bothered washing them.

He turned on the television. A group of carol singers stood on O'Connell Bridge. They had the excessive enthusiasm people usually showed at Christmas.

Bartley started to talk in his sleep. He was having a nightmare.

'Teresa!' he shouted, 'Teresa!'

His voice grew louder. Brian remembered the days when he'd abuse her, when he was so drunk he wasn't even aware he was abusing her. She'd go up to the bedroom and cry.

He stayed watching the television. After a while he put a blanket around Bartley. The lights on the Christmas tree kept twinkling. There were pine needles all over the floor.

He put the dishes in the sink. He buttered a slice of bread and put some turkey on it. The cuckoo clock chimed midnight.

The carol singers finished. Then the news came on. There was a car accident in Westmeath. It had numerous fatalities, most of them young people. Why were there always car accidents at Christmas?

The news ended. A continuity announcer appeared. He had a smile on his face. He gave details of the following day's programmes.

'May I take this opportunity to wish you all a very happy Christmas,' he said, signing off for the night.

The screen went blank. Brian listened to the static, to the clock ticking on the wall.

He was thinking of going to bed. He decided not to wake Bartley. It was better to leave him there. He probably wouldn't come to again until the next morning.

He heard a car on the gravel outside. A horn beeped. He was hoping it was Angela coming back for something she forgot but it wasn't.

'Anybody home?' said a voice.

He opened the door. Declan and Yvonne were standing there.

'Guess who?' said Declan with a grin on his face. He put his arm around him.

Yvonne looked at him helplessly.

'Happy Christmas,' she said, 'Sorry for arriving so late.'

'Don't worry about it.'

'It's just a flying visit,' Declan said, 'We had all sorts of problems getting here.'

'So I believe. What do you mean a flying visit?'

'We're going to Jackie for a few days.' Jackie was Yvonne's sister. She lived half an hour away.

'I feel terrible about this,' Yvonne said.

'Don't be crazy. It's great to see you.'

Declan looked over Brian's shoulder.

'What's wrong with the old lad?' he said.

'He's asleep.'

'Are you serious?'

'He's been drinking.'

'Uh-oh. And Angela?'

'She went home. It's been a bit dramatic here. She waited till the drink took over.'

'Oh God,' said Yvonne, 'Now I feel even worse.'

Declan went over to Bartley.

'Look at him,' he said, 'As quiet as a baby.'

'You should have seen him a few hours ago. He wasn't too quiet then.'

'What else is new?' Declan said.

'God love him,' said Yvonne.

Declan reached into his pocket. He pulled out a packet with gift-wrapping around it. He left it beside Bartley. 'That's in case we don't get to see him tomorrow,' he said.

'Is there a question you mightn't?'

'It depends on Jackie.'

'Sorry about this again,' Yvonne said. Brian shrugged.

'How's yourself?' Declan said to Brian.

'Brilliant. It's the best Christmas I've ever had.'

'This is terrible,' said Yvonne, 'Maybe we should go.'

'Would you like a bit of turkey?' Brian asked her.

'Thanks but we're fine that way, Brian. We had something on the road.' Declan handed him an envelope.

'We got this for you.'

He took it.

'Thanks, Declan.'

'Open it.'

He didn't want to. It was like when Angela gave him the laptop. He never liked unwrapping things in front of people. He always thought you had to exaggerate your gratitude.

He opened it. It was a book token for a hundred euro. Why did people always give him things to do with books? Did they not think there was anything more to him?

'You're far too generous,' he said, 'Thank you both so much.'

'It's nothing,' Yvonne said, 'I feel so bad going off like this. I wish we could stay longer.'

'I'd feel better if you had something to eat.'

'Maybe we'd have the turkey then,' Declan said, 'I can smell it.'

'What about you, Yvonne?'

'Okay. I'll have some too.'

They sat down. Declan couldn't stop grinning at Bartley. Yvonne poked him in the ribs to stop.

Brian boiled the kettle. He gave them the sandwiches. He could see they were glad to get them. The speed at which they ate them suggested they hadn't had much to eat on the road after all.

'These are lovely,' Yvonne said.

'That's what Dad said. He wasn't able for the turkey. Maybe we won't bother with one next year. We can just make sandwiches for everyone.'

Yvonne laughed. Declan tried to wake Bartley.

'I'd prefer if you didn't do that,' Brian said.

'Why not?'

'He'll be like a bull in a china shop with the booze that's in him.'

'But we'll only be seeing him for a few minutes.'

'That's the whole point. Angela and myself will have to pick up the pieces.'

He sighed in frustration.

'I don't know what to do now.'

'Maybe Yvonne is right. Maybe you should just go.'

'Without talking to him?'

'There wouldn't be any point. He'd hardly know you. He hardly knows himself.'

'What a day,' Declan said, 'The exhaust pipe started to pack up at Mountrath. Then we got a puncture. We're lucky we got here in one piece. If it wasn't for the kindness of – '

'Do you know what time it is?' Brian said.

Declan looked perplexed.

'We apologised, Brian. I hope you don't think we wanted things to work out like this.'

'I didn't say that.'

'Why did you interrupt me then?'

'Don't argue,' Yvonne said, 'Please.'

'Is there any chance of a drink?' Declan said, 'I'm parched.'

'How can you think of drink at a time like this?'

'How can I think of drink? Because it's Christmas Eve, Einstein, and the whole country is elephants except me. That's why.'

'I don't think it's a good idea.'

'Why?'

'You said you're going to Jackie's.'

'So?'

'You wouldn't want to be driving with drink, would you?'

'Let me worry about that.'

'He's right, Declan,' Yvonne said, ''we better just go.'

'Keep out of this,' he told her.

'He's turning into Bartley,' Brian said to Yvonne.

'What was that?' Declan said.

'I said you're turning into Bartley.'

Declan's face became red with rage.

'Why are you getting so aggressive when all I asked for was a simple drink?'

'Do you ever think of anyone besides yourself?'

'Fuck you, you patronising shit.'

'The same to you, loving brother.'

He shook his head frustratedly.

'Come on, Yvonne,' he said, 'We're being refused a drink so we might as well go. I didn't realise I was barred from this pub.'

He stormed out the door. Yvonne was crying.

'Come back, Declan,' she said, 'He didn't mean it like that.'

He continued to walk.

'Are you deaf? I said. 'We're going.'

She put her head in her hands. Brian put his arms around her.

'Oh Brian,' she said, 'This is awful for you.'

'I'm more worried about you being stuck with that article.'

'I've never seen him like this before.'

'I have. Why do you think we never meet up?'

They heard the engine revving up outside.

'I don't know what to do,' she said.

'Go out to him. We can talk tomorrow.'

'Are you sure?'

He nodded.

'I'm sorry,' she said, 'again.'

'And I'm sorry you had to be a part of this. You don't deserve it.'

She went out. Brian followed her. She stood at the car for a moment looking back at him.

'Get in,' Declan said.

When she opened the door the car had already started to move.

'Jesus, Declan,' she said, 'I'm not in yet.'

She threw herself into the seat. He didn't say anything. The car roared off. The exhaust pipe was loose. It made sparks when it hit the road.

Brian went back inside. Bartley was still asleep.

He plugged out the Christmas tree. Everything was quiet suddenly.

He sat in the dark. Rusty came over to him. He patted him. 'Happy Christmas old buddy,' he said. Rusty gave a whimper.

He turned off the lights and went upstairs. His room was dark except for the dim sheen of a streetlamp outside. He looked out the window. Down the road he heard some revellers singing. He listened to them until they were out of range.

He threw his clothes into a ball on the floor and got into his pyjamas. The bed felt cold. He pulled the duvet around him. It was too late to put the heater on.

He found it hard to sleep. He tried not to be angry with Bartley but the past kept coming into his mind. All the old resentments he had towards him re-surfaced. He found himself hating him, hating the way he used to be when his mother was alive even if she didn't have any resentment towards him herself. 'He isn't responsible,' she'd say, 'He doesn't know what he's doing.'

When he finally fell asleep he had bad dreams – dreams of accidents and death and cruelty. He woke up in the middle of the night and lay there in the darkness. He thought of how it used to be when that happened in his childhood, the calm after the storm, listening to nothing but the lowing of the cattle.

When he woke up the next morning it was a few seconds before he remembered what happened. When he did he felt a strange sense of relief. He wasn't shocked or even disappointed. The day reminded him of too many in the past. There was no surprise. The only thing that annoyed him was his foolish expectation that it might be different this year. He knew now that nothing ever changed in life. Things always went on as they'd done before.

He heard a sound downstairs. He presumed it was Bartley but when he called down from the landing it was Angela's voice that answered.

'Is that you, Brian?' she said.

'Yes. I'll be down in a minute.'

He dressed himself and went down. Bartley was still asleep on the sofa. Angela was tidying the kitchen.

'How did you get in?' he said.

'Bartley gave me a key a few weeks ago. I hope you don't mind me letting myself in. I knocked but you must have been asleep.'

'I can't believe you came all this way over.'

'I was worried about Bartley. He was on the floor when I got here. I put him back up on the sofa and put a blanket around him.'

'He must have been a ton to lift.'

'I managed it somehow. What happened after I left?'

'Declan and Yvonne called. They didn't stay long when they saw the state of him.'

'Can I get you something to eat?'

'No thanks.'

'This is terrible, Brian,' she said. 'How did Declan and Yvonne take it?'

'They have their own problems.'

'You mean the car?'

'Yes.'

'Did they get it sorted?'

'Not really. It's just about going.'

'Where are they staying?'

'With Yvonne's sister. She doesn't live too far away.'

'I see. Will they be here today?'

'I don't know.'

'What about you? What are your plans?'

'I'll probably head back to Dublin later.'

'I'm sorry to hear that. Bartley will be disappointed.'

'I don't think I could stick another day here.'

'You might feel different in a few hours.'

'I don't think so.'

He sat down at the table. She looked at him intently.

'Are you sure you're all right?'

'I'm fine. You can go now, Angela. I'll take care of him.'

'Am I in the way?'

'It's not that. You could be doing something with your day.'

'Sure what have I to do?'

She sat down beside him.

'Can I get you a cup of tea before I go?'

'Okay.'

She poured it out. They sat without talking.

She looked at the tree.

'There's nothing sadder than a Christmas tree the day after Christmas,' she said.

'There's one thing,' Brian said, 'The person who put it up.'

She gave a wry laugh.

'That was probably you,' he said.

She nodded.

'Catch that fellow lending a hand. His idea of decorating a room for Christmas is putting a few cards on the mantelpiece.'

'Well it's over now for another year anyway. Once Christmas Day is gone I always feel that.'

'Me too. And next year we'll wreck ourselves again with the whole hullabaloo.'

'Now you're beginning to sound like Bartley.'

'What time do you think he'll wake up?'

'That's anyone's guess. No matter what time it is he'll probably nod off again a few minutes later.'

'That's it.'

'You're good to put up with him.'

'He makes it up to me when he's sober.'

'Whenever that is.'

'He's not as bad as you think. He has that country thing that says you have to be drunk for the whole twelve days of Christmas.'

'I'm afraid it's not confined to the country.'

'I know. Maybe they should write it into the Constitution.'

'Now you've said it.'

'Well I'll be off now. What time will you get the train?'

'I haven't thought about that.'

They stood up.

'Thanks for everything,' he said.

'I did nothing. It was good to see you. I hope it won't be long before you get down again.'

She gave him a hug. She got her coat.

'I'll drop in later to see how he's doing.'

'That would be a good idea. Goodbye, Angela.'

'Goodbye. Mind yourself.'

She went out. He expected to hear the car starting immediately but it didn't. He looked out the window. She was sitting there crying. He turned away. After a few minutes he heard her going off.

He went upstairs and got his things. Bartley was still snoring when he came down.

Rusty wagged his tail. He was hoping to be brought for a walk.

'Sorry old friend,' he said, 'Maybe next time.'

He picked up his case and went out.

16

The term hadn't started when he got back to Dublin. He spent the next few days hanging around Ranelagh. He tried to ring Jennifer but he couldn't get through. The phone signal was too bad in Kerry. Maybe it was for the best, he thought. He didn't want to be unloading his problems on her. She'd heard it all before anyway. Alcoholics were very predictable, especially at Christmas.

Bartley rang him that weekend.

'I'm not going to give a big speech,' he said, 'What's done is done. I just wanted to let you know I'm on the dry now. I hope you're not going to stay away for other holidays because of what happened.'

'Not at all.'

'Good. Anyway, I wanted to say what I said. I'm very sorry.'

'Thanks. I appreciate it. How are you feeling?'

'Bad because of what I did to you.'

'Forget it. It's over.'

He tried to keep his mind off him when the term began. There was a flurry around Belfield. Everyone was full of stories about Christmas. Most people, apparently, were glad it was over.

Adrian and Dominic were absent from the lectures. Someone said they'd been expelled but he doubted that. It was difficult to get expelled from a university. It was more likely they'd dropped out. He had no way of contacting them to find out what happened. In one sense he was glad they weren't there. The break in Loughrea changed his attitude to things. He didn't think he'd be able to continue roughing it up with them like he'd done before.

He didn't go back to the security firm, knuckling down to his work instead. This wasn't so much from love of it as to ensure he passed his exams. Doing that, he knew, would buy him time for another year. It would also keep Bartley off his back.

Jennifer rang him when she got back from Kerry. She was short on the call, telling him she had a lot to catch up on. She said she'd ring in a few days to tell him all her news. It wasn't like her to be so offhand. He was wondering if it was a strategy. Maybe she was afraid of sounding too dependent on him. She did that sometimes when he hadn't called her for a while. It was a nice gesture really, adopting his own attitude to things, or at least pretending to.

He ran into Jamesie Gildea now and again. He always felt he was being vetted when he was talking to him. Anytime he said something to him he felt it was being processed in Jamesie's brain for recycling. 'How is the study going?' he'd say, or 'How is the writing?' He had an insatiable appetite for gossip. He also had the knack of being around when things were happening, popping up when you least expected him to.

Like most people who asked a lot of questions, he rarely volunteered anything about himself. He just stood there with his ears stuck out. Brian tried to avoid him but it wasn't always possible. He seemed to be permanently patrolling the corridors like a sentry.

There was no point telling him to butt out. That would only have motivated him further. Instead he pretended he enjoyed his company. If he found himself sitting beside him in the cafeteria he tried to make the best of it.

Jamesie always finished the conversation by saying, 'Tell Declan I was asking for him.' He'd been in his class at school. No more than Bartley, he liked him for his confidence. Brian was too quiet for him. Declan had never been threatened by Jamesie's curiosity because he liked blabbing. Jamesie seemed to enjoy hearing things more when you didn't want to tell them. He knew that was the case with Brian, that he might say too much when his defences were down.

The more he studied, the more he got to hate what he was doing. It became mechanical. He felt he might as well have been studying Higher Mathematics. If the first term was bad, the second one was ten times worse. The French course wasn't too different but in English he had to study Old English. It was like a foreign language to him.

Martin Geraghty called over to him one day. He asked him how he'd enjoyed the Christmas.

'Not too bad,' he said.

'Same here. It goes on too long, doesn't it?

'Now you've said it. How was Bartley?'

'On his ear, I'm afraid.'

He guffawed.

'Why does that not surprise me? He reminds me of the joke about the guy who says, "They tell me I had a good Christmas." I'm sure Bartley would enjoy that one.'

'It was probably made up with him in mind.'

'Probably. I hope you told him I was asking for him.'

'I did.'

'I know he's out with me but there's no harm in being civil with each other.'

'Exactly.'

His days settled into a kind of uniformity. He was looking forward to his book of poems coming out. He tried to write some new ones on the laptop Bartley gave him but he couldn't. It inhibited him. He preferred manual typewriters. He missed putting the paper in, missed hearing the clack of the keys. Even better was writing in notebooks with a biro. That was the way he'd always worked before. Sitting at a computer gave him writer's block. Some days he felt like throwing it out the window. Maybe one day he would.

Bartley phoned him every few days. He said he was honouring his promise to stay off the drink.

'Is the muse flowing?' he asked him on one of his calls.

'I'm taking a break from writing at the moment.'

'That's a pity. They're comparing you to Famous Seamus down here now.'

'Who?'

'Famous Seamus – as in Heaney.'

He was surprised he'd even heard of him.

'If my inspiration comes back you'll be the first to know.'

'Do that. We can't have your success reaching everyone's ears except ours.'

He was bored with the call and cut it short.

He rang Jennifer as soon as he put down the receiver. He felt she wasn't going to contact him.

'Is everything all right?' he said.

'I'm sorry. It's been on my mind a hundred times a day to ring you. I've been up to my ears.'

'Don't feel you have to. That was part of our arrangement.'

'You're good to see it like that but I still feel bad. I know a bit about what happened with you.'

'Who told you?'

'Angela.'

'There was nothing new really. He always breaks out at Christmas.'

'I'm sure he's trying his best to stay off it. Did it bother you a lot?'

'It wasn't just him, it was Declan as well. He arrived with Yvonne after midnight. He started an argument with me.'

'Angela didn't say anything about that.'

'She wasn't there.'

'God help you. I believe you only stayed a few days.'

'I couldn't take any more than that. I would have gone out of my tree. I doubt I'll go down again for a while. What about yourself? How did things go in Kerry?'

'I slept through most of it. The lectures have me wrecked. I've made a decision to get back to Loughrea as much as I can now. Mam wants to spoil me and I'm not going to resist it. If I didn't have her I'd probably be in the funny farm by now.'

'It's no less than you deserve.'

'It sounds like we won't be seeing one another for a while so, with you up in Dublin and me in Loughrea.'

'Don't worry. We'll work something out.'

Declan rang him the following day. He said Jennifer had been on to Yvonne and told her all the news about him. It was almost like a network. Each person rang the other one with the latest updates on what was happening in their lives. The less that was happening, the more phone calls there were to be made, every tiny event being stretched out until it became important in the re-telling.

'Sorry about the blow up,' he said, 'I behaved like a right tool.'

'Don't worry about it. I wasn't very nice either. Christmas brings out the worst in people.'

'You might have something there. Too much drinking and too much time to do nothing. Anyway, we'll move on.'

'Agreed. That's a good new year resolution for both of us.'

'Has Dad been on to you?'

'Every other day.'

'I'm sure that cuts in on your work.'

'He doesn't stay on long.'

'The important thing is that he's off the gargle. Anyway I just wanted to say sorry for throwing the head. There was no excuse for it. I was under pressure because of the car and all that. It wasn't fair on you.'

'It's okay. I've forgotten about it. But you should be nicer to Yvonne.'

'Don't worry. We had a little talk. I've been in the doghouse with her too.'

'Did you apologise to her?'

'Grovel would be a more appropriate term.'

'Any luck?'

'I'm still trying. So far not even flowers and chocolates worked. I even offered to bring her to a Brad Pitt film with a meal in Eddie Rocket's thrown in. I think she's still in shock. I even shocked myself.'

'How did you get on afterwards? Did you stay with Jackie?'

'We didn't, believe it or not. When we got there she was asleep. We couldn't wake her up. We almost battered the door down. Then we started throwing stones at the window.'

'I bet she was delighted with that.'

'She slept through it. When Jackie sleeps, a tornado wouldn't waken her.'

'Was it not the middle of the night by that stage?' '

'That didn't help either. We ended up in a dive of a hotel in the middle of nowhere. It didn't even have hot water. You can imagine what herself thought of that. She washes her hair about eight times a day.'

'I'm sure you had a great time there.'

'Mighty. And after we left we didn't even bother going to Jackie. We were too worn out. It was probably the worst Christmas of my life. Next year we're probably going to stay put.'

'I think I'll do that too.'

'How is the university treating you?'

'Okay. It's not really my thing.'

'I never thought it would be. You need to get out of there and back to real life. There's a job here for you anytime you want it. You know that.'

'Thanks. I'll think seriously about that possibility if things continue to go downhill here.'

'Whatever works for you. Sorry again about being such a fuckwit. I totally lost the plot.'

The apology gratified him but he wondered how long it would be before the next argument. There always seemed to be this seesaw between them. What was important was not to let the flare-ups get to him. They took more out of him than they did out of Declan. He hated a bad atmosphere.

It was also important to have Declan's offer in the background if the university went belly-up. If it did, he wouldn't put it that way to Declan. He didn't want to have to go to him with his tail between his legs. He knew he'd rub his nose in it if he did. He had a subtle way of exerting power over him. It was only slightly camouflaged beneath his charm.

He tried to get to know the other students better at the university when the new term began. That was easier said than done. His time away from the campus, brief and all as it was, made him less inclined to interact with people.

He had a reputation of being stand-offish by now. When people had an opinion of you they tended to hold on to it. Even when he drank with the other students they kept their distance from him. It looked like they were doing to him what he'd done to them the previous term.

Having few social contacts meant he had more time to devote to his work. He spent most of his time in the library now. He tried to turn himself into the kind of person he hated: a literary critic. He told himself it would be just for a brief period, that after graduation he could revive his love of books without any conditions.

In between his studies he continued to write poems. He wrote stories too. There was even a stab at a novel. Every time he finished something he sent it off to a publisher for a reaction. Often they didn't reply. He knew half the country was writing books. Publishers' desks were crammed with the scribblings of geniuses and fools. A few of them said they were considering his work but that it would be months before they got back to him with a decision. At least that gave him something to hope for.

Jennifer rang him more often than usual as the year went on. She became more relaxed with each call. He was glad about that. She kept him entertained with stories about her experiences in classrooms on teaching practice. She was up and down to Loughrea all the time.

Bartley rang him coming up to Easter to ask him if he'd be going down to them for the break.

'It doesn't look like it at the moment.'

'I'm sorry to hear that. Is it because of the way I was at Christmas?'

'No.'

'Then have a think about it. '

'I'm busy cramming for the exams.'

It wasn't true. Bartley's drunkenness had left a mark on him. Besides, what was there for him at home anymore? The farm would soon be gone. Angela would be anointed as his stepmother. He needed to plan another life for himself.

He spent a lot of his time checking out places where he might go for the summer. He'd always wanted to see Europe. Bartley kept ringing him nagging him about going home for Easter. Every time he put him off he became more pushy.

'I can't imagine you doing much studying over the holidays,' he said on one call, 'Why don't you take a break for yourself?'

'I have to catch up.'

'Could you not do that here? It'd be much quieter for you without all the razzmatazz of the city. You wouldn't have to help me on the farm in case that's what you're thinking. I'll ask the few remaining cows I have not to moo when you're around. Just jump on a train. What do you say?'

'It's not as simple as that.'

'Of course it is. We'll meet you at the other end. Otherwise you'll be the only culchie in Dublin that week.'

'Let me think about it.'

He had no intention of doing that. For the next few weeks he burned the midnight oil. Easter came and went but the calls kept coming from Bradley. On one of them he put Angela on.

'You'll *have* to come down,' she squealed. That made him even more determined not to.

He didn't get much study done but he was grateful for the break all the same. Sometimes it was nice to hang around Rathgar chatting to Denise and going out walking. In the evenings he played music and read.

When the new term started he rang Jennifer.

'We missed you over the Easter,' she said.

'I couldn't get away. What about you – how did you enjoy it?'

'What can you do down here except unwind?'

'That's important too. Have you anything planned for the summer?'

'I'm burned out from the kids. I was thinking of just staying at home.'

'They shouldn't take that much out of you. Is it a bad school you're in?'

'It's mainly my own fault. I work them up with all these ruses I have to make them enjoy learning but I tend to overdo it. They become like wild animals.'

'You must be a masochist.'

'I probably am. Anyway, what's happening with you over the summer?'

'I don't know for sure yet.'

He wanted to invite her to go to Europe with him but he didn't think it would be fair to either of them. Before doing something like that they had to make a decision about their future.

'How is the study going?'

'I'm making a push for the exams.'

'Sure. Or else you're in the throes of a passionate romance with some luscious damsel.'

'Thanks for that. What about you? Are you seeing any men these days?'

'The school principal. The parish priest. That's as good as it gets for me.'

'Why don't you go out on the odd date?'

She went quiet when he said that. He knew it was a mistake. Her tone changed.

'That's hurtful. It's as if you're trying to break it off with me.'

'Don't take it that way.'

'What other way is there for me to take it?'

'Sorry. I just thought it would be a bit of diversion for you.'

'That sounds too sensible.'

'How can someone be too sensible?'

'Okay, maybe I just don't want to. I can't help thinking you're trying to get rid of me.'

'Don't be ridiculous.'

'It really hurts me when you try to fob me off on other people.'

'I don't want you to feel trapped with me.'

'How could I? But maybe you do with me.'

The call ended tensely. He didn't ring her again before the term ended. Instead he wrote to her telling her he was going to Europe for the summer. It was a cold way to do it but it was the only thing he could think of.

When summer came around he wrote what was expected of him in the exams to get the grades he needed to qualify for his second year. Any unorthodox views he'd expressed in the tutorials he kept to himself. He became one of the sheep he despised for the short term gain, parroting the words of the eminent critics from their prestigious theses. After they were over he tried to put everything about his past on the back burner – Jennifer, his mother, all the things that happened since she died.

He hung around Dublin for July. The grape-picking season didn't start until August and that's what he wanted to do. He told Bartley he was going down to Wicklow with some friends to do up a house. He thought that would keep him off his back. He hadn't told him when he'd planned to go to France. He knew it would get back to Jennifer and that he'd be expected to go down to Loughrea to see her. He was too uptight about going away to have to deal with that. She might even have talked him out of going.

But then Bartley rang him. He said Jamesie Gildea heard he was in Dublin.

'I'm just back from Wicklow,' he said.

He sounded surprised.

'When are you off to France?'

'Tomorrow.'

'Did you not tell Jennifer?'

'I was planning to ring her later tonight.'

'Okay, mystery man.'

He cut the call short. Jennifer rang him within the hour.

'Bartley was on to me,' she said.

'I thought he might be.'

'So you're off to France.'

'Sorry for the confusion. I'm not looking forward to it.'

'I wish you wouldn't go.'

He was annoyed by her drama. It unsettled him.

'Why are you saying that? Tonight above all nights. Do you realise I'm off tomorrow?'

'Bartley told me. I was disappointed to hear it from him instead of you. Is that all I mean to you? Were you not going to ring to say goodbye?'

'Of course I was.'

'You didn't even contact me from Wicklow and now you're going to Europe.'

'It's only for the summer. I'm not going there to live.'

'I don't care. It was bad of you.'

'Sorry. I'm going through a lot of stuff at the moment.'

'So am I. That's why I wanted to talk to you. Didn't we always do that in the old days?'

'You make us sound ancient.'

'I feel I've known you forever, Brian.'

'And me you.'

'I don't know why you don't want to spend the summer in Loughrea. What are you going to Europe for? You don't even know any languages.'

116

'The only words you need to know in any country are, 'Please, 'Thank you' and 'How much?'

'Very funny. Who told you that joke – one of your university friends?'

'I'm sorry if I sound flippant. I don't mean to. Even if I wanted to I couldn't cancel at this stage. All the preparations have been made.'

'Okay. Off you go then.'

'Don't be like that.'

'Like what?'

'You know what I'm talking about. Don't pretend you don't.'

She put the phone down. He wanted to ring her back but he stopped himself. His heart was pounding. He knew he'd have one foot in Galway as well as one in Europe for the summer. She'd spoiled it by ringing him. Why did she always try and knock him out of his rhythm?

17

He decided to make Paris the first stop on his trip. As a result of his studies he'd got to know the works of some famous French writers as well as the language. That was going to be a help to him now.

He didn't have a work plan but that didn't bother him. Nobody else he knew had either. They were all just going on spec – to friends or friends of friends. The money they were going to be earning was small. Jobs were more plentiful because of that. He still had some of Bartley's money left. He planned to eat into it if he couldn't get a job. When it ran out he thought he might ditch the university. There was no point paying fees for qualifications he never planned to use.

He spent his first few days trying to get his bearings. It was his first time outside Ireland but he felt strangely at home there. His love of anonymity kicked in. He walked the promenades and sat in the coffee houses. Life was easy. He could have imagined himself doing that forever. Other people might have felt lonely but for him it was bliss. It was self-indulgent, he knew, but so what?

One day he saw an ad for a job picking grapes in a nearby vineyard. It gave a phone number at the end of it.

A caretaker answered when he rang it. He was able to explain in his pidgin French that he was a student looking for a job. The man said he'd try him out. He gave him directions for how to get there. The next day he took a train to the farm. It was outside the city of Sucy-en-Brie, not too far south of Paris.

A genial old man called Marcel ran it with his wife and son. They were less friendly than he was. He was put working with five other students from various countries. None of them spoke English. They were given overalls to wear. They had secateurs to cut the bushes.

Marcel's son was full up of himself. He rode a motorcycle across the vineyard every day, barking instructions at the workers. His girlfriend sat behind him. She was good-looking, as pretty as any film star.

Everyone was assigned to a particular row of vines. If they were slow with their cutting, workers from the other rows came over and helped them. That guaranteed everyone worked as fast as they could. They didn't want to be embarrassed by being last. 'C'est communisme!' Marcel's son exulted.

Brian played football with them during their breaks. He had his work cut out trying to get the ball. The others passed it to their friends. They loved showing off, especially Marcel's son, at least if his girlfriend was on the sidelines. He tried to impress her with moves he saw on television from the professionals. Most of the time they didn't come off but that didn't stop him. Brian thought he looked ridiculous. After the game was over, Marcel would shout something in French and they'd all go off to the showers.

It was heaven letting the water flow over him, especially if the day was hot. They rose at dawn every day. They were brought to the vineyard on the back of a truck. The mornings were as cold as ice, the dew hanging on the bushes like jewellery. It melted when the sun came out.

Brian wasn't able for the heat after eighteen years of Irish weather, It sapped his energy. He preferred it when the wind blew. They called it the *mistral*.

He moved like a minesweeper across the land, his secateurs poised like a weapon. Everyone worked until their arms ached. Sometimes he bled from the prickles on the bushes. There were huge meals in the evenings. He'd often heard it said that the French lived to eat. Now he believed it. It was like sitting at a smorgasbord. One day he counted over a dozen types of cheese on display on the table.

Marcel always sat at the top. He told stories as he ate. Brian never had a clue what these were about. He didn't think the other workers had either but they all laughed if he did. They knew it would put him into good humour. His son wasn't bothered either way. He just ate his fill and then went off with his girlfriend.

Brian left the job for a fortnight. It was too draining and the pay was poor. He decided to do some travelling. The family weren't pleased that he was leaving. They thought he was going to be there until November. 'Pourquoi,' they kept saying, 'Pourquoi?'

He pretended he didn't understand what they meant. He didn't feel guilty because they hadn't been nice to him. Marcel gave him a warm handshake as he was leaving but his wife and son didn't say goodbye. He was glad to see the back of them.

Over the next few weeks he saw little but the entrances and exits of towns. Trains swallowed up the landscapes. He booked tickets to exotic-sounding destinations. The constant mobility was a contrast to him for all the years when so little happened in Loughrea, or happened so slowly.

He took casual labour wherever he could find it. He hadn't planned working on farms but it was what he knew best. Not being proficient in French cut down his options.

On one of the farms he shared a room with the sons of the man who owned it. At first sight they didn't seem to be friendlier than the boy from Marcel's vineyard. They didn't ask him any questions about himself and answered his own ones with monosyllables.

He was given menial chores like slopping out barns. They worked him to the bone. They didn't do much more than grunt when he presented his work to them for their approval. By teatime every day he felt he was almost ready for bed. It was probably just as well because there was precious little else to do on the farm. It was miles from any town.

He liked to read in bed but that was frowned on. One night when he had his head dug in a book the sons told him to turn off the light.

'As soon as I finish the page I'm on,' he said. He wasn't sure if they understood him or not. A few seconds later the older son turned the light off. Brian wasn't having this so he turned it on again. This went on for some time until the older boy dragged him out of the bed. He started punching him. Then the younger son joined in. He fought back as much as he could but he couldn't match them. At the end of it he was black and blue. The older son took the bulb out of the socket. He put it sitting in a box beside Brian's bed.

The next morning at breakfast he had scars on his face. The farmer asked him what happened. 'I fell,' he said. The sons appreciated that. They became friends afterwards.

They began taking him places. He became like one of the family. His French improved and so did their English. They spoke to one another in a mixture of both languages. One night they brought him to Paris to see a strip show. The feature act was a belly dancer from Brazil. All she was wearing was a smile.

'Now you'll have something to tell the people at home,' the older brother said to him on the way out.

'You mean *not* tell them,' he replied.

Their poor English just about allowed him to get the joke.

For the rest of his time there he started to enjoy the work. The tension went out of it. That made the time pass fast. In the end he was almost sorry to be going.

The younger son asked him if they could take a photograph of him on his mobile phone before he left. As he got ready for it, the son went up to the bedroom and brought the bulb down. He held it over Brian's head for the photo. He laughed when he saw it. It was like one of those drawings in children's comics where a character was getting an idea.

He got a reference from that job for another one nearby. That was a surprise for him considering the events of the previous few days. The pay wasn't great. He was given meals and accommodation in compensation but you couldn't accumulate savings on things like that. It limited his plans for further travel.

He tried not to think about the past on his first day. It was easy enough in the daytime when he was busy but that night his mind was like a cauldron. He tossed and turned in his bed, brooding about all the things that had happened in the past few years. The next morning he threw himself into his work, activity blocking out thought just as it did anytime he broke into a sweat in Loughrea.

He was allowed use the *patron's* phone to call home. He rang Jennifer to see if things were okay between them.

'Sorry for hanging up on you the night before you left,' she said a few seconds after picking up.

'And sorry for being so secretive.'

The line was bad but she was as natural as ever. She talked non-stop about the things that were happening on her course and in her life and he lapped it up. It was so refreshing to hear an Irish voice. After the call was finished he felt like a flower that had been watered.

A later call to Bartley proved to be less felicitous. He was drinking, which caused him to make fun of everything Brian said. At the end of the call he said, 'Do you say "Pardonnez moi?" to the cows before you milk them?'

He seemed to resent him telling him anything about the kind of work he'd spent his own life at. Did he envy him being in a foreign country when he'd never got outside Ireland himself?

People said travel broadened the mind. He wasn't sure if that was true or not. If somebody had a narrow mind to start with, it was hardly likely to be expanded no matter what corner of the globe they went to. You could put lipstick on a pig, as someone said, but it was still a pig.

He forged on, leaving jobs with the casualness of all migrant labourers. in love with change for its own sweet sake. What was to stop him being the Irish Jack Kerouac, the Irish Woody Guthrie?

He had a Walkman with a CD in it. He kept playing it over and over. It was *The Circle Game* by Tom Rush. It had a song on it called 'The Urge for Going.' He played it so many times he thought he'd burn it up. The song tapped into the way he was feeling at the time, what he was going through in his search for something indefinable.

When he was between jobs he kept travelling. The chaos of the motorways appeared in his mind in tangled dreams. When he hadn't the money for trains he hitched. This was prohibited on most of the motorways. If the gendarmes passed by they used to take him into their cars and threaten to arrest him. They always drove him in the opposite direction to where he was going as a punishment. After a while he thought up a way to escape this. Whenever he saw them coming towards him he ran across the road to make them think he wanted to go in the opposite direction. When they took him away they'd be driving him where he wanted to go without realising it.

Ninety nine out of a hundred cars passed him by without stopping. It was draining standing there in the searing heat. One day a man who stopped for him told him he'd done what he was doing when he was young too. 'Maybe when you are my age you can do thees for someone too,' he said in broken English. He even gave him a handful of euros as he was getting out of the car.

The sun beat down. Towns with unpronounceable names flew by. He sat with drivers trying to make conversation in a language he only half understood. If another hitcher appeared on the road they were competition for him and he for them. He tried to keep as far away from them as possible. Everyone was always looking for the best spot to hitch from.

Sometimes the person driving him had to make a detour down a side road. If that happened he'd be left in the middle of nowhere. He wouldn't know whether to go back or forward or stay where he was. If night was coming on he'd think the worst – he was going to be left where he was. People didn't usually pick up hitch-hikers in the dark. If the night was fine it was all right. He'd just lay down on the grass and sleep, or try to. If it was raining he had to seek shelter. He'd go to petrol stations, shopfronts, even trees. If he was lucky there'd be a town near him and he could stay in a cheap hotel or a boarding house.

One night the driver of a car he was in started to fall asleep. He was a commercial traveller who'd been driving all day. He thought he was going to crash. In a panic Brian gave him a shove to prod him awake. 'Maybe we should pull over,' he said. The driver's eyes blinked open. He said, 'Que?' After that he revived himself.

The days passed by in a blur. He was entranced by the scenery, so much so that sometimes he forgot where he was going. He didn't want the month to end. Could you travel forever and not have to stop? It often seemed that way to him. The sun spilled through the windscreens of the cars, blinding him and exciting him. He felt the wheels lifting him off the road into it, carrying him like a magic blanket into its whiteness.

For a few weeks this was his life. People became no more to him than their appearance behind steering-wheels. He didn't speak to them much. He just nodded blankly ahead of him in half-acknowledgement of their comments as their vehicles ate up the miles.

He often fell asleep. when that happened he had to be woken up by the drivers when he reached his destination. He never told Jennifer or Bartley things like that. He knew what he'd say – that he was leaving himself open to being robbed or even murdered.

Sometimes he slept in the backlots of petrol stations. He rose at dawn on the following mornings to catch the trucks that were on the road then. The light would be opaque, the sun not out yet. Every town he came to offered new excitement for him. His personality changed with each of them. He'd always been private with people he knew well but that changed with strangers. He opened his heart up to them, telling them things about himself he wouldn't even have told to Jennifer.

He wondered how he'd be with her when he got home. Would the time away change his feelings for her? Or hers for him? The memory of his mother gnawed at him. It was a scar he either indulged or blacked out. For sanity's sake he tried to forget the way she died, to bury the anger he felt towards Bartley for the way he'd treated her.

He unloaded his anger on Jennifer. She always cooled him down. He wished he had her temperament.

'She wouldn't have wanted you to carry a grudge,' she'd say whenever he opened up to her. He wasn't logical enough to think like that. When he felt the anger he couldn't contain it. 'Concentrate on where you are,' she'd say to him, 'You're doing something he's never done – and never will.'

Every time he came to a new town he told himself this was the one he'd settle in. It was the one that had everything he wanted, the one where he'd reach a kind of epiphany. He rarely experienced that but no matter how many times he failed he left himself open to the possibility of it.

He went to Italy after France. Everything felt strange to him there – the lush rains of Tuscany, the trees that stood like soldiers standing to attention, the mountain peaks glowering ominously in the dusk.

He liked the Italians more than the French. They were more natural, but work was harder come by there. There weren't as many vineyards. Tthat was where he'd done most of his work up to now.

He tried bar work for a while but learning how to mix cocktails proved too complicated for him. Unskilled labour was easier. At least there he could turn his mind off.

In Genoa he was taken on by a company that repaired churches. He never knew where he'd be on a given day. His boss dressed him in a boiler suit. He gave him a can of paint and a spray gun. He had to wear a mask on his face. He was put standing on a trolley. A group of men wheeled him down corridors so he could spray the walls. Masking tape was put on the window sills and the edges of the stained glass windows.

He got a cheap apartment. It was located in a tiny street down a flight of stairs. There was a fruit market further down the street. Every morning he woke up to the sound of the sellers calling out their prices or haggling with the customers. Sometimes they gave him their unsold fruit for nothing.

It was strange coming home from the splendour of the church to his dingy little room. The walls were practically falling down but he didn't mind. Whatever he earned in his jobs he spent almost as soon as he got it. The cost of living was expensive. So was travel but he liked being on the move.

The weather was mild in Genoa but there were flash floods that came without warning. Two elderly people died one day after being caught in them. Cars were abandoned in the middle of pools. The streets were like rivers. It was what he imagined Venice to be like.

The summer moved on liked a tide. He enjoyed being busy but doing nothing had a value too. It wasn't like doing nothing in Loughrea. Even walking down a street was an experience. Everything was so strange.

He kept a diary of what happened to him. He even put his dreams into it.

He got the idea that he wanted to write a novel. He'd put everything into it, even the most trivial detail. The writers he studied at the university had too many layers to them. He wanted to get back to simplicity.

He wrote mainly at night-time. That was when his imagination kicked ni. something that happened during the day might trigger it, something someone said, or the way they expressed themselves. The next morning he'd look at what he wrote the way a woman might look at a stillborn child, as a creature he'd flushed out of himself, something that came from nowhere and would probably go nowhere.

One of his co-workers was from Clare. His name was Damian. He kept asking Brian questions, kept trying to find people they might both know to give them a connection point. He didn't want that. He made excuses to cut the conversations short. This made the atmosphere tense between them.

He rang Jennifer one night. The phone was in the hall of the apartment block. It was shared between all the residents.

'I won't be able to stay on long,' he said, 'There's always a queue of people waiting to use the phone.'

'How are you getting on?'

'Well enough. I'm doing up a church. What about you?'

'I have no news. The lectures are as boring as ever. I have good crack with the girls in the class though. They make up for them.'

'I wish I was as sociable as you.'

'Are there not any Irish people working with you?'

'Just one. He's from Clare.'

'I suppose you see him more than the other people.'

'Not really. If I wanted to spend time with Irish people I'd have stayed in Ireland.'

He wasn't sure if Damien was listening to the call or not. The next day he said to him 'Have you something against me?' He couldn't convince him he didn't. He left the job soon afterwards. He had a girlfriend in Padua. He was meeting her there to go to Spain with her. That was where her parents lived. Brian was relieved.

Towards the end of his time in Italy he spent a day in Rome. He never enjoyed tourist spots no matter how elaborate they looked. St. Peter's Square bored him. He preferred finding places on the back streets where the ordinary people were. Historical ruins left him cold. He avoided these until night-time when there was nobody there. Looking at them then gave him a sense of how he might have felt seeing them as natural places rather than something to be photographed.

One night he went to a film. It was a western with John Wayne. He couldn't stop laughing when he started to speak. His voice had been dubbed into Italian. He sounded like a bulldog with a sore throat. Nobody else was laughing. Maybe they didn't know what the real John Wayne sounded like.

His next stop was Switzerland. In Zurich he met a postman and became friendly with him. He was staying in a boarding house the man came to with a delivery. He didn't know where to go with it so Brian helped him. When they started talking they found they had a lot in common. The man had an Irish grandparent. He was also interested in books.

He asked him round to his place for tea that evening. His partner was there. She had no English at all. She just kept smiling at Brian all the time.

He ended up staying the night with them. He couldn't understand how they weren't discommoded by him. He even got him a part-time job. It was in a nearby delicatessen. He knew the owner.

The Swiss were friendly to him without being over the top. He felt he had an implicit understanding of them and they of him. Their relaxed attitude to him made him feel he'd lived there all his life.

Like most people he was captivated by the scenery in Switzerland. On his first weekend there he took a train trip a few miles into the country. They stopped at a village that was so small you could hardly even call it that. Apart from a café all you could see was snow. It was like being in a Walt Disney film. It was at the foot of Mount Uetliberg. There were funiculars that went up and down every day. He joined a queue of people waiting for it. He usually avoided doing tourist-like things but he made an exception for that. The view from the peak was unbelievable. He sat for ages looking down on the little villages, their lights twinkling like the fairy lights of Christmas trees. Some of the people he talked to found the expanse of snow monotonous but he felt almost spiritual in it. In the silence he sensed a presence of something watching him.

One night he stayed in a hostel that was built at the foot of a mountain. It didn't have any heating in it. People were jumping up and down trying to keep themselves warm. The bedroom was like a dormitory. Hordes of students poured into it with backpacks. The man who ran it told him to keep a tight hold on his money. 'The scenery may be beautiful here,' he said, 'but the people aren't.' He was even advised to put his shoes into the legs of the bed so they wouldn't be stolen. He thought that was a bit extreme.

The temperature dropped so low that night he thought he was going to get frostbite. He couldn't imagine the North Pole being any colder. It was all right to admire the beauty of the landscape from a warm room but this was different. When he woke up the next morning he found himself longing for the central heating of home.

A boy in the bed across from him was crying. He'd drifted away from a tour group. His mobile phone had been stolen during the night and he had no way to contact his relatives. As he tramped out of the hostel later in the day he saw the boy surrounded by a group of men in uniforms. They were all on mobile phones. He was shivering beside them.

There was a blizzard later on in the day. Everything seemed to turn white with it, not just the snow and the mountains but even the air itself. All he could see was a few inches ahead of him. It was what he felt heaven might be like or at least a childhood vision of it. He let the wind blow in his face for what felt like an eternity. Then it stopped. The air cleared and the village below him came into view again. It was as if someone had sprinkled angel dust over it.

Back in the city everything moved like clockwork. Nobody broke the rules and everything was done at a particular time. It didn't surprise him to learn that the Swiss invented the cuckoo clock. Someone said to him one night that they washed their rubbish before putting it out. Another person told him it was illegal to flush a toilet after 10 p.m. He wasn't sure if they were joking or not.

Many of the people he met there were fascinated by Ireland. They kept asking him questions about it. Most of these he had trouble answering. He became ashamed of his ignorance of Ireland's history and geography.

He wasn't sure where he'd go after leaving Switzerland. His funds were so low he had to swallow his pride and ring Bartley. Angela found a way of wiring bank drafts to a Swiss bank for him. She was good at things like that. He hated the fact that she was being brought in on everything now.

The next few weeks flew by. He went from cities that deafened him with the noise of traffic to valleys where there was nothing to be heard but the hooves of horses cantering through forests. Change enlivened him. The longer he was away the more he fell in love with it. He couldn't imagine settling back on the farm or even in the university.

His money continued to run out even with Bartley's help. He hated the idea of doing any more work. He was exhausted but what could he do? It was back to job-hunting again. He didn't want to go to Bartley again for another loan. His pride wouldn't let him.

He got a job handing out the equipment in a ski resort for a week. It wasn't much fun looking out at the skiers hurtling down slopes as he sat behind a desk bored out of his mind showing wooden statues to potential buyers. Better jobs were denied to him because of his inability to get a work visa. That hadn't been a problem with the farm work or the casual jobs that didn't require him to be on any books. He stayed mainly in hostels now, crammed up against backpackers in overcrowded bedrooms. If the weather permitted, he slept 'under the stars.'

He had little sense of time while he was away. He didn't read newspapers or watch television. Often he didn't even know what day it was. He went on dates with women sometimes but he didn't become closely involved with them. He wasn't aware he was keeping them at arm's length. It was an invisible distance for him. Bartley used to say, 'He travels fastest who travels alone.' It was true. Or was he saving himself for Jennifer?

'You like cowboy in American *feelm*,' a woman said to him one night, 'You always on move.' What was he running from? Maybe himself.

He went back to France at the end of the trip. He'd gone to Europe to improve his French but it was worse than ever as October drew to a close. That was mainly his own fault. He found it impossible to study. Neither did the people help much in the way they put things. Many of them spoke at a hundred miles an hour. He was lucky if he made out a word in every sentence. Any kind of detailed conversation was impossible unless there was someone there who understood both languages. Most French people had fairly good English but that was defeating the purpose.

When he didn't understand what they were saying he often communicated with them through gestures. Sometimes even the tone of their voices made him understand them. He learned to gauge their moods the way a dog might gauge anger or friendliness from the modulation of his master's words.

His lack of proficiency led to an embarrassing situation. One night at a party he found himself insulting a woman when a friend of hers told him to say something to her that he didn't understand. It turned out to be a curse against her mother. When he found out, Brian thought she was going to hit him but she took it in good part. She knew what happened so it became a joke between them.

He spent one of his last nights in France in a village at the bottom of a mountain. A festival was taking place in it. There were barmaids dressed up in smocks and multi-coloured scarves. Their dresses billowed in the wind.

A lot of preparation went into it. Jets of water splurged out from a fountain. Lanterns dangled from terraces, bathing everyone in pools of light. A troop of singers and dancers were recruited for the night. He listened to their heels clacking on the pavements, their voices ricocheting through the square. He found himself dancing with a woman who had the strangest eyes he'd ever seen. She kept staring at him like she knew him. He was half afraid of her.

The festival continued the next night. The dancing was even more frenzied. There were guitars and castanets and tambourines. The woman with the strange eyes sang. Her singing was as mysterious as everything else about her. As soon as she opened her mouth everyone went quiet. She had a weird fascination.

As the summer drew to a close he tried to tie up all the loose ends. He wanted to talk to his friend from Zurich to thank him for everything but he couldn't get through to him. He didn't have an address for him either. He'd probably never see him again now. Part of the summer's attraction was its transience but it had its downside too.

He'd been in Europe for just four months but it felt like as many years. Another grape-picking job presented itself to him as he was about to leave France. It was only a few miles from where he'd had his first one. He wasn't sure whether to take it or not because the time was so short but in the end he did. One of the fringe benefits of it was the fact that it gave him enough money to ensure he wouldn't be broke at the airport. He'd feared that possibility. There were always extra expenses at the end of things.

He picked his last grape in early November. On the way back from the vineyard there was much cheering and back-slapping. He sat on top of the truck and looked across the land. For the first time it reminded him of Loughrea. He felt a combination of elation and emptiness. When anything ended it always brought up these two emotions in him. It was like a little death.

The mixed feelings hit him again as he said goodbye to his co-workers a few hours later. He exchanged phone numbers with them but he doubted he'd contact them again. The time away had achieved its objective. He didn't want them to be a part of his other life.

As he got ready to go home he felt strangely nervous. He started thinking about Jennifer again. She was always at the back of his mind no matter how much he tried to pretend he'd outgrown her. Maybe she'd outgrow him sooner.

She could even be with someone else now. He had no control over that. If she was, good luck to her. He'd made a choice and he'd have to live with it. If she hadn't gone to Limerick he mightn't have had the courage to go to Dublin or Europe. They were both seeking other lives to strengthen their own one together if they went back to it. But travel created an appetite. It was a double-edged sword. Most people were happy with what they had because they never had an alternative. Others hungered for that something else when it was already beyond their grasp. Maybe he'd gone away for no other reason than to try and find out if he could live without her. But you could be too independent. He didn't want to end up a bachelor.

The four months away helped him grow up. His time with nature had made him feel like nature himself. Anything that went against him in his life from now on, he felt, would be as easy for him to deal with as anything that happened to the sky, the sea, the land.

18

When he got back to Ireland it was like being in another country. Everything seemed strange to him - the weather, the buildings, even the accents of the people at the airport.

There was nobody to meet him because he hadn't told anyone the day he'd be arriving back. That was how he wanted it. It allowed him to keep being free, tto bring something of Europe's anonymity back with him.

He got a shuttle from the airport to the city centre and a taxi from there to Ranelagh. It was lashing rain. The holiday atmosphere was gone. People bustled about with worried looks on their faces as they went to work. Maybe he'd be like that himself one day too, he thought. Most people were, no matter how much they fought against it. All he could do was try and postpone it for as long as he could.

He wondered what he was going to do for money now. Probably ask Bartley again. Europe drained his finances. Travel always seemed to do that, even if you worked. He had less than a hundred euro in his pocket

He stopped at an ATM machine on the street. He didn't expect to find much in it. When he put the card in, it was gobbled up. That said it all.

Denise wasn't there when he got to Centra. A new girl was filling in for her. He was relieved. He didn't feel like talking to anyone.

He climbed the stairs. When he turned the key in his door it wouldn't open at first. There was something blocking it. Then it moved. When he went in he saw what it was – an avalanche of post on the floor.

There were a few letters from Jennifer and one from Bartley. Declan had sent some bumpf about his firm in a jiffybag. Another envelope had the UCD logo on it. He imagined it was his exam results.

He didn't care enough about them to open it. He sat on the sofa and looked around. Everything seemed the same. He felt strangely at home – even on the jumpy sofa.

He decided to call Jennifer. She picked up on the second ring. It was as if she'd been expecting the call. She sounded happy to hear his voice.

'Well,' she said, 'You got back in one piece.'

'How are you?'

'Trundling along. More to the point, how are you? I can't wait to hear your news.'

'Sorry I couldn't have given you more from Europe.'

'Half the time when you rang I wasn't sure where you were.'

'Neither was I, to tell you the truth.'

'It was very hard to hear you on some of the calls.'

'I had the same problem with you.'

'You seem to have had a lot of jobs.'

'They were hard come by sometimes. I'd have donated a kidney to get one. Money was scarce.'

'You should have sold your blood for a few quid. That's a bit less dramatic.'

'I didn't think of that.'

'Did you bring me home any grapes?'

'I'm afraid I ate them all.'

'That's nice of you. You probably picked about five million.'

'They're very addictive. If I go back next year I'll stamp on a few for you and make you some wine.'

'I'll hold you to that. How have you been otherwise?'

'Not too bad. I don't really feel like going back to the university.'

'Did you pass your exams?'

'I don't know yet. There's an envelope with the UCD logo on it but I haven't opened it yet.'

'You're unbelievable. I'd have torn it apart even before I got the door closed.'

'It might have meant something to me once.'

'Open it this instant. That's an order.'

'You're funny.'

'I'm deadly serious. Open it or I'll go up there and make you.'

'Anything to keep you happy.'

He opened the envelope. He'd passed. She let out a screech.

'Well done, lazy genius,' she said. .

'I'm far from that I'm afraid All you need is a good memory for these things.'

'You're always playing yourself down. I can see you running the English department yet.'

'And pigs might fly.'

'Why do you always debunk things you've worked hard to achieve? Sometimes I think you're a masochist.'

'I'm not trying to be dramatic. Maybe the time away changed my attitude.'

'No, you were always that way. Anyway, well done. Take a bow. Or better still, open a bottle of bubbly.'

129

'I don't think so. I'm not feeling very well today. It's probably the travel.'

'You need a woman to look after you.'

'Is that an offer?'

'Maybe. For now, all I want is to hear everything that happened to you over the last four months. In detail.'

He told her as much as he could remember. Her mind worked in terms of facts and his in terms of sensations. He found it difficult to put things in the way she wanted. Every time he paused for breath she made him fill in the blanks until he was worn out.

'Wow,' she said after he'd finished, 'That was a summer and a half.'

'It sounds exciting when you tell it in bursts,' he said. 'There were a lot of down times too.'

'That's the way with everyone.'

'What about your own news?'

'I'll tell you everything on the next phone call. Or when I see you. When are you going to come west?'

'As soon as I get my bearings. Would Halloween suit you?'

'You don't have to be so formal. It's me, remember?'

'Sorry.'

'You're forgiven.'

'How are the lectures?'

'Terminally boring. Everyone is down in the dumps.'

'You haven't said a thing about your own summer.'

'I was at home for most of it. I went to the Gaeltacht for a week but it rained the whole time.'

'It's bucketing here too.'

'I spent most of my time saying the same sentence: *"Tá sé ag cur báistí."* You probably got sun every day.'

'I was never a sun worshipper. You know that.'

'What a waste. You should have stayed in Ireland. I could have gone to France in your place.'

'That's what we'll do next year. Then you can stamp on the grapes for me instead of the other way round.'

'It's a deal.'

She was always in such good form. It made him feel they should be together forever. Where would they go from here? Having been away from her for so long made him think he'd have to get to know her all over again when they met up. How could that be possible when he knew her almost as well as he knew himself? Some breaks did relationships good. Other ones only caused problems.

He rang Bartley then. He was less upbeat.

'The prodigal son returns,' he said.

'What's happening down there?'

'Same old same old. It's a shame there was no one at the airport to meet you.'

'I don't care about things like that. I just wanted to come back here and get ready for the new term.'

'When are we going to see you?'

'I told Jennifer I was hoping to get down for Halloween.'

'I'm glad to hear you were onto her. She keeps asking about you. Angela as well. She's beside me here champing at the bit to have a few words with you.'

'Tell her I said hello.'

'Is that all you have to say?'

'Sorry.'

'It's okay. I know you're not one for small talk. We'll spare you telling us things till you're in form for it.'

'That's good of you. I'm so tired I can hardly talk.'

'Don't then.'

'Your money was a godsend, by the way.'

'I couldn't have done it if it wasn't for Angela.'

'Tell her I said thanks.'

'I will. She's brilliant with technology. I'm better with the greenbacks in the hand than on some machine.'

'So am I. I don't know where we'll be in the next generation. There probably won't be any money then at all. It'll be all buttons.'

'I won't be around for it anyway. It won't worry me.'

He didn't do much for the weekend. There was no point going anywhere. He had no energy. Instead he hung around the flat. He got to know Denise better. She made up some snacks for him from the shop. She was all friendship asking him about France. He was able to be himself with her. It was so different to UCD where he was expected to strike poses, assume attitudes.

'It's my favourite country,' she said at one stage, 'It's a million times better than anywhere else in the world.'

'When were you there?' he said.

'I haven't been yet but I really want to go.' '

She often said funny things like that. It was what he liked most about her.

He went back to the campus on the following Monday. The term was well on but he didn't care. You could always pick up.

Most of the people he knew were anxious to hear his news but he wasn't ready to share anything with them. He wasn't unduly keen to hear their news either. One of the girls in his English class had got married over the summer. Another one had been mugged. She nearly lost an eye in a scuffle in Normandy. A third dropped out to live with a man in Bath. He couldn't take as much interest in these stories as the other people listening to them did. Their tongues were practically hanging out with excitement at every morsel.

Martin called round to see him that night. He welcomed him back like a long-lost son. He'd sub-let the flat to a friend over the summer. He gave Brian a cut as a result. That eased his financial burden.

He was more relaxed the next time he rang Jennifer. She told him a bit about her summer. He was surprised to hear she'd joined a dramatic society.

'It was a bit of fun. We rehearsed in an old school. The highlight of the week was when Mrs Cullotty – she's the director – treated us to jam sandwiches.'

He knew Mrs Cullotty. She was a friend of Bartley's. She'd never married. She had a passion for the theatre all her life.

'Somehow I can't see you on a stage.'

'Why not? The classroom is one too. That's what I've learned. The kids don't listen to you unless you perform. You have to make a big deal of everything you say even if you're only telling them to open their books. Otherwise everything goes in one ear and out the other.'

'The more you talk about it, the less I think I want to go into that kind of job.'

'You'd probably be thinking of secondary, wouldn't you? That's a different ballgame.'

'I'm not thinking of anything at the moment. I'm having a hard enough time wondering if I'll see the B.A. out.'

'Don't if you don't want to. There's nothing worse than being somewhere you don't want to be.'

'Why do you think I went away?'

She went quiet when he said that. Was she thinking it was an excuse to get away from her?

'Are you still annoyed with me for suggesting you see other men?' he said.

'Not at all,' she said, 'It was good advice.'

'Are you putting it into practice?'

'There are a few guys in the dramatic society. Some of them see it as a dating bureau.'

'Are you one of them?'

'That's for me to know and you to find out.'

'Don't be coy.'

'You seem to want to push me into the arms of other men.'

'Why would I want to do that?'

'I don't know. Maybe it would free you up to go out with other women without feeling guilty about it.'

'Nothing could be further from the truth.'

'I wonder.'

He wasn't sure if he meant that. The call ended hanging in the air.Why was she always reading into situations? He thought he'd made a reasonable suggestion. Did she have to make a gangster movie out of it?

As if to spite her he started seeing a girl. Her name was Sinead. She was in his English class. She had red hair and freckles. She wore granny glasses that gave her a look of being distracted. She said she was short-sighted but he wondered. He thought she wore them for effect.

He didn't think of her as a girlfriend at first. She was just someone to pass the time with. She was from Killiney. Her father was a solicitor.

'I was surprised you had a tongue in your mouth,' she said to him the first time they went for coffee.

'I have one but it doesn't work very well. Sometimes I think the term "tongue-tied" was invented for me.'

'That's a good excuse for not talking to anyone.'

She had a sunny personality that he found refreshing. She dressed waifishly, wearing things like ponchos and espadrilles. They gave her an exotic look.

She was her own woman, refusing to use the clichés othe other students did when they were talking about the books on the course. Any insights she had were her own.

Sometimes he saw her leaving lectures in the middle of them. He followed her out once.

'Why did you do that?' he asked.

'He was boring me. I don't do boredom.'

He liked her cynicism. It mirrored his own. She didn't have the lecturers on pedestals like most of the other people he knew.

'They're just eunuchs in the harem,' she said. That put it in a nutshell for him. Their immersion in other people's lives denied them their own ones.

She was only 21 but she'd already had a string of romances. Most of them had ended badly. She blamed herself for that. Her problems started when her father left her mother for a younger woman. She went on drugs to try to inure herself to the shock. There were syringe marks on her arms. All of this gave her a dangerous attraction for Brian. It was so different to anything he was used to. Her casualness about the drugs excited him. 'I wasn't addicted,' she explained, 'I was experimenting.' That seemed to make it all right for her. She'd had an abortion too. From another woman that kind of revelation would have stopped him in his tracks but from her it was almost expectable.

In her presence he became less inhibited. The relationship between them moved fast. None of their nights together were the same. She was a dynamo of energy, unable to sit still for more than a few seconds at a time. Whenever she came over to his flat for an evening she kept moving about. Even when she was sitting she was moving – taking things up and putting them down, doodling with beer mats, chewing her fingernails down to the quick. She drank too. Some nights she didn't bother with it but when she did she didn't know when to stop.

'Why do you drink so much?' he asked her one night. It was a comment he could have made to his father any night of the year.

'I don't know,' she said, 'I don't even know I'm doing it. Maybe I was born drunk.'

They attended art exhibitions together, abstruse affairs with paintings he couldn't make head nor tail of. Sometimes he wasn't even sure if the exhibits were hanging upside down or not.

One night they went to a sculpture exhibition.

'Why does everything look like a toilet bowl,' he said to her.

'You're funny,' she said, 'You're so sarcastic you remind me of myself.'

He tried to avoid running into her friends. Most of them looked like they hadn't washed in a month. If he kept her away from them, he told himself, he might be able to reform her. Of course it could work the other way too. Maybe she'd make him go down their road.

He didn't want to tell Jennifer about her but one night her name slipped out when he was on the phone to her. .

'Who's Sinead?' she asked.

'Just a friend.'

'Are you sure?'

'Do you not believe me?'

'It doesn't matter either way. You don't have chains round you.'

'There's no need to be like that about it.'

'Like what? I'm not any way.'

'You're adopting an attitude.'

'Brian, we need to stop arguing.'

'I agree.'

She didn't speak for a few seconds. Then she said, 'I met someone too.'That surprised him. Even though he'd encouraged her to, he didn't expect her to take him up on it.

'Really? Who?' He tried to sound casual but his heart was pounding.

'A guy from the drama group.'

'Are you going out with him?'

'Not really.'

'What do you mean by that?'

'Nothing.'

Despite his pressing she wouldn't tell him his name. He wasn't sure if she brought him up to get him back for mentioning Sinead.

Their phone calls after that were tense. At the end of one of them she said, 'Are you all right? You sound a bit strange.'

'What makes you think that?'

'I don't know. You seem edgy.'

'I'm stressed from the studying.'

Guilt gnawed at him. When he was with Sinead he couldn't stop thinking of her. Sinead noticed there was something wrong. He hadn't told her much about her, just that there was a girl from his past that he saw anytime he went home.

'I thought you told me you were split up,' she said to him one night.

'We're on a break.'

'Look, sunshine, you're either in a relationship with her or you're not. There's no in between.'

'It's complicated.'

'I don't get it. Are you going to marry her? Am I stealing another girl's man?'

'Now you're being ridiculous.'

'Don't worry if you have someone stashed away in the background. I'm not the possessive type. Maybe we could have a threesome.'

'I wish you wouldn't say things like that.'

'Why are you so serious? It was a joke.'

'I'm wound up. I can't help it.'

'You're too cautious. you need to let yourself go. If you don't you might as well not live it at all.'

'You can live it to the full life without living it to excess.'

'No you can't. The road to excess leads to the palace of wisdom.'

'Come again?'

'It's a quote from William Blake. I agree with him.'

'In what way?'

'In every way.'

'Are you relating it to me?'

'Sometimes I think you're afraid of your feelings, of what giving in to them might do to you. That makes you come across as cold.'

'Just because I don't wear my heart on my sleeve doesn't mean I don't have one.'

'That's exactly what I'm trying to say to you. Put it on your sleeve and we'll see what happens.'

He tried to do that. One night he slept with her in a sleeping bag in a deserted house. Another night they lay together on a beach in Killiney under an upturned boat. It wasn't her first time doing things like that. They didn't mean as much to her as they did to him.

He wondered where they were going but for her only the moment mattered. She didn't care if things collapsed or not.

'I can love somebody,' she said, 'and then a moment later it's as if they never existed.'

It was as if there was a part of her brain missing. How could he get to know her when she didn't know herself?

'Things always work themselves out,' was her favourite expression. She used it whenever anything went wrong. Few things bothered her as a result.

'What's your secret?' he asked her one night.

'The secret is that there's no secret,' she said.

He started bringing her around to the flat more often. It was exciting being with her because of her unpredictability. One dayt she stuck her head out the window and started screaming madly. When he asked her why she did it she said she didn't know. She just felt like it.

With Jennifer he'd always known what to expect on a given day but Sinead thrived on surprising him. She was like a child in an adult's body.

She stayed with him whenever she could. Her mother was possessive. She had to make up a female 'friend' who had a flat in Ranelagh.

'I'm under scrutiny because of my past,' she said, 'She makes me check in with her all the time now.'

He was uncomfortable having her there. He told her she'd have to be quiet in case Denise heard her. She was doing overtime in the Centra. He didn't want Martin to know he had anyone staying overnight.

'Are you ashamed of me?' she said to him one night when there was a storm and he persuaded her to stay over.

'It's not that. Denise might let it slip out to Martin.'

'Martin being your landlord, right?'

'Right.'

'Are we living in the Stone Ages?'

'He knows my father.'

'Oh. So he tells your father and your father tells your girlfriend back in the bogs. Is that it?'

'You're being thick now. It might make things complicated for me.'

She burst out laughing.

'Relax. I'll behave myself. Don't worry. I'll be as quiet as a church mouse.'

After that night she stayed over more often. He left a key under the mat outside his door. She came and went when she wanted. All he asked her was that she didn't do it when she was likely to be seen.

They got closer. Then they started living together. By now she'd stopped explaining herself to her mother. She didn't care.

He was awkward when he was on the phone with Jennifer. She knew something was up. She could always tell with him. It showed in his voice. He usually liked to have things out with her but this time he was glad she didn't question him too much. He wouldn't have had any answer for her.

He was conflicted. There was no answer to the situation. Sinead told him not to think about it. She was good at not thinking. Maybe there were some things you could never work out. You just went with them until they found their own water level.

They skipped most of the lectures. The campus was irrelevant to them now. Everything they'd done before they met was irrelevant. He slipped into her world as if he was going into a pool of honey.

She took him out of his comfort zone. He developed a sense of wildness with her. 'Maybe now you know what William Blake meant,' she said.

He knew he couldn't live her kind of life indefinitely. It wasn't in him. He was able to turn himself into her for a few months but not forever. She saw that too. He began to stay in on nights when she went out. That frustrated her. The fact of him being there gave her a licence to do things. When he wasn't with her they became indulgences.

'You're no fun anymore,' she said to him. He couldn't deny it. He was afraid of becoming a slave to her addictions. When you were doing something audacious every day it wasn't audacious. It just became another kind of routine.

One day he woke up to find her gone. She hadn't left a note. He rang her but there was no answer. In her absence he reverted back to his old personality. He started going to the lectures again. He missed her but a part of him was relieved. She was pulling him into areas he didn't want to go into, areas she could probably get out of easier if she wanted.

But he couldn't stop thinking about her. During the lectures he kept staring at the seat she used to occupy, the end one at the back of Theatre L. She liked because it was near the door in case she wanted to make a fast getaway.

Then she re-appeared out of the blue. Without saying anything she sat down beside him one day. She took out a pen and wrote down what the lecturer said. She'd never done that before. He wondered if she was having him on, if she was only pretending to take notes. When the lecture ended she flashed a big smile at him.

'Hi,' she said, 'Remember me?'

She seemed sluggish.

'Are you on something?' he said.

'I'm on life.'

They started going out again afterwards. This time it was more relaxing for him. When a relationship ended once it was easier for it to end again. There was no threat because he wasn't playing for high stakes.

He didn't ask her where she'd been. He suspected she was seeing other men besides him but he didn't mind. He also suspected she was taking drugs again.

Her moods fluctuated. The dead look came back into her eyes. He'd ask her questions that she wouldn't answer. Maybe she didn't even know he was asking them.

One night when he came back to the flat he found her shooting up. He wasn't shocked. Maybe he was even expecting it.

'You promised you wouldn't do that,' he said.

She put the syringe away.

'I promise people a lot of things,' she said, 'As you know by now, I usually break my promises.'

She smiled cruelly at him. She was wallowing in it.

'I'm not able for this,' he said.

'Do you think I am?'

He let her stay with him but he didn't sleep with her. He spent the night on a mattress on the floor.

The next morning she opened up to him over breakfast. She was casual at first but then she broke down crying. She said she was struggling with her problem, that it was destroying her.

'Why didn't you tell me all this before now?' he said.

'I might never have told you.'

'Do you not think I can help you?'

'Maybe I didn't want to admit it to myself. I don't like having anything in my life that I can't control.'

He told her he'd help her if she got clean.

'Nobody ever said that to me before,' she said. She had tears in her eyes. She kissed him.

'You sound like an old woman.'

'I feel like an old woman.'

He persuaded her to go into rehab. He didn't expect her to last long there.

He brought her to the centre the first day. She was shivering from withdrawal. He wasn't sure she'd go in. They went for a coffee in a nearby restaurant to help her steady herself. She was like a child to him. He could see her wavering, telling him it was a bad idea.

'You have to want it to work for it to work,' he told her.

'Do you not think I do?'

She wouldn't let him go into the building with her.

'I won't contact you for a while,' she said, 'I can't have you asking me questions about how I'm doing. Whatever way it goes, I'll let you know.'

She was gone for a few weeks. He was tempted to ring her but he knew it wouldn't have been fair. He doubted she'd have picked up anyway. He wasn't even sure if she was allowed keep her phone.

He tried not to think of her. Did she complete the course? Was she out in the world again? Was she seeing other men? Questions swirled around in his head. He wondered if she'd reform, if she was able to. If she did, he wasn't sure it would be for long.

She re-appeared again one day just like she had the last time, coming into a lecture after it started and sitting down beside him.

She gave him a nudge. He frowned at her. She smiled mischievously.

'You're making a bit of a habit of this, aren't you,' he said.

'I'm into habits - as you know.'

'How are you?'

'Struggling. I'm off the hard stuff.'

'Where have you been?'

'It's a long story.'

They went for coffee. She told him all about it. It was pretty harrowing. They brought her parents in. She had to admit to some revolting behaviour in front of them. They went into the worst sides of her in detail. That was the idea – you were presented with your worst self to try and coax you into killing it off.

'Is it over now?' he asked her.

'It's never over. If nothing else I learned that.'

She asked him if he'd take her back into his life. He was happy to do that. He wasn't afraid of her anymore.

She agreed to attend a counsellor. He became a kind of middleman between them. She reported everything back to him that took place at their sessions.

He put her on tablets. They depleted her energy. She became quieter, more serene. At times she reminded him of Jennifer.

He never saw her happier than when she wasn't taking anything. She was relieved to be away from the university. She only went in the odd day now. She didn't go to the lectures. She just hung around the lake. On the cold days she went into the bar or the café.

'Why not try the library?' he said.

'I can't do that anymore,' she said, 'Books would kill me quicker than any drug.'

He became a kind of father figure to her, bringing food up to her and taking care of her when she got infections. She was prone to these because her resistance was low from the withdrawal. He thought Denise must have suspected he had someone in the flat because of all the food he was bringing upstairs but she didn't say anything.

She slept through most of the days because of the pills she was on. She usually took a few hours to wake up in the mornings. If he had an early lecture he didn't disturb her. He left a note on the kitchen table. It always said the same thing, 'C U at Caf.' Underneath the message he'd make a little heart.

She'd usually surface around noon. Her eyes were always falling out of her head when she arrived at the campus. They'd sit over coffee in the restaurant, often without talking.

He knew it did her good to get out of the flat. She liked being around people even if she wasn't connecting with them. After she had a few cups of coffee she'd get her personality back. She'd become excited about the most insignificant things – an unusual dress one of the students was wearing or the way a sentence was put in a book she was reading. She'd stopped reading the ones on the course now, curling up with whatever Brian bought instead.

In the evening times she'd become morose again.

'Coffee withdrawal,' she explained.

He told her she needed to get off that too. Whenever he gave her advice she said, 'You remind me of my mother.'

She hadn't told her where she was staying. She called her on her mobile sometimes. Their conversations were usually short.

She didn't really know Brian. She'd met him once at an art exhibition he went to with Sinead.

'She looks very controlling,' he said to her on the way home from it.

'Hello! Why do you think I left home?'

When she got bad with the withdrawal he was tempted to ring her up and tell her everything. Sinead sensed that.

'If you breathe a word to her about where I am,' Sinead warned him, 'That's the end of us.' He was always afraid of her going back on the drugs. If she did he knew he'd get the blame.

Her mother eventually tracked them down to the flat. She called one day and started banging on the door. Martin was with her. Brian wasn't going to answer it until he heard his voice.

When she came in she was livid.

She attacked Sinead first and then Brian. Sinead was under the weather at the time. She'd just taken her pills.

'Look at the state of her,' she said, trying to make Brian feel bad. She accused him of getting her back on the drugs. She even threatened to phone the police. Sinead was too out of it to defend him.

She said she was bringing her home then but Sinead refused to go. Then everyone started shouting at one another. They all blamed someone else for the situation.

'I can't have this sort of thing going on,' Martin said, 'There are customers downstairs.'

He went back down to serve them. It was Denise's day off.

Brian told Sinead's mother to pipe down.

'You're working her up,' he said, 'It isn't good for her.'

'Oh so you're her carer now,' she said, looking daggers at him. He wanted to wash his hands of the whole business.

'She asked me if she could stay with me,' he said, 'I took her in out of kindness.'

She stormed out of the flat in a rage.

'How do you feel now? Brian said to Sinead after she was gone. She was too stressed to answer him. After a few minutes she fell asleep.

Martin came up the stairs after he'd served the customers.

'I'm afraid she can't stay here any longer,' he said, 'I can't have afford to have a scandal on my premises. You promised me you'd be a quiet tenant.'

'I am. This is an extreme situation. It won't happen again.'

'You're on your last chance,' he said.

One night soon afterwards the police called to Sinead's home looking for drugs. It turned out one of her former boyfriends tipped them off. She'd broken it off with him a year or so before and he wanted to get his own back on her. The police ripped her mother's sofa apart and dumped everything from pressed and lockers onto the floor. They found nothing but her mother nearly had a nervous breakdown watching them. The next day she went back to the flat again demanding Sinead come home. Again she refused. Brian told her the situation was out of control now, that she'd have to go home for all their sakes.

'The cops will be ripping up Martin's sofas next,' he said.

He said he didn't want her to go but the situation was becoming too toxic for him. Eventually she relented.

They got the bus to where she lived. He walked her to the door but left as soon as she knocked. He didn't want to run into her mother. She hardly looked back at him as he was going off.

He thought they were finished as a couple after that. Martin didn't want her in the flat even for a visit and Brian couldn't call to her house because of her mother's attitude. She'd practically deserted the campus now. On the odd occasion she was there he was nervous going over to her. He saw her as a luxury he couldn't afford.

19

His poetry book was published in early December. The publisher organised a launch in a city centre pub. A lot of nervous-looking people attended it. A few of them had beards and tattoos. The publisher wore a black polo neck. He had an ear-ring in one ear. Brian thought it looked a bit posey. He wanted to get away from that image of poetry.

He imagined most of the people there were either academics or struggling poets. He didn't know which was worse. Some of them looked as if they'd just split the atom. They drank liqueurs from little glasses and spoke intensely about the state of poetry in modern Ireland. They shuffled by Brian in their faded jackets affecting an air of vague curiosity.

Some punk rocker types drifted in after a while. Brian didn't know where the publisher dug them up from. There was free beer. Maybe that explained it. The only thing they had in common with the poets was in their egos.

Sinead turned up against all his expectations. She looked as if she was on something. Brian was afraid to ask her if she'd been using. He knew she was capable of creating drama if he said the wrong thing. He offered her a glass of wine but she said she'd better not chance it.

'It'd be like a match to a flame,' she said. She didn't say what the flame was.

'How are things at home?' he said.

'Let's not talk about me. It's your night. I'll stay in the background. Let the Poet Laureate orate.'

The bar was almost full by eight o'clock. That was the scheduled time of the launch. He'd invited a few people from his French class. They were casual acquaintances who came along as a favour more than anything else. He made sure not to ask Jamesie Gildea. He knew he'd be champing at the bit to be there so he could carry some gossip home to Bartley.

A hush descended on the bar as the publisher got up to say a few words. He extolled Brian as 'an important voice of the new millennium.' There was a polite round of applause, after which everyone went back to the more serious business of getting drunk on the publisher's cheap wine..

Most of the guests went home early. Brian felt they'd be relieved to be back in their lives without having had to be pulverised by the intelligentsia. He felt guilty that people who'd never read a poetry book in their lives had to dig into their pockets and pay for his one merely because they were in the room. It was an unspoken duty. The publisher's hawk-like stares ensured that.

'You won't be able to go to the Riviera on the royalties,' he told Brian, 'but we'll be pushing the book anywhere we can.' He thought he'd be lucky if fifty people read it. He had visions of the people who bought it from duty going home to use it for firewood.

The publisher wanted him to go on Twitter to promote it but he wasn't into that.

'You're cutting off an important lifeline,' he told him.

He didn't care. He felt the same way about social media as he did about computers.

The night drew to a close.

'Well,' Sinead said, 'You've survived it. What profound speculations

142

are going on in that poetic head?'

'I was wondering where we'd get the bus home actually,' he said.

She said she wanted to go back with him.

'Then I can say I slept with a published poet.'

He wasn't sure if it was a good idea but he was tipsy from the wine and not inclined to argue with her.

She liked the book. She fell asleep with it in her hands. The next morning she was gone before he woke up. She left a note saying, 'The morn in russet mantle clad, treads o'er the dew of yon high Eastern hill. Bye bye Mr Yeats.'

He started seeing her off and on again. He found her brilliant company since she came off the drugs. Her joy of life returned. He felt they were like two babes in the wood trying to play at being adults.

She wanted them both to drop out of college and go off somewhere together.

'I can't do that,' he said.

'Why?'

'Because you'd be bored with me after five minutes. Then what would we do?'

'We'll make a bonfire of all our books and set a match to them,' she suggested.

'And be arrested for creating a public order offence?'

'You're right. You're boring.'

Bartley rang him to see if he'd be home for Christmas.

'I can't,' he said, 'I'm too busy.'

'Sorry I drank too much last year,' he said, sounding suddenly like a small boy, 'I promise I won't do it again. I'm on a clean slate now. Angela put manners on me.'

'It's not that. I'm tied up here. Let me ring you when things cool down. Tell Angela I was asking for her.'

'How are you for money?'

'All right for now.'

'Ring me if you need any. I sold another field last month. I have some to spare.'

'Did you get much for it?'

'It's the recession. Everything is going for nothing.'

'Don't decimate the place altogether.'

He kept phoning him to ask him to come down to them, refusing to take no for an answer. On one call Brian got abrupt with him and hung up. Eventually he stopped answering the phone. He just let it ring out.

He didn't know what he wanted to do now. He felt unable to go back or forward. City life became as dull as the country had once been. He didn't think he had the appetite for travel anymore.

Sinead stayed with him the odd night. He was always terrified Martin would hear her and turf the two of them out. That would have meant going home sooner than he wanted.

Some of the students from UCD heard about the launch. It changed their attitude to him. They tried to get him to join them for nights out but he refused. His absence from the university gave him a kind of allure in their eyes now. They told him they wished they had the courage to boycott the lectures the way he did.

He felt guilty about wasting Bartley's money but there was no way around that. He couldn't sit for two hours discussing whether King Lear should have been a better father to his daughters 400 years ago. Who cared? He thought Bartley was probably right about him all along. It didn't make sense for him to go to university. The only good thing it achieved was getting his mind off his mother.

Jennifer rang him to wish him a happy Christmas.

'It's a pity you're not coming home,' she said, 'I have so much to tell you.'

'Can you not tell me over the phone?'

'It's not the same.'

'Sorry for being such a Scrooge.'

'Don't worry if it's what you want,' she said.

She was trying to sound upbeat but he could see how disappointed she was. They were so different. Happiness for him was being able to walk quietly down the streets of a city full of alienated people. For her it was being able to tell every detail of her life as it happened. He felt unworthy of her.

He spent Christmas Day alone. He needed it to catch his breath. His dinner was a lunch box from the local takeaway. He played songs on his hi-fi from people like Joan Armatrading and Elvis Costello. There was something refreshing in not feeling he had to do things associated with the time of year. If you did that you conquered it.

For the next few days he hardly went out at all. Now and again he didn't even dress. He slept a lot of the time. In the street outside the flat he listened to the sounds of the season. Carols wafted up to him, sounds of people selling trees and decorations and all the other nic-nacs that proliferated everywhere he looked. When you weren't part of something it seemed ludicrous. It was like being a teetotaller in a crowded pub. He listened to the excessive declarations of love from people who were at each other's throats an hour later.

Jennifer rang him again on New Year's Eve.

'You picked up,' she said jubilantly, 'I thought you'd be out.'

'I've been living like a hermit.'

'You're going to let it all hang out tonight, though, right?'

'No. I'm going to turn in early. Let everyone else make a fool of themselves if they want.'

'You're unbelievable,' she said, 'You know that, don't you?'

'So they tell me.'

After the call he turned off the lights and went to bed. He listened to some drunks outside the flat wishing each other a happy new year. He pulled the covers of the duvet up, seeing the year out with a straight vodka and two sleeping pills.

There was a sense of gloom over Dublin as the new year began. It was like a physical thing, a black cloud of hesitancy that seemed to dominate everything. People walked with lethargy in the streets.

When he went out to Belfield he felt weird. He thought the students looked like robots, like disembodied people. He felt he was looking at them through glass, from under water.

In the spring there was a heatwave. The sun beat down on him like a weight, paralysing him and all the people around him. The crime figures dropped. There were less robberies than for years. It was as if people were too lethargic to do anything, even burgle houses.

Some days it got so warm he imagined the sun burning up the earth before his eyes, merciless in its force. People seemed to have trouble even walking down the street, becoming winded without reason.

'I can't breathe,' an old man said to him one particularly scorching day as he took off his shirt.

He sat down on the pavement.

'I spent my life wishing I'd been born in a warmer climate,' he gasped, 'Now I'm afraid of it.'

The sun was like a red ball in the sky, a laser beam cutting through people's skin. The newspapers carried photographs of holidaymakers at beaches with big grins on their faces but to Brian they looked grotesque.

Then one day everything changed. It was as if someone pulled a switch in the sky. The heavens opened, releasing a deluge of rain. It was the same down the country.

'We're glad of it for the crops,' Bartley said to him on a phone call, 'Not that I'm too bothered about that kind of thing now.'

He asked him about his poetry launch. Jamesie Gildea – who else - had told him about it.

'That was months ago.'

'I don't care. It was still a big deal.'

'Jamesie must be your chief confidante now,' he said.

'How do you mean?'

'He must be under the bed when I'm writing. I can't go a hen's race without him getting wind of it.'

'Don't have that attitude. Isn't it good he's interested? If it wasn't for him we wouldn't know what you're at up there.'

'I didn't employ Jamesie to be my publicist.'

'We like to tell people about you.'

'What's there to tell? It's only a tiny publisher.'

'I don't care. You should open up to me about that side of yourself.'

'I will when I'm ready.'

'When will that be – doomsday?'

'Don't be ridiculous.'

'You think I wouldn't be able to understand what you write.'

'That's nothing to do with it.'

'I'm sure you talk to other people about your writings.'

'Not really.'

'You didn't invite me and Angela to the launch. She'd have liked the night out.'

'That's probably all it would have meant to her.'

'Okay, leave her out of it. Your father wasn't good enough for you. Or were you afraid I'd disgrace you at it?'

'You couldn't be farther from the truth.'

'Why didn't you have it down here? I can think of fifty people who'd have been delighted to go to it.'

'It wasn't my choice. The publisher decides the location. I can see why. Who'd want to go down to Galway to toast an unknown writer?'

'You grew up here. The apple never falls far from the tree. Don't forget where you came from.'

'How could I? You know I'll be back there one day.'

'I wonder. You seem different since you went off on us.'

'What gives you that impression?'

'I don't know. It's just a sense I get.'

'That's all in your imagination.'

'You can have too much book knowledge, you know.'

'What's that supposed to mean? You paid to put me in college.'

'Don't throw that one at me. You were begging me to get away. I didn't think it would take over your life.'

Sinead laughed when he told her about the conversation.

'You're complete opposites,' she said.

'He keeps pushing my buttons.'

'Don't fall for the traps he sets. He's probably trying to pull you down to his level.'

The next time he talked to Bartley he told him he was fed up of the university. He hadn't intended to. It just slipped out.

'I can't believe what you're saying to me. What's wrong with you?'

'It's like you said. I don't belong up here.'

'What's the problem?'

'I don't know if I'm cut out for it. I wish I was different. Believe me, I've tried my best to fit in.'

'You don't have to stay there if you don't want to.'

'I couldn't do that to you after all you spent on me.'

'Don't worry about that. It's worth it if it helps you to find out what you want – or don't want. If you come home tomorrow it's no problem for me.'

'I'll give it another crack for a while more.'

'I'd love to see you back here if it doesn't work out. Now that you've tried something else you'd probably be more settled.'

'I don't know if I could ever settle anywhere the way I'm feeling.'

'Don't say that. I was like that too at your age.'

'Thanks for that.'

'Are you doing a line up there, by the way, or is Jennifer still the main attraction?'

'I'm seeing a girl but it's not serious.'

'You'll be married long enough. Spread your wings while you can.'

Such a possibility became short-lived after Sinead slipped back into her old ways. He didn't see the signs, imagining her reform was permanent. Like many addicts she was a good liar.

'I'll never go back,' she said and he believed her. But then she started injecting herself again, this time behind his back. Because she'd been clean for a while she didn't show the effects as quickly. It was only when he saw her using a rusty needle one night that he realised what was happening. She was that desperate.

It took a few moments before it registered with him what she was doing. When he did he panicked. He thought she could get AIDS.

He shook her but there was no reaction.

He didn't know who to call. He put her to bed and prayed. After a few hours she came round.

'What happened?' she said.

'You've relapsed.'

She looked at him querulously. It was all lost in the fog of her memory.

He let her stay with him for fear she'd overdose if she was left on her own. What if she died? He told her he couldn't have her there if he ever saw her injecting herself again. She promised she wouldn't. The next few days were tense. He felt as if he was living inside a volcano. She'd lied to him before. Was she lying now? He tried not to think about it. It was too much of a responsibility to have to carry.

One night they went to a party thrown by one of her friends. She was okay in the early part of the night but then she decided she wanted to get drunk. He was drinking too. When the lights went down she pranced out to the middle of the floor and started dancing like someone possessed. She was the only person on the floor. She was shaking her head wildly. Her body was quivering all over.

Everyone stopped what they were doing to look at her. She dragged Brian out onto the floor with her. He didn't want to go at first but then he fell in with her. He'd drunk half a bottle of wine. The music was at full blast, blotting out his thoughts.

'I feel like getting high,' she said to him.

'Are you not high already?' he said, She'd drunk the other half of the wine.

'Not high enough.'

What about trying something more interesting?' she said then, nuzzling up against him.

'Like what?'

She went back to where they were sitting. She opened her handbag. It had an Ecstacy tablet in it.

'Do you like E?' she said.

She popped it into his mouth.

'This will make you feel like you own the world.'

He knocked it back without thinking. A few minutes later everything became hazy. He felt he was in the middle of an earthquake. The floor rose and fell before him. He started hallucinating. The walls of the room moved. They seemed to be coming in on him. He felt he was in an elevator that was crushing him.

A few moments later he was in a zoo. He was running around with a lion behind the bars. Then he was on the top of a high building, walking along a ledge that had no barrier on it. There were people below screaming up at him not to jump. He didn't want to but he didn't know how to get off the ledge.

His feet went from under him. He fell to the floor. For a few seconds nobody paid any attention to him. They thought it was part of the dance.

Sinead knelt down beside him. When she saw his face changing colour she slapped it. When he didn't react she panicked. She turned on the lights. Everyone started screaming. They stopped dancing. By now Brian was convulsing on the floor. He was foaming at the mouth. Sinead became hysterical. 'Get a doctor!' she screamed.

An ambulance was called. It was ages before it arrived. Nobody knew what to do. They were all staring at him. He couldn't stop trembling.

He was carried into an ambulance. A man in a white jacket kept shouting, 'Stay with me! Stay with me!' He heard the siren wailing as they blazed through traffic. When they got to the hospital he was wheeled down to an operating theatre.

He saw doctors looking down at him. Above them was a light coming from a fluorescent lamp. It blinded him.

A mask was placed over his face. He wanted to sleep but they wouldn't let him. They made him stand up and walk the floor with them. Afterwards they pumped him with something. It tasted like coffee. He felt his heart going a mile a minute. Then everything went black.

When he woke up he was in a small room. All there was in it was a bed and a locker. A group of doctors came in. They stood around his bed. They started firing questions at him. What pill had he taken? Why had he taken it? Who gave it to him? He was too drowsy to answer them. They left after a few minutes.

He fell asleep. When he woke up there was a nurse beside the bed. 'Hello,' she said smiling, 'You've been through quite a time.'

'I don't remember it.'

The news reached Galway. Bartley got a train to Dublin as soon as he heard. He was in a state when he arrived at the hospital. Brian was in a normal ward by then. He had tubes coming out of him. Bartley got a fright when he saw him.

'Jesus,' he said, 'You look like Dracula.'

The nurses told him he'd have to cool down if he wanted to stay.

'He needs rest,' they said. Bartley sat by the bed. He watched him drifting in and out of sleep.

'We all love you,' he kept saying, 'You know that, don't you?'

He stayed at a hotel that night. Early next morning he was at Brian's bedside again. The nurse told him he could talk to him if he kept the conversation short.

'What possessed you?' he asked him.

'I don't know,' Brian said, 'Someone must have slipped a Mickey Finn into my drink.'

'Come on. You're not that stupid.'

'I'm not going to be prosecuted, am I?'

'Is that all you can think about. You almost died.'

'Now you're being dramatic.'

'You were in Intensive Care. Don't play it down.'

'They were just being careful.'

'Promise me you'll never do anything like this again.'

'Okay.'

'When you get better I'm bringing you back to Loughrea.'

He sat up in the bed.

'What are you talking about? I took a pill. I had a bad reaction to it. It's over now. I'm fine.'

'A pill. We read about these things in the paper every day, teenagers whose lives are ended in the blink of an eye after a pill. Do you know what you put us through? Everyone has been up the walls since we heard about it, not just me and Angela but Declan and Yvonne as well. Needless to say, we didn't tell Jennifer.'

'Thanks for that.'

'So what happened?'

'It was a mad moment. That's all I can say.'

'What do you mean a mad moment?'

'I was at a party. I was drunk.'

'I'm bringing you home, Brian. We're afraid for you. We can't take the chance you won't do something worse the next time. You're coming with me on the train.'

'No. I won't agree to that.'

'It's that Sinead girl, isn't it? I know about her. She's a junkie. She got you into this crap and she'll do it again. You need to get rid of her.'

'Did Jamesie Gildea tell you about her?'

'Never mind who it was. You're coming home when you get better and that's that.'

'No I'm not.'

'Do you want to kill yourself?'

'You better go. I don't want to fight with you.'

'You have to get away from that girl one way or another. We want you well. Is that too much to ask?'

'Don't worry, I've learned my lesson. It was nothing to do with Sinead. She just happened to be there.'

'I know that's a lie. I've talked to the doctors. They told me all about it.'

'Then why are you cross-examining me? You're the one who's the liar.'

'Get away from her, that's all I'm saying.'

A nurse came over to the bed.

'Brian is tired now, Mr Kilcoyne. It's probably best he gets some sleep.'

Bartley grunted at her. He went off scowling. Brian thanked her. He fell asleep a few minutes later.

He had a nightmare. The night of the party came back to him. He started convulsing in the bed. The nurse came over to him. She gave him something.

'What's happening to me?' he said to her.

'You can expect that for a while. Don't worry about it.'

The doctors came around again the next morning. One of them said, 'We're very happy with your progress. We're letting you out.' He couldn't believe it.

'There's no need to ring my father,' he said to the nurse.

'Will he not be collecting you?'

'No. A friend is.'

'But he told me to contact him when you were ready to go home.'

'He had to go back to Galway in a hurry. Something came up.'

He rang Sinead.

'Is there any chance you could come in for me?' he said, 'They won't let me leave without someone collecting me.'

'What about your father?'

'He knows nothing. You better come quick.'

She arrived within the hour. He was discharged without any fuss.

'I feel as if I'm after robbing a bank,' he said as they made their way through the grounds. She giggled like a child.

'Did you have trouble getting away?'

'I told my mother a lie. I'm good at that.'

'We're all good at it. I'd love to see my father's face when he comes in and finds me gone.'

'This is an unusual position for me to be in,' she said, 'Taking care of someone else.'

'You'll get used to it.'

They got a taxi back to the flat. His legs felt like jelly as he walked towards the Centra shop.

'How do I look?' he said at the door, 'Denise will probably be inside.'

'So what if she is?'

She was. He brushed by her with a wave.

'Hi, Brian,' she said, 'How are you feeling?'

'Fine. Why?'

'I believe you had a bit of a health scare.'

'It was nothing.'

So she knew. That meant Martin did too. Who else could have told her? How did he find out?

Sinead put him lying down on the bed after they got upstairs. As soon as he hit the pillow he conked out.

It was evening when he came to. She was still there.

'I can't stop sleeping,' he said.

'It's good for you. Don't fight it.'

He insisted on getting out of the bed. She walked him up and down the floor to help him get his strength back. Afterwards she got a chair for him.

'I'm not letting you out of that for the rest of the day,' she said.

'Don't be a bully.'

She made him a cup of tea. After drinking it he felt semi-normal again. He went over to the window and looked out. It was good to see people walking up and down, doing normal things. The time in hospital made him appreciate things like that.

He went back to his chair. She helped him into it.

'Why did you give me the pill?' he said to her.

'Why did you take it?'

'I don't know.'

'I do.'

'How do you mean?'

'I've been thinking about you a good bit over the last few days. I think it was because of your mother.'

'My mother? You know nothing about her.'

'I know enough from what you've told me. You still haven't recovered from her dying. I think you're trying to run away from that part of your life.'

'Since when did you become a psychologist?'

'I've always been good at analysing everyone's else's problems. It's only my own ones I'm rubbish at.'

'We're all a bit like that but I'm afraid you're off target with your theory. I was just drunk.'

'Maybe. What do you plan to do now?'

'Drink less, I suppose.'

'Did the doctors put you on anything?'

'No. They gave me the name of a counsellor. I'm supposed to see him next week.'

'Why do you need one of those guys? They're only timewasters. You can get a qualification as a counsellor now after a weekend course. They're like snake oil salesmen.'

'You can't say that out loud. I better go to keep my father quiet. He probably set it up. He's funding my education.'

'I remember you saying something about that.'

'I'll go for the first session anyway.'

'Tell him what he wants to hear. You can pull the wool over these people's eyes with bullshit.'

'That's what I was planning.'

He saw him the following week. He ran his practice from a dusty room in a cul-de-sac in Blackrock. He was a squat little man with rimless glasses and a crumpled suit. He asked the questions Brian imagined most counsellors would have asked, adjusting his glasses after each one and recording the answers on a machine. It was a pointless exercise for him. He felt he'd have got more value out of chatting to someone at a bus stop on the street.

After the session ended he was given a prescription. He couldn't really read the writing. The tablets had a Latin-sounding name.

'What are these?' he asked.

'You're probably better not to know too much about them. Just take them as directed. Come back to me in three weeks and we'll see how you're doing on them.'

'Are there any Ecstacy tablets among them?'

'I wouldn't joke about things like that if I were you.'

'Sorry. I thought it was funny that a pill caused my problem and now I'm being given more pills.'

He got them from a pharmacy on the way home. He doubted he'd take them.

He rang Sinead to tell her how it went.

'He was even worse than you predicted,' he told her.

'Do you have to go back?'

'I said I would but I probably won't.'

He went back to the university the following day. There was a ten o'clock lecture in Theatre L. That was early by his standards but he wanted to get back to his routines. Somehow he struggled out to it.

He found it hard to concentrate. He kept checking the other students to see if anyone was looking at him. He felt they all were.

Sinead came in half way through it. She sat in her familiar seat near the door. When it finished she came over to him.

'You're an early bird,' she said, 'Talk about getting back to life fast.'

'I didn't expect to see you here.'

'Someone has to keep an eye on you.'

'Thanks.'

'You look back to yourself.'

'I feel like I've just been run over by a truck.'

'Don't be impatient.'

'Look who's talking.'

'As I said before, do what I say, not what I do.'

They went for coffee.

'How are things at home?' he asked her.

'Everyone is watching me like a hawk.'

'I know that would happen to me too if I went back to Loughrea.'

'You're lucky you don't have to.'

He sipped his coffee. The students blustered around him. It was good to be back in the buzz of people. Maybe that was what he'd miss most about the university if he left.

'I was surprised to see you at the lecture,' she said, 'I thought you'd given up on the books.'

'They're like a bad habit to me. I only go back to them when there's nothing else. It's like a lover you've fallen out of love with but can't let go of.'

'Is that a reference to me?'

'Don't be funny. You've got me through this year more than anyone else.'

'I could say the same about you.'

'Now you're losing the run of yourself.'

Two people sat in beside them. He made room for them. They were talking about Proust.

'I keep thinking everyone is looking at me,' he said to her.

'Don't be stupid. They have more on their mind.'

'I even notice it in Ranelagh.'

'How do you mean?'

'The shoppers coming into Centra.'

'How would they know anything about you? You're paranoid.'

'People always know things in this country. Brendan Behan said Dublin was the biggest village in Europe.'

'People probably looked at Brendan Behan all right. He spent most of his life falling all over the place.'

'I don't feel too far off him at the moment. I'm as weak as a kitten.'

She led him out of the café.

'I suppose you'll go home now,' he said.

'Not just yet. I could manage a few more hours with you if you want me.'

'That'd be great. Are you sure your mother won't suspect anything?'

'I don't care if she does.'

They went back to the flat together on the bus. When they got there she pulled out a chair for him.

'You don't need to do that,' he said, 'I'm pretty much back to normal now. Getting out to Belfield did me the world of good.'

She looked serious suddenly.

'I feel responsible for what happened to you,' she said.

'Put that thought out of your mind. You didn't force me to take the pill.'

'Maybe not, but I put it in front of you. I feel worse for what I did to you than anything I did to myself.'

'Let's not guilt-trip one another. We've got through this.'

'Good idea. Will you do your exams?'

'I doubt it.'

He pointed to the books on his shelves.

'I feel like making a bonfire of them,' he said.

'That sounds like a good idea too.'

Sinead was 21 the following week. Brian put on a spread for her, doing the flat up with bunting and a 'Happy Birthday' banner over the mantelpiece. He asked Denise for every sandwich she had in the shop. When she brought them up to him he put them on plates all over the room. A bottle of champagne stood in the middle of them on the coffee table.

She nearly cried when she saw everything.

'Nobody ever made this kind of a fuss for me,' she said.

'It took me about five minutes.'

He opened the champagne. He always drank it too quickly. That night was no exception. It went straight to his head. She had too much too. They fell around the room together afterwards.

'We're like the blind leading the blind,' he said.

'Or rather not leading them.'

They sat on the sofa. She laughed at the jumpy spring.

'How does it feel to be ancient?' he asked her. She was two years older than him.

'I never thought I'd make it this far.'

'It's only a matter of time before you get the bus pass.'

She told him his party meant a million times more to her than the one her mother threw for her a few days before that. As he looked at her he wondered if they might start going out together again. He was tempted to but he knew it would be a bad idea even if her mother permitted it.

Instead of that they just saw one another now and again, either at the university or the flat. They kept saying they were going to drop out of college but somehow they hung on. Brian felt he was running the clock down, seeing out the term for no better reason than it would soon be over.

When summer came round they both turned up at the exams but neither expected to pass them. They giggled at one another after they went into the examination hall.

'This is insane,' he said, 'I haven't done a stroke for months.'

'Me either,' she said, 'Let's see what happens. You might get some miracle questions.'

Middle English was the first paper but the questions were more like Greek to him. He wrote his name on the top of the page and then sat back looking at the other people in the room. He listened to the sound of their pens scratching on the paper. What were they writing? Did it matter? What would Chaucer think of having his books torn apart like animals in a laboratory?

His mind felt blank. It was comforting not to want to do anything. There was a time he might have felt bad about it. Now he just felt peace.

It seemed like no time before the man at the top of the room said, 'Hand up your papers please.' Brian walked out of the hall. Sinead followed him a few seconds later.

'How did you find it?' he said to her.

'Brutal,' she said, 'And you?'

'The same.'

They high-fived one another.

'All I wrote was my name,' he said.

'I think that gets you 1%. Congratulations.'

'Tomorrow I plan to do the same.'

'Is this some kind of protest?'

'No. Maybe I'll write my name a hundred times so everyone looking at me will think I'm inspired.'

The following day's paper dealt with more modern writers. There was a question about *Watership Down*, a novel about rabbits. It was written by Richard Adams. He was a civil servant. Brian only wrote one sentence: 'I'd prefer to read a novel about civil servants written by a rabbit.' It wasn't his joke. He'd read it somewhere. Under the sentence he drew a picture of a rabbit with a pair of glasses on.

Sinead was amused when he told her.

'I can't believe you did that,' she said, 'You'll be thrown out.'

'With a bit of luck,' he said.

She'd made a stab at a few of the questions but she knew she had no chance of passing. She'd done some cramming over the past few weeks but it was too little too late, even with her mother's urging.

'I'm not going to do any more of the exams,' he said to her over coffee a few hours later, 'What about you?'

'I have to turn up for them. I'm on probation.'

'Then maybe I won't see you for a while.

'What are your plans for the summer?'

'I'm thinking of going to America.'

'Are you serious? This is a bit of a bombshell.'

'It's been at the back of my mind for a while.'

'Bully for you.'

'Would you like to come with me?'

'I'd love to but I can't.'

'Because of your mother?'

'She said if I ever went anywhere with you again I was out of the house.'

'Wise woman!'

He gave her a hug. He wondered if it was for the last time.

'Our little adventure seems to be over,' he said.

'It was good while it lasted.'

20

Ireland's economy revived itself as he prepared to go away. A country that was on life support for the past decade was resurrected. The recession had ended. There were signs in shop windows saying 'Staff Wanted' for the first time in years. Houses were being built again. Property prices started to rise. The city became a hive of activity. People breezed by him in the street in sharp suits, speaking on mobile phones about business deals as if their lives depended on them.

Some days he went into Temple Bar for no reason except to sit in a café and watch life going on. Dublin had been the style capital of Europe a few years before. Would that time come again or would it go back to the way it was?

He wandered around the streets. He liked looking at people doing ordinary things. It was like with the waitress that first day in Belfield. He needed an antidote to the life he'd just left to give him energy for the one he had yet to live.

He was on to Bartley a few times since he left the hospital. He was annoyed at him for giving him the slip but he came to accept it. Brian told him not to ask him any questions about his behaviour and he came to accept that too. He knew he was curious about the exams but he didn't talk about them. He said he was going away for the summer but he didn't say where.

He told Jennifer but swore her to secrecy.

'I bet you're dying with excitement,' she said to him on his last phone call to her before he went off.

'Not really. I can't think about a place until I'm in it.'

'Do you not have butterflies in your stomach?'

'If I do it's probably more from nerves than excitement. I'm always tense when I'm breaking away from something.'

'We all are. You'll be fine when you get where you're going.'

'Hopefully.'

'I'm mad jealous of you,' she said then, 'I've always wanted to go to America.'

'Maybe you will one day.'

He told her he'd made a mockery of his exams and wouldn't be going back to the university. She was hardly surprised. He'd been saying as much to her for months.

'See how you feel in the autumn. You might change your mind yet.'

'I doubt it.'

'Anyway, have a great summer. The next time you see me I hope to be a fully-fledged teacher.' She was about to finish her course and look for a job.

'I don't know if I'm going to be able to get my head around that.'

'How do you think I feel?'

When he boarded the plane a few days later he tried to put everything about Ireland out of his mind. It was better to concentrate on where he was going instead. That wasn't difficult.

He'd grown up with American culture as much as his own. It was like the house next door. Would the people he met over there be like the ones he knew from films or would they be nothing at all like them? Maybe he'd experience the *National Enquirer* image of America instead of the country itself.

He'd only met a handful of actual Americans in his life, Most of them tourists. They hadn't left much of an impression on him. He hoped tourists didn't represent a country. Maybe countries tended to export their worst specimens. Or did it even out in the end? 'People are the same wherever you go,' his mother used to say to him. She never stereotyped anyone. He hoped he'd be as big-hearted as she was.

Most of the other passengers on the flight were students like himself on J1 visas. They talked excitedly to one another about their plans. One girl had cowboy boots on her. A few others were wearing Stetsons. They said things to each other like 'Right on, man,' as if they'd already reached their destinations. Was it the influence of television? At times it seemed like Ireland was a mini-America.

An in-flight film came on almost as soon as he sat down. He put on his headphones. It was about the Mafia. Robert de Niro was kicking somebody's head in. He fell asleep after the first few scenes. When he woke up, de Niro was still kicking the person.

The air hostess came around with tea. He didn't really want it. He only took it to break the journey. He tried to sleep again but he couldn't. Afterwards there was turbulence. That made it even more difficult to nod off. The captain came on. He told everyone not to worry.

Brian took some tranquillisers Angela had sent up to him. He'd had the misfortune to tell her he was a bad flier when she rang to say goodbye to him. 'These are capable of knocking out an elephant,' she told him. Even so, they didn't work. Maybe his system was fighting them. That often happened him with pills. It was one of the reasons he didn't take the ones the counsellor from Blackrock prescribed.

He started to think about what might happen over the summer, what he was leaving and what he might find. Bartley hadn't been in favour of him going away but in the end he sent him a generous cheque to tide him over. He'd mellowed a lot since the hospital experience, maybe because he felt Brian was growing away from him.

He expected to find work in America. If he hadn't done that in Europe he wouldn't have been able to stay there for half as long as he did. The time would have dragged too. Work was the best way to meet people anywhere. Tourists never really saw places.

He had a relation who was living in Massachusetts, an aunt called Edie. She was Bartley's sister.

He'd never met her. Bartley talked about her warmly. 'Make sure you get to see her,' he exhorted on his last phone call, She'd emigrated years ago, having gone over there to meet up with a man she'd been dating in Galway. It was only when she got to Boston that she found out he was already married.

She was too proud to go home so she stayed on, making a life for herself even in her misery. She worked her way up in the fashion world but never married.

She cut herself off from Ireland afterwards. Brian's mother used to phone her every so often, plying her with questions about herself but not getting much back. She wrote the odd letter but never had any significant news. They got the impression she'd never recovered from her broken heart. 'She was a one man woman,' Bartley said. He heard she'd had a few other relationships in Boston that hadn't worked out, eventually making her give up on men altogether. Brian planned to stay with her for a few days at some stage of his trip.

When the plane touched down he felt a sense of exhilaration. Taking his first gulp of American air gave him an adrenalin rush.

He found himself becoming intoxicated by the atmosphere at the airport. It was chaotic. Everyone seemed to be from different countries. Birds flew overhead inside the dome. Looking at them he was filled with their sense of freedom.

As he waited for his luggage at the conveyer belt he thought he was going to be trampled. People had that intense look on their faces he often saw at airports. It was one that said, 'Don't interrupt me. I'm going somewhere important.'

His luggage took a while to arrive but it was easy to manage. He'd only brought a gymbag with him. It meant he got out of the airport quickly.

When he went through the door he felt the air was rich with promise. What did the three months on this wild continent hold for him? He was determined to leave himself open to anything.

The tarmac felt hot under him. If he'd been in his bare feet he thought he'd have been singed. As he hailed a taxi he felt like a character from a film. He'd seen so many of them where the hero got into a yellow cab and said, 'Follow that car.'

The driver was from the Bronx.

'Where are we going, buddy?' he asked him.

'The city centre,' he replied.

'You're not in Ireland now. You gotta be more specific.'

'How did you know I was Irish?' he said. The driver just chortled.

He got out at Times Square. The first thing that struck him was the noise. It was of traffic, people rushing around, road workers drilling into the ground. Then it was the size of everything. The airport was nothing on it.

The air was heavy. It was as if the skyscrapers stopped it from moving. It hung there like an invisible cloud.

His clothes were sticking to him. As he walked down the street he became swallowed up in a sea of people. He was fascinated looking at their clothes, listening to their voices.

159

A loudspeaker from one of the bars pumped rap music onto the street. A group of people danced to its rhythms. He thought of Kenneth Tynan's comment, 'The noise of New York is the sound of the city tearing up yesterday.' Could he do that too? It was often said the Irish were in love with the backward glance. Maybe that applied to him as well.

The heat of the sun burst through the trees on Central Park. It scorched him. He smelt hamburgers, hot dogs, the sweat of joggers.

People roared at each other non-stop. They roared even when they were embracing. He passed by a man standing behind a stall. He was selling everything from crucifixes to Swiss watches. Another man ran down the street wearing a long dress. Or was it a man? Four men in suits played violins at a corner. A drum with the top cut out of it was on the ground in front of them for people to put coins into.

He sat down beside a fountain. Everywhere he looked there were skyscrapers. For the first time he knew why they had that name. They were so high they darkened everything around them.

Trucks belched smoke into the air. Neon signs offered him everything from holidays in the sun to weddings in Las Vegas. A black man played the blues on a trombone. He was dressed in a tuxedo and runners. Somehow it didn't seem incongruous. The front page of a newspaper blew across the street with the headline, 'Puerto Rican Stabbed to Death in Subway Incident.'

A couple embraced on a corner. The girl was crying. Were they breaking up? Had they argued? He tried to imagine what their lives might be like as he watched them. A hooker stood outside a department store in a mini-skirt and a skimpy top. She was checking numbers on her mobile phone, looking intensely into it. Beside her a man with a beard stood on a box speaking about the end of the world through a microphone. 'Repent,' he said in a gravelly voice, 'The Lord is waiting to hear from you.' Neither of them were aware of one another.

He went into a café. The blinds were down. He ordered a coffee. As he sat drinking it he looked out at the panoply of life around him. How many emigrants before him sat like this wondering what the future held for them? Had Aunt Edie?

He listened to a busker in an Elizabethan suit crooning a folk melody. He was playing an instrument he'd never seen before. A man with tattoos up to his neck breathed fire. A juggler did somersaults. He threw three tennis balls into the air and caught them as he moved.

He sat transfixed watching them all. It wasn't as if they were demanding attention. This was ordinary life for them. They didn't seem to care if anyone was looking at them or not.

Cars raced up and down the street in front of him. The drivers showed flashes of the famous New York temper if anyone annoyed them.

160

Music from a honky tonk bar caused a ruckus in his ears. A man with a lost look in his eyes stood at a corner. He looked into the distance as if he was searching for something that had disappeared from his life.

A street vendor held a newspaper up. He shouted 'Latest!' at nobody in particular.

Brian left the restaurant. where would he go now? It didn't matter.

He passed an Irish bar. He'd heard New York was littered with them. A man with a red face was singing 'The Fields of Athenry' inside. It was the last place he would have gone into. Why did people leave Ireland and then keep talking about it and singing about it?

The image of Humphrey Bogart appeared on a billboard. It must have been twenty times bigger than life size. How many people would know him? Maybe more than he thought. He'd seen his films in Loughrea. Who could have guessed his fame would last into the new millennium?

He took out an accommodation guide he'd brought with him. It was called *America on $50 a Day*. He'd bought it in the campus bookshop one day. It had the addresses of all the cheap hostels in it. He scanned the pages, ticking off the places that didn't seem too dingy. Eventually he saw one that looked as if it might be suitable. He made his way to it.

It was at the end of a street. He entered a lobby that was so small the walls seemed to be closing in on it. A wrinkled old man stood behind a counter. He eyed him suspiciously. When he told him he was looking for a room he opened a book. It was filled with blank pages.

'This is the busy season,' he said, 'You'll have to pay extra.'

He didn't want to argue with him. 'Okay,' he said. The man slapped the book shut. He came out from behind the counter.

'Would you like to see the room?' he said. He nodded.

He led him upstairs. The steps creaked as they walked. At the top there was a long corridor. At the end of it there was a steel door. He opened it. They walked into a room with a sloped ceiling. You couldn't walk across the floor without bending.

'Here you get a brilliant view of the city,' the man said.

He went over to the window and opened it. He inhaled the dry smell of the city. All he could see were the backs of buildings. As he walked back into the room he banged his head off a beam that was coming down from the ceiling.

'Careful,' said the man, 'The roof could come in. Then where would we be?'

'How much?' Brian asked.

'$40 a night,' he said, 'In advance.'

He rummaged in his pocket. He took out two $20 bills. The man grabbed them. He put them in his pocket.

'There's your key,' he said. It was on a little key ring with The Statue of Liberty on it. 'There's the rest room,' he said pointing to a door. Then he was gone. Brian didn't ask for a receipt.

He looked around the room. All it had was a wardrobe and a chair apart from the bed. A dim light came from the ceiling. A fly buzzed around inside the lampshade as if it was trapped in it.

He went into the rest room. It was tiny. He turned on the tap in the sink. Nothing happened for a few seconds. Then some coffee-coloured liquid gushed out. It spilled on his hands. There was no soap to wash himself. He let the water run until it changed colour.

He ran the shower. The water was freezing cold. When he turned the switch the merest fraction to the right it became scaldingly hot.

He walked back to the main room. There was a cockroach on the floor. He stamped on it.

He closed the curtains. Evening was coming on. He was glad of the darkness. His eyelids felt heavy but he didn't want to sleep. He knew if he slept too soon he'd probably wake up in the middle of the night. The blanket on the bed felt damp. He wondered if it was from the humidity.

The air conditioner blew hot air into the room instead of cold. It crackled like a broken-down fan that was about to snap. If it didn't burn him to death, he thought, it was capable of electrifying him. He turned it off.

Night sounds came in through the window – sounds of music, birds, people calling one another. They whispered and cajoled, laughed and cried. Then everything was silent. It was like a television that had been turned off.

He lay on the bed. It would have been nice to go out for a walk but he was too tired. He wondered how long he could bear to live there. His head started to feel woozy.

He heard his mother calling him for school on a day long ago. Bartley was milking the cows, singing a song to himself. Jennifer was cycling to school. All the images blended into one another as he drifted into sleep.

He woke up a few hours later. There was a couple arguing in one of the rooms. A woman screamed. If it was anywhere else he'd have done something about it but he didn't.

The acrid smell was still there. He opened the window but it didn't help much. The view didn't look too bad now that it was night. Neon twinkled over the backlots.

A soft wind came through the curtains, shuffling them slightly. Car horns honked. Music blared from a club down the street. He thought he heard mice rustling behind the skirting board. Then he fell asleep.

When he woke up the next morning he found himself looking forward to the day. What was it about sunlight that seemed to act as therapy for everything?

162

But as soon as he got out into it he found it difficult to breathe. He wasn't cut out for warm climates. Even a warm day in Ireland sucked the energy from him.

He spent most of the day in Central Park. It was like any Irish park multiplied by a thousand. The hours fled by. He wandered through the streets and shopping malls. No two of them were the same. He felt like a piece of litmus paper sucking everything up and turning into it. He thought he could happily spend his life in this limbo of inactivity.

He called Jennifer that night. She was relieved to know he'd arrived safely. She said she regretted not having forced him to bring her with him. She'd finished her studies now. She was looking at job opportunities.

'Sorry for being so boring,' she said.

She asked him what he thought of New York. All he could do was quote the Neil Diamond phrase, 'Beautiful Noise.'

He phoned Bartley then. He kept asking if he was going to visit his aunt soon.

'That might be difficult,' he said, 'considering she's in Boston and I'm in New York.'

He told him to enjoy himself and not think about Ireland. That was difficult considering he'd dropped out of college without telling him. How would he take it? Would he put pressure on him to go to Newbridge? There was no point thinking about it. These things had a habit of working themselves out. Most people's lives reached some kind of water level, often without them even being aware of it.

He put Angela on at the end of the call. She said, 'Don't forget to visit the museums and the art galleries.' He'd prefer to have been dead than do that but he just said, 'Of course. They're top of my bucket list.'

The next few days raced by. He soaked up everything he saw, enjoying the feeling of being swallowed up in a blitzkrieg of activity. He felt like a cowboy in a film, staying in a place where he knew nobody and nobody knew him, feeling his way into a different culture inch by inch. Was it Sinead who said he was like a cowboy? Maybe she was right.

His money dwindled despite the hotel being cheap. He didn't know what he was spending it on. It was always the way when he wasn't working. He had too much time on his hands. For the lack of anything else to do he accumulated junk. He'd see something on a window and buy it. Then a few hours later he'd decide he hated it. Most of the stores had loud music blaring out of walls. That put extra pressure on him to buy things. It was probably the reason behind it. He found himself trying to match its pace, quickening his steps around the aisles as he browsed through books and CDs he wouldn't have thought twice about buying at home.

The longer he spent doing nothing the less inclined he was to break the cycle. Maybe that was good for him. Jennifer always told him he was too intense. She was the opposite. Sinead said it too. She recognised it because she was that way herself.

He missed her being with him. He missed Jennifer too but in a different way. Sinead excited him but he knew she was bad for him. Jennifer was a stabilising influence but he wasn't sure he was ready to be stabilised yet. Life did that to you anyway.

He started to think back on the past two years, what they'd represented for him. He couldn't tell Bartley he'd made a farce of the exams. He knew it would become public as soon as the results came out. He'd want to know what happened, why he fell so far in his second year after doing so well in the first one. That was the problem about any achievement. You set a standard and you were expected to live up to it.

He had no interest in the repeats. How could he go back to the university now? The years in Belfield had been little more than a holiday from life. After the summer was over he'd try to get back to that life, either in Dublin or Galway.

He went to Central Park nearly every day. He liked going there for a jog. It made him feel more normal to do something like that. He sat on benches watching businessmen on lunch breaks from their offices, munching sandwiches and drinking coffee from flasks. People in tracksuits walked dogs. He felt envious of them, envious of everyone who had something concrete to do. One day he sat down beside a girl on a bench. Thy chatted for a minute but then she moved away from him. It wasn't like Ireland where you could do that without anything being thought of it.

Being bored made him feel guilty. How many people chained to desks in Ireland would have killed to be in his position? What would they have given to have enough dollars in their pocket to be able to sightsee without getting a job? But what good was freedom when it had nothing at the end of it? Wandering around the streets of New York wasn't too different from wandering around Dublin or Galway. You had to have goals. He seemed to have lost his ones.

He started sleeping late and doing less with his days. He looked at himself in the mirror one morning and hardly recognised what he saw. He'd been growing his hair long since Christmas. Now he had a stubble as well.

Towards the end of the week he rang Jennifer.

'I'm bored,' he said.

'It's a sin to say that. He who's tired of New York is tired of life.'

'Isn't that London?'

He said he was living like a hobo.

'In the great tradition of bohemian travellers,' she said.

'I suppose so.'

'How are you feeling?'

164

'Confused. The days are running into each other.'

'How long are you there now?'

'A part of me feels I just arrived yesterday. Another part feels I've lived here all my life.'

'Are you going to get a job at any stage?'

'I suppose I'll have to.'

'Why don't you buy a guitar and head for Greenwich Village?'

It didn't sound like a bad idea. The only problem was, he was fifty years too late to run into Bob Dylan.

After he put the phone down he started to think back to Dublin. Was it really only two weeks ago that he'd left all those blank pages on his sheets of foolscap back in the examination hall?

The university seemed like another world. It was only when he got away from it that he saw how crazy it was, how crazy he'd been to enter it in the first place.

Authors swam in his head: Flaubert, Balzac, Genet. What did they mean to him now? Nothing. He expelled them in the same way you might remove material from a computer by pressing the Delete key. He might as well have been in a space capsule for the two years. His supposed love of learning was really just a need for escapism. Europe had been a brief respite from it. Now he needed a longer one. Maybe he needed a new identity altogether.

His pretensions to being a poet were even more unfathomable to him. Who did he think he was bringing out a book? It gave him an exaggerated sense of his importance.

Here in this vibrant city he felt more like a dwarf. The height of the buildings did that to him. So did the huge number of people swirling around him.

New York lost its allure for him. The heat killed his energy. He continued to retreat from it into the cafes and the shaded areas of Central Park, emerging only when the sun went down. In the evenings he cruised the bars. He sat at counters gazing into space as he sipped strange-sounding cocktails. Some of them played havoc with his system. One night a barman asked him what he was having. 'Surprise me,' he said. After he drank it he became violently sick. He couldn't remember the rest of the night.

The following morning he checked out of the hotel. The man behind the counter looked more pathetic now than intimidating. How could he live in such a hellhole? Maybe if you spent long enough in a place like that you didn't notice it anymore. You became like it, like a human cockroach.

He went out onto the street. The air was more humid than ever. It made walking difficult. He went down to the Greyhound Bus depot. A list of destinations were exhibited on a grid. Places he'd previously only heard mentioned in films were there. They sounded romantic to him. Idaho, Tucson, Wisconsin, American places always sounded romantic to him. Maybe if he went to them he'd find they were as banal as anywhere else.

He went up to a counter. A woman with butterfly glasses sat behind it.

'Where are we off to, sir?' she asked.

'Rockaway Beach,' he said. He might equally have said Santa Barbara or Poughkeepsie. He picked it for no better reason than it was the first name he saw on the grid.

A bus arrived within the hour. When he went into it he noticed most of the other passengers were foreign. They weren't talking to one another. They just looked into space, as exhausted from the humidity as he was. After a few minutes a group of students boarded. They looked like part of a tour. A man in a uniform followed them in.

When the bus moved off he started to feel guilty about Aunt Edie. Why hadn't he picked Boston? There was no reason not to. When would he see her now? As far as she was concerned he was due to visit her after New York. Bartley thought that too but it was too soon for him. He'd only left Ireland. He needed to do something different. If he went to her now he'd only have Irish news for her. It would be like visiting her in Loughrea or Dublin. He wanted to blood himself in America first.

He'd spoken to her a few times on the phone. She was friendly to him but they didn't have much to talk about. She said she was looking forward to seeing him but the tone of her voice was tense. She kept asking him for the time of his arrival and how he was going to get there. She wanted to know so she could have food in. Such things weren't important to him.

When he thought about it, what would there have been in the visit for either of them? Maybe he'd be doing her a favour by not calling. He might have made her uncomfortable. She might have feared too many pressing questions about her life in America, especially since it had begun on such a bad note. Or was he just thinking like that to give him an excuse not to go to her?

21

When the bus reached Rockaway Beach he wasn't sure if he wanted to stay there or go on to the next destination. He only got off because the students did.

The man in the uniform was leading them somewhere. He gave them instructions in a stern voice as if they were children. They headed to a bar. Brian assumed it was part of the tour. It looked pretty. In the distance he saw a boardwalk with a rollercoaster behind it. Beside it there were a horde of sailboats on a marina. Seagulls cawed above them like predators.

When he got inside the bar he saw it was full of historical artefacts. He knew then he was right about it being part of a tour. The man in the uniform started talking about something that took place in the 1880s. The students followed him out to a back room.

A barmaid stood in front of him. She was dressed in an orange trouser suit. She was beautiful looking.

'Are you with the tour?' she asked him.

'Yes and no,' he said.

'Are you Irish?'

'What makes you think that?'

'Your accent – and the fact that you don't seem to be able to answer a straight question.'

'I can answer that one. I am. The name is Brian.' He shook hands with her.

'I'm Mia. What would you like to drink?'

He ordered a whiskey. When she brought it to him he asked her about the tour. The voice of the guide drifted in from the back room.

'You're not missing much,' she said, 'All he talks about are centuries-old battles nobody gives a shit about.'

He was a weedy little man with a thin face. They watched him waving his arms as he made some point.

'At this stage,' she said, 'I think he believes he fought the battles himself.'

'By the look of him, he'd more likely have been under the bed.'

'I agree.'

'Does he give these talks much?'

'Too much. I could almost finish his sentences for him at this stage. I'm probably the best educated barmaid in America about the founding fathers of our country.'

He asked her for another whiskey.

'Already?' she said.

'Get one for yourself too,' he said. She surprised him by agreeing to.

There were only a few people in the bar so she wasn't busy. She started to open up about herself. She said she was from Arizona. She'd been brought to New York as a child.

'After that everything went downhill,' she said.

'I know how that must have felt. I was the same when I went to Dublin.'

'Where were you coming from?'

'Galway. I grew up on a farm.'

'You're a farm boy?'

'For my sins.'

'I suppose you're over here for the summer.'

'Yes. What about you? Do you work here all the time?'

'No, they let me home at night.'

'That's a good joke. Do you tell it to all your customers?'

'Only the Irish ones,'

She said she was only there part time, that her main interest was social work in Africa. She was involved in a scheme to get water for a tribe in Ghana that was threatened with dehydration.

He had another glass of whiskey. He felt it going to his head as he listened to her. He couldn't stop staring at her. When she finished he told her bits about his own past – his mother, the farm, his relationship to Bartley. He'd never thought of Americans as great listeners but she took it all in. The time sped by. Words started to pour out of him under the influence of the whiskey and her beauty. He surged along on a tide of infatuation, telling her how he felt about American politics, about its music, its films, anything he could think of to try and interest her. He finished by getting onto the subject of money.

'America worships the dollar,' he said.

Some of the other people in the bar turned their heads.

'Cool down, soldier,' she said, 'We have a lot of Old Boys in here. They might get you deported for that – or worse.'

He looked at the clock on the wall. An hour had elapsed. In that time he felt she got to know more about him than he did about some people he'd known since childhood. What quirk was it in human nature that people talked more to strangers than intimates? There was a freedom in telling things to a stranger. You felt it wouldn't go back.

When she moved away to serve another customer he went into the toilet. He doused his face with water to try and sober himself up.

One of the students from the tour came in when he was there. He spoke in an Australian voice.

'Okay, mate?' he said.

'Yeah, and you?'

'She's nice. You have good taste.'

'How do you mean?'

'The barmaid. She's a ten.'

'Thanks. I thought you were in the other room. How did you notice me?

'Mate, you were undressing her with your eyes.'

When he got back to the bar she'd finished serving the other customer.

'Where were you?' she said.

'In the toilet. I needed to cool off. I think the heat is getting to me.'

'Or the whiskey maybe.'

She left him to serve some of the other customers. He watched the ease of her movement as she got the drinks and brought them to the tables. She was at one with her body. It was perfect. He knew what the Australian meant.

The more he drank, the more he found himself becoming turned on to her. He watched the way she swayed her hips, her trim figure. There wasn't an ounce of spare flesh on her.

She came back to him towards the end of the night.

'You're a stayer,' she said, 'I'll give you that.'

'Thanks.'

'But now the bad news. We're closing.'

'You can't be. I'm only getting warmed up. Get me another whiskey.'

'I think you've had quite enough, young man,' she said. She looked at the row of empty glasses on the counter. 'You've reached your limit.'

'I'm Irish. We don't know the meaning of that word over there.'

She put her hands on her hips. A sternness appeared in her face that only served to accentuate her beauty.

'Is that childishness supposed to impress me?' she said.

'Come on, just one more.'

'You're the last man in the bar. I don't want to lose my job. If I don't have you out of here in five minutes, both of us are in trouble.'

'That's not true. Some of the tour people are still here.'

'Not for long,' she said.

She went over to them. She told them the bar was closing. Then she came back to him

'There,' she said, 'Does that help?'

He decided he might as well be hanged for a sheep as a lamb.

'Would you meet me sometime for a drink?' he asked her, the words coming from a crazy part of his brain.

She sighed but he could see she was flattered.

'Look,' she said, 'Give me your glass and sit at that table over there. When everyone is gone I'll talk to you.'

She ushered the last few students out. As she did so, the Australian winked at him. She spotted it.

After they were gone out she said, 'What was that about?'

'I met him in the toilet. He saw me talking to you. He said he admired my taste.'

'You were talking about me?'

'He knew I liked you. Can we talk some more?'

She looked confused.

'Hold on a minute. I'm going to take off my uniform.'

She went into a room. When she came out she was in a black leather skirt and a white blouse. She took his breath away.

'Now,' she said, 'What did you want to say to me?'

'I was wondering what your plans were for tonight.'

'To go home and get some sleep. Anything else?'

'You're beautiful.'

'Am I? Well you're drunk. I think you need to go home and sober up.'

'I don't have a home. I'm a student – remember?'

'You don't have anywhere to stay?'

'No.'

'Then you need to go to a motel.'

'How do I do that?'

'There's one down the road. Did you not think of booking in before you got here?'

'I was going to do some travelling. I haven't organised an itinerary yet.'

'So you were going to sleep on the bus?'

'I hadn't thought about it. I just followed everyone else in here.'

'You're even crazier than I thought. Do you realise it's eleven o'clock.'

'I was so busy looking at you I forgot the time.'

'That's the worst come-on line I ever heard.'

'Will you see me tomorrow night?'

'Are all the Irish boys this forward?'

'Only when we're drinking. What do you say?'

She paused for a few seconds.

'Okay,' she said, 'but only if you behave yourself.'

'I will. What's your phone number?'

'I know I'm gonna regret this,' she said, 'I must be crazier than you are.'

She wrote it down on a beer mat. He put it in his pocket.

'Goodnight,' she said, ushering him out.

He walked down the road in a dream. He kept taking out the beer mat and looking at it. A part of him wondered if she was having him on or not. What had he done? He'd never asked a stranger out before. What came over him?

He got to the motel. When he went inside he saw the other students were staying there too. He went up to the desk. A pleasant man with a round face booked him in.

'You must be following me,' said a voice behind him. It was the Australian.

'Or you me.'

He went upstairs to his room. The door had to be opened with a card. He didn't know how to do it. It took him ages to get it to click into place.

He didn't bother to turn the light on when he finally got it to open. He flopped onto the bed and fell asleep in his clothes.

22

When he woke up the next morning his head felt like it was about to lift off. He wondered if the night had happened at all.

He rummaged in his anorak for her number and found it after a few minutes. It was only now he realised her writing was almost illegible. He could hardly make it out.

He didn't know if he had the courage to ring her. Drunkenness had made him brave enough to ask her out but now it was morning and he was sober again. Was it all a big mistake? Falling for a woman wasn't in his plan. It would mess everything up at home. He was meant to be unwinding, not developing extra tensions. He didn't want to be attracted to her. Sinead had been a casual flirtation, something to make him feel there was a world out there that wasn't Jennifer. This was in a different league.

He dialled her number but hung up after it rang once. After taking a deep breath he re-dialled.

She picked up.

'It's me,' he said.

'Did you ring just a moment ago?'

'Yes. I wasn't sure I had the right number so I hung up.'

'Oh. How are you feeling?'

'As if a small army of people are drilling a hole inside my head.'

'I'm surprised you're still alive after what you drank last night.'

'In Ireland that's what we do for a living.'

'More like for a dying, you mean.'

'It's all your fault for filling me up with that rotgut.'

'Thank you. I tried my best to get you to stop but you wouldn't listen.'

'Did you mean what you said about meeting me tonight?'

'I always mean what I say.'

She gave him directions to where she lived. It was within walking distance of the bar. After he hung up he got sick in the bathroom. He didn't know if it was from nerves or the drink.

There was a kettle in the room. He made himself a cup of tea. Afterwards he went for a walk. As he passed by the bar he wondered if she'd be inside. He thought of going in for a moment but then decided not to. It would have ruined everything.

He spent most of the day in his room trying to work off his hangover. Bartley used to say a hair of the dog was the best cure. There was a bar in the motel so he went down to it. He had another whiskey. It burned inside him. Then he asked the barman for a half bottle to take out with him.

He wondered what he was getting himself into. Already he felt he was in over his head. He thought she was the most beautiful woman he'd ever seen. He didn't know if she was interested in him or just humouring him.

He went to her apartment that evening. There was a Land Rover parked outside the door. He was nervous as he walked up the driveway. How was she going to be to him? It was anyone's guess.

She opened the door with a smile on her face. She was dressed in jeans that were cut at the knees. She had her hair in a ponytail.

'You got here,' she said.

'Yes. In one piece.'

'How have you been all day?'

'Hellish.'

'Come in and we'll try to do something about that.'

He went into the hall. There was a load of unopened mail on the floor.

'Come on,' she said, 'I'll show you the kitchen.'

They went down to it. It was furnished simply. A large window looked out over a field. It reminded him of home. He saw the ocean in the distance.

She took a concoction out of a cupboard and mixed it in a glass. She served it up to him. He wasn't sure whether he wanted to drink it or not.

'What's that?' he said.

'Don't ask questions. Just drink it. I got the recipe from a tribe in Africa. They don't mess around out there.'

 He knocked it back.

'It tastes terrible,' he said.

'It's supposed to.'

'Will it work?'

'Your guess is as good as mine.'

She led him down a corridor. There was some gym equipment there. He might have guessed she was into working out from her figure.

The living room was at the end of the corridor. The furniture in it was sparse: a bare table with four chairs around it. Propped against one of them was a painting of a woman with her face blacked out.

'Who did that?' he asked.

'Me.'

'Who's the woman?'

'Same answer.'

Was she trying to tell him something? Did she even know herself? He didn't pursue the point.

There were lithographs of Tanzania on the wall, postcards from places like Croatia and Turkey. On a coffee table there were booklets about Africa.

'You've been around,' he said.

'It's the only thing that keeps me sane.'

There was a poster on the wall showing a man and a woman walking along a beach as the sun was going down. The inscription on it said, 'I'm not in the world to live up to your expectations and you're not in it to live up to mine. You are you and I am me and if we happen to meet, it's beautiful.'

'I like that idea,' he said.

'I thought I did too when I bought it. It looks a bit cheesy now.'

Clothes hung from tables and chairs. There were boxes all over the room with books in them. She started lugging them across the floor. Every few minutes she took some duct tape from a cupboard and roll it around one of them, marking it with an address label.

'Are you moving in or out?' he asked her.

'In. I never stay long anywhere. It's a three-month lease this time. That's long for me. I don't like to get too comfortable.'

He sat down.

'How is your head?' she said.

'A bit better. Your cure must have worked.'

'They say if you don't die after five minutes you'll probably survive.'

'Thanks. It's good to know that.'

She took her phone out of her handbag.

'I have to make a few calls,' she said, 'I won't be long. When I'm finished I'll sit down with you.'

She talked to someone about the water project she was involved in. It was mainly technical language so he couldn't really follow it. All he could understand was when she said the names of places – Nairobi, Ghana, Zimbabwe.

When she hung up she made another call. She sounded angry. She was giving out about a job that hadn't been done. Then she dialled a third number. She had the phone on speaker for a lot of the time. She was moving the boxes as she spoke. After she was finished she let out a big sigh.

'Is someone not doing things the way you want them to?' he said.

'Do they ever?'

She started pulling things out of presses, stacking them on top of the boxes.

'That's the end of the calls but you'll have to be patient with me. I need to knock this place into some kind of order before I sit down. You can talk to me while I'm working if you like. I'll give you a minute to tell me the story of your life.'

'You mean all the bits I left out last night?'

'That's right.'

'Here it is so. I was born. I went to America. Then I met you.'

'Very interesting. It got a bit complicated in the middle. Could you not make it a bit shorter?'

'I'll work on editing it down.'

'Good.'

She continued moving the boxes. He got the impression her life was always this chaotic. It made him feel awkward, like a fifth wheel.

When she went next door with one of the bigger boxes he reached into his pocket for a slug from his hip flask of whiskey. He'd promised himself not to do this but he couldn't resist it.

She came back in.

'Okay,' she said, 'Everything is sorted. I'm done.'

'I bet you're relieved. I can't think straight when things are in a mess.'

'My whole life is a mess. I create it and then I have to get rid of it.'

'I'm like that too.'

'So what do you want to do now?'

'Whatever you want.'

She sniffed him.

'Do I smell drink off you?'

'Maybe.'

'Oh no. Please. Not after last night.'

'I needed it. You make me nervous.'

'How could I make you nervous? We're just talking.'

'I can't explain it.'

'Are you trying to kill yourself?'

Bartley had said the same thing to him in the hospital.

'I'm sorry.'

'Promise me you won't take any more.'

'Okay.'

'Would you like to go for a walk? It might clear your head.'

'Why not.'

They went outside. The night was so clear it might have been the first night of creation. There were sailboats on the marina. The moon darted in and out of the clouds. Tourists walked up and down in Bermuda shorts. The rollercoaster looked like something out of a science fiction film. Seagulls shrieked above it like angry old women.

They walked along the promenade, the rollercoaster skulking behind them. The blue of the sky seemed to merge with that of the sea.

'You're lucky to live in such a beautiful place,' he said.

'I probably won't be here long enough to enjoy it.'

His head buzzed with questions he wanted to ask her, questions about what she'd done in the countries she'd visited, why she'd visited them.

'Where do you plan to go next?'

'I don't know. I don't want to talk about it. We're out for a walk. Let's just enjoy the night for what it is.'

He looked down at the beach. There were some people playing volleyball on it, high-fiving one another every time one of them got a slam dunk.

The sun was on the rim of the horizon. It was huge and red, like a giant football. Her face was silhouetted against it, merging with it into the night.

She took a camera out of her handbag.

'Can I take a few shots of you?' she said.

'I'd prefer if you didn't. I hate people photographing me.'

She put it down. They sat on a wall. She smiled at him. He tried to kiss her but she pushed him away.

'Not with that stuff in you,' she said. The bottle of whiskey was sticking out of his pocket.

'I only had a drop.'

'I'm afraid you'll carry on where you left off last night.'

'There's no danger of that.'

'Didn't you say your father had a problem with drink?'

'So what?'

'Give me the bottle.'

He took it out of his pocket. She looked at it with disdain.

'Do you mind if I throw it away?'

'Yes.'

She took it off him He asked her what she was going to do with it.

'Watch,' she said.

She lifted it high in the air.

'You'll thank me for this tomorrow,' she said.

She threw it as far as she could. He watched it shattering on a bunch of rocks that were jutting out into the ocean.

'That's not very ecological for someone who cares about the environment.'

'I make an exception for people who abuse drink.'

She looked at him tauntingly, willing him to take her on.

'Why are you a barmaid so?'

'Don't give me that one. It's just a temporary job. I'm not making the stuff.'

'And I'm just temporarily being drunk.'

'Shut up.'

'Do you always say that to people who argue with you?'

'Maybe by being a barmaid I can keep my eye on idiots like you who do their best to destroy your insides.'

They sat looking out at the sea. It slushed against the rocks. There was a sheen on the sand from the sun. The ships glinted.

'We better go back,' she said, 'It's getting late.' He wanted to kiss her but he didn't want to be pushed away a second time.

They walked back to the apartment. The night was black. Everything was quiet, even the seagulls. He linked her and she let him. He felt frozen

175

in time. There was no need to talk.

When they got to the apartment she stepped away from him.

'Do you mind if I don't ask you in?' she said, 'I'm going to turn in early.'

'No problem,' he said, 'Sorry again about the drink.'

'And sorry for throwing your bottle away. All the seagulls can get drunk on it.'

'Can I see you tomorrow?'

'I suppose so. At least if you arrive sober.'

'I have to. I have no whiskey now.'

'Go away,' she said, 'You're too much.'

23

He met her again the following night. In his excitement he cut himself shaving as he got ready to go out. She laughed when she saw him. His face had little bits of tissue paper all over it.

'You look like you've been in the wars,' she said.

'Active pilot duty in Afghanistan,' he said, 'Shot down by terrorists in the heat of battle.'

He produced a bunch of flowers. She groaned as she accepted them.

'You should know I'm not the type of woman men give flowers to. I usually throw these sorts of things in the garbage.'

'Don't this time. As a favour to me.'

'This is a first for me.'

'And for me.'

She'd prepared lasagne for him. As they ate it he told her she looked even more beautiful than the day before. She didn't react to the compliment.

'You must have been out with a lot of men,' he said.

She looked bored.

'How do you deduce that?'

'Because of your looks for one thing.'

'Is that all you think women represent?'

'I didn't mean to offend you.'

'You shouldn't think that way.'

'What way?'

'Good looks plus personality equals boyfriend plus flowers. Isn't that the way the dating scene works?'

'Why are you blaming me for it?'

'I shouldn't. Maybe I've met too many men who thought a bunch of flowers would get me into bed with them.'

'I'm not like that.'

'I believe you but don't think looks are the be-all and end-all. I don't care about things like that.'

'Maybe if you didn't have them you would.'

'I can't believe you said that. You're a sexist pig.'

She took the dishes off the table and threw them in the sink. He thought she was going to break them. She started washing them feverishly. He'd learned his first lesson: Don't argue with her.

She was more relaxed with him after her outburst. Maybe it did her good to let her feelings out.

Why was she so angry? He wondered if there was something in her past. He wanted to ask her about it but he didn't dare to. He was afraid she'd flare up again.

'Sorry for rearing up on you,' she said after everything was put away, 'You didn't deserve it.'

She put her arms around him. This time she let him kiss her without pulling away.

He looked at her intently.

'What are you thinking about?' she asked him.

'I was wondering if the reason you let me kiss you was because I didn't smell of drink.'

'Of course. Is it different in Ireland?'

'It used to be.'

'How do you mean?'

'In the old days the dance halls would be full of women until the bars closed. Then the men would come in drunk and the dancing would begin.'

'It sounds lovely. What changed?'

'Now the women are as bad as the men.'

'Great. So now everyone comes in drunk together.'

'Something like that. We don't have dancehalls anymore but women feel liberated enough to be able to do what they want.'

'What's liberated about them behaving as badly as men?'

'Good point.'

She asked him how many girlfriends he'd had.

'Only a few,' he said.

'I'm surprised.'

'Why – because I'm good-looking?'

'Don't try to be clever.'

'Ireland isn't like America. We start later over there.'

'Not from what I hear. Do you live with your mother?'

'I used to but she died.'

'I remember you saying that. How did it happen?'

'I'd prefer not to talk about it if you don't mind.'

She didn't speak for a few seconds.

'Do you live at home when you're not in college?'

'Of course. All Irish boys live with their parents until they get married. It's written into the Constitution.'

'I believe it used to be like that over there.'

'In some places it still is.'

'That would be a nightmare for me. Do you plan to move out when you graduate?'

You mean *if* I graduate.'

'I wouldn't have thought you'd have a problem that way.'

'So you think I'm brainy?'

'I'd say so. Maybe I'm wrong.'

'I've lost the will to study.'

'I'm sorry to hear that. Maybe it'll come back when you go home.'

'I doubt it. I'm going to drop out of college when I get back.'

'Are you serious? When did you make that decision?'

'About ten seconds ago.'

She put her hand under her chin.

'You're a bit of a comedian, aren't you?'

'There's some truth in what I said. I've been thinking about it for a few months but now I'm sure.'

'If you leave, will you go back to your farm to live?'

'I don't know. I don't get along that well with my father. I think I told you about that.'

'How is he coping with your mother's death?'

'He has a new woman now.'

'Is he living with her?'

'He may be. I'm not sure. They seem to be heading that way.'

'Would that bother you?'

'Maybe.'

'Do you think he'll marry her?'

'Probably.'

'How do you get on with her?'

'Not very well.'

It always bored him to talk about himself. He changed the subject to her, asking her about how she got on with her own parents. She said she had a bad relationship with both of them but didn't go into any detail. He decided not to delve. She looked upset when she brought it up.

'We're talking too much,' she said, 'I need a drink.'

'That makes a change.'

'Would you like to go out for one?'

'I'd love to.'

'There's a nice place near here. It's much more respectable than where I work.'

'Lead the way.'

It was nearby so they didn't bring the Land Rover.

'We're turning into a right pair of athletes,' she said as they made their way towards it.

They got to it within a few minutes. It looked as attractive as she described. As soon as they went in, he heard some people saying, 'Mi-a! Mi-a!'

'Ignore them,' she said, 'If you give them any attention it only makes them worse.'

He sat at a table. One of them started talking to her when she went up to the counter to get a drink. She didn't appear to be too interested in what he was saying. She called Brian over.

'Meet my Irish friend,' she said, 'He's just off the plane. He brought a leprechaun with him, and a few four-leaved shamrocks.'

'Well begob and begorrah,' the man who'd been talking to her said in a stage-Irish voice.

'Top of the mornin' to ye,' Brian said.

They went back to the table he'd been sitting at. Another man she knew was at the next table. He was quieter than the people at the counter.

'Why aren't you with the others?' she asked him.

'They don't think I'm good enough for them,' he said.

When she heard that she put her drink down.

She went back to the counter. Brian could hear her having an exchange with the men. When she came back her face was red with rage. There was a vein on her forehead that looked like it was going to split open. He was almost afraid of her.

She sat down beside the man at the table next to them.

'It's okay now,' she said, 'You can go back to them if you want.'

'Why would I want to drink with people like that?' he said, 'I'm sorry you had to go to such trouble over me.'

She stood up.

'Come on,' she said to Brian, 'Let's get the hell out of here.'

'What's wrong?'

'Nothing. This goes on all the time.'

They left the bar. Outside he asked her what she'd said to them.

'You don't want to know. The man that was sitting beside us is one of the nicest guys I know.'

'Why didn't they want him with them?'

'He's from the wrong side of the tracks. This place is reeking with snobbery. It makes me want to puke.'

They walked back to the apartment. The vein on her forehead was still

179

jutting out. Her lips were pursed tight. He tried to talk to her but she didn't answer him.

Her quietness continued when they got back to the apartment.

'Sorry for being anti-social,' she said, 'You got me on a bad night.'

'I'd say every night is like this with you.'

'You know what? Maybe you're right.'

'With your kind of energy I can see you getting everything you want in Africa.'

'I don't know. It pisses some people off.'

She told him to help himself to a beer. She turned the television on. Adam Sandler appeared in one of his comedies.

It made her laugh. She sat watching it with her feet up. He was flattered that she was being herself with him. He felt he knew her a lot longer than a few days.

They watched a political programme after the Adam Sandler film. Every few minutes it stopped for ad breaks. That caused her to go into another tirade.

She started throwing cushions at the television.

'You're impatient, aren't you?' he said.

'I can't help it. I want everything yesterday.'

When the programme was over she yawned.

'I should be going,' he said.

'Why don't you stay the night? It's late.'

He couldn't believe what he was hearing.

'Are you serious?'

'Of course. Don't worry, I won't molest you. You'll be sleeping on the sofa.'

She went out to the room next door. When she came back she had a duvet in her hands. She threw it on the sofa.

'Pleasant dreams,' she said, blowing him a kiss.

'Pleasant dreams.'

She went into the bathroom to wash her teeth. He listened to the tap gushing.

After a few minutes he heard her going into her room. He took off his clothes and lay down on the sofa, throwing the duvet over himself. His heart was thumping, his pulse racing.

He couldn't stop thinking of her. She was only a room away from him and yet he couldn't have her. He wanted to go in to her but he knew if he did it would be the end of them.

He couldn't figure her out. One part of her was staving him off and another part drawing him into her web. What was her game? Or did she have one? Maybe she was just being herself.

24

The next morning she pottered around the kitchen in her nightie. As he looked at her he tried to pretend he didn't notice her curves. She had no make-up on but that didn't make her look any the less beautiful. By the way she carried herself he got the impression he wasn't the first man who would have spent the night in her apartment – and not on the sofa either. She was throwing her sexuality in his face but it was natural to her to do it rather than a game.

'How did you sleep?' she said..

'I'm not that good in strange places. I'd say if I got two hours it was as much. How about you?'

'Not good either. I couldn't stop thinking about James.' He was the man she tried to help in the bar.

As they sat down to breakfast he asked her about the literature on Africa that was on the table. She talked about the project for digging wells that she was involved in. The tribe she was trying to help were going through a dry season. The crops had failed as a result. She'd been out there once to survey the damage. She hoped to go back again in a few months as a volunteer.

'What do you think you can achieve?' he said.

'Not much. I'm only putting my finger in a dam that keeps bursting. The problems of Africa can never be solved. Everyone has a vested interest.'

'Can you not cut through that?'

'Better women than me have tried. The system was there long before me and it'll be there long after me. All you can do is work inside it. It's like a high level game of chess played by members of government. I do my best to stay one step ahead of 'em.'

She was talking at a fast pace. He tried to listen but he was too busy taking in her beauty to concentrate. He watched her face forming words, her hands slicing the air when she became agitated.

'That's very interesting,' he said at one point.

'Be honest. You haven't heard a word I've said. I can tell by your expression. Your mind is a million miles away. What are you thinking about?'

'Sorry if I'm not taking it in. I'm groggy from all the tossing and turning last night.'

'That's fine. Just tell me the next time so I don't get hoarse cackling to thin air.'

'I won't.'

She started to tidy the table. He was afraid to ask her if he could see her again in case she thought he was putting pressure on her. In the event, though, she brought the subject up herself.

'Why don't you drop into the bar tomorrow?' she suggested, 'We could go for another walk.'

'That sounds like a good idea. I really enjoyed last night.'

'Maybe you should go now so. As usual I have a hundred things to do.'

He went over to the sofa to tidy it up.

'Leave that to me,' she said.

'Sorry it's in such a mess.'

She grabbed the duvet cover and threw it in a cupboard.

'There. Mess gone. Be off with you now.'

Everything was on her terms but he was happy to play it like that.

He put on his coat and went out. As he closed the door she was already going upstairs to do something. She didn't say goodbye to him.

Later on he phoned his aunt. She nearly went through the phone with excitement when she heard his voice. Was it really him after all these years? She'd spent years hoping to see Bartley and then gave up on it.

'We spent years hoping to see you too,' he said.

She said that was impossible, that she was a bad traveller.

'So when are you coming up?' she said, 'I'll roll out the red carpet for you. We have twenty years to catch up on.'

'I'm afraid I'll be a bit delayed getting to you,' he said.

'Oh.'

'It's nothing major, just a slight change of plan.'

'I hope there's nothing wrong.'

'Nothing at all.'

'I'll be seeing you sometime, though, won't I?'

'Definitely.'

'Don't let me interrupt your holiday if it's inconvenient. Come to me when it suits you. I don't want to put pressure on you if you're doing anything more interesting.'

'I'm not. I can't wait to see you.'

'And me you. I'll tell Bartley I was on to you.'

'That would be great. He never stops talking about you.'

'I hope you're not coming to me because of that.'

'Absolutely not.'

'I still feel Irish no matter how many years I've been here.'

'Then I'll definitely be up to see you.'

'You might get a fright when you see my little shack.'

'I'd prefer a shack to an elaborate place.'

'That's a relief.'

After putting down the phone he went back to the motel. He couldn't think of anything to do so he went for a walk on the beach. It looked different to the night before. It had no atmosphere now.

He made a brief call to Bartley to tell him he'd touched base with aunt Edie.

'I know, he said, 'She's getting the place ready for you.'

He didn't like to hear that. It put pressure on him.

'Have you been on to Jennifer?' he said then.

'Not for a few days.'

'She was up to us last night. We talked about you. We're all curious about what's happening. Are you still in New York?'

'Yes.'

It wasn't really a lie, just a part one.

'Tell her I'll be on to her.'

He couldn't say any more than that.

The time crawled by. He kept thinking about Mia, how she'd be with him that night. He tried to convince himself he wasn't falling for her, that it was only an infatuation. But deep down he knew it was much more than that.

He went down to her bar after tea. As soon as he got in the door he saw her deep in chat with a group of drinkers. She was like a queen bee with her drones flocking around her.

When he went up to the counter she barely acknowledged him, continuing to talk to the men. He recognised a few of them from the previous night.

Most of them were dressed in speedos. One had a surfboard. There was some diving gear beside him. They all had tanned bodies. He couldn't compare with them with his milky white skin. Their raucous laughter made him imagine they weren't too intelligent. What was she doing with people like that?

'Hello, Mia,' he said eventually, realising she wasn't going to make the first move.

She looked vacantly at him. for a moment he wondered if she was even going to acknowledge him.

'Howdy stranger,' she said.

The men looked at him as if he was interrupting something. One of them made a comment he couldn't make out. Was it another leprechaun one?

'You know Brian, don't you?' she said. They didn't show any reaction. He didn't know what to say.

'I'm not off duty for a half hour yet,' she said to him, 'Why don't you find yourself a seat and I'll bring you a drink so you won't be too lonely without me.'

'That sounds like a good idea.'

'What will you have?'

'Give me a whiskey.'

One of the men whistled.

'This early in the day?'

'Why not.'

'Righteo,' she said, 'The man said he wants a whiskey so a whiskey he shall have.'

He sat down at one of the tables. She poured it slowly. The man who whistled smiled at her.

She brought it over to him.

'There you go, tough guy,' she said. propping it down on the table.

'What do I owe you?'

'It's on the house.'

'Thank you.'

He took a drink of it.

'What does it taste like?' she said.

'It tastes like whiskey.'

She gave a little laugh. She went back behind the counter. She stayed there talking to her friends.

Now and again she looked over at him. She waved at him once but that was all. Why was she keeping him at arm's length? Did she think he was getting too involved with her?

He nursed his drink as he waited for her to finish her shift but it did nothing for him.

Every so often she passed by his table with a tray of drinks. She winked at him once. For the rest of the time she was behind the counter mixing cocktails or laughing with the customers. Most of them were drinking soft drinks. He couldn't imagine any of them ever getting drunk. They were too fond of their bodies.

It seemed ages before she came over to him.

'I'm sorry,' she said, 'Sadie got delayed. She's my replacement. Have I ruined your day?'

'Not at all. I had nothing better to do. I enjoy watching you having fun with your friends.'

'You call those guys friends? They're just horny bastards who think they have the right to grope me after they've had a few beers.'

He couldn't believe what she was saying. She'd appeared to be enjoying herself hugely with them.

'Look,' she said, 'It's too late to do anything now. Would you mind if we left it till another night? I'm just about ready to pass out. I'll be gone before I hit the pillow. I don't know why we were so busy tonight. It's a feast or a famine in here. You have to roll with the punches.'

'Get some shut-eye,' he said, 'I can see you anytime that suits you.'

25

He spent the next few days wondering if he'd go up to his aunt or not. Bartley was putting pressure on him to. Angela even got in on the act. She spoke on most of the calls now. He hung up on one of them, apologising afterwards by saying the phone slipped from his hands. He talked to Jennifer once but she sensed his tension. She didn't stay on the line.

He felt excited and depressed at the same time. He knew he was getting in over his head with Mia. Most likely there'd be nothing at the end of it for either of them. He was sorry he didn't go straight to Boston from New York and see where the summer took him. Maybe it was a bad idea to go to America at all, or at least to go without Jennifer. He liked to think of himself as independent but he didn't feel like it now. He felt rejected.

When he rang Mia she was friendly to him.

'How about coming for a meal with me and some of my friends?' she said, 'You'll love them. They're almost as intelligent as you.'

He'd prefer to have seen her on her own but he knew better than to say no to any of her suggestions. When he met her she was back to herself. She chatted in a more casual way about everything.

She drove him to a nearby restaurant. It was a plush place. All the waiters scurried around in fancy uniforms. She introduced him to her friends. The man, Preston, was an insurance salesman. He looked like a West Point cadet. His wife was more handsome than pretty. She was an executive in one of the organisations Mia was affiliated to. They were polite to Brian in a way that made him feel they were working at it.

The menu was mainly sea food. He hated that. He'd have been happier with a plate of chips. He ended up going for a lasagne. It was one of the few things that looked familiar.

'Good old lasagne,' she said as he ordered it. He felt she was being disparaging. Her friends laughed. They laughed at almost everything she said. She had oysters. He almost got sick watching her eating them.

The conversation at the table was peppered with the kind of dry wit that passed for insight. They knew it all about the economy, the environment, even literature. Preston gave a kind of throaty cackle every time he said something profound, or quasi-profound. His wife tittered along.

Brian tried to act relaxed but he was never much good at that. His exchanges with them were forced. They noticed that. They also noticed that he had eyes only for Mia.

He didn't participate much in the night. When the couple left to go to the toilet she pulled her chair over to him.

'Why are you being so rude?' she said.

'I don't mean to be. This isn't much fun for me.'

She gave him a hard look.

'Do you think it is for me?'

'I'll try to mix in from now on.'

'Don't bother. It's too late.'

The couple came back. They had forced smiles on their faces.

'I'm afraid I have bad news,' Preston said, 'The sitter has to go home. Something happened. We'll be leaving early.'

'Oh no,' Mia said.

They gathered their things together. Brian tried to look disappointed. They threw some money on the table to put towards the meal.

'Awfully nice to have met you, Brian,' Preston said.

He mustered up a smile. His wife gave something resembling a smile. He tried to remember her name but he couldn't.

They went off. Mia looked at their half-eaten food.

'Are you happy now?' she said.

'I told you I was sorry. Surely you can meet these people any time. I thought this was going to be our night.'

'Don't try to own me,' she said, 'You hardly know me.'

She paid the bill. He sat waiting for her to come back but she didn't. She went straight out to the Land Rover and drove back to her apartment alone. He walked back to the motel.

He rang her to apologise the next morning. He expected her to give him the third degree but instead she said, 'There's nothing to apologise for. I was thinking about it afterwards. I see where you're coming from. You didn't know these people from Adam. They probably weren't your type anyway.'

'Have you been on to them since?'

'Of course. Everything is hunky dory.'

'I didn't believe the sitter story, by the way.'

'You're impossible.'

She said she was going to a different restaurant that night and that he was welcome to come along. It was a more easy-going one. She was going to be with friends there too – the people who'd been in the bar the day he called to it. He didn't want to go but he couldn't say no. Seeing her with other people was better than not seeing her at all. If he had any chance with her he had to work it that way. He was surprised she hadn't cut him off altogether. This time she arranged to meet him in the restaurant itself.

Everyone was eating when he got there. They looked at him as if he was a creature from another planet.

'Oh my God,' she said as he walked in, 'I got the time wrong. Can you forgive me?'

Was it another one of her little games?

'How could you have?'

All he had to eat was a sandwich. Most of the conversation went above his head. A lot of it was like High School banter, the kind of talk he thought she'd be a million miles from. It was like a carbon copy of the day in the bar.

He moved away from her to the other end of the restaurant as she entertained her friends. There was much empty laughter. Towards closing time one of them put his arms around her and she didn't stop him. Brian grew enraged. Maybe she sensed it. She came over to him shortly afterwards with an apologetic expression on her face.

'He's just a casual friend,' she said, 'Don't panic.'

With another woman he might have thought she was trying to make him jealous but that wasn't her style. She was too direct.

'What have you been up to all evening?' she said then.

'Waiting for it to be over.'

'This is the second night in a row I've deserted you. I feel terrible.'

'I'm getting used to it.'

'I'll tell you what,' she said, 'I've had enough of these idiots here. Why don't you go out to the Land Rover and wait for me there. Then we could do something. Would you like to go for a swim?'

'A what?'

'You've heard of swims, haven't you? They're things people do in the water.'

'Do you know what time it is?'

'I do. I happen to be in possession of a watch.'

She gave him the keys of the Land Rover. A mobile of a buffalo hung from the mirror beside his head.

It had all her chaos in it. There were empty coffee cartons on the floor. The back seat looked like the inside of a sofa. It was as if someone had emptied the contents of a handbag over it. There were pieces of paper, keyrings, lipstick holders, perfume bottles.

She came out after a few minutes. She hugged a few of the men as she said goodbye to them. They went off amid much cheering and laughing.

She opened the door.

'There,' she said, 'Didn't I keep my promise? Move over in the bed.'

He got into the passenger seat.

'I like your buffalo mobile,' he said.

'Thanks. It's from one of the trips to Ghana.'

She turned the ignition on. Suddenly he started to feel good again. The engine wheezed into life. A few seconds later they were speeding down the road. The night stretched before him with endless possibilities.

He watched the speedometer needle climbing. Every time she passed an amber light she went through it.

'Where's the fire?' he said.

'Am I going fast? I didn't notice.'

187

'You remind me of the drivers back home. They think a yellow light is a signal to accelerate instead of to slow down.'

'Then you shouldn't be surprised.'

She had an answer for everything. A part of him enjoyed the fact that she had to be in control of things. It defined her.

The beach came into view. It looked glorious in the twilight, an eternity of sand. The tide was in, crashing off the rocks.

She screeched to a halt by the dunes and they got out. The night was full of stars. There was a wind blowing in from the sea.

She started to take off her clothes.

'You'll freeze to death,' he said.

'Don't worry. I'm used to it.'

She got into her swimsuit. It clung to her shape. She could have been a model, he thought, though he suspected the idea of doing something like that would probably have made her throw up.

As she walked down to the sea she reminded him of a leopard, stealthy and graceful in her strides. The waves unfurled themselves, combing the coast with spray.

'Why don't you join me?' she said, 'There's a pair of men's trunks in the jeep.'

'Do you realise it's after ten o'clock?'

'This is the best time. You avoid all the sunbathers.'

'Do you avoid the sharks as well?'

'Don't worry about them. Even sharks have to sleep sometime. Anyway, I hear they're allergic to barmaids.'

'What about university students?'

'Students they eat without salt. Especially drop-outs.'

She dived in.

'By the way, a shark gobbled the foot off a tourist here last week. You might have read about it in the papers.'

He didn't know if she was having him on or not.

'Really?'

'Yeah, really. What do you need two feet for anyway? You can do just as well with one.'

She dived into the water again, her hands slicing the waves. She disappeared for a few seconds and then sprung up again.

'How cold is it?' he asked.

'It's like a sauna. Come on in.'

'No.'

'Don't be such a chicken. Get the trunks.'

He knew she wouldn't take no for an answer so he went over to the jeep. They were displayed prominently in the trunk. He took off his clothes and put them on. They were at least a size too big for him. He had to double them over at the waist to make them stay up on him.

'Where did you get these?' he said, 'I'm swimming in them, if you'll pardon the expression.'

'They're from my last boyfriend. I got rid of him but kept the trunks. They were all that was worth preserving.'

He went into the water. It was ice cold. .

'Liar,' he said, 'You told me it was warm.'

'Throw yourself under it quickly and you won't feel it.'

He did that. It was agony for a few seconds but then his body acclimatised to it.

'You're right,' he said. 'It's as if there are two temperatures to it.'

'I'm right about everything,' she said. 'The sooner you realise that the happier you'll be with me.'

He waded over to her.

'Thanks for coming in,' she said, 'I know it wasn't easy for you.'

She wrapped herself around him. She started kissing him. Then she was gone again, swimming away from him like an eel.

'Watch this,' she said when she'd got a certain distance away.

She put her hands in the air and threw herself under the water. Then she came back up again like a creature from the deep. The waves swirled around her as she swam towards him. He felt her body against him. The moon came down on the water. She seemed to sink into it. Suddenly there was nothing else in life he wanted but look at her.

'What are you staring at?' she said, 'Have you never seen a woman before?'

'Never one like you.'

'Shut up and swim.'

'I never learned how.'

She looked at him as if he was having her on.

'That's unthinkable.'

'We don't have your warm water back home.'

'That's nothing to do with it. We learn to swim almost at birth here. It's part of growing up. You don't have that?'

'That's right, Keep pumping up your country at the expense of mine.'

She started to splash him.

'Two can play at that game,' he said, splashing her back.

'Try a few strokes and let me see if I can help.'

'I can't. I'd drown. I nearly need a lifebelt in the bath.'

'Just try it. I'll be here if you get into trouble.'

'You can't learn to swim in a few minutes.'

'There's nothing to it. It's all about convincing yourself you're not going to drown.'

'That would never work for me. Drowning is the only thing I think of when I'm in the water.'

He tried a few strokes but he didn't have much success. Waves were coming at him from nowhere. He lost his footing and fell under the surface. She went over to him to stop him thrashing about. When he stood up he started coughing, his lungs full of water. .

'I've just drunk half the ocean,' he said.

'Lucky you. Stop boasting.'

He was shuddering. She couldn't stop laughing at him.

'You remind me of an octopus trying to do a rain dance,' she said.

'Thank you.'

'The fun is over. From now on I want you to make a genuine effort.'

She crinkled up her eyebrows.

'Would you mind telling me exactly what you're doing?'

'I wish I knew.'

'You're mad. Do you know that?'

'So they tell me.'

'You have to do a particular stroke for it to be effective.'

'Okay.'

'So which one do you want to learn?'

'Could I leave that up to you?'

'No.'

'I really want to get the hang of this.'

'Just swim. Swim like your life depended on it.'

'Doesn't it? I mean if you stop you die, right?'

'I think we'll suspend the lessons for tonight,' she said, 'I agree with you. You're unteachable.'

She swam away from him again, going so far away this time he almost lost sight of her. When she was little more than a speck he shouted at her to come back.

She didn't reply and he didn't expect her to. She always ignored him when he said something she didn't like.

She swam back eventually.

'I'm annoyed with you,' he said.

'Why?'

'You could have drowned.'

'I don't think so. I've been swimming almost as long as I've been walking.'

'You were out of sight for a long time. I was worried about you.'

'That was stupid of you.' She pronounced it 'stoopid.'

'Why is it *stoopid*?' he said, mimicking her.

'I come down here all the time. I know what I'm doing.'

'What if you got cramp?'

'What if Moby Dick swam by and gobbled me up? You worry too

much. It's a waste of time bringing you down here. You're a landlubber.'

'A very cold landlubber at the moment. Will we be long more here?'

'Seeing as you're that miserable I'll come out now.'

She swam to the shore. When she stood up the water dripped off her. Her hair was matted to her head. She got a towel from the jeep and wrapped it around herself. After she'd dried herself she gave it to him. His teeth were chattering.

After getting into their clothes they sat on the sand watching the sun go down. Within a minute it was on the horizon.

'The sky is pink,' she said, 'That means a fine day tomorrow.'

'Isn't every day fine over here?'

'Who told you that?'

'It's common knowledge. That's why I don't know if I could ever live here.'

'And in Ireland you get the four seasons every day, right?'

'Right. Actually every few minutes.'

'I couldn't get used to that either.'

'So maybe we're destined to be apart.'

The waves licked their way along the shoreline. He watched a trawler chugging out to sea. A dog chased a seagull up and down the strand.

'What profound thoughts are going through your mind now, Mr University Student?' she asked him.

'I was wondering about your past. I know very little about you.'

'My past. Wow.'

She dragged the word out. It seemed to ricochet across the bay. He wondered how much she was going to tell him. Probably as little as possible.

'Let's see,' she said. She took a deep breath.

'Well first there was my birth on Mars. Then I had my juvenile delinquency phase. That began at about eight. Afterwards there was the correction centre - and then that spell in San Quentin after a spate of murders. Is there anything else you'd like to know? It's all been rather boring really. Your typical mid-West rich bitch sophomore type of thing. What about yourself?'

'My past was much more interesting,' he said, 'I stole a bar of chocolate from a sweet shop once. That's the only exciting thing I can think of.'

'Cheater. You get all the good stuff out of me and then you wimp out.'

As he looked at her he felt she was like someone from another planet. He was a child in comparison to her. There was only a few years between them but it seemed like decades.

They walked back towards the Land Rover. The sun was almost out of sight.

'Now,' she said as they got to it, 'Aren't Aren't you glad you came down here with me? Isn't this the best feeling in the world, looking up at the sky after feeling your insides totally cleaned out?'

'I suppose so.'

'It beats looking at another Adam Sandler film, right?'

'I can't argue with that.'

'Will you come down with me again? To stave off the boredom?'

'You always need to have something happening, don't you?'

'That's right. It's been a fairly typical night in the frenetic life of Mia Schroeder.'

It was the first time she said her name. It added another dimension to her.

She turned on the ignition. They sped off. He imagined sparks coming from the road as she took the bends.

He must have shown shock because she said, 'If you don't like the way I drive you can walk home.'

'It's you I'm concerned about. You're working yourself up.'

'Don't worry about me. I'm fine. Driving fast relaxes me. Sometimes I feel like driving this baby off a cliff.'

'The next time you feel that way, tell me. Then maybe I'll be happy to walk home.'

She turned off the ignition when they came to the top of a hill.

'What are you doing?' he said.

'Freewheeling.'

'Isn't that against the law?'

'So are most things I do behind the wheel.'

'What happens if someone blindsides you coming round a bendl?'

'We die, brother, we die. But we die happy.'

At times like this he knew there was nothing he could say to her. He just had to sit quietly and turn his mind off – or pray.

He wanted to ask her a hundred questions about herself but he feared her anger at his curiosity. They drove along as she pulled the gears this way and that. He felt he was in the middle of a hurricane.

The last light faded from the day. Clouds gathered over the surrounding hills. The lights of the town radiated around them like constellations of another sky.

26

After they got back to the apartment she was elated. She made spaghetti bolognese and washed it down with wine. She talked about everything – Africa, her friends, her job, the swim. He couldn't get a word in. She was like a clock someone wound up, elated merely to be alive.

They finished a bottle of wine between them. Then she opened another one. When they got to the bottom of it she started to tell him the real story of her teenage years. It was the first time he'd seen her totally relaxed. She sat on the floor with her head propped against a cushion and her legs crossed.

'I was sent to a finishing school in Paris by my father but I disgraced myself there. He wanted me to be Audrey Hepburn but instead I turned into Jane Fonda. In the second semester they threw me out. That was my proudest moment.'

He loved her bravado, the way she turned everything into a joke.

'What happened then?'

'After I got back here I was arrested for drunk driving. Dad pulled some strings with the local judge to get me off with a warning. Since then he thinks he has me in his thrall.'

'Have you ever been seriously involved with a man?' he asked her.

'Just once. I actually came close to marrying him, believe it or not.'

'I could never imagine you marrying anyone. It doesn't jibe with you.'

'It was my father who was behind it. It wasn't long after the driving offence. There were a few stories going around about me being wild in France. He wanted to steer me in a different direction. That's what he does when something isn't to his taste. He thought I was going to end up as Patty Hearst.'

'You don't seem to like him very much.'

'That's a brilliant deduction.'

'Is there any particular reason?'

'He's a lawyer. Isn't that enough?'

'You don't like lawyers, I take it.'

'He treats me like someone he has on the stand. I'm on trial all day every day. It was years before I realised how controlling he is.'

'In what way?'

'In every way.'

'Even with your boyfriends?'

'Especially with them. I used to let him set me up on dates when I was a teenager. That stopped when one of them died. Do you want to hear about him or would it be too upsetting for you?'

'I want to hear everything.'

'Okay. He was an architect. Dad is very big on architects. He thinks the world would be a much better place if everyone married one.'

As she spoke he thought the classic chauvinist thought: All feminists have frustrated relationships with their fathers.

'So you broke it off with him.'

'As soon as I realised what was happening. Dad told me I was in love with him and I believed him. When the penny dropped that I wasn't I was out of there like greased lightning.'

'What happened to him afterwards?'

She paused.

'He killed himself.'

'You're joking.'

'I wouldn't joke about something like that.'

'How did it happen?'

'After we broke up he fell in love with another woman. Or at least he thought he did. One night he found her in bed with someone else. He was so devastated he shot himself. It was as simple as that.' Everything in her life seemed to be as simple as that – life and love and the death of love.

'You had a lucky escape.'

'I probably had but you don't see it like that at the time. I had a kind of breakdown after it happened.'

'Even though you didn't love him?'

'Maybe I thought I was responsible for his death. I told him he was throwing himself away on the woman he was with. It was a stupid thing to say. Maybe in some crazy part of myself I wanted to protect him from her. I actually went round to her place one night and told her what I thought of her. That probably led to a few arguments between them.'

'Do you blame yourself for what happened?'

'The only thing I blame myself for is thinking I could cure him of his delusions. He had this idea that life was like a jigsaw and every piece had to fit. The rest of us know most of them never do.'

'How do you feel about him now?

'Relieved. It was like being in jail when I was with him.'

'Do you ever feel that way with me?'

'Don't take this the wrong way but I don't feel any way with you. I hardly know you. Do all the Irish get this heavy with their women this fast?'

'No, only this one.'

'Well now I'm ordering you to stop, Speedy Gonzales.'

Her moods fluctuated. One day she got some bad news about the water project. She'd filled in a form looking for a grant to have a reservation installed in the village she was involved with but she left out one of the letters in her email address and it wasn't processed as a result. The upshot was that her trip was delayed.

She was fit to be tied when she heard that.

'These people are capable of killing off a tribe because I missed a digit,' she said to Brian, 'Doesn't that say it all?'

'You told me you were going to be ground down by red tape,' he said, 'Where's the surprise?'

194

She looked at him as if she was seeing him for the first time.

'You know something?' she said, 'You're right. I did say that.'

'See? I listen after all.'

He found he was able to relax her by common sense. She was so involved in her life she couldn't see what was happening in it. He was outside it so he could.

It brought them closer.

'Look,' she said to him one night, 'You're spending a lot of time in the apartment. Maybe you should move in with me.'

He couldn't believe what he was hearing.

'It makes sense,' he said, trying to conceal his excitement at the offer.

After that everything moved fast. He was so excited he couldn't remember the train of events. He didn't have much to move anyway. All he could think of was the luxury of being with her all the time. It was as if life would be a permanent holiday.

The first time he slept with her he felt guilty.

'What's wrong?' she said, 'Is it that girl in Ireland you're thinking of?' He'd mentioned Jennifer to her.

'No,' he said, but it was. Even though they'd given each other a blank sheet to be with other people when they were apart he felt he'd betrayed her.

'How many girls have you been to bed with?' she asked him.

'I'm not telling you,' he said, 'How many men have you been with?'

'257,' she said.

When he woke the next morning she was gone from the room. He didn't know for how long but when he put his hand on her side of the bed it was still warm. He moved over to it and lay there.

He heard her moving around the kitchen but when he called out to her but she didn't answer.

He looked out at the sky, the mountains, a palm tree across the road that was blowing in the wind. It made him feel good to see the first things she saw each day. It gave him an immersion in her life.

When he went out to the kitchen she already had breakfast ready for him. He ate it as if it was the most normal thing in the world to be sitting with a woman who'd suddenly become his lover.

Were they a couple now? Would she drop him as soon as she invited him into her life? There was no point worrying about that. She probably didn't know herself.

He stayed in the apartment after she left for work. In the afternoon he went for a swim. It was like another part of his immersion into her.

When she came home that evening she asked him what he'd done with the day.

'Nothing,' he said.

195

He didn't tell her he went swimming. Maybe he was getting like her. The best way to make the relationship work was for both of them to have secrets from one another.

Was he falling in love with her? What was love? Was he in love with Jennifer? Could you be in love with two people at the one time? Or even more than two? Maybe you could love different things about people. If that was the case you could love hundreds of women simultaneously.

The more time he spent with her the more he felt his past being swept away. It became welded to hers like cement.

Sometimes she seemed only half real to him. He thought if he took his eyes off her she'd disappear.

The days became warmer, the sun burning like blood in the sky. It made everything under it sizzle.

He told her he was uncomfortable with it.

'What's wrong with you?' she said, 'You're supposed to be happy after all that Irish rain.'

'I can't breathe'

On the really hot days there were so many people on the beach they could hardly see the sand. There were deck chairs everywhere.

They sat under gigantic umbrellas to shield themselves from the sun. He tried to get chairs for himself and Mia but they were usually snapped up by the tourists. Some of them got up at dawn to be first in the queue for them.

It was even too hot to walk on the sand sometimes. When it got like that they waited inside until the sun went down.

'We're like vampires,' she said.

They sat on the verandah drinking cocktails as the days unfolded around them. They listened to the drone of traffic, the crashing of the waves. They tasted the salt of the sea in their nostrils.

She spent a lot of her time making arrangements for her African trip. He went jogging or down to the local McDonalds to kill time.

At the weekends they didn't go out at all. Often they didn't even dress. They sat around the apartment like two slugs. She was a treasure trove of anecdotes and he hung on her every word.

'You're the best listener I ever met,' she said to him one day. 'I go on for hours and you sit there like a bump on a log.'

'That's because you've lived such an interesting life.'

'I don't see it that way. I just do what feels right at the time.'

'That's the point. Most other people don't. We do what we feel we have to do because we're afraid not to.'

'Do you include yourself in that description?'

'Probably.'

'We'll you're out here, aren't you? You broke away from Mother

Ireland.'

'This is only a blip on the radar. I didn't come out here to live. When I met you I was supposed to do nothing but see some sights and visit my aunt in Boston.'

'She's the woman who was unlucky in love, right?'

'Right.'

He couldn't even remember telling her about her. There were so many stories, so many nights.

'Are you going to go see her at any stage?'

'I know I should.'

'Don't let me stand in your way.'

'That's not the point. She came out here to live. I'm only here for the summer.'

'Maybe I'll even go up to her with you.'

'I'd love that.'

He wasn't sure if she was teasing him or not. Was it possible she was falling for him?

A few weeks earlier he'd have laid bets they'd murder each other rather than become a pair but now, strangely, they were almost stable. He didn't allow himself become smug but she seemed to accept him more now, even accept his outdated attitudes.

She had the innocence of a child. There were days when she'd wake up flushed with excitement as she regaled him with the details of a dream she'd had. Often it would be something like driving a car close to the edge of a cliff for a thrill or surfing the waves in a storm. It wasn't only in her waking life that she was taking risks but in her sleep as well. Could he compete with her in any department?

She continued planning her trip to Africa, trying to salvage it from all the glitches surrounding it.

She went to seminars on outreach programmes some nights, giving presentations if she was asked. A different woman to the one he knew took over when she did that. Even her voice changed.

Which was the real her? He didn't know and he didn't care. Back at the apartment afterwards she'd ask him how he thought she did.

He always praised her but she wasn't good with compliments. Occasionally he'd see a glow of radiance emanating from her but she never admitted to being satisfied with herself. It was like a block she had.

'Be specific,' she'd say, 'What do you think I did well?'

He could never tell her that. The topics she talked about were over his head. He'd stutter some half-comment that made no sense. It usually caused her to go into all sorts of hysterics.

He was profoundly ignorant of politics. He knew he'd demonstrate that the more he talked so he tried to say as little as possible if he could get away with it. He often said things he knew to be wrong merely to fill up a silence. His hands would grope the air looking for a word as he hung on the edge of some obscure insight that never came out. Or worse, did.

'Do you not care about the Third World?' she asked him once, her eyes almost leaping out of her head.

'Of course I do,' he said, 'I just don't know what to do about it.'

'That's a cop-out.'

'Okay, so. I'm copping out. You save the world and I'll try and keep the apartment tidy.'

Even at that he was useless. One night when he was trying to put her books in order he hit the shelf with his elbow and everything tumbled to the ground.

When his nerves were on edge he fumbled the simplest of tasks. Reaching for the sugar bowl during a meal he'd tip something over with his jacket-cuff. If he cooked anything it was usually burned to a cinder.

'Don't worry about it,' she'd say, 'You should know by now that your clumsiness is the thing I like most about you.' If only he could only have believed it.

One night he went to one of her presentations without telling her. She was giving it to a delegation of foreign dignitaries in a nearby hotel. Her professionalism didn't surprise him. It was the same Mia he saw in the bar the time the scuba divers were around her.

She had the audience in the palm of her hand. He looked up at her with pride. After she finished speaking there was a big round of applause. Then everyone dispersed into groups.

He watched her holding forth in one of them. He wasn't sure if it would be a good idea to announce himself to her.

She was chatting to a few men in sharp suit. Her hands were going in all directions as she made some point. He walked towards her with his stomach churning.

'Well done, Mia,' he said when he got to her, 'That was fantastic.'

She stopped talking. Her mouth hung open as she looked at him. For a second he wasn't sure if she recognised him or not. Was she that much lost in her world? After a few seconds her natural expression returned.

'Brian,' she said, 'What are you doing here?'

She introduced him to the men she was talking to but he felt out of sorts. He didn't stay long with them, excusing himself to go to the toilet. She kept talking for a while.

Eventually the lights went down. The room was empty. He was sitting at a table at the back of the room. She went over to him.

'That was a surprise,' she said.

He knew she was upset and also that she wasn't going to admit it. She put on a good act of talking normally going home in the jeep and also back at the apartment over a midnight cocktail but he knew he'd infringed on some unspoken law. He'd entered her Holy of Holies without seeking her permission.

He feared the consequences.

27

A few nights after the presentation she asked him if he'd like to meet her parents. He'd heard her talking to them on the phone a few times but he didn't sense much warmth in the conversations. Anytime he brought them up she cut him short. Her mother she described as a victim. She only talked about her father the night she was ranting on about him.

'Have I been invited?' he said.

'I'm afraid so. I told them about you a while ago. Since then they've been mad to meet you. I can't keep putting them off forever.'

They lived in a lavish house a few miles away. He was a bag of nerves all day. As she drove into the grounds he told her he'd probably need a tranquilliser to get him through the evening.

'What am I going to talk to them about?'

'There's no "them," there's only him. You're not allowed to talk to my mother. He doesn't approve of it.'

'Okay, I'll rephrase that. What will I talk to him about?'

'If you have a few hours to spare, ask my father about how he got where he is. He'll tell you about the first dollar he made and how that made way for the second one and then the third and so on until he finally got to his present exemplary status. He thinks of nothing but money. He's unapologetic about that fact.'

'Do you not think he's entitled to be if he made it the hard way?'

'Like a lot of people who were born poor he's embraced capitalism with both hands. I think the expression is "self-made man." I've often wondered what that means. Isn't God the only person we should credit with this - unless there are new forms of eugenics I'm not aware of.'

'I think we better get on to another subject. I can see your blood pressure rising.'

'He brings out the worst in me just like I bring out the worst in him. It's like a bad marriage.'

'With the advantage that you don't have to look for a divorce.'

'Thank Christ for that.'

They reached the house. He was breathing heavily.

'Relax,' she said as he got out of the Land Rover, 'If he attacks me I have a Swiss knife in my back pocket.'

She parked in a gravelled circle beside a fountain. There was a Greek statue in the middle of it.

'I feel like I'm entering the world of *Gone With the Wind*,' he said.

He came out to the porch. He was a large man, someone you might expect to see in a Country Club. He spoke as if his mouth was full of marbles.

'Welcome,' he said, 'Welcome to our humble abode.' They walked towards him.

'I love Ireland,' he said as soon as he saw Brian, 'I keep promising myself to get over to the Emerald Isle sometime soon.'

He was dressed in a coloured shirt and a pair of check trousers. They reminded Brian of the kind golfers wore. Mia told him he had ambitions to take it up as a career when he was a young man. He could imagine him at Augusta dreaming of donning the green jacket.

His wife was more subdued. She was a willowy woman, graceful and delicate. She looked like fallen grandeur. Her face bore the experience of pain. He could see she would have been very beautiful once.

'I can see where you got your looks from,' he said to Mia.

Dinner was lavish. It was served in a dining-room large enough to feed an army. The maid who looked terrified.

As they ate he told stories about his life growing up, how he fought his way from poverty to where he was now. apparently he had the classic Huckleberry Finn youth, foraging for a living for years before he hit paydirt. Various shady characters were introduced as part of his story, soe of them helping him along, some plotting his destruction.

He told Brian how proud he was of Mia, how she'd achieved so much in such a short time. He had big dreams for her but he wasn't in favour of the African trip. A social worker had been murdered in Ghana the previous year. 'I'm afraid she'll go too far into the interior,' he said, 'She always goes too far everywhere.'

His wife stayed silent as he spoke. Maybe, Brian thought, she was as frightened as the maid. Or was she just broken?

He continued to hold forth after they'd eaten. His eyes were dead. They didn't move as he spoke. All that moved was his Adam's apple. His wife wrung her hands out of one another.

Brian imagined his stories had been recycled often over the years with only minor variations. He tried his best to look impressed. He gazed covertly at his watch whenever he could, wondering how much longer the torture was going to continue.

They adjourned to a side room which was even more ornate than the one they'd been in. A buffalo's head was mounted on the mantelpiece. Books lined the walls. They all had similar colours, similar bindings. They looked unread.

Mia and her father started to exchange banter as cocktails were served.

'We usually wait until the second martini,' she'd said to Brian in the apartment. She wasn't far wrong. One insult followed another. Brian watched them going at each other like two prize-fighters who knew all the rules of combat. It ended in a draw. The weapons were put down after the martinis were finished.

'We're going outside for a few minutes,' she said to him then. She gave her mother a kiss before leading Brian outside.

'He's an unashamed right-winger,' she said to him at the fountain. She was speaking loud enough for him to hear. He suspected this was intentional.

'It was my right-wing money that put you through college, darling,' he said, coming up behind them.

'Yes,' she replied, 'and I threw it back in your face when I dropped out.'

He would have been embarrassed by these sparrings if it was anyone else but he got the impression they were common currency between them. He also felt they didn't care who was listening. As a result they weren't as dramatic as they might have been in another kind of family.

Back inside they had more cocktails. He started to drink faster. The stories became more *risque*. His wife squirmed in her seat. Politics, inevitably, came up. Mia attacked him for his views. He seemed to enjoy it. He baited her just as Bartley baited Angela. It was like theatre.

The evening ground to a close. Mia said, 'Brian and myself are going out for a breath of air.'

'So soon after the last outing?' her father said, 'Is it to badmouth me again?'

She led him out to a bench that was beside some rose bushes.

'I was Daddy's little darling right through my childhood years,' she said, 'That's probably why I turned against him when things went wrong. I fell off the pedestal he had me on. He wanted me to stay forever as his Jon-Benet Ramsey.'

'Did your mother never try to patch things up between you?'

'She was never a match for him. I watched her crumble under him too many times. She was the one who made me tough more than anyone else.'

'She doesn't look too happy.'

'She had a heart scare a few years ago but she's okay now. She doesn't get involved.'

'What does she think of you?'

'She thinks I'm looking for love, that this political stuff is a cover. She imagines Sir Lancelot will ride over the horizon one day in his shining armour and knock all the nonsense out of me.'

Could that person be him? He doubted it.

'In some ways she's worse than my father. She knows he's a bully but she lets him away with it. That's what I can't accept. He believes what he's saying. I give him a kind of a pardon for that.'

'Did she ever think of leaving him?'

'How could she? She loves him. The worse he treats her, the more that love grows. She must have Irish blood in her somewhere.'

'It sounds like she's a glutton for punishment.'

'That's the way it's been since the day he met her. He got his way then and it continued after he walked her up the aisle. Her wishes never counted. She just learned to accept him as the crazy man he was. She told me the first year of the marriage was the most turbulent. That was when I was conceived. It probably explains why I'm so fucked up.'

They went back to the house. Everything was quiet when they got there. Her parents were sitting like statues. He could tell by their expressions that they'd been talking about them. They would have known they'd been talked about too.

Her mother sat tensely reading a magazine. Her father looked up for another fight.

'Well,' he said to Mia, 'What are you going to do with yourself after you save Africa from the conglomerates?'

'Murder you, probably.'

'Don't say things like that, honey,' her mother said, 'You know it upsets me.'

'Sorry, mom. He drives me to it.'

She walked away from him. He turned to Brian.

'How are your studies going in Ireland?' he said. He muttered some kind of an answer.

'Say hello to Dublin for me when you get back, won't you?'

He said he would. Mia shook her head. She was almost on the point of laughing now.

The rest of the night was tense but there were no more sparks. It ended on an anti-climax. Everyone was happy about that except her father. He kept gunning for more drama.

Brian hadn't expected this level of tension even with Mia's warnings. He felt his head about to explode as they put on their coats to go home.

'I hope we'll see you again,' her father said to him at the door, 'You have all the charm of the Irish.'

He wondered why he said that. He'd hardly talked to him for the whole evening.

'Thank you. I'll do my best to come back.'

He shook hands with him and with his wife.

She put on a pained smile. She looked like the saddest woman he ever saw in his life.

'Take care of my little girl,' she said.

He couldn't wait to get out the door. Mia kissed her mother on the cheek. She didn't wave to her father.

They walked towards the Land Rover. Her father waved as they sat in. She beeped the horn.

'Your father is smiling,' Brian said.

'Yes,' she said, 'through gritted teeth.'

She drove out of the grounds.

'That was an interesting evening,' she said, 'Maybe we'll do it again soon when we're in need of more entertainment. What did you make of it?'

'It wasn't exactly Walt Disney.'

'You could say that.'

The journey home was sweet because of what came before it. How many things in life, he wondered, did people evaluate because of what preceded them? The same landmarks he'd looked out at a few hours before in dread were now like paradise to him – the mountains, the sea, the setting sun.

He rolled the window down. The wind blew in his face, driving the tension away.

'It's like getting out of prison, isn't it?' Mia said, 'I must have had the worst father in Christendom.'

'Mine was no picnic either,' Brian said.

'Of the two. I think I'd prefer a soak to a Grade-A bastard.'

His head was lifting. He stuck it out the window.

'You'll get decapitated if you're not careful,' she said, 'Trucks come along this stretch at the rate of knots.'

'It might be worth it,' he said, 'It's ready to explode.'

It was one of the few nights he wanted her to drive fast. She bombed along, skidding at the bends, appearing to take some of them on two wheels.

'You can get away with murder in a mother this big,' she said.

'I hope you don't mean that literally. I feel I'm being knocked six ways from Sunday.' That was one of her own expressions. He was around her so much he'd started talking like her.

The thought of her father was stuck in both of their heads.

Back at the apartment he said to her, 'I think I know now why you left home so early.'

'It's a two-way street,' she said, 'Maybe I'm as much the problem as he is. I goad him. I'm also aware he paid for most of the things I have in life. I can hardly forget. He keeps reminding me.'

'I have that problem too.'

'Then you know what I'm talking about. We shouldn't have to pander to these people. It's not even the money. It's the way he wallows in it. It's his God.'

He'd railed against America's glorification of the dollar the night he met her. Little did he know then she was the antithesis of that. Her father would have been a more appropriate target for his comments.

A wistful look came into her eyes.

'My regret is that he could have been so different. I'd love to have known him when he was my age. Did I tell you he was kicked out of college in his final year?'

'What for?'

'He hung one of the other students over a balcony after he insulted him one night. He threatened to let him go if he didn't apologise.'

'I thought you disapproved of drunken behaviour.'

'He was sober at the time.'

'That puts a different complexion on it. He sounds like someone I wouldn't like to have tangled with.'

'At least it showed he had fire in his belly. That disappeared when he graduated.'

'Was he not expelled for what he did?'

'They were going to. They took him back after a lot of grovelling. That was the beginning of the end as far as I'm concerned. He's been grovelling to people ever since. That's what graduation does to you.'

'Maybe I was afraid it would happen to me in UCD.'

'Maybe. You were wise to get out. Somehow I can't see you lecturing pimply adolescents on *The Canterbury Tales*.'

'That makes two of us.'

She didn't want to let the night go. The encounter with her father gave her a burst of energy. He knew what was coming. just before midnight she suggested they go down to the beach again.

'Do you ever do anything besides swim?' he said.

'The weather is too muggy here. It's the only thing you can do to cool off.'

'I don't know if I'm in the mood for it.'

'You're never in the mood.'

She got her way as usual, running out to the Land Rover before he had a chance to say no.

He followed her in. She gunned the engine, driving even faster than usual as the night came down.

'I know you'll start complaining about the cold unless I hurry,' she said by way of excuse.

'Don't forget you've been drinking,' he said but she didn't reply.

They were there before he knew it. She parked in a No Parking zone to be nearer the sea.

'Are you not worried about being clamped?' he said.

'At this hour? You must be joking.'

204

She took their swimming gear out. They walked to a spill of rocks that stood on the edge of the sea. She climbed up to the top of them and gazed into the distance.

'Is there anything in the world as beautiful as the sea?' she said.

'Come down or you'll fall,' he said.

'You're always afraid of something, aren't you?'

She jumped down.

The wind was blowing. They walked along the beach. It blew the sand into their faces, stinging their eyes.

There were a few fishermen farther down the shore. They stood beside them watching them tug their rods. They had them buried in the sand.

'Look at those lazy slackers,' she said.

'It's the way everything is these days. There'll probably come a time when you can fish by remote control.'

'I'd love to see something come out of the water and drag them in with it.'

'That's a bit dramatic.'

'Do you approve of fishing?'

'I don't have any strong views on it. I believe in saving the whale all right. I'm not so sure about the fish.'

'No?'

'Have you never eaten fish for your dinner?'

'You just accept everything in life don't you?' she said, 'Could you not have a bit more anger in you?'

'Why would I want that?'

'I don't know.'

'There's too much anger in my past already.'

They started to take their rods out of the sand. They'd caught nothing. She was glad.

'Ha!' she said, 'An empty haul. Fish 1, Fishermen zero.'

They carried their tackle towards a parked truck.

'Tough shit,' she said as they passed.

'Thanks, honey,' one of them replied. She laughed at him.

He stuck his middle finger up at her. She did the same thing back.

'Bastard,' she whispered under her breath.

A few minutes later they were in the water again. He found it freezing until he got out of pain but then he started to enjoy it.

When he looked at her body now he saw it as the body of a mermaid. She was so much in tune with the water she might have been a part of it. She glided along almost without appearing to move, looking as if she was propelled by an invisible engine.

The waves rode to the shore like horses trying to race one another. She waited for them to get as high as they were going to and then dived under them.

'You really love this, don't you?' he said.

'I'd live in the sea all the time if I could. I'd only come out to eat.'

The lights of the promenade glinted. A foghorn droned somewhere in the distance.

He watched her moving along the necklace of the bay, swimming parallel with the tide. She was oblivious of him, oblivious of everything. All she needed was to breathe, he thought, to coast along in that rhythmic way she had. She didn't even seem to be moving her muscles. The water was doing the work.

Waves curled around her. She enveloped herself in them. They pounded like thunder as they crashed on the rocks.

He stayed longer than usual in the water. He was able to swim a few strokes now because of the times he went down to the sea on his own. He never told about these.

They dressed quickly to get back to the Land Rover as soon as they could. As he walked to it he saw something yellow on the back wheel. He suspected the worst.

'You're not going to like this,' he said, 'We've been clamped.'

Her face went white.

'I don't believe it,' she said, 'I've never had to pay for parking here before.'

There was a sheet of paper gummed to the side window. She ripped it off. It said, 'You Have Been Clamped. Do Not Attempt To Drive The Vehicle.' She tried to pull off the clamp but it wouldn't give.

There was a number to ring under the message. She rang it.

'What the hell is going on here?' she said after it was answered.

'You're at the beach, right?' said a voice.

'Right.'

'There are parking charges. Did you not pay them?'

'How can I? There's no machine.'

She was trembling with rage.

'You need to text your car registration number to the number on the sign.'

'What sign?'

'You'll see it on a pole. Look to your right.'

She looked up. It was beside a palm tree.

'You mean the one that's trying its best to hide behind the tree?'

'The charge is a hundred bucks. You can pay in cash or by credit card. Which will it be?'

She was speechless with rage.

'Take the phone from me,' she said to Brian, 'before I break it.'

She walked up and down trying to calm herself.

'Just pay it,' Brian said, 'There's nothing we can do. We'll know for the next time.'

'They'll be putting a wall around the waves next, telling us we can only swim out so far.'

She gave the man her credit card number.

'Someone will be along to de-clamp you as soon as possible,' he said.

She started biting her nails. A few minutes later a man arrived in a truck. He got out and removed the clamp.

'Why don't you get a real job?' she said to him as he went back to his truck.

'I don't make the rules, lady. Next time, open your eyes.'

'Fuck you, you piece of shit,' she yelled at him as he drove off.

28

Over the next few weeks she became more tender towards Brian. They settled into a mellowness together.

She rose at the crack of dawn every morning to shower and do her Pilates exercises. Afterwards she had what she called a 'killer' cup of coffee to get her going for the day.

When he got up she was usually on the phone to Africa. He'd slumber out to the breakfast counter and she'd already be adrenalized. Then she'd get into the orange uniform she hated so much. 'It makes me feel as if I'm in Guantanamo Bay,' she'd say.

After she went to work he might go back to bed if he hadn't slept well the night before. If he stayed up he'd either read or watch some show on the television. Every so often he went out for a jog or tidied the apartment. His day really only began when she came home.

He often left the television on all day. That drove her mad.

Sometimes he'd be in the middle of watching a programme and she'd just turn it off.

He knew better than to argue with her at times like that. She'd sit in the silence, letting the night come down as she watched the shadows lengthen on the walls

'Enjoying yourself?' he'd say, 'Philosopher Queen.'

Being under her thumb so much made him want to assert himself more with other people. He became aggressive on nights when he wasn't with her. It was as if he needed to compensate in some way for the fact that she was stamping out his spirit. Creating drama for himself took his mind off her. It was like a diversion tactic.

'I've been hearing stories about you,' she said to him one night.

It was like a parent chastising a wayward child. But she was smiling as she spoke. She said she was glad he was developing this other side to him, this sense of arrogance. He wanted to turn it on her but he was afraid to. It might have excited her but it might also have driven her away. He couldn't take the chance.

One night when they were at the beach she swam out farther than she'd ever done before. Her head bobbed up and down and then disappeared. He started to worry.

He waded out towards her looking for any sign of her. He called her but there was no answer.

When she eventually came into view his worry was replaced by anger. He knew she must have heard him calling. He walked back to the shore.

He sat looking into space. She came out of the water.

'Are you all right?' she said.

'Why didn't you answer me? I thought you were in trouble. Your head was bobbing up and down like a buoy.'

'Or even a girl,' she said, putting on a funny face.

'Please don't crack jokes like that. It makes me out to be an idiot.'

'You need to relax, dude. You'll give yourself a breakdown.'

'Do you not appreciate the fact that I care about you?'

'Caring can be suffocating.'

Even when she was in the wrong she could turn a situation to her advantage.

Now and again they went to a film. He loved the nights he spent just sitting in the dark with her but she was too impatient for them. She'd go in and out to the shop or to the toilet, anything to get out of her seat.

When they were in the apartment he felt he irritated her if he wasn't active.

'You need to get a job,' she told him one day, 'We're spending too much time together.'

He didn't want to but if it meant her being in better form it was worth it.

'Just tell me what to do,' he said.

He scoured the Situations Vacant columns of the local paper that evening. The next day he answered one of the ads. It was for a job in a pizza parlour.

The interview was a joke. He was hardly asked any questions at all. But at least they didn't want him to go on the books. He suspected it had a rapid turnover of employees, most of them probably there out of desperation.

He enjoyed the mindlessness of it. Little was expected of him. He spent most of his time putting the pizzas into boxes and getting them ready for delivery. The main business was takeaways. A few customers were served at a table in the parlour but that was all. The pay was low. So was that of the couriers. They made most of their money on tips.

'I won't stay long at this,' he said to her after coming home the first day, 'It's soul-destroying.'

'Nobody is happy at their job,' she said tiredly, 'We work to pay the rent.'

He continued to postpone visiting his aunt. Would he see her at all now? He didn't want to ring Bartley because he knew he'd keep nagging him about her.

He rang Jennifer one night when Mia was asleep. It was ages before she answered. When she did he didn't know what to say to her. He was afraid Mia would wake up.

'It must be the middle of the night over there,' she said, 'What are you doing ringing me when every sane person is asleep?'

'I just wanted to say hello. How are things?'

'Not too bad. Why haven't you been on to me? I can't remember the last time you called.'

'I've been busy.'

'Where are you?'

'With a friend. I better not stay on too long and run up the bill.'

Mia started moving. She called out his name in her sleep.

'What was that?' she said, 'Is there someone with you?'

'No, it's the television.'

His voice must have sounded tense because she said, 'Are you okay?'

'I'm fine,' he said, 'Sorry for being in a rush. I have to go now.'

He could see she was taken aback. He felt more awkward with her than he would have with a stranger.

'Why did you ring if you don't have time to talk to me?'

'To hear your voice,' he said, putting the phone down.

Mia was awake when he got back to the bed. He wasn't sure if she heard him. If she did she didn't say anything about it.

The days surged on like a tide. Sometimes he felt as if he'd been with her forever. He wanted to be but he couldn't see it happening. They were like night and day. She had so many things going on in her head and he had so few. He never knew where he stood with her.

He kept asking her about herself. It frustrated her.

'There's nothing left to tell,' she said, 'You've heard it a hundred times before. Why do you keep asking me the same things?'

'Because you seem to have lived ten lives in one.'

'I disagree. Anyway, all that stuff is in the past.'

The summer became warmer. They watched tourists buying nic-nacs at the flea markets, watched them lying head-to-head along the sand like burnt animals. He felt his youth slipping away from him as she became the centre of his life. She never looked more beautiful. Construction workers wolf-whistled at her as she walked past them in her flimsy tops.

'You must be flattered,' he said to her when a man jumped up and down on the roof of a building as he looked at her.

'I'm bored,' she said.

He didn't know how long it would be before she got bored with him too. She told him she'd gotten rid of other men in the past without warning. If something wasn't working, she said, you had to spit it out like poison. There was no reason for him to think he'd be treated any differently no matter how much she was thawing out with him.

She talked about moving out of the apartment. If she did, he didn't know if he'd be invited to go with her. She never mentioned that part of it. Many nights she'd come back from the bar and say, 'I hate this dump.' Was it a kind of hint to him that one day she'd be gone from his life as suddenly as she came into it?

Every day he woke up beside her was a bonus. The fact that it could end any time made the hours he was with her all the more precious. He waited for her to go to Africa, a place where she could be fulfilled without having to be dragged back to earth by his predictability. He felt like her plaything, someone she could dangle on a string and then dispense with when she went away. If that happened he'd be left floundering in her wake like a meal that went down the wrong way. He'd be discardable, like yesterday's news.

'I know I'm holding you back from your travelling,' he kept saying to her, trying to suss her out.

She assured him that wasn't the case, that when she was ready to blow she'd blow. He asked her if she'd ever consider going to Ireland with him but she just laughed. He felt like a fool for even suggesting it.

What they had was nothing more than a holiday romance, he told himself. It had advantages as well as disadvantages. They could do different things each day without having to worry about the responsibilities other people had. If they got on each other's nerves for whatever reason they could go their separate ways. Who else had such freedom?

The pizza parlour started to get him down. He rang in sick sometimes but it wasn't the kind of job where you could do that. He knew he'd be easy to replace at a moment's notice. There were any number of people queueing up to take his place.

His boss rang him one day when he was lounging in bed .

'Do you want this job or don't you, buddy?' he said. He went in later in the morning but the atmosphere was bad. He started to be ordered around like a 12-year-old. After a few hours he snapped, banging a pizza down on the counter for a customer when the boss was watching.

'I think you better go,' he said.

He was almost relieved. A few days later he was in another job. It involved selling advertising space over the phone for a tourist magazine. It paid even less than the pizza parlour but it passed the time for him. They allowed him work flexi-time. That made it more bearable. He asked Mia if she could get him work in her bar with her but she didn't think that was a good idea.

Her father rang one night when she was at a conference.

'How is she?' he said, 'Beth and I are worried about her.'

'Is that your wife?'

'Yes. She has angina. I don't like to see her worked up.'

'I didn't know that.'

'She probably didn't tell you in case it weakened her position with me. She's capable of putting anyone's health second to gain ground.'

He didn't know what to say to that. Was he making it up? Anything was possible.

'Why are you ringing me?' he said, 'Why don't you talk to her yourself?'

'You know how she is. She goes ballistic when I say anything.'

'I don't know how I can help.'

'You seem like an intelligent young man. You must have seen the tension between us.'

'Can you not work things out between yourselves? I'm sure she'd appreciate a call from you.'

'She hangs up on me every time I phone.'

'That's nothing to do with me.'

'Is she still set on the trip to Africa?'

'I think so.'

'Are you going with her?'

'I doubt it.'

'We're worried she'll get into trouble with the government over there or even with some of the tribes. She has no sense of danger, as you might have noticed.'

'I'm worried about that too.'

'Have you tried asking her not to go?'

'She doesn't listen to me either.'

'Please try again. For all our sakes.'

'I'll tell her you rang but I doubt it will have any effect on her.'

'So do I. You saw the way she was with me the night you visited us. I know I've made mistakes with her in the past but she's not a teenager anymore. She can't keep living like one.'

She came home from the conference in a bad mood. Things hadn't gone her way and she'd let everyone know it.

'I gave them all a piece of my mind,' she said.

'Sometimes I think you're fighting the world.'

'What's wrong with that?'

'Nothing, I suppose.'

'I like a challenge.'

He wasn't sure whether to tell her about her father's call. In the end he did. She got as angry as he expected.

'That son of a bitch,' she said, 'He's getting on my last nerve. I'm going to ring him right now and tell him what to do with himself.'

'He said your mother is worried about you. You didn't tell me she had angina.'

She looked at him with her eyes blazing.

'He told you that?'

'He sounded worried about it. He said you worked her up.'

She gave a dry laugh.

'That's always been the card he's played against me. "Don't work your mother up, she has a bad heart." It's the oldest one in the book. I'm surprised you fell for it.'

'Are you saying it's not true?'

'I'm saying he's exaggerating it out of all proportion. He's capable of sabotaging her health to get his way with me.'

'That's exactly what he said about you.'

'Whose side are you on?'

'Yours, obviously, but you can't play around with your mother's health even if he's making it up.'

'If anyone is playing round with her health it's him. He doesn't give a rat's ass about her. The angina is just a stick to beat me with.'

'Maybe you're going a bit far there.'

She banged a cupboard with her fist. She always hated him disagreeing with her, even about the smallest thing. He shuddered.

'Did I tell you he left her a few years ago?' she said when she cooled down.

'No. What happened?'

'I don't know the details but it blew her mind. Up till then he was like Mr Sensible for her. She didn't think he'd do something like that in a million years. He never gave a sign.'

'How was she with him afterwards?'

'She could never feel the same about him.'

'But she didn't throw him out.'

'No, but she can never forget it. It eats away at her. She won't talk about it and that makes it worse. It probably brought on the angina.'

'What about the other woman?'

'That was over before it began.'

He didn't know what to say.

'This is a bit of an eye-opener for me. I shouldn't have been making pronouncements about a man I don't know.'

'It's all right. I know you're trying your best to resolve things. I can't believe he rang you. He hardly knows you.'

'He sounded desperate.'

'That's another act he puts on. Don't fall for it. Did he say anything else?'

'That you keep hanging up on him when he calls you.'

'That bit is true.'

'He asked me to try and knock some sense into you.'

'Be my guest.'

'He seems to have this idea that I have a good head on my shoulders because I'm at college. Maybe I remind him of your architect friend. Little does he know how mixed up I am in my own life.'

'He had no right to ring you no matter what way he feels about you. I'm still fuming. Let me ring him. I need to talk to him.'

'Please don't. Not now anyway. It'll rebound on me if he finds out I told you. Maybe he's just lonely for you.'

'Lonely? That's a laugh. He'd prefer to have a grizzly bear visit him. You're far too nice about him.'

'I never said I liked him. I don't want to make things worse.'

In the end she didn't make the call. The next morning she was glad. She thanked him profusely for stopping her. She was in such good form she even took the day off work. They lazed around by the marina for the day. In the evening she made quiche.

'I wish I was more like you,' she said as they ate it.

'If you were, you'd wish you weren't.'

'Maybe I should bring you to Africa with me. Every time I'm about to explode you make me count to ten.'

'Thanks for saying that. I think we're good together. You have a hundred sides to you. I only have one.'

She became like a drug to him. His logical mind was outside himself. Time felt irrelevant. He was like a watch somebody forgot to wind.

They strolled along the boardwalk feeding the pigeons. Occasionally she stopped people walking by and asked them to take photographs of them. He hated that.

'It makes me feel like a tourist,' he said.

'You *are* a tourist,' she insisted.

Afterwards they sat on the wall watching surfers riding the waves. They bought ice cream cones from vendors in multi-coloured vans, licking them off one another's faces like adolescents. Now and then they went to a show in a local hall, one of those summer acts put on by comedians who couldn't get work any other time of the year. The standard was usually poor. The jokes were so bad they were almost good. They found themselves laughing at them for that reason. Or maybe just because it was summer, the silly season.

He got better at swimming but never came anywhere near her ability. She stayed in the water much longer than him, making him nervous as he watched her going out further and further in rough tides. When she came back he'd berate her, telling her it wasn't fair to him.

'You remind me of my father,' she'd say

The next time she'd go out even farther and stay longer. He had to beware of her rebellious side of her so he had to pretend not to care, or at least not as much as he did

The summer ended almost without warning. Before they knew it the leaves were turning brown and falling from the trees. Heavy winds blew down the street and across the harbour. The nights came in early, turning the water in the bay from blue to grey. When they were foggy the lamps from the nearby lighthouse combed the sea for boats that were in trouble, sending beams of light over the waves like pyramids.

They didn't go out much now, contenting themselves with cooking experiments and mindless television shows. She experimented with exotic dishes. Some of them almost poisoned him. He had conservative tastes while she wanted to be adventurous. He was afraid to say anything if he didn't like her food but if she didn't like it he was afraid to say he did. Everything was on her terms.

She put a plan in place to get him a visa for the African trip and he became excited by that, seeing it as a kind of commitment from her, maybe even a permanent one. He felt Ireland calling him back to it but he ignored it, ignored it as he ignored everything about his past life. He could live with her forever, he thought, could become immersed in the elixir of her and not miss anything he'd known before her, not Jennifer or Sinead or any of the other things he once imagined were important to him.

29

As the days went on she talked less about the idea of him going with her. Whenever he brought it up she changed the subject. He thought she regretted suggesting it in the first place. It put a demand on her, a demand she couldn't fulfil. In some ways he regretted she made it too. If she hadn't, there might have been more of a chance of her coming back to him after her work was finished.

He felt her growing away from him but she denied it when he said it to her.

'Sometimes I think your experiences with your father made you distrust all men,' he said.

'Oh,' she said, 'We're getting Freudian now, are we?'

'It's not Freud, it's just common sense.'

'Well it's bullshit. Believe it or not, his horriblenesss made me appreciate men more. I don't take their nice sides for granted.'

'Does that include me?'

'You more than anyone.'

'But you still refuse to commit yourself to me.'

'You'd regret it if I did.'

'Why can't you let me be the judge of that?'

'Because I know myself. It's not you I don't trust, it's me.'

'That sounds like a line from a bad book.'

'Whatever it sounds like, it's true.'

She started doing overtime in the bar. She said it was because her money was low but he took it more as a sign that she wanted to be away from him. He hardly saw her at all now.

She reared up on him when he offered to collect her from work one day.

'Why would you want to do that?' she said, 'It only takes me a few minutes to drive home.'

'It would give me something to do 'Otherwise I'll just lounge around the apartment like a beached whale.' He was clocking off work in mid-afternoon now in his own job now.

'Okay,' she said, 'If you want.' But there was no enthusiasm in her voice.

He wanted to get their relationship back on track. A bottle of wine might work, he told himself. He cooked lasagne as well, the old faithful. He left it simmering in the oven before leaving the apartment that night. The wine sat in the middle of the table surrounded by candles.

He had mixed feelings as he walked to the bar. Maybe he was invading her space. When he got there it was closing; she was serving her last few customers. He didn't announce himself but he felt she saw him out of the corner of her eye as he sat down. She didn't acknowledge him.

As he watched her finishing her shift he was shocked by her appearance. For the first time since he'd met her she looked all of her 26 years. Up until now he'd seen her more as a precocious child than a woman but in the harsh light of the bar she looked almost haggard. She'd been losing weight for a few weeks now. She had bags under her eyes from sleepless nights.

She was trembling when she came over to him.

'What's wrong?' he said.

'We had some difficult people in tonight. It took me all my willpower not to lay one of them out.'

'You should throw in the job now that you have so much going on.'

'If only life was that simple.'

She marched towards the exit, nodding for him to follow her. He felt like her lapdog.

She broke every red light she came to on the way back to the apartment. When they reached it she parked the Land Rover on the kerb at a diagonal angle.

'Is that wise?' he said, 'Having it like that all night?' but she just shrugged.

As soon as she got inside she smelt the lasagne.

'You cooked a meal!' she said.

She saw the wine and the candles.

'Is this Valentine's Day?'

'I wanted to do something special for you. I know how hard you've been working.'

She threw herself into a chair.

'Sorry for being such a bitch. I shouldn't be taking my bad moods out on you.'

'Don't worry about it. Things go in one ear and out the other with me. Why don't we just sit down and have a quiet evening together?'

'I wish I could but I'm bunched. I feel ashamed I can't show my appreciation for this. Would you forgive me if I went to bed? Can it keep till tomorrow?'

He put his head in his hands.

'I know this is bad of me,' she said, 'I'm touched by what you did.'

'Would you not even stay up for a few minutes?'

'I'd probably fall asleep if I did. I know that's terrible of me after all the trouble you went to.'

'It's not just the meal. You're different.'

'You think so?'

He couldn't take her dismissiveness. It goaded him into a confrontation.

'Are you seeing someone else?'

'What are you talking about? Don't be crazy.'

'I want to know.'

'I'm not going to answer that dumb question.'

He took the lasagne from the oven. He shovelled it into the bin.

'What did you do that for?' she said.

'What was the point of keeping it?'

She shook her head as if she was the one who was hard done by. A few seconds later she went into the bedroom. He followed her in. She got into the bed.

'Are you okay?' he asked but she didn't answer.

She put her head under the duvet. He knew from previous experience there was no way she'd talk to him when she did that so he went back to the kitchen.

He picked at bits of the lasagne that were left in the oven but it had no taste. He gathered the plates up and put them in the cupboard. He scraped the remaining food into the bin.

When he went back into the bedroom she was sweating.

'What's wrong?' he said.

'I don't know.'

'You're run down. You need to see a doctor.'

'I've never been to one in my life. They only put you on pills and I don't take pills. I know what's wrong with me. My resistance is shot, that's all. It's a bug. I'll ride it out. It usually takes a few days. That's all there is to it.'

He slept on the sofa that night. He hadn't been on it since the first night. Maybe, he thought, things would end as they began.

When he woke up the next morning he saw her uniform hanging on a peg. It was never there at that time. Had she not gone to work?

He went into her room and saw her lying there.

'Would you be an angel and make me a cup of tea?' she said.

He made it and brought it into her. She started coughing as she drank it. She took a handkerchief from under her pillow and blew into it. She was getting up phlegm.

'Would you mind ringing in sick for me?' she said.

'I wish you'd let me call a doctor. That's what you need.'

'We've already had this conversation.'

He spent the morning watching television. She was asleep most of the time. After a few hours she emerged in her bathrobe. She mixed a concoction that reminded him of the one she'd made for him the day he'd had the bad hangover. She knocked it back in one swallow. He didn't ask her what was in it.

She went back to her room. He lay down on the sofa but he couldn't sleep. After a while he heard her snoring. It was ages before he nodded off. He woke up briefly and heard her moaning. She seemed to be having a bad dream. He wondered what tangled emotions were in her head. He couldn't make out the words she was saying.

He woke at dawn. She was already up, moving around the kitchen in her uniform.

'How was your night?' she said.

'Not too good. I was awake for most of it.'

'People always think that. I came out around three or four and you were snoozing like a baby.'

'How are you?'

'Cured. Doctor Mia's concoction worked.'

She started doing herself up at the mirror.

'Don't tell me you're going to work. You'll get a relapse of your bug.'

'It's gone now. I know this bug. We're almost on first name terms now. It's a 24-hour one. You could almost set your clock by it.'

'Maybe you don't know yourself as well as you think you do.'

She blew him a kiss.

'I'm off now. Don't do anything I might.'

She gave him a wave and then she was gone. How could she do a 360-degree turn like that and expect him to accept it?

Maybe because she'd been doing that all along. And he'd been doing that all along.

He didn't know what to do with the day. He wasn't able to go to work. His boss rang but when he saw his number he didn't answer the phone. What was the point? He'd be leaving America soon anyway. One of these days he'd give the job up. He'd just go in and collect whatever money was owed to him. They'd have his position filled in the blink of an eye. It would be like the pizza job.

He wandered round the apartment in a daze, half-watching television as he button-hopped from channel to channel. She rang him at one stage to say she wouldn't be home till late that night.

'Another conference,' she said, 'Dullsville.'

'Okay,' he said in a dead voice. The conversation was over within a minute.

It was after midnight when she came home.

He'd sat up waiting for her. When she came in she hardly looked at him. He watched her putting a manuscript away in a drawer.

'How did it go?' he said.

'It was diabolical.'

'Did you speak?'

'No.'

She shuffled around the room taking things out of folders and putting them into other ones. It reminded him of the first night when she was moving her boxes around.

'You're not really here, are you?' he said when he realised she wasn't going to talk to him.

'Sorry?' she said. She always pretended she didn't hear something when she was in a bad mood.

'You're not really here.'

'What's that supposed to mean?'

'I talk to you but you don't answer me. Sometimes you're not even aware you're doing it. That's what worries me most.'

'Maybe I have that attention deficit thing,' she said.

He couldn't take any more of her sarcasm.

'Why do I always feel I'm on a string with you,' he said, 'no matter how long we spend together?'

'Easy on,' she said, 'You work me up when you talk that way.'

'I need to know where we're going?'

'You mean as regards Africa?'

'You know what I mean.'

She stopped what she was doing.

'Look,' she said, 'There are 101 things on my mind at the moment. When I get them sorted we'll sit down and have a talk.'

He suggested going out for a drink with her but she said she'd prefer a swim. He should have known.

They drove down to the beach again, her perennial haven when things got too much for her. The journey was like a blur to him. He was so focussed on what was happening between them they might as well have been driving to the moon.

'Wake up,' she said when they got there, 'You were in a trance.'

They walked along the strand. The sun shone on the water, making the waves look like so many diamonds.

'Am I getting too possessive of you?' he said.

For once she took his question seriously.

'I'm feeling down. It's nothing to do with you.' He felt down too but it was everything to do with her.

In the next few days he tried to figure out a way to hold on to her without her feeling he was crowding her. She was on the phone a lot about her trip. Whenever she rang the airport she didn't tell him if she was booking seats for one person or two. Did it matter? She could drop him just as easily in Ghana as on Rockaway Beach.

He phoned home. He told lies about where he was, lies that weren't believed because he didn't tell them with any conviction.

'Where are you?' Bartley said to him on one call, 'Your visa must be close to running out by now.'

'I haven't checked.'

'What are you doing with yourself?'

'Moving from place to place.'

'What about Edie?'

'I'm still hoping to see her.'

He told Mia he was thinking of giving in his notice to the advertising job.

'Don't do that,' she said, 'Hang on to it for a while more. It's easy money.'

'I can't see the logic of that. I'll be going back to Ireland soon anyway.'

He was saying it to see if she'd try and stop him but she didn't. She was in her own world now. They were like two magnets that drew away from one another, two trains hurtling in different directions.

September ran on. His visa would be running out soon. He felt he should take the bull by the horns and leave her. He could go up to his aunt for few weeks and then fly home. That was what a sensible person would have done. But he didn't want to be sensible. He was still clinging to his dream.

He gave a week's notice to his boss. As he expected, he wasn't too bothered. Now that he was gone in his mind he found it difficult to concentrate. He had to quote page lengths to customers, differing rates for colour or black and white ads. His mind was miles away. He could have been giving away the space for half nothing for all he knew. The people at the other desks were intrigued by him. It was a blessed release when he walked out of the building for the last time. He thought they must have been relieved to see him go.

She gave up her own job the next day.

'Was it because of me?' he said.

'No. I need a get myself organised before I leave.'

She didn't say 'before *we* leave.' It was all he needed to hear.

'We're like two hoboes now,' she said. It reminded him of the time with Sinead after they started boycotting the lectures in the university.

When October came in they were around one another more than ever but communicating less. She refused to answer him anytime he asked her if his visa had come through for Africa. He did so only from a vague curiosity.

Maybe the application had been rejected, he thought, and she hadn't told him. Or maybe it was accepted and she told them not to bother, that things had changed. Anything was possible. Either way he didn't care much.

One day in the second week of October she collected all her luggage and put it in the corner of the bedroom. It was his signal to lgo.

But he didn't.

Her father phoned the next day. He pleaded with her not to go. She was polite to him but she told him she'd made her mind up. He offered her a large sum of money to stay but she only laughed.

'You should have taken the money and still gone,' Brian said, 'It would have come in handy now that you're not working.'

'I couldn't have lived with myself if I did that.'

She sold the Land Rover. Now they had to walk everywhere. Their tempers grew short with one another.

They argued about nothing. Maybe, he thought, most of their arguments were about nothing. Maybe all arguments were.

He always felt their relationship would end when the summer did. He was her seasonal fling. When the weather got bad she'd fly to Africa like the migrant birds. She'd leave him teetering in her wake.

She started inviting her friends around to the apartment. There were farewell parties thrown by people he didn't know. This was the other side of her life, the one she only half-invited him into. A few of the customers from the bar were at them, people she liked to act the diva with. He felt she pretended to be in better form than she was on these nights, putting on an act for them that everything was fine. And maybe for herself as well. He usually went to bed early on these nights, burying his head under the pillow as the noise became more raucous.

Sometimes things would get broken if people got too drunk. One night the police were called after a neighbour complained. The following morning she acted as if nothing happened, fending off his questions her about how the night went.

Their conversations became banal. They talked about small things to avoid having to discuss big ones. He felt irrelevant. He was like a man returning to a port after a pointless odyssey to a foreign land. He searched her face for signs of emotion but he couldn't see any. She even stopped talking about Africa. Was Jane Fonda turning into Audrey Hepburn?

He went down to the sea without telling her where he was going. He swam up and down the coast angrily, trying to burn his desire for her out of himself. He wavered between leaving and staying, between a life of adventure and one of routine. At the beginning of the summer life had opened out for him like a flower but now that flower was being stamped into the ground.

He felt they were heading for a confrontation but he shied away from it. The pain of being with her seemed marginally better than that of being alone. Did she feel the same way? Hardly.

Each day he waited for an explosion but when it came it was a silent one.

'I've decided to go to Africa alone,' she said one evening after they'd had their tea, 'for both our sakes.'

He smiled to himself at the inevitability of it all.

'I was expecting that,' he said.

'You were? That's funny because I wasn't.'

'I don't think you ever really wanted to bring me with you.'

'That's not true. It's that things have been ganging up on me lately. I'd be no company for you.'

'You know I wouldn't mind that.'

'It wouldn't be fair to you though. And I'd be gone a lot of the time.'

'You are here too,' he said.

She laughed. Maybe she was relieved he was being frivolous. But it was only a cover. She had to have known that.

'Is there nothing I can do to change your mind?'

'No.'

'I thought not.'

'I'm sorry if I haven't been myself these past few weeks. Everything has been getting to me – the bar, planning the trip, even my father's phone call to you. I feel bad you were caught in the crossfire.'

'What's going to happen with us after you get back?'

'That's up to you,' she said but he knew it wasn't. Nothing ever had been since the day he met her.

She was out most of the time coming up to her flight date. He felt she wanted him to go to Boston but she didn't say anything. Was she afraid of hurting him? If she was it was too late. He'd gone beyond that into another place now.

She started selling her furniture. One of her friends from the bar bought the sofa. Another one bought some chairs. She rang her landlord to tell him she was leaving. He called one night to return her deposit.

'You're one of the best tenants I ever had,' he told her.

'You should see it when you're not here,' she said.

She was jocose with other people but serious with Brian. Her face was telling him to go but she wouldn't voice the words.

The tension was killing him. He decided to bring things to a head. One night when she was at yet another farewell party – he hadn't been invited – he put his things into a gymbag. He left it in the hallway.

The hours crawled to midnight. He sat in the darkness of the living-room waiting for her to come home.

He felt his heart going fast as he finally heard her footsteps coming up the drive. The key turned in the door.

When she got in she tripped over the bag. She started laughing. He came out of the living-room.

'Have you been in the dark?' she said.

She was drunk.

'Yes.'

'Why?'

'I don't know. It felt pleasant.'

She burped. Her eyes looked glassy.

'Have you been drinking?'

'A bit. Why did you leave your bag there?'

He didn't answer. She looked him up and down, wobbling on her feet.

'Are you going somewhere?'

Again he didn't answer. She held onto the wall for support.

'What's going on?' she said, 'You look strange.'

He stood in front of her, feeling confident with her for maybe the first time since he'd met her.

'I'm leaving,' he said.

'Don't be ridiculous. Sit down and have a drink with me.'

He didn't move. She looked at him intently.

'Jesus, you're serious.'

'Yes.'

'May I ask why?'

'I can't take your uncertainty anymore.'

'About what?'

'Everything.'

She wobbled from foot to foot.

'I have to pee,' she said.

She went into the bathroom. He heard the toilet flushing. When she came out she'd sobered up.

'Maybe now you'll tell me what this little performance is about.'

'It's not a performance.'

She screwed up her eyes in that way she had.

'I'm coming back to Rockaway after Africa. I'd like you to be here for me.'

'You didn't say that before.'

'Well I'm saying it now.'

'What am I supposed to do while you're gone – pine for you in an apartment without furniture?'

'I thought you were going to see your aunt.'

'And then what? Wait for my visa to run out? Do you want me to be arrested? Would you visit me in jail when you get back?'

'Don't be dramatic. You're not going back to the university. You can stay in the States on a visitor's visa.'

'What am I supposed to do for money?'

'What's wrong with doing the kinds of jobs you've been doing when you're not on anyone's books?'

'You've sold your furniture. How can I believe you when you say you'll be back?'

'I didn't say I'd be back to this apartment. You know me, I live life on the wing. If you're willing to take a gamble with me somewhere else maybe we can make a go of things. I'll have my head together better then.'

'No. It's too late.'

'Why?'

'For a hundred reasons. You know them and I know them.'

'No I don't.'

'Why don't you admit it? It's written all over your face.'

'I don't know what I'm meant to say. Can you not just leave things as they are?'

'How can I? You're like two people. Only one of them is with me.'

He felt he was double-bluffing her, forcing her to an ultimatum.

'That's just your perception of things.'

'No, it's the way things are.'

She went into the kitchen. He heard her shuffling around. When she came out she had a glass of vodka in her hand.

'Want some?' she said, holding it out to him.

'Are you trying to get the courage to tell me it's over?'

'Come on. You know I never needed courage for anything like that.'

'Then put the drink down.'

On their first night together she'd tried to stop him drinking. Now he was trying to stop her. The wheel had come full circle.

She went into the bedroom. with her drink. It was over.

He took up his bag and walked out the door. She stayed in the room as he went out. He didn't look back.

He could feel her eyes burrowing through him as he went down the driveway. He felt sick but free, alive and dead at the same time.

He walked towards the motel. He felt in control of the situation for the first time. His head felt light. He could hardly feel his feet touching the ground.

She was gone. He kept saying it to himself to make it sink in. If he said it enough it would be something he could deal with, something in the past that couldn't be changed.

He got to the main road. The day was hazy, the sun beating down on him. It looked huge, like a neon moon. He felt tiny under it. He felt like a midget in a vast landscape of strangeness.

He tried to walk fast. He knew if he didn't he'd be tempted to go back. An intangible force propelled him on.

The hotel looked different when he reached it. He hardly recognised it as the place he'd stayed in before. It was empty except for the man behind the desk. He was the same man who'd been there that first night, the man with the round face. He remembered him. 'Welcome back,' he said smiling. He gave him the same room he'd been in before.

He walked up to it. The first time he went up these stairs he'd been flushed with excitement. Now he was flat. He thought of the morning years ago after he'd been with Jennifer for the first time, how flat he'd felt then too. He threw his bag on the bed. There was a phone on the bedside locker, the same phone he'd used to ring Mia that morning. He lay on the bed looking out at the darkness of the night.

He didn't expect to sleep but he did. He dreamt of her in the sea, swimming away from him to some distant place as he called after her, her head bopping up and down in the water until it became little more than a dot on the horizon.

30

He rang the airport the following morning to make the arrangements to go home. It was easy enough to do because he had an open ticket. It was just a matter of filling in the date.

He wasn't sure how to fill the day. He watched television for a while and then went out for a walk. It rained in the afternoon. The people in the room next to him were having a barbecue. He watched them laughing as they ran for cover with their cocktail sausages in their hands.

The past and the future merged in his mind. He thought about what happened to him and what might happen next. Ireland meant nothing to him now. It stretched before him like a blank canvas. He would be returning to it only in his body. His mind would be with a woman he'd probably never see again.

The rain continued. It was so torrential it reminded him of Irish rain. Was God trying to prepare him for going back? It came down in sheets. He looked out at the deserted balconies of the other apartments. The barbecue people were nowhere to be seen. They were probably hunkering down inside. they left the lingering smell of burnt food behind them.

He didn't make any contact with her over the next few days. He knew she wouldn't have expected him to. He thought he might make a call to her before he got on the plane but he wasn't sure. He wondered if things could have worked out differently for them. If he'd chosen a different destination than Rockaway Beach that day at the Greyhound bus station would there have been another Mia in it? Was there a Mia in Maine? Or Memphis? Was it his self-destructiveness that created all the problems?

He rang Bartley.

'We were beginning to give up on you,' he said, 'What's happening?'

'I've bought my ticket,' he said, 'I'll be home next week.'

'I'm delighted to hear that. Did you visit Edie?'

'I'm afraid not.'

'Oh.'

He could hear the disappointment in his voice. He knew he should have felt guilty but Edie was the last thing on his mind now.

'I'm not going back to the university either,' he said then. It was as well to get everything out when he was in the frame of mind not to be awkward about it. There was a pause on the line. He sensed the disappointment again.

'That surprises me,' he said, 'You were doing so well.'

'I'll tell you everything when I get home.'

He rang his aunt then. It wasn't an easy call for him to make. A wave of guilt passed over him as he dialled her number. It was only slightly erased by her warm tone as she answered.

'I thought it might be you,' she said, 'You're probably ringing to say you don't have enough time to see me.'

'You read my mind. I'm so sorry. I have no excuse.'

'Don't worry about it. I know how things happen. I was young once too, believe it or not.'

'You still are. I know that from all the stories I've heard about you.'

'I don't know about that but thank you. I've heard stories about you too.'

'Probably bad ones.'

'On the contrary.'

'Anyway I have to apologise to you again. You're very good to forgive me. I had great intentions of going up to you but everything just caught up on me.'

'It's always the way. You should have come earlier.'

'That was the plan. I should have stuck to it. Things that are put off often never get done. Maybe I'll see you next summer. If you'll have me.'

'Nothing would please me more. I've enjoyed our chats over the phone, brief and all as they were. I can hear Bartley in your voice.'

'I don't think he'll be as understanding as you about me not getting to see you.'

'I told him not to put pressure on you.'

'It wasn't pressure. I really wanted to see you.'

'I'm afraid I'm rather boring.'

'I doubt that. From what Dad tells me, you've led quite a life.'

'Most of it the wrong way, sad to say.'

She paused for a moment. He wasn't sure whether to say anything or not. How could he? He'd never even met her. If they sat down for a four hour conversation maybe they could have talked personally. He could have told her about all the things that were going on in his life and she could have told him the things that were going on in hers. It would have been ludicrous to attempt anything like that on a phone call made to cancel a meeting.

The moment passed.

'What about you,' she said, 'Did you have a good summer?'

'Fantastic. Maybe I'll get to tell you about it someday. It would have been even better if you were in it.'

'You're too kind, Brian. I wish I met you.'

'We'll do it sometime. Goodbye, aunt Edie.'

'Goodbye. Mind yourself. Give my love to Bartley and Declan.'

After he put down the phone he felt better. How was it that some people had a way of relaxing you without even trying? If he'd gone to Boston instead of Rockaway he might have had the summer of his life. Or at least one free of pain. But maybe pain was necessary in life. Maybe it was what made a man of you. Maybe Mia made a man of him.

He thought she might contact him in the next few days but she didn't. Then one night he saw her on the pier with another man. He owned one of the shops in the area that sold scuba diving gear. He was a jock, one of those types for whom life seemed to come easy. He'd only had a few conversations with him. His mind unpolluted by thought, he gravitated pleasantly from surfboard to surfboard, from one gorgeous woman to another. They'd talked about him a few times over the sumer. She always said she didn't care much for him.

They were laughing. A week ago it might have upset him to see that. Now it didn't. He hadn't expected her to miss him.

He saw her once more before he went home. It was by arrangement. He rang her. He was surprised at how relaxed he was dialling her number. She was relaxed too as she answered. They talked about all the practical things – his flight date, how he felt about going home, her own African plans

He asked her if she'd like to meet him for a coffee. She waited a few seconds before saying yes.

They met in a café they used to frequent in the early days of the summer, one of the places tourists went to for light snacks. It was beside the beach. There was no talk of swimming now or anything else that once excited them. She was wearing sunglasses even though there wasn't much sun. Her hair was tied neatly in a bun. She had an anorak on her. When she took it off he saw she was wearing her white blouse and her black leather skirt, the combination she'd worn that first night after she got out of her uniform. He was in a shirt he'd bought from a stall a few days before, one of those gaudy ones tourists tended to buy to put them in the holiday mood. Maybe he was trying to appear upbeat, to fool himself into thinking he had his mind set on other things than her.

'You look different,' she said.

'In what way?'

'More assertive maybe.'

'My future beckons. I have to dress accordingly.'

'Is this the new and improved Brian Kilcoyne?'

'To be sure. Onwards and upwards to world domination.'

'So when are you off to Africa?'

'Tuesday, God willing. Or maybe I should say the devil.'

'How are the preparations going?'

'They're manic. Everything is haywire.'

'Are you looking forward to it?'

She took off her glasses. She started fiddling with them, rubbing the lens with the corner of her blouse.

'Now that it's finally happening I'm getting apprehensive. What about you? Will you find it difficult to get a job in Ireland if you don't go back to your studies?'

'I'll probably find it difficult to stay in one even if I do.'

'I suppose you've been on to your father.'

'I have. He's giving me grief about not going to Boston.'

'I felt he would.'

'I talked to her. She was fine about it. What about you? Have you heard from your own father?'

'He keeps ringing off the hook. He must have me on repeat dial. He won't give up.'

'Who does that remind me of?'

She gave him a punch.

They walked down the promenade towards the beach. The sun was starting to sink. It was the same walk they'd always gone on, the same sights they saw, the same smells of seafood they got from the roadside cafes. But none of it seemed real to him now. They were finished with one another. He was seeing it from a dream, from someone else's past.

The sun fell lower. Clouds hovered along the ridges of the mountains. The moonlight fell on her face. They sat on the pier watching the sun go down. As the last glint of it disappeared he felt a sensation. It was like a key closing in a lock.

A breeze got up. She shivered. The waves thrashed.

'The sea looks wild tonight,' she said.

'I love it when it's like that.' It was almost turquoise in colour.

He put his arms around her. He didn't know why. Maybe he was trying to encase her in a cocoon one last time.

'That's nice,' she said. But she said it as a sister might, not a lover. Or even an ex-lover. He didn't mention that he'd seen her with the other man. Maybe she knew.

'What now?' he said.

'This is where the string quartet comes in.'

She mimed the playing of a violin. He smiled.

'You'll have a lot to tell them back home,' she said.

He thought of Ireland, of a future he once imagined he could escape with her. Maybe she was another element of that foolishness.

'You mean *not* tell them.'

'Does your father know you're dropping out of college?'

'Yes. He's probably lining up a few fields for me to plough as a punishment.'

'The cows will have missed you.'

'There are only a few left. It's not much fun on the farm these times.'

'Take off again if you're not happy. Life is too short for doing what you don't want.'

'Don't worry. If nothing else, you've cured me of compromising.'

'I'll take that as a compliment.'

The sun disappeared below the horizon. It was like a light being switched off. She stood up. He thought she looked sad suddenly, but even more beautiful for that.

'I'll never forget you,' he said, 'You know that, don't you?'

'Easy on the schmaltz. Crying ruins my mascara.'

'You might remember me too.'

'How could I not?'

'Will there be anything that stands out?'

'Probably that first night in the bar.'

'Please, not that.'

'Of all the gin joints in all the world,' she said, mimicking Humphrey Bogart's voice from *Casablanca*, 'he walked into mine. '

He tried to laugh but he couldn't. The conversation was over. She was back to her efficient self as she zipped up her anorak.

'I'm not good with goodbyes,' she said, 'so I'm going to go now. But before I do I want to say one thing. You're the only man I could ever have loved. Maybe that's why it didn't work out for us.'

'You don't want to fall in love?'

'It wouldn't work for me. Love takes over your life and I couldn't have that.'

He wasn't sure if she was giving him a line or if she meant it.

'Say hello to Dublin for me,' she said.

'Hello, Dublin,' he said.

'And whatever you do, don't ever get old.'

'That might be a bit harder.'

He looked at her a last time to make sure he'd remember her forever. But he knew he would.

She walked away from him. He was hoping she'd look back but she didn't.

He thought of the way she'd ended her other relationships - quickly, like an executioner. A part of him was glad. You had to tear the plaster off quickly or it hurt more.

He kept looking back to see would she turn but she didn't. She got smaller and smaller as she went farther away from him. It was just like the way she was in the sea. This was a different kind of drowning.

It got dark. He wanted to drink himself stupid in some bar but he knew that would be the coward's way out. He had to face up to what had happened, face it now and tomorrow. And all the tomorrows.

He started to walk back to the motel. Seagulls screeched above him as they skimmed across the sky. They seemed to be serenading his departure from this blessed, cursed place.

He sat on a bench trying to collect his thoughts. Everything looked different without her. It was as if he was seeing the world without its clothes on. Nothing tried to be attractive. The sky was dull. There was nobody on the streets. The buildings looked like deserted film sets being photographed by a bad camera-man.

He stood up. His legs felt heavy. Ahead of him a couple were embracing. He was jealous of them, jealous of two people he didn't even know. Was this normal? Was he always going to be this mean-minded?

He imagined her back in her apartment, relieved maybe that the meeting had gone well, that he wasn't too clingy. He'd acted as if he was over her but he knew he wasn't. Maybe she did too.

He walked through the streets they'd been in over the summer. The ice cream man was gone. Everywhere looked barren. The sailing boats were empty.

The journey back to the hotel was made worse by the sight of more landmarks, more triggers to memories that were nothing now but that, pale re-treads of what he once had, what he took for granted as people always took for granted what was easily had.

When he got back to the motel he told the man at the desk he'd be checking out the next day. He said he'd make up the bill.

He went up to his room and sat on the bed. He had a pain in his stomach. He was too awake to sleep and too tired to do anything else. He knew he couldn't ring her again. He felt the emptiness more now than on the night he left her. He was angry with himself, angry that he'd played a game with her, a game of pretending he didn't care as much as he did.

The room was dark except for the chinks of light that drifted in from the moon. He sat listening to the roar of the waves, the tinkling of the sailboats. They were like billiard balls clicking together.

He went over to the window. He looked out at the bay, at the houses that surrounded it. What lives were lived in them, he wondered, what dreams dreamed? How many hundreds of people would go through what he what he went through and conquer it – or not conquer it?

The thought relaxed him. It made him feel clean and clear in his head. He told himself he was a member of something now, the club of those who'd loved and lost, the club of the human race. He thought of the first night he saw her, watching her cleaning the glasses as he tried to work up the courage to ask her out. If she said no would he have been better off? Was an appetite never indulged better than one that was satisfied and then taken away?

It would be difficult to go back to Ireland, he knew, difficult to sober into the future. But it would happen. It would happen with the same ease with which his departure from it had happened.

What did it matter that she was gone? That was life. It was like snakes and ladders. One day you were excited about something and then the next it went away. You put up skittles and knocked them down again and when they were all gone you were more content than you could have been any other way. It was need that was the enemy. If you had no needs you wouldn't be disappointed. You would be pure.

His flight was for the following evening. He'd get the bus to New York and get the shuttle from there to the airport. He found his eyes becoming heavy.

As he drifted into sleep the words of a song came into his head: 'Where do you go to, my lovely, when you're alone in your bed. Tell me the thoughts that surround you, I want to look inside your head.' He'd never got inside that head because she'd never let him. Maybe he hadn't wanted to for fear it would destroy her mystery.

He woke up at dawn. It was too early to have breakfast. The bus wasn't leaving until the early afternoon. He'd probably get a taxi to the station.

He decided to go down to the beach. Was there a chance she might be there? Would they have had anything to say to each other if she was?

The wind was up when he got there. It blew the spray from the waves onto the wall that ran along the promenade, scaring the seagulls away. It was so strong he could only take small steps.

Every few minutes he had to stop to catch his breath. The waves thundered in on the strand, slushing their way to the dunes. Big globs of foam lay along the coastline like yellow candy floss.

He sat at the rocks thinking about the other times he was there – the first night he watched her swimming, the night the Land Rover was clamped, the times they came down because they were feeling good and the nights they came down to make themselves feel good. Thinking about it didn't help him. It was gone. It might have never happened, all of it.

There was nobody on the strand. When he was with her they always wanted it to be like that. 'It's our beach,' he used to say to her, 'We own it.' But now the emptiness made him feel lonely.

The sand looked more grey than gold. Or was that just the way he was seeing it? He looked out at the driftwood thrown up by the departing waves. The wind was blowing them towards the dunes, making little necklaces of foam. Seaweed lay in clumps around him like dirty grass.

He remembered the way she used to be as she swam by his side, merging with the water or dunking him under it when she felt playful. She would swim on some other beach now with a different partner as she developed other needs, as new affections took the place of old ones. So it was and so it would always be, like the changing face of the sea or the sun, like the changing face of love and the death of love.

The boardwalk was deserted. Seagulls shrieked above it, swirling around in the sky like so many buzzards. Everything in front of him shimmered: the road, the beach, the sky. He felt he was seeing things

231

through a gauze. His eyelids became heavy. He wanted to sleep, to forget everything that happened.

Driftwood blew onto the shore. A flock of swallows scudded across the waves like a tiny squadron of planes. In the distance was the rollercoaster. It looked forlorn now that there were no tourists on it. It was like a dead beast from some primitive kingdom.

There was a carousel beside it. Behind it a tent advertised a dinosaur-like creation It excited a group of children standing beside it. He watched them queueing up for tickets to get in. They jumped up and down with anticipation. There was a time he would have been happy for them. Now he was just neutral. They might as well have been characters from a film he was watching.

A seagull flew above him. He had a shell in his mouth. He dropped it onto the sand. He was trying to crack it but the sand was too soft. He picked it up with his beak and flew over to where the tarmac was. Then he dropped it again. He swooped down, reaching the ground almost as soon as it did. This time it cracked and he was able to eat what was inside it.

The day was warm. He took his shoes off and went into the water. It felt pleasant. There were stones under his feet. They slushed as the waves eddied back and forth around him. Once or twice he thought he heard her voice whispering through them. She was still the mermaid he'd once compared her to.

Would she be with someone else now? Might there even be someone on the plane to Africa? She'd been secretive about her plans. Maybe the man he saw her with on the promenade was going with her. Maybe that had been the intention all along.

She'd be more natural with one of her own, someone with the same toughness, someone who wouldn't be awed by her.

He was. That was his mistake. Idolatry was boring.

He thought of her beauty, her shapeliness, a dress she used to wear that showed too many of her curves for the good of his heart. It all wound up to an impossible formula. Was she real or had he dreamt her up? If he hadn't met her he wouldn't have believed she could have existed.

She was beyond him now. Maybe she always had been. He'd get over her in time but for now he didn't want to. He wanted to wallow in the memory of her. Thinking of her prolonged her existence in his life no matter how painful that might be. It was like the aftershock of an earthquake. She was there but not there, a presence to be indulged as the first step to his expulsion of her.

The day grew misty. The mountains in the distance were only vaguely visible. A plane flew overhead. It left a plume of smoke that seemed to bisect the sky. That would be him tomorrow.

He came out of the sea. He put his shoes back on. He walked back towards the hotel.

Her voice came into his head, a vague sound at the edge of memory. He imagined her digging wells in Africa, standing up to governments, creating havoc anytime she saw injustice. He didn't know if she'd achieve as much as she thought. If she didn't it wouldn't be for the want of trying. Maybe it didn't matter. Her failures would have been more exciting than most people's successes. She'd fight tooth and nail to get what she wanted. The only battle she could never win would be the one against herself, against her restlessness. He had that in common with her.

As he passed her apartment he stopped for a moment. He looked in at it. He thought of her making her last preparations, her mind already on the next challenge, the next frontier. The driveway looked empty without the Land Rover. The blinds were down. It was like another part of the closure.

He got to the hotel. The man behind the desk smiled at him.

'You're up early,' he said.

'The early bird gets the worm,' he said.

He asked him to prepare the bill.

'It's been nice having you,' he said.

He looked like a lonely man. Nobody ever talked to him. They just signed in and out.

He went up to his room. It was as quiet as a graveyard. Everything looked mechanical suddenly. It looked like nothing, the nothing that was his life. He looked out the window. The sky was pale. It was cloudless. Trees swayed in the wind. People walked up and down like ghosts.

He rang for a taxi. As he was waiting for it to arrive he went down to pay his bill. They were serving breakfast in the restaurant but he didn't want it. He brought a cup of coffee up to his room.

He sat there looking at some photographs he had of her in his wallet. She was in the water in one of them. In another one she was serving a customer in the bar. She was laughing. A third one had the two of them together. They were eating ice cream on the promenade.

He spread them out before him on the floor. Were they a record of their time together or a few insignificant snaps? He looked at them with a mixture of fondness and regret. They lay scattered around him on the carpet like a worn-out deck of cards.

31

A few hours later he sat in the airport in New York waiting for his flight to be announced. He didn't feel tired even though he hadn't been sleeping much in the last few days. He rang Bartley during one of the delays that seemed to be unpreventable in airports.

'You're good to call,' he said when he heard his voice, 'It seems like years since we saw you.'

'I hope you don't mind about the university.'

'Whatever you decide is fine by me.'

'Are you sure?'

'It's only a piece of paper.'

'Can you meet me at the airport? Would it be too far for you?'

'It would make my day. And Angela's too. Just give me the time.'

Angela's name had been coming into the conversations every time he talked to him now. He didn't know why that should have surprised him. No doubt they were together all the time now. It shouldn't have mattered to him but it did.

It was raining when he got on the plane. In a way it relaxed him, making him feel he was home already. It was great to hear the Irish accent again. There was something comforting in that too.

He sat in his seat. He looked out the window at the clouds above him, the sea below. It was like an infinity of space. An air hostess came around with a meal after a while but he didn't feel like eating. The man in the next seat started to talk to him. He was from Philadelphia. He was on his way to Kerry to look up his Irish roots. He didn't feel like getting into it with him. If he did, the conversation would probably last for the whole journey.

An in-flight film came on. It was a comedy with Jennifer Aniston. He put on his headphones to watch it. The air hostess came round with drinks. He asked for a whiskey. He looked at the film vacantly. The whiskey made him sleepy. He nodded off with the earphones still on him.

It seemed to be only seconds later when the person sitting beside him poked him awake.

'We'll be landing soon, buddy,' he said, 'You better get your ass in high gear.'

He was groggy. As they approached Ireland he felt a rush of excitement. He looked down at the fields below him. They were spread out like a canopy, like a chessboard in green. A child in the next row to him was crying. His ears popped, making everyone's voice sound far away.

The disembarkation was delayed because of a bomb scare. Everyone started to panic but then it was discovered to be a hoax. After that the panic turned to boredom. People looked around themselves with a bewildered expression on their faces. When were they going to land? Nobody knew. The pilot apologised for the delay. Passengers who were worried about losing their lives a half hour before were now just cranky.

The sky was foggy. The plane had to circle the airport for ages before it cleared. Afterwards the pilot came on again. He said they were about to land.

The plane started its descent. An air hostess came around. She asked everyone to put on their seatbelts. Brian grimaced. He always hated the moment before the wheels hit the ground. He became a white knuckler for those moments. Maybe other people were the same. He sensed a relief from them all after the plane stopped moving. For a moment he thought they were going to applaud. He'd seen that happening in films.

Some of them stood up. They stretched their arms. Others started to take their hand luggage down from the racks. He looked out the window. The day was clear.

The pilot said, 'We've landed.'

'Really?' one of the passengers said, 'Who'd have guessed.'

Everyone moved fast. They gathered their belongings in that sudden surge of activity that often followed a lengthy period of immobility. As soon as he got out of the plane he felt his energy beginning to come back. People were running everywhere around him with frantic expressions on their faces.

He watched tourists with golf bags, backpackers with burnished faces. He wondered what happened to the people he saw on the plane when he was on the outward journey, the ones with their Stetsons and cowboy boots. Had their dreams of the summer been realised? Did they have a rollercoaster like him? Would he ever see them again?

At the duty free he bought a bottle of whiskey for Bartley and some perfume for Angela. He walked out to the luggage area. Travelling cases whirled around the conveyor belt, all shapes and sizes tumbling in on top of one another. People clambered across it to get their luggage before everyone else.

After a few minutes he saw his gymbag. It was so small by comparison it looked like something a person might bring away for a weekend. It had all his memories in it. A weekend case for a life.

Customs was easier to negotiate than it had been on the journey out. Everything was more relaxed and low key.

'Don't lose your buffalo,' the customs lady said to him as he hoisted his bag over his shoulder.

'Sorry?' he said.

'Your buffalo. It's falling out.'

It was only when he took the bag off his shoulder that he saw it. It was the buffalo mobile from the Land Rover. She must have slipped it into his bag one day when he wasn't looking. How had he not spotted it before now?

He thanked the Customs lady. She smiled.

When he got out to the Arrivals area he saw Bartley and Angela waving at him. He went over to them.

Bartley was going mad with excitement.

'I can't believe you're here!' he said, 'Is it really you?'

He hugged him. Then Angela did.

'Maybe I should put my finger into the wound,' he said.

Brian had to laugh.

'You mean like doubting Thomas?'

'The very man. Come here to me.'

He hugged him again. Brian was shocked by his appearance. He'd aged noticeably since he saw last. He'd also lost a lot of his hair. He ran what remained across the top the way people did to try and camouflage the baldness but it really only accentuated it.

He was dressed in a tweed suit instead of his more familiar torn jacket and corduroy trousers. It looked all wrong on him. He imagined Angela stuffing him into it. He had a multi-coloured tie on him that looked like it came from a Hollywood film from the 1930s. There was a blood stain on the collar of his shirt. He often had one after he shaved. It was the only thing that seemed the same about him.

'Well,' Brian said, 'Am I supposed to kiss the ground like the Pope used to?'

'No, just kiss the people who came out to meet you.'

Angela had a big smile on her face. She was dripping jewellery. She had a Burberry coat on her. She held her handbag in front of her like a child she was minding.

She looked different. She had no neck at all, he thought. Her chin seemed to fall into her shoulders.

She'd had her hair done for the occasion. It was lacquered to within an inch of its life. Her lipstick was blotched as if she put it on in a hurry.

'Look at you,' she said to Brian, 'You've turned into a man. All the women will be after you.'

'You look great yourself.'

'Thanks. I'm afraid most of it came out of a bottle.'

'I like the coat,' he said. It was what she called her 'good' one.

'She only puts it on for state occasions and bonfire nights,' Bartley said, 'She thinks she's the Queen of Sheba in it.'.

'I'm flattered.'

Brian looked at her. Before he left for America she'd had a great figure. Now it bore the evidence of too much easy living.

'Go on,' she said, 'Say it.'

'What do you mean?'

'You're staring at me with a look of shock in your eyes. You think I'm putting on weight.'

'That's not true. I was looking at your coat.'

'You're a bad liar,' she said.

He blushed.

'How are you feeling, travelling boy?' Bartley said.

'Exhausted. I'm still on American time.'

'We were about to give up on the plane landing. What was that about a bomb? You haven't joined the IRA or anything, have you?'

'No. Sorry to disappoint you.'

'Welcome back to the old sod anyway. It looks like we still can't get the planes to run on time. It used to be just good old-fashioned inefficiency. Now it's terrorism or some other malarkey. Isn't that progress?'

'The Gospel According to Bartley,' said Angela, 'Next thing he'll be running for Taoiseach.'

'A damn sight better job I'd make of the job than the present fella.'

'That's enough about that,' she said.

She stared at Brian.

'How do you think Bartley looks?'

'Mighty.'

'He's anyone's fancy in the new suit.'

'I can't stop admiring it.'

'His stomach is going on for a career of its own though.'

'I'm six months pregnant,' Bartley laughed, 'I think I'm about to have twins. What do you think I should call them?'

'Johnny Walker and Arthur Guinness if they're boys,' she said.

'Don't be smart.'

'Maybe you should lease it out and charge people to have a look.'

'You're not much better yourself,' he said, 'Am I right, Brian?'

He got awkward.

'How is Declan?' he said to change the subject.

'Very well. He sends his best.'

'So he didn't drive up.'

'No. too much pressure at work.'

Even though Newbridge was a much shorter drive than Galway he wasn't surprised.

He handed the whiskey to Bartley.

'I'm sure you'll make short work of that.'

'Never let it be said.'

'Here's something for you, Angela,' he said.

He handed her the perfume. Her eyes lit up.

'My favourite!' she gushed, 'I can't believe you got this for me.'

'It was nothing.'

'I know what this stuff costs.'

'You get a cut in the duty free.'

'Not much.'

She put a dab of it on her wrist.

'Sniff it,' she said to Bartley.

'I'm not into that sort of thing,' he said. He pushed her away.

'What about you, Brian?'

He smelt it.

'It's very nice.'

'It's a pity this latchiko here wouldn't agree.'

'I'm getting a whiff of it. Not too bad. But I still prefer cowdung.'

'Caveman.'

'Thanks very much.'

The noise around them subsided. People started to move towards taxis, waiting cars.

'Let's go for a bite to eat,' Angela said.

'I'm on for that,' Bartley said, wiping his hands.

'I knew you would be. It was Brian I was thinking about.'

They walked to a McDonald's that was beside them. Bartley went up to the counter to order. Angela sat down beside Brian at a table.

She quizzed him about the summer. He told her he'd been all over America. He couldn't bring himself to say he'd spent the whole time in one place. It would have led to too many questions. She seemed content with his clichéd delineation of the country's good and bad points.

'When did you start growing your hair so long?' she said after a few minutes, 'You look like a hippie.'

'It's been like that for a few months now.'

'Were you that badly off that you couldn't afford a haircut?'

'It wasn't the money. I was too lazy.'

Bartley came over with tea and chips.

'I heard you talking about your hair,' he said, 'It suits you.'

'At least you have something to work with,' Angela said, 'Not like Baldyboots here.'

'Thanks for the compliment.'

They started to eat.

'How do you feel to be back?' Bartley said.

'A bit strange, to be honest.'

'That'll go away once you get back into the swing of things.'

He wondered what that meant. Were there any things left to swing on the farm? Even if there were he'd hardly be the right person to swing them.

'Anything new in Loughrea?' he said.

'Nothing much,' Bartley said, 'The crops are still coming up bad. The weather is still atrocious and every day I curse my arthritis more than I did the day before. But that's enough about me. What was America like?'

'As I told Angela, it was pretty much what you'd expect. Lots of fat Yanks buying Big Macs and looking at stupid programmes on the television. For a while I thought I'd turn into one of them.'

'Did you spend most of your time in New York?'

238

'All of it.'

'It's a pity you didn't get to visit Edie. She was on to me a good few times about you.'

'She's a lovely woman. I feel really bad about mucking that up.'

'Don't worry. She understood.'

'My head was all over the place for most of the summer.'

'So I gathered from your phone calls. That's what America does to people. You're welcome to it. The land of opportunity my arse. More like the land of burn-out.'

'Now you've said it.'

He stuffed the chips into his mouth.

'Is there any ketchup to go with these?' he said to Angela.

'Look under your nose.'

There were a few packets of it on the tray. He tried to open one of them but he couldn't.

'Why do they have to pack these fucking things so tight? You'd want to be Arnold Schwarzenegger to open them.'

'Give it to me,' Angela said.

She opened one for him. He squirted it over the chips.

'You didn't bother the postman too much,' he said to Brian.

'I'm not the type to write letters. You know that. By the time you write them and get the stamp and the envelope your day is half gone.'

'The next time you go away I'm going to get someone to chain you to a letterbox. Or a phone.'

'That should be fun.'

'It's the only way we're going to hear from you.'

'When you were my age I bet you were caught up too.'

'He's still your age, Brian,' Angela said.

'The two of you should have come with me,' he said, 'You'd have loved it.'

Angela perked up at that.

'What do you think, Bartley?' she said, 'Next time?'

'I suppose you think the cows would milk themselves.'

'We could have found a way around that. All work and no play makes Bartley a dull boy.'

She winked at Brian.

'The problem with this fellow is, he doesn't want to fly. Right, Bartley?'

'Would you blame me?' he said. 'It's bad enough worrying about crashing but now you have this terrorism business. I think we'll stick with Bundoran.'

'Jesus, not Bundoran again,' she said. 'The most exciting thing you can do there is play Crazy Golf. I'll get you to the Canaries if it's the last thing

I do.'

'So what's next for you?' Bartley said to Brian, 'I mean now that you're not going back to the university.'

'I didn't expect you to take it that well.'

'Why wouldn't I? Most graduates I know are unemployed anyway as far as I can see. They're walking around the place with half the letters of the alphabet after their names and no jobs.'

'Thanks again.'

'How does it feel to be back to the bonnie shores of Erin?'

'It's a tonic. The second we touched down it brought it all back to me. It does you good to see the fields.'

'You'll be seeing a lot more of them if you hang around Loughrea.'

'I've seen the forty shades of green already.'

They stood up.

'Thanks for the money you sent me, by the way. I'd have been lost without it.'

'No problem. Money doesn't go far when you're on the move, especially in America. I was talking to a man the other day and he opened my eyes about that. His son spent the summer in Texas. He said he went into a restaurant one day and was charged twenty dollars for a coffee and a slice of cake. What do you make of that?'

'It doesn't surprise me.'

'It would want to have been a nice slice of cake,' Angela said.

'It's the atmosphere you're paying for.'

Bartley stopped suddenly as they started to walk towards the car park.

'I almost forgot,' he said, 'We have a little bit of a surprise for you.'

'A surprise?'

'We weren't going to tell you until we got home but now is as good a time as any.'

'Put me out of my suspense.'

'Okay,' he said. He took a deep breath.

'Are you ready, Angela?' he said. She giggled like a schoolgirl.

Brian knew what was coming. Maybe he knew from the moment they started waving at him. Maybe he knew from the first day she came into his house.

'We got married last month.'

His mouth went dry as he heard the words he always feared. Had he any right to expect not to hear them?

His chest constricted. He couldn't speak for a moment. There was a sinking feeling inside him. It brought back all the memories of his mother again. It felt like the last nail on her coffin.

His heart was beating fast. He found it hard to breathe.

'Congratulations,' he said.

The two of them went quiet. They looked at him. waiting for more. He didn't know what to say. How was he expected to react? With jubilation? She had to have known he didn't like her. So did Bartley.

He started stuttering. His voice went.

'Are you okay?' Angela said, 'Is it that much of a shock to you?'

'It's not a shock at all,' he said, 'I'm delighted. I expected it to happen. I just thought you'd wait for me to come back before it did.'

'Don't worry about it.'

He hugged Angela.

'Welcome to the family,' he said.

'Thank you, Brian. I'm proud to be a member of it.'

She showed him her ring. It was an extravagant one with a huge stone.

'It's beautiful,' he said, trying to sound enthusiastic.

'Sometimes I think I should have put it round her nose instead of her finger,' Bartley said.

'Shut up you.'

'Sorry I wasn't here for your big day.'

'There weren't that many people there,' Bartley said, 'Just Declan and Yvonne and some other dossers that'd go to the opening of an envelope. We didn't want to be too ostentatious.'

'That was the right way to do it.'

'Mind you, I'm surprised you didn't read about Angela's wedding dress in the papers. It was bigger news here than the 1916 centenary.'

'I must have missed them that day.'

'Don't mind him,' Angela said, 'It was nothing special. He'd have had me going up the aisle in any old rags.'

'Was it Fr. Finnerty who performed the ceremony?'

'The very man.'

'I'd say he made a nice job of it.'

'It was very dignified.'

'Weren't you very sneaky to do it so quietly?'

'We should have told you about it on the phone but you were always in such a hurry.'

'Did you have a big reception?'

'Average, I suppose, at least for the crowd that was there.'

'A great time was had by all,' Angela said, 'We danced the night away.'

'You mean *you* danced the night away,' Bartley corrected, 'At my age it's more a case of wondering if the knees are going to hold out.'

'Stop making yourself old before your time. You're not that bad.'

'Would you have come back for it,' Bartley asked Brian, 'if you knew about it?'

'It would have been awkward for me.' The truth was that he wouldn't have wanted to be there anyway even if he'd been in Galway.

'We should have told you though, or at least delayed it. It's not as if Angela was in the family way or anything.'

'What's he going to come out with next?' she said.

'Only having a laugh, dearie, only having a laugh.'

Brian didn't know why he was taking it so badly. He knew she was good for Bartley. That should have been his priority. What right had he to deny them? Everyone spoke of her as being a godsend to him rather than someone crawling into a widower's heart.

'I know I can never replace your mother,' she said. 'All I can do is my best.' It was as if she read his mind.

'Don't think like that. Just be yourself. It will be great for both of you.'

'For the three of us,' Bartley said.

They stood there awkwardly. Brian didn't know what to say. How could you follow the news of your father's wedding?

He looked around him. There were crowds of people waiting on planes. They held up boards with names like 'Hamil' and 'Zoe' on them. Once it would have been 'Sean' or 'Maura.' This was the new Ireland. When a familiar face was spotted they dropped the board and rushed towards them. He felt sorry for the people who had nobody.

'Well,' Bartley said slapping his hands together, 'I suppose we better make our way to the car.'

They started to walk. There was an escalator beside them so they got onto that. Brian's ears were still popping from the plane. He was relieved when they got outside.

'Good Irish air once again,' Angela exulted, giving him a smile.

'You mean filthy Irish air,' Bartley said.

He had a card for the parking. He put it into a machine and paid the fee. It was five euros.

'Jesus,' Angela said, 'The amount they charge these days for an hour or two. You'd imagine we were here for a week.'

They walked towards the car park. Bartley put his arms around Brian.

'We've given you our news,' he said to him, 'Now it's time for you to give us yours.'

'I don't have very much.'

'Come on, you must have something to tell us.'

'A lot of the time I was doing nothing.'

'Give me a break. You were in America, for God's sake. It's not like going to Bonniconlon.'

'You can't have excitement day in day out even if you're on the moon.'

'So that's all we're getting after you being gone for four months.'

'It's hard to think of things when people put you on the spot.'

'Leave him alone,' Angela said, 'He'll tell you in his own good time.'

'Thanks, Angela.'

They got to the car. It wasn't the Austin. It was a Hyundai.

Bartley put his chest out.

'What do you think?' he said.

He kissed the windscreen like a child.

'Where's the Austin?' Brian said.

'Did I not tell you? I put it in the shed. I haven't turned the ignition in months. It's on its last legs.'

'I wouldn't say that.'

'How would you know? You're not down here drying out spark plugs on wet Monday mornings.'

'So you dumped it and got the Hyundai.'

'Do I need your permission to buy a car now? Maybe I should have phoned you every time I was going to the bathroom to ask you if it was all right.'

The old Bartley was back.

'Stop it,' Angela said, 'The boy hasn't even got out of the airport yet and you're on his case.'

'Brian understands the way I think. Don't you, Brian?'

'Yes, but maybe I'll do it up. There might be some life in the old dog yet.'

'There isn't. I know what I'm talking about.'

'I'm not thinking of long journeys, just round the fields maybe.'

'I can't see the logic of that. By the time you pay the tax and insurance you're only throwing good money after bad. Why bother with a dying beast when you can have this glorious animal?'

He tapped the bonnet with his knuckles.

'He's proud of his Hyundai is Bartley,' Angela said, 'He practically sleeps in it.'

'It has lots of stuff in it I couldn't be bothered with, like that satnav crap.'

'I love satnav,' Angela said.

'I wouldn't give you tuppence for it. I heard of a fella last week who wrapped his car round a lamp post because of the delightful satnav. He had his eyes peeled on it instead of looking at the road ahead of him. We'll get to a time people won't know how to go down to the letterbox without checking it out. They'll go out to buy a loaf of bread in Eyre Square and end up in Timbuktu.'

Brian felt strange looking at it. It completed the strangeness he felt about everything else. Did the new car go with the new wife?

He wasn't looking forward to the journey home. He remembered some of the trips into the hospital when his mother was there. If he let Bartley take the wheel when he had drink on him they'd all have been patients. He still saw him as a liability even though he was sober today. He knew he'd be showing off in the Hyundai, pushing it to its limits like a teenager in his first car.

'I'll put your bag in the boot,' he said.

He popped it open with his remote. Brian handed it to him.

He sat in. Angela got in beside him. On previous journeys she'd stayed in the back, leaving the passenger seat for Brian. Now he was the one in the back. It was a sign of her new status. She didn't seem to be aware of it. Neither did Bartley.

The seat was wet. The back window had been left open and rain got in. There was a newspaper on the floor. He put it under him.

The smell of wet leather reminded him of days when they travelled to Galway when he was a child. It was usually raining then as well. Bartley would be cursing it. his mother would have her head out the window, looking for a break in the clouds. He'd go swimming with Declan if the day brightened up. His mother would sit on the sand watching them like a hawk, terrified they'd go out too far. Afterwards she'd warm them with a flask of tea. Bartley would have his own flask with something more 'interesting' in it.

There was a box beside Brian. It had photographs of houses in it.

'What are these?' he asked.

'Nothing,' Bartley said, 'Push them out of your way.'

'You're not thinking of moving, are you?'

'Far from it. In fact we've just done the house up. Wait till you see it. you'll hardly recognise it.' That's what he was afraid of.

He started the car. It made a deafening sound when he revved it. He threw his eyes to heaven.

'That's the latest crack,' he said, 'Noise for the sake of it. Sometimes I feel I'm in a space capsule.'

He drove off. He wasn't wearing his belt.

'Put your seatbelt on,' Angela said.

'I don't feel like it.'

'Don't be stupid.'

'I'm a good driver. I don't need it.'

'What if you meet a maniac on the road? I mean someone even worse than yourself, if that's possible.'

'I'll deal with that problem when I come to it. If it's your time to go it's your time to go. And thanks for the compliment, by the way.'

'You're behaving like a child.'

They got onto the motorway. He went into the fast lane where the trucks were. He put an important look on his face as if he was unaware of the speeds he was hitting.

He started to talk about recent events in Loughrea. A man they knew had got divorced. A business closed down. A young girl committed suicide as a result of Facebook bullying.

'He makes it sound like it's all go down there,' Angela said. 'Believe me, it's not. These things happened over a long time. In the ordinary course of events the only thing that ever happens in this place is a cow calving out of season or some poor *lúdramán* winning a few bob on the Lotto.'

She loved running down Loughrea but he sensed she was more than content to be living there. Maybe she was trying to downplay her elation at her new married status.

'There was a rape in Connemara last month,' Bartley said out of the blue.

'That's terrible.'

'It's happening everywhere.'

'Is that supposed to make it right?' Angela said.

'I didn't say that.'

'You seem to be condoning it.'

'Just because I say it's happening everywhere doesn't mean I condone it. I think it's a despicable crime. There's only one cure for it. Get the man who did it and do a little job on his family jewels to make sure he doesn't do it again.'

'Don't be so crude,' Angela said.

'There's no pleasing you today.'

'Let's talk about something pleasant.'

'Okay. Mrs Delahunt got a new hat. Are you happy now?'

'Stop it, Bartley. I'm warning you.'

'All right, I'll be quiet. You two can have a chat.'

'You're impossible.'

The journey drained him. He hated the monotony of the motorway. Most of the small towns had been bypassed by it. He missed going through them and watching people going about their business. He missed the country roads as well, the *boreens* that had cottages on the roadsides with smoke coming out of the chimneys. There were no roads that climbed and dipped anymore, no stragglers or angry dogs or farmers peering out over walls with pipes in their mouths, gazing aggressively at you for no other reason than that you were a stranger. There were no crops, no plants, no bales of hay piled like giant sugar lumps on the rolling fields. Now it was just tar and cement. He even missed the potholes.

They came to a toll booth. It was four euro. Bartley started cursing. He spent an age rooting in his pockets for the right change as the traffic built up behind him. One driver honked him. That made him delay longer.

'Nobody ever honked Bartley Kilcoyne and got joy out of it,' he bragged.

When he got back on the motorway he screamed at other drivers for minor misdemeanours. Nobody could do anything right in his eyes. They were guilty until proved innocent. Brian was amazed at the anger in him. His knuckles were white on the steering wheel from gripping it so tightly. He held onto it as if he had a personal vendetta against it.

He flashed his headlights at one driver who changed lanes without indicating and then overtook him. The man reacted by rolling down his window and swearing at him.

He shook his head in disbelief.

'These guys drive me nuts,' he groaned. 'First they try to ram into you and then they tell you to fuck off.'

'Ignore him,' Angela said, 'You'll live longer that way.'

'How can I? My blood is boiling.'

'Then tell it not to boil. Forget it happened and in a few minutes it will be as if it didn't.'

'Why wasn't I born a woman? You have a genius for not caring about things.'

'It goes back to when we were in the caves. We didn't beat our breasts like men did. You guys had to keep showing off even then.'

'Do you think so?'

'Yes. If you were there you'd probably have wanted a bigger cave than the next fellow. And a bigger car.'

'There were no cars then,' he said.

'Freddie Flintstone had one,' she said.

He laughed. As Brian listened to them they reminded him of two teenagers bantering with one another.

'You're not going the old way home,' he said.

'I know. It's not practical.'

'I miss them.'

'So do I. At least you saw some living creatures on them. All you get here are speed merchants. If you drop your concentration for a second you'll end up with your guts splattered onto the road.'

'Not if you travel in the slow lane,' Angela said.

'Why should I? I'd lose any advantage the other drivers have.'

'Then you're as bad as them.'

He ignored her.

'Then you have all these bloody tests to make sure your car is roadworthy,' he said. 'Last year I failed the NCT because of a bald tyre. Don't tell me a bald tyre is responsible for the carnage we see on the road every day of the week. It's more likely from sixteen-year-olds off their faces on drugs. They plough into ditches at a hundred miles an hour in the middle of the night with seven or eight people in their cars.'

'Good speech,' Angela said, 'Now shut your trap.'

She started singing: 'Keep your mind on your driving, keep your hands on the wheel, and keep your filthy eyes on the road ahead.'

'What's that?' he said.

'A song. Would you like to hear the rest of it?'

'Not particularly.'

She sang it anyway.

'We'll have fun sitting in the back seat, kissing and a-hugging with Fred.'

'Is that Fred Flintstone?'

'Don't be stupid. It's a song.'

'You were talking about him earlier.'

'So what? I'm not even in the back seat.'

'If you're in form for songs I could sing one for you.'

'No thanks. Concentrate on your driving. You're talking too much. You won't be happy till you kill us all.'

'I have to talk or I'll get woozy. That's what happens me when I sit behind the wheel. It's worse than being drunk. I feel my eyes going unless I do something.'

'Let's pull over and get a bite to eat then. It's not the end of the world if we're late home.'

They spotted an exit with a restaurant sign on it so they took it. After a while they came to it. It was a pokey little place with a roof that looked like it was going to cave in.

'Jesus,' Bartley said when he saw it, 'It looks like something out of a horror film.'

They went in. He said to Angela, 'We're probably the first customers it's seen all year.'

'Shut your whist,' she said.

There was a woman standing behind the counter. She put a plastic smile on her face when she saw them.

'Can I help you?' she said, blinking her eyes.

'Do you have any food here?' Bartley said.

'It's a restaurant. That's the general idea.'

Angela sat down at a table near the door.

'Just get me a sandwich like a good man,' she said to Bartley, 'Any type of a one. But make it fast. I'm starving.'

Bartley went up to the counter. Brian followed him. They stood before a display case. It had some sandwiches in it. They looked like they'd seen better days.

'Are they last year's?' Bartley said to the woman.

'They're today's. Do you want one?'

'I'll take three,' he said, 'as long as you can assure me they don't poison us.'

'We don't give those kinds of guarantees,' she said, 'If anything happens, we'll inform the emergency services.'

They walked back to the table.

'What was all that about?' Angela said, 'She doesn't look too happy.'

'He met his match,' Brian said.

They sat down.

'This bread looks like it's made of cement,' Bartley said, 'There's something inside it that's either lettuce or grass, I'm not sure. It could be a combination of both.'

'Stop complaining,' Angela said, 'They'll stop a gap.'

'They'll do more than that. They'll probably stop us bloody breathing.'

'Why did you order them so?'

'You told me you were hungry. There's no pleasing some people.'

The waitress came over. She slapped the sandwiches down beside Bartley.

'Enjoy,' she said.

A moment later she brought a tray over. It had a teapot and three cups on it.

'Did you ever hear of milk?' Bartley said.

'Is that the stuff that comes out of cows?'

'Now you have it.'

She went back to the counter.

'Stop it, Bartley,' Angela said, 'You'll have us all turfed out.'

She arrived with the milk. Bartley threw a 20 euro note on the table. She picked it up.

'Thank you,' she said.

She walked up to the counter with it. A moment later she came back with the change.

'Two euros and 30 cents,' she said.

'Keep it,' Bartley said, 'for the friendly service.'

She put the plastic smile on again. Then she went off.

Brian stood up.

'What's up with you?' Bartley said.

'I'm not hungry. I'm going back to the car.'

'Now look what you've done,' Angela said.

He looked at Brian.

'Sit down and have your sandwich.'

'You said it was uneatable.'

'Drink your tea then. It'll sustain you.'

'I don't want it.'

'You're leaving because of me, aren't you?'

'Why do you always have to disgrace yourself?'

'She started it. You have to put these old biddies in their box.'

'You're not safe to let out,' he said.

He went towards the exit. Angela followed him. She brought his sandwich with her.

'Do you want this?' she said, offering it to him.

'No thanks.'

She sat into the car. The two of them gazed into space. They didn't speak. Bartley joined them a few minutes later. Angela scowled at him.

'I hope you didn't say anything else to her,' she said.

'Absolutely not,' he said, 'We kissed and made up. We're best friends now. In fact I'm thinking of inviting her to my Christmas party.'

He turned on the ignition. The interlude had put him into good form. He threw his sandwich out the window as soon as they got moving. Two crows descended on it. They tore it apart.

'Watch them dying slowly,' he chirped.

'Now you've put me off my one,' Angela said. She put it in the cigarette tray.

Bartley sped up. Brian watched the needle getting higher. He thought of Mia in the Land Rover.

'What are you in such a hurry for?' he said, 'Where's the fire?'

'We've lost twenty minutes in that kip. I'm forced into it with these motorways. You have to go fast or someone will plough into the back of you. I don't know why they ever built the bloody things.'

'To get rid of traffic jams,' Angela said.

'Bullshit,' he said, 'All they do is transfer them to the next town. Then that gets blocked. It down the road again to some other poor bastard stuck in it. The only bypasses that I'm interested in are heart ones. That's probably on the cards for me next.'

'If it's not your arse it's your elbow,' Angela said, 'You haven't stopped moaning since you got into the car.'

Brian sank into his seat. He'd only been in Ireland a few hours but already he saw nothing had changed. Bartley had been so friendly on the phone he thought he was going to be different. He saw now that there was no chance of that. His friendliness was due to Angela. He wanted to see how he'd take the news of the wedding. It was a kind of trade-off for him leaving the university. Now that he'd accepted the marriage, Bartley was fre to go back to his old self.

He asked him about the farm.

'It's beyond me at the moment,' he said, 'Apart from everything else it's bankrupting me. Every time I sell a cow there's some fucking tax on it from the EU.'

He kept up a rant about one thing and another for the whole journey home. If it wasn't the farm it was the town. If it wasn't the town it was the people in it. Complaining was like a drug to him. It made him elated. Brian knew better than to interrupt him when he was in full flow. It would have been pointless. He'd just keep arguing him down, talking over him.

Eventually they arrived in Loughrea. After America it looked like a ghost town to Brian.

'As you can see,' Bartley said, 'it's as exciting as ever.' There wasn't a sinner on the streets.

'Where's everyone?' Brian said.

'In Dublin,' Bartley replied, 'if they have any sense.'

'Don't say things like that,' Angela said.

'I believe in calling a spade a spade. What did it ever do for me?'

'It gave you a living.'

'So would every other godforsaken place on the planet if you happened to be born there.'

'Don't be too sure of that. Some people slave for fifty years and have nothing to show for it.'

'Do you think I have?'

They passed the river. As they rounded a hill he saw the first roofs of the town. It brought back memories of days they went on drives to Galway. He always felt sad coming home. Today it was different. It was tinged with anticipation.

They drove into the town centre. He started to see activity now. Crowds huddled at corners. Some new shops had opened up.

'This is more like it,' he said.

'What?' Bartley grunted.

'It looks lively.'

'It might for five minutes. After that you'll see it's the same old tuppence ha'penny. You'll be screaming to get back to America.'

'Don't be too sure,' Brian said, 'America isn't all it's cracked up to be.'

'You don't think so?'

'No.'

'The savage loves his native shore, I suppose.'

'Don't call him a savage,' Angela said.

'It's an expression, my dear, an expression.'

'I never heard it before.'

'That's because you don't read. Except for those stupid women's magazines you refuse to take your head out of.'

'And I suppose you're Shakespeare with your racing sheets and the sports pages of the local rag.'

'Stop it, both of you,' Brian said, 'I'm hardly off the plane.'

'Sorry. Brian' Angela said, 'He started it. He always does.'

'No I didn't but I'll finish it if I have to.'

They passed a row of bungalows. They looked out of place with everything else.

'When did these go up?' Brian said.

'A few months ago,' Bartley said, 'Do you like them?'

'Yes.'

'That's good because you might be living in one of them some day.'

'Why do you say that?'

'Let's just say I have an interest in them.'

'What kind of an interest?'

He gave him a wink.

'Your father is getting another string to his bow,' Angela said.

'What kind of a string?'

They looked at one another.

'I can't talk about it now,' he said.

'Why not?'

'Because I can't, that's the why.'

'Don't say you bought one of them.'

'I didn't say that.'

'Well, did you?'

'I can't tell you.'

'Why?'

'You above all people should understand when information is confidential. You're so private.'

'I'm only asking about a house. You either bought one or you didn't.'

'It's not as simple as that?'

'Why? What are you hiding from me?'

'My lips are sealed.'

'I don't know why you're being so secretive about it.'

'Everything will be revealed in due course,' Bartley said, 'as the cat said when she came out from behind the dresser.'

32

Brian was surprised to see electronic gates had been installed when they reached the farmyard. They were between the two large pillars that stood on the driveway.

Bartley took out a remote he had in his pocket. They opened when he clicked it. He drove in, the tyres crunching on the pebbled drive.

'As you can see,' Angela said, 'we've gone up in the world.'

'Everyone has them nowadays,' Bartley said. 'There are too many nutcases around. Gone are the days when you'd hear a noise and it would be a cat squawking on the top of a bin. Now it's more likely to be someone who'd come in and slice you up.'

'That's a bit of an exaggeration,' Angela said.

They got out of the car. Bartley opened the boot. He took Brian's bag out.

'Is that all the luggage you've got?' he said, 'I'd have brought that much to Maam Cross.'

'I travel light.'

'I'll give you that much. You certainly do.'

'I bought a lot of junk and got rid of it. If I brought it with me it would probably have taken the train down.'

'I'd like to have seen some of it.'

'Sorry. I should have brought presents for yourself and Angela.'

'Don't worry. It wasn't a hint.'

He looked around him at the cowsheds, the farmhouse. the driveway. He thought of the games he used to play on the hawthorn tree with Declan.

'What's the matter?' Bartley said, 'You're in another world.'

'I was just thinking.'

'About what?'

'I don't know. It's good to be home.'

'That's the spirit.'

Rusty jumped all over him when he got inside the house. He almost licked his face off with excitement.

The kitchen was different. There were pine presses everywhere. A new fridge and washing machine had been installed. They were integrated.

'What do you think?' Angela said.

He didn't know what to say. He might have been in Declan's house in Newbridge.

'It's nice,' he said. He always said something was nice when he didn't like it.

The fireplace was gone. A stove stood in its place.

'What happened here?' he said.

'Nobody has fireplaces now. They're too expensive.'

'What's the idea with the stove?'

'It saves a mint on fuel.'

Angela put on the kettle. He sat at the table. Bartley was at the top. Angela sat beside him. She was in the chair his mother used to sit on.

He looked around him. Whatever changes had been made two Christmasses ago seemed minor now. The piano was gone as well. Playing it had been his mother's favourite hobby.

'Where's the piano?' he said.

Bartley looked guilty.

'It was out of tune. I sold it.'

'You should have told me you were going to do that.'

'I didn't know you wanted it. Teresa liked it but – '

'It was the thing she loved most in the house. You knew that.' He was shouting.

'That's why I had to let it go. It was too painful to have around.'

He walked over to the door.

'Are you all right?' Angela said.

He went out. Bartley followed him.

He went over to the tree.

'I'm sorry ' he said, 'It brought her back to me too much.'

'Did you not want her brought back?'

'She's gone, Brian, there's no pretending she isn't. It's not healthy. She wouldn't have wanted it.'

'You left my room as it was. Why not be consistent?'

'That's different. I wasn't married to you.'

He stood looking into the distance. The wind blew through the tree.

'Would you mind leaving me alone for a while?'

'No problem. I'm sorry.' He went in.

There was a bench beside the tree. He sat down on it. The wind blew onto his face.

Why had he come home? It was a bad idea. It wasn't home anymore. It was someone else's house.

He should have stayed in America. Mia would have been home in a month. They could have re-ignited their relationship. The break might have changed her attitude to him. They could have done the simple things again. They could have swam, walked the promenade. She might even have married him. If she did, he'd have had citizenship. He could have stayed there forever.

He went back in. Angela was at the cooker. She looked tense.

'Sorry, Angela,' he said, 'I didn't mean to ignore you. I think you said something to me before I went out.'

'No problem. Can I get you a cup of tea?'

'No thanks.'

The kettle boiled. She made a cup for Bartley and herself.

'You can't beat the old cup of tea,' she said, 'It sustains you.'

'What else have you done?' Brian asked Bartley.

'I'll show you the other rooms if you like,' he said.

'Okay.'

They walked down the corridor. The living-room was to the left. It had been converted into what looked like an office. The carpet was replaced by a pine floor. There were filing cabinets everywhere. The bookshelves didn't hold books anymore. There were business folders in them.

'What's all this about?' he said.

He started riffling through the folders. One of them contained information about the bungalows he'd seen in town. The cover of it said, 'See Our Fantastic New Development.' It had Bartley's name on it.

Underneath was the name of an auctioneer.

Angela came in with Brian's bag.

'Would you like me to bring this up to your room?' she said.

'No. I'll do it.'

She put it beside him.

'What the hell is going on?' he said to Bartley.

'I was going to explain everything to you tomorrow.'

'Is there anything else?'

'Not really. You've seen most of it. The other rooms are the same, by and large.'

'In that case I think I'll go to bed.'

'Do you not want to hear about the office?'

'Not tonight.'

'Would you like to have a drink with me?'

'I didn't sleep much last night. It wouldn't do anything for me.'

'Suit yourself.'

'Why didn't you tell me about the changes when we were in the car?'

'They were supposed to be a surprise.'

'Surprise? They're not surprises. They're abominations.'

'Brian, I have something else to tell you, and by your reaction to the house I don't think you're going to like it.'

'What is it?'

'A party is being held for you in the pub.'

'Tonight?'

'I'm afraid so.'

'Why are you springing all these things on me?'

'Some people might like the fact that a party was being thrown for them.'

'Do you not know your son? I always hated things like that.'

'You haven't been home for a long time. I thought you might have changed.'

'Does Jennifer know about it?'

'We told her but I doubt she'll come. I think she wants to see you on your own.'

'She can, because I'm not going to any party.'

'Please don't say that. It would be like Hamlet without the prince.'

'I told you, I'm fit to drop. My eyes are falling out of my head.'

'It would mean a lot to us if you came. You could have a lie-down before it if you're tired. I could call you in an hour or so.'

'I told you, I'm not going.'

'Come on, it's only a small shindig.'

'I know your small shindigs. They usually involve half the town.'

He remembered birthday parties thrown for himself and Declan when they were growing up. Any excuse for a drink was good enough in those days. Maybe it still was.

'Please, Brian. Some people have gone to a lot of trouble organising this. You can disappear after a while. It's just to make an appearance.'

'You shouldn't have done it without telling me.'

'I mis-read the situation. I see that now. Believe me, if I had it to do it again I wouldn't.'

'How many people are going to be there?'

'I'm not sure. You know this place. It could be 2 or 102. It depends on who's busy or not. I know how hard it is for you but try and suffer it. It'll be over tomorrow.'

'And if I don't go it'll be over tomorrow too. What's the difference?'

'Nobody will bother you. They know you're shy.'

'They'll be wanting news. Their tongues will be hanging out of their mouths.'

'If they are, tell them to fuck off. You need to grow a pair. If you're going to be spending your life here you'll have to set down some markers with these people.'

'I don't want a lecture from you. I want to go to bed.'

'Have a lie-down then. I'll call you in an hour. You'll be refreshed.'

'I don't need an hour. I need a month.'

'Nonsense. You're young. You have a bit of jet lag, that's all. Your system will re-adjust before you know where you are.'

'If I meet people tonight I'll be giving them a message that I want to see them. They won't leave me alone.'

'You're ahead of yourself as usual. Come on, you're not Elvis Presley. It's not like they're going to be battering the door down.'

He was tired arguing. Bartley always got his way. With his mother, with the other farmers, with everyone. He looked at Brian with a smile of victory.

'Before you have your snooze,' he said, 'I have another surprise for you.'

By now he was beyond caring.

'What is it?' he said tiredly.

Bartley went over to a chair. A suit was hanging over it. He lifted it up. 'Ta-dah!' he said.

Brian looked at it in a daze. It was about two sizes too big for him.

'I hope you didn't buy that for me.'

'We can't have you going to your coming-home party looking like a hippie, can we? Do you like it?'

'I'm too tired to talk to you anymore. Just let me go to bed.'

'It was Angela's idea. We know you're not exactly a clothes horse but if you're going to this bash tonight...'

'I didn't say I was.'

Angela came in. She looked as if she'd been listening to the conversation.

'Brian, you have to,' she said, 'We've been setting it up for weeks. What do you think of the suit?'

'It's very nice, thank you, but it wouldn't fit me.'

'It looks like it might be a bit on the big side all right.'

She put the jacket up to his chest.

'Yes,' she said, It's at least a size too big.'

'Good. Now you can bring it back to the shop you got it in and tell them it didn't suit.'

'The suit didn't suit. That sounds funny.'

'Maybe it'll fit Declan,' Bartley said, 'He has a larger frame.'

'Declan wouldn't be seen dead in anything that was bought for someone else. He wouldn't wear it to the bog.'

'What makes you think that? How do you know?'

'It was me who got the hand-me-downs growing up. That's how.'

'I'm sorry. I didn't think. So much for my talent at picking things.'

'Stick to the auctioneering,' Angela said.

Brian's ears peaked up.

'Auctioneering?' he said.

'I meant farming.'

Brian looked at Bartley.

'What's going on?' he said.

Bartley gave an awkward smile.

'I've been dabbling a bit in the other business,' he said, 'That's what I wanted to talk to you about.'

'So that's what the files in the car were for. They're yours, right?'

'Guilty, Your Honour. I did a course with the NPSRA.'

'What's that?'

'The National Property Services Regulatory Authority'

'With a view to what?'

'There's an auctioneer in town I'm going to hook up with. He was trying to get a loan from the bank but they said no. He rang me one night and asked me if I'd like to invest a few euros in his company. I thought it sounded like a good idea.'

'Is it Arthur Finlay?'

'Yes. Do you know him?'

'I remember you talking about him in the old days. So you were doing the course when I was in America?'

'I didn't want to tell you about it in case you thought I was selling the farm.'

'I see. To go with all the other things you didn't want to tell me about.'

'Blame Angela. She was the one behind it.'

'He's right, Brian. I felt he needed to get away from physical work for his health.'

'This is a bit too much for me to take in at the moment. You never tell me anything.'

They mumbled apologies to him. He picked up his bag.

'See you both later,' he said, 'I'm going to bed.'

'Does that mean later tonight?' he said expectantly.

'I don't know.'

His head was spinning. He thought he'd be coming home to the familiar but the way things were he might as well have been in someone else's house.

He was expecting his room to be ravaged like everything else in the house but mercifully it wasn't.

It was still his shrine. Everything was the same as when he was there last − the bed, the wardrobe, the bedside cabinet. An old skateboard he used to have had even been kept.

He went over to the bed. Angela had left a chocolate on the pillow the way they sometimes did in hotel rooms. Things like that annoyed him. She still wanted him to be the baby of the house.

He set the alarm to wake him in an hour. Then he lay down. He heard them whispering downstairs. Were they hatching another plan?

He didn't think he'd sleep but he did. He dreamt of Mia, of the airport, the journey home. When the alarm went off he didn't know where he was for a moment. He thought it was a phone ringing.

He jumped up suddenly. He went out to the bathroom.

Bartley heard him moving about.

'Are you up?' he said, 'I was going to call you. Are you coming to the party?'

Suddenly he didn't care one way or the other.

'Probably.'

'Fantastic! You're a star!'

He looked at himself in the mirror. He felt old suddenly. He turned on the tap. He put his head under it to try and wake himself up. He held it there for a long time.

He dried himself. They were whispering downstairs. He went down to them. Bartley looked cowed, almost afraid to speak.

'If you really don't want to go to this you don't have to,' he said.

He always said things like that when you'd agreed, when it was a *fait accompli.*

'It's okay. I'll go.'

'I could make some excuse that you're not well.'

'You don't have to. I'm ready for it now. '

'I have a snack for you,' Angela said.

He sat down. They stared at him as he ate. He was surprised at the way they were tiptoeing around him. Maybe they realised they'd gone too far.

Angela sat half way down the table instead of at the top of it. The position she'd held earlier in the evening, like her position in the car, suggested she'd taken on his mother's role. Now she was backtracking. What had been taken for granted earlier was now being revised; she was putting her new status on hold. To Brian it was as if Bartley was Hamlet and she was Gertrude. The wicked stepmother. They were trying to orchestrate a scenario that would make him feel comfortable to be around them in their new set-up.

Their pandering to him made him nervous. He'd have preferred if they were like iron. There would have been some authenticity in that.

She'd made egg sandwiches. The conversation was stilted as they ate. They just talked shop. They'd obviously decided to keep the subject of the auctioneering until another day.

Mattie O'Connor had bought a new tractor. Joe Foley's son was off in Russia. Gertie Donnelly died. Angela made made twittery comments. Bartley sat more quietly.

When they were finished eating, Brian said he was going out for a walk.

'A walk?' Bartley said querulously.

'To clear my head.'

'Of course, Bartley said. He seemed almost afraid of him.

'Good.'

'You need to stretch your legs after the sleep,' Angela said, 'It'll get rid of the cobwebs.'

He felt better as soon as he stepped outside the door. It had been raining. He got the smell of wet grass from the fields. They always smelt lovely after a shower.

The rain was one of the things he'd missed most in America. Its uncertainty matched the uncertainty of people's moods, an uncertainty he liked. It was probably why he'd stay in Ireland. Irish people drove him mad but they were never predictable. That was their saving grace.

He walked onto the main road. They called it the main road but it was still very much off the beaten track. He felt the tar sticking to his feet. How many hours had he stood there in childhood, waving at the drivers as they passed?

He was a man now, not a child anymore. Or was he? He remembered the day Jennifer told him he was a man. It was after spending the night with her in the field. What did being a man mean? That you were able to deal with things better? That hardly applied to him. He'd been more like an adolescent with Mia. Looking back on that time now he found it hard to believe he'd got so worked up about her. At one point he'd almost imagined himself taking an overdose if things went wrong between them. Now it was as if she'd passed into another realm.

He wondered what the American trip had achieved. Had he been trying to 'find himself' as Bartley put it? Maybe he was just buying time to avoid having to go out into the world. Now that the time was bought, what was he going to do with it? He owed a debt to himself. There was a life to be lived, either here or somewhere else.

He didn't know if he'd stay in Loughrea. Life with Bartley wasn't going to be like he expected. He imagined Angela worming her way more and more into his mother's shoes. It would be done subtly. She was too clever for anything else. And it would be done apologetically. She'd stoop to conquer.

What was going to happen with Jennifer? He wasn't ready to ring her yet. Bartley said something about her having got a job on one of his calls. She'd be waiting for news of whether he was going to get one. Or maybe not. He wondered if having a job would have changed her. Maybe she wouldn't be as happy-go-lucky as she used to be now that she had to get up at a set time every day.

He didn't know whether to ring her or not. Why hadn't she rung him? Was she waiting for him to take the first step? Surely she wasn't playing games with him after all the years they spent together. That would have been childish. He didn't know how he was going to say he spent the summer. It was easy enough to bluff his way through it with Bartley and Angela.. She'd be a tougher nut to crack.

He went back to the house. Bartley was standing at the door like a child waiting for his mother to come home.

'Well,' he said, 'Did that do you any good?'

'I think so. Where's Angela?'

'Where do you think? Upstairs admiring herself. Are you settled back yet?'

'I think so.'

'I'm delighted to hear that.'

He started to sing.

'Home, home, where the buffaloes roam.'

He hadn't a note.

'Stop that squawking,' Angela called down from the landing, 'You're deafening me.'

'Maybe I'll try on that new suit after all,' Brian said, 'I could wear a jumper under it to fill it out.'

'That's a good idea. It would mean a lot to Angela if you wore it.'

'I'll do that so.'

'Thanks. At least one of us will look respectable. Angela always tells me I look like something the cat dragged in.'

'That's because you do,' she said, putting her head over the banisters.

'Jesus,' Bartley said looking up at her, 'What have you done to yourself?' She had cream all over her face. 'You're like a waxworks dummy.'

'It's easy for men. They can go out looking as ugly as the day they were born.'

'It beats spending five hours preparing yourself to have a pint.'

He took out a hip flask of whiskey he had in his pocket.

'Like a drop?' he said to Brian, 'while the devil isn't looking?'

'No thanks.'

He started talking to Brian about the farm, about the stock he'd let go. He hadn't wanted to do it but they were getting unmanageable. He didn't have the energy for farming that he used to have. He talked about the way he used to be when he was young, the enthusiasm he had every morning going about his chores. Now it wasn't a question of enjoying them so much as wondering whether he'd be able for them.

'I'm at a bit of a crossroads in my life at the moment,' he said, 'Having Angela around the house makes me want to be here but as the day goes on I feel like a spare part having nothing to occupy me.'

He asked him about America. He told him a bit about it without saying anything specific. Brian could see him getting woozy. He wondered how many drinks he'd had, how many more he'd have. He didn't think he'd last the night. He had a low tolerance for it now.

Angela came down after a while. She had high heels on her. She was wearing a dress that looked like it was made out of curtain material.

'Am I over-dressed?' she said. She did a little curtsy before them.

'You're always over-dressed,' Bartley said. 'Let's see you in the nip. That'd be more interesting.'

'You can never resist the temptation to act like a ten year-old, can you?'

'You look lovely, Angela,' Brian said.

'At least we have one gentleman in the room,' she said.

Bartley's phone rang. It was Declan.

'I thought it might be you,' he said.

They talked for a few seconds. Then he whistled over to Brian.

'He wants to talk to you,' he said.

'Can it not wait till tomorrow?'

'No.'

He took the phone from him.

'How is Wandering Aengus?'

'Not too bad. A bit groggy with the jet lag.'

'You'll get over that soon enough. How was your trip?'

'Pretty good.'

'Did you work?'

'A bit.'

'I can see you're bubbling over with enthusiasm to tell me how it went.'

'I'm exhausted.'

'Why did you go to America anyway? Abu Dhabi is where you should have been. That's where the money is nowadays.'

'I didn't go to make money.'

'Of course. How are Dad and Angela?'

'Well.'

'A little bird told me you're off to a party.'

'So I believe.'

'There's no end to the action in your life. Will Jennifer be there?'

'I hope so.'

'Are you still going to marry her?'

'Yes. In fact we're on the altar at the moment.'

'Great. How many women did you get pregnant in the U.S. of A.?'

'About ten.'

'That's disappointing. You're letting the side down.'

'I'll try harder next year.'

'That's my boy. By the way, Yivvy said to tell you she was asking for you.'

Yivvy was his pet name for Yvonne.

'Tell her I said the same. I'm looking forward to seeing her.'

'I hope that'll be soon. Anyway, just checking in with you. Have a great night.'

'I'll try to.'

'Before you go, can you put me on to Dad for a second?'

'Okay.'

He handed the phone to Bartley.

'You should be here for your kid brother,' he said.

'I'd love to but I can't. No rest for the wicked.'

The pair of them discussed business. From what Brian could gather, Declan seemed to be in on the auctioneering too but he couldn't say for sure. Bartley was whispering. He was also using a lot of technical language.

'Men,' Angela said, 'Why can't they talk English?'

'Is Declan going to be in on the auctioneering too?' he said to her.

'You're asking the right person now,' she said, but he felt she knew more than she was letting on.

Bartley hung up. He put the phone in his pocket.

'Okay, folks,' he said, 'It's time to hit the road. There are precious pints waiting for us.'

'I presume you're not bringing the car,' Angela said.

'Are you joking? You'll lose your license now if you have more than a pint. Gone are the days when you could give twenty quid to a copper when you were twisted and expect him to keep quiet.'

'Let's go then. I hope the heels hold out.'

She tested herself on them, pacing up and down the floor. She was wobbling.

'What are you bringing those for?' Bartley said, 'You'll destroy your feet with all the potholes.'

'I like them.'

'Whatever you like.'

He went over to the sink. When the water was running for a few seconds he slicked it over his head.

'Is that your idea of preparing yourself for a night out?' Angela said, 'a bit of water to make people think you have Brylcreem on?'

'Brylcreem?' he said, 'That went out with the Indians.'

'At least it's more modern than water.'

They put on their coats.

'Mind the house for us, won't you, Rusty?' she said to the dog, 'Don't let any strangers in unless they're good-looking.'

He wagged his tail at her.

They walked down the road. Angela tottered in front in her heels. Bartley got out of breath soon. He started gasping.

'I didn't realise you were so unfit,' Brian said to him.

'It's all this sitting around since Angela turned me into a gentleman,' he said, ' I'll be okay once I get a few drams into me.'

33

It was only when they got to the pub that Brian remembered how much he hated it. It usually smelt of urine and stale beer. He thought back to the days when he had to drag Bartley out of it when his mother was fretting about him.

He checked out all the Exit signs as routes of escape if things became too much for him and he had to leave early. Bartley was amused looking at him.

'I know what you're at,' he said. 'Do you not appreciate it when people go to trouble to make you feel important?'

'I'd prefer to have lighted matches put under my fingernails than to be here. You know that. I came down because you twisted my arm. There's nothing I hate more than attention.'

'Enjoy it while it lasts. When you get to my age they won't give two fucks about you.'

He looked around the bar. It was crowded.

'It's going to be a great night,' he said to Angela. She yawned.

'I'm going to get a table for myself,' she said.

He spotted some people he knew. They signalled to him to go over to them.

'Come on, Brian,' he said.

They went over to them. More gathered before long. It was the way it always was with him in McDonagh's. He was a people magnet.

'I could murder a pint of Guinness,' he said. One of the group clicked his fingers at the barman. A minute later it arrived. He sucked on it like a baby on a soother.

'You're losing your touch,' he said to the barman. 'The last time I was here you pulled one for me in less than ten seconds. This time you were nearly twenty. What's going on?'

'Old age, probably,' the barman said, 'I'll try and make sure it doesn't happen again.'

Angela came up behind him.

'Are you going to desert me for the evening?' she said.

'Why don't you join us?'

'I don't like standing.'

'Okay.'

He excused himself from the group.

'Come on, Brian,' he said walking over to Angela's table, 'The oracle has spoken.'

They sat down.

'That's better,' she said, 'Now I don't feel like a widow anymore.'

They looked around them. A corner of the bar had been set aside for the party. There were streamers going from one end of the counter to the other. A sign in red marker said, 'Welcome Home Brian.' There were bowls of finger food on the tables. Taytos and peanuts were placed in little dishes on the counter.

A group of young people sat at the far end eating cocktail sausages. Some of the men were wearing football jerseys. They'd obviously come from a match. They had glamorous-looking girls with them. Bartley's eyes were out on sticks as he looked at them. They had plunging necklines. Their skirts showed more of their legs than Angela liked.

'Why do they wear them that short and then spend most of the night pulling them up,' she said.

'If you don't know the answer to that one,' Bartley said, 'You've never been a teenager.'

'Stop looking at them' she said, 'You're a married man now, in case you forgot.'

'Just because I'm on a diet doesn't mean I can't look at the menu.'

263

Some of the people from Brian's class came over to him. They stood in front of him with big grins on their faces. A few of them bear-hugged him.

'I hardly recognise most of you,' he said.

'We could say the same about you,' a young girl said. He couldn't put a name on her. He'd never seen her out of her school uniform. She'd turned into a woman in the two years since he'd seen her.

She took his photograph.

'Please don't do that,' he said. It reminded him of the night with Mia.

'Why?'

'I'm camera shy.'

He put his hands over his face. She took them away. He grabbed her wrist but she wriggled free. She started laughing.

Her friends started to get in on the act.

'Make sure you get his best side,' she told them.

A hush descended on the bar. A man stepped forward. Brian didn't know him. He turned his face to the crowd.

'Give us a B,' he shouted.

'B!' they chorused.

'Give us an R! Give us an I! Give us an A! Give us an N! What do we have? Brian!'

They stamped their feet as each letter was roared out. Brian wanted the ground to swallow him up. Then they sang 'For He's a Jolly Good Fellow' to him, banging their glasses on the counter.

'Speech!' they shouted but he waved away their requests.

The more they persisted, the more he dug his heels in. After a while they stopped, drifting away to their little groups. They started talking to one another. He was relieved. Maybe Bartley was right, he thought, maybe the worst was over.

He walked towards the counter to get a drink. As he reached into his pocket for his wallet he found his hand being gripped.

'Your money is no good here,' said a voice. He looked up. It was Gabriel Hoey. He'd had been in his class too. He had the reputation of being a snob. His father was a surgeon in Galway.

'So our latterday W.B. Yeats has come home,' he said.

He put on a deep voice.

'And what dumb beast,' he pronounced, 'his hour come round at last, struggles toward Bethlehem to be born.'

'Very nice,' Brian said, 'If I knew what it meant.'

'How does it feel to be back from exile?'

'Exile? I was away for a summer. It was hardly that.'

'How are you?'

'Good. I thought you might show up.'

'Show up? I organised this little get-together.'

'Are you serious?'

'I couldn't let your return go unheralded. If it was left to any of the other fuckfaces around here, nothing would have been done.'

Gabriel wasn't liked at school. He was always piping up the answers to everything. It got him the name of being a smart alec. 'If you told him you were on the moon,' Bartley said to Brian once, 'He'd say he was there the week before you. If you said you were in Tenerife he'd say he was in Elevenerife.'

Brian looked at him. He still had the same baby face. He seemed to be dressed in the same suit he had the last time he saw him. It was a size too small for him.

'I believe you wrote a book,' he said.

'Who told you that?'

'I have my spies. I haven't read it yet but I'm looking forward to.'

'Do yourself a favour and don't. It was a momentary aberration. I'm sane again now.'

'Sane? And you came back here?'

'Don't be sarcastic.'

'I believe you lived the high life in America.'

'I wouldn't say that.'

'And now it's back to porridge.'

'Something like that.'

'Have you traded in the Hush Puppies for a pair of wellies yet?'

'I'm getting around to it.'

'I can't believe you organised a party for me.'

'It was easy.'

'I don't know whether I should thank you or punch you in the face. The only way I'm going to be able to get through the night is to drink myself senseless.'

'I feel like that every night.'

Bartley whistled over at him.

'My father must want something.'

'He's probably going to give out to you for talking to me.'

'Why do you say that?'

'He doesn't approve of how I live my life.'

'Why not?'

'Probably because I never got a job.'

'I'm sure that's all in your imagination,' he said but he knew it to be true. Gabriel was living off his father – and the dole – since he did the Leaving Cert.

He went over to Bartley. He had a face on him.

'What are you talking to that fellow for?' he said.

'Why shouldn't I?'

'What was he on about?'

'Nothing much.'

'I wouldn't have anything to do with him if I was you.'

'Why not?'

'I always feel he's sneering at me.'

'I don't know how you think that.'

'He's wasting his life. I'm told he sits around all day watching DVDs.'

'So what?'

'When you consider how hard his father works it's a disgrace.'

'I don't think I'd like to be cutting up bodies for a living. Give me the DVDs any day.'

'I can see you're in the mood for a fight. Is that what America did to you?'

'I don't like being told what to do.'

'Talk to him all night if you like but he's a waste of space. Everyone around here has his number. I don't know how he swings it. I'm amazed he works up the energy to go down to the dole office to collect his cheque. Maybe the old man drives him down in his Merc.'

'You really have it in for him, haven't you?'

'I make no apology for it.'

'I wanted to stay home tonight. You dragged me down here. When I try to socialise with someone you give out to me.'

'Keep your voice down. He's coming over.'

Gabriel arrived beside them.

'Hello, Mr Kilcoyne,' he said, 'I bet you're glad to have this little urchin back.'

'I am, to be sure. How are you, Gabriel?'

'If I was any better I'd be worried about myself.'

'It looks like it's going to be a good night.'

'I hope so.'

'They went to a bit of trouble setting it up.'

'Guess who the "they" is?' Brian said.

'Who?'

He pointed at Gabriel.

'Are you serious?'

Gabriel smiled shyly.

'It didn't take long. I just put up a few streamers.'

'You're very good.'

'I never turn down an opportunity to get plastered.'

'Join the club.'

'Brian is looking well, isn't he?'

'Why wouldn't he be?' he said, glugging back his Guinness, 'He's been on his holidays for the last four months.'

'I beg your pardon,' Brian said, 'I hardly ever stopped working.'

'Relax. I'm joking.'

'Do you think he'll stay home this time,' Gabriel said, 'now that he's got the taste of travel?'

'I'll be putting him under lock and key until further notice.'

'Once they get a taste of gay Paree,' said Gabriel, putting on a Deep South accent, 'How you gonna keep 'em down on the farm?'

'Now you have it,' Bartley said, 'I'm sure he'll be off to some other where in no time.'

'And why shouldn't he?' Angela said, 'He has the world at his feet.'

'Indeed,' Bartley said, 'The world at his feet. All the rest of us have is bunions.'

Brian laughed.

'I'm going to get another drink,' he said, 'Let me know if you need anything.'

'Don't worry about that,' Bartley said.

He went back to the counter with Gabriel. The bar was noisier now. Some of the people from his class were dancing. The ones who didn't take to the floor were knocking back shorts.

'Your parents look happy,' Gabriel said.

'Don't call them my parents.'

'Sorry. Your father and stepmother.'

He looked around him. He wondered if Jennifer would turn up. He didn't know if he should ring her or not. He'd be self-conscious if she came down. Everyone would be looking at them. There might even be a round of applause when she came in. He'd have to kiss her.

Gabriel poked him in the ribs.

'Did you ask your father why he doesn't like me?' he said.

'He never said he didn't.'

'I know he doesn't. He thinks I sit around all day doing nothing.'

'Do you not?'

'Fuck off.'

Brian sipped his drink. Gabriel put on an important face.

'If you must know,' he said, 'I'm writing a novel.'

'Like everyone else in the country.'

'Thanks. I thought you'd be interested.'

'Sorry. Tell me about it.'

He cleared his throat.

'It concerns the son of a surgeon who spends his time trying to save his sanity in a one horse town.'

'So it's an autobiography.'

'Not quite. He's been abused by a priest as a child. He suffers from depression as a result. He's made a few suicide attempts. Cries for help.

267

You know, that sort of thing. So he goes for counselling. The counsellor tells him a problem shared is a problem halved. Then he does a course on mindfulness.'

'You have everything in there.'

'At the end it gets a bit crazy. He goes off potholing in South America.'

'It sounds fascinating.'

'Thanks. I'm going to donate the royalties to one of those Adopt a Pet charities. I'll go on *The Late Late Show* to promote it. Ryan Tubridy will get canaries with excitement. What do you think?'

'It'll be a best-seller,' Brian said, 'No doubt about it. I can see it being translated into 33 languages. You'll become so famous you won't be able to get in your front door without being mobbed.'

'That's exactly what's going to happen. Maybe your father will think of me differently then.'

Brian looked over at Bartley. He was sinking into his seat. He wondered how long it would be before he became senseless.

A man came out of a back room. He had an accordion in his hand. He was tuning it. Nobody noticed him for a few seconds. They carried on singing and dancing. Then they stopped.

'I'm going to sing a song,' he said, 'I accompany myself.'

'Good for you,' someone said.

He started singing. Even from the first few notes it was obvious he hadn't a good voice.

'I wish I was in Carrigfergus,' he sang.

'I wish he was too,' Gabriel said.

It got worse as it went on. People started laughing at him.

'I hope he doesn't give up the day job,' Brian said.

The song went on forever. When it ended everyone clapped.

'I'd say that was more from relief than anything else,' Brian said. They went back to their conversations.

By now the people from his class seemed to have forgotten he was there. Or that he was the reason they were there. Many of them were getting amorous with the drink. Bartley couldn't keep his eyes off them.

'So this is what the dating scene is like these days,' he said, 'the women behaving like trollops.'

'The men are hardly monks either,' Angela said. 'Look at them eating the faces of one another. Wouldn't you think their mothers would have given them a bit of food before they came out?'

'They're probably all living together,' Bartley said. 'A girl in transition year had a baby a few months ago.'

'I didn't hear that.'

'She'll probably bring the little fellow into class with her after he's born.'

'There was a time she'd have been sent to one of the laundries,' Angela said, 'Now they put them on pedestals.'

Every now and then someone came up to her asking if they could shake hands with 'the new Mrs Kilcoyne.' She lapped up the attention as she sipped at her sherries. She started getting merry on them.

'Would you like a dance?' she said to Bartley.

'Are you joking? At my age? I'd be laughed out of the place. Ask Brian. I'm sure he'll do the honours.'

'I don't know.'

'Go on. He'd be delighted.'

She went over to him.

'What would you say to taking an old daisy like me around the floor?' she said.

'Why doesn't Bartley?'

'He says he isn't up to it.'

He took her onto the floor. Everyone stopped what they were doing to look at them. They started a slow handclap. The accordion player struck up his instrument.

She was a brilliant jiver. Brian tried to imagine what she'd been like in her prime, wowing the men. She was light on her feet as she danced. It was as if they had a life of their own. He trailed after her faintly.

'There's life in the old girl yet,' she said.

'I can't match you.'

'You're all right. You just need someone to lead.' He was out of breath in no time.

The song finished.

'Will we go again?' she said.

'I'm afraid that's it for me. You have me worn out.'

She gave one of her curtseys.

'Thank you, young man,' she said, batting her eyelashes at him.

'I should be thanking you. You should be on *Strictly*"

'Oh my God. That's a bit excessive.'

She went back to Bartley. He followed her.

'You'd want to watch that one,' he said, 'There are some young fellas here tonight that have their eye on her.'

'Don't I know it,' Bartley said, 'and she had the cheek to stop me looking at the pretty ladies earlier on.'

He was slurring his words. The Guinness was only half drunk but there were a few empty glasses of whiskey on the table.

'That's women for you,' Brian said.

'Stop it the two of you,' she said, 'It was just a dance.'

Bartley rested his head on her shoulder. She tried to push him away but he was too heavy.

'Look at this fellow,' she said, 'He's going asleep on me and the night only beginning.'

Brian suddenly felt sorry for her. He remembered Bartley whizzing her around the floor one night in the kitchen before he went to the university. It hadn't taken anything out of him then. He'd aged dramatically in the two years.

'Can I get you a drink?' Brian said to Angela.

'Not at the moment thanks. Go back to the young people. You don't want to be spending the night yapping to us old fogies.'

'I'll be back and forth,' he said. 'Let me know if you want anything.'

'Maybe I'll help myself to his Guinness.'

He went back to the counter. Gabriel had a grin on his face.

'Angela sorted you out on the floor,' he said, 'You looked like you were getting multiple coronaries out there.'

'She left me for dead.'

More dancers took the floor. The music got louder. The man on the accordion was more out of tune than ever but nobody noticed. It was like the old days when he'd be there with Bartley as a schoolboy, everyone doing their own thing without a care in the world.

He looked at all the crinks in front of him, drinks that were being brought to him almost non-stop without him asking for them since the night began.

'I won't live long enough to drink these,' he said to Gabriel.

'Just leave them to me,' he said, 'I'll sort them out.'

He was drinking something interesting-looking himself.

'What's that you have?' Brian asked him.

'I don't know what it's called,' he said, ' I just know what it does to me.'

Brian laughed.

'Don't end up like my father,' he said.

'That's a distinct possibility,' he said, 'My head is on fire. Who knows where the night will bring me.'

'Why don't you dance with one of those young ladies over there?' Brian asked him.

He blushed. He always got embarrassed when that subject came up. He was awkward with women behind all the banter. Some people even thought he was gay.

'I know what I'll do,' he said, 'It's time for a speech.'

'What do you mean?'

'A speech. You can't have a party without a speech.'

'No, Gabriel, don't. Please.' He tapped the counter.

'Is everyone listening?' he said. Nobody heard him.

'Is everyone listening?' he said, louder this time, but there was still no response. He jumped up on the counter.

'Come down, you fool,' Brian said.

He stomped his foot.

'Shut up everyone,' he said. They stopped talking.

'I have a proposal to make,' he said. 'I put it to the house that we take a vote on whether Brian Kilcoyne, whom I have in front of me, should be kept in this jurisdiction for the rest of his natural life by general decree.'

Brian remembered him in the debating society at school. He was the auditor of it. Maybe he was picking up where he left off.

A voice from the crowd said, 'I second that emotion.'

'If he departs the boundaries of the county,' he went on, 'he will be arrested and taken back to these borders and detained at the government's pleasure until such time as he sees reason.'

'Hear hear,' said the girl who'd taken his photograph. She tugged at his trouser cuff to indicate her approval of what he was saying.

He looked down at her.

'I declare the motion carried,' he said.

He came down from the counter.

'Well,' he said to Brian, 'Does that influence you?'

'I wish you wouldn't do things like that.'

'Why not?'

'I don't like attention.'

'So that's why you came to a party with thirty-plus people at it.'

'I didn't know there'd be thirty-plus people here.'

'You knew there'd be some.'

'I was forced into it.'

'Stop backing into the limelight.'

The man with the accordion started to play louder. A few more couples stepped out on the floor. A girl tapped Brian on the shoulder.

'Fancy a jive?' she said.

'I'm no good at it,' he said.

'I noticed.'

She tried another person further down the counter.

'That's Fergus Donnelly,' Gabriel said to Brian, 'Do you remember him?'

He was one of the wildest people in the school. When he had enough drink taken he was capable of anything. Brian remembered him at a party one night trying to take his trousers off over his head.

'Unfortunately,' he said.

He started doing some kind of exotic dance with the girl.

'She's nice,' Gabriel said, 'You missed a trick there.'

'Who is she?'

'Virginia Sweeney. We used to call her virgin for short – but not for long.'

'I heard that one before.'

A girl passed by them in a mini skirt. Gabriel whistled at her. She glared at him.

'Why do they wear their skirts up to their arses,' he said, 'and then get snotty with you when you admire them?'

'You can't whistle at women, Gabriel.'

'Why not?'

'Because it hasn't been acceptable for about twenty years. What stone were you buried under?'

'I don't care about being acceptable.'

'Then be prepared to accept the consequences.'

He poked Brian in the ribs.

'I suppose you had lots of women abroad,' he said.

'No I didn't.'

He laughed as if the idea was ridiculous. He kept pressing him for information. No matter how many times he said there was no one, Gabriel remained unconvinced. Eventually he wore him down.

'Okay,' he said after being grilled incessantly, 'There was someone.'

'I knew I'd get it out of you. What did she do?'

'She was a cocktail waitress.'

'I'm impressed. Lots of free pints, eh?'

'She didn't drink much.'

'What did you do then?'

'She liked swimming.'

'Swimming? That's a new one on me. Is that where they go dating in America these days?'

'Are you seeing anyone yourself?'

'The female population of Loughrea has thus far have escaped my lustful clutches. Lucky them. Or me, depending on your point of view.'

Brian knew he was all talk and no action when it came to women. The common perception of him was that he'd have preferred to kiss the Barney Stone than a woman. He warded off personal questions with quips. It meant nobody ever really knew much about him.

'What's the story with Jennifer?' he said.

'How do you mean?'

'Are you two going to hook up again?'

'I don't know.'

'Is that because of the cocktail waitress?'

'Don't be ridiculous.'

'Have you seen her yet?'

'No.'

'That surprises me.'

'I'm only back.'

'She's up at the farmyard a lot.'

'We've been on the phone to one another all summer.'

'But yet you're home now and you haven't laid eyes on her.'

'Gabriel,' he said, 'Does the expression "Go fuck yourself" mean anything to you?'

'Yes, but it's physically impossible. I've tried it.'

Angela called over to him.

'I'll be back in a minute,' he said.

'You're trying to get away from me. Okay. I'm being too nosey as usual.'

'Shut up. It's nothing to do with that.'

He went over to her. Bartley was lying against her. He was half asleep. .

'I'm trapped,' she said, 'I can't move.' She was laughing.

'How did he get so bad so quick?'

'He was on it before we came out. You saw that.'

He started to wake up.

'Where am I?' he said.

He looked at Angela.

'Who are you?' he said, 'What are you doing here?'

'I'm going to have to bring him home,' she said to Brian.

'Do you think so?'

'He's only going to get worse.'

'I'm sorry for you.'

'And me for you. I hope this doesn't spoil your night.'

'It won't.'

'Maybe you all can be more yourselves when we're not here. '

'I don't intend to stay long. I've already had more than my limit.'

Bartley gaped up at her.

'Get me a cup of tea,' he said. And the paper. I haven't read it yet.'

Brian smiled at her.

'How are you going to get him back?'

'I rang for a taxi. It should be here any minute.'

They heard the sound of a car outside.

'I bet that's him,' she said, 'Speak of the devil.'

He came in.

'What did I tell you?' Hello, Gerry. Gerry, this is Brian, Bartley's son.'

'Hello.'

They shook hands.

'That's what I call service'

'I can see he's in a bad way.'

They lifted him up.

'What's wrong?' he said, 'Where are we going?'

'Home,' she said, 'home to bed and sleep.'

They got him walking. After a few seconds he found his balance. He walked towards the Ladies. Angela stopped him when he tried to open the door.

'You don't want to go in there,' she said, 'unless you've developed some new organs I don't know about.'

He sobered up for a second.

'I want to go to the toilet.'

'You'll have to wait till you get home.'

'Is that a good idea?' Gerry said, 'I don't want him going in the car.'

'Don't worry. He's toilet trained.'

He started to slip from Angela's arms. Gerry grabbed him.

'Is he always this heavy?' he said.

'Only when he's drinking.' In other words, yes.'

'He's like a dead weight.'

'The worst will be over when we get him into the car.'

'How are we going to wake him at the farm?'

'Let me worry about that.'

They bundled him towards the door.

'Up the republic!' he roared as he got to it.

He tripped on the saddle.

'Fuck it,' he said.

'He's a caution, isn't he?'

'Nearly there now,' Brian said.

They got him outside. The taxi was only a few feet away.

'Open the door,' Gerry said to Angela. As soon as she had it opened, Brian and Gerry dropped him in. He fell into the seat like a sack of potatoes. A few seconds later he was snoring again.

'Go back in now,' Angela said to Brian, 'Enjoy the rest of your night, party boy.'

34

Gabriel was standing at the door when Brian went back inside He'd been watching everything. He was obviously enjoying it. Brian could see what Bartley meant by him being a sneerer.

'I'll say one thing for that father of yours,' he said, 'He knows how to empty a bottle.'

He started talking to someone on the phone.

'The coast is clear now,' he whispered, 'You can come in.'

He hung up.

'Who was that?' Brian said.

'You'll find out soon enough.'

'Is it something to do with me?'

'You better believe it.'

Just then a woman came in the door. She strode over to Brian.

'Who are you?' he said.

She had a leather coat on her. Her hair was hair tied up in a topknot.

'Okay,' Gabriel said, 'Off you go.'

She unbuttoned her coat. She threw it on the floor.

She was dressed in a bra and thong. A pair of fishnet stockings were fastened by a suspender belt.

'Is she a Kissogram girl?' Brian said. Gabriel didn't answer him.

Everyone in the bar gaped at her. The accordion player played stripper music. Brian looked around at the people beside him. Everyone's eyes were glued to him.

'If you're responsible for this,' he said to Gabriel, 'You're dead.'

Gabriel was doubled up laughing. He gave a fist-pump. The girl licked her lips as she looked at Brian. Then she started kissing him.

'I can't breathe,' he said to her.

'That's the idea,' she said.

He tried to disentangle himself from her but he wasn't able. He loosened the top button of his shirt. People stamped their feet.

She ran her hands over her breasts.

'Do you like me?' she said.

'What kind of a question is that?'

'A yes or no one.'

'Yes.'

She started to massage him.

The crowd shouted, 'More!'

He drew himself away from her.

'What's wrong, sunshine?' she said.

'There are too many people watching.'

He walked towards Gabriel.

'Come back,' she said.

'Sorry. It's too much.'

She looked at Gabriel. He put his hands out helplessly.

'Okay, honey, if that's the way you want it. I get paid the same whether I get kissed or not.'

Brian pointed his finger at Gabriel.

'Don't ever do anything like that again,' he said to him.

'Why?'

'I felt as if I was being strangled by a boa constrictor.'

'It's meant to be fun.'

'What if Jennifer walked in?'

'Never mind Jennifer. You'll have this to remember for the rest of your life.'

'If I live past tonight.'

The Kissogram girl came over to Brian.

'Hello again,' she said, 'Do you still love me?'

'Passionately.'

He looked at her properly for the first time. He thought she was beautiful, as good as any film star.

'You have a fantastic figure,' he said.

'I bet you say that to all the girls.'

'You better get some clothes on you soon or you'll come down with pneumonia.'

'That's a new angle. Most people want me to take everything off.'

'Brian is unusual,' Gabriel said.

She put on her coat.

'So your name is Brian?'

'Yes.'

'Then you're a gentleman, Brian. I don't always get that. But don't be so formal.'

'Sorry.'

She blew him a kiss.

'I wish we did more,' she said.

'So do I.'

She collected her things. Before she left she did a little swivel for the crowd. They whistled again.

'How come they get away with it and I don't?' Gabriel said. A moment later she was gone.

It all seemed unreal to Brian.

'Did that really happen?' he said to Gabriel.

'You bet your boots it did.'

'I feel I dreamt it.'

'She was something else, wasn't she?'

'A woman and a half.'

'Did she give you a French kiss?'

'I don't know what country it came from but I felt it in my toes.'

'So did I and I was only watching. What did you think of her get-up?'

'She didn't leave much to the imagination.'

'It's just as well Bartley and Angela went home.'

'Don't worry. They'll hear every detail. Word is probably getting back to them even as we speak.'

'Thanks for that.'

'What did you think of her thong?'

'I don't know how they wear those things. It must be agony. There's not enough material in them to blow your nose.'

'I wouldn't worry about it if I were you. You're never going to have to face that problem. At least I hope not.'

'Even if I was a cross dresser I think I'd draw the line at that.'

'I'm betting that's the last time anyone ever organises a Kissogram girl for you.'

'Hopefully.'

His heart pounded harder than ever.

'I need another drink,' he said.

'I have a short here that I'm not drinking. Do you want it?'

He nodded. Gabriel handed it to him. He knocked it back.

'Feel better now?'

'I'm still in shock. She was like a character out of a comic book.'

'You should have seen your face when she grabbed you. I wish I had my camcorder with me.'

'I'd have broken it over your head if you had.'

The bar got quieter. Some people started to go home. Brian kept drinking without really wanting to. Gabriel pushed him to say more about Mia. His defences were down now and he talked too much, telling him how much she got in on him.

'So she's in Africa now,' he said.

'I suppose so.'

'You're better off without her. Women are bitches. They specialise in trying to destroy us.'

'You think so?'

'Jennifer is more your style.'

'Hopefully.'

'You know what they say. The best way to get over a woman is to get under another one.'

He waited for him to laugh but he wasn't in the mood for laughing.

'Or maybe just get drunk with your old buddy,' he said.

'Maybe that's a better idea.'

Gabriel hugged him. Then he stared at him. It wasn't just an ordinary stare. It lasted so long he started to wonder if Bartley was right about him being gay. Gay-briel.

Already he was sorry he went on so much to him about Mia. He always hated himself when he talked too much to people, especially people he wasn't that close to, like Gabriel. It usually only happened when he had drink taken.

He asked him what he thought about America in general. He wasn't interested in pursuing the subject so he fobbed off his questions. Gabriel took the opportunity to tell him his own feelings about the country. He could have predicted what was coming. He'd heard him at enough debates to know how he felt. He went on a rant about everything from Donald Trump to the invasion of Iraq. It was beyond boring.

'Is there any sign of you to get a job, Gabriel?' he said for something to say.

'Now you're beginning to sound like my father. The only steady job I've ever had is analysing the heads on the top of pints of Guinness.'

'You could do worse.'

'Agreed. It's a dying art.'

'The problem is, who's going to pay you for it?'

'Good point. Hardly the barman.'

'Especially if you say bad things about his heads.'

He hugged Brian again. By now he was starting to feel uncomfortable with him.

'Easy,' he said, releasing himself, 'I have to go to the toilet.'

He walked away from him. He didn't really need to go. His main purpose was to get away from him.

The toilet smelt rank. His head was whirling from the drink. He knew he'd have a massive hangover in the morning.

Gabriel looked fed up when he came out. He was staring at the people from the class. They were huddled in a group in one of the snugs. Some of them were holding their phones in the air to take photos of themselves.

'Look at those eejits,' he said, 'taking their bloody selfies.'

'What's wrong with that?'

'It makes me sick, that's what's wrong with it.'

Was there anything in life that didn't make him sick?

'Why?'

'Because who wants to see a photograph of those losers? Whether it's taken by themselves or anyone else.'

'They're on a night out, Gabriel. They're having fun.'

'You can have fun without taking selfies. They probably don't know whether they're having fun or not until they look at their stupid faces on a screen.'

'It's not a crime.'

'I have a thing about that people like that.'

'Well you better get over it because they represent about 90% of the human race.'

'That's the problem.'

'Why is it a problem?'

'Do you know how many accidents occur every year from people at that lark?'

'No.'

'A lot, that's how many. And you know what?'

'You're probably glad.'

'Right. Anyone who's that much in love with themselves deserves what's coming to them. It might wipe the smile off their faces.'

He found himself becoming annoyed by Gabriel's negativity. It was draining. He needed to get away from him.

'Would you be upset if I went over to talk to these selfie people?' he said.

'I don't know why you'd want to do that. What would you have to say to them?'

'I just want to thank them for turning up.'

'I'm sure a lot of them just came down for the crack. They're not all from the college, you know.'

'Off you go then.'

He went over to where they were sitting. Some of them were still taking the selfies. One of the girls was checking her lipstick. She was doing a trout pout.

'Thanks for coming along,' he said to nobody in particular.

They looked up at him like he was a stranger. Maybe Gabriel was right. Maybe they'd only come along for the crack.

'How is the guest of honour?' said the girl who was doing the trout pout.

'I almost forgot that's what I was.'

He tried to talk to them but it wasn't easy. He didn't know any of them well. They'd moved on with their lives since doing the Leaving Cert just as he had.

When you were thrown into a school with somebody for five years a relationship was automatic. You didn't have to work at it. They were just there. Out in the world it was different. There was nothing obvious creating a compatibility. You had to work at it.

He sat down beside a girl who was dressed like one of the cast members from *The Rocky Horror Picture Show*. She was wearing a dress spattered with fake blood. Her eyes were caked with what looked like black paint. She seemed to be crying. Or was it the mascara?

She looked into her phone.

'I've just unfriended my cousin from my Facebook app,' she said.

'Sorry to hear that,' he said. Are you going to a fancy dress party?'

'No. I always dress like this.'

She didn't smile as she said it. He wondered if she was trying to make a fool of him. The girl beside her burst out laughing.

'Don't mind her,' she said, 'We're having a Frankenstein-themed night.'

'So that's it. I thought I was in the wrong pub for a minute.'

'Did you have a good time in America?'

'Brilliant.'

'I bet you don't remember me.'

'What's your name?'

'Joanne Connolly.'

It didn't mean anything to him.

'I was in the class behind you. How are you settling back?'

'I feel a bit out of things to be honest.'

The girl with the fake blood opened her mouth to reveal a set of fangs. They were the kind you got in theatrical shops. She made a grunting noise at him. Her friend giggled.

'I hope I'm not interrupting anything,' he said.

'Don't worry.'

'How are you enjoying the night?'

'Majorly. The main problem now is finding out how much beer we can squeeze into our bellies without vomiting.'

The girl with the fake blood stared at him.

'Did you ever hear of Bram Stoker?'

'Yes, he wrote *Dracula*.'

'He was my father.'

She was looking at him as if daring him to contradict her.

'Really?'

'That's right. We used to have Bloody Marys for breakfast.'

'Lucky you. You're looking very well. He died almost a century ago.'

'It's the make-up.'

'My mother was Mary Shelley.'

'Very interesting. She was even older than Stoker.'

'Maybe it was my grandmother so. She wrote *Frankenstein,* you know.'

'Is that right?'

'Yes. We were quite a literary family.'

'Well enjoy the rest of the night.'

'Are you going? Would you not like me to bite your neck?'

'Maybe later on.'

He went back to Gabriel.

'You were right,' he said, 'It wasn't a good idea to go over. They're all a bit crazy.'

'They're from the dramatic society. They're doing Frankenstein.'

'It makes sense now.'

'They didn't bother coming out of costume for you. Are you insulted?'

'Highly.'

He was starting to get bored. He wondered how long he'd stay. The whole point of the night was gone.

The barman clinked two glasses together.

'Closing time;' he said, 'Hand up your glasses.'

Almost immediately there was a stampede for the counter. It amused

Brian, bringing back a memory of days with his father. It hadn't been the case in Europe or America. Irish people panicked when they were told they'd have to stop drinking soon. It brought out their love of the forbidden fruit.

'Have they never heard of takeaways?' Gabriel said.

'People like drinking in pubs more than at home,' Brian said, 'You can't see the evidence here because the barman takes the bottles away. At home they sit there in front of you as if to say, "Look how many of me you had last night?"'

'What gets me about pubs is the fact that you can't have a smoke in them anymore.'

'Is there not a place in the back?'

'You'd get frostbite out there.'

He started chuckling to himself.

'What's so funny?'

'I was thinking of the old days. Going into the jacks with a cigarette in my mouth and dropping it into the urinal. I used to try and split the fag from the filter when I pissed on it. Sometimes you didn't have enough piss to do it but usually you did.'

'You've obviously had a very interesting past,' Brian said.

'I miss things like that. Do you ever think we could have those days back again?'

'I don't know. Maybe you should bring it up with the County Council.'

He wanted to be away. The night had gone on too long. Obviously Jennifer wasn't going to turn up now.

He put on his coat.

'Don't say you're going,' Gabriel said.

'If I stay any longer I'll just drink myself sober.'

'That would be tragic.'

'I didn't put my hand in my pocket all night.'

'Don't worry. We'll get you the next time. Tonight was just to hook you in.'

He walked towards the door.

'See you soon, Gabriel,' he said, 'Thanks once again for your thoughtfulness.'

He gave him that gay look again.

'Elvis has left the building,' he said.

He felt the rush of air as he opened the door. It was comforting. The night was balmy.

He didn't want it to end just yet. He'd have stayed longer in the pub if he wasn't stuck with Gabriel. He enjoyed him for the first half of it before he started his rants. He knew why he got on people's nerves. A little bit of him went a long way.

He was hoping Bartley would be asleep when he got home. He wondered if it was too late to ring Jennifer. Would she even come down? They could have one for the road. It would be a relaxing way to break the ice with her.

He knew he should have rung her sooner. He wasn't sure why he didn't. Maybe he thought she'd surprise him by appearing out of the blue.

He decided to text her instead of ringing. He took out his phone. He started spelling the words.

The drunkenness made his fingers slip on the keys. The message went, 'Can I rrrrrrring you?'

A few seconds later his phone buzzed.

'Jennifer?' he said.

'Welcome home.'

'Sorry I didn't ring earlier.'

'I thought you might have. How are you?'

'Good. Things have been a bit crazy since I got back.'

'I can't wait to hear.'

'I believe you got a job.'

'I'll tell you all about it when I see you.'

'You didn't make it to the party.'

''I thought I might be in the way. You might have felt you had to stay with me.'

'What would have been wrong with that?'

'That's a stupid thing to say. Why don't you come down now?'

'Is the pub not closed?'

'Not quite. We could squeeze in a quick one. I left about five pints behind me on the counter. People were buying them for me as if they were going out of fashion.'

'I don't know if that's a good idea. I have work in the morning.'

'It sounds weird to hear you saying that.'

'How do you mean?'

'Work. We're getting old.'

'Look, Brian, you've obviously had a few. Get a bit of sleep for yourself. I'll see you soon. We have all the time in the world to catch up.'

'Okay.'

'Welcome home again. I can't wait to see you.'

35

Bartley was sitting in the kitchen when he got back to the house. He looked the worse for wear.

He had a bottle of whiskey in his hand. There was a cigarette in his other one. An inch of ash was on it.

He looked more sentimental than drunk. There was a photograph album on the table. It lay open at his wedding page. He looked like he'd been crying.

'Did you enjoy the night?' he said.

'It was great.'

'There you go. Telling the two of us you were dreading it. These things are never as bad as you expect.'

'Agreed.'

He took a swig of the whiskey.

'Sorry I fell asleep.'

'Don't worry about it.'

'And sorry about the Gabriel business. You're old enough to decide you who you want to be your friend.'

'He's not really that. I just felt I owed him because he organised the night.'

He stubbed his cigarette out.

'Brian,' he said, 'You have no idea how much it means to me that you came back to us.'

'Where else would I go?'

'When you didn't home at Christmas I thought we might have seen the last of you.'

'That's ridiculous. I just got caught up with the books.'

'What did you do in the pub after I left?'

'Not much. There was a bit of singing.'

'Did you talk to many people?'

'No. It's hard to pick up the threads when you've been away. Is Angela gone to bed?'

'She was exhausted. Probably from lifting me into the taxi.'

'Do you remember that?'

'I sobered up as soon as I got in the door. I don't know why I drank so much. The atmosphere went to my head.'

'Would you not go to bed now?'

'I don't know. My mind is active. I don't like being alone with my thoughts. Would you have a drink with me?'

'If I have any more I'll explode.'

He put the bottle down.

'Sorry about the piano,' he said.

'That's your third "sorry" since I came in.'

'We could get another one if you wanted.'

'Do you mean another "sorry" or another piano?'

'Don't make jokes. I'm not feeling well.'

'What's wrong with you?'

'I've been doing a lot of thinking since I got home.'

'About what?'

You. Me. Your mother.'

'Why now?'

'I don't know. Maybe because you're home. And because I married Angela. I don't know if you approve of that or not.'

'I never said I didn't.'

'You seemed upset at the airport.'

'How did you get that impression?'

'I know you. You put on a good show. It might have fooled Angela but not me.'

'What was I expected to do – jump through hoops?'

'All I want is for you to understand me.'

'What's there to understand?

'How I mess everything up.'

'Like what?'

'The Christmas. Tonight. Your childhood…'

'This is getting a bit heavy. Why don't you go to bed. We can talk about it in the morning.'

He gripped Brian's arm. His eyes were blazing.

'You blame me for Teresa's bad health, don't you?'

'What are you talking about? You're mad.'

'Did you know you can get cancer from stress?'

'Are you trying to tell me you think you caused her death now. Is that it?'

'I don't know. I don't know anything anymore.'

'Go to bed.'

He took a gulp from the bottle.

'I want to say something else.'

'Please – '

'You think I was seeing other women while she was alive, don't you?'

'I think you're drinking too much. That's what I think.'

'Answer the question.'

'People say that.'

'Do you say it?'

'I don't know.'

'Tell me one way or the other.'

'No.'

'You have to.'

He paused.

'Okay, I think you were sleeping with the entire female population of Loughrea. And every other town in Galway as well. Are you happy now?'

'I need to talk about this. I've needed to for a long time.'

'What do you want to say?'

'What I want to say is that they're right.'

'About what?'

'Me seeing other women.'

'Are you serious?'

'Yes.'

'Okay. You've confessed. I forgive you. Now go to bed.'

'Don't be like that. what I'm trying to say to you is that I didn't do anything with them. They were just friends.'

'Why are you bringing it up so?'

'Because I want you to understand me.'

'Well that's fine then. I understand you. Is there anything else?'

'They were just company, Brian. I needed to unload my problems on them. Do you believe that?'

'If you say so.'

'You don't sound as if you're convinced.'

'I am.'

'It's the God's honest truth. We weren't getting on, Brian. She turned her back to me every night in the bed. That's why I started seeing Angela. There was never anything in it even though Teresa always thought there was. In the end I had to bring the vegetables to her father's shop. You might remember that.'

'Can we talk about this some other time?'

He looked up at him pleadingly.

'I just want you to know that I've changed, Brian. I was bad in the past but I'm different now. You know that, don't you?'

'Yes.'

'We'll never be able to bring her back but I want you to know it.'

'It's okay. Honestly. You don't have to do this.'

'I need to. I'm sorry. I was stupid.'

'There's no need to say that. You made your point. I get it.'

'For the first five years with Teresa I was a married bachelor. I wasn't ready to settle down. And we were so different. I didn't know what was going on in her head. Maybe we got married too young. Today it's different. People live together. Do you know what I'm saying?'

'Yes.'

'Then talk to me.'

'What do you want me to say?'

'Anything. I need closure.'

'Then you have it.'

'Maybe you're just saying that.'

'Stop it. Stop this now. I can't take any more of it.'

'I wish you wouldn't be so confrontational with me.'

'I'm not being confrontational. You're the one who's bringing all this stuff up.'

'That's because I feel a distance between us. I want to eradicate it.'

'There's no distance.'

'We're all each of us has left now.'

'Are we?'

'What do you mean?'

'You have Angela.'

'I didn't mean it like that. I mean we're…family.'

Family. It was the thing that always meant most to him. Like the Mafia. Blood was thicker than water. Blood was thicker than everything.

'We're a broken family now,' Brian said, 'One of us died. Have you forgotten that? All the talk in the world can't bring her back.'

'I wish you wouldn't think of things that way. She's still alive to me in my memory. I think of her every day.'

'Is that why you married Angela - to help you to think of her some more?'

He had to say it but as soon as it was said he regretted it. Bartley sobered up momentarily. He stared at Brian with his eyes bulging.

'That was below the belt.'

'Sorry.'

'Jesus, Brian, is that the way you feel? That's why I wanted to talk to you tonight. I know what you think of me. You think I put her in the ground. You don't know how hard the last two years have been for me.'

He thumped his chest.

'I'm saying this to you now because I have drink taken but that doesn't mean it's the drink talking. It means it gave me the courage to express myself in a way I probably won't again.'

He looked defenceless, almost like a child.

'So you forgive me?'

'There's nothing to forgive.'

'You were her favourite by a mile, you know that. Declan was supposed to be mine but I never saw it that way. I tried to give the two of you exactly the same attention.'

'It didn't look that way to me.'

'We think we had Declan too early in the marriage. He wasn't planned. When he came along I showered attention on him. Maybe I blamed myself and I was trying to camouflage that. I don't know. Maybe she drew away from him for the same reason. Or maybe he drew away from her. He was never a child you could pick up. He was always on the go, always with mud all over him. You were quieter. When you were born she was more ready to be a mother. She took you over. By that stage I had so much built up with Declan I put you into the background.'

'It would have meant a lot to me if you said this to me a few years ago.

I knew it anyway. I didn't think you'd admit it.'

'I never thought about it. Maybe the drink brought it out.'

'In vino veritas?'

'Something like that. Do you know I got sick the day I got married to Angela? Everywhere I looked I saw Teresa. It was as if she was haunting me, telling me I shouldn't go through with it.'

'How did Angela feel about that?'

'I never told her. Promise me you won't either.'

'Of course.'

'Don't think life is any party for me.'

'I never thought that.'

'People look at me now and they think: Happy wife, happy life. It isn't like that. We struggle like everyone else. I feel I've stolen her life in some ways. I looked at her dancing on the floor with you tonight and I felt a fraud. I felt like an old man who married a teenager.'

'She's a bit beyond that.'

'She has a lot of life in her. I can't fulfil that.'

'Maybe if you went off the drink.'

'Don't think I don't try. Teresa spent the first half of our marriage begging me to cut down on it.'

'Did you listen to her?'

'In those days I didn't listen to anyone. After Declan was born we went in opposite directions. We were like oil and water.'

'I didn't know it was that bad.'

'We put on an act when you were around.'

'I saw it when I got older.'

'There wasn't as much need to lie then. You could take it.'

'What about Declan?'

'He was made of tougher stuff than you.'

'Sometimes I thought you resented my closeness to her.'

'I was frustrated. You gave her things I never could have. Everyone knew you two had a special thing going on. I could never break into it. It was like an invisible wall around the pair of you.'

'Did you try?'

'You have no idea how many times. Anytime I accused her of spending more time with you than me she said what you said - that I resented your closeness to her. She'd stop the conversations there. I wasn't allowed make my point.'

He went quiet. They heard movement upstairs. Angela came out of the bedroom. She stood on the stairs in her nightie. Her breasts were hanging out of it.

'What's going on down there?' she said, 'Are you two going to stay up all night?'

She sounded stressed. Had she been listening?

'I'll be up in a minute,' Bartley said.

The bottle of whiskey was nearly empty.

'We can continue this some other time,' Brian said.

'Maybe. Or maybe not.'

He stood up. He was swaying on his feet.

'Isn't she a beautiful woman,' he said, 'Did you see her? I love it when she wears things like that.'

'You're wobbling. Be careful.'

'Please try to like her.'

There were tears in his eyes.

'I know the way people talk about her being a social climber and all that. They probably think she married me for this.'

He swept his hand around the room.

'Don't,' Brian said, 'You'll fall.'

He grabbed the edge of the table to balance himself.

'Do you think she's beautiful?' he said, 'Did you see her figure in that nightie?'

'Of course.'

'I can't satisfy her that way, you know. I want to but...'

'We better go up. It must be the middle of the night.'

'Do you resent her getting the farm? Is that why you can't be yourself with her?'

'She's welcome to it. I never wanted it.'

'It's coming to you after her time. You know that, don't you?'

'I couldn't care less if it is or not.'

'Well I'm just telling you it is. She wants that. So does Declan.'

'Do you realise what you put me through tonight? I'm sick with tiredness. I need to go to bed.'

He raised the bottle to his lips but there was nothing in it.

'Fuck it,' he said.

He threw it on the sofa.

'She has a heart of gold. She'd give you her last penny.'

'I never said she wouldn't.'

'She knew I had problems with Teresa but she never came near me while she was well. It was only when she got sick that things changed. I'm not good with sickness. You know that.'

'Do you think I am?'

' I crumble. I'm a coward. Everyone who drinks is a coward. We have to find some way to deny it.'

'Stop beating yourself up.'

'I could never hold a candle to Teresa that way. Or any other way. Angela was understanding of my weaknesses. She has a few herself.'

'I don't want to hear this.'

'There was too much of a gap between me and Teresa. It was like living with a saint. She was a saint and I was a devil.'

'You're not too bad of a devil. Go to bed now.'

The comment seemed to bring him back to the room. He smiled. His eyes were full of tears.

He lurched towards the stairs.

'See you in the morning, son,' he said.

He frowned as if he didn't know what he'd said.

'Son,' he said. 'Son. It feels good to say that word.'

He started to go up the stairs. Angela appeared again.

'I came out to go to the toilet,' she said, 'I can't believe the pair of you are still talking.'

'I'm coming up,' Bartley said.

She came down a few steps for him.

'Are you not coming up yourself?' she said to Brian.

'In a while.'

He listened to her dragging him across the landing and into the bedroom. He continued rambling even after they went inside.

He sank into a chair. Outside a cow bleated. A car screeched on a bend. He tried to collect his thoughts. Everything was happening too fast for him. The party meshed with Bartley's ramblings. A part of him was still in the airport, in Rockaway Beach. He couldn't separate what was happening from what was in his mind.

Who was to blame for the neglect of wives, children, lovers? Maybe everyone and maybe no one. He searched inside himself for answers but deep down he knew there were no answers.

There was only the living of it.

36

When he woke up the next morning he felt sicker than he'd ever felt in his life. How much had he drank? It was impossible to tell. People had slipped him shorts in between the pints. He was mixing them without even realising it.

It could have been worse. He'd have stayed longer if Gabriel hadn't bored him so much. He had him to thank for that now. The drinks he didn't finish were his saviours.

He thought about the conversation with Bartley. Why had he become so emotional? Was it looking at the wedding photographs that did it?

He feared it would be continued over breakfast, continued even in Angela's presence. If that happened he wouldn't be able to take it. He'd have to leave.

Daylight crept into the room. He heard Angela pottering around downstairs. He didn't want to go down to her, to have to listen to her post mortems about the night.

The bedroom door was open. He heard Bartley snoring. Angela would probably have the breakfast ready by the time he surfaced. 'Angela is a multi-tasker,' he used to say, 'She could cook for an army and clean the kitchen at the same time.'

He wondered what to take for his hangover. Bartley's hair of the dog wouldn't work. Neither would anything else. You just had to tough it out.

He stood on the floor. His body felt numb. It hurt when he walked. He had to move slowly or it hurt more.

He showered. The cold water felt good on his skin, driving away the headache. He stayed inside it for a long time.

Angela called up from the kitchen.

'Are you coming down? I hear you moving around.'

'In a minute.'

Why wouldn't she leave him alone? He'd have to make small talk with her now. It would be harder because of the way he was feeling.

He went down the stairs. He expected to see her in the kitchen but she wasn't there.

'Come in here,' she said from the room next door.

He went in. She was sitting behind a table. It had a laptop on it. There were files beside it. Rusty was standing beside her. He had his head resting on her lap. She patted him.

She had some auctioneering literature in her hand. She was reading it through a pair of horn-rimmed spectacles.

'You look secretarial,' he said.

'Thank you – or maybe it wasn't a compliment.'

'It was'

'Well I'll accept it as one so. Actually I've been on the phone to clients earlier.'

'You have? After all the activity last night?'

'Someone has to do it.'

'Do you think it's going to work out?'

'If we survive the first year. That's always the worst one in any business.'

'What kind of feedback are you getting from the clients?'

'The usual. They make out like they're interested until it comes to putting their hands in their pockets. Then you can't see their heels for the dust.'

'That sounds familiar.'

'Everyone wants something for nothing. They go out of their way to annoy you. They spend all day asking you questions about places and then buy nothing.'

'That doesn't surprise me either.'

'A great hobby of the Irish is picking your brain.'

'You sound like Dad now.'

'We spend so much time together maybe we're turning into one another.'

'So you've actually started showing places to people?'

'I wasn't supposed to let that out of the bag.'

'You seem to know a good bit about it.'

'I worked at this kind of thing for a while before I met Bartley. Did you not know that?'

'There are a lot of things I don't know about you, Angela.'

She gave him a look.

'What's that supposed to mean?'

He wasn't sure why he'd said it. He couldn't resist baiting her. He wanted her to take offence but she was too clever for that.

'Who thought up this idea first?'

'Both of us really. He was looking for something to take him away from the farm. I thought it would be a good antidote.'

'See how it goes anyway.'

'It'll keep us off the streets. The devil finds work for idle hands.'

She stood up.

'I have some rashers in the kitchen. They're already cooked. I just need to heat them. Or would you like a toasted cheese sandwich? I have a machine that makes them but I don't use it much. You can't beat the natural food, can you?'

'No.'

'I've never bothered with those bloody microwaves. Bartley says we're the only house in the country without them but I've never gone for them.'

'You're right. The fry would be great.'

'How are you feeling after last night?'

'Not too clever.'

'Did Jennifer turn up?'

'I spoke to her on the phone. It was too late for her to come down. She has work today.'

'That's a pity.'

'I'll see her as soon as she has a minute.'

'I'm sure you have a lot to catch up on.'

'Buckets.'

Did you enjoy the dancing?'

'You put me to shame on the floor.'

'I still have a few moves left in me, don't I?'

'More than a few.'

'I shouldn't be trying to be as good as the young people.'

'You're better than them. You were a real hit.'

'Come on now. I couldn't hold a candle to them.'

'How was himself when you got back?'

'He woke up, as you know. I was hoping to get him into bed before he did. That was some session you had with him.'

'Is he awake yet?'

'He made a few grunts when I was getting up. I'd say he'd be down soon.'

'Did he keep you awake when he went up?'

'I hardly closed an eye all night.'

'You should go into the other room when he's in that condition. Mam used to.'

'She did?'

He was sorry he said that. He didn't want to share anything about his mother with her.

'Occasionally. Not often.'

'I thought the pair of you were on for an all-nighter.'

'It would have been if you didn't appear.'

'I hope I didn't interrupt anything.'

'I didn't mean it like that. We were finished.'

'Okay, so let's have some breakfast, will we?'

'That'd be great.'

They went out to the kitchen. Rusty was there. He ran over to him.

'Hello, buddy,' he said.

He was hoping Bartley would be down soon. They'd exhausted their conversation. If it went on any longer she'd probably start asking him questions about his plans for the future. He wasn't sure he'd be able to take that.

She stood at the cooker. For a moment he saw his mother in her. It was the way she was standing with her hand on her hip as she fried the eggs. Her face was reflected in a mirror on the opposite wall. It reminded him of a photo he had of her, a photo in a cameo brooch.

'What's wrong?' she said, 'You look like you've seen a ghost.'

How close she was to the truth.

'It must be the hangover. Don't mind me.'

'You probably had a few too many. Don't worry about it. If you're not entitled to that after two years I don't know what to say.'

'People were buying them for me right left and centre. That's always dangerous.'

She turned on the kettle.

'I hope you didn't mix the grape with the grain.'

'I'm afraid I did.'

'That's always treacherous. You need some blotting paper to soak it up. Wait till you have a few rashers and eggs inside you. You'll feel like a new man.'

She continued frying the eggs. The rashers sizzled beside it. She started singing. She often sang as she cooked. That reminded him of his mother too. Rusty looked up at her expectantly. Every few seconds she threw him a piece of bread.

The kettle boiled. She gave him the tea. Afterwards she poured a cup for herself. She must have put five spoons of sugar into it.

He started drinking. It was only then he realised how thirsty he was. He was gulping it.

'My God,' she said, 'Slow down or you'll choke. You remind me of himself with the other stuff.'

'It's the dehydration.'

'At least it won't give you a hangover.'

'I'll be thankful for that small mercy.'

'The latest I hear is that the caffeine in it is bad for you. They'll be telling us water is bad for you next.'

'You're probably right.'

She gave him the egg.

'The rashers will be done in a minute.'

'This is fantastic. You're like Darina Allen.'

'Darina Allen my granny. You're losing the run of yourself there. It's just basic food, I'm afraid. Be an angel and get the plates out of the dresser, would you?'

He got them. She ladled the food on. There were more rashers and eggs than he expected.

'I don't think I'll be able to do justice to this,' he said.

'Of course you will. Just gobble it up.'

He started eating, started to feel vaguely human again. Before he knew it he had half the food gone.

'You look like you're enjoying that,' she said.

'I feel like someone who just came off a hunger strike.'

They heard Bartley moving upstairs.

'He's awake,' she said, 'I wondered when he was going to surface.'

'He'll probably be in a bad way. He fairly laid into it last night.'

'If he could only have stayed on the Guinness.'

'Some hope.'

'Did you have a job getting him out of the taxi?'

'It was like lifting a sack of potatoes. Thank God I have Gerry. He did most of it.'

He tramped down the stairs.

'Here he is. God love him, he'll probably have the mother and father of all hangovers.'

He came in.

'Good morning to you both,' he said.

His eyes were bloodshot. When he went to sit down he almost missed the chair.

'Be careful,' Angela said, 'You'll kill yourself.'

'I'm fine.'

He sat in more carefully this time. .

'I thought you were going to end up on the floor.'

'The situation is under control now. What's for breakfast?'

'Have a bit of patience. You're hardly in the room.'

'I see the two of you eating. That looks nice what you have, Brian.'

'It's delicious.'

'Okay, Angela. Some of that if you wouldn't mind.'

'It's already done. If you don't pressurise me I might be good enough to get it for you.'

'Do you hear, that, Brian? She's making me work for it.'

She went over to the cooker. The rashers were still sizzling. She put a few on a plate. She plonked it down in front of him.

'There,' she said, 'Eat that up and stop complaining.'

'Thank you.'

'You look desperate, by the way.'

'Thanks.'

'What do you expect? You drank the bar dry.'

'Loving words from a loving wife,' he said, looking at Brian.

'How is your head?' he said to him.

'Falling off me.'

'It's always the way.'

He started eating.

'In the old days I'd have had a day's work done by this time.'

'Never mind your day's work. Just get some rashers into you.'

She handed him a glass of orange.

'What's that?'

'Orange juice. I squeezed it myself.'

He looked at it as if it was something from another planet.

'She gives me the good stuff in the morning,' he said to Brian, 'to take away the taste of the bad stuff I put into myself at night.'

'That sounds sensible.'

'Hopefully it evens itself out. Piss away the whiskey to make room for the juice. Maybe it'll ferment it.'

'Stop that talk,' she said, 'It's disgusting.'

'It's true, though, isn't it?'

Brian finished his meal. He stood up.

'Thanks for listening to me last night,' Bartley said to him.

'And thanks for what you said.'

He looked out the window. Everything was peaceful. He felt restless. The day yawned in front of him. He didn't know what to do with it. He wondered what time Jennifer would be off work.

'I think I'll go out for a walk,' he said.

'Not again,' Bartley said.

'What do you mean?'

'Didn't you go for one last night?'

'I've been known to take two walks a year.'

'You're right,' Angela said, 'Get away from us two old cronies.'

'Where will you go?' Bartley said.

'Nowhere in particular.'

'That usually means a woman,' he said. 'Tell Jennifer I was asking for her.'

'I'll probably just go up through the fields.'

'I left my keys in the tractor. If you see them you might bring them back to me.'

'It's not like you to forget them.'

'My son was coming home from America,' he said, 'I was all excited.'

37

It was a warm day. The air reminded him of America. His footsteps crunched across the gravel of the driveway. He listened to the chickens cackling in the barn. He remembered Bartley telling him on one of his phone calls that a fox had broken in while he was away. He'd reinforced the lock since.

He went into the shed where the Austin was. It looked bad. There was rust everywhere. The tyres were flat.

The door creaked as he opened it. He sat in. The keys were on the dashboard. He gunned the engine but nothing happened. Maybe Bartley was right, he thought, maybe he should drive it into a scrapyard. On the other hand it was one of the few links to the past that were left.

He went back outside. What would he do with the day?

He jumped over the wall beside the cowshed. He could go any way he wanted. He thought of times when every day was like this, when things just happened in their own sweet time. It was a good way to live.

He walked up by the north field. It was the biggest one they owned. Only a few cows remained on it. They looked forlorn.

He crossed into another field. He wasn't sure if it was one they owned or not. What had Bartley sold and what had he kept? Sometimes he didn't even seem to know himself. A lot of his deals were sealed by handshakes under the influence.

He wondered if he'd continue doing farming on the side if he went into the auctioneering in a serious way. They hadn't got round to talking about that yet. Would he stay on the farm himself? He didn't know if he wanted to or if he was expected to. Maybe he was expected to go into the auctioneering fulltime.

He thought of Sinead in UCD, Mia in Africa, Jennifer in her school. Everyone was busy except him. Was life passing him by? A part of him wanted to go back to Dublin Airport and jump on a plane somewhere. The adrenalin of coming home had taken his mind off Mia. Now that things were quiet again he thought of her. Maybe Jennifer would take his mind off her. Maybe she'd take his mind off everything.

He went from field to field. Farmers waved at him. He didn't know most of them but they seemed to know him. It was always the way with him, being greeted by people he didn't know. It was even the way iat the party in the bar.

He got to a field where there used to be a bull when he was growing up. Declan and himself used to aggravate it to get it to chase after them. They always kept a safe distance from him, climbing over a wall when he got close, but one day he moved faster than usual after them. He started gaining on them before they reached the wall.

Declan got there first. He screamed at Brian to hurry up. He was running as fast as he could but when he looked behind him he saw the bull was practically beside him. He could feel his breath. He had to jump into a ditch to avoid him. They laughed about the incident for years afterwards. His ankle got twisted in the fall. He was hobbling around for the next few weeks on crutches. That spelt the end of his bull-baiting days.

The wind got up. He tightened his coat around him. He wanted to walk until all his worries were gone. That always got rid of them for him. When he walked he forgot everything.

He stopped at a cowshed they owned. When he went inside the smell almost took his breath away. It was rancid.

He looked out the window or what passed for a window. It was really only a hole in the wall. Outside it he saw Bartley's tractor.

He went up to it. The keys were in the ignition all right.

He turned it on but the engine just spluttered. He kept turning it but nothing happened. He knew what Bartley would have said if he was there: 'Stop it for fuck's sake, you'll flood the engine. That fuckin' thing will be the death of me. It's clapped out - like everything else in this place.'

He decided to ring Jennifer. He thought she'd be a work but she picked up immediately.

'Sorry about last night,' she said.

'It wasn't your fault. Are you not at work?'

'I rang in sick. I couldn't get back to sleep after your call. I think I'm coming down with something. I'd have been worthless if I went in. The kids crawl all over you if you're below par.'

'I feel responsible.'

'Don't. You did me a favour. We have a bitch of a principal. I needed a break from her.'

'So when am I going to see you?'

'I don't want to give you my dose. Wait till I pick up a bit. How is your head?'

'You're the third person who's asked me that today. I'm starting to feel it's a topic of national interest.'

'Maybe it is. What are you doing with yourself?'

'Just wandering around the fields.'

'I envy you.'

'Call me as soon as you feel up to it.'

'I wish I could be with you.'

'You will soon.'

He didn't know what to do after he hung up. It was pointless going back to the house. They'd only pump him with questions all day long.

He decided he'd go into town. Would he walk in? The decision was made for him when he saw a bus coming.

He hailed it. The driver waved to him. He thought he recognised him. It stopped beside him like a car would. When the door opened he saw it was Joe Ruddy inside. He was another classmate of his.

'This doesn't look like an official stop,' he said.

'Fuck the official stops. How are you, me old segotia? Long time no see.'

'Not too bad.'

'I heard you were home. Sorry I couldn't make it to your bash last night.'

'You didn't miss much. So you're a bus driver now.'

'How did you guess? Get in.'

It started moving before he was properly inside it.

'Jesus,' he said, 'Are you trying to kill me?'

He laughed.

'No,' he said, 'Just testing your reflexes.'

He reached into his pocket for the fare but Joe stopped him.

'Sit down, for fuck's sake. I take it you're going to town.'

'To be honest with you I don't know where I'm going. I have a bad hangover. I was trying to walk it off when I saw the bus. I took it as a sign not to take too much out of myself.'

'Good thinking.'

He sat down. He was the only one on the bus. Joe started to sing. He was glad he wasn't interested in putting up chat on him.

He drove like a maniac, screeching on the bends in a way that made him feel they were on three wheels. He'd always been something of a show-off. He remembered him imitating the teachers in the college when they were out of the room.

They got to town in a matter of minutes.

'Thanks, Joe,' he said getting off, 'even if you're a liability to Bus Eireann.'

'You're welcome. It's always nice to see an old face. Be seeing you around. Take care of that head. A large Southern Comfort usually does the trick.'

'You sound like my father.'

He walked down the street. It was empty of people. He used to like it that way but now he thought there was something desolate about it. America had given him an appetite for activity. Maybe Gabriel was right about travel creating a need that had to be nourished.

He wondered how many people lived in Loughrea. Was it more or less the same as when he was growing up? Why were there so few people on the streets? Could Bartley make a living trying to sell houses in a town with such a small population? Did he intend to branch out to other ones? Maybe it wasn't about that. Maybe it was just about having a reason to get up in the morning. If nothing else it might help him to go easy on the bottle.

Could Brian live with him in Loughrea? Could he make his life in Dublin either? Maybe he belonged in neither place. Jennifer said to him once, 'You're in love with change.' He hadn't thought of himself like that before she said it. Sometimes other people knew you better than you knew yourself.

He liked Loughrea's intimacy but it was too small-minded. Joe Ruddy had been friendly but he still felt at a distance when he was talking to him. There was something in his expression that said, 'You think you're better than us because you've been away.'

Was that the real reason he didn't talk to him? Coming back to Loughrea to live meant people would always be looking at him, taking him in. He preferred being the watcher rather than the watched. He wanted to take in everything that was happening without being a part of it. That was why the coming home party didn't work. He wasn't able to milk it like Declan would have.

He passed gardens overgrown with weeds. JCBs lay in disused lots. Many of the people he passed were overweight. A lot of them were on their phones. Was that the reason? He expected that in Dublin but not here. Two years ago it wasn't like that. Could things change that fast?

Everywhere looked neglected to him. What made it worse was that nobody seemed to be aware of that fact. The town, he thought, had a low self-image. He'd felt that way himself growing up. Anything showy was regarded as a fault. Humility was the great virtue in all things.

He felt people were looking at him as he walked. Was it his imagination? Now and then someone said hello. They were respectful but distant, like Joe Ruddy. Did they know who he was? Maybe they thought he'd got notions about himself since he went to Dublin. That was always the expression they used for someone who was out of Loughrea for any length of time. They had 'notions.'

The sun beat down on him. He went in to a pub to escape its glare.

It was one of those spit-on-the-floor places that hadn't changed since he was a child.

He felt as if he was entering a tomb as he walked up to the counter. There was an old man a bit further down. He had a half-drunk pint of Guinness in his hand. He recognised him as Eddie Culkin, a retired shopkeeper. He used to see him out walking with his wife. They were inseparable.

He was looking at the television as if his life depended on it, the way people did in bars. The News was on. There'd been a car crash.

Brian sat down beside him. He took his eyes off the television.

'Soft oul' day, thank God,' he said.

'It is.'

'You're Bartley Kilcoyne's lad, aren't you – the one that went away?'

'That I am.'

'Welcome home. How's she cuttin'?'

'Fine, thanks.'

'When did you get home?'

'Yesterday. '

'And you're out on the town already.'

'I wanted to see the place. I haven't been here for a while.'

'Good man. I'm glad you chose here as one of your stops. It's my haven. Can I buy you a drink?'

'That's very kind of you.'

'What's your poison?'

'I'll have a pint of Guinness.'

He put his hand up.

'Two pints of Arthur G, Seamus,' he said to the barman. And to Brian, 'I believe you were in the U.S. of A. The Land of Opportunity.'

'So they say.'

'How did you enjoy yourself?'

'I had a good time. I moved around as much as I could.'

'Why not? You might as well enjoy life while you can.'

The drink arrived. He sipped at it. Eddie drained the last of his other pint.

'That was terrible about your mother,' he said, 'I was very sorry to hear it.'

'Thank you. It's a while ago now.'

'I know, but the hurt doesn't go away.'

'Maybe not, but you learn to deal with it better.'

'Hopefully. It was an awful tragedy though.'

'Awful.'

'I used to see her taking you to school when you were a lad. She used to hold onto your hand as if her life depended on it.'

'It's nice to hear that.'

'Your father has been in a bad way since she died.'

'He's doing better now.'

'I'm glad to hear that. I'm sure Angela is a great comfort to him.'

'She is.'

He licked the froth off his drink.

'I believe you're getting into the property game,' he said.

How did he know about that? Maybe everyone did. Nothing would have surprised him now.

'We haven't made a decision on it yet.'

'Don't leave it too long. That's where the money is. There's a lovely set of bungalows going up outside the town.'

'So I believe.'

'You might even think of getting one for yourself.'

'You'd never know. What about you? Would you be interested?'

'That'll be the day. They cost a king's ransom. I think I'll stick with my little *shebeen.*'

He hadn't been drinking his pint but now he lowered it in one swallow. Brian was mesmerised watching him. It was as if it was water.

'How is your wife?' he asked him.

He paused.

'I buried her last winter,' he said.

'I'm sorry to hear that.'

'She was sick for a long time.'

'That doesn't make it any easier.'

His eyes welled up.

'Do you have any children?'

'Two, Sean and Paddy. They're abroad in England now. I don't see them much.'

'That's a pity.'

'They have their own lives now.'

'I'm sorry to hear that.'

'That's the way.'

He looked into the distance.

'Young people,' he said. He gave a chuckle.

'Anyway I better be off. I have a few things to do.'

'It's good to have met you.'

'You too. We need more young faces around here. Are you planning to stay?'

'I hope to. For a while anyway.'

'Say hello to Bartley for me.'

'I will.'

He stood up.

'Well, *go n'eírí an bóthar leat.*'

'The same to you.'

He was slow making his way to the door. It was only when he started walking that Brian realised how infirm he was.

He went out. The barman took his glass.

'Nice man,' Brian said.

'He's here every day,' he said, 'He should probably take out shares in the place.'

'I'm sure that could apply to more than him.'

'He beats the main contingent to the door every morning. After that he just drinks all day, God love him. He can't get over Ann.' That was his wife.

Brian looked out at the day. It was darkening.

The barman turned on the television. He watched Sky News. The same item kept repeating itself – an accident on a motorway in Athenry.

He could have sat there all day watching it, watching the same images repeat themselves, the same wording on the tickertape. How many people like Eddie Culkin did that. Would he too if he lived there?

'I think we're promised more rain,' the barman said. Why did people say promised when they meant threatened?

'We probably wouldn't recognise anything else.'

He stood up.

'I'm off.' he said.

'Are you not finishing your pint?'

There was two-thirds of it left.

'I thought I'd be able for it but I wasn't. I had a few too many last night.'

'I know the feeling,' he laughed.

'See you again.'

'Thanks for your custom.'

Everywhere seemed to be bathed in a haze when he got out to the street. It took him a while to get used to the daylight. It was always the way after coming out of somewhere dark.

He looked around him. The shopfronts had a worn-down look. A pane of glass was broken in a newsagent's window. A board had been placed over the hole. Flies buzzed around the newspapers.

A car outside the door had a flat tyre. The tax disc on the windscreen said 2008. He had a vague memory of seeing it there before he went to Europe. A bicycle with its tyres missing lay chained to a lamp-post. Only the frame was left. The chain was probably worth more than anything else there now..

A shop with 'Mocha Coffee' written on the window had closed down. Beside it was an auctioneer's office. There was a 'For Sale' sign on it. Would Bartley buy it? There was a JCB parked beside it. He wondered if it was going to be demolished.

Many of the shops in the street had closed down. Some were in the process of doing so. They had signs saying 'Bargains' and 'Clearance – Everything Must Go' in the windows. Others were taken over by the conglomerates. The ones that survived had 'Sale!' splashed over their windows. They were offering goods at knockdown prices. It looked like an attempt to avoid the same fate. There were only one or two very few customers in them. He was reluctant to go in to any of them for fear of being nabbed by an over-zealous proprietor.

The Capri café was gone. It was just a boarded-up shack now, another victim of the recession. He thought back to the day he'd spent there with Jennifer and Tommy Glynn. He hadn't seen Tommy since. Bartley said he was on the buildings in Kilburn.

A car slowed down in front of him. The horn beeped. A face smiled out at him. Who was it? He thought it might have been someone else from his class. Why did people in cars always think you recognised them? They could be gazing at you from behind a dirty windscreen and they'd still assume you knew who they were even though you hadn't seen them for years.

People walked by him giving him the kind of look that said, 'I know you but I can't put a name on you.' It made him feel self-conscious. Two years of anonymity were being replaced with sudden exposure. Last night had increased that. As he said to Bartley, he couldn't go back on that now. He didn't know if he'd be able to deal with it in the long term. As a child he was just another person. He could have done a somersault up and down the street and nobody would have noticed. It was different now. Would that difference eventually get him down? Would he have to go away to get rid of it?

Travel was exotic. Routine wasn't routine in a foreign country. It wasn't just the people or the scenery that was different, it was everything. But if you spent long enough in a place there had to be repetition. It was impossible to avoid it. That's what he was trying to tell Bartley and Angela when they assumed all of his time away was exciting. Nothing could be. No matter where you were it was somebody's home place, somebody's dullness.

If he stayed in Loughrea he knew it would be better for him to get away from the farm even if he wasn't going to marry Jennifer. Maybe he'd move into an apartment. Joe Ruddy might know of a cheap one. It would mean getting a job to pay the rent. What would that entail? He had no qualifications. If he went back to UCD he'd have some but that was a remote prospect now. He'd lost all interest in the idea.

If he got a steady job he might be able to afford to buy a house sometime in the future. That would be a million times easier if he got back with Jennifer. They could even have moved into one of the bungalows Eddie Culkin was talking about. Bartley would help them get on their feet if that transpired. Was it on his mind? Was it on Jennifer's?

He needed to see her, to find out how she was thinking about things. He knew he'd be self-conscious talking to her because of Mia. She'd be expecting him to call to her house when she got over her dose. He'd have preferred to meet her somewhere neutral like a café. He didn't want her to come up to the farm. That would have meant Bartley and Angela earwigging everything they said.

His life would be simple if he married Jennifer. She'd probably stay in the job she was in even though she wasn't too keen on the school. He could apprentice himself to the auctioneering business and do a bit of farming on the side. The transition from his old life wouldn't be too sudden. Jennifer could move in with them until they got the deposit together for a house. He imagined Bartley and Angela showering them with presents and nine months later serenading the entry of a grandchild into the family.

Would he be happy with that or would he always be looking outside it? Would his mind drift back to Europe, to America? Could he immerse himself in the kind of life most people lived, the kind of life they didn't even have to work at tolerating because they had a higher threshold of routine than him?

It started to rain. He tried to cross the road but he couldn't. The cars on the road speeded up. Why did they always go faster when it rained? Maybe it just seemed that way.

He pulled up the collar of his coat. The rain came down in sheets. It stopped when he sheltered in a doorway. By that stage he was drenched. It knew how to catch you at your most defenceless.

He felt a hand on his shoulder as he tried to shake himself dry.

'Jaysus,' a voice said, 'Is it yourself that's in it?'

It was Paudie Gleeson. He'd been in his class at school too. Was he going to run into the whole class before the day was out?

'How's the goin'?' he said.

'Not too bad. It's good to see you.'

'You too. You're looking well. It must be all that American sun.'

'How did you know where I was?'

'We have nothing better to talk about round here. Maybe we need someone to be jealous of – especially when it's raining its guts out.'

'You don't have to be jealous. The sun is over-rated.'

'Don't say that or you'll bring a curse on us. It'll be like St. Swithun's Day. We're bad enough as it is.'

'How are you keeping yourself?'

'Middling. I haven't seen you since the Leaving Cert.'

'How did you get on at it?'

He gave a wry laugh.

'They gave me three Honours,' he said, 'The honour of doing it, the honour of failing it and the honour of being kicked out of the college.'

'Very funny.'

'It's closer to the truth than you might think. Have you been back to the place yet?'

'I'm only home. I might drop down sometime.'

'I believe you went to the university.'

'For a while.'

'What's that supposed to mean?'

'I doubt if I'll go back.'

'Did you fail your exams?'

'No. I just got fed up.'

'That's a pity. You had the brains. All I have between my ears is sawdust.'

'Me too. It's just a different kind of sawdust.'

'Don't be modest.'

What are you doing with yourself?'

'I got a job in Leahy's.' It was the local hardware shop.

'You could do worse.'

'It's the only thing that's out there now. The Latvians have all the good jobs got. There aren't many leftovers.'

'That can't be true.'

'It is. This is the town that time forgot. Every building that's standing is on borrowed time. Once the excavators get in from Dublin they won't be happy till they blitz the last one of us off the face of the earth. That's why you have to grab the first thing going.'

'I thought you might have got a few quid during the boom.'

'Now and then you'd see a few trendies buyi ng SUVs to let you know how well they were doing. They were the exceptions. Most of us were pulling the devil by the tail.'

He took a hammer out of his pocket.

'Need any old wardrobes fitted, sir?'

'Not at the moment,' he laughed, 'but I'll keep you in mind.'

'What will you do if you don't go back to the university? Will you stick at the farming?'

'I haven't made up my mind yet. I'm between the devil and the deep blue sea.'

'You won't get much blue sea around here. Just mucky water.'

'That'll do.'

'Did you ever think you'd stay away for good?'

'Maybe I'd have been better off to.'

'I'd love to get out of this kip.'

'Don't be so hard on it. There are worse places.'

'Name me one.'

'Dublin.'

'I doubt that. Take my advice and feck off back there again even if you don't go back to the university.'

'Why do you say that?'

'Nothing goes on here. The only thing that changes is the weather. We farm in the summer and fuck in the winter. Beyond that we just sit around the house and look out at the rain.'

'Are you still living with your parents?'

'Unfortunately. The old lad isn't well.'

'I'm sorry to hear that. I hope it's nothing serious.'

'We're keeping the fingers crossed. He's having tests at the moment.'

'I'll say a prayer for him.'

'Thanks. I believe your own father got hitched again.'

'That's right. To Angela Curley.'

'Angela has the head well screwed on. She's great crack too. She'll be good for him.'

'I hope so.'

He looked up at the sky.

'It's getting ready for another shower. I better be pushing on. If I don't get back to this dosshouse they'll give me my P45.'

'It was good to see you.'

'If you're staying around you'll be seeing a lot more of me. I'm up and down this street a hundred times a day.'

He slapped him on the back and went off. Brian watched him as he swung round the corner. He envied him. His life was free of tension. Maybe that was more important than anything else.

The day darkened. He started to walk again. He went towards the bus stop but then changed his mind half way to it. He didn't want to run into Joe Ruddy again. He decided to take Paudie's advice and go down to the college.

He passed by houses he remembered as a child. Many of them were boarded up. A dog barked at him from behind a gate. Two men sitting at a porch gave him a half-wave.

He walked faster. Every so often someone hooted a horn at him. He waved at them without knowing who they were.

He got to the college. How many times had he cycled up the avenue to the huge front door? He knocked but got no reply. Then he noticed that it was slightly open. He pushed it in.

The first thing he was aware of was the smell of chalk. He walked down the corridor. Photographs of former students lined the walls. He wasn't among them.

He walked along by the classrooms, stopping for a moment outside his own one. When he looked in he realised it wasn't a classroom anymore, it was a laboratory. The benches were piled on top of each other in the corner. As he went further down the corridor he noticed other classrooms had been converted too. A strange sense of nostalgia hit him. How could he be nostalgic for something he didn't like when it was happening?

He went outside again. The day had cooled. He walked down by the river. A few fishermen were in the middle of it in their waders. He watched fish jumping up to catch flies in their mouths. The water gurgled under the bridge.

As he approached the main road he saw Fr Finnerty coming towards him, his cassock blowing in the wind. He was hoping he wouldn't notice him.

'That wouldn't be Brian, would it?' he said.

'I'm afraid it would,' he said, 'behind all the hair.'

'Welcome home,' he said shaking his hand. 'Yes, you have quite a mop, haven't you? You haven't joined a rock band or anything?'

'Not quite.'

'You've been gone from us for a while.'

'Two years.'

'My, my. Where does the time go? I believe you've been touring around the globe.'

'I saw a few places all right.'

'You're at the university in Dublin now, aren't you?'

'Not anymore I'm afraid.'

'Why so?'

'I wasn't cut out for it.'

'But I heard you passed your first year with flying colours.'

'I did. Second year was different.'

'Could I ask why?'

'It's complicated.'

'Try me.'

'I can't really explain it. I just gave up the ghost.'

'So you failed your exams.'

'Yes.'

'Oh Brian, you must repeat. It would be so much of a waste with your brains. The teachers here talk about you as our great hope for the town. They want you to put us on the world's stage.'

'That's a laugh. I'm afraid the only stage I'll be on is the one out of town.'

'Please, Brian, no jokes. I beg you to do the repeats.'

'I'd only fail them again.'

'No you wouldn't. Remember Robert Bruce. He succeeded at the seventh attempt.'

'I don't think so, Father. I failed because I wanted to.'

He gave a bewildered look.

'That I don't understand.'

'As I said, it's complicated. I just realised I wanted something different.'

'Let me get this straight. You deliberately failed an exam your father paid you to sit.'

'That's it.'

He shook his head frustratedly.

'You were one of the brightest boys in your class. Are you going to throw all that away?'

'Brightest? That's the first I heard of it.'

'We might have been a bit hard on you. If we were, it was to get the best out of you.'

'It doesn't matter now anyway. The university just wasn't for me.'

'Have you told Bartley you failed the exam deliberately?'

'No, and I'd appreciate it if you didn't either.'

It was the first time he'd ever said anything assertive to him.

'This is very upsetting to me. I don't know what else you have in mind. You have to see your degree through. I'm sure everyone tells you that.'

'They do but I don't listen to them.'

'We all go through periods like that, Brian. The good Lord understands. Why not give yourself a break from it, even for a year. You'll go back refreshed then.'

'I've already had a break. That's what made up my mind for me.'

'I think you're making a big mistake. I'd hate you to come back to me in five years saying you regretted your decision.'

'If that happens I'll tell everyone you warned me about it.'

'Brian I –'

'I'm sorry but I don't want to talk about it anymore, Father. My mind is made up. Wild horses wouldn't drag me back to UCD. I've done a lot of thinking over the last two years. It wasn't a decision I made lightly.'

He was silent for a few moments. Then he said, 'How is Bartley?'

'He's fine. Full of praise for you about how you handled the wedding.'

'It was my pleasure. We all deserve a second chance at life. And Angela?'

'She's fine too.'

'I was glad for them. Love works in strange ways. I'm sure your mother was smiling down at both of them from heaven.'

'I'm sure she was.'

'Well anyway I won't go on about your studies. I'll just say a prayer that you find what you're looking for in life.'

'Thank you.'

'Say a little prayer for me too, won't you?'

'Of course.'

He paused, looking him up and down.

'I suppose you never thought of the priesthood. Do you remember the days when you were my altar boy?'

'How can I forget them?'

'I had you pegged for the cloth at that time.'

'I've changed a bit since.'

'Not too much, I hope.'

'I don't think I'd have made much of a priest.'

'I beg to differ. Did I hear you lost your vocation after your mother died?'

'It wasn't as simple as that.'

'But it had something to do with it, right?'

'Maybe.'

'That would be a pity.'

'Do you not find it difficult to believe in a God who'd make such a perfect person as my mother suffer like she did?'

'Of course. That's the real tester for our faith, isn't it? I know that sounds like a cliche. Even though it was terrible how she died, I firmly believe the good Lord took her that way for a reason. Maybe he took her like he took his own son, so she could be with him, so she could pray for the rest of us.'

'That's a nice way to think about it.'

'But you find it too convenient.'

'I'm afraid so.'

'He'd want you with him too, you know.'

'Me? You mean God wants me to die?'

'No, I was thinking of you being a priest. Your mother often conveyed to me her wish that you'd join us in the seminary.'

'That was when I was a boy. Her dying wish was that I'd marry.'

'It was?'

'Yes.'

'Ah. I presume she was thinking of Jennifer Coyle.'

'She was.'

'Jennifer is a fine girl. I know her family well. I used to see the pair of you out walking before you went away. You made a lovely couple. If you ever decided to go up the aisle I'd be more than happy to perform the ceremony for you.'

'That would be very nice. If it happened.'

'Thank you, Brian. How does she feel about your decision to leave the university?'

'She said she'd go along with whatever I decide.'

'Isn't she teaching now?'

'She is.'

'I'm sure she'll be a credit to the profession. You would too if you decided to go down that road.'

'That's unlikely.'

'Have you any idea what you might do?'

'Not really.'

'I believe Bartley is winding down at the farm now. You won't have that to fall back on if you persist in your decision to drop out of college. With a degree under your arm, all sorts of doors would open for you.'

'Let's not get back into that.'

'Okay, Brian. I can see you have your father's stubbornness.'

'Is my old classroom gone?' he asked, trying to divert him, 'I was down at the college.'

'Yes, they're closing a lot of the rooms down. Very few pupils now, you see. There are no boarders either, only day boys. They're all deserting us.'

He gave a little laugh.

'I suppose it's happening everywhere.'

'It is. They got rid of me last year. It appears my teaching methods were too conventional. Did you ever hear the like of that? Talk and chalk is dead, I hear. It's all audio-visual aids now.'

'I didn't know you'd retired.'

'That's a polite way of putting it. I'm still on the Board of Management. It helps me to keep my hand in. I need that. Life can get lonely for someone who lives on his own.'

'I thought you had a housekeeper.'

'What planet have you been living on? Priests don't have housekeepers anymore. They'd be afraid we'd molest them.'

'I'm sorry to hear that. Are there still priests there now?'

'A priest is almost a dirty word now as a result of the scandals. Lay people are running the world these days, aren't they? They'll be saying Mass yet.'

'Do you miss the classroom?'

'I did when I left it first but you get used to being out of it. I'm nearly seventy now, you know.'

'You don't look it.'

'Thank you.'

He couldn't think of anything else to say. Fr. Finnerty suddenly looked old. He felt sorry for him.

He looked at the fishermen across the road. They were putting away their catches. The sky was starting to darken.

'I better let you go now. I don't want to take up your day on you.'

'It was good to meet you.'

'And you. Give my best to Bartley and Angela. And of course Jennifer. I'd love you to come down and see me sometime. I want to ask you about the things you did while you were away. I promise not to nag you about UCD.'

'I'll do that.'

'And don't forget the prayers. We all need them.'

'I won't.'

'Goodbye, Brian.'

'Goodbye, Father.'

He watched him walking down the road. Despite his age he was able to move quite fast even in the wind. Brian had a grudging respect for him, for his survival instincts.

He wasn't surprised that he'd been removed from teaching. He remembered him for his sarcasm in the classroom, his outmoded attitudes. He liked his pupils to be smart but not too smart. If they were, the sin of pride entered the fray.

Bartley had lots of stories to tell of his toughness in the classroom since Brian went to Dublin. He said to him one night, 'Some of them would make the hairs stand on the back of your neck.' He looked so harmless now as he waddled off. Why was it, he wondered, that so many teachers only showed their humanity outside the classroom? Was it something toxic in the walls?

38

When he got back to the farmhouse the car was gone. That was unusual. The main door was unlocked. He walked inside. Everywhere was quiet.

There was a note on the kitchen table. It was on the back of a Cornflakes packet in Angela's scrawly handwriting. It said, 'Gone shopping. Sambo in fridge if you're peckish. Wrapped in tin foil.'

He opened the fridge and looked inside. She'd made him a salad sandwich. He took a few bites out of it.

He was tired from the drink. It felt strange to be in the house on his own. He went upstairs.

It was early to go to bed but he still undressed. He tried to sleep but he couldn't. There were too many thoughts drifting round in his head. When he finally drifted off he dreamt about being married to Jennifer, about living on the farm with her.

The night was black when he woke up. He looked out the window. The car was in the driveway.

He went downstairs but there was nobody there. He saw another note on the kitchen table. Again it was written by Angela. It said, 'We didn't want to wake you. See you in the morning.' He was relieved. Now he wouldn't have to talk to them.

He went back upstairs. He didn't expect to sleep again. He sat at the window for a while looking out at the night. The moon was huge, scudding between the trees. A light wind was blowing.

He left the window open. He lay on the bed. As soon as he closed his eyes he started to get dizzy again. He thought it must have been the drink. Sometimes it acted as a sleeping pill for him.

The next thing he knew it was morning. He wiped the sleep from his eyes. For a few seconds he thought he was still in America. He tried to think of the people he'd met yesterday. They were all jumbled up in his mind.

He looked out the window. It was a fine day. The sun blinded him. A sheep bleated in a distant field. Everything seemed to be the way it always was. By the time he'd dressed and washed he felt more at home.

He went down to the kitchen. Angela was there before him. She was a morning person in contrast to himself and Bartley. She looked as efficient as ever.

'Ready for brekkies?' she said. He hated the baby talk she used with him. It nauseated him.

'Is Dad not down yet?'

'Are you joking? Maybe after a few hours.'

The toilet flushed. His voice came down from the landing.

'Did you speak or did my ears flap?'
'Is that you?'
'Either me or someone who sounds suspiciously like me.'
'Are you coming down?'
'It might be a good idea seeing as it's morning.'
'You were out for the count when I was getting up. I thought you'd lie on for a while. How did you wake up?'
'By opening my eyes. It's been happening since I was a child.'
'Don't be smart.'
'Why did you get up so early? Do you never lie on?'
'It doesn't suit me. You know that. I thought it would be a better idea to entertain the pair of you with my delightful company.'
'Come down as soon as you're decent. Your son wants to tell you about his day. Right, Brian?'
He didn't reply.
A few minutes later he clumped down the stairs. He had a towel in his hand. He was drying his hair with it.
'Where's the breakfast?'
'Patience is a virtue. Sit down. If you're good I'll give it to you.'
He was breathing heavily. He gave her a peck on the cheek.
'Last of the great romantics,' she said. 'What did I do to deserve that?'
'Maybe I should have reserved it till I had the breakfast.'
'Maybe you should.'
'Good morning, Brian,' he said, 'That must have been some walk you went on yesterday. We thought you'd gone off to America again.'
'It did me good to get the air.'
'I suppose you went to town.'
'Eventually.'
'What's that supposed to mean?'
'He probably went by the scenic route,' Angela said.
'Did you meet anyone?'
'Just a few of the lads from school. I went down to the college afterwards.'
'What were you doing down there?'
'Nothing in particular.'
'They're only taking day pupils now. The boarders are gone.'
'So I gather. I ran into Fr. Finnerty. He was asking for you.'
'I hope you complimented him on the fine job he made of the wedding.'
'I did.'
'Did he ask you about the university?'
'Yes.'
'I bet he tried to get you to go back.'

'He didn't get far with that.'

'That's the style. It's time we stood up to those old demagogues.'

'So the two of you went shopping,' he said.

'Just to kill the day. We didn't buy much. When you take Angela to a clothes shop make sure you have nothing else to do for a few hours. She tries on everything they have at least once and then decides not to buy it. That's women for you.'

'No wonder you were gone a while.'

'We had a couple of jars after. Did you have a few too?'

'One or two. I met Eddie Culkin.'

'Eddie? The poor man. He lost his wife.'

'So he said.'

'One of nature's finest.'

Angela came over with the breakfast. Bartley's eyes lit up when he saw his.

'Angela's fries are mortal sins,' he said, 'You have to go to the next parish to have them forgiven.'

'It looks very nice.'

'Very nice? That's like saying the Hanging Gardens of Babylon are very nice. Gordon Ramsay is only in the ha'penny place.'

'Do you hear that *ráiméis* he comes out with, Brian? It's only a few rashers and eggs, for God's sake.'

He wondered if it was a daily occurrence or if she was making the extra effort because of him coming home.

'It's a bit more than that. You must read books on cuisine to get them this tasty for us.'

'I just put them on the pan. The cooker does the rest.'

'Don't be modest. There's enough criticism in life. Take the compliments when they come your way. Amn't I right, Brian?'

'You are.'

'Are you not having something for yourself?' he asked her.

'In a minute.'

He started munching.

'I don't know how she does it,' he said. 'They call the washing-up liquid Three Hands. Angela must have five.'

'You can finish the compliments now. You'd do me a bigger favour if you didn't wolf down your food.'

'What's wrong with that? I like to show you I'm enjoying it – not like those wimps who put little morsels into their mouths as if they're half afraid of them.'

She took some knives and forks from the drawer. She put them on the table.

'Do you ever give her a hand?' Brian said.

Angela laughed.

'He hardly knows where the cooker is,' Angela said, 'His mother ruined him that way.'

'Like all the mothers in this country,' Bartley said.

'Not mine, let me tell you.'

'It only happens with boys. You should take a rest now though and join us.'

'Who's going to do the washing up if I do? The fairies aren't going to come down the chimney and scrub the plates.'

'True enough.'

'It wouldn't do you any harm to get up off your bottom and help me once in a while.'

'Did you hear that?' he said, 'I married a feminist. We better all watch out.'

'You better. I might go on strike.'

'Keep your mouth for eating,' Bartley said to Brian, 'You're after putting bad ideas into her head.'

He attacked the plate like someone who hadn't eaten for a month. He spilt various bits of food on his jumper in a rush to get it down.

'Be careful,' Angela said, 'Some of that is getting into your mouth.'

'Hangovers always make me hungry.'

'You must be hungry a lot of the time then.'

'She's in fighting form this morning,' Bartley said to Brian.

'You bring out the worst in me.'

Brian felt their banter was harmless. It was almost as if they were showing off for him. They were like two young people on a date.

Bartley finished his meal. He wiped the grease off his plate with a leftover piece of bread.

'I hate when you do that,' she said.

'Why? Amn't I saving you from washing it?'

'It looks primitive.'

'I've been doing it all my life. Why should I change now?'

'There are a lot of things you've been doing all your life that you should change.'

'Like what?'

'How much time have you got?'

There was a coffee cake on the table. He stuffed a slice of it into his mouth. Angela shook her head.

'That sweet tooth will do you in one of these days,' she said.

'It's nice to have something to wash the tea down with.'

'What about you, Brian?' she said.

Bartley gave her a look.

'He gets offered it and I get given out to. Where's the logic in that?'

'He doesn't eat sweet things for breakfast, dinner and tea.'

'No thanks, Angela,' he said, 'I've had more than enough.'

'See what I mean?' she said.

Bartley stood up.

'I'm going into the office,' he said to Brian, 'Would you like to join me?'

'Office, mind you,' Angela said, 'Is that what it is now?'

'We've created it,' he said, 'We might as well put a name on it. What do you say, Brian? Maybe it's time we had a chat.'

'You mean about the auctioneering?'

'Yes.'

'Okay.'

'Don't let him rope you into anything you don't want,' Angela said.

They went out. It was the last thing Brian wanted but he felt he couldn't say no. Maybe it was better to get everything out in the open.

'I'll bring ye in a cuppa in a few minutes,' Angela called after them.

Bartley sat behind his desk. He drummed his fingers along it.

'Grab a seat, young man,' he said to Brian, putting on a serious face. Brian sat down.

'This could be a whole new future for us.'

'Does that mean the farm is finished?'

Bartley laughed.

'You amuse me when you say things like that. You wouldn't milk a cow to save your life a few years ago.'

'A few years ago they weren't in danger of being let go.'

'The land is dead, Brian, you know that. You could hardly raise weeds on it now. Neither am I convinced your new-found enthusiasm for it will last. You've been known to change your mind about a few things in the past.'

'Are you referring to the university?'

'That and everything else. Because you've picked a few grapes in France you've developed a romantic attitude to the land. That's fine but there's nothing romantic about raking shit out of a farmhouse on a Monday morning when it's raining cats and dogs. Try writing poems about *that*.'

'Don't worry. I won't.'

'As you mention, I've sold a lot of the stock. You'd have to buy them back again if you were serious about what you're saying. If you'd like to build things up again I'd help you but I wouldn't recommend it. We can't go back to the way we were.'

'I didn't say I wanted to. I just think getting rid of everything so suddenly mightn't be wise.'

'Suddenly? Do you realise how long you've been away? I've scraped the dirt out from under my fingernails. I don't see any future messing about on dead land for the sake of having a few cows to look at in the morning.'

'You got your living out of them.'

'There was a time they were viable. That was back in the good old days when you'd get a grant for blowing your nose. Such things are gone for their tea now. The government has seen to that. Your long-suffering father has been elbowed out as a result.'

'What will you do with your time now?'

'You mean apart from the auctioneering?'

'That's hardly going to be a fulltime job.'

'What does anyone do? Enjoy the idleness. Vegetate.'

'You might miss the farming.'

'I don't think so. I don't think I'll miss mucking out stables. Or praying for wet weather. Or fine weather. Or having to get up at the crack of dawn smelling shit when everyone else is sleeping their arses off. Or worrying about foxes killing your chickens. Or crops failing or prices dropping or who's going to be around to save the hay with me when you're tripping the light fantastic in New York with your gymbag over your shoulder.'

'Steady on there. only made a comment.'

'Sorry if I sound like I'm getting at you but I'm fed up to the back teeth of everything. I'm getting on, Brian. It's time to put the feet up. I'd like to enjoy what years are left to me with Angela.'

'You're entitled to that.'

'So what do you say? You can be as involved in this new caper as little or as much as you want. I won't push you either way.'

'I need time to think about this.'

'Take all the time in the world. There's no rush on anything.'

'Would I have to do the same course you did?'

'Probably, at least if you were serious about it in the long term. Afterwards you'd have to serve your time with Arthur. I'm still doing that. Strictly speaking I'm not allowed sell anything for him yet.'

'He's probably more interested in you for your connections than anything else.'

'Maybe. Anyway I'm a wee bit excited about it all. He's going to let Angela in on the secretarial side of things, by the way. She might have mentioned something about that to you.'

'She did. It'll save you a few bob employing someone.'

'Why buy a dog when you can bark yourself?'

Angela came in with a tray. She had the knack of appearing at just the right moment. It was as if she was listening outside.

'Are you calling me a dog?' she said.

'You know what I mean.'

'Of course. Don't take me too seriously.'

He could imagine her sitting behind a desk, fawning over the farmers with their big wads of cash. Even flirting with them.

'You might be able to help her with the typing,' Bartley said, 'You're good at that kind of thing, aren't you?'

'I wouldn't say that.'

'Do you not use the computer we gave you?'

'Not as much as I should.'

'Okay. Well that's the story anyway. With you and Angela on board we'll have few enough overheads. All in the family. We'll be like the Mafia yet.'

'Or the Murphia.'

'Ha ha.'

Angela put the tray on the coffee table.

'Tea for the businessmen,' she said.

'We'll really look the part now,' Bartley laughed, 'I might ask you to take a letter later.'

She went over to him. She tugged at his jumper.

'Did you know you have a hole in that?' she said, 'A fine sight you'd be selling houses. You'd scare the customers away.'

'It's not my jumpers they'll be concerned about as long as I have good properties to put on the market.'

'God love your innocence if you don't think image isn't important.'

'It's my business how I dress.'

'It's my business too if it affects our livelihood.'

Comments like that made Brian realise how involved she was in it all, how hungry she was to make a go of things.

When they got together at first he thought she'd be happy just to be with him but now she was more like his manager. People in the town spoke of her as a gold digger. Did they know her better than he did?

39

He rang the university the next day to say he wouldn't be returning to it. The person who took the call didn't seem to care one way or the other. All he said was that the results of his exams had been sent out in the post. He didn't bother telling them he hadn't attempted any of the papers.

He had no regrets about his decision. It sickened him even to think of the place now. He knew a lot of the reason was his failure to make a go of it. He hadn't made much of an effort to get to know his classmates either. His defences had been up from the start, both with the curriculum and them. There were only a few of them he'd miss. He didn't think he had even one of their phone numbers to tell them. The only number he'd kept was Sinead's. He wondered if she was still clean.

He rang her to tell her he wasn't going back. He didn't think she'd be surprised. Maybe she wouldn't be going back either. She told him once that she'd be happy selling sweets in a corner shop in the middle of nowhere for pin money. Her life really only began at night.

Her mother answered the phone in a frosty voice.

'Could I speak to Sinead?' he said.

'Who will I say is calling?'

'Brian Kilcoyne.'

'Hold on,' she said coldly

He heard her saying, 'It's that Kilcoyne boy. Do you want to talk to him?'

She came on immediately.

'You're back!' she said excitedly, 'I was wondering if you might stay in America.'

'Believe me, I thought about it.'

'I bet you did. How have you been?'

'So-so. What did you do for the summer?'

'Not much. I spent most of it cooped up here.'

She lowered her voice.

'Mum is in the next room so I can't say much.'

'It's good to hear you anyway. You sound well.'

'I am. How are you? Are you back in Loughrea?'

'Yeah. I'll probably stay here.'

'I told a few people about your *Watership Down* joke. We had a laugh about it.'

'How are you doing with the other stuff?'

'I haven't touched it since I saw you.'

'That's good.'

'I wouldn't have had a chance to even if I wanted. They practically have me under house arrest here.'

'Poor you. What happened to the fountain of excess?'

'I'm afraid it's gone a bit dry at the moment.'

'I'm surprised your mother let you speak to me.'

'She's not that bad. How did you get on in America?'

'I'll tell you about it sometime. I just wanted to ring you to let you know I was back. How did you get on at the exams?'

'Believe it or not I scraped through.'

'What?'

'I know. Nobody was more surprised than me.'

'You cute shot. You've been holding out on me. Probably getting secret grinds without letting on.'

'I couldn't believe it. One of my friends must have been correcting the papers.'

'So you're going to go back for the last year.'

'I have no choice. I'll be thrown out of the house if I don't. What about you? Will you repeat?'

'No, I'm through with that side of things. If I never see Belfield again it will be too soon.'

'I figured that. Are you ringing from home?'

'Yes.'

'How is your father?'

'He's okay.'

'And Jennifer?'

'I haven't seen her yet.'

'I miss you.'

'And me you. I'll look you up the next time I'm in Dublin.'

'I hope so.'

'I'll call in advance in case your mother sets the dogs on me. Thanks for kidnapping me from the hospital, by the way.'

'It was the least I could do. If it wasn't for me you wouldn't have been in there.'

'I wouldn't be too sure of that.'

'Thanks for getting me back on the straight and narrow.'

'You did that yourself. It's staying there that's the hardest part.'

'I know. Keep in touch, won't you? In case I slip.'

'You won't. I know it.'

He was glad he rang her. She was one of the few real people he'd met in Belfield. When he thought about his time there now it wasn't the books or the lectures he remembered but all the other things that happened to him when he was there – Sinead, the music he listened to, even the night life of Ranelagh that he'd sampled from his window in the flat.

He decided to ring Martin Geraghty. He hadn't told him he wasn't going to be staying in it. He wasn't sure how he'd take the news about him defaulting on his lease.

His voice was friendly as he answered the phone.

'Long time no hear,' he said, 'What part of the world are you calling me from?'

'I'm back at the ranch. I have some bad news for you, I'm afraid.'

'I bet know what it is in advance. You're not coming back.'

'How did you guess?'

'I felt you'd stick around down there once you got some bogdirt behind your ears.'

'Is that going to give you a problem with the letting?'

'Not really. I have a lad there at the moment. I think he wants to stay on. He'll be delighted. Rented properties are pretty rare in the capital these days.'

'He must have thought he was going to be turfed out.'

'When I didn't hear from you for a while I thought something must be going on so I told him to sit tight.'

'You must be psychic.'

'I felt things were coming apart for you in the university.'

'I was thinking of staying in Ranelagh even if I didn't go back there. That's why I didn't ring you till now. Sorry about all that stuff with Sinead.'

'It wasn't your fault. I knew you were just trying to help. How is she now?'

'She seems to have sorted herself out.'

'I'm glad to hear that.'

'What's the position on my deposit?'

'I'll send it down to you.'

'Are you serious? That's very kind of you.'

'You were a good tenant. I don't think you broke any of my prize furniture.'

'I hope not. I bought a few bits and bobs too as you might have seen. They're harmless. You can tell the other tenant to keep them.'

'That's nice of you. All I could see were books the last time I was there. You have the place looking like the National Library.'

'I doubt the new guy will share my tastes. He'll probably want to use them for firewood.'

'I might have a read of some of them myself and expand my mind.'

'Take my advice and don't. They'll only shrink it.'

He chuckled.

'I see you're leaving the academic world with some bitterness.'

'It didn't do much for me.'

'I can see that. Anyway I better go now. It's good to talk to you. Let me know when the chicken's neck arrives.'

'Will do. I hope Bartley doesn't intercept it. He might want to keep it as a hostage for the money I owe him.'

'I'll mark it "Private and Confidential" to stop him putting his grubby paws on it.'

'I wouldn't do that if I was you. You know Bartley. It would only make him more curious.'

'Good point.'

After he left down the phone he felt his faith in human nature had been restored. He could never understand why Bartley had it in so much for him. Was he jealous of his success since he left farming? Was he afraid he wouldn't be able to go anywhere near it himself?

The cheque arrived two days later with a 'Good Luck For the Future' card with it.

'Look at that,' he said, showing it to Bartley, 'You told me he'd find some way of holding on to my deposit.'

'I have to admit I'm surprised,' he said, stroking his chin thoughtfully, 'All I can deduce is that he was afraid I'd beat the lard out of him if he tried to pull a fast one.'

'Anyway I have it now. I should give it back to you.'

'Hold on to it. You'll need it to keep you going until you decide what to do with yourself.'

'Does it bother you that I haven't made my mind up yet?'

'Actually it bothers Declan more than me.'

'Why is that?'

'He thought the travel would have got your restlessness out of your system.'

'What business is it of his?'

'He's coming in on this too. He's been on to Arthur about opening a branch in Newbridge. We could all be a part of it yet.'

'This is turning into a bit of a dynasty.'

'I know. He's really excited about it.'

'Does that mean he's going to be nagging me as much as you are?'

'Probably more.'

He rang that very night and got straight into it.

'Dad says you're still shilly-shallying. Did he tell you I was going to be in on the Finlay thing.'

'Just today.'

'That's good because things are moving fast down here.'

'In what way?'

'I should have the office open soon.'

'What office? I don't know what you're talking about.'

'I bought the shop next door a few years ago. It went to the wall during the bust. Since then I've been wondering what to do with it. I was going to put some more computers in it but this is a better proposition - for both of us.'

'How do you make that out?'

'You could move down here. I'd be happy to have you as my wingman after you get a bit of experience where you are.'

'You must be having me on. I've hardly unpacked my bags'

'I heard you only brought one.'

'Okay, my bag. That's not the point.'

'Isn't that what you like, being on the move? What's to keep you in that dump.'

'I don't know a soul in Newbridge.'

'You know me, don't you? And Yvonne. We'll introduce you to all the best people. There's a brilliant social life here. It would be great for you.'

'I don't think so.'

'Why not? You've tried travel as well as the university. Neither of them floated your boat. Time is ticking. You have to stop hopping from Billy to Jack.'

'You're throwing this at me out of the blue. I couldn't even begin to think about it now.'

'Why not? What's to stop you?'

'About a hundred things. The most obvious one is working for a stranger instead of someone I know.'

'Are you talking about Arthur Finlay?'

'Yes.'

'He's a pussycat. You'll love him. Anyway you wouldn't be working for him. You'd be working for me. You're hardly afraid of that, are you? Arthur might even make you a sleeping partner down the road.'

'What's that?'

'A bit like what it says. You'd get big bucks for doing fuck all. If you were good at it you'd get a big slice of whatever profits the firm made. That wouldn't be today or tomorrow, of course, but it would be something to aim for.'

'What about today and tomorrow?'

'You'd be learning the ropes. You wouldn't have the authority to make deals but it would be a cushy number for you. There are lots of tasty birds coming into the office as well. You might be interested in doing a bit of overtime with them, if you know what I mean.'

'What are you talking about?'

'Let's put it this way. You're not the ugliest-looking specimen I've ever seen in my life. You can even string a sentence or two together when you're put to it. If you play your cards right you could have your pick of the women down here. There are a lot of broken hearts looking for a knight in shining armour to ride over the hill and sweep them off their feet.'

'I'm sure Jennifer would love that.'

'Is she still on the scene? I thought you two broke up.'

'We were *on* a break. That's a different thing.'

'Now you have me confused. I'll have to get my dictionary out.'

'Look, Declan. I don't like to cut you short because you're obviously high about this but the timing is bad. I'm just off the plane. I'm not sure if it's for me in the long term.'

'Don't say things like that. It's the chance of a lifetime. You're always moaning about the fact that I got the silver spoon when we were growing up. Now I'm offering one to you and you're throwing it back in my face.'

'Why does it mean so much to you that I join you? We don't get on particularly well. I'm sure you could get someone else to fill the bill.'

'Would it be too hard for you to accept the fact that I'm trying to do you a favour? I told you I'd look out for you when Mam died. Yvonne is always going on about the fact that you're the greatest thing since sliced bread. I obviously missed something when we were kids.'

'I appreciate your concern. If I feel it's right for me I'll get back to you. Don't try to strong-arm me into it.'

'This offer won't be there forever, buddy. You need to know that. You have to move fast in this life or you'll get left behind.'

'Not all of us are as good as you at making snap decisions. We're built differently.'

'The only difference between us is that I grab opportunities by shooting from the hip. You spend forever looking at the ins and outs of everything and then doing nothing.'

'Are you trying to tell me you never made a mistake by jumping into something too soon?'

'I'd prefer to make that kind of a mistake than your kind.'

'Let's agree to differ on that.'

'So what's it to be?'

'We've talked enough for tonight. I know your position and you know mine. Let's leave it at that for the moment.'

'At what? We haven't sorted anything out yet.'

'If I decide to go for it you'll be the first to know.'

Declan sighed.

'Once again I'm breaking my back trying to do something and you fob me off.'

'Once again you try to play God and expect me to fall in with it.'

He started shouting.

'You're going to be humming and hawing for the rest of your natural. Stop sitting on your hands. Wake up and smell the coffee.'

'Don't talk to me like some sixteen-year-old you're interviewing for your computer business.'

'I'm not talking to you any way. You have all these defence mechanisms built up whenever I try to give you a piece of advice. You're driving me crazy.'

'And you're driving me crazy. You can talk about auctioneering till you're blue in the face. It won't make a bit of difference to me. I told you I'm putting it on the back burner.'

'That back burner must be almost burned up by now.'

'What's that supposed to mean?'

'You can't keep putting off things forever.'

'Why does it matter so much to you what I do or don't do? You're always trying to control my life.'

'Control? Did I control you when you went gallivanting off to Europe examining your bellybutton? Did I control you when you were wasting thousands of euros on a crap Arts course in UCD and then throwing your hat at it?

'I'm not listening to any more of this. You're doing my head in.'

'Come down from the cross, little brother. We need the wood.'

He was going to say something to him but then he thought: What was the point?

Instead he hung up. .

He'd never done that on him before. He surprised himself by doing it. His heart was pumping.

He went out to the living-room.

Bartley was sitting there reading the paper, or pretending to.

'Was that Declan?' he said.

He obviously knew it was. He probably had his ears cocked for the whole call.

'Did you ask him to ring me?'

'No. What was he on about?'

'The fact that Arthur Finlay is thinking of opening a branch of his business in Newbridge.'

'Is it going ahead?'

'From what he says I think so. Are you sure you're telling me everything you know?'

He put down the paper.

'Declan moves fast. He's always been looking to do something with that place he bought next door to his office.'

'I didn't even know he owned it.'

'You didn't? That's because you never listen. He's always talking about it.'

'Not to me he isn't.'

'What did he say?'

'He thought I might like to work with him.'

He jumped out of his seat.

'You mean leave here?'

'Yes.'

'Holy Moses, that sounds like a great idea.'

'Are you trying to get rid of me?'

'Not at all. Wouldn't it be a novelty for you? You seem out of sorts lately. I'm sure Declan would fix you up with a nice flat. Maybe you could even move in with him and Yvonne until you got settled.'

'What about Jennifer?'

'She could go down too.'

'And leave her job?'

'They have schools in Newbridge, believe it or not.'

'Now you sound like Declan.'

'What's the problem? She might like to get out of this place. She often tells me she's fed up of it.'

'You're talking as if we're living together, or married. Neither of us have a clue where we're going with each other. Why is everyone trying to live my life for me?'

'We're not. We're just suggesting things.'

'My head is lifting.'

'Have a whiskey.'

'That's your answer for everything, isn't it?'

'I've heard of worse ones.'

He knocked it back.

Bartley looked at him with that mischievous expression that came into his eyes sometimes.

'Yvonne would do her nut to get you to move down there. She has a real soft spot for you. And for Jennifer too, needless to say. They don't go out much these days. Declan is cooling down on the social scene. They'd be glad of the company.'

'Stop it. Please.'

'What's up with you?'

'Just stop.'

'I know Declan and yourself spark off one another. That's life. He sparks off me too. It's the way he is with everyone. Don't let him get to you. It wouldn't be a fulltime commitment. You could come back here at the weekends if Jennifer didn't want to up sticks.'

'You have it all worked out, haven't you? It's a wonder you haven't bought my train ticket. Maybe you'd like to tuck her into bed the nights she's not with me.'

'Okay, I can see we're not getting anywhere. Let's talk about something else.'

His headache got worse.

'Pour me a drop of whiskey,' he said.

'I knew you'd give in.'

He knocked it back.

'I hung up on him, you know.'

'You what?'

'I hung up on Declan.'

'Fair dues to you. I'm glad you're standing up to him. I always wanted you to when you were young.'

'He probably won't talk to me for six months now.'

'That's not true. He'll forget about it tomorrow. He doesn't hold things in. He's given you food for thought anyway.'

'I don't know about that.'

'Have you ruled out bringing Jennifer down?'

'It's not for me to rule anything in or out. She has her own mind. Why would she want to go hauling herself down to a place where she has no connections?'

'You'd be her main connection. Why would that be different here than in Newbridge?'

'You're far too ahead of yourself. I haven't even seen her yet. We don't know if we're going to be together in the long term. Are you not aware of that?'

'Of course I am. I'm just thinking out loud.'

Brian walked around the room biting his nails.

Bartley put on that mischievous look again.

'You're in a rut here, Brian,' he said, 'Any eejit can see that. I know Angela and myself get on your nerves sometimes. A boy your age needs to be with the young people. you need to get into technology. That's where the future is.'

'Why do you keep going on about that? I don't know one end of a computer from another.'

'Do you think I do? A few months ago Declan told me I'd have to go online. I thought he was talking about the clothes line. He meant the internet.'

'You have to be joking.'

'You know me and technology. I'd eat it first. The first time Arthur told me he had his properties on a site I thought he was talking about a building site but it was a website he meant.'

'You must have been living on the moon for the last decade if you don't know what websites are.'

'He didn't say website. He said site. I'm not thick.'

'Who said you were?'

'I've heard people talking about them but it wasn't until he sat me down one night that I realised how sophisticated they are. You click a button and you see the outside of whatever house you're after. Then you click another one and, bingo, the inside pops up. It saves a lot of time.'

'Well done. You've been dragged kicking and screaming into the 21st century.'

'Relax. I'm just telling you what he showed me. He has all this stuff on his phone. It's one of those Smart ones. Maybe you think I'd be better off with a stupid one seeing as I'm so thick.'

'Stop saying that. What I meant was that you were out of date.'

'He said it does everything but make the dinner. He even gets emails on it.'

'I wouldn't be bothered with one of those. He'll be asking you to tweet him next.'

'I'll leave that to the birds.'

'Or Angela maybe.'

'She'd be the one for it all right but I have to ease her in gradually. He has his own staff. I don't want to come on too heavy.'

'That's good thinking. You don't want to scare him off.'

'I have to make him think I'm doing him the favour instead of the other way round. He runs a much bigger operation than I thought.'

'How many houses has he on his books?'

'A lot. Have you seen them? I think you did the day you came home. They're the dog's bollox. I was almost tempted to buy one myself. Maybe I will some day.'

'You said you wouldn't when I asked you before.'

'I wasn't thinking that way then. This place is getting too big for Angela and me. Everyone is downsizing these days. There's too much upkeep on this hacienda. I could do with not having to climb a staircase with my bandy knees. A nice little bungalow would suit me.'

'I don't like bungalows. I'd feel too exposed in one. Some madman could be looking in the window at you in the middle of the night.'

'I suppose you're right. Anyway we'll see how the land lies before we make any decisions. I know he'd give us a good deal on a house if it ever came to it. Declan is thinking that way too. If Arthur goes well in Newbridge he could branch out to other places.'

'You mean outside Ireland?'

'Who knows? Declan said it could go viral, whatever that means. I told him I didn't want a virus.'

'He meant it could be worldwide.'

'Imagine the Irish-Americans looking for a little bolthole down in Loughrea. We could charge them a small fortune for a tip.'

'Don't get ahead of yourself.'

'Wouldn't it be nice to be rich all the same?'

'Now you're starting to sound like Declan.'

'What's wrong with a bit of money? If you married Jennifer it would be nice to be on your feet that way.'

'Maybe we're moving too fast.'

'Declan thinks the opposite. He thinks it's now or never.'

'He's that way about everything.'

'I know.'

'Are you sure you didn't ask him to ring me?'

'On my honour.'

'I have my doubts about that.'

'Look, Brian, nobody is trying to force you into this against your will. I hope you know that.'

'Sorry if I sound uptight. This would be a big move for me.'

'Why don't we go for a pint and discuss it more casually.'

'That might be an idea. When were you thinking of?'

'What's wrong with now?'

'Are you serious?'

'Why not? There's no time like the present. You're not doing anything else, are you?'

'No.'

'We could bring Angela too. She's very good on the practical side of things.'

He paused.

'You don't sound too happy about it. If it's a problem for you we can just go on our own.'

'No. Bring her.'

He wondered if this was going to be the shape of things to come, if she was going to be a part of everything that happened.

'Are you there, Angela?' he called out.

She came in without missing a beat. Had she been listening again?

'What is it?'

'We're going down to McDonagh's for a chinwag about the house business. Would you like to tag along?'

'Maybe I'd be in the way.'

'Would she, Brian?'

'Of course not.'

'Let's go then.'

As she was putting on her coat she said, 'I hope I'm butting in on your scene.'

'How could you be? You're going to be as much a part of it as any of us.'

They decided to walk down to McDonaghs. Bartley was in talking form on the way. He got excited telling them about how he was going to develop the business.

'I thought retirement was going to mean sitting by the fire drinking Horlicks,' he said, 'Who could have imagined this?'

'Don't count your chickens,' Angela said, 'We haven't even got on our feet yet.'

When they got seated in the pub he took out a file with various properties listed in it. It was too dark to read them properly.

'I can't see a damn thing,' he said, 'Will we move to the other end?'

'No,' Angela said, 'It's nice and cosy here.'

He looked up at the barman.

'Dessie,' he said, 'You wouldn't mind throwing a bit of light on the subject, would you? I feel like Dracula here.'

He turned on a fluorescent light over his head. Bartley winked over at him in appreciation.

'Now all we need is something to wet our whistles.'

'The drinks are on me tonight,' Angela said.

She was almost as high as Bartley. It was as if everything was coming together for her, Brian thought, the business and her marriage and now him home to complete the Blessed Trinity.

She got a sherry for herself and a pint of Guinness for Bartley. Brian was on Smithwicks.

'I'm going to speak to you about the business in general,' Bartley said to Brian, 'Whatever you do about Newbridge is separate. You can make your own mind up about that in time. You might prefer to do your apprenticeship here.'

'I don't care where I do it. I might decide not to do it at all.'

'Fair enough but don't knock it till you've tried it., as the man said.'

'I doubt I could make a living out of it whatever way it goes.'

'That's not true, Now that we're crawling out of the recession the property market is starting to grow again. You can see the twinkle coming back into people's eyes.'

'I wonder how long that'll last. I wouldn't put it past us to crash a second time.'

'That won't happen. Not even the Irish are that stupid.'

'You have a lovely view of your customers.'

'You can't reason with the people around here. You have to out-think them.'

'How do you plan to do that? By selling substandard properties?'

'You'd get the same thanks in this country if you're selling a cowshed or a luxury penthouse with a jacuzzi inside. I've broken my back trying to help people over the years. It means fuck all to them. They'll go through you for a shortcut afterwards if it suits them. That sort of thing hardens you. It makes you suspect everyone.'

'Thanks for your charming insight into human nature.'

'I'm just trying to prepare you for the worst. Most of the people around here are addicted to complaining. They're not happy unless they're miserable.'

'Do you think you can reform them?'

'I don't know about that but I'll have a go at charming them anyway. That's something I've always been good at.'

'That and humility,' Angela said. Bartley smiled sarcastically at her.

'Most of the auctioneers in Ireland don't know their arse from their elbow. They couldn't sell insulin to a diabetic. And do you know why? Because they don't understand the basic rule of business.'

'What's that?'

'It's the fact that how you sell something is 90%. The thing you're selling is the other 10%.'

'Tonight I'm more interested in the 10%.'

'Okay. Let me give you an example. Arthur says the most important room in a house today is the kitchen. Don't ask me why. These days kitchens have to be half the size of O'Connell Street to satisfy people. God only knows what that's about.'

'Maybe it's about food,' Angela said, 'People have been known to eat, from what I hear.'

'Eating is one thing. Filling their bellies like there's no tomorrow is another.'

'Do you hear that?' she laughed, 'I haven't noticed you going on any hunger strikes lately.'

'I never denied I have a sweet tooth. That's not what I'm talking about. We live in the country. The kitchen is big anyway. What's different now is that people in cramped housing estates want big kitchens as well. That means cutting corners in the other rooms.'

'Okay,' said Angela, 'So we're all going to become millionaires by telling Arthur Finlay to sell houses with big kitchens. Well done. Is is the extent of the Kilcoyne plan for the expansion of his business?'

'That's just the first step. The next one is what I was talking to Brian about earlier – the tourist market. Especially the American one. Yanks are always sniffing round for somewhere that looks like it came out of *The Quiet Man*. Put a garden leprechaun in a shack and you can charge a king's ransom for it. It's the same philosophy farmers use for mushroom-growing: Keep them in the dark and feed them lots of bullshit.'

'I hope it keeps fine for you,' she said.

'What do you think, Brian?' he said, 'Am I a genius or a fool?'

'Maybe a bit of both.'

He gave a guffaw at that.

Afterwards they talked about other things. It was a pleasant night. Bartley went easy on the drink. Maybe his new interest would keep him off it, Brian thought.

He spent most of the next day wondering if he'd take him up on his offer. He still wasn't sure if he was interested in it or not. Bartley kept pushing him for a commitment but he couldn't give him one. He tried to be out of the house as much as he could to keep him off his back.

He rang Jennifer to ask her what she thought but she didn't want to venture an opinion one way or another in case it blew up in her face. If she gave him any advice she thought he might blame her if it didn't work out.

'Don't commit yourself until you're 100% sure,' she said, 'and don't let them rush you.'

'When are we going to meet?' he said to her at the end of the call, 'It's getting ridiculous at this stage.'

'What's wrong with today?' she said, 'Mam and Dad are gone to a wedding in Dublin. You'll have me all to yourself.'

'That sounds promising.'

40

He was nervous as he walked up her driveway later that day. He didn't know why. It was crazy considering they'd spent so much of their time together in the past.

Was it because there were so many postponements? It was the only thing he could come up with.

It was raining as he got to the door. He thought of the night he walked her home after spending the evening with herself and Tommy Glynn. How far away that seemed now. It could have been another life.

He unlatched the gate. It creaked as he opened it. He was always telling her to get some oil for it.

'I'm getting around to it,' she used to say every time he asked her about it. That always amused him. He knew she never would.

The doorbell was broken. That was another thing he liked about her. She'd never bothered getting that fixed either.

He tapped on the window. That was what he used to do when he was calling for her in the old days.

She looked out at him. She was smiling when she opened the door.

'I was wondering when you might show up,' she said.

She was dressed in a tank top with matching tracksuit bottoms. He couldn't stop looking at her.

'What's wrong?' she said.

'There's something different about you.'

'You only think that because you've been away so long.'

'No, there's something else.'

'Are you going to come in or would you prefer to stay on the doorstep all day?'

He went inside. They hugged.

'The returned Yank,' she said.

'Please, I have enough problems without that hanging over me.'

She had earplugs on. They were from a device hooked to her waist. She put them in her pocket.

She reached for them with her left arm. Her right one was in a cast.

'Jesus,' he said, 'What happened you?'

'Basketball accident. Someone thundered into me. '

'That's terrible. You should have told me.'

'I hate talking about it. It gets boring telling the same story over and over again.'

'You've never liked people fussing over you, have you?'

'You can say that again.'

'It must have been agony when it happened. Were you out cold?'

'I wish I was. The pain was pretty bad for a while.'

'How are you now?'

'Fine. It's just the inconvenience of everything. You have no idea how much you use your hand until it's crocked.'

'Why don't you sit down and let me make you a cup of tea?'

'I'm not that bad. Do me a favour and talk about something else. That way I can forget about it.'

'All right. Sorry for not coming sooner.'

'No problem. Take off your coat. It's wringing wet. You'll catch your death.'

He took it off.

'I'll put it over the rad. Is your jumper wet?'

'I don't think so.'

She felt it.

'It's wringing. Don't let it dry into you. Take that off too.'

'You shouldn't be doing things like that. You'll make your arm worse.'

'I'm fine. Stop fussing over me.'

She put it on the radiator beside his coat. For a moment he felt like the old days when they were doing things like this, when they had a natural ease with one another. He forgot how much he'd missed it.

'Sit down and tell me all your news,' she said, 'You must be sorry you came home. It's done nothing but lash rain in the last few weeks. Which reminds me...'

She went over to the radiator to check his jumper.

'You could probably chance it now,' she said, handing it to him.

He put it on.

'It feels nice and warm. Thanks.'

'The rain is terrible, isn't it?'

'I don't mind it too much.'

'That puts you in a minority of one in this country.'

'Maybe it's different when you've been away. I got a break from it.'

'It was fine yesterday. That was probably our summer.'

He stared intently at her. Her eyes looked greener than ever. They were like the sea.

'I meant it when I said you look different,' he said.

'In what way?'

'I'm not sure.'

It was a few seconds before it registered with him. She had her hair in a bob. It had highlights in it.

'I know what it is,' he said, 'You've got your hair styled.'

'You noticed. That's observant. For a man, I mean.'

'Was it getting too long to manage?'

'It was like Niagara Falls. Men don't have to worry about things like that. All you do is cut it.'

'Or in my case, don't.'

'Yes, I noticed. When did you decide to go for the hippie look?'

'That's what Angela said. It wasn't a decision. It just happened. I like being untidy.'

'How do you feel about her marrying your father?'

'I wasn't that surprised really. I hope they make a go of it.'

'So do I.'

She looked at him as if she had something on her mind.

'I'm probably calling at a bad time,' he said.

'How could you be? I really wanted to see you.'

'You could have come to the pub that night.'

'I explained that. I didn't want to cut in on your scene.'

'It wasn't my scene. It was a public event.'

'Maybe too public. I didn't want everyone gawking at me.'

She asked him if he'd like a cup of tea. He said he would.

As they waited for the kettle to boil she asked him to autograph her arm. There were lots of messages on it, messages like 'Luv U Jen!' scrawled everywhere in various pens and markers. He found himself being jealous of all the friends she had.

The kettle boiled. She got up to make the tea. When she brought it over he noticed that it was herbal.

'Herbal tea? Where did you get that?'

'In the health shop. They say it's much better than the other stuff.'

'I have my doubts. I never experiment with things like that.'

'Will I get you an ordinary cup?'

'It's okay. I'll try it.'

He sipped it. It tasted putrid but he didn't want to say anything.

She laughed.

'Your face is a sight,' she said, 'You're obviously just about ready to throw up.'

'Don't say that. It's fine.'

'Liar. I can see you gagging on it.'

They listened to the rain pelting on the roof.

'You must have loads to tell me about America,' she said, 'Do they say things like "Have a nice day" over there?'

'That's a cliché you get from films. Most of them are pretty normal.'

'I bet you met your share of ladies over the summer.'

'One or two. Nothing serious.'

'Your phone calls meant a lot to me.'

'There should have been more of them.'

'I feel I know Rockaway Beach backwards now.'

'I didn't know I talked that much about it.'

'Did you mean to go there all along or did you just end up there?'

'It was circumstances really. One thing led to another.'

'It's a pity you didn't get up to your aunt .'

'It was unforgiveable of me.'

'Thanks for phoning me from the pizza parlour.'

'I almost forgot that. I was going out of my tree there.'

'Is that the only reason you rang?'

'I didn't mean it like that.'

'It sounded better than selling advertising space.'

'There wasn't much between them. Summer jobs are mainly about money.'

'I wish I could have gone with you.'

'I wish you could too. Maybe we'll do it yet.'

'This place gets so dull. Nobody is adventurous like you.'

'Adventurous? I don't think so. The real test would have been if I stayed in a place longer than the summer. I always had the university to come back to.'

'You still got away. So many people around here haven't been beyond the county line.'

'I know. Like my parents.'

'And mine.'

'Did your mother never go abroad?'

'She wasn't the type.'

He went quiet.

'Does it upset you when people talk about her?'

'A bit. Sometimes you remind me of her.'

'It's probably the green eyes. I really loved her.'

'She always wanted us to be together.'

She looked distressed for a moment.

'Tell me about college,' she said, 'I believe you're not going back.'

'I should never have been there to begin with. It almost killed my love of books.'

'Aren't universities supposed to do the opposite of that?'

'In theory maybe. I spent two years rehashing things other people said, gobbling them up and spewing them out in exam halls.'

'It sounds horrible.'

'It was. Anyway, it's over now. I want to forget it. Reading a book now would be harder for me than digging a quarry.'

'Did you work hard in America?'

'Only as hard as people made me.'

'They say Paddies make more of an effort abroad than here.'

'Not this one.'

'I don't believe that for a second. You're always hammer and tongs at something.'

'That's not true. I can be as lazy as the next man if I'm not interested in what I'm doing.'

'That's the secret.'

'So how are things here? You said your parents were in Dublin?'

'They're at a wedding. It's a big treat for them. They never go anywhere.'

He looked around the room. It was furnished simply. There was a photograph of the two of them on the mantelpiece. She was sitting in the sea with her clothes on.

'I see you kept the famous photo,' he said.

'How could I not?'

He remembered the day he took it. They'd been at the beach together on their bicycles. They decided to cycle into the sea. A freak wave knocked her off her bike as soon as she went in. He snapped her as she sat there soaking wet. She exaggerated her discomfort, pretending to be in agony. Then she dragged him down on top of her. The pair of them roared laughing as they sat in their clothes. They were drenched to the skin. They were lucky they didn't catch pneumonia. The camera was the only thing that stayed dry.

'Are you home for good?' she said.

'I don't know. I'm confused about what the future holds for me.'

'Now that you've got itchy feet you'll probably be off again in no time.'

'That's what Gabriel Hoey said.'

'It has to happen so. Gabriel has never been wrong about anything in his life.'

'Poor Gabriel,' she said, 'He's the target of everyone's jokes.'

She clicked her fingers.

'I haven't offered you anything to eat or drink since you came in. Are you hungry?'

'Not particularly. Don't go to any trouble for me.'

'Don't be silly. It's no trouble.'

She put something in the microwave.

He started to relax. He wanted to say, 'Why don't the two of us go off together?' The dreamer in him thought he could do things like that. He thought he could just kick off the traces without preparation. She'd always been impulsive too. It was one of the things he liked most about her. He remembered how she used to be as they went on their first dates together, always urging him to do wild things.

'I'm having stew,' she said, 'Will you join me?'

'That would be lovely. It's been a while since you cooked anything for me.'

'An eternity.'

The microwave pinged. She took out the stew .It was sizzling. She ladled it into a bowl. She was as good with one hand as two.

They sat at the table. As he ate he got a strange feeling, a feeling that they were a married couple. He'd been away all those months but ten minutes in her company blotted them out,. They returned him to his other self. His mother used to say happiness in marriage was doing the ordinary things together. The comment came back to him now.

'It's delicious,' he said, 'You never lost your touch.'

'I only do the simple dishes. Anything out of a bag suits me. Especially now that I'm working.'

'How is the job?'

'As I probably told you about a hundred times, I don't think I'll stay long in it. One good thing about breaking the arm was the time off.'

'Teaching jobs are like hen's teeth now.'

'What good is that if you're not happy at it? I don't really like the people in the school. They're not that friendly.'

'If you left, where would you go?'

'Maybe Europe or America. Recommend somewhere for me. You should know. You've been to so many places.'

'I didn't stay too long in any of them.'

'That would be my ambition too. I hate getting into ruts.'

Suddenly he didn't know what to say to her. The conversation was too sensible, too mature. He wanted to get back to the crazy things they did together, the things that had no meaning.

He looked at her hands.

'I see you still bite your nails,' he said, 'I suppose it's the job that's doing that.'

'Try spending all day with 37 screaming kids and see what it does to you. I'm lucky I'm not in a straitjacket.'

'Are they that bad?'

'They drain you with their demands. I don't know whether I'm meant to teach them or be a second parent to them.'

'What's wrong with a bit of both?'

'Nothing, I suppose – as long as they don't start inviting themselves home with me.'

'The holidays will keep you sane if you stay.'

'That's what the other teachers say.'

'Do you still visit your cousin in Kerry?'

'Now and again. Do you remember the year I brought you down with me?'

'How could I forget it? She had designs on me.'

'Had? She's still nuts about you. She says if the pair of us don't marry she's going to nab you for herself.'

'If you see her, tell her I'm flattered she remembers me.'

She got up from the table.

'Have you made up with your father?' she said.

'We're never going to be bosom buddies but we probably understand each other better now.'

'He told me he's getting out of the farming to become an auctioneer.'

'He's always got some crazy idea on the go.'

'Are you going to join him in it?'

'I don't know.'

'Why not? It'd be a soft landing for you.'

'I couldn't see myself lasting longer than five minutes in any job with him.'

'Did he tell you he came up here a few times after you left.'

'He did. You were up and down to him too, weren't you?'

'We had some good chats. He's a nice man.'

'When he wants to be.'

'What about Angela?'

'I have my problems with her too.'

'It would make your life much easier if you all got on.'

'I can't help the way I feel.'

'Stubborn to the last. That was always you.'

She looked at her watch.

'Am I staying too long?' he said.

'I have to get the cast off at some stage but there's no rush.'

'I'll be off soon anyway.'

She jumped up suddenly.

'Your coat!' she said, 'It's probably burned to a cinder. That's me all over. If my head wasn't tied on to me I'd probably forget it.'

She went over to the radiator.

'It seems okay. Do you want to try it?'

He stood up. She put it on him. It was bone dry.

'You did a great job on it.'

'It's all part of the service. Jennifer's Laundermat.'

She smiled at him. It was the smile that made him fall in love with her in the first place. He felt the old attraction to her coming back. It blotted out everything about Mia.

'What's wrong with you?' she said, 'You're looking at me kind of funny.' He felt his heart beating fast.

'Would you like to come out for a drink with me tonight?' he said suddenly.

It was like the offer someone would make to a stranger, not a girl he'd known almost as long as he'd known what it was to breathe. But it felt like that. It felt like a request for a date.

She didn't reply immediately.

'A drink?' she said.

'Yes, why not? We're still a couple, aren't we? I mean, sort of.'

'Are we?'

'You're not seeing anyone else, are you?'

'No.'

'Then what's to stop us?'

'Are we not on a break?'

'I thought that ended when I came back.'

'That's right but...'

'What?'

'I wasn't sure how we stood that way.'

'Do you not want to come out with me?'

'I didn't say that.'

'Then let's do it.'

She stood away from him.

'Sit down, Brian. I have something to tell you.'

'What do you mean?'

'Just sit down. I wasn't going to say this.'

'Say what?'

He sat down. She pulled over a chair beside him.

'Are you ready?'

'Ready for what?'

'I don't know how to say this to you.'

'Tell me, for Jesus' sake.'

She paused. Then she took a deep breath.

'I'm pregnant.'

He felt as if someone stabbed him. The feeling went from his body.

'What are you talking about? What are you saying to me?'

'I'm sorry,' she said, 'I've never been sorrier for anything in my life.'

'I don't believe you. This is a joke, right?'

'I'm serious.'

'It doesn't make sense. You can't be.'

She looked at him helplessly. He felt his pulse racing. He looked at her but he couldn't see her. Everything in the room clouded up.

She was pregnant. He'd felt guilty being with Mia and she was with someone else. She of all people. How could she have done it? It was the ultimate betrayal. It was worse than Bartley getting married, worse than anything.

'I wasn't going to tell you.'

'You weren't going to tell me? What's that supposed to mean? Until when?

'Please don't be like that. I'm very confused at the moment.'

'I'm not getting this. We've been talking for the last hour and everything seemed normal. Then you drop this bombshell on me.'

'I didn't want to.'

'So you were going to let me leave here today and not tell me? Was I going to find it out from someone at a street corner?'

'I wanted to see you and talk about ordinary things. I knew it would be too much for you to take in. It's a lot for me to take in as well.'

'My heart bleeds for you.'

'I wasn't ready to tell you. But when you asked me out...'

She stopped talking. Time seemed to stand still. Everything stopped, even the rain.

'How long?' he said.

She didn't answer. She just looked at the ground.

'Do you know who the father is?'

'Please, Brian, don't do this to me.'

'Do what?'

'What kind of a question is that? Who do you think you're talking to?'

'Don't you know?'

'Maybe you should go, Brian. I can't take these kinds of questions.'

'Are you with another man? Is that what this is all about? Is he here now? Hiding in the back room while your parents are away?'

'Please go, Brian, just go.'

'I want to know if you're with someone. You owe me that much.'

'No, I'm not with anyone. The man in question is gone out of my life. In fact he was never in it.'

'So it wasn't planned.'

'No.'

'When is it due?'

'In a few months.'

'A few months? So this hasn't just happened.'

'No, it hasn't just happened. You were away, as you might remember. You told me you wanted some time apart from me. You said we weren't right for one another.'

'So I'm to blame. Is that what you're trying to tell me?'

'No.'

'Then why did you put it like that?'

'Because you're interrogating me.'

'I'm not interrogating you. I'm asking you questions. There's a difference.'

'I can't talk about it anymore now. You'll have to understand that. I've told you. Now please leave me alone. I have a headache.'

'Okay, I'll go. But I need to talk to you.'

'I need to talk to you too.'

'Can we still meet tonight?'

'No. That wouldn't work for me. Let me get the cast off and I'll ring you.'

'All right.'

He didn't move for a moment. It was as if his body was paralysed. She was staring at the floor. He didn't look at her. His coat still felt warm from the radiator.

He went out the door. As he walked down the avenue he remembered the night Mia called out his name from a half-sleep when he was on the phone to her. Was that the night she decided to have done with him? Was that the night the baby was conceived?

41

He couldn't think straight over the next few days. Bartley kept asking him about Arthur Finlay until he was ready to scream. He stayed out of the house most of the time.

'What's wrong with you?' Bartley said to him, 'You're going around the place like a headless chicken.'

'I haven't settled back yet,' he said.

He felt guilty about the way he'd reacted to the news of Jennifer's pregnancy. He realised he'd been too dramatic, especially in view of the way he'd been with Mia. He realised he had a double standard. It was wrong of him to expect her to save herself for him when he hadn't saved himself for her. Looking back on it, it was the shock of the news rather than anything else that worked him up. Now that he'd had time to let it sink in he felt ashamed of himself.

She got the cast off. When she got the strength of her arm back she went back to her job. He rang her a few times but she didn't pick up. Then one day she did.

'I'm sorry about the way I reacted to your news,' he said.

'I understand why you did. I should have told you sooner. It was on my mind to do it all summer. I didn't know how to break it to you. I couldn't say it over the phone.'

'I shouldn't have turned on you. It was the shock more than anything else.'

'I didn't think badly of you for it.'

'Thanks for that. Have you told them in the school?'

'I had to. I'll be showing a bump soon.'

'How are they about it?'

340

'Not too pleased. I'm only in the job a wet day. It will mean maternity leave.'

'Who else knows?'

'Only Mam and Dad.'

'How did they take it?'

'They've been very good. They're glad I'm going to keep him.'

'Him?'

'It's going to be a boy.'

He asked her if she wanted to meet him but she said not for a few days. Work was manic and there were hospital appointments. He was more accepting of it when they met up, His shock subsided. The fact that the father wasn't involved with her helped him deal with it.

It helped her deal with it too. She told him she didn't want a hands-on father. There were so many of them now. It was a total contrast to the way things were in the old days where fathers of children headed for the hills when their girlfriends told them they were pregnant. She wasn't sure which situation was worse. Life was always full of extremes. Today they almost wanted to cut the cord.

'So you're still not going to tell me who he is,' he said.

'You won't believe it when you hear.'

They had some good nights together but also ones when they argued. During the course of one of them he told her he'd never have gone to university if she hadn't gone to Limerick first. That was where all their problems started, he said, when they parted.

'You were still in school when I did the Leaving Cert,' she said, 'What was I meant to do? Hang around the college every day waiting for you to come out? I'd have been like a stalker.'

She went on maternity leave shortly before Christmas. Bartley was having high level negotiations with Arthur Finlay about the auctioneering at the time. He went through the finer points of every possible scenario until Arthur was getting ready to pull the plug on the whole deal. Declan stepped in as an intermediary just as the situation was about to explode.

Brian stayed on the sidelines. He kept things ticking over on the farm. That was what Bartley wanted rather than him thinking about what his long term plans were. Things would take their course.

He was relieved to have got Mia out of his system. It was like an illness he'd been cured of. Jennifer's pregnancy pushed her into another part of him, the part that wasn't real.

He slopped out the stables and turned his mind off. He didn't know if his future was going to be with Jennifer or not. He knew the baby was going to change things between them. Would it be an extra noose around his neck if they decided to marry?

He didn't know if he was ready to be with her all the time. They didn't talk about it. Conversations about the baby filled the space. He was amazed at the way she was dealing with it. Instead of it making her insecure it made her proud.

He wanted to be with her through it all. He drove her to her medical appointments in the Hyundai when Bartley wasn't using it.

That wasn't always the case. One day he decided to get the Austin up and running again. Bartley told him he was mad but he didn't listen to him. He rang a garage and asked a man to come out and see if he could get it going. By some miracle he did after a number of tries.

'It'll need major surgery,' he said, 'I won't be able to do it here obviously. We can't move it until we get new tyres onto it.'

He put them on the following day. Brian went with him as they drove to the garage. He spent a while looking at the various options. Eventually he came up with a plan that didn't cost an arm and a leg.

'I can get her going for you,' he said, 'but there are no guarantees. It'll be on your own head.'

'I'll settle for that.'

Bartley wasn't pleased when he told him what he'd done.

'It makes nonsense of me buying the Hyundai.'

'I don't agree. What's wrong with having two cars?'

It was worth it to him even if it didn't make much practical sense. He enjoyed bringing Jennifer for drives in it on days when she hadn't anywhere specific to be. They went to the old haunts, places they'd driving to when they were going out together first.

He loved the feeling of timelessness driving gave him. It made him forget all his worries, forget Bartley and Angela putting ideas into his head. When he was away from them he felt as free as he did when he'd been in Europe or America.

One day Jennifer said to him, 'You'll probably be off on your travels again one of these days.'

'Are you trying to get rid of me?'.

They were more relaxed with one another now, coming back to the way they were before she went to Limerick. Maybe the pregnancy helped that.

She still wouldn't tell him who the father was. For a joke he said he thought it might be Gabriel Hoey. She almost lost her reason.

'Not if you gave me a million pounds,' she said.

He kept asking her if he could tell Bartley and Angela about it.

'Not yet,' she said.

'But they'll hear it around the town surely.'

'Let them.'

Early in the new year she finally felt ready to tell them. She announced it one evening when the four of them were in the pub. Brian felt Angela already knew. She kept looking at Jennifer's stomach every time she saw her. He wasn't sure about Bartley.

They threw a party for her at the farm. Her parents even came. Everyone got on really well together. Brian hadn't realised Jennifer's mother went to school with his own one. They were only a year apart in age. Why hadn't she mentioned that to him before?

He saw a lot of Jennifer in these months. Even though he wasn't the father of the baby he acted like it. He loved looking at the ultrasounds. He got excited whenever he kicked There were many appointments with the gynaecologist. One day the Austin broke down so he had to ask Bartley to drive them. He was happy to do it. He sat patiently in the foyer until they came out. He was so different to how he'd been when Brian's mother was alive.

'What time does,' Brian said.

'I told you,' she said, 'He's a good man.'

The baby was born in April. She couldn't take her eyes off him as he developed his features, his mannerisms. She called him Stephen after her father. Most people in the area thought he was Brian's son. A few people at the christening said he even looked like him.

'It just shows you what the imagination can do,' Jennifer said.

'I must be a miracle of nature,' Brian said, 'being able to impregnate someone from 3000 miles away.'

42

After he finally signed along the dotted line with Arthur Finlay, Bartley was on the phone to him morning noon and night checking on properties. Angela usually served him tea and biscuits as he spoke to him.

'I can see you're getting ready for your secretarial role,' he said to her one day as he brought them in on a tray.

'I hope I'll be doing more than this,' she said.

She continued to wait on him hand and foot, drooling over him like a child. Some days she even brought him his breakfast in bed. He took it in his stride. Brian wasn't surprised. He'd been used to it with his mother over all the years.

Spoiling him made Angela feel as good as it did him. He repaid her with his cheque-book. In the afternoons he drove her to town to buy her anything she wanted in the shops. She'd always dressed elaborately. Bartley didn't mind shelling out on clothes but he drew the line at the necklaces and bracelets Angela put her eye on.

'The only piece of jewellery I ever had time for,' he liked to say, 'is the ring in the barm brack. And that's because you get the brack as well.'

Other than that he was unusually generous with her. They planned to go to Alicante in the summer. It was a far cry from the fortnights he'd spent in a caravan in Spiddal in years gone by.

A maid came in to do the housework every few days.

'Do you really need her?' Brian said to Bartley.

'Angela has asthma,' he said, 'She's not as strong as she looks. She takes too much on herself. I have to stop her doing things she's not able for. Now that she's going into the office we need to give her all the help we can.'

Brian would have preferred if Angela stayed at the housework instead of joining them in the business. When he said this to Bartley he laughed.

'So you'd have her chained to the sink,' he said, 'I don't think the feminists would take too kindly to that.'

He spent the following days lounging around the house. Sometimes he went down to the pub and joined the local hard men pontificating about the ills of the world. He remembered the party that was thrown for him the night he came home. He felt important then. Now he was just another returned emigrant.

To get away from Angela he walked the land. When he left America he'd been looking forward to recapturing memories but it felt different now. It felt like someone else's land. He was an interloper.

One day Bartley asked him if he'd like to go into the office with him. He'd been in there a few times to get the feel of the place. He went in for a few hours the next day but he didn't have much to do. Arthur was polite to him but distant. He'd known Bartley for years but he didn't look overly excited about having all the Kilcoynes taking over his business. He sat in a back room for most of the day with his head buried in files. He only came out when he had to leave the office altogether.

It wasn't as busy as Bartley had led Brian to believe. Only a handful of people called in. Some of the properties were advertised on a revolving screen in the window. People stopped to look at this but that was usually it. If they came in, Brian felt it was more out of curiosity than anything else.

Bartley's phone didn't ring once. He made a few calls himself but his exaggerated enthusiasm wasn't shared by the people he was talking to. His rough accent hadn't the polish Brian imagined would have been expected for someone trying to sell houses. Angela would have performed better, he thought, but she was off on a whist drive that day. Arthur promised her a job down the line. For now she was just filling in for a secretary who was on maternity leave.

Brian wondered if the whole thing was going to come a-cropper. He spent most of the day reading the paper and looking out the window. Arthur left in mid-afternoon to attend a conference. He barely glanced at him on his way out.

'That was fun,' he said to Bartley as they put on their coats to go home at the end of the day. Bartley wasn't amused.

'Could you not look a bit more interested when you're talking to Arthur?' he said sternly.

'I wasn't aware that was how I was coming across.'

'It was. You had a face as long as a wet week on you all day. If you were selling me a mansion for a song I probably wouldn't have bought it off you. You looked like you'd have preferred to be washing dishes.'

'I can't sell my soul to sell a house. Arthur Finlay hasn't been canonised yet, to my knowledge. I don't think I should have to genuflect every time I see him.'

'Don't be so high and mighty about it. Every job involves a bit of brown-nosing. Is it asking too much of you to be civil to him? He could fill his office with people your age if he wanted. He's going out on a line for you because of me.'

'I'll make a bigger effort the next time.'

He did that the following week but he didn't feel it worked. He thought the change in his attitude made Arthur tense. Maybe he knew it was fabricated, that Bartley had had a word with him.

Arthur gave him some literature about the course he'd have to attend. When he leafed through it he thought it looked very boring. There was no attempt to enthuse the customer.

Arthur said it might do him good to show people the occasional house to get him used to the procedure. He didn't think that was a good idea. He'd never been a salesman. He wasn't good at 'talking a property up,' as Bartley put it. He was more likely to alert them to a problem.

His frustration boiled over one day after he showed a woman from Foxrock a five-bedroom property in Bearna. After she'd seen it she said, 'Is this everything?'

He said, 'Did I not show you the swimming pool out the back?'

Luckily she took the remark as a joke rather than him being sarcastic. He was fuming after he got back to the office.

'People raised families of ten in houses the size of horseboxes in the old days,' he rasped at Bartley.

'These aren't the old days,' Bartley said, 'You can't let your disapproval of people show. They're our bread and butter.'

'I'd prefer to starve than suck up to bitches like that.'

He stayed in the office after that. It was just as well. He was able to be himself more there, telling people exactly what was on offer rather than embellishing it like Bartley did. He thought people backed off if you sounded too eager about something. They smelt a rat.

The best properties sold themselves. The auctioneer was just the middleman. He was the person who did the paperwork and asked them to sign along the dotted line. The crunch issue for the buyers was getting approved for a mortgage or a bridging loan. Once they got to that stage they didn't usually haggle about the kind of details Bartley made such a song and dance about. Getting the keys to a house was like a holy grail for most of the young couples Brian knew in Loughrea, people of his own age who were struggling to get jobs or to stay in them.

He went to some NPSRA classes over the next few weeks but without much conviction. Arthur's business fluctuated because the economy was uncertain. Interest rates rose and fell without any pattern. He read reports of tracker mortgages, variable rates, uncertainties in stock market shares. Nobody seemed to know if they were going to have a roof over their heads for life. Most people rented because they couldn't get mortgages.

'They don't like doing that,' Bartley said to him, 'It's not in our culture. We can't forget the days when the Brits were our absentee landlords.'

Sales often collapsed after they put down deposits. Arthur would put a 'Sold' sign outside a house and a few days later he'd have to take it down again. The reasons were many – the breakdown of a relationship, the loss of a job, a health problem.

No matter how persuasive Bartley was he couldn't sway buyers who found a better place than Arthur was offering. It might have a smaller mortgage or no stamp duty or possibilities for an extension out the back. There was always a catch. Either that or the government brought in some new legislation that robbed Peter to pay Paul. Meanwhile Arthur worried about the expenses he was racking up. They were in the leases on his offices, his advertising, even his electricity.

'I'm having a hard time keeping my head above water,' he said to Bartley one day, 'What would you do if I had to shut up shop?'

'Maybe I'd go back to ploughing fields,' Bartley grunted, 'At least the plough doesn't change its mind half way through the job.'

43

The business went on in fits and starts. Weeks would go by without anything happening and then a few sales would happen at once, lifting all their spirits. Brian was bored a lot of the time but he decided to stick with it until he knew what was happening between himself and Jennifer. They settled into the kind of stability they'd had before he went off on his travels.

As sometimes happened with older people who try something completely different to what they've spent their lives at, Bartley became fascinated by the internet. He was a slow learner but once he grasped it he started to enjoy it like nobody's business. He started looking up auctioneering sites and graduated from there to farming programmes. Once he got in on it he started googling everything from animal studies to the circumstances surrounding the 1916 Rising.

'I've become a geriatric nerd,' he said.

'It's as if I don't exist anymore,' Angela complained, 'He's married to that computer.'

'She's exaggerating as usual,' he said, 'Angela can be very demanding as you know. When she wants your attention nothing is allowed get in the way of it, even an earthquake.'

'Don't try to talk your way out of it,' she said, 'I don't see you from one end of the day to the other. I'm getting worried you'll forget what I look like.'

'Would that necessarily be a bad thing?' he said.

She gave him a punch.

'Do you want to sleep on the sofa tonight?' she said.

'No.'

'Then be nice to me.'

'What do you want me to do?'

'Admit that you spend too much time on that computer.'

'All right.'

'It's a waste of time.'

'I know. You sit down for five minutes at it and before you know where you are the day is gone.'

'I rest my case.'

'On the other hand, it could make us rich, dear. Very, very rich.'

'Has it given you any ideas about the houses?' Brian said.

'Hundreds. The only problem I don't know if I'll live long enough to put them into practice.'

Brian sat down beside him. He said he was fed up working for Arthur. There was too much drudgery and the money wasn't anything to write home about.

'Why don't we break out on our own and try something completely different?' he said.

'Like what?'

'We could do up houses and sell them at a profit. I've heard of people making a killing at that.'

'Where would you get the money to buy them?'

'We'd just get one at a time and plough the profits back into the next one.'

'It sounds good in theory. Maybe if I was sweet sixteen again. Let's hang on with Arthur for a while more.'

The business started to pick up over the next few weeks. Arthur had to go to a conference in London. In his absence Bartley saw an opportunity to get Brian more experience without having someone looking over his shoulder all the time. He also prevailed on him to buy a suit and get his hair cut.

Arthur's secretary was still out on maternity leave so Angela's job was secure for a while yet. She sat across from Brian, smiling over at him and giving little waves that infuriated him.

Arthur phoned every day from London to find out how things were going. He told Bartley to show the houses to anyone who asked to see them until he got back. Bartley jumped at the chance to act like the owner of the company.

He dropped in with potential buyers every few days to collect sets of keys. He drove them around to properties and tried to work his charm on them. He always made a big flurry of asking Angela for the catalogue before going off with them, clicking his fingers at her as if she was a menial. When he showed a house to them he'd act as if they were about to see the Taj Mahal. During a particularly spirited encounter Brian heard him saying to one of the Americans he loved entertaining, 'I'm not offering you a *papier maché* shack like some of the other buckos are pedalling where the phone rings next door and you think it's your one. No, siree, this is the real deal.'

He usually didn't bring them back to the office after the viewing unless he wanted to give them what he called 'The Treatment.' One day he arrived back with a man from Montana who was thinking of settling down in Clifden. His name was Winston. He was obviously rolling in money. Bartley practically genuflected in front of him.

'That house we just looked at wasn't insulated!' he fumed at Angela, 'and there's dry rot. We're going to have to knock walls down all over the place if this gentleman is to be interested. Do you agree, Winston?' Winston nodded his head. A few minutes later the pair of them went out to Bartley's car to continue their discussion. When he came back in he said to Angela, 'I think I'm after hooking a big fish. That guy is so rich he could buy Áras an Uachtaráin and use it for a summer home.'

Angela was in a sulk.

'Why did you shout at me for the house not being insulated?' she said, 'I'm not a builder.'

'You don't realise. We have to look like this is a major catastrophe. I like to respect my customers.'

'What about respecting your wife? It annoys me the way you lick up to anyone who has a few dollars in their wallet.'

'What would you have me do – spit in their faces? These people are paying our wages. Don't forget that.'

'Winston looks to me like a major pain in the arse.'

'So what? You're not married to him.'

'Thank God.'

'I can swallow his bullshit if he lines our pockets.'

'Do what you have to but don't bring him back here anymore if you don't mind. I shouldn't have to swallow it too.'

'All right.'

'My guess is you'll probably never see him again.'

'Don't be so negative.'

'He was like one of those people who view houses without having the slightest interest in buying them. They just look at them to get ideas about re-designing their own ones.'

'Do you think I came down in the last shower? I can spot a time-waster a mile off.'

'I don't want you wasting your sweetness on the desert air.'

'Have no fear of that, my lady. If anyone pulls a fast one on me they'll live to regret it. If I see their interest slipping I whip out a form and get them to give me some kind of a deposit like hot snot. That sorts them out quick enough.'

Brian was amused at their bickering. They always made up afterwards.

One day he watched Bartley sitting two clients down and going through brochures with an air of great self-importance. He flashed through pages muttering 'Gone, gone, gone' about properties that were still available. He gave the impression the company was much busier than it was. After they left, Brian said to him, 'You're some chancer, lying through your teeth about houses we can't sell. Is this the same man who gives out about Martin Geraghty selling you bad cattle?'

'There's a difference,' he said, 'I'm not trying to flog bum products. I'm just putting a gloss over our little establishment.' He could argue his way out of a paper bag.

Whatever his secret was, his tactics bore fruit. The company showed a profit when Arthur did his annual audit.

'What did I tell you?' he exulted after being in the bank one Friday. He came into the office brandishing a cheque from his American friend – a deposit for the house in Clifden that had to be insulated. To Brian he was like a child in a sweetshop. He couldn't stop looking at the cheque.

'Maybe you'd like to frame it,' Arthur said.

He told Angela he didn't need her anymore when his secretary came back from maternity leave.

'It's pointless having two secretaries in such a small office,' he said.

Angela was enraged. She'd been enjoying having the extra money for buying clothes for herself.

'It's ageism,' she fumed, 'pure and simple. Or should I say *im*pure and simple.'

'Keep your hair on,' Bartley said, 'The other lady has been with him since she left school. He could hardly give her the chop now.'

'I hear she spends half the day doing her nails,' Angela said, 'or blabbering to her friends on the phone. He just wants a pretty little thing at the desk, batting her eyes at the customers.'

'Tell him to send her down to Newbridge,' Brian suggested, 'That's what Declan is looking for down there - someone to wave their boobs in the customers' faces so they'll buy any old house that's falling apart.'

Bartley stiffened on the spot.

'Give Declan a break, will you? He works bloody hard for what he gets.'

The Newbridge branch of the business didn't do well. Declan employed a few whizzkids to get things going for him. They had some early success but after a few months he fell foul of another auctioneer in the town. He'd had a virtual monopoly before Declan opened his office and he didn't take too kindly to the competition. They locked horns immediately. Both of them lost money chasing the same buyers. They usually had to climb down on the prices they were looking for as a result. It frustrated Declan so much he told Arthur he was thinking of baling out. It was more work to him than it was worth. It also cut in on the time he wanted to devote to the computers. They were his main mealtickets.

The fact that he was thinking of getting out of things got him off Brian's back. He stopped asking him to join him now.

'I suppose you're glad,' Bartley said to him.

'For me,' Brian said, 'not for him.'

Jennifer was glad too. She laughed out loud when Brian told her Declan had suggested she go to Newbridge with him. 'As if I could just up sticks like that,' she said, 'with a baby in tow.'

Stephen continued to be a handful to her but she knew she was lucky to be in a job that gave her a lot of free time to mind him – and to have a mother who filled in when she couldn't be there with him.

The relationship with Brian stayed steady. They didn't talk of marriage anymore or even of moving in together. They couldn't have afforded to anyway.

'We're semi-detached,' Brian joked.

He didn't know if she wanted more in the long term. She didn't give any sign that she did. He knew some women who became closer to their child than their husband after they got married. He didn't want that to happen to him. The fact that she had Stephen before they committed to one another helped in that way. Maybe when he got bigger she mightn't be so possessive of him.

'Do you not want a man in your life?' her father said to her.

'I have one,' she replied.

Brian didn't regret throwing in the towel with Arthur. Apart from everything else it gave him the time to do the jobs around the farm that

Bartley wasn't strong enough for anymore. He had more of a stomach for these now that he saw what the alternative was. He brought Rusty out in the tractor with him and played with him when it broke down. That happened more often than it didn't.

'Are you thinking about getting another job?' Bartley asked him one night.

'When my money runs out.' He hadn't earned much with Arthur but living at home meant he had few enough expenses. Bartley also slipped him a few euros anytime he was short.

One day he answered an ad in the paper for a job in a sweet factory outside the town. They were looking for someone to do the books. He had no experience in that area. He wasn't even sure he wanted the job. The only reason he applied for it was because he was bored.

The interviewer was a man called Joe McSweeney. He smelled of stale cigarette smoke.

He took him on immediately. That made Brian suspect Bartley put in a word for him. He'd done the same with Arthur Finlay. He knew him well. Was there anyone he didn't?

He was from a poor family in Mayo. When he arrived in Loughrea as a young man, Bartley put him herding cattle.

'I gave him his start,' he boasted.

Joe could hardly spell his name at that time. He came out of his shell at school and became a top student. After the Leaving Cert he did a course in business management in London. It went to his head. He came back to Galway acting like royalty. He got married but it broke down in no time. He was in his thirties now, living with a girl not much more than half his age

'Where did he get the accent?' Brian asked Bartley.

'Don't worry about that,' he said, 'After a few jars the bogman comes out.'

He had a lackadaisical attitude going into the interview. That was because he didn't expect to get the job. He was surprised when that proved not to be the case.

'The position is ideal for a young man like you,' McSweeney told him almost as soon as he sat down, 'Someone with an imaginative spirit.'

It hardly seemed like that once he started. The work was soul-destroying. They called him a cost accountant but he was really just a glorified clerk.

The hours were long. Figures swam before his eyes until he could hardly see them. He sat in on meetings where he tried to ask important-sounding questions. 'Good point,' Joe said almost every time he opened his mouth. Maybe Bartley told him to do that too.

At the end of the month he was given an office. Everyone on the assembly line seemed to know a favour had been done from upstairs. One of the other staff members who'd been interviewed for the job had much more experience than Brian. Passed over for promotion, he left the company soon afterwards. Brian felt responsible for this but he couldn't show it. It would have been a slap in the face for Joe.

He felt like a paper man sitting behind his desk trying to look busy. He had a conscience about the size of the pay cheque he got every Friday. He was presiding over people who were working twice as hard as he was and getting double the money they were.

His position had a degree of prestige attached to it. After serving his apprenticeship he was put on the monthly staff instead of the weekly one. He was also given a parking space with his name on it. There were other perks too, like not having to come to work until ten instead of nine like most of the other workers. All of this alienated them from him. Maybe he was alienated anyway.

He went out for lunch so he wouldn't have to sit in the canteen with them. The atmosphere was too tense. He joined them for coffee breaks but it didn't work. He had nothing to say to them. Some of them knew Bartley. He thought that might have helped but it didn't. There was always the unspoken knowledge that he'd got him the job.

Neither did it help that he'd been in America. If he spoke about his travels he knew it sounded as if he thought he was above them. Some of them had hardly been outside the town, never mind the country. He tried to play it down but that only made it worse. It came across as false modesty. The fact that he'd been in the university was another bugbear.

The harder he tried to be one of them, the more awkward he became. He sensed their resentment of him even when they weren't speaking. It was in their eyes, the way they moved, the way they said things to him. . He had some chance with the people in the other offices but not on the factory floor.

In the end he came to realise that people were going to feel about him the way they wanted regardless of how he behaved towards them. The bottom line was that he wore a suit and they wore boiler suits. That was the only thing that mattered. It over-rode class, money, everything. There were days he couldn't wait to get back to his office. Ten minutes in their company seemed like as many hours. He could almost see them thinking: You're making twice as much as us for half the work.

He spent his money almost as soon as he got it. There was no reason not to. It burned a hole in his pocket.

Every pay day after he cashed his cheque he threw the money onto the dressing table in his bedroom. He picked at the crumpled-up notes as if they were liabilities to be gotten rid of. He bought clothes he didn't need. He got a plasma television but he didn't watch it. It sat in his room mocking him with its uselessness.

He knew he was just marking time in the job until something better came along. What was that likely to be? He didn't know. The position with Arthur had become as unbearable as the university. Would this one too? Declan told him he was impossible to satisfy.

He asked Jennifer what she thought he should do

'It's down to what you want yourself,' she said, 'How can I get inside your mind?'

His emotions were in turmoil a lot of the time. He felt the same as when he went to Europe. That was allowable. It was a phase, the experimental phase most young people went through at his age. This was more serious. It could go on all his life if he didn't do something about it.

He had too much time on his hands. That was the case with the factory workers too. It was especially the way at the end of the month when the orders had been processed and they were waiting for new ones to come through. They spent a lot of time smoking in the toilet. It was the only place in the building where an alarm didn't go off. It was broken and McSweeney showed no indication of having it fixed. He was lax like that. Brian was supposed to root them out but he couldn't. He'd have preferred to be in there with them than sitting at a fancy desk looking out at the mountains.

One day McSweeney told two of the factory workers their jobs were gone. There was no notice. They got the news in a circular delivered to their desks at 9.05. They hadn't even had a chance to take their coats off. If they'd been there longer they might have had some redress but they were new recruits. They had no rights. All they got was two week's pay to send them on their way.

Brian felt guilty. When he went down to the canteen later that day the atmosphere was worse than ever. Nobody said hello to him. They hardly even acknowledged his presence. He could see they were tense. Whose name was going to be on the bullet next?

He went in to McSweeney. His girlfriend was beside him. She was sitting on his desk in a mini-skirt.

'What do you think of those legs?' he said to Brian. It was like something Bartley would have said, or Gabriel. He didn't seem to realise people didn't talk about women that way anymore. But she didn't mind. She smiled.

'They're very nice.'

'What can I do you for?' he said. He always put it like that.

'I need to talk to you.'

'Is it about the jobs?'

'Yes.'

'Don't worry. You're bulletproof.'

353

'What about the two people you let go?'

'What's that got to do with you?'

'I work here.'

'Brian, if you don't mind, I'm busy.'

'I can see that,' he said.

The girl giggled. He left the office.

One of the men who was let go had just got married. He'd been struggling with a mortgage. Later in the day Brian found him crying his eyes out in the canteen. He said his bank manager was demanding the keys of his house.

'I'm going to be homeless,' he said, 'We have a child on the way.' Brian didn't know what to say. He went back up to his office. For the rest of the day he couldn't do any work. At one point he banged his hand on the desk.

When he went home he told Bartley but he wasn't interested. It was like talking to McSweeney all over again.

'It's happening every day of the week,' he said, 'Welcome to the human race. You can't be taking responsibility for these people's lives. You don't know them from Adam. Everyone has their own shit to deal with. What's wrong with your hand, by the way?'

'I hurt it moving some machinery.'

One Friday as he was getting ready to leave the factory he was accosted in the corridor by one of the factory hands, Frank Flannery. He was a rough diamond. He'd been a few years ahead of him at school. He'd left under a cloud. Declan told him once that he'd been expelled.

'Your old man got you the job,' he said, grinning at him. Brian stopped in his tracks. It was the first time anything had been said to him. Maybe this was better than the silent resentment. It didn't bother him. But his next comment did.

'How did he manage to sober himself up long enough to lick McSweeney's arse?' he said.

He felt an anger rising inside him, an anger he didn't know he possessed.

He threw Flannery against the wall. He started punching him.

'Stop, you fucking bastard,' he said. Blood spilled out of his mouth.

'The next time you say anything about my father you're dead,' Brian told him. He looked at him with hate in his eyes. Brian thought he was going to spit at him. Instead he just rubbed the blood from his mouth.

'This isn't over,' he said.

He was surprised he backed off. He was bigger than him. Brian wasn't used to having fights. He could hardly remember any at school apart from the one with Tommy Glynn. That was for the same reason.

McSweeney's secretary saw it happening. She was at the coffee machine. It wasn't too far away. She looked almost amused as Flannery slunk off.

Brian went up to her.

'I'd appreciate it if you didn't say anything about this to Mr McSweeney,' he said.

'I saw nothing,' she said. She zipped her fingers across her lips the way children did sometimes.

'Are you okay?' she said. He nodded.

'He's a trouble-maker,' she said, 'You did us all a favour.'

He felt angry for the rest of the day. Was that how people saw Bartley, as nothing more than a drunk? Were they right? He'd said it himself. It was different when someone said it in public, especially someone outside the family.

Flannery didn't come in to work on the following Monday. McSweeney's secretary told Brian he rang in sick. He came in on the Tuesday but he was subdued. Brian didn't think he'd do anything. He had a bandage over his mouth. The other people on the assembly line slagged him about it. Brian didn't think he told them what happened. He wouldn't have minded if he had.

His mind went to sleep as he did his chores in the following days. Anytime he made a mistake it was covered up by McSweeney. He felt like a protected species.

'Just get the books to balance,' he kept saying, 'That's all that matters. I don't care whether you get there by the scenic route or not.'

He began going in later in the mornings and leaving before everyone else. Most days on the way home he stopped by an off-licence and bought himself a six-pack. When he got to the house he nearly always went straight to his room. He put Jennifer off whenever she rang. He didn't think he'd be any company for her.

He spent most of his time watching television. Sometimes he didn't even turn the sound up. He flicked buttons on the remote without knowing what he was looking for. Images of war blended with those of girlbands, political debates, chefs with big hats on them. He usually had music playing in the background. It was as if he was trying to stop himself from thinking. It was easy to do that with the beer inside him.

He watched films on Netflix and idiotic game shows. He often fell asleep during them. He'd wake up in the middle of the night not knowing where he was. A few hours later the alarm would go off. He'd go down to the car in a daze. He'd drive to the factory with the windows open to try and get himself into the day.

He did his work on auto-pilot now. McSweeney didn't seem to notice. His girlfriend was his main focus. He often went off on holidays with her somewhere. He put a lot of them down to expenses. Brian felt the factory was heading for a crash.

He tried to live each day for itself but it wasn't easy. He felt he was becoming old before his time. When he was a boy he loved not knowing what was going to be happening on a given day. It didn't even have to be exciting. The surprise was enough. That was gone now.

He felt detached from his experiences. It was as if he was in a film about his life – or someone else's life. He was outside himself, watching himself having experiences with people who were characters in the same film. They were like figures on a landscape, ciphers he could make not exist if he wanted to.

Bartley's moods were up and down.

'Did you ever ask yourself what's the point?' he said to Brian one night when he was lounging in the kitchen.

'The point of what?' he said.

'Of anything. Getting up in the morning.'

'We all get thoughts like that. I wouldn't worry about them'

'What do you do when you get them?'

'I don't know. I just wait for them to pass, I suppose.'

'And do they?'

'More often than not.'

'With me they don't.'

'Do you get them a lot?'

'No, but when I do they stay a long time.'

'Are you feeling that way now?'

He paused.

'Yes.'

It was unusual for him to be this personal. He wondered if things were going badly with Angela. She was out a lot now.

'They passed before,' he said, 'They will again.'

'Every time I get them they last longer.'

'Did you mention them to Angela?

'No.'

'Have you thought of seeing anyone about them?'

'Like who?'

'There are a lot of people out there. Trained people.'

'How could they help?'

'You'd be surprised.'

'I'm not into that kind of thing.'

'How are you at the moment?'

'Pretty bad.'

He sat down beside him. His eyes were burning in his head.

'They say the darkest hour is before the dawn,' he said.

He gave a wry laugh.

'Is that the kind of shit you learned in UCD?'

'I know it sounds like a cliché.'

Bartley's eyes became glazed. He looked as if he was about to cry.

'I shouldn't be turning on you. It's myself I'm annoyed at.'

'Don't be. You're fighting it. That's the main thing.'

He went to bed that night without drinking. When he was this depressed it didn't do anything for him.

He was in better form the following morning. Brian asked him how he was. He just said 'So-so.' He didn't mention the conversation they'd had. He had to go to town for some things Angela asked him to get. After he was gone Brian said to her, 'He was pretty low last night.'

'He's that way a lot of the time,' she said, 'What can you do about it? It's life.'

Curiosity took him out of it. It always had. when he was thinking about other people he forgot about himself. It happened on a night when Brian was on the phone with Gabriel Hoey. He'd rung him out of the blue to ask him if he'd like to go out for a drink with him.

'I enjoyed that night in the pub,' he said, 'Where have you been hiding yourself since?'

'Keeping a low profile mainly.'

'I heard you left the auctioneering.'

'I couldn't wait to get out of it.'

'And now you're in another job.'

'Sort of.'

'Would you like to meet for a jar some night?'

'Sorry Gabriel but it's not really my thing.'

'If you change your mind you know where I am.'

Bartley came into the room as he was hanging up.

'Who was that?' he said, 'A secret admirer?'

'Gabriel Hoey.'

'Ah, Lord Muck. What did he want?'

'He asked me if I'd like to go for a drink with him.'

'I hope you told him what to do with himself.'

'I did, more or less.'

'Good. You don't want to get sucked into a boozing scene with that loser.'

'We've had this discussion before. He's not as bad as you say he is.'

'He's the greatest arse this town ever threw up. I'd avoid him like the plague if I was you.'

'You seem to be against me having any kind of a social life.'

'How do you mean?'

'You keep telling me I should meet more people but when someone asks me out for a drink you tell me to say no to them.'

'I make an exception for Hoey. I can't stick him.'

'Why do you come down on him so much? All he wants is a bit of company.'

'I've never liked him. Just because his old man is a sawbones he thinks his shit smells like Christmas cake.'

44

Brian was tense in the following days. He couldn't concentrate on even the simplest tasks at work. He picked fights with Bartley. He comfort ate and comfort drank. The days ran into one another without him having anything to show for them. It didn't rain and he missed that. The sky was a kind of off-white. It drained everything from it.

Driving to work became one of the few pleasant tasks in his day. Sometimes it seemed as if the car was driving itself. When he got into his office he locked the door and looked out at the mountains. That always relaxed him. It was his favourite time of the day, sitting there with a coffee and his head empty. But then his phone would ring or he'd have to go to his computer to print out a document or something.

He felt as if he was in suspended animation. As soon as he unlocked the door his secretary would come in with a sheaf of papers and go through them with him. Most of the time he only half-listened to her. She could have been speaking to him in a foreign language. Sometimes he felt as if he was back in Europe again, scanning people's features for clues to what they were saying. The job became his home from home, a place he needed to get away from Bartley and Angela so he'd be able for them in the evenings.

He still found it difficult to sleep at night. When he did he usually dreamt. Many of his dreams were about his childhood, about the early years when his mother was happy and Bartley wasn't drinking too much. Some of the dreams were strange. In one of them he was walking along a road that had a building at the end of it. The faster he walked, the smaller the building got. Then he started to run. The road seemed to move under him. Eventually he reached the end of it. By then the building had disappeared.

Jennifer wondered why he wasn't meeting her more. He said it was just a phase he was going through, that he'd get over it.

'Is it because of Stephen?' she said.

'I don't know what makes you think that,' he said, 'I love being with him.'

She said the job was still driving her crazy, that she'd do anything to get into another school. One day she rang him to say she'd been at an interview for one, that she wanted to talk to him about it.

'Are you free tonight?' she said.

'That would be great. Name a place.'

'What about Brennan's in two hours?' It was a slightly more upmarket pub than McDonaghs.

'Perfect. I'll see you there.'

He was glad he didn't have too much time to think about it. If he did he mightn't have gone. He put on the suit Bartley bought him for the coming home party. He hadn't worn it since. The factory demanded a more severe black one.

'So it's getting a second exhibition,' he said when he saw him in it, 'Is this some kind of date you're going on?'

'It's only Jennifer.'

'Why do you say "only" Jennifer?'

'I didn't mean it like that. Does the jacket still look ridiculous on me?'

'It's not too bad. You'd get away with it if you put a jumper under it.'

He was tense driving to Brennan's. There was no reason to be but being out of the groove of meeting people made any rendezvous a challenge.

She was there when he arrived. She was sitting in a corner with a glass of vodka in front of her. There was a pint of Smithwicks beside it. There was a candle stuck into a wine bottle beside her. It lit up her face, giving her a Madonna-like look.

'I like the jacket,' she said when he got to the table.

'It's about two sizes too big for me.'

'Not at all. You wouldn't notice.'

He looked at her glass.

'I see you're drinking vodka. That's unusual for you.'

'I need it after the day I've had. I got a pint of Smithwicks for you. Was I right?'

'It's just what I need. Tell me about the interview.'

She puffed out her cheeks in exasperation.

'They really grilled me. It was like a court martial. They wanted to know everything about me since the day I was born. You'd think I was running for the president of Ireland.'

'All the interviews are like that nowadays. It's because jobs are like gold dust.'

'The funny thing was, only about 1% of the questions were about teaching.'

'What were they about?'

'Debates, doing sports with the kids, that kind of thing.'

'Beyond the call of duty stuff.'

'Exactly. If you can say anything is beyond the call of duty nowadays. We'll see what happens. I'm tired talking about it. Mam says to put it out of my mind until they call – or don't call. I'm probably in a queue of about twenty for it.'

'I'm sure you'll walk it.'

'It would be great to get away from where I am.'

'Is it still as mad as ever?'

'I'm on tranquillisers now.'

'I believe a lot of teachers are.'

'The doctor said to take one every time I get stressed. I said, "That means about 47 a day." The funny thing is, the first thing you see on the bottle is a message saying, "Keep Away From Children." I can't – they're my job.'

'Very funny.'

'It's not too funny when you're in the firing line.'

'Better you than me.'

'It's like being a lion tamer in a circus sometimes. The longer I do it, the more I'm in danger of turning into a child myself. That's the problem with spending all day with six year olds. Eventually you become one of them.'

'Didn't George Bernard Shaw say something like that?'

'If he didn't he should have.'

'I know how hard you work.'

'I wish everyone did. Teachers have a bad image in a lot of people's eyes.'

'I've heard a few stories all right.'

'Most people only see the short hours and the long holidays. They don't think about the extra stuff we do that eats up our time. I often just flop into the bed after coming home. Anyway that's enough about me. Have your spirits picked up since I talked to you last?'

'A bit.'

'I suppose the job is as boring as ever.'

'Worse. I'll probably run out of the place screaming some day.'

'Are you getting on any better with your father?'

'Slightly. How is Stephen?'

'Driving me quietly insane with his energy levels.'

'Who's minding him tonight?'

'Mam, needless to say. I don't know what I'd do without her.'

'He must think he has two mothers at this stage.'

'I know. I wasn't sure how she was going to be when I broke the news to her about being pregnant but she's really come up trumps.'

'Was your father harder to win round?'

'You could say that. He's more old-fashioned. Men often are, contrary to what people say.'

'Would you put me into that bracket?'

'Not really. I understand why you got so worked up the day I broke the news to you.'

'I suppose you're still not going to tell me who the father is.'

'Maybe I should. At this stage I know you're never going to stop asking me.'

'It's a natural thing to want to know. I've heard lots of rumours flying around about who it might be.'

'Well let me tell you they're wrong.'

'So you've heard them too.'

'How could I not? It's all people have to talk about.'

'So who is he?'

She didn't look as if she was going to say but then her expression changed. She took a gulp of her vodka.

'Okay, here it is. I've kept you waiting long enough. You probably won't believe it when you hear.'

'Go on.'

She put down her glass.

'It's Billy Sheehan.'

For a second he thought she was joking. He looked at her to see if she was going to break into laughter. Billy couldn't get a girl to save his life. People used to make jokes about him. They used to say he wouldn't get a kiss in a brothel, that the tide wouldn't take him out. He lived with his mother out the country.

'You're having me on.'

'I knew you wouldn't believe me.'

'This is worse than you telling me you were pregnant.'

'These things happen, Brian. We may not want them to but they happen.'

'But you don't even know him.'

'He's in the drama group I joined. Do you not remember me telling you about Mrs Cullotty and her jam sandwiches?'

'He couldn't be. How could he know anything about drama?'

People thought he didn't know anything about anything. Brian used to think he was mentally slow when he was growing up. There was a story that he'd been deprived of oxygen when he was born.

'The standards of our group are hardly up to those of the Abbey. Mrs Cullotty rarely rejects anyone.'

'So you were in a play together?'

'It was one of those John B. Keane things. He played a farmer. I was the local piece of skirt. I was supposed to swoon every time he looked at me because he had a few bob. It was probably the worst production of a play this century.'

'But you continued the relationship with him offstage.'

She sucked in her breath.

361

'One night we substituted the jam sandwiches for large whiskeys. It was the last performance. We were both hammered. The prompter was very busy that night. I can't believe we got through it without everyone walking out.'

'Go on. I'm still in shock.'

'We had a drunken fumble in the dressing room. It was a poky little place where all you could smell was Pond's cold cream. That's what we used to take our make-up off.'

'I don't know if I want to hear any more.'

'I put it out of my mind almost immediately after it happened. It was as if that would somehow make it *not* have happened. Then two weeks later I had the test and boom, I got the bad news. Bambino on the way. I couldn't believe it when I tested positive.'

'Please tell me you're making all this up.'

'I wish I was. It was the only time I was with a man besides yourself. You mightn't believe that.'

'At this stage I don't know what I believe.'

'It was the night after one of your phone calls to me. You'd said you thought it would be good for us to see other people. In a strange way it helped me get over you. Anyway, that was the end of my single life. And the play.'

'Has he an interest in the baby?'

'He pretends he has but he isn't a very good actor. I knew that already from the play.'

'Do you see him much?'

'Only about things to do with Stephen. He keeps asking me to go out with him but I always say no.'

'So he's interested in you that way.'

'He's been lusting after me since I was a child. Surely you know that.'

'I didn't.'

'He keeps asking me to marry him.'

'What?'

'I'm serious.'

'Did you ever think you might have made a go of things with him?'

'Absolutely not.'

'Why didn't you tell me this before?'

'What would have been the point? I don't even know what the point is now.'

'I'm glad you did.'

'I kept putting it off. It was stupid of me.'

'Does he give you any financial support for Stephen?'

'He's good that way.'

'He works in the Co-Op, doesn't he?' It came to him out of some kind of fog.

'That's right. It's a dead end job but Billy was never the type to let that kind of thing bother him. He'd be happy to stay there till he's seventy. I could see him having a dozen kids in his mother's house.'

'And a wife, presumably.'

'Yes, as a kind of extra to the mother and kids.'

She took a drink of her vodka.

'You know everything now. How do you feel?'

'Shocked. Bewildered.'

'Have another drink. That'll help the shock sink in. You can get me one too.'

He went up to the counter. His head was pounding.

Billy Sheehan. The town joke. Was that who he was in competition with? It was almost surreal.

He came back with the drinks.

'I think we should talk about something else,' he said, 'It's too much for me to get my head around.'

'Agreed. When you wake up tomorrow you'll see it all makes perfect sense.'

'I doubt that but maybe you're right. Things hit me like a ton of bricks when I hear them first. I don't have shock absorbers in my head like cars do.'

'Sorry to have laid this on you. I really only asked you to come out with me so I could talk about the interview.'

'You'd have told me sooner or later. I'd have dragged it out of you.'

'I'm glad you got it from me instead of a stranger.'

'So am I.'

'Not that there's anyone else who knows. Billy said he wouldn't tell either but it could have come out from his parents.'

'Or yours.'

'That would be unlikely.'

As he started on his second drink he found himself relaxing. In a way, what did it matter who the father was? It relieved him to know that she wasn't interested in him romantically. That was all that mattered. The child was there anyway.

'So he contributes to Stephen?' he said.

'As much as he can. He isn't on much of a salary in the Co-Op.'

'No wonder you're pulling the devil by the tail every time I see you.'

'I'm okay as long as I have the job.'

'Teachers don't earn much.'

'That's why Mam is so important. She saves me a fortune on babyminders by spending so much time with Stephen.'

'Are they still a bit funny about him in the school?'

'Unfortunately. To my face they're all sweetness and light but you know what goes on behind closed doors here. I've only brought him in once or twice. I know they resent me going on maternity leave so soon after getting the job. But that's enough about me. I've hardly asked you a thing about yourself. How are things at the farm? Do you think your father will stay at the auctioneering?'

'That's in the lap of the gods. It's not really him but I'm sure he'll make the best of it. I think Angela is pushing most of his buttons. She always saw farming as beneath her.'

'I thought it was all about him trying to wind down.'

'She makes it look like that. She has the ability to decide on a course of action and make it look like someone else's idea.'

'Does he listen to her that much?'

'She has him round her little finger. He'd move to the moon if she asked him.'

'You seem to dislike her more every time I see you.'

'It doesn't matter what I think of her. He's the one who's married to her. The chemistry was never great between us from the word go but we tolerate each other. That's probably as good as it's going to get. She makes him happy. I can't ask for more than that. And she's probably stopped him drinking himself to death.'

'Does she know you don't like her?'

'If she does she doesn't act like it. If I say anything even half-funny to her she goes into these silly fits of laughter. She thinks that pleases me but it drives me up the walls. She's afraid to be herself with me.'

'I get that in the school too. You'd prefer if someone just told you to fuck off.'

They started laughing. For a second it was like the old days.

He stared at her.

'What's wrong?' she said.

'Nothing. I was just thinking how beautiful you looked.'

She blushed.

'Now you're embarrassing me.'

He wondered what might have happened if he married her instead of leaving. Did she feel the need of a father for Stephen? If she did, could that person be him? Maybe she'd find another man, someone with more optimism about life than he had, someone less bruised by it.

A pip came from her mobile.

'Sorry,' she said, 'That's probably Mam.'

She read the message.

'Oops,' she said, 'I have to go. She's getting panicky. Stephen is acting up.'

'No problem.'

'This is terrible. After me asking you out.'

'What a tragedy. We might never see one another again.'

'Don't be facetious. I was enjoying the chat.'

They walked out of the bar. There was a full moon out. He wanted to kiss her. It lit up her face the way the candle had done in the bar.

'I'm sorry about this,' she said.

She swiped the message from her mobile.

'It's nothing.'

'Well, see you soon. Next time I promise to have the little fella safely in the land of nod before I see you.'

As they embraced he felt all the old emotions he had for her returning. For a moment it was like he'd never been away. The other women in his life disappeared, the ones he once thought could fulfil him when he didn't know who he was.

He kissed her. She looked at him with love in her eyes.

'I'm really glad we met tonight,' she said, 'even though it was short.'

'So am I.'

They stood there under the light of the moon. He didn't want her to go and yet he couldn't say anything to stop her.

'Can I tell you something?' she said.

'Of course.'

'It was you I was thinking about the night I was with Billy.'

'I don't know what to say to that.'

'How do you mean?'

'Whether you were thinking of me or not it's still his child.'

'I know. Please don't get annoyed with me. I just wanted to say that to you.'

'I'm sorry for giving you mixed signals. You did nothing wrong.'

'You don't think so?'

'No. I was the one who changed everything. You were only reacting to that.'

'You have no idea how much your phone calls meant to me when you were away.'

'Really? I thought you were having the time of your life in Limerick.'

'A lot of the time I was waiting by the phone.'

'You should have told me.'

'I didn't want to spoil the time for you.'

'You wouldn't have.'

He kissed her again.

'Do me a favour,' he said, 'Don't see Billy anymore. Let me fund Stephen from now on.'

'Do you mean that?'

'Yes. I don't want him in your life.'

'This is very sudden.'

'You know me. I'm a mixed-up fool.'

'No you're not.'

She smiled at him.

'Does this mean we're an official couple again?'

'If you want us to be.'

'Of course I do. It's what I've wanted all along.'

'Me too. I was too stupid to admit it to myself.'

She hugged him.

'I better go home,' she said, 'If we stay here any longer we'll probably end up in bed together. Then you'll have two children to contend with instead of one.'

He laughed. Maybe that's what they needed, he thought. A laugh. To take the tension out of everything.

'There's one thing I want to ask you,' he said.

'What?'

'If we're serious about being an official couple again, let's keep it between ourselves. You know what this place is like.'

'I couldn't agree more.'

45

When he got home that night Bartley and Angela were merry. He could see they'd had a few drinks.

'We heard it's back on with Jennifer,' Angela said.

He couldn't believe what he was hearing.

'Who told you that?'

'Maureen. She bumped into Jennifer at the shops.'

She was a teacher in Jennifer's school.

'So what?'

'She told me all about it.'

'About what?'

'She was on the phone to Jennifer. Apparently she told her she'd met you.'

'And?

'She said the pair of you are going steady again. Is it true?'

His blood boiled.

'Of course it is. In fact we're getting married tomorrow. Buy a hat.'

'I'm sorry,' Angela said, 'Is this confidential?'

'It's okay. I know you mean well.'

She shuffled out of the room. He went up to his room and rang Jennifer.

'What's going on?' he said, 'Have you been talking to Maureen?'

'How do you mean? I ran into her in Spar after I left you.'

'Angela said you told her we were going steady again.'

'What?'

'She could only have got that from you.'

'She didn't, Brian. Honestly.'

'What did you say to her?'

'I can't remember the exact conversation. Whatever it was, it was nothing like that.'

'Why would she say what she said?'

'You know Maureen. She lets her imagination run away with her.'

'Come on. You must have said something.'

'Nothing of any consequence.'

'You shouldn't have said anything at all. You told me you were going to keep it under your hat..'

'I was.'

'So what happened?'

'She knew about us going out together in the past and that you were home.'

'So what did you say to her?'

'Just that I met you and that we got on well. It was a totally ordinary conversation.'

'That we got on well. That was it?'

'As far as I can remember. God, Brian, now I feel terrible. I know I should have kept quiet but obviously Maureen added two and two and got five. I'll have to have it out with her. She can't keep anything to herself. She's always bursting to tell things to people. She'd tell the Third Secret of Fatima if she could.'

'Since you know that, you should have been more careful with her.'

'I can't tell you how sorry I am.'

'You must have met her straight after leaving me.'

'I dropped into Spar to get some baby wipes for Stephen. She was in the next aisle. Her eyes were out on sticks when she saw me. You know what she's like.'

'Why didn't you text me?'

'I didn't think there was any need to. I was rushing back to Mam.'

'Are you sure you're telling me the whole conversation?'

'All I said was that we got on well and that we'd probably be seeing each other more regularly now.'

'It was wrong to say that. You know how private I am.'

'She dragged it out of me. I was high. I know I put my foot in it. How many times can I say I'm sorry?'

'We might as well put it on Facebook now.'

'Brian, you're over-reacting to this. We live in a goldfish bowl. Sooner or later everyone finds out everything about everyone.'

'That's the point. I wanted it to be later.'

'I know how sensitive you are. I won't tell anyone else. Please don't go on about it. We'll keep a lid on the situation.'

'If Maureen has it you can bet your bottom dollar the whole town knows.'

'I'll call her tonight and swear her to secrecy.'

'It's too late for that.'

'What can I say, Brian? I can't take it back.'

'That's the problem.'

He was annoyed with himself for getting annoyed but he couldn't help it. Everything was back to square one for him now.

He didn't make contact with her over the next few days. Angela noticed him being in on himself but she knew better than to pry. Bartley kept asking him what was wrong with him but he didn't say. Then one night Jennifer rang him in tears. For a few seconds she could hardly speak. It made him feel guilty.

'Sorry about the other night,' he said, 'I was out of order.'

'Don't be. You were in your rights.'

'No I wasn't. I shouldn't have upset you. It seems like nothing now. Is that why you're crying?'

'No.'

'Why then?'

'I don't know. I'm at a very low ebb these days. Anything is capable of setting me off.'

'There must be something specific.'

'I had a terrible day at work. Every day is terrible now. They're ganging up on me in there.'

'Is it about Stephen?'

'I'm not sure. His name is never mentioned but it could be. I think they heard I went to the interview.'

'That's more likely the reason.'

'There's a deafening silence every time I walk into the staff-room. It's driving me bonkers.'

'Have you heard anything back about the interview?'

'No. I'm presuming I didn't get it. How are you keeping?'

'Not much better than you, I'm afraid. I feel trapped here as well.'

'We should go away somewhere together. Then we'd both be free.'

'It sounds great in theory but what would we live on - fresh air?'

'We'd find a way. I could get a job easily enough and you probably could too. If you couldn't I'm sure your father would help you out, or even Declan.'

'I'm surprised to hear you talk like that. You weren't exactly jumping out of your boots with enthusiasm to go down to Newbridge when he mentioned it.'

'That was different. We wouldn't have been in our own place. I'd love to break away from everything I know – to do what you did. Sometimes I see a city in my mind. I don't even know which one it is. It's like a place out of a fairytale.'

When she talked like that she reminded him of Mia. Maybe they had more in common with one another than he had with either of them.

'I wish I could be as spontaneous as you. I'm too tense to think of anything like that at the moment.'

'I'm sorry that's the way you feel about things.'

'We made a breakthrough a few nights ago. Are you not happy with that?

'Of course, but it was only a first step. Since you got back from America we've been like two people who hardly know one another.'

'That's because I can't make up my mind where my next move is coming from.'

'Will you ever be able to?'

'That's a bit cruel.'

'I don't mean to be. I'm just tired of all these baby steps we're making. I need a break from my job, from Loughrea, even from Mam and Dad, no matter how good they are to me.'

'So do I at the farm. I hate being beholden to anyone.'

'Then you know what I mean.'

'Of course I do, but something is stopping me acting on it.'

She frowned.

'Look, Brian, I love you and I want to be with you but our relationship is no good to me the way it is with this constant see-sawing. I'd prefer not to see you at all if we're going to be in this permanent limbo. If you don't love me enough to want to be with me all the time I'd prefer if you walked away from me this minute.'

'Where is this stuff coming from? Is it because of Maureen?'

'Maybe there's a bit of that in it. The way you went on about her really worked me up. It made me think you were looking for an excuse not to commit to me.'

'That's ridiculous.'

'It was bad enough you going to Europe and then America. If I'm going to lose you a third time please tell me in advance so I can start to plan my life without you.'

He went quiet for a long time when she said that. When he spoke again it was in a strong voice.

'You're right in most of the things you say,' he said, 'but it isn't true that I manipulated the Maureen situation to get away from you. I love you as much as you love me. I'm just not ready to live my life with you yet.'

'Why not? Is there someone else you're not telling me about?'

'No.'

'Why then? Are you waiting for the shining light of Damascus to descend on you to tell you I'm the one for you?'

'Nothing as dramatic as that. My head isn't in a good place now. Sometimes I wonder if I even know who I am.'

'You're Brian Kilcoyne. Look in the mirror.'

'I deserved that.'

Her phone vibrated with a text. She took it out of her handbag and read it.

'I have to go now,' she said, 'Stephen is crying. We've said everything we have to say. I have to go now.'

'Okay, Jennifer. Goodbye.'

He didn't talk to her for a week after that. When he did it was to ask her if she'd bear with him for a while more until he got himself sorted out. Reluctantly she said yes. Afterwards they drifted back into the situation they'd been in since he came back from America, meeting once or twice a week to go for a drink or to a film if Jennifer's mother was able to mind Stephen.

She continued to go for interviews for other schools but she didn't have any luck with them. She had a few run-ins with her principal. She only stayed where she was because she liked the children so much.

Sometimes Brian passed her on the way to work. He used to beep the horn as he overtook her. One day she got a puncture and flagged him down. He put her bicycle into the boot and drove her to her job. She was tense for the whole journey, totally unlike the girl he remembered from when he got to know her first.

'I should have checked the tyres before coming out,' she said, 'I was late leaving the house and everything was up in a heap. The alarm didn't go off for some reason and Mam wasn't well either. I had to ring a babyminder service to arrange for Stephen to be taken care of for the day. They didn't answer for ages. I was going out of my tree when I was finally able to get up on the bike.'

'Relax,' he said, 'You're talking like a clock.'

'I know. I'm up to ninety with everything. If something goes wrong in the morning it upsets me for the whole day. I hate being late. It gives the kids the upper hand with you.'

'Is it as manic as ever in there?'

'It's worse, if that's possible.'

When they reached the school he thought he saw a kind of pleading in her eyes, a pleading that asked him to take her away from it all. He wanted to say, 'Let's go away together to that city you talked about' but the words wouldn't come out. Every so often he found himself wondering what marriage with her would be like. He supposed he loved her but if he did why didn't he want to be with her permanently? Was it only affection he had for her? Was Mia still at the back of his mind?

If he married her, he though, he'd probably have qualified for assisted housing in one of the estates Arthur Finlay was selling outside the town. He could stay in the sweet factory and she could stay in the school. That would mean there'd be two salaries coming in. It wouldn't be too bad of a life. They'd get on well together. They'd be as happy as anyone else he knew. They could have other children besides Stephen and go off on drives in the evenings or maybe to films in Galway or to the beach in Salthill. In the summers they'd probably be able to afford a fortnight somewhere like Lanzarote. The years would bring acceptance of what they had as age gained on them, affection hopefully growing into love with the passage of time.

46

Life took on a pattern of bearable boredom. At times it seemed like he'd never been away, that he was like everyone he knew who were content with bad jobs and didn't think too much about them, like Billy Sheehan in the Co-Op or Paudie Gleeson or anyone else. He did his forty hours and looked forward to the weekends when he could put his feet up and watch the soccer on the television, or download some of the latest films from Hollywood on his computer.

He pottered around the garage on Saturdays. It was a relief to get out of the suit he was required to wear at work. On Sundays he watched car racing on the television and gorged himself on food.

Angela's Sunday dinners were legendary. They took her half the day to prepare. One Sunday when Bartley tried to sample a piece of food from the pot he was given a sound rap on the knuckles. He accepted the punishment without a whimper.

'It's not like you to take something like that lying down,' Brian said to him, remembering his tempers of old.

'Don't ever go into the ring with that lady,' he said, 'She makes Conor McGregor look like a pussycat.'

Brian knew he was expected to go into ecstacies about the food when it was eventually served. He did his best to do that even if it wasn't to his taste. Afterwards he usually went up to his room for a lie-down. 'Going for our little siesta, are we?' Bartley would chide. As he lay on his bed he remembered the Sundays of his childhood, days in which little happened but Mass and hanging around the kitchen afterwards. He'd have a chat with his mother as Bartley and Declan played football outside. After tea he'd start to get a knot in his stomach thinking about the following day at school. The teachers were always in bad form on Mondays, getting worked up about trivial things. It was as if they were making him pay for having the weekend off.

Something similar happened in the sweet factory. It was almost mandatory to have glum faces on Mondays. McSweeney was always like a bull in a china shop. There was never much work to do. Brian tried to look busy if he came into his office. A lot of the time he was sending personal emails to people to pass the time. He'd have to close down the lid of the computer in case he looked at it, or click onto the facesaver.

Machines always seemed to pick Mondays to break down as well. He'd have to make phone calls to find a technician to come in and fix them. There were also absentee problems with a lot of the workers on Mondays. It was hard to know who was on the level and who was sleeping off a hangover. Brian had the unenviable job of trying to find out which was the case. The last thing he wanted was to accuse anyone in the wrong but he didn't want to look like an idiot either if someone was pretending to be sick and then bragging about a soccer game they watched in the pub the day afterwards.

The biggest challenge he had was a sex molestation charge from one of the office girls. That happened after he was only a few months in the job. She said she was being made feel uncomfortable on a daily basis by one of the men on the assembly line. Brian wasn't sure how to deal with it. When he mentioned it to Bartley he said he knew the girl. 'Isn't she the one who wears the dresses up to her arse?' was his only comment on the subject. Eventually the man had to be let go.

In the autumn McSweeney put him on a training course. It meant he was away a lot. After he finished it he was promoted. That made him feel even more alienated from the workers than he already was.

He had a week's leave due to him at the beginning of October but he didn't take it. He didn't like being around the house with Bartley and Angela. When he asked Jennifer if she'd like to go somewhere with him she said she'd prefer to wait until Halloween. She had a mid-term break coming up then.

They decided to go to Tramore that weekend. Brian would have preferred to spend the whole week there but Jennifer felt that would be too long to leave Stephen with her mother. He was acting up a lot and she wasn't as able for him as she used to be.

They'd been there once before, when they started going together first. Because it was Halloween, most places were booked out. They could only get a second-rate hotel.

'Sorry I didn't make the booking sooner,' he said to her as they checked in. The carpet was threadbare and paint was flaking off the walls.

'Who do you think you're talking to,' she said, 'Beyonce? I didn't expect the Ritz. You've roughed it in your time too, haven't you?'

'You're good to think of it like that.'

'Sometimes you can have more fun in places like this. We can spill stuff on the carpet and not worry about the fact that they might fine us.'

He booked a double room even though they hadn't slept together since he came back from America. There was a single bed in it as well as the double one. He didn't know which he should sleep in.

Jennifer's mother rang after they'd unpacked their things. Brian was in the shower. He heard her saying, 'Just do your best. I'll be back in a few days.'

'What's wrong?' he said when he came out, 'Is it Stephen?'

'He's been crying his eyes out since I left.'

'I wouldn't worry too much about it. Babies are always crying.'

'It's my first time away from him for any length of time.'

'Are you sorry you came?'

'Not at all. we'll make the best of it. Mam will quieten him down. She's brilliant with him.'

They looked around the room. It was old-fashioned in the way it was furnished but neither of them cared too much about things like that.

The television was so high up it was practically on the ceiling. 'Watching that would nearly give you whiplash,' she joked. They hung their clothes in separate sides of the wardrobe.

'It's as if we're married,' she said, laughing nervously. She boiled a little kettle that was sitting on a shelf. They had tea and biscuits. Afterwards she suggested going down to the hotel bar for a drink but Brian was too tired after the journey. He said he was going to turn in early.

'Okay,' she said, 'We'll probably have more energy to do something decent tomorrow that way.'

He decided to sleep in the double bed with her. They were both shy undressing.

'Do you mind if I sleep with my back to you?' she asked when they got into bed. He felt she was uncomfortable lying beside him, He was uncomfortable too. He listened to her breathing after he turned the light off. Her body rose and fell under the sheets as she snored gently. She was like an infant. What wouldn't he give to be her, he thought, looking at her curled up in her foetal calm.

Her mother rang again the following morning. She said Stephen was off his food, that she thought he was coming down with something.

'It's just as well we only came for the weekend,' Brian said, 'Imagine what it would have been like if we were here for the whole week.'

'I'd never have left him with her for that long,' she said, 'Sick or well.'

If he was married to her, he thought, would she be always be like this, obsessing about the child and putting him into second place?

Over breakfast they talked about what they might do for the day. The weather wasn't great. Brian longed for the old days when they used to go camping together without a thought. He remembered one time when the camp blew away in a storm. All they could do was laugh about it. Getting pneumonia would even have been a joke. Were they really only a few years younger then? It seemed more than a decade ago to him. His travels had speeded time up for him. It was like a film in fast motion.

In the end they just walked around the town. Jennifer bought a dress in one of the boutiques while he walked along the promenade. They met afterwards in a café where they had coffee and scones. In the afternoon they walked the beach. A strong gale was blowing. Jennifer was wearing a hat to keep her hair out of her eyes but the wind kept blowing it off. They had fun chasing it down the strand and over the dunes. After tea they went for a drink in one of the local bars.

They were the only two people in it.

'Welcome to Las Vegas,' the barman said as he served them.

'He's funny, isn't he?' Jennifer said after he went back to the counter.

Brian didn't like the way he looked at her. He thought he was flirting with her.

'I don't see any sign of Elvis yet,' he said. She smiled.

Was this what marriage would be like, he thought as they sat there, going out for walks with someone you knew for so many years, having a drink with them afterwards and trying to think of witty things to say to them to entertain them?

The night before they left they went for a drink in the hotel bar. It was full of witches masks and pumpkins. There were candles lit up inside them. A sign on the window said, 'Come In And Have A Spooktacular Time.'

There was a cabaret act on. It was a singer who used to be big once but was now relegated to out-of-season venues. He played his old hits but without any great passion. He belted them out knowing they were what the people had come to hear, no doubt feeling the melodies were enough to make the night a success even if he couldn't sing them properly anymore. It was difficult for him to get the audience going because he didn't have his old band members with him, just a keyboard player who looked past it. The music sounded fabricated to Brian, not much better than karaoke.

'We might as well be listening to a CD,' he said.

There was no attempt to create even the slightest imagination in his phrasing, no suggestion he'd even rehearsed his set.

'What age would you put him at?' he asked her at one point as he appeared to crack on a note.

'He'll never see sixty again. That's for sure.'

'I'd say he's using something in the hair,' he said then. That made her laugh.

374

'I'm surprised to hear you coming out with that kind of comment.'

'Why? You've said yourself he's over sixty. What sixty-year-old man has jet black hair?'

He interspersed his songs with jokes. That made things even more pathetic.

'He's trying to turn himself into a comedian,' Brian said, 'to cover up the fact that he can't sing.'

'Give him a chance,' she said, 'It's only Tramore, for God's sake.'

After the show was over they walked the beach. It was a glorious evening. The moon shone on the water. He thought she looked beautiful. Her skin was as clear as the first day he met her. Her hair was hanging down over her shoulders like a horse's mane.

He rolled up his trousers and paddled in the sea. There were stones at the edge of it. As the waves crashed against the shore they kicked them onto his heels.

'Look,' he said, 'I'm being stoned to death.'

She was lost in thought and didn't hear him. He came out of the water.

'What are you thinking about?' he said.

She didn't reply. After a moment she said, 'Would you like to be married?'

'Why do you ask that?'

'It just came into my mind.'

'I don't know. So many marriages break down these days, don't they? What about yourself?'

'I don't know. Most of the time I don't think about things like that but sometimes I get these moods where I feel all old-fashioned and it seems like a nice idea.'

They left the conversation dangling, dangling like the relationship itself. Maybe they could go on like this forever, he thought, having their dates and their times away and maybe they'd last longer that way than many couples who married and split up, or even couples who moved in together without getting married, or ones who lived together off and on when it suited them. He wasn't sure if Jennifer would go along with that in the long term. Maybe her old-fashioned nature would kick in and make her look for more.

He slept in the single bed that night. He wasn't sure why. Maybe he felt if he joined her in the double one she'd start talking about marriage again and put pressure on him. When he woke up the next morning he went over to her bed. He lay under the covers with her.

'I hope you didn't mind me not being with you last night,' he said.

'Don't worry about that. It was worth it if it helped you sleep better.'

'I was tense. I thought I was going to be tossing and turning all night. I didn't want to keep you awake.'

'I wouldn't have minded.'

'Sorry I haven't been myself down here,' he said then.

'Have you not? I didn't notice.'

'Oh come on. You must have.'

Over breakfast he thought she looked worried. He stared at her bitten fingernails and the lines on her face. He felt a million miles away from her. As they ate she started to tell him some story about her teaching but he couldn't concentrate on it.

She was talking about the difficulty she was having trying to control a child in her class who was autistic. He was physically hearing her words but he wasn't really listening to them. He wasn't even looking at her as she spoke. He was looking over her shoulder at a waiter who was giving out to a young employee of the hotel who hadn't set a table properly.

He thought of Mia, of how she'd been on the day when they met to say their final goodbye. When he looked at her now he saw Mia's face. He was upset about that because he didn't want to. He wanted to leave Mia behind but she was stuck inside him, stuck inside him like a wound. He cursed the day he ever met her, the day she created an appetite in him that he'd never be able to satisfy.

47

He felt pangs of guilt after Tramore. He thought he'd been unfair to Jennifer, leading her on with promises and then withdrawing them. He didn't know what he wanted. Would a life with her have given him fulfilment? Maybe he'd always be looking over his shoulder at what had been, what might yet be with someone else.

Sometimes he drove out to the beach. He often sat in the car for hours waiting for the night to come down. As he looked up at the moon racing through the clouds he felt a great serenity descending on him. He listened to the waves coming in and then slithering back as they sucked the pebbles from the shore. He loved the way the seagulls flew over the pier as they waited for the fishing boats to come in. It reminded him of Rockaway Beach.

Christmas was uneventful. Bartley promised to stay off the bottle but Brian doubted he'd be able to. Jennifer came down with Stephen on Christmas Eve and stayed the night. Declan and Yvonne visited on Christmas Day. The conversation was forced at the dinner table. Brian wasn't sure if that was because Declan was annoyed with him for not going into the auctioneering with him or because he hadn't done well out of it himself. When he was alone with Yvonne he asked her how it was going for him.

'He's sorry he ever got involved in it,' she told him.

'I'm sorry to hear that,' he said.

'He's thinking of cutting off ties with Arthur Finlay and going back to the computers.'

'That's terrible. Arthur knows the business back to front. He could make a fortune for him in the long run.'

'Declan never thinks that far ahead. With him it's always about how he feels like at the minute.'

'That's what drives me crazy about him.'

'Me too but what can you do about it? It's his nature.'

He admired Yvonne's attitude. She never let things get to her. It was just as well she was like that, being married to someone whose mind was like a tornado most of the time.

Everyone sat around glumly after the dinner. Nobody knew what to do or say once the rituals of opening presents and wishing each other the compliments of the season were over. It always seemed worse to Brian being unhappy at Christmas than any other time of the year. It was almost as if you weren't allowed to be. That made it that much harder to be yourself. You felt you had to paint on a smile to get through the day. Conformity to tradition demanded it.

The house looked empty after Declan and Yvonne went off. Yvonne's presence always lifted Brian. Bartley obviously missed Declan more. Angela tried to cheer the two of them up by making sandwiches from the left-over turkey. After finishing them they dug into the endless boxes of chocolates that seemed to sit on every table.

Bartley said he was going to make a New Year Resolution to go easy on the whiskey. Brian had his doubts about how long that was going to work. Most of his New Year Resolutions in years gone by hardly made it to mid-January.

Brian tried not to drink in his presence for fear of tempting him. He went up to his room with Jennifer listening to music. She loved Leonard Cohen. As they played him he thought back to the time he was listening to him in UCD. One night he put his music on for Adrian and Dominic in the dilapidated house he shared with them. His voice had come through the walls like an echo then. It was less pronounced in the house but it still created an atmosphere.

'What are you playing that miseryguts for?' Bartley when he came into the room, 'Do you want to make me more depressed than I am?'

They went for a drive in the car to get away from him. Jennifer had Stephen on her lap. She dandled him up and down the way Brian's mother used to do with him when he was young, pulling his hands back and forth until he giggled. He could see how much she adored him. It should have made him glad but he couldn't help feeling left out.

One day they went out to the ruins of an abbey they used to visit when they were going out together first. It was beside the sea. He remembered a particular day he'd been there with her in late summer. A group of swallows had swooped around them. They were getting ready to fly off to Africa as they did every year at that time. A feeling of restlessness came over him as he watched them clucking. They shrieked wildly above him, moving up and down on the telegraph wires. They seemed fanatical in their desire to be away.

'They're like you,' Jennifer said to him. Even then she'd known he had 'the urge for going' as Tom Rush put it in his song.

Some of them pecked at the nests they'd built until they fell from the trees. It reminded him of a book he'd read once where the residents of a city burned down their houses before they evacuated them. They kept shrieking on the wires, all in a line like soldiers, switching from foot to foot as if they were on hot grids. The sun speared through them like fire. Then they took off, blackening the sky momentarily as they rose to the zenith in a V formation.

As they flew away he watched them becoming smaller and smaller. After a few minutes they were no more than dots in the sky. Jennifer said, 'Look at the nests. Don't they look like crowns of thorns?'

He agreed with her. After they'd gone they sat down on the grass. She'd brought a flask of coffee with her and they drank from it. Her hair tumbled down over her shoulders. As he looked at her he thought there was no way he could be happier than he was at that moment.

What he wouldn't have given to be able to recapture that feeling now. What took it away? Was it Mia? Or Stephen? Maybe it was just time, time and his travelling. He wondered if he'd ever get it back.

When the new year came in he often saw her cycling to school as he was on his way to work. He always stopped the car when he did.

'Any sign of a puncture?' he said to her one day.

'No,' she said, 'but that doesn't mean I won't ask you for a lift one of these days. My legs aren't what they used to be. Every day the journey seems longer than the day before.'

'Stay at it,' he said, 'Otherwise you'll end up like me – a fat excuse for an executive behind a steering wheel.'

He liked passing her house on the way home. Her bicycle was always propped up against a tree outside the front door. Every so often she'd see him and give him a wave. If she wasn't busy she'd signal to him to stop the car and go in. They'd usually have tea.

Afterwards he'd bring her back to the farm. Angela was always a bit stiff with her, Brian thought as if it was work to make her feel at home. Bartley would take Brian aside and talked horses with him, or how the auctioneering was going.

Declan kept asking him if he had any interest in the Newbridge offer.

He did it so much, Brian said to him, 'Now I know why you're such a good salesman. You never take no for an answer.'

Yvonne told Brian she was worried he was getting an ulcer from the stress of the job. She said he was desperate to get out of his arrangement with Arthur Finlay but that he was legally blocked from doing that. Apparently he'd signed some document that tied him to him for a number of year. Arthur was holding him to it unless he paid him a large sum of money to negate it.

'That was so unlike Declan,' Yvonne said, 'He always reads the small print on documents.'

She had a part-time job with the HSE now. It suited her down to the ground. She loved getting out of the house even if it was only for a few hours every day. 'I don't do much more than answer the phone,' she said, 'but the few bob comes in handy.'

Declan was always making arrangements to meet Brian to talk business but nine times out of ten he broke them. Some of them weren't even in Loughrea. If he was going to Galway for work he'd tell Brian to meet him there. He always liked swinging by 'the city of Tribes' for a chinwag.

'It'll be a break for you,' he'd say, 'We'll go for a few pints and see the city.' Declan never minded if these arrangements fell through. He always enjoyed going to Galway and roaming around the streets. It was better than trying to make conversation with Declan, better than pretending he was interested in what he was talking about. He welcomed his absence.

Then something happened that threw them into contact in a different way. After years of fertility treatment, Yvonne finally got the news that she was pregnant.

She'd had trouble conceiving since they got married. Brian knew she wanted a child more than anything in the world. She was sensitive about not being able to have one so she didn't talk about it but he knew how much it meant to her from comments she'd made to him over the years. Bartley was aware of it too.

'Everyone else on their estate is producing sprogs,' he'd say, 'Think how she must feel.' Brian remembered one of the telegrams that were read out at her wedding. It said, 'May more than railings run around your front lawn.' Until now nothing had. He knew the child would be that much sweeter to her because it was so long delayed.

'She's preggers!' Declan boomed down the phone to Bartley the day he got the news. He was practically catatonic.

'A bun in the oven at last,' Bartley said. He was relieved too. Brian knew he would be. He'd taken Declan aside once and asked him if there was some problem with his 'equipment,' as he called it. He told him he thought every man should have a child to prove he could do it. After that it was up to himself whether he bothered having any more or not.

He took the opportunity to toast the occasion with a bottle of bubbly.

'Where did you get that from?' Angela asked him.

'It was in the cupboard,' he said. It just 'happened' to be there. He was able to produce alcohol from oblique places on occasions like this.

'Champagne for my real friends,' he chirped as he popped the cork, 'and real pain for my sham friends.' The foam gushed all over the floor. Angela rushed into the kitchen for the mop.

'Don't bother,' Bartley advised, 'Rusty will lick it up. He's partial to it. I've trained him well.'

Brian expected her to share in the happy mood but she was subdued. When he thought about it, he wasn't sure if she'd ever got on that great with Yvonne over the years. They never had words or anything. It was just a feeling he got. There didn't seem to be any reason for it. Was it a clash of personalities or did it go deeper than that? If it did, Yvonne's pregnancy wasn't going to help. Until now they had childlessness in common. That would be changing soon.

'I'm delighted for you,' Brian said when he rang Yvonne, 'How is it going?'

'Kicking almost non-stop,' she said.

'I'm sorry to hear that. It's bad enough being kicked from the outside in life, never mind the inside.'

'Now you've said it. Keep your fingers crossed everything goes to plan for the next nine months. It's taken us so long. We'll be on tenterhooks.'

'I'm sure everything will be fine. Prayers from a heathen like me probably won't be much good but I'll say them anyway. If God exists he'll probably put a block on them as a result of the bad things I've been saying about him all my life.'

'Maybe he likes the fact that you challenge him. In my opinion a heathen's prayers are the best ones.'

She was on the phone every other day for the next few months with updates about doctor appointments. Declan filled in any blanks she left.

Bartley and Angela went down to them often on visits. Brian and Jennifer joined them if they were going at a weekend, Everyone was always in good form. Yvonne looked radiant as she showed off her bump. Declan was much friendlier than usual to Brian. He even stopped hassling him about the auctioneering.

Angela told Yvonne she'd be more than happy to babysit for her anytime she wanted a break. She said, 'Let me have the baby first, Angela!'

Jennifer made that offer too. She said it was as easy to mind two babies as one.

'Or as hard,' Yvonne said.

48

The months rolled on. Before anyone knew where they were it was June. Every summer up to now had been some kind of watershed for Brian but not this one. He had nowhere to go. There was no Europe or America to recharge his batteries. He was just a factory manager now.

Jennifer continued to have problems in her job but she became philosophical about them. Stephen kept her going. She rang Brian to tell him all the funny things he said and did. 'Better you than me' was his reaction..

She didn't talk about marriage anymore. To him that suggested she was happy for things to go on as they were between them. When he asked her if she still felt restless she said she did. Having Stephen, unfortunately, made her realise she probably wouldn't be able to do much about it.

'I don't know if that's resignation or dour acceptance,' she said.

She made plans to go to Amsterdam with one of her friends from the training course during the summer holidays. The thought of that kept her going. Brian was glad she didn't ask him to go with her. He felt Tramore hadn't gone well. A prolonged trip away could well have been worse, especially with Stephen on board. He was glad he'd done his travelling when he did. He didn't think he'd be able for it now. He found it hard to believe how he'd done some of the things he had in his past, not only in Europe but the time with Sinead when he was basically living in squats.

He rang her one day to find out how she was doing. He was pleasantly surprised to hear she was still 'clean,' as she called it. When he asked her what she was doing she said, 'You're not going to believe this. I'm studying for a degree in Economics.' She laughed as she said it. She couldn't believe it herself. He was amused. Everyone, it seemed, was drawing in their horns.

'What about you?' she said, 'What's your story?'

'I'm just a country bumpkin now,' he said, 'I spend my time roaming over the land like a gentleman farmer.'

The days were mild. That made it look more attractive to him but he was sad whenever he got to thinking it would soon be gone.

The cattle became more sparse as each week passed. There were days when he felt he was part of an empty domain. A world was passing from him and he was powerless to do anything about it.

Bartley made good on his promise to cut down on the drink. It was torture for him but he did it. Part of that was due to Angela's urgings and part due to fear for his liver. 'I'm going to donate it to medical science,' he proclaimed one day, 'for research purposes.'

Two of his friends from down the road had died in the spring. Both of them had been ill for a long time but their passing still shook him. He was subdued at the funerals, telling Angela on the way home from the second one, 'I'll be next.'

Whether it was from the drink or not, he grew more confused in his behaviour. One morning when he was shaving he put the brush into a cup of tea he was drinking instead of into the shaving mug.

'Are you drunk again?' Angela said when she saw the colour of his face.

'It's my new look,' he said, 'Do you like it?'

'Not too bad for an early Alzheimer patient,' she said.

He became depressed about his age. 'Everyone I know is dying,' he said to her one day. There was no point trying to console him. Once he got an idea into his head that was it. If she told him he looked well he'd say, 'I bet you a pound to a penny I'll be gone within the year.'

'The problem with that kind of bet,' she said, 'is that if you're right you won't be there to collect.'

Even Bartley had to laugh at that. She amused him with her bluntness.

He was 65 in July. To try and take his mind off himself she decided to throw a surprise party for him, inviting everyone she could think of in the area. There were lots of hushed phone calls in the weeks preceding it. Bartley suspected something was going on but he didn't know what it was. The penny only dropped on the night itself. She'd given him the usual cake and present earlier in the day. He thought that was that but after tea there was a ferocious pounding on the door that caused him to leap out of his seat and Rusty to go into a mad frenzy of barking. When he opened it, a crowd of revellers poured in, most of them already well on. He stood looking at Angela with his hands on his hips as they descended on him with birthday hugs.

'The Special Branch needs people like you,' he said to her as more and more people barrelled past him, 'How did you keep it from me?'

'The same way I keep everything from you,' she said. 'It comes from a lifetime of living in a place where too many people want to know what you had for breakfast.'

There were knocks on the door every few minutes. People lined the walls. A few of them could hardly stand. They'd been tanking up in McDonagh's for some hours beforehand. When everyone was settled she brought Bartley out to the middle of the floor. She told him he'd have to give a speech.

'At this short notice?' he said, 'You must be joking. 'I couldn't say "Hey diddle diddle, the cat and the fiddle."'

'I never knew you to be stuck for a word. Just say whatever comes into your mind. It doesn't have to be Robert Emmet's Speech From the Dock.'

'Has anyone got a pen?' he said, warming to the task without the need for too much further encouragement.

Brian fished one out of his pocket for him. He went into the kitchen.

The door rang every few minutes with more arrivals. Most of them were from Brian's class. There were a lot of faces he didn't recognise. He wouldn't have been surprised if half of them didn't know Bartley from Adam. It could have been just somewhere to go for a lot of them.

Angela had asked him if there was anyone he wanted to invite. Apart from Jennifer and a few people like Paudie Gleeson and Joe Ruddy he said no. He knew Gabriel Hoey would be there whether he was invited or not. He could smell a party from a hundred yards away.

He arrived with Jennifer. They'd met on the way. She was wearing a satin dress. Brian hadn't seen her since she came back from Amsterdam. They'd been on the phone a few times about it.

'You look exquisite,' he said as he gave her a kiss at the door, 'Welcome home.'

She'd brought him a windmill from Holland. It played 'Tulips From Amsterdam' when you wound it up.

'It's beautiful. I'll treasure it.'

Gabriel and herself went over to the drinks cabinet. Brian tried to organise seating for the late arrivals. Many of these were of Bartley's vintage.

He was glad to see Eddie Culkin there. He thought the night might cheer him up a bit. He brought him into the dining room. The younger set were next door with their potions. Gabriel positioned himself in the middle of them for maximum attention. Brian hadn't seen some of them since his coming home party. Before long they were in full swing. They danced to rap music.

Bartley finished his speech. He came out of the kitchen with the pages flapping around in his hands. For a moment he looked dazed at what he saw before him – the gyrations of the new generation. He shook his head in amazement.

'I hope you're not thinking of trying to copy them,' Angela said.

'Wait till I have a few jars in me.'

He went over to the cabinet. He poured himself a glass of whiskey.

'Is it not a bit early for that?' Angela said.

'It's never too early for whiskey.'

He couldn't stop looking at the young people throwing shapes on the floor.

'You'd think you never saw anyone dancing before,' Angela said.

'They're like baboons trying to break out of a monkey cage.'

'It's called interpretive dancing.'

'What?'

'It's all the rage nowadays.'

'Is it another way of saying, "I haven't a clue what I'm doing"?'

'Probably.'

'Give me an old-fashioned waltz any day of the week.'

'Whenever I tried to do one of them with you it was like carrying a sweeping brush around the floor.'

'I never said I was good at it. I just said I liked it.'

Angela had the house looking like a new pin. All the rooms had been done up. That was something Bartley should have copped onto in the preceding weeks. Maybe he was so used to her power cleaning over the years he didn't think anything of it. Now that the secret was out she put streamers on the walls.

There was a 'Happy 65' poster over the fireplace.

'Too many reminders,' Bartley sighed, 'Too many reminders.'

She kept buzzing around the place like a hen on a hot griddle asking people if they were all right for drink.

'I wish she'd take a back seat from now on,' Brian said to Jennifer, 'it puts everyone on edge when she fusses like that.'

'Let her be herself. I never heard of anyone complaining about being asked what they'd like to drink at a party.'

'What about yourself? What'll you have?'

'Is there any martini? I developed a taste for it in Amsterdam for some reason.'

'That's probably the one drink we don't have. Trust you to be awkward.'

'Don't worry about it.'

'I'll see what I can do.'

He went into the room where the young people were. Gabriel came up to him.

'What's up with you?' he said, 'You look as if you found a penny and lost a pound.'

'You wouldn't know anyone who has martini with them, would you?'

'That's a woman's drink. Don't insult us.'

'It's for Jennifer.'

'That's different.'

He cupped his hands to his face as if he was speaking through a loudspeaker.

'Is anyone in this building drinking martini?' he roared.

'Shut up, Gabriel,' Brian said, 'You'll wake the dead.'

'I'm only doing what you asked me.'

Everyone looked at him blankly.

'I'll try Angela,' he said.

'Don't bother.'

He went back to Jennifer.

'No joy,' he said.

'It doesn't matter. Was that Gabriel's voice I heard?'

'I hope he's not going to embarrass me. Remember the oming home party?'

'Don't be always thinking the worst.'

Angela came over with sandwiches. She offered one to Jennifer.

'No,' she said, 'If I take any more I'll burst.'

'We're more interested in booze at this stage,' Brian said.

'Sorry about the martini,' Angela said to Jennifer.

'It wasn't important. I can have something else.'

'How did you know about it?' Brian said.

'Gabriel.'

'He should have kept his mouth shut.'

Angela went back to the kitchen. Bartley followed her in.

'Can you think of anything funny about being 65?' he said to her, 'I was looking for a joke to round off my speech.'

'There isn't much to laugh about when you get to 65,' she said.

'Thanks a lot.'

Brian and Jennifer sat down on the floor. People drifted back and forth in front of them. A lot of them were already the worse for wear.

'I love watching people at parties,' he said, 'They always have that expression on their face as if they're going somewhere important.'

'It's usually the toilet,' Jennifer said. They both laughed.

'Do you remember those ones you used to have when your mother was alive?' she said.

'I try not to think too much of those times.'

'Sorry.'

'Don't be. It was nice of you to remember her. She thought the world of you.'

'And me of her.'

Fr Finnerty tapped on the window when everything was in full swing. Bartley let him in.

'You were the last person I expected to see here,' he said.

'I'm just putting my nose in to convey my good wishes. I can't stay very long. I have a wedding tomorrow.'

'Not your own, is it?' Bartley said

'God forbid.'

Jennifer heard him.

'Have you got something against women, Father?' she said.

'That came out the wrong way, Jennifer.'

'I was only joking.'

Bartley led him into the back room. Angela poured him a whiskey when they got inside.

'Is that all you're giving him?' Bartley said. The glass was half full. He filled it to the top.

'If I drink that,' Fr Finnerty said, 'There'll be no wedding tomorrow.'

'They might be better off,' Bartley laughed.

'That's enough out of you,' Angela said.

Bartley's glass was full too.

'That stuff will kill you one of those days,' Fr Finnerty said to him, 'You know that, don't you?'

'At least I'll die happy.'

Fr. Finnerty sipped the whiskey as if it was poison.

'Why did you give me this?' he said. 'More importantly, why did you give it to yourself?'

'It's my birthday, Father,' Bartley said, 'I'm on a day off from sermons.'

The kitchen door was open. Brian and Jennifer looked in at them. They saw Fr. Finnerty wagging his finger at Bartley. He put his glass down a few moments later.

'The good priest seems to have achieved something Angela hasn't been able to do in three years,' Brian said.

Bartley looked out at them with a defeated expression on his face. He motioned them in to him.

'I need help,' he said, 'This man is trying to get me to take the pledge.'

'That I am,' Fr Finnerty admitted.

'Better men than you have tried and failed,' Bartley told him.

He threw his eyes to heaven.

'How do you stick him?' he asked Brian.

'By the grace of God,' Brian said.

'I can tell you now you're wasting your breath, Father,' Bartley said, 'I'm too far gone down the road to hell now.'

'A journey of a thousand miles begins with one step,' Fr Finnerty said.

Bartley took a deep breath.

'The way it is with me, Father,' he said, 'If it's that long, I think I'd prefer not to start it at all.'

Fr Finnerty had enough. He buttoned up his coat.

'I'm off,' he said, 'I hope you all enjoy the rest of the night.'

'Don't say you're going already,' Bartley said, 'You're hardly here.'

'I told you, I have a wedding.'

'Feck the wedding. It's my birthday.'

'Let him go,' Angela said, 'There are more people than you in the world.'

'Are there?' he said, screwing up his eyes, 'I hadn't realised that.'

Brian and Jennifer went back to the room where the young people were. Gabriel was stumbling around the place trying to engage someone in conversation. Brian avoided him. He talked to Joe Ruddy instead. He wondered who was going to create the most trouble before the night was out, Bartley or Gabriel.

Martin Geraghty arrived at the door not long after Fr Finnerty left. Brian had an inkling he'd be there but he wasn't fully sure he'd make it. Angela told him she'd invited him without telling Bartley. She'd been texting him to his car to make sure she got to the door before Bartley knew he was there. She could see he was nervous about how Bartley was going to be with him.

He'd brought a bottle of Paddy as a peace offering.

'Is he on the warpath?' he asked Angela, 'Do you think he'll go for me?'

'I know he will,' she laughed, 'When he does, just pass it off. If you don't rise to the bait he'll drop it.'

'I wish I could be as confident of that as you are.'

'Come in now and let me close the door.'

'I'd prefer to stay here until I see how he is.'

She went into the kitchen. Brian heard raised voices. Then he heard something breaking, a cup maybe.

He came out after a minute. He looked daggers at Martin.

'What are you doing here?' he said.

'I wanted to wish you a happy birthday.'

'You're barred from this house.'

'Stop that talk,' Angela said, 'I invited him.'

'You what?'

'I invited him.'

'I don't believe you.'

'You can believe me or not. I don't care. Just shut your trap. It's your birthday. You're supposed to be in good form.'

'I was until a few minutes ago.'

He turned his back on Martin. He went back to the kitchen. Angela followed him. He sat at the table.

'Why did you do this to me?' he said. His face was beetroot red. He took the cork out of a bottle of whiskey and raised it to his mouth.

'What are you doing?' Angela said.

'What does it look like?'

'Are you not going to go out to him?'

'To lay him flat, you mean?'

'Don't be funny. You can't leave him at the door like that.'

'This is my house. I can do anything I want.'

'Go out to him. Please.'

'I will in my hat.'

She dropped her shoulders in disappointment.

'What will I tell him?'

'Tell him to drop dead for all I care. He's here without my wanting him. That's the long and the short of it. You invited him here behind my back. He robs me in a cattle deal and now he's standing in front of me as large as life. What do you expect me to do? Roll out the red carpet for him? '

'Don't be such a cry baby. He doesn't want the red carpet. Just be civil.'

'You've landed my worst nightmare on my doorstep and you want me to be civil. Where's the logic in that?'

'I thought –'

'Well *don't* think. That's where you make all your mistakes. Do you realise how much he cheated me?'

'That's ancient history. You love harping on the past.'

'It's called justice. People look for it when they've been wronged. Did you ever hear of the Birmingham Six?'

'Dear God, he's comparing himself to the Birmingham Six now. You're talking about a few head of cattle.'

'Many head of cattle, my dear, many head of cattle. And their bodies too.'

'What's done is done. It's time to move on. Be nice to him. It'll create a bad atmosphere for the night if you don't. You can't leave him out there in the cold.'

'That's not my fault.'

'It's not his either. I asked him here.'

'You did, damn you.'

'Don't be so dramatic. You're making it worse by going on about it. Go out to him. He needs to be asked in.'

'Why don't you ask him to move in with us while you're at it?'

'Tell him to vamoose, pronto.'

'I can't do that.'

'If you don't I will.'

'Don't, Bartley, please. He's driven all the way from Dublin. We can't ask him to just turn his car around and go home.'

'That's exactly what I plan to do after I kick his arse out the door.'

'Try to be a human being for once in your life. You might get to like it.'

He drummed his fingers along the table. It was a long time before he spoke. Angela looked at him expectantly.

'Okay,'he said, 'You win. I'll let him in - but only for a few minutes. After that I don't want to see his ugly mug again for as long as I live. If he looks sideways at me I'll kick him into the middle of next week.'

'Good on you. I knew there was a heart beating in there somewhere.'

'I don't know why I'm doing this but I'm doing it.'

He walked back to the front room. Martin was still standing at the door.

'You can come in,' he said, 'but I'm not sure for how long. You can thank my wife.'

'Sound man, Bartley. I appreciate it.'

He handed him the bottle of whiskey.

'What's this – bootleg?'

'No. I'm going straight now. Finally.'

Bartley grunted.

Martin stepped inside the door. Bartley went into the kitchen with the whiskey. Angela was standing there with her hand under her chin.

'Thanks, Bartley,' she said.

'Don't mention it. And don't bank on the fact that I won't lay him out before the night ends.'

'Please don't say things like that.'

'You're after throwing me under a bus. I was looking forward to being with the people I'm close to tonight and he turns up. You must be trying to kill me off before my next birthday.'

'No, Bartley, I'm trying to see that you reach it. Anger isn't good for you.'

'So you're going to let him away with everything. That puts the tin hat on it.'

'I'm a woman. Women go for harmony. Men prefer to spend your lives tearing strips off one another.'

'You're right. Women know it all. Men are from a primitive stage of evolution.'

'Exactly.'

Brian watched the two of them sparring with one another from a distance. He was glad he had Jennifer to keep him away from them. If she wasn't there he knew he'd have been roped into it.

The atmosphere lightened afterwards. People started to mingle more. The tension went out of the night. It was as if a cloud had lifted.

Brian knew Martin would want to talk to him. He waved over at him. Martin smiled back, wiping imaginary sweat from his brow.

Angela watched him talking to Bartley. She looked relieved. Brian gave her a thumbs-up. She went back to serving people drink. People guarded their supplies like precious cargo.

'It's like having a family of thirty,' she said to Jennifer, 'I'm flattened.'

'You seem to be coping pretty well.'

'You must be joking. I had this thing planned like a military operation but it never works out like that. As soon as the first person steps through the door, all your plans go out the window.'

'Why is that, do you think?'

'Because they always want the one thing you don't have. In your case it was the martini.'

'You're too much of a perfectionist,' Jennifer said, 'I hardly think civilisation is going to crumble because of that.'

<h1 style="text-align:center">49</h1>

Angela hovered around Martin and Bartley for the next half hour or so. She had a special reason for that. On one of her phone calls to Martin she'd asked him about a house he owned in Oughterard that had fallen into disrepair. It was a huge one with five bedrooms. He thought it should fetch well over a quarter of a million euro if it was put on the market, maybe more if it was done up. He asked her if she thought Bartley would be interested in selling it for him through Arthur Finlay. Angela felt he would. She waited until the two of them got talking before she mentioned it.

She called Bartley into the kitchen. His eyes lit up as she talked.

'Why didn't you tell me all this before now?' he said, chewing his lip, '250,000 euro isn't to be sneezed at.'

'I thought you'd blow a fuse if I brought up Martin's name.'

'Didn't I blow one anyway?'

'I felt it was better to wait till now.'

'You cost me precious talking time. I'll squeeze the bastard for every penny he owes me. '

'Don't do that.'

'Why not? I've been waiting for something like this for years.'

He went out to Martin. Angela watched him intently. He had a cross face on him for a few minutes but then she saw him laughing. He poked Martin in the ribs but it seemed to be more in jest than anger. At the back of it all, Angela thought he missed his company over the years.

She stayed in the kitchen until he came back in.

'Well,' she said, 'How is it going?'

'He wants jam on it. I'm going to have to make him eat humble pie. Either we do it my way or not at all.'

'Don't look a gift horse in the mouth. I worked hard to get things this far. Do you not realise that?'

'I'm not going to give him a soft deal. If he thinks I am he has another think coming.'

The two of them spent the rest of the night hammering out the details of the percentage Bartley would get if the house sold. Angela told Brian and Jennifer her plan had worked.

'Good on you,' Jennifer said, 'You have a wise head on your

shoulders.'

'You have to be ten steps ahead of that fellow to get anything done.'

'Is it safe to talk to them now?' Brian asked her.

'Probably. Just bring your bullet-proof vest.'

'I know. I'll probably need it.'

He stood up. They seemed to be getting on well. He went over to them. Martin was all smiles when he saw him.

'So the two old rivals forgive and forget,' he said, putting his hand on Bartley's shoulder.

'Forgive, not forget,' Bartley said.

'He's still not giving me an inch,' Martin said.

'Why should he change the habits of a lifetime?' Brian said. Martin guffawed at that.

'How is life outside the university?' he asked Brian.

'Good enough. Who's in the flat now?'

'Two head-the-balls from Sallynoggin. They spend most of the day playing heavy metal music. It's like Chinese torture to myself and Denise. God knows what they're on but it's not Horlicks.'

'Are you going to keep them?'

'I doubt it. Those kinds of people eventually wreck your place. You were an angel by comparison.'

'You're only praising him,' Bartley said, 'to get me to agree to the Oughterard deal.' He could never accept the fact that a compliment could be given by someone who didn't have an ulterior motive.

'That's not true. Brian and myself got on like a house on fire. Didn't we, Brian?'

'For sure. How is the trampoline?'

'The what?'

'I'm remembering the sofa that sent you into outer space if you sat on it too fast.'

'Oh that. I'm sure the two new buckos are having lots of fun with it. They're probably taking lumps out of the ceiling with it.'

Martin dug Bartley in the ribs.

'I believe you paid his university fees,' he said, 'You mustn't be all bad.'

'Don't be trying to *plámás* me.'

Brian went into the kitchen to get a drink. Angela was sitting at the table smoking a cigarette to catch her breath.

'They're like old friends again,' he said to her, 'Well done for coming up with the idea.'

'It was nothing. Anyone could have engineered it.'

'I doubt that. The wounds went very deep.'

'Every man has his price – even Bartley.'

After the pair of them finalised things they gave one another the traditional spit on the hand that cattle dealers did. Martin went off to talk to some people he knew from the old days.

Angela gave Bartley a kiss.

'What's that for?' he said.

'For curbing your temper. I know how hard it is for you.'

She went over to the hi-fi and turned down the volume. The room came to a standstill as everyone stopped dancing.

She called for hush.

'And now,' she said, 'The moment you've all been waiting for – Bartley's speech.'

There were a few groans from the young people.

'Not now,' Bartley said, 'I have too much on my mind.'

'What could you have on your mind? Aren't things sorted with Martin?'

'I still have stuff I need to go through with him.'

He took some papers from his pocket.

'Look at these,' he said.

They were legal documents.

'This isn't the night for that kind of thing,' she said, 'You have the rest of the year to read those.'

'I don't want him to do me again. I have to sign them. There's probably a catch.'

She grabbed them from him.

'The only thing you need to read now is your speech. Where are your notes?'

'I don't know.'

He looked through his pockets.

'I've lost the fucking things. Maybe they're on the table in the kitchen.'

She went in to look but she couldn't find them.

'They're probably in one of your pockets,' she said.

She rummaged through them. Everyone started laughing.

'She's pickpocketing him,' Eddie Culkin said.

'It's the only way to get money out of that lad,' someone else said. There was more laughter.

'My head is all over the place,' Bartley said.

'That's what happens when you get to 65,' Angela told him.

'Give your speech,' Eddie exhorted, 'You're wasting drinking time.'

'Okay,' he said, 'You asked for it.'

'Keep it short,' Angela said.

'Don't worry.'

He cleared his throat. The room went quiet.

'I'm going to say a few words,' he said, 'emphasis on the few. The woman beside me is responsible for all this nonsense tonight. Blame her if you're not enjoying yourself.'

There was a round of applause. Angela bowed.

'I'm delighted you could all be here,' he went on, 'especially those of you I thought were dead. Or even hoped were dead.'

Everyone laughed.

'I should be dead myself too,' he said. 'I've tried my best to shorten my life for the last 65 years but for some reason God doesn't seem to want to let me go.'

'He has a lot to answer for,' said a voice from the back. There was more laughter.

'If I knew I was going to live this long,' he said, 'I'd have taken better care of myself.'

'That's an old one,' Brian said to Jennifer.

'An oldie but a goodie.'

'My doctor,' he said, 'tells me I'm at the age where I should take up a hobby like golf. It sounds like a good idea in theory but the problem is I don't like golf. I find drinking much more enjoyable for two reasons. The first is that you don't have to leave the house for it. The second is that you don't have to buy a pair of trousers everyone is going to laugh at.'

'Good on ye, Bartley!' an old farmer shouted up, 'Ye never lost it' Some people stamped the floor.

He went on to talk about his health problems. He started to tell a joke about a rectal examination but Angela stopped him.

'That's enough,' she said, pulling him aside.

'I'm not finished yet,' he said.

'Oh yes you are.'

A palpable sense of relief went round the room. People began to move away.

'I was only getting warmed up,' Bartley said to Angela, 'Why do you ask me to do something and then drag me off the floor when I'm in full flow?'

'Because you give me panic attacks,' she said.

He looked down at the crowd.

'You can all go back to what you were doing,' he said, 'My speech has unfortunately been cut short.'

Most of them already had. Angela went over to the hi-fi. Music blared from it as she turned it up to full volume. Bartley put his hands over his ears. The young people went back to the other room.

Brian tapped Jennifer on the shoulder. .

'Like to dance?' he said.

'I'd love to.'

They went out to the other room. She glided around the floor like a butterfly. He felt he was watching a movie queen from Hollywood's golden era. She had that serenity about her, an untouchable beauty.

A slow song came on. They danced closely. It was good to feel her body against him. He smelt the perfume she was wearing. He felt his desire for her growing.

'I'm really happy to be here tonight,' she said.

'Is it better than Amsterdam?'

'Much better.'

When the music ended they went back to where they'd been on the floor.

It was like the old days. Angela had left a bottle of wine for them. Brian poured glasses for the two of them. She started to talk about Amsterdam but the music drowned her out.

'Let's just enjoy the night,' she said, 'I can tell you everything later.'

Martin came over to them.

'You never introduced me to your girlfriend,' he said to Brian.

'Sorry, Martin, this is Jennifer. Jennifer, this is Martin.'

They shook hands.

'So this is the famous Jennifer,' he said, 'I've heard a lot about you.'

'Not all bad, I hope.'

'Quite the contrary.'

'I'm glad it went well with Brian's father.'

'I can't tell you how relieved I am. Here's hoping he keeps a cool head from here on.'

'We'll be keeping our fingers crossed,' Brian assured him.

'Well I better be hitting the road then,' he said, 'Mission accomplished – sort of.'

'Safe home,' Brian said, 'Sorry about the bit of tension early on.'

'I expected it to be much worse.'

Angela came over to let him out.

'You did great,' she said.

'I've aged five years tonight. Please don't invite me to any more birthday parties, will you?'

'The way he's going, there won't be too many of them.'

'Do you mean with the drink?'

'What else?'

'He has a good woman to look after him.'

'I don't know about that.'

'Tell him I said goodnight. I was trying to get his attention but he was in the middle of a group. I didn't like to disturb him.'

'Goodnight, Martin. Thanks for keeping a cool head.'

'I'm glad you thought I was cool. I was shivering underneath.'

'Off with you so. You can get your composure back on the journey to

Dublin.'

She went back into the kitchen after he was gone. Bartley was sitting there deep in chat with another farmer. He was a childhood friend as far as she could make out. He was regaling him with some yarn from long ago.

'You made a show of yourself with the speech,' she said, 'After all the work I did to get things right for the night.'

'Cool down,' he said, 'Everyone enjoyed it except yourself.'

He took a slug of his whiskey.

'I was hoping you'd go easy on that stuff tonight,' she said.

'I have a chest infection,' he said, 'I'm trying to burn it out of myself. Whiskey is a powerful potion, as you know.'

'Yes, to send you quicker to the grave.'

She went back out. Some of the younger people were leaving the living room. They had their overcoats on.

'I hope you're not leaving already,' she said, 'The night is only getting on the road.'

'We're going to another party,' one of them said, 'No offence.'

'Go on out of that. I get the message. We're too dull for you here.'

'Not at all. We had a great time.'

They went out to their cars like a herd of cows. Gabriel cut a forlorn figure as he brought up the rear.

'Poor Gabriel,' Brian said, 'No one wants him.'

He wandered off alone, not being asked into any of the cars.

They revved up. There was lots of laughter and shouting.

'I hope they don't get pulled by the law,' Angela said to Brian, 'Most of them are three sheets in the wind.'

She stood there with the door open. The tail lights of the cars disappeared into the night.

'I suppose the other shindig will see them through till dawn,' she said, 'Isn't it great to be young?'

'That's a matter of opinion,' Bartley said.

As she was closing the door she saw a car coming towards her.

'Uh-oh,' she said, 'I think I know who that is.'

It pulled into the driveway.

A horn honked.

'Guess who's here?' she called in to Brian, 'It's Declan. I was wondering when he'd show up.'

'Johnny Come Lately,' Brian said.

'Better late than never.'

'He'd be late for his own funeral.'

They got out of the car. Yvonne waved in to Brian. Declan opened the boot. He took out some packages. He brought them over to Angela.

'For Dad,' he said.

'You're too good,' she said, putting them inside the door.

'It's nothing.'

'Where were you both till now?' she said, 'You missed all the fun. I thought you weren't going to come.'

'We wouldn't have missed it for the world,' Yvonne said.

'We passed a few cars on the road,' Declan said, 'The drivers were looking pretty excited. Did they come from here?'

'It was the younger set,' Angela said, 'Things were a bit too quiet for them.'

Brian and Jennifer came over. They hugged Yvonne. Declan gave Jennifer a kiss on the cheek. He shook Brian's hand.

'You took your time,' Brian said.

'The computer crashed. If it's not sorted soon the whole company could collapse.'

'Why are you not there now?'

'I stayed with it as long as I could. Then I just said, "I'm out of here." Where's the guest of honour?'

Bartley appeared from the kitchen.

'At your service,' he said. He was holding a glass of whiskey.

'They brought presents,' Angela said.

'The liquid kind, I hope.'

'We didn't think we'd be let in otherwise,' Declan said.

He started clapping his hands.

'Happy birthday to you,' he sang, 'Happy birthday to you, happy birthday dear Daddy, happy birthday to you.'

'Keep it down,' Yvonne said to him, 'You're giving me a headache.'

'Always the showman,' Brian said to Jennifer.

He stopped singing.

'I heard that,' he said.

'You were meant to.'

'Do you ever do anything but give out? I thought you'd be glad to see me.'

'I am. Just tone it down a bit.'

'Hello Yvonne,' Bartley said, 'How long more till Junior arrives?'

'Not too long. How did the party go?'

'Well enough. I gave a nice speech even if some people don't agree.'

He gave Angela a look. She put out her tongue at him.

'How are you?'

'We had a bit of a nightmare getting here. I didn't think we'd make it for a while.'

'That's always the way with you two. There must be a curse on the road from Newbridge to Loughrea.'

'I agree. Some nights I expect to be ambushed at a crossroads by someone with fangs and a cape.'

'Bring a crucifix the next time.'

'I will – and a clove of garlic.'

'Anyway you're here now. What are you drinking?'

'A beer for me,' Declan said, 'Yvonne isn't allowed to drink.'

'Then she's not welcome here.'

She laughed.

'Maybe I'll try a small one,' she said to Declan. He nodded gruffly.

'Of what?'

'Anything.'

'Good girl,' Bartley said.

He went into the kitchen.

'Are you sure this is a good idea?' Declan said, 'The doctor won't be too pleased.'

'Let him get it. I don't have to drink it.'

Bartley came back with a bottle of something that didn't have any identification on it.

'What's that?' she said, 'It looks funny.'

'Someone gave it to me for a present. They thought I was into cocktails.'

'Are you sure it's safe?'

'There's one way to find out.'

She took a sip.

'Well,' he said, 'What's the verdict?'

'It's nice...I think.'

'Of course it is. A few more of those and you won't know yourself.'

'That's what I'm worried about.'

Declan punched Bartley on the shoulder.

'Well,' he said, 'How does it feel to be 65?'

'Not as good as 64,' he said, 'but probably better than 66.'

'Good answer. And now to more important matters. Where's the drink?'

'Why don't you have some of this?'

He gestured the whiskey.

'No thanks. That stuff plays silly buggers with my head. I thought you were on the wagon.'

'I was, sort of, but then it got to be my birthday. The plan became temporarily derailed if you know what I mean.'

'I understand. If you can't have a tipple on your birthday, when can you?'

'Tell that to Angela, will you?

Declan looked at her.

'Angela,' he said, 'I believe you masterminded everything.

Congratulations.'

'I'm not sure masterminded is the word. It's been a bit chaotic to be honest.'

'The best laid plans of mice and women...'

'I believe you had your problems too.'

'Don't talk to me.'

'I thought you were a wizard with computers.'

'So did I. There's always something you don't know and that's always the thing that gets into your hard drive.'

'What's happening at the moment?'

'God only knows. I'm not going to think about it till Monday.'

'You're right.'

She went over to Yvonne.

'Is the baby still kicking?' she said.

'Like Maradona,' she said.

'Come over here with Jennifer and me,' Brian said to her, 'We have a corner all to ourselves.'

'I can't,' she said, 'I'm in a rush for the toilet. If I don't go now I'll burst. Is it still in the same place since you did the renovations?'

'First door on the left when you go down the corridor. If you get into any trouble send me a telegram.'

She scuttled off.

'You might like to join us,' Brian said to Angela.

'I'd love to. To get away from all the men.'

They went over to their spot. Bartley started dancing around the floor with Declan.

'Look at that pair,' Angela said, 'You'd think they were two gay boys.'

Bartley heard her. He jigged around like a woman, putting his hands on his hips and making pouts.

'I hope this isn't the beginning of another binge,' she said to Brian.

'Try not to think about that.'

'You're right. One day at a time.'

'I thought that was for people going off the sauce instead of going onto it.'

'Maybe we'll have to invent a new Twelve Step Programme for that fellow.'

Yvonne came back.

'That was quick,' Angela said, 'Park yourself on the floor with the hoboes.'

She sat down.

'Maybe she should be on a chair,' Brian said.

Angela got one for her.

'Thanks Angela. Thanks, Brian. You have no idea of the relief that little trip to the loo gave me. My insides are all knotted up since I got pregnant. I don't know what they're going to do from one minute to the next.'

'I'm like that too,' Brian said, 'and I'm not even pregnant.'

'Maybe you are without knowing it,' Jennifer said.

'Thanks, Jennifer. You say the nicest things. What do you think I should do with her, Yvonne?'

'Banish her to the wilderness,' she suggested.

'Good idea. Depart from me you cursed into the everlasting darkness. Expelliarmus!' He made a mime gesture like Harry Potter.

'Okay,' she said, 'I'm gone. Now can I have a drink?'

'You don't deserve one.'

Angela tapped Yvonne on the shoulder.

'I feel sorry for you with all that stuff going on with your body. Thank God I was spared it.'

'You don't know how lucky you are.'

'Believe me, I do. My heart goes out to you.'

'Actually I'm getting used to it a bit. God knows I should be. I'm half way there now.'

'How long have you to go?'

'A bit over four months.'

'You're as thin as a whippet.'

'If you swallowed a pea you'd look pregnant,' Jennifer said, 'I hate women like that.'

'Go on out of that,' Yvonne said, 'You're a skinnymalink yourself.'

'I wish.'

Bartley and Declan finished their dance. They came over to where everyone was sitting. Bartley was out of breath.

'You didn't wish me a happy birthday yet,' he said to Yvonne, 'I'm annoyed with you.'

'Happy birthday,' she said, 'Sorry I can't sing it like Declan.'

'That's all right. I shouldn't even be reminding you of it. I'm trying my best to forget my age these days.'

'Sure,' Declan said, 'That's why you threw such a big party.'

'It wasn't my idea.'

'Good point, ' Declan said.

Bartley looked at Yvonne.

'Show us the bulge,' he said.

She opened her coat.

'What do you think?'

'Very small,' he said. 'Declan, you'll have to start feeding this woman.'

'What are you talking about?' he said, 'I never stop.'

'I'm eating for two now,' she said.

'You always did,' he chided.

'Don't mind him,' Brian said to her, 'I wouldn't know you were pregnant unless you told me.'

Declan tipped Bartley on the shoulder.

'I must have a chat with you about Martin Geraghty before the night is out,' he said.

'It's a bit noisy here,' Bartley said, 'Come into the kitchen and I'll give you all the details.'

They went off.

Angela sat down beside Yvonne.

'Are you hungry?' she said, 'You haven't had anything to eat since you got here.'

'I'm fine, Angela, honestly. We had something before we came out.'

'That was hours ago. I could rustle up a few sandwiches for you if you want. I'm afraid most of the good food is gone.'

'If you insist. Knowing you, they'll be delicious.'

'I wouldn't be too sure of that.'

'Just give her two loaves and five fishes,' Brian said, 'and she can feed the multitudes.'

'Flattery will get you nowhere,' she said. She went off. Brian turned to Yvonne.

'How is the job going?' he asked her.

'What job?'

'Aren't you still in the HSE?'

'Not any more.'

'What?'

'I left it ages ago. Did I not tell you?'

'Not that I remember. Were you let go?'

She took a few seconds before answering.

'Declan was afraid I'd miscarry. He made me give it up.'

'That's ridiculous. When did he do that?'

'About a month ago.'

'I'm shocked. Or maybe not. Nothing that fellow does would surprise me at this stage.'

'Don't be too hard on him. He's so into the baby you wouldn't believe it. He has the room done up like something out of *Charlie and the Chocolate Factory*. Some people might think he's a chauvinist but you have to understand him. The pregnancy has changed his life.'

'*His* life? What about yours?'

'I can see why you'd say that.'

'Jesus, Yvonne, this is bad. He's a control freak. You can't let him go on like that. He'll be having the baby for you yet.'

Angela came out with the sandwiches. The way Yvonne laid into them made her realise how ravenous she was.

'I'm going to make some more now,' she said.

'Please, Angela, don't,' she said but she was already gone.

Yvonne started talking to Jennifer. Brian was in his own world.

He went into the kitchen. Declan was deep in chat with Bartley. He was showing him the document Martin gave him to sign.

Brian stood over him.

'I don't like what you did to Yvonne,' he said.

Declan looked up at him as if he didn't know what he was talking about.

'Come again?'

He rasped the words out this time.

'I don't like what you did to Yvonne.'

He backed his chair away from the table.

'In what way?'

'Making her give up her job. She said you made her leave the HSE.'

He looked at him as if he was going to hit him.

'And that's suddenly your business?'

'Insofar as I care about her, yes.'

He took a sip of his drink. He left the document down.

'Okay,' he said, 'Because it's Dad's birthday and because I'm in a a fairly good mood I'm going to pretend I didn't hear what you just said. But that only applies if you fuck yourself off within the next five seconds.'

Brian grabbed him by the shirt. He pulled him out of his chair.

'Holy mother of Jesus,' Bartley said, 'What the fuck is going on between you two?'

He separated them. His natural strength enabled him to do that despite the fact that he was drunk. Declan was sweating fiercely. His chest was going in and out. He pursed his lips.

'Get out of here,' he said, 'Get out before I flatten you.'

Brian went out to Jennifer. She'd heard the noise.

'What went on in there?' she said.

'Nothing.'

Declan came out. He went over to Yvonne.

'Get your things,' he said, 'We're going.'

'What are you talking about?'

'We're going. Now.'

'What happened in there?'

'Your delightful brother-in-law attacked me. He's insane. He needs help.'

She looked at Brian.

'What's he talking about?' she said.

'Just go, Yvonne, ' he said, 'before I do something I'll be sorry for.'

Declan came over to him. He put his face up to his.

'What might that be?' he said.

'You wouldn't want to know.'

Angela came between them.

'Stop it the pair of you,' she said, 'You'd think you were both ten years old.'

'No, Angela,' Declan said, 'Only one of us is.'

'Don't keep it going, Declan. Please.'

'I'm tired protecting him. He came into the kitchen gunning for me. It's time someone told it like it is. He's been mollycoddled since the day he was born. He's pissed on every opportunity that ever came his way and yet he acts like King Shit.'

Yvonne started crying.

'You promised me you weren't going to argue with him tonight,' she said.

'I didn't want to. He pushed my buttons. Why did you go moaning to him about the HSE?'

'Is that what this is about?'

She looked at Brian.

'Is this about the HSE, Brian?' she said, 'Because if it is, it's cracked.'

'No, Yvonne,' he said, 'It isn't about the HSE. It's about the fact that you're married to a fucking bastard.'

Declan made for Brian. Angela intercepted him. Yvonne went over to Brian.

'I'm very disappointed in you,' she said, 'If you're out for my good you have a strange way of showing it.'

She put on her coat. Declan led her to the door.

'Sorry for upsetting you, Yvonne,' he said.

She didn't reply. Declan looked at him with disgust.

'I feel sorry for you,' he said.

They went out. Jennifer came over to Brian.

'Are you okay?' she said.

'Sorry for ruining your night,' he said.

Bartley came out of the kitchen. His eyes were groggy.

'Her night?' he said, 'The last I heard, tonight was *my* birthday.'

They heard the car starting outside.

'They were supposed to stay,' Angela said, 'That's the second time Declan left in a temper.'

Nobody spoke for a long time.

Everyone was just standing there as if they were paralysed.

The only sound was the ticking of the clock.

Angela went over to a cupboard.

Inside it was a Black Forest cake.

There were six candles on it and a half one in the middle of them. 'Happy 65th' was written on it in red icing.

'I made this for Bartley,' she said, 'Anyone fancy a slice?'

50

Opinion was divided over the next few weeks on who was responsible for the blow-up. Bartley thought it was Brian's fault. Angela said it was Declan's. She said he had no right to do what he did to Yvonne and that he was even worse to have turned on Brian when he confronted him about it. Brian didn't think her support of him was genuine. He saw it as an attempt to sweeten him up. If it was, it backfired. It had the opposite effect, turning him against her more than ever.

Bartley signed the form Martin gave him but he was on the phone to him every other day complaining about its terms. The tentative peace of the party night was followed by endless haggling. Declan backed Bartley up on a lot of it. 'He doesn't trust me,' Martin said to Brian, 'That's the bottom line.' Eventually he dropped out of the whole business. 'It wasn't worth it for my mental health,' he said. The house was sold for a song in its unkempt state.

Brian spent a lot of time with Jennifer. He went up to her house any chance he got after he finished work.

'I don't mind falling out with Declan,' he said to her one day, 'because I don't care about him. What I'm more annoyed with is upsetting Yvonne. That could go deeper in the long run.'

'It won't,' she said, 'Believe me.'

'How do you know?'

'Because I've spoken to her.'

'You have?'

'Yes. More than once.'

'Is she still angry with me?'

'She knows you did it out of concern for her. I don't think she'll stay mad at you for long. It's not in her nature. But you need to keep your nose out of her relationship with Declan. At the end of the day she loves him. That's all that matters. How many people that we love do things that we don't like and we put up with them?'

'If only I had your logic,' he said.

A part of him was glad his problems with Declan had come to a head. Most of the arguments they'd had in the past were behind closed doors. The fact that this one had been conducted in public meant everyone was aware of it. Brian needed that to happen so people would understand how deep things went. He didn't mind that he came off worse in it.

If anyone asked him about it he said, 'This goes back to the cradle.' If they were interested he showed them a photograph of the two of them as children. It was one he found in a drawer Bartley hadn't cleared out after his mother died. It was taken a few years after they'd been married. Already he could see the sadness in her face. She tried to conceal it behind a smile but it was there nonetheless, maybe even more so because of that. Brian was just a baby at the time. She was holding him in her arms. Bartley was smiling at Declan. Declan was sitting on the grass in a romper suit. Even this early the allegiances were being forged.

Brian always felt Angela would have preferred if it was Declan who'd stayed at home and him who moved to Newbridge. They'd have had more banter together. As things stood, Declan was like the prodigal son. She'd look forward to killing the fatted calf for him whenever he visited.

Her days were busy now. She was out a lot. Sometimes she met her friends for bridge. She also organised coffee mornings for cystic fibrosis. A cousin of hers suffered from it. In time it became a kind of cause for her. People commended her for her energy. She could focus it on anything – her fundraising outside the house and her multi-taking inside it.

'Angela is a powerhouse,' Bartley used to say. Brian thought she'd have made a brilliant politician if she was interested.

She sat at the table every morning before he went to work, smoking a cigarette and listening to the radio. She'd comment on all the titbits she heard and try to draw him into conversation with her about them. She made the tea so strong you could trot a mouse across it.

Every time she gave him a cup she'd watch him drinking it as if her life depended on it. If he left it for a minute to do something in another room she'd be in after him with it, following him like a lover.

'Your tea is going cold, love,' she'd say if he left it on the table, 'Will I heat it up for you?' He'd always say no even if it was freezing.

It was the little things she did that infuriated him rather than the big ones.

She sat too close to him at the table, so close that if he moved his elbows he'd bump into her. The fact that she was unaware of it annoyed him as much as the fact that it happened at all. It annoyed him that he didn't have the kind of relationship with her that permitted him to say things like that to her.

If he moved away from her to the other side of the table she took it as a snub. She became quiet. Her hurt feelings were used as a kind of weapon against him. She was good at playing the victim.

She took it as another snub that he didn't divulge personal things about his life to her. She'd complain to Bartley and he'd report back to Brian.

'She tries too hard,' Brian would say, 'but don't tell her that. If you do, she'll try not to try and that will make her try harder than ever.'

The distance between them grew. It was made bigger by the fact of them not talking to one another about it. The silence deafened Brian.

One day he stormed out of the kitchen after cutting himself with a bread knife.

'You're pumping blood!' she screamed even after he'd stanched its flow.

'It's a flesh wound,' he said, 'It needs a piece of plaster, not open heart surgery. Why do you have to get so hysterical about everything?'

She went in to Bartley. He was in the next room taking it all in. She told him Brian was picking on her again.

'Don't pass any heed on him,' he said, 'He'll be back to himself in a few hours.'

'Something is always rubbing him up the wrong way,' she said, 'I keep having to tiptoe around him in case I upset him. No matter how careful I am I still seem to mess things up. I wonder if it's worth the bother. Life is hard enough without having that to contend with.'

'Have you tried asking him what the problem is?' Bartley said.

'He wouldn't tell me if I did. Most of the time I can't get a word out of him. It's like talking to the wall.'

'He finds it hard to show emotion.'

'You could have fooled me, the way he was with his mother.'

'That was different.'

'What has he against me?'

'Nothing. It's your imagination.'

'No it's not. I feel even by being in the house I get under his skin. I'm doomed before I start.'

'His life has been uprooted in the last few years. You have to understand that. He went everywhere with Teresa. She was like his twin. I used to joke that he saw more of her than I did. Maybe it wasn't a joke. When he lost her it was like losing a part of himself.'

'It makes me feel worse hearing that.'

'Just stay with the situation. He's very sensitive.'

'If I hear that word again I'll scream. We're all sensitive. It's another word for selfish.'

'That's a bit harsh. I'm trying my best with him. I neglected him for too many years.

'His mother wrapped him in cotton wool. Do you not think you're continuing that?'

'If I am I don't mind . He always thought I ganged up on him with Declan when Teresa was alive. It was two against two then but after she died it became two against one as far as he was concerned. I've spent the last few years trying to convince him that isn't the case.'

'Are you succeeding?'

'To an extent.'

'Do you not think it's time you cut the cord?'

'He's raw at the moment, Angela.'

'He's permanently raw as far as I can see. He'll be a middle-aged baby if the two of you carry on the way you're going.'

'You're not making too bad a job of babying him yourself from what I can see.'

'I'm in an awkward position here. Blood is thicker than water. I've been competing with a ghost since I married you. It's not easy. I can't tell Brian what I think of him for the same reason he can't tell me what he thinks of me.'

She said an unusual thing to him then.

'Do you ever think of Teresa when you look at me?'

'I don't let myself think of Teresa too much,' he replied, 'If I did I wouldn't be able to live with myself. I was a bad egg when I married her.'

Her eyes narrowed.

'It hurts me to hear that,' she said.

'Why?'

'It makes me feel Brian is right in everything he says.'

'That's not the way to think about it. You bring out the best in me – the man I should have been for Teresa. With you I have the chance to redeem myself from the way I was with her. It's only now I'm ready for marriage, now that I have one foot in the grave.'

'Don't say things like that. If you go easy on the drink you can live for years.'

'And if your aunt had balls she'd be your uncle.'

'Stop that language or I'll walk out of this house.'

When Brian came down for tea that night the conversation was forced. Bartley and Angela tried to inject a levity into it that wasn't there. Levity didn't come easily to Bartley unless it was tinged with sarcasm. With Angela it tended to be over-exaggerated.

Angela had made tagliatelli, her speciality, but he hardly touched it. As he got up to leave the table, most of it was still left on the plate. She couldn't resist saying, 'You're not rushing for a train, are you?'

'Sorry,' he said, 'I'm not hungry tonight. The meal was lovely. I wish I could have done it justice.' With that he was gone.

'There you go,' she said to Bartley, 'Once again Rusty gets his leftovers.'

'I'll have a word with him when he gets back.'

'Don't. That'll only make it worse.'

She put the tagliatelli into Rusty's dish. He gobbled it up. Afterwards she sat down and smoked a cigarette. Her foot shook as she lit up. It always did that when she was nervous. There was a game show on the television that she sat half-watching. Bartley was reading a farming magazine, casually flipping over the pages as he watched her. Eventually she turned the television off.

He went over to her.

'Don't let him get to you,' he said.

'I feel he's coming between us. He's affecting my relationship with you. I can't be happy when he's around anymore.'

Later that night Bartley went up to his room. He asked him what the problem with Angela was.

'I can't put it into words,' he said, 'I'm sure it's my fault instead of hers. I'm sorry if it's getting to her.'

The following day he was even quieter than usual with her. She asked him if he'd like a cup of tea and he said no. Then she asked him if he could help her with a clue of a crossword she was doing.

'I'm rubbish at crosswords,' he said, 'even the Simplex ones.'

She went up to Bartley. She threw her hands in the air in despair.

'I'm out of ideas,' she said.

Brian would have preferred it if she left him to his own devices but she couldn't do that. She saw him as a mountain to conquer, a bridge to be crossed. She already had Bartley in her grip; he was the one to be won. But as time went on it became an ambition too far for her. She decided to take Bartley's advice and try and forget about him.

She watched television almost non-stop after she finished her housework. Quizzes were her favourite types of programmes, especially if there were prizes offered. She entered competitions with the zeal of an incurable romantic, not appearing to notice that she never won any of them. When she witnessed other people doing so she jumped up and down on the sofa screaming with excitement. 'They got a car, Bartley!' she'd scream, 'and a holiday!'

Reality TV was another favourite of hers. She formed her views of psychology from *Dr Phil* and *Jeremy Kyle*, screaming at the screen during these shows if an item upset her.

She loved the soaps too. The characters in them became like real people to her. Sometimes she got so worked up at the way a character was behaving in an episode she'd have to leave the room. If it was an emotional scene she was capable of breaking down in tears.

'You're an old softie, aren't you?' Bartley would say amusedly to her. He said to Brian, 'I don't understand that lady. If the butcher tells her he's giving her his best meat she insists on going inside the counter to double-check it but if someone in *Eastenders* was captured by aliens she'd swallow it wholesale.'

Murder films provided another type of fascination for her. She was brilliant at guessing the identity of the killers in them. 'I have a suspicious mind,' she admitted, 'My problem with whodunits is that for a lot of the time I think everyone "done" it. I spend most of the film trying to narrow down the bad guys to a figure under five.'

Brian tempered his anger at her with a bewilderment at her contrasting sides. He enjoyed seeing her excited about things outside his world - her bridge, her coffee mornings - because it kept her involvement with him at bay. If she was idle in the house her temptation to collar him got the better of her once again. She fastened on to him, quizzing him about everything and nothing.

His answers to her were usually brusque but she always came back to him for more punishment. As soon as he walked in the door at six o'clock she was all over him for news. How had the day gone? Who had he met? Had he worked hard?

Bartley was the opposite to that. He'd hardly have noticed if he came home with a leg missing. One day he told her he'd been invited to lunch with a company director. She went mad with excitement.

'Did you hear the news?' she said to Bartley, barely able to control herself, 'He's having lunch with one of the big knobs at work.'

Bartley looked at her as if she needed her head examined.

'So what?' he said, 'I couldn't give a monkeys if he's eating with Enda fucking Kenny;'

51

He came home late a lot of nights. 'Got waylaid by some lady, did we?' Angela would say when he came in, especially if she smelt drink off him. She'd usually have his dinner on the table. She'd sit beside him as he ate it, watching him digest every morsel. Bartley tried to draw her away from him, distracting her any way he could. If he succeeded it gave Brian an opportunity to go up to his room.

As soon as he got inside he locked the door to stop her coming up. He knew she'd appear on the tiniest pretext. She'd have some figary about whether he wanted a jumper washed or a shirt ironed. He'd put his transistor on loud to deter her. If he was going out he'd run down the stairs so fast he'd be in the car almost as soon as she heard him going out the front door.

'He'd give Sonia O'Sullivan a run for her money,' she said one day as she heard the engine turning.

'That sounds like a very bad pun,' Bartley said.

He spent many of his weekends hanging around the town. It was like when he was in the early years in the college, not long after he started going out with Jennifer. If Bartley ran into him he'd be amused. 'How is

James Dean?' he'd jibe if he was wearing his cords.

Bartley and Angela went on frequent trips down the country after Bartley applied for the free travel. He was getting himself in training, he said, for 'an old age of perpetual motion.' If Angela behaved herself, he told her, he might let her ride shotgun.

They always asked Brian to go with them. He usually refused but one week he decided to join them. He wasn't sure why. They went to Lahinch on the train. Angela was high about the fact of him going with them. She talked non-stop all the way.

When they got there Bartley decided he wanted to play a game of golf. He'd never been on a course before. The closest he'd got to it was a few games of pitch and putt as a young man. For Brian the idea of him playing golf was about as likely as Brendan Behan taking up crocheting but when he got an idea into his head it was impossible to get it out of it. He imagined it was the same determination that made him an alcoholic.

He took clumps of grass out of the ground with almost every shot. Brian thought there'd be nothing but clay visible by the time they were finished the eighteen holes. The captain of the club was watching. He told him he'd have to leave after he saw the devastation he'd wreaked. Bartley accepted the decision with uncharacteristic meekness.

That night in the pub he was back to himself.

'I know I'm not Tiger Woods,' he said, 'But it was a bit of a laugh, wasn't it?'

'For you maybe,' Angela said, 'You nearly took my eye out with a few of your drives.'

She was in better form the following day. They went shopping. She had a joint account with Bartley and didn't stint on eating into it with her credit cards. When she came back to the hotel she was laden down with bags of clothes. Bartley was livid.

'We'll probably have to sell the farm to pay for that lot,' he said.

'Wait'll you see me in them,' she chirped, 'It'll be worth it.'

'You can spare me that delight,' he said drolly.

Brian was bored most of the time. One morning when he was sitting in a park with them he heard a passer-by saying to the person he was with, 'Your man is a bit old to be on holidays with his folks, isn't he?' It was said in a whisper but he picked it up. He thought Bartley and Angela did too but they didn't let on. He made a decision that day never to go away with them again. The week cemented him in his decision that he needed to get away from them altogether soon.

Back home he found himself going into a downer. He did as little as possible around the house. If Angela was out he didn't even cook, preferring to eat in McDonalds. If she asked him to do a job he'd give some excuse and put it off. More often than not that meant he wouldn't do it at all.

There was a leak in the shower one day. Another day a window wouldn't close properly. Angela asked him if he could fix it. When he said he couldn't she went after Bartley. He wasn't much better. In the old days he used to enjoy doing jobs like these but now they were just headaches to him. His concentration was off.

Things came to a head the day she asked him to paint the living-room. He wore himself out getting the job ready, taking down his overalls from the attic and sanding down the walls.

After that everything went downhill. He told her the paint wasn't worth a curse, that it kept flaking off.

'It's a bad workman that blames his tools,' she said.

He made a few stabs at it but patience was never his strong point when something wasn't going his way.

'Fuck this for a game of cowboys,' he said.

He went off to the pub, leaving Angela with a half-painted wall.

'That man does my head in,' she said to Brian, flapping her arms up and down, 'I'll swing for him yet.'

He wondered if she was fabricating her frustration to deflect attention away from the problems she was having with himself. She was slow to show disappointment with him even if he walked away from a task. He would have preferred if she did.

He wanted her to show the kind of anger with him that she did with Bartley. He deliberately tried to work her up sometimes to find out if another person – the real Angela maybe – would come out. But it never did. The most she'd do was throw her hands in the air or blow her cheeks out in frustration. It made him think she was either a very good actress or she had the patience of a saint.

One day Bartley was trying to repair a clock that was losing time. It tumbled out of his hands after he opened it up.

'You won't be happy until you've destroyed it,' she said, looking at all the pieces of steel rolling around the floor.

'You made me nervous,' he said, 'standing over me like a Gestapo merchant.'

He allowed her to boss him. She even had him washing the dishes after meals. He wouldn't have washed a dish to save his life when Brian was growing up. He hardly knew where they were kept. Now, as he grimly remarked, 'I'm turning into one a New Man. I'll be wheeling Yvonne's pram yet.'

Old habits died hard with him. He still got up at the crack of dawn even though he wasn't stravaging the farm anymore. 'A shit, a shave and a shampoo is what gets me going,' he'd say on his way into the bathroom. He'd worked off his hangovers by exercise as a young man but that was impossible now. Getting himself ready for the day was exercise enough. He'd strip himself down to the waist at the sink and douse himself with cold water. He'd try to get the alcohol out of his system for a few hours before he put it back in again.

He went through the horrors when he woke up. He had the shakes of most alcoholics even if he hadn't been drinking the night before. He tried to quell them by slipping whiskey into his morning coffee. That worsened his hangover in an attempt to cure it.

After having his breakfast he read the paper. Then he'd ramble down the road going nowhere in partocular. He'd usually run into someone he knew. If he stayed talking to them he'd be late back for his dinner. Angela hated that. She ran the kitchen like a military barracks. Everything had its place and its time. Bartley preferred eating when he felt like it rather than at a prescribed hour. After lunch he went to bed for an hour or two. In the evenings his energy levels would go up again. That was what Angela called 'the mad time of the day.' She always went to bed before him.

In her absence he drank. He'd be hungry for conversation as the night went on. He tried to nab Brian for chats. He did his best to avoid these. He knew they'd go on into the small hours if they began at all. Bartley would relay an old yarn he'd heard a hundred times before. A lot of the time he wouldn't even remember he'd told it to him already.

Sometimes Brian found him wandering around the kitchen in the middle of the night. Often he wouldn't know what he was doing there. Angela said to him one day, 'Why is it that if I send you down to the shop for a loaf of bread you come back three or four hours later with a pint of milk?'

'To quote Fr Finnerty,' Bartley replied, 'Man cannot live by bread alone. We're in touch with the higher things of life.'

'Like what?' Angela said, 'Getting drunk on the way home?'

He always insisted drinking was a hobby for him rather than an addiction.

'I could give it up in the morning if I had something decent to do,' he'd say.

One morning Angela suggested he bring Rusty for a walk to give himself a bit of exercise.

'I get enough exercise,' he said, 'carrying the coffins of my friends.'

'Don't talk like that,. You'll only tempt God.'

'God is beyond being tempted. Didn't he prove that in the desert when the devil tried a few tricks on him?'

'Now you're being sacrilegious.'

His health deteriorated rapidly in a short time. He developed arthritis in both of his knees not long after his birthday. Then an old shoulder injury started acting up again. He'd got it years ago in a fall from the tractor. He was in and out of hospital with it. Now and again he went to hospital to dry out. He didn't talk to people about these stays.

'I have a dicky ticker,' he said whenever anyone asked him what was wrong with him, That part was true. He had an irregular heartbeat.

His doctor told him it was a miracle he was still alive. Bartley didn't have much confidence in him. He missed most of the appointments he made with him.

'He knows fuck all,' he'd say to Angela, 'and charges you through the nose to emphasise that fact.'

He enjoyed telling people he could drop dead at any moment. Brian thought he dramatized his ailments for attention. He was a creaking gate and the creaking gate got the oil.

'I'm a ticking time bomb,' he liked to say, a comment that drummed up the kind of sympathy he fed off.

Brian used to go down to McDonagh's with him some nights if he wasn't seeing Jennifer. He'd only be in the door when a group of people would surround him. He'd show Brian off to them but he knew they were only interested in talking to him. They were his type of people and the conversations they had reflected that. They ran down the government and went on about the cost of living. Anecdotes about farming went back to the year dot.

If his knees were bad and Brian wasn't available to drive him to the pub he'd often chance driving there himself. When he did that he'd take the two sides of the road with him on the way home. One night he almost got killed at a bad bend a few hundred yards from the farm. It was an accident black spot that claimed many lives in the past. He took a perverse delight in speeding up as he approached it instead of slowing down. There was always that devilment in him.

Angela was in the passenger seat at the time. A truck came at them from nowhere when they got to it. It missed them by inches. He swerved at the last second. They ended up in the ditch. Amazingly, neither of them sustained anything but flesh wounds. For Angela it was a wake-up call, especially in view of how her parents had died.

'That's it,' she said, as she watched a tow truck digging the car out of the ditch, 'I wouldn't get into a car with you again even if you had a thimbleful of beer on you.' Her resolve cut in on his daytime driving. She used to enjoy him bringing her shopping but some of the time she wasn't sure he was even sober for that.

To get some independence for herself she started taking driving lessons. Like most things she did in life she proved to be a quick learner. Brian was amused the first time he saw her behind the wheel. It was like Part Three of her progression from the back seat to the passenger seat. Now this.

Before long she was driving Bartley out the country during the day.

Sometimes they stayed in B&Bs. Other times they visited her grandmother. She was in a nursing home in Sligo. Angela hadn't got on with her. It was more a duty visit than anything else. She had dementia.

She never talked much about the visits. If Brian asked her how she was she'd say something like, 'She's as good as you could expect a woman of her age to be. They're charging enough for her anyway.' She was footing the bill for the nursing home herself. That made the situation worse for her. 'I'll be joining her soon,' Bartley used to say after they came back from these trips. He could never resist the opportunity for some drama.

Autumn came in with a vengeance. The days were bleak and wet. Leaves fell from the trees and lay curled up in the gutters. Bartley sat at the stove reading cheap detective novels. Angela watched more television than ever. If it went on the blink, Bartley would stamp his foot on the floor to get it going. He felt that worked better than ringing a repair man. He hated having to pay for things like that. He enjoyed watching a programme more on a fifth-rate set that was falling apart than a new one that would have knocked him back a few pounds.

He bought a lot of products on the black market. Deals were made with a nod and a wink with shady individuals in McDonagh's. The things he bought usually let him down but he continued to buy them. He loved bargains. He was happier coming home with ten useless objects for the same price as one good one. His attitude was, 'We'll get a go out of it anyway.' Angela thought it went back to his childhood. It had been lived in near-poverty.

At the weekends they pored over the papers. Bartley pontificated on the sad state of the world from his favourite chair as Angela yawned. It had foam sticking out of it. She tried to keep it wedged in with safety pins. She had huge ones she'd kept from the days when she did Irish dancing as a girl. Bartley would be solving Ireland's political problems as she positioned herself at his feet stuffing the foam out of sight in case someone called. 'What are you doing?' he'd say as she went down on all fours, 'Are you trying to molest me or something?'

He hadn't much more joy with his prognostications in McDonagh's. The people there grew weary of him over time, the recycling of old prejudices like a broken record. 'I don't think I'll bother voting anymore,' he said to Brian one day after watching a documentary on the recession. 'They're all the same. Once they get their arses planted in a Rolls-Royce they forget the people who put them there. The country is bankrupt but they're still raking in the millions. It's always the same. Only the people suffer. They're talking about burning the bondholders. I know where I'd burn them – in a vat of tar.'

She was happy to let him rant. Her fatalism helped her. 'Things either come right or they don't,' she'd say. There was no point losing sleep about dirty deals in high places.

'You'll only drive your blood pressure up going on about stuff like that,' she'd tell him.

'I suppose having your eye on a new coat is of more significance to you than the country falling apart,' he'd shoot back.

If Brian was with them on their trips he usually stayed in the car when they went shopping. If he joined them he knew he'd be driven demented by their bickering. He listened to music to pass the time. Bartley tended to grow impatient if Angela was trying on clothes. He'd head for the bar. She'd meet him there when she was ready.

That made the day work for him. If there was a bookie's nearby it was even better. The drink gave him an excuse to bet and the betting gave him an excuse to drink. If he passed the car he'd whistle for Brian to join him. Brian watched him looking at the TV screen with excitement as his horses took off. More often than not they bit the dirt but he never lost hope. He had the naïve optimism of most gamblers. When Angela came back he'd be well on. No matter what she bought he'd praise it excessively. It was the drink talking.

If she wasn't looking for clothes they might just do the weekly shop for food. At these times Brian felt he was back in the past. He remembered the days Bartley drove his mother to similar shops for similar things. It gave him a warm feeling thinking of those days, at least for a while. If he dwelt on them too long the memories became painful.

He tried not to spend too much time with them. He couldn't forget the comment of the woman in Lahinch. He knew she was right. It didn't look good for someone like him to be seen out with ageing parents. If he had hobbies, he thought, or if he was sociable, there would have been a way around it. Otherwise it was difficult. There was nothing to do but wander round the shops.

When he did that it was impossible not to run into someone he knew. They always asked him the same questions. What was happening with Jennifer? Was he going to go away again? Would he stay in the sweet factory or was he going to go back to the auctioneering? Many people even knew about the proposed move to Newbridge, something that now looked well dead and buried.

If it was an older person talking to him they tended to reminisce about the past. Maybe that was inevitable. He'd been away so often they didn't have much else to talk to him about. But he hated the packaged image they had of him: the dependence on his mother, the globetrotter, the frustrated farmer.

If they knew Fr Finnerty they might even throw 'spoiled priest' into the mix. It gave them comfort to be able to put him into a box. It reminded him of the way the students in UCD drew comfort from putting books into different kinds of boxes. It was a way of owning him, of imagining they could control him because they had him safely installed in these definitions.

He always made an excuse to get away. It was difficult if the person was persistent. In his desire to cut the conversation short he often said something he shouldn't have. It was a bit like Jennifer with Maureen when she buttonholed her in Spar that night. Whatever he told them he knew would be related to another person within the hour. An hour on from that someone else would have it, and someone else an hour on again. In no time at all it would get back to Bartley and Angela. Then there'd be more interrogations from them.

One day when he got back to the car Bartley said he'd met a woman they both knew. She told him Brian had been rude to her.

'I don't know what you're talking about,' he said, 'I had a few words with her and she went off.'

'That wasn't the way she saw it. According to her you had your head in the clouds. She said it wasn't the first time it happened either. She said you're always in a rush to be away when you see her.'

'I'm that way with everyone.'

'Would you not consider giving her a bit of time seeing as it means so much to her?'

'I have better things to do than waste my day talking rubbish to some old biddy who has nothing on her mind but idle chat.'

'That's not a very Christian attitude.'

'Sorry for upsetting you. I know you always speak so tenderly of the people of Loughrea.'

'There's no need for that. I'm just making a comment.'

'Too many people in this town want to carve me up into little pieces. It's like emotional rape.'

'Emotional rape? That's a good one. In my day we used to call it being interested in someone.'

'There was a time you used to be like me. Do you not remember the days when you told me you were living in a backwater?'

'Different things become important to us as we get older. Life is tough without friends. It's nice to know people care about you.'

'There's a thin line between interest and interference.'

'If there is, you can be sure you'll find it.'

Being given out to like that made him retreat more and more into himself. One night he turned on Bartley after he told him he needed to get out of the house

'If I do,' he said, 'You'll probably accuse me of meeting Gabriel. I'm damned if I do and damned if I don't. It's like the way you were about UCD. You told me to become a student and then you were all for me dropping out. You get worked up about the auctioneering for a while and then you decide it's all bullshit. I don't know what you want.'

'Maybe it's you that doesn't know what you want. Get out and meet the people.'

'The people. What people? Out of work losers in love with the sounds of their own voices.'

Bartley got a laugh at that.

'Do you hear him, Angela?' he said, 'We'll have to invite some Hollywood stars down here. They'd give you a bit of excitement. Obviously we can't match up to the standards of New York.'

'Don't throw that at me. You seem to forget I grew up here.'

'You could have fooled me. You stayed away long enough.'

He went up to his room and put on some rock music. He turned the volume up to high. He was trying to annoy Bartley. He knew he hated rock music.

He came up and asked him to turn it down. 'Do you enjoy breaking the sound barrier?' he said, 'It sounds like someone drilling the street.' He put it higher when he said that.

'Now you're behaving like a teenager,' he said.

'You're turning into Angela,' Brian roared back at him, 'I need to get out of here.'

The obvious thing would have been to move in with Jennifer but he couldn't bring himself to do that. He didn't know if she wanted that anymore. She didn't say one way or the other anytime the subject came up now. It created tension. It was the elephant in the room.

The longer they went on as they were the more comfortable he became in the routine of being with her when he wanted and then going back to his other life. It was like marriage without the responsibilities. Was she as comfortable with that as seemed? She might have been afraid of pushing him away if she asked for more. Instead she talked about Stephen, about her pupils, her problems with the principal. Sometimes he thought their nights out had the predictability of marriage itself. Was that what made him shy away from it?

Gabriel called to the house every now and then. There was no love lost between himself and Bartley but Angela always put on a cup of tea for him. Afterwards Brian would go to a film with him or maybe for a game of snooker. He was still on the dole. He didn't show any signs of coming off it. His father supplemented what he got from the government with generous hand-outs whenever he asked. Brian was amazed at his casualness. It seemed to border on irresponsibility.

'He's too busy chopping people up to give out to me,' Gabriel said, 'He just keeps throwing money at me.' The two incomes enabled him to live quite a comfortable life while inching his way towards the completion of The Great Irish Novel.

He kept asking Brian to call up to him but he didn't like the idea of that. He could only take him in small doses.

One night he said he would, finally giving in to the endless invitations he threw out every time he met him. It went as he thought it might. Gabriel never shut up for a minute. Most of his comments concerned the fact that he thought he was a genius surrounded by dullards in Loughrea. At one stage he said, 'I can do the binomial theorem but I can't parallel park. That's all that matters to people around here.'

'Don't be an intellectual snob,' Brian said.

Gabriel burst out laughing.

'What's up with you?' he said.

'I'm thinking pot kettle black.'

'Just because I've read a few books doesn't mean I look down on anyone.'

'But you never connect with people.'

'That doesn't mean I feel superior to them. Maybe I feel inferior.'

'Now you're rationalising,' Gabriel said.

Afterwards he went on a rant parochialism. Brian had a headache. It was like an extension of the night in the pub. He remembered him sticking to him like glue and boring a nest in his ear about everything from his love life to Donald Trump.

At midnight he retrieved the precious novel from under his bed. He started to read passages from it. Brian didn't think much of them. They ranged from pretentious drivel to purple prose.

The main thread of the book was that Gabriel was a genius surrounded by goons. One day 'the little people,' as he called them, would come to realise that.

Brian tried to humour him. He knew it was all he had but he couldn't resist surreptitious glances at his watch. It looked like the dawn was going to come up before Gabriel reached the end of his recital.

As he finally stood up to leave he said, 'What do you do when you're not writing your book?'

He remembered Bartley's comment about him spending all his time watching DVDs. There were dozens of them scattered around the floor.

'I have so much stuff going on in my head,' he said, 'I can't answer that question.'

'I hope you invite me to your canonisation,' he said.

Gabriel's face went puce at that. Brian thought he was going to spontaneously combust.

'Fuck you,' he said, 'You've obviously been listening to the crap everyone in this dump have been spreading about me.'

'I've heard it,' Brian said, 'but I didn't believe it until tonight. You need to come down to the planet Earth, Gabriel. That's where the rest of us live.'

'It's time for you to go,' he said, 'I took you for someone else.'

'Likewise.'

He walked out of the house leaving the door open. Gabriel slammed it shut behind him.

'Have a nice life, shithead,' he called after him as he went down the road, 'See you on the other side.'

Brian didn't relay the details of the night to Bartley. He knew it would have been all round the town if he did. He just said he'd been to see him and that they'd had a pleasant night.

'I hope he didn't make a grab for you at any stage,' Bartley said.

'What's that supposed to mean?'

'Everyone knows he's as gay as Christmas. Even a blind man could see that.'

'I'm not blind and I don't see it.'

'He's never had a girlfriend, has he?'

'He talks about girls a lot.'

'That's probably a cover.'

'You have an over-active imagination. So what if he is? Would it make you think any the less of him?'

'Gay or straight, I never thought much of him anyway.'

52

Declan made a lot of calls to Bartley during Yvonne's pregnancy. One day she came on the line herself. She asked to speak to Brian. They hadn't talked since Bartley's birthday party. He felt nervous taking up the phone despite what Jennifer said about her. They talked small talk for a few minutes. Then he said, 'I'm really sorry about the way I behaved that night at the party.'

'Don't worry about it,' she said, 'Everyone was a bit crazy that night. That's what happens at parties.'

'I wanted to ring you to tell you how bad I felt but I thought you had enough on your plate with the pregnancy.'

'I wanted to ring you too.'

'You should have. I know Jennifer was on to you. So we're good again, are we?'

'We always were.'

'Thanks, Yvonne. I needed to hear that. I suppose that husband of yours will take longer to thaw out.'

'No. He's good too. He just thinks you don't want to talk to him.'

'That's not the case. If Dad put me on any of the nights he was on to

418

him I'd have apologised.'

'Maybe you should have said that to him.'

'I probably should. Arguments in Ireland go on for too long. Everyone is afraid of making the first move.'

'You're right. Declan was a bit that way too. He told me he had nothing in for you but it might have been harder for him to say it to your face. Or even through your Dad.'

'We'll get it sorted. Drink is a terrible thing. That's what it was all about really. I had more taken than I thought.'

'I'll tell Declan what you said. I'm sure it will mean a lot to him.'

'We're never going to be best friends but I respect him, strange as that may sound. He must have something going for him to make a lovely girl like you fall for him.'

'I better get off the line now, Brian. I burn up when I get compliments like that. I could set the phone on fire.'

She was nervous about the baby coming. She did everything she was told, following her doctor's orders to the letter. Declan oversaw everything. He even put one of the ultrasounds of the baby on Facebook for his friends to slaver over.

Brian tried not to let things like that bother him. He didn't want another argument.

Jennifer was delighted when he told her he'd talked to Yvonne.

'I knew she was going to be fine about everything,' she said.

'I probably knew she would myself too. I just had to hear it from the horse's mouth.'

She was up and down to the farm all the time now. She always got on great with Bartley. Brian thought there was an atmosphere between herself and Angela but he didn't say anything to her about it.

One day the four of them went on a picnic to Spiddal. The chemistry between Angela and Jennifer seemed even worse there. Brian drove. Bartley sat in the passenger seat. That was a mistake because it left Jennifer and Angela in the back. They hardly exchanged a word for the whole journey.

The downbeat mood continued when they got to Spiddal. Angela had packed sandwiches. As soon as they stopped the car she took a picnic basket out of the boot. They walked towards a field that was beside the beach. She put a blanket down on the grass for them to sit on. A few seconds later she let out a shriek.

'Bartley! You have mud on your shoes!'

It got on the blanket too. That was what freaked her out. Brian was shocked at her reaction. He put it down to the fact that she was in a bad mood. He thought it went back to having to sit beside Jennifer for the journey instead of being with Bartley.

What she didn't say to him wasn't worth saying but he took it.

'Let's make ourselves scarce,' Jennifer whispered to Brian as the furore erupted.

He told Bartley they were slipping away for a bit. They went off down the beach as Angela bundled the blanket into the car. She dabbed at it furiously with a cloth to try to get the mud off it.

'The sandwiches will be in a nice condition now,' Jennifer said, 'I can't see anyone eating them now.'

'Don't worry,' he said, 'They'll make short work of them once they get back to the car.'

'If they're still talking to each other.'

'I've seen them at this lark before. Angela blows hot and cold. She rears up and then it's over.'

'At least for her.'

'I know what you mean. Don't worry. Bartley understands her. That's why they're good for one another.'

'If only we could all be like that.'

'It's worth it to him. If he argues with her she gets worse.'

'The poor man.'

'Don't fret too much over him. There are a lot of times he's in the wrong too and she makes allowances. It evens out over time.'

'You're a good psychologist, Brian,' she said.

'I wouldn't say that. It's just common sense.'

'Maybe, but as my father said to me once, common sense isn't too common.'

She was quiet for a few moments. Then she said, 'Do you ever psychoanalyse us?'

'How do you mean?'

'I don't know. I suppose the way we've been on and off with one another over the years.'

He was taken aback by her change of tone. It was months since they'd talked seriously about themselves. He regarded these kinds of conversations as things of the past. But maybe they weren't for her.

'I thought we agreed not to talk about things like that.'

'I'm sorry. It just slipped out.'

'You shouldn't have to apologise for it. There's no crime in having a conversation.'

'We're getting on well together. That would be enough for most people.'

'But not for you.'

'I didn't say that.'

'Do you want to get married? Is that what this is about? Or to live together?'

'I don't know what I want. I feel we're drifting away from one another. I thought something was going to happen when you came home.'

'So did I. I know I've been in on myself a lot these times. You deserve better than that.'

'I'm not complaining. I love seeing you. I just feel there's something missing.'

'Like what?'

'I don't know. Sometimes it seems we've only met.'

'That sounds pretty bad. Is it my fault?'

'It's nobody's fault. It's just the way things are.'

She sat down at a bench. He watched her biting her nails.

'Maybe we fell in love too soon,' she said.

'Why are you being so dramatic?'

'Maybe you want to want me more than you do.'

'That's a bit obscure for me. What do you mean?'

'Women are different to men. They make their minds up sooner about what they want.'

'I don't know about that. Aren't women always changing their minds?'

'Not about relationships.'

'The modern woman might disagree with you on that.'

'I never claimed to be modern.'

'You're in a funny mood today.'

He was uncomfortable with the conversation. Why was she bringing things like that up now when they'd been getting on so well over the past few months?

They came off the beach. He looked at Bartley and Angela up the road. They were outside the car. Bartley waved at him.

'I think Bartley is calling us,' he said.

'I don't want to go back yet. Let's get a coffee.'

'All right.'

They went across the road. There was a cafe at the end of a cobbled path. A group of gift shops were beside it. Brian stopped at one of them.

'Let's go in here for a minute,' he said. She agreed half-heartedly. When they were inside he saw a brooch he thought was nice. He asked her if she'd like him to buy it for her.

'Okay, if you want.'

He went up to the counter to pay for it. She put it on.

'It looks nice on you,' he said, 'It really goes with your dress.'

'I like the Celtic design. You're very good to have got it.'

He thought it would put her into good form but it didn't.

'I don't think I feel like the coffee after all,' she said as they left the shop, 'If you want to go back to them I don't mind.'

'Are you sure?'

'Yes.'

Neither of them talked as they walked back to the car. When they got to it, as Brian predicted, Bartley and Angela had made up.

'Sorry about the way I went on earlier,' Angela said to Jennifer, 'I've ruined the day for everyone.'

'Don't say that,' Jennifer said, 'We had a nice walk.'

She held out a plate to her.

'Have a sandwich,' she said, 'You'll be glad to hear it doesn't have Bartley's footprints on it.'

She nibbled at it. Angela produced a flask. She gave them cups of tea. Bartley cracked some jokes. They were as corny as most of his jokes. He was the only person who laughed at them but he laughed enough for the four of them.

Angela tidied up when everyone was finished. Brian told Bartley he bought the brooch. Bartley said, 'Fair play to you. That's the way to sweeten them up. Don't tell Angela though. She'll only want one too.'

He was in great form on the journey back to Loughrea. He talked to Brian the whole way. Jennifer was quiet with Angela in the back. Angela thought it was because of her performance with the blanket.

'I know you wanted to get away from me,' she said to her, 'I can be a right tarter at times.'

'Sometimes,' Jennifer said, 'I want to get away from everyone.'

53

.

The weeks went on. Brian's job kept him from thinking too much about the conversation with Jennifer. He brought it up with her once or twice but she said she didn't want to talk about it.

He did what was expected of him at work and then came home and watched television or went for a drive until it was time to turn in for the night. His conversations with Bartley were more relaxed now. It was almost as if the two of them were getting too tired to argue about things anymore. Bartley told him he was confident he'd get further promotions if he stayed where he was and in that way avoid having to go back to Arthur Finlay or move to Newbridge.

Angela made sandwiches for him every night to save him having to go into the canteen at work the next day. As he got more adept at his work he found he was able to do the accounts in a way that kept everyone happy without having to make too many compromises.

Jennifer brought Stephen in to see him in his office some days and he ran around the desk playing hide and seek. Now and then she talked about leaving teaching. For a while there was a suggestion she'd go down to Newbridge and set up a beauty salon with Yvonne. She was on to her on the phone about the idea a lot. It had always been a dream of Yvonne's to do something like that. She said she was going to think seriously about it after the baby was born.

Brian made up with Declan. The two of them agreed to count to ten the next time they felt an argument was brewing. He also made up with Gabriel.

Gabriel rang him one day in floods of tears. His father had finally got tough with him. He told him he'd have to leave the house if he didn't get a job, The way Gabriel wept into the phone made Brian realise how much of a child he was at heart. For the moment the completion of The Great Irish Novel had to be postponed.

Yvonne's baby was born later than she expected. Brian was delighted. It was a boy.

It was perfectly healthy. Declan rang Bartley to tell him the news. He'd been sitting by the phone all day waiting for it to ring. He knew Yvonne had been taken into hospital to be induced. Declan talked to him as if a royal birth had just taken place.

Brian took the phone after a few minutes.

'Congratulations,' he said, 'Can I speak to the lady of the moment?'

'Is that all I get?'

'You'll get more when you start reproducing.'

'You're an awful man.'

Yvonne came on the line. Brian told her he was delighted to hear there were no problems with the delivery.

'I took the coward's way out,' she said, 'I had an epidural.'

'That's not cowardice. It's using your head.'

'I don't know. Declan says you miss out on the experience.'

'That's a nice one. I'd like to see him in labour. Anytime he had a runny nose growing up he was almost into A&E with it.'

She asked him to be the godfather. It was a surprise to him.

'How does Declan feel about that?'

'It was his idea.'

He rang Jennifer to tell her.

'You should be honoured,' she said.

'You know me and things like that. I prefer to stay out of them.'

'You can't go through life with that kind of attitude.'

'Would you like to come down to Newbridge for the christening? They're having it next week.'

'That soon? Most people wait months for it.'

'Not this pair. They're too excited. What do you say?'

'I'd love to.'

Angela bought an elaborate outfit for it. Bartley dug out his wedding suit and dusted it down. That was a big deal for him. Angela insisted he bring it to the cleaners.

'Will nothing satisfy you, woman?' he said, 'I haven't worn it since the wedding.'

'Really? I thought you might have had a few marriages since.'

'I'd prefer to go in my duds.'

'I know you would. That's why I have to watch you like a hawk. You'd disgrace me – and yourself.'

'They'll be too busy looking at His Lordship to bother with me.'

'That's a handy excuse for going around looking like a tramp.'

Everything was chaotic over the next few days. It was as if it was the only baby that ever had a christening. Thankfully it was being held on a Saturday so Brian and Jennifer didn't have to worry about taking the day off work. Declan was on the phone to Bartley ten times a day with the preparations.

'You'd think he was getting married again,' he said to Angela. He put just as much preparation into it. It was as if the job didn't exist now that he'd become a father.

Bartley was a bag of nerves on the day itself.

'I believe there's going to be a huge turn-out,' he said.

'So what?' Angela said, 'I thought you liked crowds.'

'I don't anymore. I must be getting like Brian in my old age.'

'Well you better get over it. Declan never does things by halves.'

'I'd say the presidential inauguration will be small by comparison,' Brian said.

'He's been waiting long enough,' Angela said, 'He's entitled to make a splash.'

'No pun intended,' Brian said. That drew a muffled laugh from Bartley.

They got into the car. Brian was driving. He was as apprehensive as Bartley about the day but he tried not to show it. He had to collect Jennifer from her house. That was working him up too. He didn't want to run into her parents. He thought they were getting a bit frustrated about the way things were going with her in his recent visits up there. Maybe she'd said something to them. Her father was old-fashioned. The fact that Yvonne was having a 'legitimate' baby was important to him.

Bartley was in a philosophical mood as he got into the car.

'Everyone I know is either having coronaries or grandchildren,' he said.

'I think I'd prefer the grandchildren,' Angela said.

They weren't long getting to Jennifer's house. Brian beeped the horn and she came running out. Her parents stood at the door waving. Brian thought she looked really elegant in her new outfit. It was a grey and white tartan dress.

'Wow,' Bartley said when he saw it, 'It suits you down to the ground.'

'It only goes to the knee,' Brian said.

'Smartarse.'

'It's lovely,' Angela said to her.

'Yours is lovely too,' she replied.

'That old thing? I've had it in the wardrobe for years. I was wondering if I'd ever get a wear out of it.'

She was sitting in the back of the car with Bartley. Jennifer got into the front. Angela didn't look too pleased. Bartley thought it was because of Jennifer's outfit.

'She's in a sulk,' he said, 'Your dress is nicer than hers.'

'Don't mind him,' Angela said, 'He's trying to get a rise out of me.'

'Maybe you'd prefer to sit in the front,' Jennifer said to her.

'Not at all,' she said, 'We have to keep the young lovers together.'

'How is the job going?' Brian asked Jennifer.

'Worse than ever. I think my days are numbered there now. It's getting too hard to juggle things with Stephen. What about you?'

'Not much better. At this stage it's just a question of hanging in there.'

He spent most of the journey talking about how the people on the factory floor resented him, how Joe McSweeney seemed to be more interested in his girlfriend than how the company was doing.

'Maybe we'll both be out of a job before the new year,' Jennifer said at one stage.

'Stop it the pair of you,' Bartley said, 'You'd think ye were going to a funeral instead of a christening.'

They decided to stop at Declan's house to see the baby. It was on the way to the church. The Skoda was in the driveway when they got there but there was no sign of either of them. Brian had to beep the horn a few times before he came out. He was holding the baby in his arms.

Jennifer got out to look at him.

'He's gorgeous,' she said. Declan beamed with delight.

'I'll be looking for some parenting tips from you,' he said. 'How's Stephen?'

'Basically an eating machine at this stage,' she said.

'This guy will probably be the same. Look at the size of him.' He was over eight pounds.

Angela got out. She drooled over him.

'What are you going to call him?' she asked.

'Harry,' he said, 'after Yvonne's father.' He'd died young of a heart attack a few years before.

Bartley was having trouble getting out of the car.

'It's the arthritis,' he said.

'More likely the laziness,' Angela said.

'Harry,' he said, 'That's a nice name. Is there any chance I can have a look at him?'

Declan paraded him in front of him.

'Well,' he said, 'What do you think?'

He stroked his chin.

'He looks a bit Winston Churchill,' he said, 'All he's short of is the cigar.'

'Ben Elton said every baby looked like the last tomato in the fridge,' Brian said.

'I think Ben Elton looks like a tomato,' Jennifer said. Everyone laughed.

'He has your eyes,' Declan said to Bartley.

'I wish he'd give them back to me,' Bartley said, 'Mine are fucked.'

'Stop that language,' Angela said.

'Where's Yvonne?' Brian said.

'Chasing her tail as usual,' Declan told him, 'No matter what time she has to be at an event she manages to find a way to be late.'

She came out as he was speaking.

'You should be married to some of my friends,' she said to him, 'Then you'd know what late was. You're the most impatient man I ever met.'

She was wearing a mini-skirt. It must have been six inches above the knee. Angela looked shocked. Yvonne spotted her expression.

'Is it too short, Angela?' she said, 'I know it's not very appropriate to the occasion.'

'It's fine,' Angela said uncertainly.

'If you've got it, flaunt it,' Bartley said, 'You have great legs. you can get away with it.' She blew him a kiss.

Brian looked at the baby.

'How could something that big come out of something that small?' he said to Jennifer.

'Are you calling the baby a thing?' Jennifer said.

'You know what I mean.'

'It's been happening since the dawn of time. Your mother should have explained the facts of life to you.'

Yvonne laughed.

'I think he's trying to compliment me,' she said, 'as usual.'

'I know,' Jennifer said, 'I'm only trying to wind him up.'

Declan looked at his watch.

'I'd love to stand here jabbering for the day,' he said, 'but tempus is fugiting. We better be making tracks.'

'You're right as usual,' Yvonne said. She hugged everyone again.

'See you later, alligator,' she said to Brian.

'After a while, crocodile,' he replied. They always said that to each other when they were going somewhere.

The cars sped off for the church. They got there within minutes. Declan was momentarily quicker. Such things mattered to him. He screeched into the grounds and parked the Skoda prominently near the door.

'I don't think he's supposed to be there,' Brian said to Jennifer.

'It's not our business to tell him,' she said.

The church was thronged. Most of the people there were Declan's workmates. They were scattered in various pews. Yvonne's mother was in the top one. She had a sad smile on her face.

She waved to Yvonne. Jackie, her other daughter, was beside her. She was the godmother.

Yvonne walked up the aisle holding Harry. Declan was beside her with a big grin on his face. Bartley and Angela walked behind them. Brian and Jennifer were behind them again.

Yvonne and Declan went on to the altar with Harry. The priest welcomed them. He tickled Harry's chin. He giggled. Yvonne beckoned Jackie to her. She stood beside her. Then Brian went up.

The ceremony began. The priest had only a few words said when Bartley took a babypower of whiskey from his pocket. He had a sip of it when Angela was looking the other way.

Brian spotted him.

'I don't believe this,' he said to Jackie.

He continued to drink as the prayers were read. Brian tried to get Angela's attention but he couldn't.

As the priest was sprinkling the baby with water, Bartley piped up, 'I hope you're putting a drop of the hard stuff in that, Father.'

He laughed nervously. Angela glared at Bartley.

'You're not with Fr. Finnerty now,' she said, 'Do you want to get us thrown out?'

There was a round of applause when the ceremony finished.

The priest put his hand on Harry's head.

'You behaved brilliantly,' he said, 'Not a tear.'

Declan stuck his chest out with pride. People rushed out of their seats to get a better look at the baby. They made a great to-do about his every expression.

Yvonne was awkward with the attention but Declan basked in it. He couldn't wait to take out his camera phone.

He made everyone stand in a ring around the baby while he snapped them.

They had to say "Child" instead of "Cheese."

'I can't take this,' Brian said to Jennifer, 'I'm going outside.'

'Don't,' she said, 'You'll only attract attention to yourself. Remember your mother's funeral.'

'I can't pretend I'm amused,' he said.

'Put on a plastic smile for a few seconds. It won't kill you.'

Declan took photo after photo. Everyone had to stand to attention like Brown's cows. Brian yawned. Jennifer dug him in the ribs.

'Stifle it,' she said, 'It doesn't look good.'

'I'm already dreading the day he takes his first step,' he said, 'He'll have it out on his webpage as if he's the new Neil Armstrong.'

'Don't be too hard on him.'

'I'm sorry. I promised myself I wouldn't let him get to me. I can't help it.'

Finally it was over.

'Before we leave,' Declan said, 'I want you to be very quiet while the choir sings.

'Choir?' Bartley said, 'At a christening?'

'Should it not be the priest who says that?' Brian said.

They sang a haunting hymn that made everyone very emotional. Declan went into a rhapsody listening to it. As Brian looked at him he found himself thinking of how Harry's life would go from here, how much Declan would keep him under his thumb just like he did Yvonne.

He'd probably be enrolled in a fee-paying school, he thought, before he was properly out of the cradle. He'd grow up surrounded by neat houses with well-trimmed lawns. When he left school he'd probably follow his father into the family business. He'd marry a girl from the 'good' end of town and have a small, well-behaved family who'd have all the creature comforts Declan himself enjoyed.

It seemed a long time before the hymn ended. Jennifer came over to him. He had his eyes closed. She waved her hands over his face.

'You're gone from us,' she said, 'What were you thinking about?'

'Wasn't the music lovely?' he said, 'It took me over.'

54

There was a do afterwards in the local hotel. Brian wasn't looking forward to it. He always felt these sorts of things went on forever. He had visions of a repetition of his coming home party. Was Declan going to bore everyone to tears with a saccharine speech? Would Bartley make a fool of himself by drinking too much? He decided he'd keep as low a profile as he could. At least he didn't have to go back to the house.

The hotel was done up as if for a wedding.

'I've got a bad feeling about this,' he said to Jennifer as they went in.

'Don't put the mockers on it,' she said, ' It'll be fine.'

'You were lucky to be born an optimist.'

Everyone's names had been written on elaborate cards. 'Brian and Jen' was on one of them. The names were in the shape of a heart.

'That's probably Yvonne's doing,' Jennifer said, 'She's such a sweetie.'

'Either that,' Brian said, 'or a gentle hint from Declan that we should be tying the knot.'

Bartley and Angela were seated at a table with Yvonne's mother. As Brian looked over at them he could see that Bartley was already trying to work his charm on her. Angela looked worried that he was coming on too strong. By now, Brian thought, she'd probably spotted the whiskey. Maybe she'd got the smell of it off his breath.

She asked Yvonne's mother if she was seeing more of Yvonne since Harry was born.

'Almost every day,' she said.

'I believe you're a great help to her with him.'

'I do a bit. He's already a ball of energy.'

'If either of you need a break anytime I can fill in.'

'That's very kind of you.'

'Me too,' Bartley piped up.

'A fine help you'd be,' Angela said, 'You'd probably give the poor child a six pack to get him to sleep.'

Some of Declan's contacts from the computer world were at another table. Brian didn't take to them. A lot of backslapping was going on. As he listened to their banter he imagined what Declan's social life was like in Newbridge. Friday nights in the boozer joking adolescently about nothing with people whose main ambition was to get rich quick.

'I don't think much of that shower,' he said to Jennifer.

'Why would you let a bunch of strangers bother you?' she said, 'You don't have to meet any of them, do you?'

'No.'

'Then put them out of your mind.'

Declan tapped a glass with a spoon. He stood up.

'I'd like to thank everyone for being here today for our little celebration,' he said, 'It took us a while to get there but it was worth it in the end.' There was a round of applause.

He paused for a moment. He looked across at Bartley.

'When Mam died, all our worlds fell apart. Some of us didn't know how we were going to be able to go on. Now we're starting to move again. One world stops and another begins. Here's to the future.'

He raised his glass in the air. There was more applause.

Bartley gave a fist pump. Angela waved jubilantly.

'That was perfect,' Yvonne said.

'I did it for him,' he said, tapping Harry on the head.

Bartley came over to them.

'Well done,' he said, giving Declan a hug, 'I couldn't have put it better myself.'

Declan looked over at Brian's table. Jennifer waved to him. Brian put his hands in the air. He mimed a handclap. Declan smiled in appreciation.

Yvonne came over to Brian and Jennifer. She had Harry in her arms.

'What did you think of the speech?' she said.

'It was lovely,' Jennifer said.

'Short and sweet,' Brian said.

'Harry liked it too,' she said, 'Didn't you, Harry?'

Harry gurgled as if he knew what she was saying.

'He's having the time of his life with the attention,' she said.

'It's all downhill from here on,' Brian said.

'Listen to cheerful Charlie,' Jennifer said. She asked Yvonne how she was feeling.

'Not too great,' she said.

'Why not?'

'I don't know. Maybe it's post-natal depression. I feel all frumpy. I shouldn't have worn the mini-skirt. It's far too revealing for someone who just had a baby.'

'Not at all,' Jennifer said, 'Knowing you, you'll get your figure back in no time.'

'It's a pity I couldn't get someone else's.'

'What are you talking about? You haven't a pick on you.'

'You need to go to Specsavers.'

'I mean it.'

'You're a great liar, Jennifer. I feel like Ten Ton Tessie.'

'Nonsense.'

'Ask Declan. He sees all the hidden bits.'

'Nothing is hidden today,' Jennifer said, 'Not with that sexy skirt you have on.'

'The pair of you are making me embarrassed with your compliments,' Yvonne said. 'Let's change the subject.'

Brian felt himself relaxing into the day. Maybe it wouldn't be so bad after all.

'Do you need clothes for Harry?' Jennifer said to Yvonne, 'My little fellow is growing out of everything.'

'Not at the moment, thanks. We could stock the parish with all the things people are giving us. At the rate they're coming in I won't have to buy anything for him till he's about 27.'

Declan's voice boomed over at them from the other side of the room. He was holding court in his little circle.

'Will he ever grow up, do you think?' Yvonne said.

'Hardly,' Brian said, 'He's his father's son.'

'Like you,' Jennifer said.

'I'll get you for that.'

'He's been like a hen on a hot griddle since I got pregnant. A woman from the estate we're on had a cot death. Since he heard that he's been in an almost constant state of panic. Every time Harry burps he almost has a nervous breakdown. He's like, "What's that? Is he supposed to do that?" I know I'm not going to get a minute's rest for the next few years.'

'It's supposed to be the baby that keeps you awake, Yvonne, not the husband.'

'I know. He's already reading up about bottle feeds.'

Jennifer put on a look of horror.

'I hope you're joking.'

'I wish I was. Sometimes I feel I'd be better off with one of those old-fashioned fathers who didn't bother too much with the baby side of things.'

'Dad is one of them; Brian said, 'He wouldn't know an umbilical cord if it hit him in the face.'

'Is Declan putting pressure on you to have more children?' Jennifer asked Yvonne.

'Yes, but I'm not biting. One is enough for me, thanks very much.'

'Who was it that said when you have one child you're a parent but when you have two you're a referee?'

'Whoever he was, he made a lot of sense,' Brian said.

'Why do you assume it was a man?' Jennifer said, 'It was much more likely to have come from a woman.'

'Why do you say that?'

'Because were the ones who spend most of our time with children.'

She was staring at him as she spoke. Was she getting at him?

'Do you think I should spend more time with Stephen?' he said.

She grimsced.

'That's not what I meant,' she said, 'He's not your son.'

'You said once that I made him feel like I was.'

'Did I? I forget.'

'I'd say Brian would make a great father,' Yvonne said.

'Thanks, Yvonne. It's nice to know someone appreciates me.'

'I wish your brother was more like you.'

'Seriously, though,' Jennifer asked, 'Is he demanding more kids?'

'You better believe it. Now that we've set the ball rolling he wants a hatful. He doesn't realise how much the nine months took out of me.'

'Was he there for the birth?' Jennifer said.

'Yes but he wasn't really able for it. When he came into the delivery room he started to feel faint. I said, "Who's having the baby here, me or you?" I wanted him out of there. It was hard enough on my own. God be with the days when fathers just got drunk across the road from the hospital. Now they nearly get morning sickness.'

Jennifer looked at Brian.

'You wouldn't be like that, would you?' she said.

'No. I'd be the guy getting drunk across the road.'

They all laughed.

'Did he leave when you asked him to?' Jennifer asked Yvonne.

'He practically had to be carried out by security. He kept saying, "Breathe, breathe." I said, "Shut up, Declan. I know the routine. If I stop breathing I'll die." He got that stuff from the pre-natal classes.'

'Don't say he went to them with you.'

'Just once. I was mortified. He was the only man there. It might be trendy to do things like that in Galway but in Newbridge you're looked on as a big girl's blouse.'

'You would be in Galway too,' Jennifer said.

'I shouldn't be moaning. I know he means well.'

'It's over now anyway.'

Thank God. It's great to *unpregnant*, if you know what I mean. Long may it continue.'

'Make him sleep on the sofa,' Brian said. 'Either that or lock the bedroom door.'

'What about investing in a chastity belt?' Jennifer suggested.

She laughed.

'I never thought he was going to be so much of a family man. When we were dating in the early days it was the pub every night.'

'It's the old story,' Jennifer said, 'When they have a child of their own they change.'

'I suppose. When I wasn't getting pregnant over the years he got very frustrated. I felt I was letting him down bigtime.'

'It could have been worse,' Jennifer said, 'You could have been married to Henry the 8th.'

'That's true. He's one man you definitely wouldn't have said "Not tonight, darling, I have a headache" to.'

'If you did, he'd have organised a different kind of one for you!'

'He never had to pay his exes alimony, that's for sure.'

Brian said, 'I heard of this guy in Africa the other day who cut his wife's hands off because she couldn't bear children. At least he's not that bad.'

'Give him time,' Yvonne said. She burst out laughing.

'That's the first time I've laughed in ages,' she said. 'You two make me feel so good. 'I'll kill you if you don't come down to see us.'

'We promise we will. Won't we, Brian?'

'For sure.'

'I need people like you two. It's been nothing but baby talk since I got pregnant. All the yummy mummies.'

'I had that too,' Jennifer said, 'It's like a clique you get into.'

'They just jabber on about the same old stuff all the time.'

'Baby bores are the worst kind. They only have one subject.'

'If anyone says "Breast is best" to me one more time I'll scream.'

'I can identify with that.'

'You can be too sensible, can't you?'

'Definitely. Sometimes I feel I want to go crazy. Declan has me living like a monk for the last nine months. I can't wait to get drunk some night. Maybe even tonight. Though on second thoughts no.'

'Why not?'

'It wouldn't look good in front of Brian.'

'To hell with that,' Brian said.

'He's so old-fashioned. He thinks drinking is something men do.'

'You'll have to disabuse him of that notion.'

'I wish I could. I'm not looking forward to staying in every night with the baby. I know it sounds terrible to say that when I wanted it so much. Before I got pregnant I was a bit of a gadabout. You get very selfish when you have only yourself to worry about.'

'I can't imagine you ever being a gadabout.'

'Then you don't know me. I could show you how to lower a bottle of Campari in record time.'

'Go on. Give us a demonstration.'

'No way. I'd have to get into training for it. I've turned into such a couch potato recently. Ever since I – '

She stopped.

'Ever since what?' Brian said.

'I was going to say about giving up the HSE but I don't want World War Three to break out again.'

He put his arms round her.

'Don't worry, I've learned my lesson. I'm not going to there again. Is there not some way you can get back into it?'

'It's dicey. They weren't too impressed when I told them I was leaving. I didn't give them any notice.'

'That's a pity. You need to be get away from that house.'

'I'm out of the habit.'

'What's stopping you?'

'I don't know. It's like everything else, isn't it? You start doing something and before you know it, it's your life. I'm probably suffering from cabin fever. Declan expected me to stay put during the pregnancy. Now I can't break out of it.'

'That was bad of him.'

'He said it was because he was afraid of losing the baby. I think it goes deeper.'

'He's always been a chauvinist,' Brian said, 'I bet he expects you to have his tea on the table the minute he gets home from work.'

'Now that you mention it, he does.'

'I know the tea I'd give him.'

'It's all very well to say that when you're not in the situation. I'm dependent on him every way now, including for money.'

'You don't have to be. The HSE isn't the only job in the world.'

'He keeps telling me my life will change irrevocably now. That's the word he keeps using. Irrevocably. I'm not sure what it means but it scares the daylights out of me.'

'Don't listen to him. As for going out, have they never heard of babysitters down in Newbridge?'

'I should consider that. So far it's been mainly my family helping out.'

'Families are great,' Jennifer said.

'This lady lets her parents do all the dirty work,' Brian said.

'He's right.' Jennifer said, 'I'd be lost without them.'

'Jackie offered to come up from Sligo anytime I want,' Yvonne said, 'I don't know if she's just saying it.'

'I'm sure she'd love to do it. Take her up on that for sure.'

'Mam said she'd pitch in too but I don't think she's up to it. It's so far away.'

'Could you not go down to them?'

'I don't know. Everything is up in the air at the moment.'

Harry started crying.

'He must have heard us talking about him. I don't think he wants to go to Sligo.'

'Can I hold him?' Jennifer said.

She rocked him in her arms. After a few seconds he stopped.

'You're good at this,' Yvonne said, 'How much do you charge?'

She asked Brian if he'd like to hold him.

'No thanks. I'd be afraid I'd let him drop.'

'I'm like that too,' Yvonne said, 'Every time I lift him up I'm terrified. I've always been a butterfingers.'

'After a few weeks it'll be second nature to you,' Jennifer said.

Brian looked around him. Declan beckoned him over but he shook his head. The noise from his table was deafening him. Bartley was getting noisy too.

'Why don't we have another drink?' Yvonne suggested, 'Are you ready for one, Brian?'

'You better believe it.'

'What about you, Jennifer? There are bottles of wine just waiting to be drunk. If we don't have them, someone else will.'

'Why not? Let me hold Harry while you get them.'

'It's okay. I think he's ready for a snooze.'

She put him in the pram.

'I'll get the drinks so,' she said.

She went off.

'She's looking great, isn't she?' Jennifer said to Brian.

'Like a million dollars.'

'It's been such a long wait for them.'

'That makes it all the sweeter.'

'I'm sure Declan will spoil Harry rotten.'

'Like you with Stephen.'

'I suppose so.'

'Do you find yourself thinking of him?'

'He's in and out of my mind all the time. I can't help it.'

'Is your mother minding him?'

'Yes. I don't know if she's able for him anymore.'

'Of course she is. It's fulfilment for her.'

'That's easy for you to say. He's a 24-hour job.'

Yvonne came back. She had three glasses in her hands.

'This is a bit of a challenge,' she said, 'at least for a butterfingers.'

'It's easier than holding a baby,' Brian said. He took two of the glasses from her.

She looked like she was in heaven as she raised the glass to her lips.

'That really hits the spot,' she said, 'The three of us should get quietly drunk together.'

'Good idea,' Brian said, 'Or even noisily drunk.'

'Declan will go mad if he sees me. He's got so sensible since I got pregnant.'

'I wouldn't call it sensible. I'd call it selfish.'

'If only he gave me some confidence in myself. He thinks I don't know one end of a baby from the other.'

'At this stage,' Jennifer said, 'there's not much difference!'

Yvonne laughed.

'I shouldn't be giving out about him,' she said, 'He's very stressed out at the moment.'

'You could have fooled me.'

'That's the point. He fools everyone.'

'What's he stressed about?'

'Money mainly.'

'I thought you were rolling in it down there.'

'We were until I gave up the job. Then the auctioneering stuff happened. That knocked us sideways a bit. He's working 25 hours a day to make up. Sometimes I wonder what's the point of being married to him. I never see him.'

'Lucky you,' Brian said.

'Seriously though, I worry about his health.'

'Don't. He thrives on that kind of thing.'

'I don't know. His blood pressure is going through the roof.'

'Things will cool down now that you've had the baby.'

'You must be joking. I don't think he'll be able for Harry being awake at night. He wanted him more than anything in the world but he doesn't realise all the things that come with it.'

He appeared behind her as she said that. She wasn't sure if he heard her or not.

'How is my little treasure?' he said. His eyes were glazed.

'Do you mean me or Harry?'

'Both of you.'

'Yvonne says you're thinking of expanding the family,' Brian said to him.

'Yes,' he said, 'We're going to have 247 children.' He was slurring his words. 'We're in negotiations at the moment, aren't we, Yivvy?'

'Is it not a bit soon for another one?'

'On the contrary. Now that I've learned it all works I'm all on for it. It's very simple. The man fertilises the woman and nine months – here's the surprising bit – a little human being comes out of her. Try it sometime if you don't believe me.'

'Thanks for the information,' Brian said, 'You've really opened my eyes on where babies come from.'

'Mine too,' Jennifer said, 'even though I've had one already.'

'Think nothing of it. You can pay my fee to the secretary on the way out. I'm thinking of giving classes on babymaking.'

'Maybe you could even have a go at having one yourself,' Brian suggested.

'Maybe I will.'

'If men could have babies,' Jennifer said, 'Every child would be an only child.'

'And if men could get pregnant,' Brian added, 'Abortion would be a sacrament.'

'The problem with sayings like that,' Declan said, 'is that they overlook one thing. It's men who bring home the bacon.'

'It's a pity they wouldn't cook it more often,' Yvonne said.

'The only reason they do,' Brian said, 'is because when their wives they jobs, their husbands –'

Yvonne gave him a look. He stopped.

'Yes?' Declan said.

'Most mothers have jobs today,' he said.

'And the ones who don't, work twice as hard,' Jennifer said.

'You better admit defeat on that subject, Declan,' Brian said, 'You're being outvoted two to one.'

'Three to one by the looks of it.'

'All right,' Brian said, 'Three to one. I have no problem being called a feminist.'

Declan started to walk away.

'He hates losing arguments,' Brian said. He stopped.

'Don't be so childish,' he said, 'I see you have your women to protect you. Maybe sometime we'll just go *mano a mano*.'

'I'd like that. Anytime. Just name the date and the place.'

'Stop this childishness,' Yvonne said, 'Both of you.'

'The reason I had to leave you beautiful people,' Declan said, 'is that I'm having to keep an eye on Joe Devlin. Take a look.'

Devlin was standing on a chair. He had a bottle of vodka in his hand.

'Who's he?' Jennifer said.

Brian knew about him. He was a friend of Declan's from school. He had a drink problem. Declan gave him a job in his business after it took off. Now he was sorry. He hadn't made use of it. It wasn't long before he went on the tear. He'd been barred from most of the local pubs.

'I knew it was only a matter of time before he started acting up,' Yvonne said, 'It's a pity you invited him.'

'You don't invite Joe to things,' he said, 'He just turns up. It's always the people you don't want at a function who make a special effort to be there. They know they have the power to make the day a disaster.'

He went over to him. He tried to take the bottle from him but he fought him off. He started to orate.

'Congratulations to Declan and Yvonne,' he said, 'And a big welcome to Prince Harry. Welcome to Earth from a fellow earthling.'

Some people laughed nervously. He fell off the stool and came tumbling down to the ground. By some miracle the bottle didn't shatter. Declan picked him up.

'Are you all right?' he said. He had a gash on his forehead.

'Did you like my speech?'

'It was fantastic. Now let's get someone to look at your forehead.'

He looked at Declan as if he didn't know who he was. His eyes were going in all directions. Declan led him back to his table.

He went over to Bartley.

'What are we going to do with him?' he said.

'I know what I'd do if it was up to me,' Bartley said.

'It's all right. As long as we can keep him in his seat.'

Yvonne was still chatting to Brian and Jennifer. He went over to her.

'I think the crisis is over,' he said, 'At least for the moment.'

'You handled it well,' Brian said.

'He's fine most of the time. Drink makes him into another person.'

'Who does that remind me of?'

'Don't say things like that. Dad's been very good today.'

'It's not over yet.'

'What an optimist. How do you put up with him, Jennifer?'

'He's just being cautious.'

'Yes. That's his middle name, isn't it? I keep telling him he needs to throw caution to the wind. Don't I, little brother?'

'You do. You always give me brilliant advice.'

'I do, don't I? If more people listened to me the world would be a better place.'

'Infinitely better,' Brian said.

Declan looked at Jennifer.

'When are you going to take this fine lady down the aisle?' he said.

'I'm afraid that item is off the agenda at the moment,' Jennifer said.

Declan told a joke about an old country couple who'd been dating since they were teenagers. They were both in their sixties now. One day the man said to the girl, 'Bridget, don't you think it's time we got married?' She replied, 'I don't know, Packy, sure who'd have us now?'

Yvonne laughed.

'You wouldn't want to get to that stage, would you, Brian?' she said.

'Don't say you're going to start now, Yvonne.'

'I've always thought you two should tie the knot. I can't think of a nicer couple.'

She looked at Jennifer.

'You're like an extension of Brian's mother,' she said to her.

'That's a lovely thing to say, Yvonne. Thank you.'

'Anyway, that's the end of that topic. Sorry, Brian'

He looked awkwardly at Jennifer. She was staring at the ground.

Bartley and Angela wandered over. Yvonne's mother was with them.

'You're all very quiet here,' Angela said, 'Have we interrupted something?'

'Of course not,' Yvonne said, 'We were nattering away to beat the band till a few seconds ago.'

'Maybe we should go,' Brian said, 'The day is getting on.'

'I wouldn't mind another drink,' Bartley said.

'Where have I heard that song before?' Angela sighed.

Declan joined them.

'Sorry about the situation with Joe,' he said.

'Don't worry about it,' Yvonne's mother said, 'No christening would be complete without a bit of drama.'

'He's gone now, thank God. One of the other guys is driving him home. He'll probably wake up in about five days if I know anything.'

Jackie appeared. Jennifer gave her a hug.

'Where have you been all day?' she said, 'We hardly saw you.'

'I got waylaid by some of Declan's friends. They're very jubilant.'

'I can think of another word for it,' Brian said.

Jennifer gave Jackie a nudge.

'I'm sure you're proud of your sister,' she said.

'As proud as punch. I almost feel as if I've had the baby myself. It's been a worrying time.'

'That's why everyone is so relieved.'

Declan's eyes started to fill up.

'I wish Mam was here,' he said, 'She always wanted a grandchild.'

Bartley put his arms around him.

'She's here in spirit. Maybe her prayers got Vyonne pregnant.'

'I never thought of it like that,' he said, 'You've hit the nail on the head.'

'I think that calls for another drink,' Bartley said.

'I don't know if that's a good idea,' Brian said, 'We don't want you turning into Joe Devlin.'

'Come on. I've been a good boy today.'

'You have, but time is getting on. We're all a bit tired. Maybe we should think about hitting the road.'

'Already? I feel things are just warming up. You only get christened once.'

'Look around you, Bartley,' Angela said, 'There's hardly anyone here.'

People had started to drift out. The only full table was the one Joe Devlin had been at.

'Don't be too sensible. It's a celebration. Right, Declan?'

'Right, Dad.'

'Declan looks tired,' Angela said to Bartley.

'Are you tired?' Bartley asked him.

'Absolutely not.'

'He's just saying that to be polite.'

Bartley slugged back what was in his glass. Brian buttoned up his anorak. 'I think we should go,' he said.

Bartley looked crestfallen.

'Why is nobody any fun anymore?' he said.

'Come on, Bartley,' Angela said.

She started to walk him over to where the coat racks were. Brian couldn't believe he was giving in. He looked at Jennifer.

'History in the making,' he said to her.

'He's a changed man.'

Yvonne hugged Brian and Jennifer.

'Before you go,' she said, 'I'm going to make both of you swear you'll honour us with your presence in Newbridge once all the excitement dies down.'

'You're just looking for cheap babysitters,' Jennifer joked.

They made their way over to Angela and Bartley. He was having trouble getting into his coat. In the end Angela put it on her arm.

They passed the table with all the people from Declan's job.

'Look at them,' Angela said, 'Drinking themselves good-looking. I can imagine what they'll be like in a few hours.'

'Lucky them,' Bartley said.

It was dark when they got outside. Bartley did a little dance, tipping an imaginary hat as if he was on stage.

'Little things mean a lot,' he sang. He put his arms out to a woman who was passing with her shopping. Angela shook her head.

They sat into the car. Brian asked Angela to drive. She'd had the least drink of all of them. She was glad to oblige. Bartley got in beside her. That left Brian and Jennifer in the back.

They didn't talk much on the journey home. Jennifer tried to make conversation with Brian but he wasn't in the mood for talking. What Yvonne said about him marrying Jennifer kept going through his mind. They made him feel both guilty and angry.

Angela was too busy keeping her eyes on the road to talk. Bartley was annoying her anyway. He kept singing snatches of different songs out of tune. Then he got sleepy. He started falling into her shoulder like he did on the night of Brian's coming home party.

'Is there any way you can keep him off me?' Angela said.

She had trouble seeing ahead of her as the night darkened. The lights of other drivers were blinding her. Then it started to rain. The roads became skiddy. Bartley kept bumping against her unless Brian kept his hands on him all the time. Jennifer tried to help but she was too far away on the other side of the car.

'I suppose there's no way you could wake him up,' Brian said to Angela at one point.

'That's the joke of the day. It would be easier to wake an elephant.'

The journey drained everyone. Brian felt he'd been on the road forever when they got to Dublin. The time in the car seemed even longer than the day in Newbridge. He supposed that was because of Bartley - and because Jennifer didn't feel like talking.

When they got to her house he gave her a kiss. She didn't return it. She grabbed her bag and got out of the car.

'I'll ring you later,' he said.

'Maybe we should leave it for a few days,' she said.

She walked slowly from the car towards her house. Angela gave the horn a beep. She didn't look back when Brian waved.

'Jennifer seems a bit in on herself,' Angela said as they drove off.

'She's just tired,' Brian said, 'We all are.'

As soon as they got in the door they all made for bed. Usually they'd have had a nightcap and a post mortem about the day but that wasn't on. They were too tired.

As Brian lay in bed his brain whirled with all the events of the day – the priest blessing Harry, Bartley having his secret whiskey, Declan's speech, the chats with Jennifer and Yvonne. All in all he supposed it was a success. For some reason, though, he couldn't get it out of his mind what Yvonne said about himself and Jennifer being suitable for marriage.

Was he a fool not to land himself on her doorstep and ask her to spend her life with him? He couldn't do that even if it was the right thing to do. He felt more confused than ever.

Yvonne rang Bartley a few days later to thank them all for coming down. She said Harry was a handful but not as bad as they thought. Declan was going a bomb at work and getting more sleep than he expected.

When she was finished chatting with Bartley she asked to speak to Brian. He didn't want to come to the phone but Bartley made him. It was the first time he'd ever been that way with her.

She sounded subdued when she started to talk.

'I hope I didn't upset you with what I said about you and Jennifer,' she said, 'I didn't mean to put pressure on you.'

'Don't even think about it,' he said.

'I noticed you went a bit quiet when I said what I said. It was none of my business. At the end of the day it's your decision, not mine.'

'Don't worry about it, Yvonne. honestly.'

A few days later Gabriel Hoey rang.

'I believe Yvonne had her baby shower,' he said.

'Christening, you mean.'

'I prefer to think of it like a shower. I hope everyone got suitably pissed.'

'Well the baby did anyway.'

He asked him if he'd like to meet but he said he wasn't up to it.

'What's the story with yourself?' he said then.

Gabriel's answer surprised him.

'Not too good,' he said, 'The old lad is twisting the knife.'

At the end of the call he mentioned that he'd seen Jennifer with Billy Sheehan at the shops one night. Brian acted casual when he said it but it disturbed him.

'What's so strange about that?' he said.

'They looked pretty cosy with each other.'

'Fuck off, Gabriel,' he said.

He hung up. A few minutes later he rang Jennifer. He got straight into it.

'Gabriel said he saw you with Billy Sheehan,' he said.

'I see Billy now and again,' she said, 'So what?' '

'Is there any specific reason?'

'As I told you before, it's usually because of things to do with Stephen.'

'You used to tell me you met him because he was giving you money. I thought you didn't need to when I started helping out that way.'

'I don't most of the time but there's always something.'

He felt there was more to it but he didn't delve. What right had he to? He was either with her or he wasn't. And yet he couldn't stop the anger rising inside him every time he thought of him.

He tried to keep his mind off him in the following days. He was upset at the way the call ended. He knew he'd been confrontational. The last thing he wanted to do was throw Jennifer into Billy's arms from anger. Could that happen? Anything was possible.

He drove down to her house the next day. He wanted to find out how she was feeling about everything. She hadn't been the same since the christening.

He walked in through the creaky gate. He rang the broken doorbell. Her father came out. .

'Hello, Brian,' he said, 'We haven't seen you for a while. How are you keeping?'

'Fine. Is Jennifer around?'

'She's working at something in the kitchen. I'll get her for you.'

She came out. He thought her face looked tired.

'Hi,' he said, 'I was wondering if you'd like to go for a drive.'

'I don't know. I'm correcting copies.'

'So your father said. Can they not wait till tomorrow?'

'If you let them pile up it just gets worse and worse.'

'I need to talk to you.'

'About what?'

'Everything.'

'I'm not in form, Brian. It's too late.'

As she closed the door he wondered what she meant by that. 'Too late.' The words struck a chill through him. It was the first time she'd ever said no to a drive. Why hadn't he pushed it? He didn't know. Maybe the copies were only an excuse.

He went for the drive on his own. He drove through the night without knowing where he was going. He drove faster than he ever had in his life, pushing the needle up the way Bartley used to do when he was angry. He rolled down the windows and let the air in at him, blowing all over his face until it hurt. It blotted out his thoughts.

Over the next few days he spent more time in the Austin than anywhere else. It became a kind of sanctuary to him. He ate in it, he read in it, he used it to sleep. It became like a friend to him, a friend the Hyundai could never be. But it couldn't last forever. Like anything else it had a finite life span.

He pushed it beyond its limits and one day shortly afterwards it broke down on him. It just stopped in the middle of the road when he was on his way to work. No matter how many times he gunned the ignition, nothing happened. He had to ring for a tow truck to get it to a garage. When he asked the mechanic what was wrong with it he said, 'How long have you got?'

He could hardly complain. It owed him nothing. How many journeys had he taken in it? Too many to count. His mother and himself used to speak of it almost as if it was a person. When they'd get to a destination without the radiator overheating or some other mishap he'd almost be surprised. 'When is it having its check-up?' ' she'd say, 'I hope the blood pressure is good.' Now there would be no more check-ups.

He drove it to a scrapyard on its last journey. It almost felt like bringing a cow to the slaughterhouse. The exhaust pipe scraped off the ground the way Declan's had the night he had the problem with his baffler. There was steam coming from everywhere. He had to push it the last few yards.

What he got for it would hardly have filled the tank with petrol but it was a fair price for what was left of it. He'd almost have paid to have had it taken away. It was an anachronism now.

'What happened?' the mechanic asked him when he saw its decrepit condition, 'Has it been in a war?'

'It died,' he said. He couldn't think of any other way to put it.

55

Just like that it was November. The evenings became shorter. the sun lower in the sky. The land looked sad to him as if it was missing the animals that used to graze on it.

Bartley complained about everything. There was a blackness in him that he kept blotting out with his drinking but it always came back worse than ever the next morning. He hid it like the actor he was but sometimes the thirst got too much for him. When it did he became like a child in his need, searching frantically for the bottles he would have in his old hiding places, the cupboards and presses Angela was always aware of but didn't mention in case it caused a row. If he couldn't find them he'd go out to a pub or an off-licence to slake his thirst.

One morning Brian saw him slumped over the steering wheel of the Hyundai with a naggin in his hand. He wasn't sure if he'd been there all night or not. Angela didn't say. There were other days when he had to go

443

to bed to ride out the shakes. His hangovers became more unbearable than ever.

Angela was slowing down too. Brian watched her struggling with jobs that once came easily to her. He listened to her groaning with the pain of arthritis as she tried to climb the stairs on the wet evenings. The fact that she was so much younger than Bartley made him think age would never catch up on her but now it seemed to be doing that.

It depressed him to be surrounded by two people who were losing their power in life. Angela didn't complain but he saw the pain in her face. Bartley made complaining almost into an art form.

To get away from them some nights he drove into Galway. He dropped into pubs and just sat there soaking up the atmosphere. It was like on the nights when he used to drive in to meet Declan – or rather not meet him. It was always bubbling with life when he was there. The sound of people's laughter stimulated him. He sat watching throngs of students going down the streets singing, embracing one another, play-fighting. At the Claddagh there were usually buskers. There were often Ceili dancers as well, or people in dreadlocks with strange musical instruments. He couldn't imagine these kinds of people ever worrying about jobs or mortgages or even long-standing relationships. He envied them their capacity to lose themselves in the moment.

He found it difficult to settle back to the quietness of the farm after nights like that. He often considered moving to Galway with Jennifer. It was the obvious place, he thought, close enough to both of them and yet far enough away to be able to lose themselves in the hustle and bustle.

'I suppose you'd never think of bringing me on one of your jaunts,' Bartley said to him one night. It was true. He'd never thought of it.

'The next time I'm going I'll let you know.'

The following week he made a point of asking him to go along with him. He jumped at the opportunity but it turned out to be a flat night. They sat in a pub without having anything to talk about. Bartley wasn't drinking. He'd just come out of hospital after having some tests. He wasn't feeling well. He said it would have turned his stomach.

'I'm boring when I'm sober,' he said at one point of the night. Brian was afraid to agree with him. Were alcoholics people who drank to make themselves more interesting? Or to make the world more interesting? They left the bar early. He imagined that was a first for Bartley.

'I suppose that's the last time you'll bring me with you,' he said on the way home.

'Don't be stupid,' Brian said, but inside himself he was wondering what was the point. If he'd been drinking he might have made a commotion. That would have been worse.

He drove to work in a half daze, barely noticing the roads he travelled on. He was in the Hyundai all the time now. Sometimes he thought it could have found its way to the factory on its own. When he got there he parked in the same place, walked up the same stairs to his office, said hello to the same people on the corridor, turned the same key to his door, put his coat on the same rack, sat down at the same desk, asked for a cup of coffee from the same secretary and looked out the window at the same fields. Then he took a heap of files from a cabinet and tried to make sense of figures that meant nothing to him.

Business continued to get worse even though firms around them were thriving in Ireland's second boom. He'd been sworn to secrecy about that fact by McSweeney. 'A rising tide lifts all boats,' he told the staff during their fortnightly meetings. It was a statement made more in hope than in expectation. Until that day arrived, he was told to be 'creative' with the figures in case an audit was ordered.

He didn't mind cooking the books. With a stroke of the pain he could make 100 into 1000 or 1000 into 100 depending on which side of the page it was on. The only thing that mattered was that the figures balanced. Because of his magic touch the emperor could still have all his clothes and nobody would be any the wiser. People went home on Friday evenings with their salaries in their pockets and didn't question how they got them. Those who were worried about paying their bills got stays of execution. So did the growing numbers who worried about having their houses repossessed. Meanwhile he drew a salary for telling pleasant lies. His conscience had long stopped bothering him about that. He convinced himself he deserved the money he was getting because of the torture he endured sitting at his desk trying to look busy. Trying to hide the fact that he didn't know what he was doing took more out of him than what he was doing.

The worse he felt, the better an act he had to put on. He developed a slick manner that impressed those above him, parroting the jargon of corporate texts to camouflage his ignorance. Maybe everyone was at it, he thought. It would either go on forever or the house of cards would come tumbling down without warning and they'd all be out of a job.

Bartley loved telling people his son was a manager. 'You'll be as good as Declan yet,' he'd say excitedly. And Brian would think: Could a worse fate be imagined?

Jennifer called in one day with Stephen.

'You're looking more the part than ever,' she said to him as he sat behind his desk in a new suit. He was annoyed by the comment. It suggested he was selling himself out to the job.

'Please don't insult me,' he said. I'm playing a part here. I deserve an Oscar for acting.'

She took Stephen out of the pram. He crawled around the floor. There was a stapler under the desk so he started playing with it. He was amused at the sound it made when he clicked it. Jennifer laughed.

'Obviously he's going to follow you into the business world,' she said.

Brian went down on his hunkers. He made faces at him but Stephen ignored him. He continued to play with the stapler.

Brian found it an effort trying to appear jolly with him. He wasn't in good form. He was trying to impress Jennifer but she saw through it. She always knew when he wasn't being natural.

'Would you like a coffee?' he asked her to break the tension.

'Why not.'

She put Stephen back in the pram. They got the lift down. There were only a handful of people in the canteen. They stared at Brian as he ordered the coffee. He thought it might make them more friendly to him to see him there with someone from the outside world but it had the opposite effect. They looked through him when he nodded at them.

He tried to pass it off but Jennifer noticed.

'Are they always like that?' she said as they sat down.

'Unfortunately yes.'

Every sip he took of his coffee made him more tense. Eventually he said, 'I better get back to the desk. McSweeney is around.'

They went back up in the lift. McSweeney was in the corridor as they got out.

'I don't believe I've had the pleasure,' he said to Jennifer.

'Sorry,' Brian said, introducing them to one another.

They shook hands. 'Lovely baby,' he said, looking into the pram. 'What's his name?'

'Stephen.'

'He's the image of you,' he said to Brian.

'I better get back to the office,' Brian said, 'I have a report to do.'

'I'll be in to you later,' McSweeney said, 'There are a few things I want to talk to you about.' .

'That sounds serious,' Jennifer said when he was gone.

'He's probably going to give me the sack.'

'Or a promotion. You'll be like Joe Lampton out of *Room at the Top* yet.'

'Who?'

'It was a film with Laurence Harvey. Did you not see it?'

'No.'

'It's about this guy who'll do anything to get where he wants. He even marries the boss's daughter.'

'That definitely sounds like me. If you buy the firm off McSweeney I'll be all yours.'

'No problem. Anyway, I hope the rest of your day goes well.'

446

'You too.'

'Goodbye little fella,' he said, clucking his tongue out at Stephen.

Everyone knuckled down to their work as Christmas approached.

'They're scared shitless they mightn't get their bonuses,' McSweeney said to Brian, 'It's the same every year.'

There were few absentees now or even latecomers. Machines whizzed all day every day, their cacophony drowning everything out, making people have to roar to be heard above them. Some days Brian found himself overcome by it. He locked himself into his office and put mufflers over his ears.

A man came into his office one day in overalls. He had a requisition form for a battery charger that Brian had to sign. He knew his face from school.

The man stood there covered in oil and grease as he waited for his signature.

'You were in the class ahead of me in the college,' Brian said, 'Weren't you?'

'Mark Cadden,' he said, 'We never really got to know one another.'

They shook hands.

'How's Deccie?' he said.

'Getting richer by the minute.'

'I always felt he'd go places. He couldn't wait to get out of school.'

'I know the feeling.'

He felt awkward sitting in front of him, thinking he admired Declan more than him. He remembered them playing football together, coming up to the house sometimes.

'How do you stick the noise?' Brian said.

'You get used to it.'

It was the great Loughrea phrase, the phrase of Paudie Gleeson and Joe Ruddy and others who hadn't done much with their lives but didn't seem to mind. 'You get used to it.' But he couldn't. He couldn't get used to the noise or the people or the way of life. It was why he had to get away.

He scrawled his name on the form and handed it to him. He looked at it quizzically.

'I can't make out your signature,' he said.

'It's like the doctors,' Brian joked, 'The more important you are, the more illegible you have to be.'

'Aye. Except in their case it's usually because they fucked up some way and don't want to be identified.'

He went off smiling. Brian was envious of him. He was content with his job and his lot, an uncomplicated man who knew what he had to do and didn't need to jump above that or challenge it. It was the order of things. One person sat on the top of the hill and another one was below him, either trying to leapfrog over him or not bothering to.

The days bled into one another. He worked and came home. Or at least he pretended to work. Often he just stared out the window instead of at his computer until McSweeney came in to chat about his girlfriend or how wretched the weather was. Maybe the day would come when he'd cotton on to the fact that he hadn't a clue what he was supposed to be doing and throw him out. By that stage the company would probably be bankrupt.

People started talking about Christmas. Brian tried to avoid the hysteria that surrounded it. He wasn't able to take the gaiety they seemed able to summon up so easily at this time of the year every year.

He dreaded the thought of the party. Everyone would go around with ridiculous hats on them telling everyone else they loved them after drinking themselves senseless.

In a factory in England, he read in a newspaper, a man was sacked for refusing to put on a Santa costume in October. Maybe Ireland would become as insane with time. Maybe the sweet factory would too. Would he still be there if it did? He felt he was just marking time, waiting for something to happen to ease him away from it and from everything else he knew that gave him a false security. But nothing did. He was trapped.

The year narrowed into the hardness of winter. Sheep shivered in the few fields they still owned. The landscape was like a frozen shell, the trees shredded to nothing.

The sun shone down almost grudgingly. A film of frost covered it some days. People pulled their coat collars around them as they walked the roads, their breaths fogging the air. Rain was almost constant. It thundered down in sheets, ushering the last fallen leaves into the drains.

Angela said the house was like an icebox. She wore two or three jumpers to try and keep herself warm.

'I can't get any heat out of these radiators,' she complained, jiggling at the dials repeatedly.

'That's because they're on timers,' Bartley said, 'Timers are the holy grails of the ESB. They mean you freeze your nuts off unless you're in the habit of getting up at 5 a.m. when the booster kicks in.'

'They wouldn't be much use to you then,' she said, 'You're only turning around for the second time at 5 a.m.'

56

Donald Trump beat Hillary Clinton to the American presidency towards the end of the year. She'd been an odds-on favourite to win but this was the year of surprises. In the Brexit referendum in Britain the polls were wrong too. They forgot about the people in the small towns.

Brian felt Trump was going to drive America off a cliff. Leonard Cohen had died the day before he won the election. It seemed like an omen, the great liberal checking out as the racist right-winger prepared to take the reins of power. Maybe he intuited it. He thought of Cohen's famous line, 'First we take Manhattan.' That was where the Trump Tower was located. It was appropriate. The next line of the song was, 'Then we take Berlin.' That might have been even more appropriate. Some of Trump's rantings reminded him of what it must have felt like to be under the Nazi jackboot in the 1930s.

He wondered how Gabriel would have taken the news. He hadn't spoken to him since the night he told him about seeing Jennifer with Billy Sheehan. Maybe he liked Trump. You could never tell with him. He was capable of saying he admired someone if everyone else hated them. He liked being different for the sake of it, for the shock value.

He had arguments with Bartley about Trump, about rising crime figures, anything that was in the news. They argued to keep their minds off themselves, off the fact that so little was happening in their lives. Angela stayed out of the discussions. She felt the two of them would turn on her if she said anything.

The weather got mild in mid-December. Nobody knew why. In the past a sudden change in climate would have caused people to talk but not now. On news channels they watched programmes about tsunamis, flash floods, rivers breaking their banks in every corner of the globe.

'It's those bloody ice caps,' Bartley sad, 'They're melting. We'll all be fried soon. I saw a picture of a penguin at the North Pole the other night and he was wearing sunglasses.'

One day shortly before Christmas Brian noticed the answering machine blinking when he came home from work. When he turned it on he saw it was a message from Jennifer. She said just two words, 'Ring me.' She sounded bothered. He hadn't seen her since the day she called in to see him in his office. He'd asked her down to the farm for Christmas but she hadn't said whether she'd go or not. She seemed removed from him on their last few phone calls. He was going to ask her if there was anything wrong with her but he didn't. If he had he felt it might have led to another conversation about where their relationship was going.

When he rang her she picked up immediately. As soon as she started speaking he knew she wasn't herself. Her voice sounded strange. She was breathing very fast.

'What's wrong?' he said.

It was a long time before she spoke. Her voice sounded hoarse when she did.

'I have something to tell you,' she said, 'I was going to suggest meeting but I don't think it would be a good idea now.'

'What are you talking about?'

'I have something to tell you about Billy Sheehan.'

'What about him?'

She paused.

'He asked me to marry him.'

He got a shock. It was the same feeling he had when she told him she was pregnant. He felt like screaming but he couldn't. The news went into a part of him that didn't react anymore, that learned how not to react.

'So what?' he said, 'Isn't he always asking you that?'

She paused again..

'Brian, I told him I would. I hope you'll understand.'

He didn't properly hear what she said so he had to ask her to repeat it. When she did he still didn't think he'd heard her correctly. Or maybe his mind couldn't take it in.

'You're going to marry Billy Sheehan?'

'Yes.'

A nerve in his ear started to pulse. He was losing the town beauty to the town joke.

'I don't believe you,' he said.

'I'm sorry,' she said, 'We were going on too long without anything happening.'

He left the phone down on the table, stepping away from it as if it was somehow responsible for the message it conveyed. He walked around the room with his hands on his head, trying to bring the blood back to it. When he got back to the phone he could hear her saying, 'Are you there?' in her light voice.

He picked it up.

'You can't do this,' he said, 'You can't do this to me.'

He wanted to stamp on the phone, to throw it out the window so it would be destroyed along with its words.

'Are you at home now?' he asked her.

'Yes.'

'Can I call over?'

'That wouldn't be a good idea.'

'Why not?'

'Because he's here.'

'Is he listening to this conversation?'

'He's talking to Mam in the kitchen.'

'So you're upstairs.'

'I'm putting Stephen down.'

She was putting him down. It sounded like a term a vet might use for an animal he couldn't cure.

'Would you do me a big favour, Jennifer, and come over here now?'

She took a while before she replied. He thought she might be going to agree but she said, 'I don't think that would be a good idea either.'

'I need to talk to you. You're making a big mistake.'

'I've thought it through, Brian. I've thought it through a thousand times and it's what I want.'

'You told me it was me you wanted.'

'You don't love me enough to make it work.'

'I do. You know that.'

'I wish I did.'

'Please believe me.'

'You're making this very hard for me, Brian.'

'I don't want to do that. I'm saying it because I want you.'

'You could have had me five years ago. You could have had me before Europe, before America. If I hadn't been proposed to you probably wouldn't even be on the phone to me tonight.'

'So what you're telling me is you don't think I love you.'

'Not enough.'

'Do you think Billy loves you?' It hurt him even to say the name.

'He says he does. That's good enough for me.'

'But you don't love him back. You told me you didn't.'

'We've been seeing each other a lot over the past few weeks. We've become close.'

It was getting worse.

'Seeing one another?

'Yes.'

'Behind my back?'

'I wouldn't call it that.'

'Why didn't you tell me then?'

'I was afraid of what you might do. I was afraid you'd offer to marry me from guilt, or maybe from the fear of losing me. I wouldn't have wanted you to be with me for the wrong reasons.'

'Do you not think you'll be with him for the wrong reasons?'

'No.'

'Why not?'

'He's kind to me. I know he'll take care of me. And of Stephen.'

A penny seemed to drop for him.

'You're marrying him because you want a father for your baby.'

'That's part of it. I don't deny it.'

'Is another part the fact that you're on the rebound from me.'

'You can put it whatever way you like. I never liked that expression. I've loved you since the day I first set eyes on you but I don't think you'll ever be able to make up your mind about me even if you live to be a hundred. I could break it off with Billy and you could marry me in the morning but I don't think you'd be happy with me. What good would you be to me? You've said it often enough yourself when we were on our breaks. I felt the breaks were going to be going on forever and we'd just get tired with the situation. Or with one another.'

He felt his head pounding. It pounded so hard he felt it was going to burst open. .

'That might have been true the way things were but it isn't now. Your call tonight woke me up. It made me aware of how much you mean to me. I can't face the thought of life without you.'

'That's not love, it's desperation.'

'Everyone knows you're the woman for me. Ask any of them.'

'It's no good them knowing it. *You* have to know it.'

'I do.'

'I don't believe that. You haven't loved me for years. You might have said the words but you didn't mean them.'

'Do you think I'm saying them tonight to stop you marrying Billy Sheehan?'

'Yes.'

His head began to throb now with a new kind of pain. It felt as if an object was pressing on it, crushing the two sides of it together.

'I need to see you,' he said.

'Why? To try and talk me out of it?'

'No. Just to see you.'

'That wouldn't be good for either of us. We might fall back into one another's arms like we did that night in Brennan's pub. We might even convince ourselves we were still the two people who met as children and felt a connection. But it wouldn't be real. Afterwards we'd have times like the terrible weekend in Tramore. That would be the way it would always go. We'd be trying to convince ourselves it was going to work because we'd be too afraid of it not working.'

'You're wrong, Jennifer. I know why you're saying what you're saying but you're 100% wrong. Please give me another chance. I've been obsessed with myself since my mother died. Maybe I had to be shocked into that realisation.'

'I've made my decision, Brian. Please accept it. We've been going round in circles for too many years and it was killing what we had. At least now we'll have happy memories.'

'I won't have any happy ones. The only ones I'll have will be of what you said tonight. The worst things you've ever said to me in my life. And the most untrue.'

'I don't think they're untrue. I think you went off me. You went off me a long time ago but you wouldn't admit it, not even to yourself.'

'What makes you say that?'

She paused.

'Gabriel Hoey said you had an affair with a woman when you were in New York.'

'When did he tell you that?'

'We were at a party. He was drunk. He probably wouldn't have said it if he wasn't. I think he was trying to protect me.'

'Protect you? He wouldn't know the meaning of the word.'

'It's true, though, isn't it?'

'Yes. I didn't intend it to happen but it did. Does that make me a bad person? She's out of my life now. She has been ever since I set foot on Irish soil.'

'I wish you'd told me about her.'

'It wouldn't have done either of us any good.'

'I told you about Billy.'

'You could hardly not have after you got pregnant.'

'I would have anyway.'

'I would have told you about Mia too.'

'Mia. Was that her name? It sounds nice. Was she good in bed?'

'Don't do this to me, Jennifer.'

'You haven't played fair with me.'

'I have. We told one another that we could meet other people.'

'I never wanted to. I only said I would because I didn't want you to feel trapped by me.'

'So that's why you got pregnant.'

'That's not fair. It was a one night stand. We were drunk. It was different for you.'

'How do you mean?'

'I think you still have feelings for her. That's probably why you haven't been the same with me since you got back.'

'That's not true. I thought you were the one who changed.'

'Maybe we both did. That's why it's better we part.'

'Don't say that. Don't twist the situation to make an opening for that fool.'

'Please don't call him that. You're talking about the man I'm going to spend the rest of my life with.'

'I'm sorry. I just want you back with me. At any cost.'

'There's no point, Brian. I could never be sure of you. You're always going to be going off somewhere, or wishing you were.'

'I could go from here to the end of the earth but you're the woman that would always be in my heart.'

'That speech might have worked last year. It might even have worked three months ago. But not now. You've hurt me too much.'

'It's not a speech. It's me.'

'I know you believe that but you're not ready to settle down yet. I am.

Maybe women reach that stage sooner than men.'

'I thought you'd always wait for me to be ready for you.'

'I would have if I thought such a day would come. Now I know it won't.'

'What do your parents think about all this?'

'Dad thinks it's for the best. Mam is against it. She knows how I feel about you. Or should I say felt about you.'

'Can you not see things from her point of view?'

'Maybe I could have until recently. Too much has happened since.'

'What if it doesn't work out with …him.'

'If it doesn't it doesn't. I'm going into it with my eyes open. I know he loves me. For now that's enough.'

'So it's more important to be loved than to love.'

'It's not that simple, Brian. Please don't try and talk me out of it.'

'I can't believe you're able to walk away from everything we had.'

'It suits you to think that's what's happening but it's the other way round. You want me on a string. You want to know I'm available for you but not to do anything about it. That's not enough for me anymore.'

'I'd marry you tomorrow.'

'Maybe, but you wouldn't have done it yesterday. That's the point.'

The baby started crying.

'Hold on a minute,' she said.

She went to see what was wrong with him. Brian heard him being pacified with her hushes as he settled down to sleep. When she came back her voice was stronger.

'Let's not kid one another,' she said, 'We haven't been going anywhere for a long time now. I'm leaving you because you left me. You left me when you went to Europe and again when you went to America.'

'It was mutual. We were on breaks for those times.'

'Maybe you were. I was nursing a broken heart.'

'Going to these places wasn't about leaving you. It was about finding myself.'

'Finding yourself. The great cliché to excuse desertion. Wasn't that what the hippies used to say when they wanted to get out of a relationship? You're always going to be in love with change. If it wasn't that girl in America it would have been someone else. You want to love me but you can't. It took me a long time to accept that. Maybe it's time you accepted it too.'

'I can't and I never will.'

'We're going round in circles now. Needless to say I'll give you back every penny you gave me for Stephen.'

'Keep it. You'll need it for the other eleven children you're going to have with Billy.'

She put the phone down again. This time she was a longer time away.

'I'm not going to talk for long more,' she said when she came back, 'I just want to say one thing. I put off making this call for a long time because I didn't think I'd be able to. I was sick to my stomach thinking of it. Now that I've done it I'm even sicker. But I'm not going to go back on my decision. Please forgive me for that. One day you might thank me for it. You might thank me because you'll know it's the right thing for both of us. For me to let you go and you to let me go.'

'No, Jennifer, that will never be the case.'

'I have to go now,' she said, 'They'll be wondering why I'm so long up here. I hope you'll be happy at whatever you decide to do in life or whoever you spend it with. I'll always care very deeply for you.'

He started to talk to her about Mia, about the farm, about the trauma he went through with his mother. He talked for a long time without her saying anything. Then he realised that she'd already hung up. He was talking to static.

He looked into the dead face of the phone. He let it drop onto the floor. The silence that followed deafened him.

57

He wasn't able to sleep that night or any of the nights following. His heart hammered in his chest. He spent most of his time in his room, only venturing out of it to eat.

He felt the past receding from him like a wave. The things he once held dear to him suddenly didn't matter anymore. He felt dead inside. Daily chores took his mind off himself but when he wasn't doing anything his mind was like a cauldron. It was like a person inside him hitting him with a hammer.

All his old regrets came back. He found himself wishing he'd stayed in Europe, in America, anywhere things were happening. Like a coward he'd come back to Ireland with his tail between his legs when Mia left him. Trying to pick up with pieces with Jennifer was never going to work. He'd retreated to the old sanctuaries of the land, the home, the family. But the family wasn't there anymore. Neither was the land or the home. All that remained in their place were shells of his old life. He tried to embrace those shells now, to make something of them that might grow into new structures, structures that could sustain him for whatever future he might have.

Bartley woke up with a barking cough most mornings. His lungs were in bits. Angela was in denial about it. There was a time he would have been too, a time he'd have run away from it. He couldn't run now because there was nowhere to run to. He'd burned his boats.

Jennifer was gone out of his life for reasons he still couldn't understand. He'd destroyed the only valuable thing that had ever been given to him.

He rang Gabriel.

'I believe you shot your mouth off to Jennifer about Mia,' he said, 'She's after dumping me.'

He sensed his nervousness at the other end of the line.

'Jesus, man, I'm sorry,' he said, 'I didn't think it was a secret what you did or didn't do that way after she had the child. I thought the two of you were doing your own thing.'

'That wasn't the way it was, Gabriel. Don't try to defend yourself.'

'I'm not. If I did anything wrong I'd admit it. She didn't act like it was any big deal.'

'Well it was. It's over between us now.'

'I don't believe that for a second. She's probably just putting you on the cooler for a bit. She'll come back when she's made you suffer.'

He didn't want to get into it.

'How are you keeping yourself?' he said.

'Not good. The old man kicked me out. I'm gay.'

He said the three sentences as if they were one long one, running the words into one another. It was as if the last two words were a discardable addition.

So Bartley was right.

'You're what?'

'I've been fighting it for a while. Maybe you copped it.'

'I must say the thought crossed my mind now and then.'

'Anyway I'm with a guy now. We're in Claregalway. Maybe we'll meet up sometime. I'll tell you about it all. In the meantime I hope it works out with Jen.'

'Thanks. Good luck, Gabriel. I hope you find what you're looking for.'

'I always knew you'd understand. Thank you.'

He was surprised, but not as much as he thought he'd be. It put a lot of things in perspective.

He understood him better now. The denial was probably behind a lot of his bad behaviour. He should have seen through it, all the crude jokes and the pretence of confidence with women.

It was so obvious. He was glad he was able to admit it to himself. It would make a lot of things easier in his life from now on. Maybe he'd even add a new character to his novel.

He rang the factory.

'I'd like to give in my notice,' he said.

Maybe Gabriel's call gave him the courage to make his own one. It was the day for change.

A secretary he didn't know took the call. She didn't say anything. McSweeney came on the line an hour later. He thought it was a joke.

'What the hell is going on?' he said, 'I got some kind of garbled message about you leaving us.'

'I am.'

'You can't be serious. You were going a bomb. What's up?'

'I can't talk about it now. There's a lot happening. I'll drop in to the factory after Christmas and have a chat with you.'

'Don't go, Brian. It would be a big mistake. I have plans for you in this place.'

'I know that, Joe. You've been very good to me. As I say, it's complicated. I need to sit down and talk with you in the new year.'

'Do that. I'm not taking this call seriously, by the way. I'll be keeping the job open for you.'

'I appreciate that. Happy Christmas.'

'The same to you. We want you here. Remember that. You're a breath of fresh air to the place. Becky thinks you're great too.' That must have been his girlfriend.

Bartley was listening to the call.

'What's all that about?' he said, 'Did I hear you resigning from the factory?'

'You shouldn't be listening to other people's conversations.'

'I just happened to be passing. What's going on?'

'I don't want to go into it.'

'This is crazy.'

He tried to get him to talk about it in the next few days but he fended off his questions.

His evasiveness led to a more searching one.

'What's happening with Jen?' he asked him one day, 'Is she coming down for Christmas?'

'I don't know.'

'You haven't seen her for a while, have you?'

'No.'

'Is everything okay between you two?'

'Of course.'

'Make sure you tell her we'd like her down.'

He kept ringing her but she didn't answer. Eventually he stopped trying. After a while he didn't know if he wanted to talk to her or not. What was the point? She'd made her mind up. There would be no changing it.

He was angry with her but more angry with himself. He wanted to visit her but he knew there was no point in that either. He'd have been running into her parents – and probably Billy Sheehan as well.

Declan rang to say he wanted to spend Christmas in Loughrea.

'Yvonne can't wait to show Harry off to everyone,' he said.

Bartley took the call. He said that would be a great idea but when he ran it by Brian he said, 'No way.'

He had to ring them back and say something came up. They didn't know what to think.

Brian broke down that night and told Bartley everything. He couldn't keep it in any longer. Bartley couldn't believe it. He was cevastated for him.

He knew Billy. He thought he was a pathetic creature, almost as pathetic as Gabriel. 'She's selling herself short,' he said. Angela said she'd have made a wonderful daughter-in-law. That made him feel even worse.

Everything was subdued in the days leading up to Christmas. Angela usually loved getting the decorations ready but this year she only put up a few. Bartley advised her to get a small tree and a small turkey. Everything was done on a minimal scale.

Yvonne rang Brian on Christmas Day.

'My heart is breaking for you,' she said.

'What do you mean?'

'Bartley told me about Jennifer,'

'He shouldn't have done that.'

'He didn't want to tell me. I got it out of him. We're at our wit's end here wondering why you wouldn't have us for Christmas.'

'I wish you hadn't rung. I'm trying to deal with this on my own.'

'I care about you, Brian. So does Declan. He really likes Jennifer. He's very sorry for you. He asked me to tell you that.'

'I don't want anyone's pity.'

'Maybe it's for the best,' she said, 'I know it might be hard for you to accept that.'

'How could it be? I'm in bits.'

'I know you are but you were having a hard time making up your mind about Jennifer. Obviously there was some doubt there.'

'Everyone knows I was always slow to commit. What man isn't? That's not the point. She needed to let me know how she was feeling.'

'The last thing she wanted to do was pressure you into marrying her.'

'I have much more pressure now that she's gone.'

'That will ease in time.'

'I don't think so. She pulled the rug from under my feet.'

'She didn't see it like that. It was the other way round for her.'

'How come you know so much about the situation?'

'She used to ring me from time to time. Occasionally your name would come up.'

'Why didn't you tell me that before?'

'I didn't think it was worth mentioning. We wouldn't be gossiping or anything but sometimes she said things I thought were important.'

'Like what?'

'I don't know whether I should say this to you or not.'

'Go on. You've said enough already. You might as well finish it.'

'All right. I think the way you reacted about Maureen had a big effect on her.'

'What do you mean?'

'You gave out to her when Maureen said it was back on between you two.'

'So what?'

'He took that very badly. Did you not know?'

'No. Maybe I blocked it out. Maybe I've spent my life blocking things out. Maybe that's why I'll never meet anyone as good as Jennifer.'

'Don't say that. There are more fish in the ocean.'

'Not for this fisherman. For me it was her or no one.'

'Don't think that way. It's not good for you.'

'I'm going to go now, Yvonne. If I stay on the line in the condition I'm in I'm capable of saying much worse things.Wish Declan a happy Christmas for me.'

'Try to get your mind off her. I know it's not easy, especially at this time of the year.'

Thoughts whirled in his head when he put down the phone. He didn't know what he wanted or what he didn't want. He was full of anger against Jennifer, against Maureen, even against Yvonne. He knew none of them had done anything wrong but he was still angry with them. He wanted to kill the messengers.

He spent most of the Christmas locked in his thoughts. Angela did her best to divert him with her treats. Bartley was on his best behaviour too. Declan even laid off his usual sarcasm when he was on the phone.

'I've reformed,' he said, 'I'm not that guy anymore. Harry humanised me. Yivvy doesn't know what to make of it all.'

The world seemed to be falling apart as the year wound to a close. Every time he picked up a newspaper or turned on the television there was some new atrocity, some new global disaster. A terrorist attack took place in Europe. A teenager shot dozens of people in a shopping mall in America. In Ireland there were drug killings, suicides, fatal car accidents. Normally he'd have been shocked at events like that but they washed over him as if they hadn't happened.

The world of show business was blitzed as well. George Michael had a heart attack on Christmas Day. David Bowie had died earlier in the year along with Leonard Cohen. The following week the actress Carrie Fisher died at the age of 60. She'd got a heart attack on a plane from London to

Los Angeles during a book tour. Debbie Reynolds died the following day from heartbreak. She was Fisher's mother. It was as if the world of celebrity was being decimated by a malevolent deity.

He couldn't properly react to any of these things because his own problems weighed so heavily with him.

He remembered reading somewhere that that was what depression was, the inability to empathise.

He couldn't stop thinking of Jennifer. Her departure from his life was even more tortuous to him than Mia's had been. The difference between them, he thought, was like the difference between a comet and a planet. Both of them had burned him in a way he could never have imagined. Maybe all the women in his life had burned him. Maybe that's what women did to everyone. They were like viruses, incurable diseases. Gabriel was better off without them.

On the last day of the year he drove to her house. If he wasn't feeling so bad he mightn't have had the courage. He'd always been shy with her there but his depression took that away now. It took everything away.

He sat in the car across the road from the house. A part of him wanted to go in and beat Billy Sheehan to a pulp.

But of course Sheehan wasn't the problem. He was. He'd created the situation. Only he could solve it.

He sat there wondering what he'd say to her. Different speeches formed themselves in his mind. Speeches with marriage proposals, speeches where he said he was going to leave the country, speeches that included having another child with her.

He wrote them down on a sheet of paper but when he read them to himself he thought they sounded ridiculous. He tore them up and threw them out the window. He watched the paper flying around the windscreen like confetti. He knew it was senseless being there in the first place, senseless thinking there was anything to salvage with her.

He drove home by a different route than usual. It meant passing the graveyard where his mother was buried. She'd been on his mind a lot over the past few weeks. Christmas always did that to him. It brought up things he thought he'd forgotten, things he'd pushed to the back of his mind.

He'd only passed it a handful of times since he got home. He hadn't stopped. He wasn't sure why. Maybe he was afraid of the memories it would dredge up. But now he felt able for it.

It was situated in a hollow. After he parked the car he walked down a stone path. It curled all the way down to the grave.

He got a shock when he saw it. There were weeds were growing up everywhere. They made her name almost invisible on the headstone. He knelt down beside it. He said a prayer for her.

He tried to remember the happy times. He thought of how brave she was in her last months, the way her personality changed after her operation and then came back to itself.

He knew he'd never recover from her death but he didn't want her back. She was better off out of life, better off not knowing how things went without her, especially things that had happened to him.

Where was she now? Was she anywhere? It was difficult to think of a spirit like hers being quelled even by death. There was one place he knew she'd always be: inside his head.

One of the last things she'd said to him was to marry Jennifer. She always got bothered when he told her they were taking things slowly. 'One day I think we'll marry,' he'd say, 'but I'm not ready yet.' 'Sometimes we don't know what we want,' she'd reply, 'until we throw ourselves into a situation.'

He couldn't do that now. It wasn't a possibility for him even if he wanted it. Did he? Maybe Jennifer was right. Maybe if they married they'd only have made each other miserable. They'd have been going up the aisle because it was the convenient thing to do, because it seemed to be a way out of loneliness. But you could be more lonely with someone who was wrong for you than if you were on your own.

The evening drew in. A fog had risen. It blocked everything out. It was so thick he could hardly see ahead of him. He listened to a car horn beeping, a sheep bleating on a hillside. A dull ache of regret gnawed at him.

He went back to the car. When he got to it he stood looking down the valley. The grave was bathed in the mist like a protective cocoon. Loughrea was another cocoon. So was his life on the farm.

His hands trembled on the steering wheel as he drove home. He couldn't get his mind off his mother. She was buried in the town where she'd been christened, the town where she'd been married. She'd hardly been outside the county limits and yet she'd lived a fuller life than anyone he knew. That was because she contained everything inside herself. Unlike him she didn't need to travel to make herself feel she was experiencing things.

What would she think of him now? She would have seen his travelling as a way of trying to escape from himself. His life at home wasn't much better. To see him living with a stepmother he didn't like would have disappointed her. She'd her life stolen from her. She wouldn't have wanted his to be stolen too. She'd have thought he lacked backbone in not getting out even if she'd have been too ladylike to put it that way.

The farmyard was quiet when he got back to it. There was a light on in Bartley's room. He heard a vague muffle of voices through the window.

He went inside. Bartley and Angela were talking upstairs. Bartley would usually have called down when he heard the door opening but tonight he didn't. He thought of going up to him, of telling him the grave could have done with being tended to but there was no point. He would have said, 'I don't think of your mother as being in that hole. That's only her body.' And maybe he'd have been right.

He went up to his bedroom. It seemed different. He sat on the bed. Someone on the road was singing 'Auld Lang Syne.' He felt strange, as strange as the first time he came home from the university. He looked around the room at his possessions, all the things Bartley kept as they were since before his mother died. He'd been glad of that once but now it meant nothing. It was just an encumbrance. He thought of a verse from the Bible, 'When I was a child I thought like a child but when I became a man I put away childish things.' It was time for him to do that too.

The room wasn't his shrine anymore. It was someone else's. He felt like a man wearing another man's suit of clothes.

It began to snow. Everything seemed suspended, washed clean. He might have been looking at the night through a gauze. The moon shone through the trees. He looked out at the hills, at the clouds that gathered themselves above them like dark balls of fluff.

He remembered a day years ago when he was lying in bed with Jennifer and it was snowing outside. They just lay there looking at it for hours. Something like that would have been impossible with Mia. One woman was like earth, the other like air. Maybe his tragedy was that he didn't know which suited him more.

The snow covered his thoughts as well as the ground. It was like a blanket over everything, a comfortable lie. It would help him get up tomorrow and go on with other lies that were more comfortable. It reminded him of his youth, of the Christmasses of long ago when his mother was alive. It fell over the land like balls of wool.

He took up the bottle that was in the shape of a dome, the one that had the snow inside it. He turned it upside down. The snow fell on Santa, on a snowman, on the toy figures inside. How magical that bottle had been to him the year Bartley gave it to him. Now it was just a keepsake.

He thought back to the days when he used to roam through the fields with him, when things were good between them. Life was simple then. Questions had answers. He knew where he was going to be on a given day and what he had to do there. His mother's life was simple too. When she spoke it was with the reassurance that everything would be well in the days to come, that everything would always be well.

He had a photograph of her on his locker. It was taken when she was in her twenties, before he was born. Her hair was jet black then. She looked out at the world as if it held infinite possibilities for her.

Why did he not have a photograph of Jennifer? Was it true that she'd always have come second to her, that no woman could live up to her as far as he was concerned? All the women who met him were up against an impossible obstacle. Her perfection robbed him of a future with any of them.

What did such a future hold for him now? Hardly marriage, or children. He could have had both with Jennifer if he hadn't ruined it. Would things have been different if he hadn't gone away? He didn't know. Maybe he had to travel to realise that other places didn't have the allure you thought they had before you went to them, or other people either. That was its main function. Not to fulfil you, just to make you realise everything was on your doorstep. It didn't matter if he lived in Ireland or picked grapes in France or worked in a post office in Zurich or lived with a social worker in New York or a drug addict in Dublin. No matter where he was he'd always be himself. Paralysed in a small town like one of the characters in Gabriel Hoey's novel.

Maybe he'd write a novel as well. If he did, that would be its theme. It might strike a chord with people. Wasn't that what everyone wanted, to break out of their traps? Maybe he'd get rich out of it. Then he wouldn't have to work. Writing could become his new job. It could become like any other one, something you started every day at nine and finished at five like in the sweet factory.

He went downstairs. It was still quiet. He opened the door. There was a stoop outside. He sat down on it, drinking in the night air. There was a mist over the valley. A dog barked somewhere in the distance. The wind blew through the trees. Clouds were banking themselves along the horizon. The sky seemed to be a million miles away.

A car alarm sounded but nobody bothered with it. It kept shrieking until he had to put his hands over his ears to block out the sound of it. It reminded him of the wailing of a cat. Nobody went to it. He imagined what Bartley would have said if he heard it: 'Nobody bothers with anything in this godforsaken place. Imagine if that was the house alarm and we were inside being carved up.'

Maybe he'd turn into Bartley if he stayed in Loughrea long enough. Maybe he'd become like those people who went down to McDonagh's every night and solved the world's problems from a barstool. They talked about things like the closure of the Garda stations in the area, the closure of the hospitals.

Nobody bothered with car alarms in Loughrea and nobody bothered with hospitals either. Country places didn't matter in Brave New Ireland. Only cities did.

Cities were where life was. They were where the young people were. Modern Ireland was no country for old men, as Yeats said. Or old women either. They could be murdered in their homes. It would be headlines for a day and then it would be replaced with the following day's news. That was the way things were, the way they would always be.

He rested his head against a frame behind the stoop. He thought of his first days in the university, the thrill of writing and the thrill of Sinead. So much had happened since. He didn't know if he was more mature now. Maybe he was less mature.

Would he be different if he went back to America? He wasn't sure of that either. It wasn't possible anyway. Donald Trump was getting rid of the Irish just as he'd got rid of everything else that was decent in life.

He started thinking about Mia, about her fractiousness, her beauty. The first time at the beach with her. The nights they spent doing nothing. Their fights.

Would she still be in Africa? Would he ever see her again? He thought he was over her but maybe Jennifer was right. Maybe he wasn't. She was like an undertow to his emotions. It was like someone who had an amputated limb still feeling its sensation even though it wasn't there anymore. But he couldn't have lived with her longer than he did. He knew that now even if it was Job's consolation to him.

His eyes became heavy. The clock crawled towards midnight. Everything was still outside. The air was pure and he felt part of it, part of that purity. His youth could be recaptured, he told himself, and with it the dreams he'd nurtured in the past when nothing mattered but such dreams. People said you outgrew your past but you didn't. You couldn't. It was as much a part of you as what you ate, as the colour of your eyes.

In a way it was more real than the present. He'd never felt a part of the present the way other people did. When he said that to them they thought he was trying to be superior but he didn't mean it like that. All he meant was that he felt removed from things as they were happening. It was as if he wasn't properly immersed in life but somewhere outside it, looking at it from a distance. He might have been a seagull flying over the beach, flapping its wings and gazing at everything with a casual eye, not bothering too much if he became a part of it or not. He was like a body within a body, a self within a self, struggling to make things meaningful.

He walked out into the snow with Rusty trotting along beside him. It covered everything now. He slushed through it, marvelling at its silence, its domination of the landscape.

He went over to the tree that had the tyre hanging from it, the one Declan and himself used to swing in when they were young. He hadn't sat inside it since the funeral. The rope was frayed. It would probably have snapped if he put any weight on it.

In the distance he heard some people singing. 'Should old acquaintance be forgot,' they sang, 'and never brought to mind, should old acquaintance be forgot for the sake of auld lang syne.' Their voices rang through the air. He felt envious of them, of their camaraderie. He wanted to be a part of it even for these few moments.

He wondered if they were from the factory. They were having their party tonight. McSweeney had invited him to it even though he wasn't working there anymore. He refused politely. He wouldn't have gone even if the situation hadn't happened with Jennifer. He'd have spent the night floating between the top brass and the assembly line workers, trying to be nice to both and ending up as neither fish nor fowl. The story of his life.

Another year had come and gone, he thought, and nothing basically had changed. The house was dying into the new year and everything in it was dying too, including himself. No matter how far he travelled he'd never left it in his mind.

He saw his life stretching ahead of him like a road he wasn't sure he wanted to travel, a road that could lead to others ones he wanted even less. Sometimes you went down a side road and it brought happiness for a while but then you went back to the main one and you couldn't relax on it because of where you'd been. Was that what happened to him? Had he taken the wrong side roads?

'You think too much,' Jennifer used to say to him, 'Can you not just live?' But he couldn't. Thinking had always been more important to him than living.

It started to rain. After a few minutes the landscape lost its whiteness. It became slushy. He looked over at the barn. It was falling apart but it still seemed entrancing to him. Night had a way of doing that. It made everything look beautiful. He felt bathed in its embrace.

He went back inside. Rusty looked up at him with his ears cocked.

He listened to Bartley and Angela moving around in the bedroom. Did they know he was there? He hoped not.

He went upstairs. Rusty scampered along beside him. When he got to his bedroom it was dark. He didn't bother turning on the light. Instead he opened the curtains. The light of the moon flooded in.

He lay down on the bed. He made a mound of the pillow and sunk his head into it. Outside the wind whooshed through the trees. It was the only thing he could hear.

He thought of Mia standing over a well in Africa, of Jennifer having a quiet night in with Stephen. Life was happening somewhere else. He'd cut himself off from involvement, from love. Only Rusty looked up to him now.

He looked out at the moon. A flight of birds skeetered across it. Everything seemed hazy to him. He found it difficult to focus on what he was seeing, what he was feeling. Rusty came over to him, resting his chin on the duvet. He looked up at him as if to say, 'Do you need to talk?' Sometimes he did that. A part of him believed he knew what he was thinking.

He tried to sleep but his thoughts were racing too much. He got out of bed and went over to the window. He looked out, soaking himself in the shadows that slipped across the farmyard and onto the fields. The tops of the trees glinted in the night light.

A chicken trotted into the barn. Somewhere far away he heard a train thundering through the night. It seemed to be calling to him, calling to him like the lights of Rockaway Beach. He felt a longing for something he wasn't quite sure of.

He looked around the room. Would he miss it if he went away from it? Could he leave it tomorrow without a thought and seek a new life for himself somewhere else? He could spend one night here, he thought, or all the nights of his life. There were fixtures in it that reassured him, fixtures that were there since childhood, things he'd woken up looking at for as long as he could remember. The wallpaper. The carpet. The wardrobe. The tallboy with the crooked drawer. Benchmarks to live by, comfort blankets in an uncertain world. Did he have the courage to leave them behind as he once did, for better and worse things?

His transistor was on the window sill. He turned it on. He always kept it on the country and western channel. The melodies relaxed him.

A singer was crooning about what country singers always crooned about: a love lost through drink. She made the theme sound romantic. She even made her hearttbreak romantic.

He thought of the Capri Café, of Priory Grove, of Leafwood Lane. Every place seemed to be one place, every person one person. He saw the past like a river flowing away from him, visible but unreachable, enticing to him in all the wrong ways. It was as real to him as yesterday. He felt the way he'd felt as a child when he took his first step in life, when he played his first football match, when he loved his first woman.

His mother was playing the piano. She was singing. Bartley was looking at something on the television. She started crying. He asked her what was wrong with her. 'Nothing,' she said.

The central heating came on. It always gave a click when it did that, the midnight boost Bartley liked to joke about, the boost that was most powerful when it was least useful. 'You have all the creature comforts here,' Declan liked to say to him. And he had.

Except one.

Jennifer would be asleep now, he thought, asleep in a house he should have been in with her, asleep beside a child that should also have been his. She'd probably marry soon. He imagined her with a large family. She'd minister to them at home and teach them in school.

He looked out at the north field, his favourite one. He thought back to the days when cows bleated on it, when tractors drove through it, when ploughs crackled over its stony soil.

His life was predictable then, as predictable as Jennifer's was now. He'd get top grades in his Leaving Cert. His mother would accept the fact that he wasn't going to be a priest. He'd marry Jennifer and go to college. Three years later his mother and father would go up to Dublin for his graduation ceremony. He'd become a teacher or maybe even a lecturer. Bartley would advise him to seek out the best-paying job.

He didn't have any job now. Would he go back to it? He could see how things would pan out if he did. His work would more or less stay the same. McSweeney would keep telling him to massage the company's figures until Ireland's 'rising tide' lifted its boat. He'd get a promotion to a bigger office in a year or two and an increase in salary, more generous than he deserved if Bartley hadn't known McSweeney. His influence would continue to make him more distant from people he was already distant from. He'd continue to eat alone in the canteen. The people from the assembly line would continue to stop talking when he entered a room because he was in with the men at the top who hired and fired.

There would be two weeks off every summer. He'd go on a package holiday somewhere because he'd be thought odd if he didn't. When he came back he'd talk about the hot sun and the poor hotel conditions, the two main subjects of conversation among the others as they chatted over coffee about previous holidays. Those who couldn't afford to take them would stifle yawns as the details were relayed to them.

Declan, meanwhile, would rave about the wonders of the computer world, at least when he wasn't raving about the wonders of Harry. Bartley would grow more infirm with the years. That would be tough on Angela but she was a survivor. She'd find other things in her life than caring for him if he became too demanding.

His own life would become more tense. He wouldn't be able to keep his feelings about Angela to himself forever. Sooner or later they'd come to the surface. There'd be some kind of confrontation and Bartley wouldn't know which of them to support.

He could avoid all that by going away again now. But where would he go? When he was unhappy in the past there was always the mystique of travel but now that mystique was gone. The faraway hills weren't green anymore. They were just far away.

He saw himself becoming trapped in the house as the years went on. Bartley and Angela would try to organise his life more for him as he got older. He'd broken away from them for a while but now he was in their clutches again. They knew he was a homebird at heart no matter how many times he went away. Now the bird was back in its cage, banging its head against the bars. Outside lay freedom but it was an empty one. It was no good to him because he didn't want it. In time he'd probably want it less and less. He might even come to fall in love with his chains. That could be the revenge Loughrea would take on him for not leaving it.

He looked out the window. It was raining over the snow. He liked when it did that, when it made holes in it. The people singing 'Auld Lang Syne' were still there. He sang along with them. Rusty gazed at him as if he was wondering what was coming next. 'Happy new Year, buddy,' Brian said to him.

He decided to have a drink to usher it in. There was a bottle of Prosecco on the floor. He lifted it up.

'Would you like some?' he said to Rusty. He wagged his tail in delight.

He poured it into a dish. Rusty licked it up. Maybe Bartley was right. Maybe he'd developed a taste for it.

'Let's get drunk together,' he said, 'Let's get so drunk we won't even wake up tomorrow. If we do, we'll have a hair of the dog. That's your hair, by the way. You're the dog.' Rusty looked delighted at the prospect.

He opened the window. The night breathed in on him. Suddenly he started to feel relaxed. The future didn't seem too bleak.

He raised his glass in the air.

'Happy New year to everyone,' he said. 'To Bartley, to Angela, to Declan and Yvonne, to Jennifer and Mia and Sinead and all the women I've loved and lost. And all the women who've loved and lost me.'

Maybe there would be other Mias, other Jennifers. Maybe he could travel again. Maybe he could go back to France or Italy or any of the other places he'd been. There were still a few more grapes to be picked, a few more mountains to be climbed.

'Right, Rusty?' he said. He barked as if he was in agreement. Or maybe he just wanted more Prosecco.

In a few hours the dawn would break. He'd wake up with a hangover, the hangover that was obligatory for Irish people on the first day of every year. He'd go down to the kitchen and wish Bartley and Angela a happy new year.

Bartley would give him a hug. Angela would fidget around him, asking him what he'd done the night before, how he'd run out the old and rung in the new. Then Bartley would say, 'We never died a winter yet.' He'd open a bottle of whiskey and they'd all have a drink from it, tinkling their glasses together as they did so.

They wouldn't do much with the day, sitting around eating the last of the Christmas leftovers at lunchtime. Afterwards they'd watch television shows that talked about delights that were to come during the new year. At some stage of the day they'd ring Declan and Yvonne to find out how Harry enjoyed his first Christmas. He'd leave them alone to chat. In the evening he'd go out for a walk or a drive in the car. When the night came in he'd go to his room and read.

His head started to buzz. He listened to Bartley and Angela laughing next door. He seemed to be tickling her. Usually she went crazy when he did that but this time she seemed to be enjoying it. She sounded as if she was drunk. It was the one night of the year she let her hair down. Bartley was drunk as well. They could have been two adolescents. He wondered if he ever tickled his mother like that. He doubted it.

He turned the volume of the radio up to block out the laughter. Rusty cocked his ears up at him, sensing his discomfiture.

Then all of a sudden it stopped. Everything became still.

The sky was full of stars. He felt himself being sucked up into them. A sense of peace descended on him. He became removed from everything, all pleasure and pain. In that moment he knew that whatever life threw at him he could cope with.

He felt Jennifer inside him. He thought back to a day they'd spent at a beach together, a day like any other. It was when they were going together first, when everything seemed so simple. She was sitting on her bicycle as she told him some silly story, her laughter cascading through the air as she tumbled off the crossbar and into the sea.